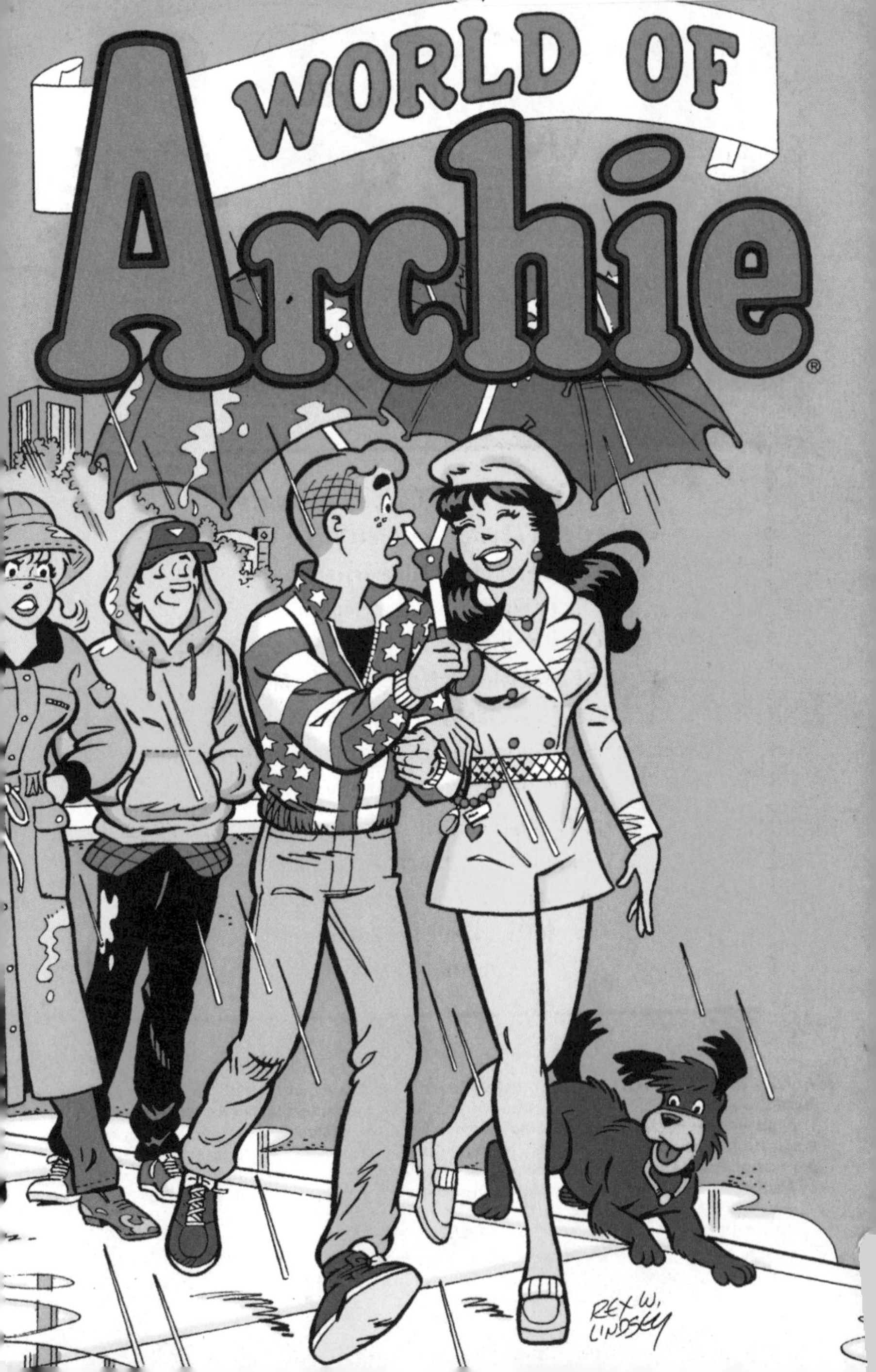
WORLD OF
Archie®
REX W. LINDSEY

Publisher / Co-CEO: Jon Goldwater
Co-President / Editor-In-Chief: Victor Gorelick
Co-President: Mike Pellerito
Co-President: Alex Segura
Chief Creative Officer: Roberto Aguirre-Sacasa
Chief Operating Officer: William Mooar
Chief Financial Officer: Robert Wintle
Director of Book Sales & Operations: Jonathan Betancourt
Art Director: Vincent Lovallo
Production Manager: Stephen Oswald
Lead Designer: Kari McLachlan
Associate Editor: Carlos Antunes
Editor: Jamie Lee Rotante
Co-CEO: Nancy Silberkleit

Printed in USA. First Printing. ISBN: 978-1-68255-795-2

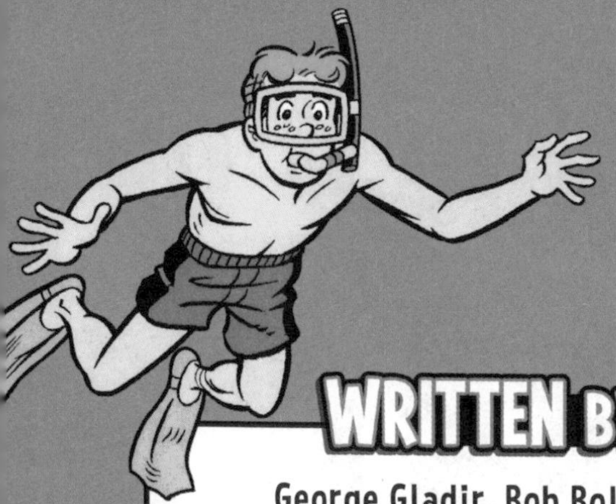

WRITTEN BY

George Gladir, Bob Bolling,
Mike Pellowski & Dan Parent

ART BY

Rex Lindsey, Henry Scarpelli, Dan Parent, Stan Goldberg,
Rudy Lapick, Bill Yoshida & Barry Grossman

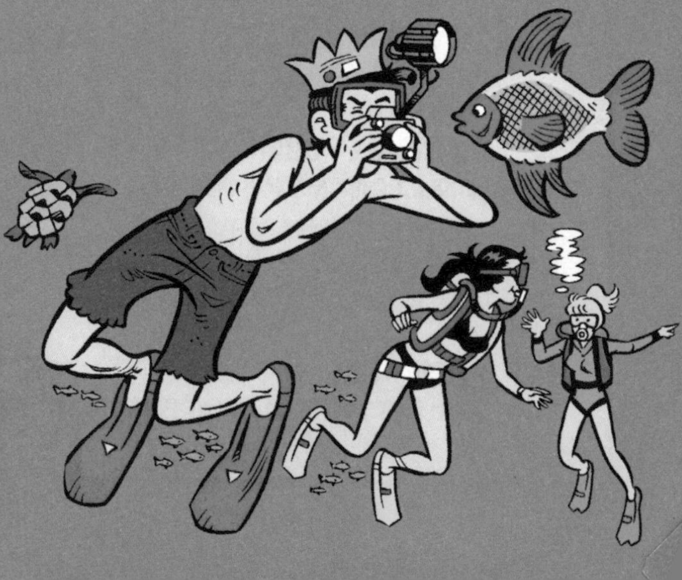

WORLD OF Archie

TABLE of CONTENTS

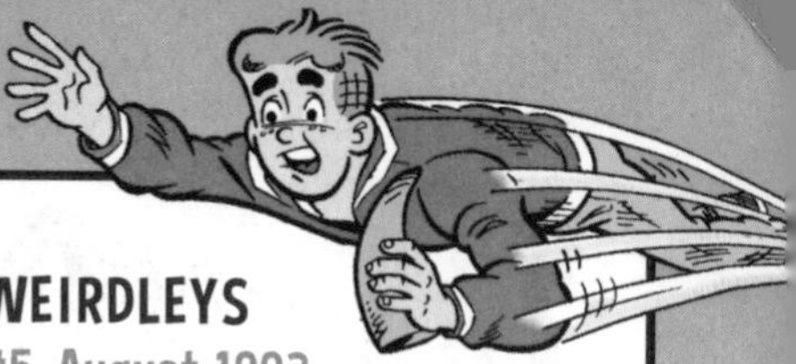

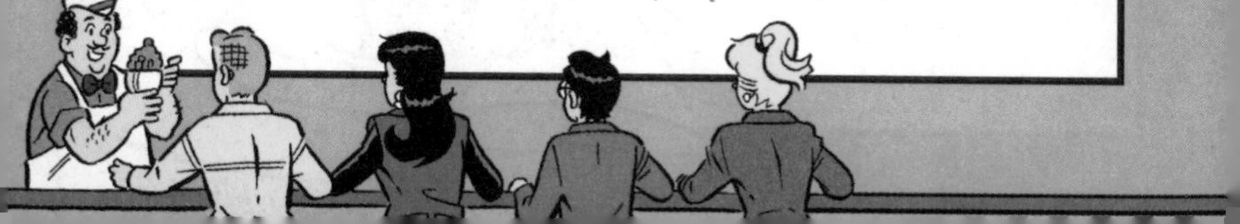

WORLD OF Archie

Archie Andrews is known for his adventures (and misadventures) in school and in the dating world—but that's not all Archie's experienced in his teenage life! The *World of Archie* series placed our red-headed hero, along with his best friends, in situations that were out of this world—like encountering dinosaurs, visiting the Wild West and taking on the Great Outdoors!

World of Archie began as a quarterly in 1992, following the end of the *Archie Giant Series.* In this series, Archie's adventures go far beyond the ordinary, like recreating the events that led to the discovery of America, learning the ropes out in the Wild West with cowboy training, and even encountering sea monsters and Vikings! *World of Archie* was jam-packed with action and adventure, but that doesn't mean you won't also find stories of humor and romance that fans have come to expect from Archie.

So don't wait any longer—turn the page and begin your journey into the World of Archie!

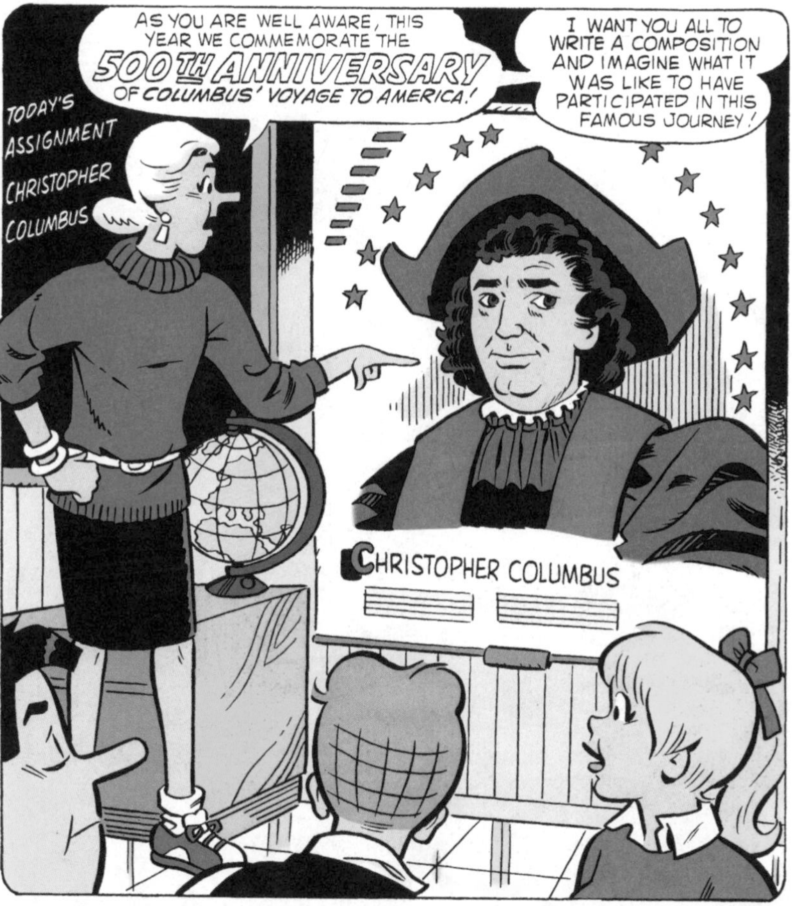
AS YOU ARE WELL AWARE, THIS YEAR WE COMMEMORATE THE 500TH ANNIVERSARY OF COLUMBUS' VOYAGE TO AMERICA!
I WANT YOU ALL TO WRITE A COMPOSITION AND IMAGINE WHAT IT WAS LIKE TO HAVE PARTICIPATED IN THIS FAMOUS JOURNEY!
TODAY'S ASSIGNMENT CHRISTOPHER COLUMBUS
CHRISTOPHER COLUMBUS

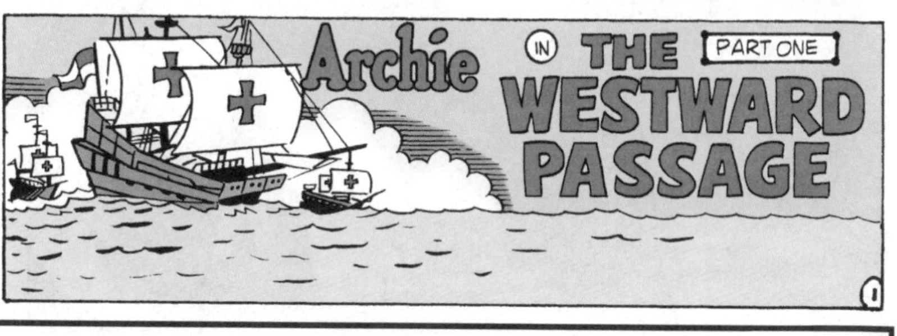
Archie IN THE WESTWARD PASSAGE
PART ONE
1

Story: George Gladir Pencils: Henry Scarpelli
Inks: Rudy Lapick Letters: Bill Yoshida Colors: Barry Grossman

Originally printed in WORLD OF ARCHIE #1, AUGUST 1992

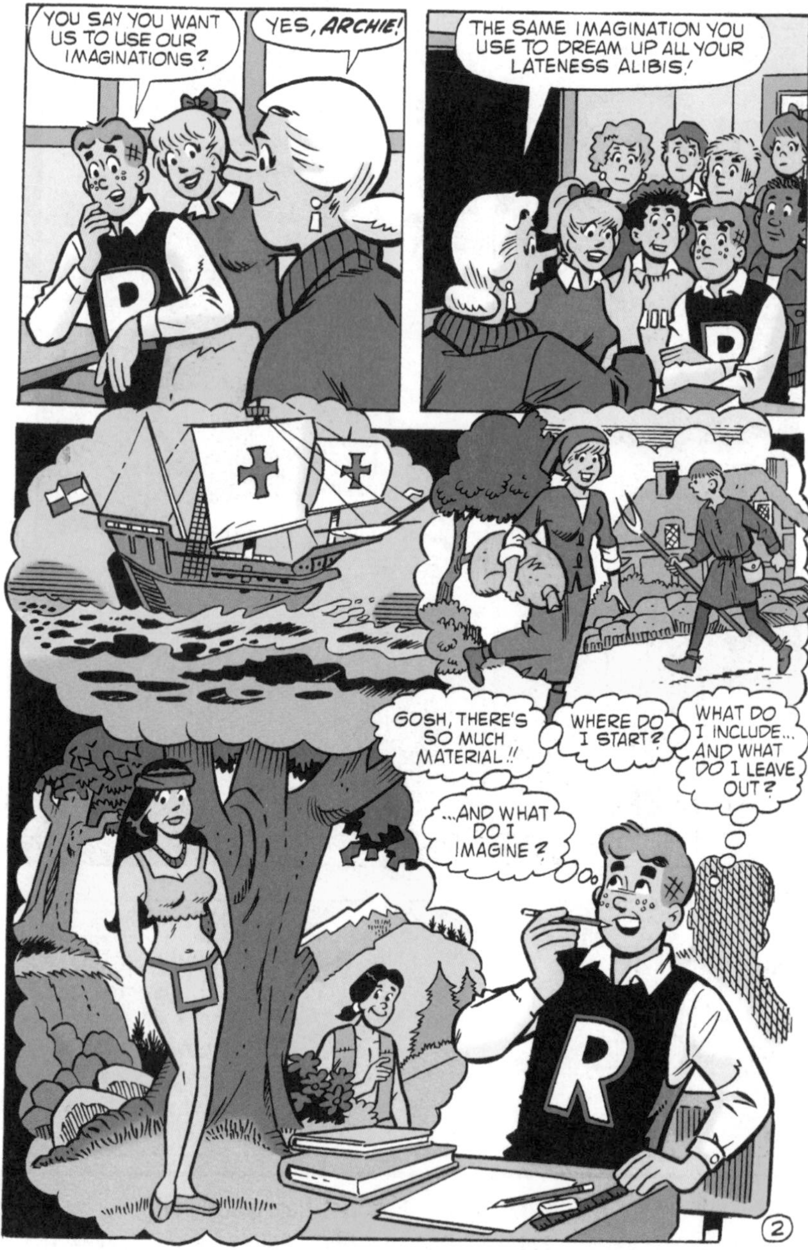
YOU SAY YOU WANT US TO USE OUR IMAGINATIONS?
YES, ARCHIE!
THE SAME IMAGINATION YOU USE TO DREAM UP ALL YOUR LATENESS ALIBIS!
GOSH, THERE'S SO MUCH MATERIAL!!
WHERE DO I START?
WHAT DO I INCLUDE... AND WHAT DO I LEAVE OUT?
...AND WHAT DO I IMAGINE?
2

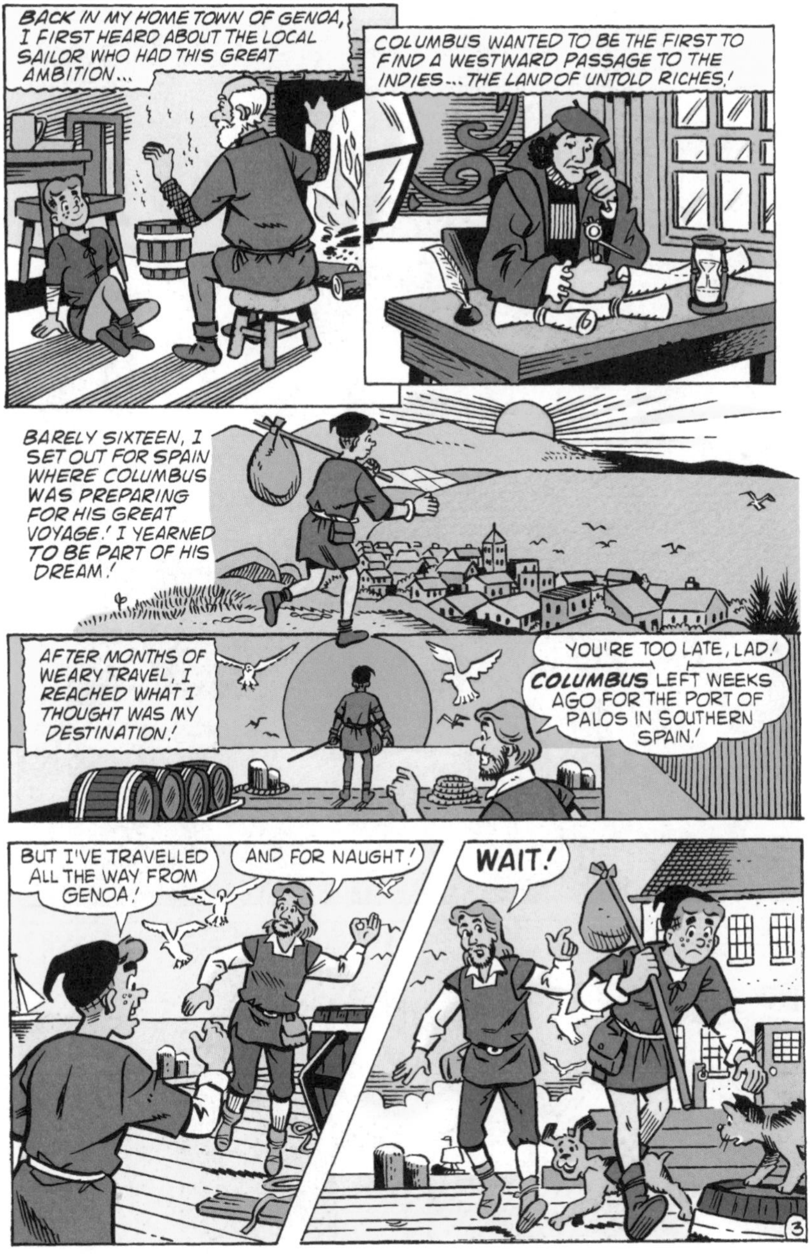
BACK IN MY HOME TOWN OF GENOA, I FIRST HEARD ABOUT THE LOCAL SAILOR WHO HAD THIS GREAT AMBITION...
COLUMBUS WANTED TO BE THE FIRST TO FIND A WESTWARD PASSAGE TO THE INDIES...THE LAND OF UNTOLD RICHES!
BARELY SIXTEEN, I SET OUT FOR SPAIN WHERE COLUMBUS WAS PREPARING FOR HIS GREAT VOYAGE! I YEARNED TO BE PART OF HIS DREAM!
AFTER MONTHS OF WEARY TRAVEL, I REACHED WHAT I THOUGHT WAS MY DESTINATION!
YOU'RE TOO LATE, LAD!
COLUMBUS LEFT WEEKS AGO FOR THE PORT OF PALOS IN SOUTHERN SPAIN!
BUT I'VE TRAVELLED ALL THE WAY FROM GENOA!
AND FOR NAUGHT!
WAIT!
3

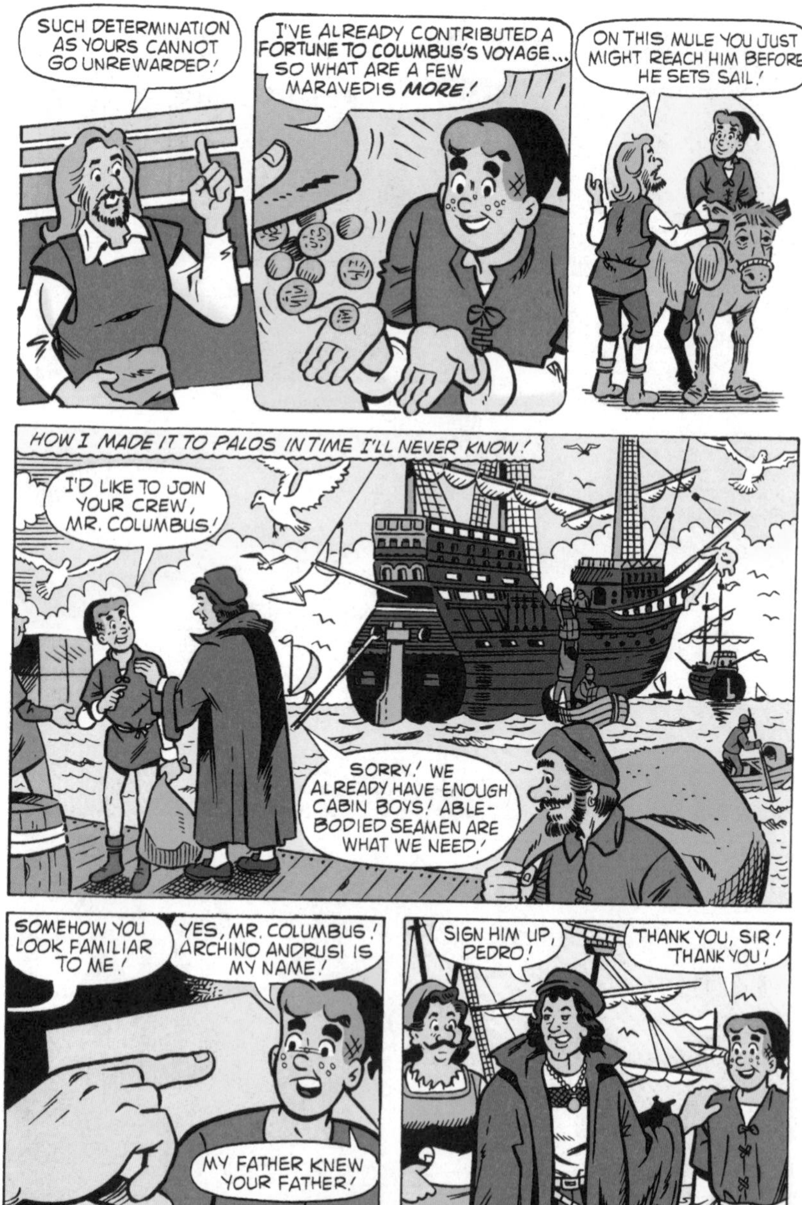
SUCH DETERMINATION AS YOURS CANNOT GO UNREWARDED!
I'VE ALREADY CONTRIBUTED A FORTUNE TO COLUMBUS'S VOYAGE... SO WHAT ARE A FEW MARAVEDIS MORE!
ON THIS MULE YOU JUST MIGHT REACH HIM BEFORE HE SETS SAIL!
HOW I MADE IT TO PALOS IN TIME I'LL NEVER KNOW!
I'D LIKE TO JOIN YOUR CREW, MR. COLUMBUS!
SORRY! WE ALREADY HAVE ENOUGH CABIN BOYS! ABLE-BODIED SEAMEN ARE WHAT WE NEED!
SOMEHOW YOU LOOK FAMILIAR TO ME!
YES, MR. COLUMBUS! ARCHINO ANDRUSI IS MY NAME!
MY FATHER KNEW YOUR FATHER!
SIGN HIM UP, PEDRO!
THANK YOU, SIR! THANK YOU!
4

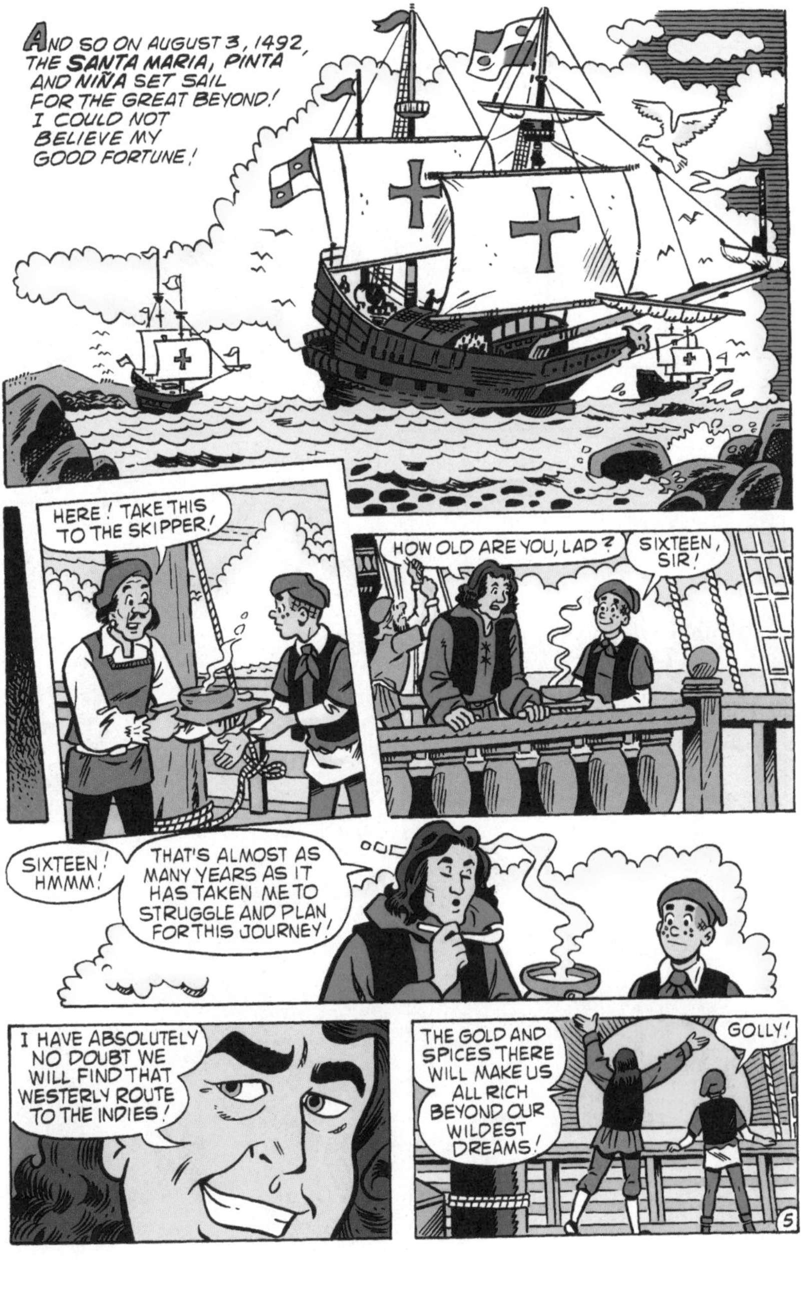
AND SO ON AUGUST 3, 1492, THE SANTA MARIA, PINTA AND NIÑA SET SAIL FOR THE GREAT BEYOND! I COULD NOT BELIEVE MY GOOD FORTUNE!
HERE! TAKE THIS TO THE SKIPPER!
HOW OLD ARE YOU, LAD?
SIXTEEN, SIR!
SIXTEEN! HMMM!
THAT'S ALMOST AS MANY YEARS AS IT HAS TAKEN ME TO STRUGGLE AND PLAN FOR THIS JOURNEY!
I HAVE ABSOLUTELY NO DOUBT WE WILL FIND THAT WESTERLY ROUTE TO THE INDIES!
THE GOLD AND SPICES THERE WILL MAKE US ALL RICH BEYOND OUR WILDEST DREAMS!
GOLLY!
5

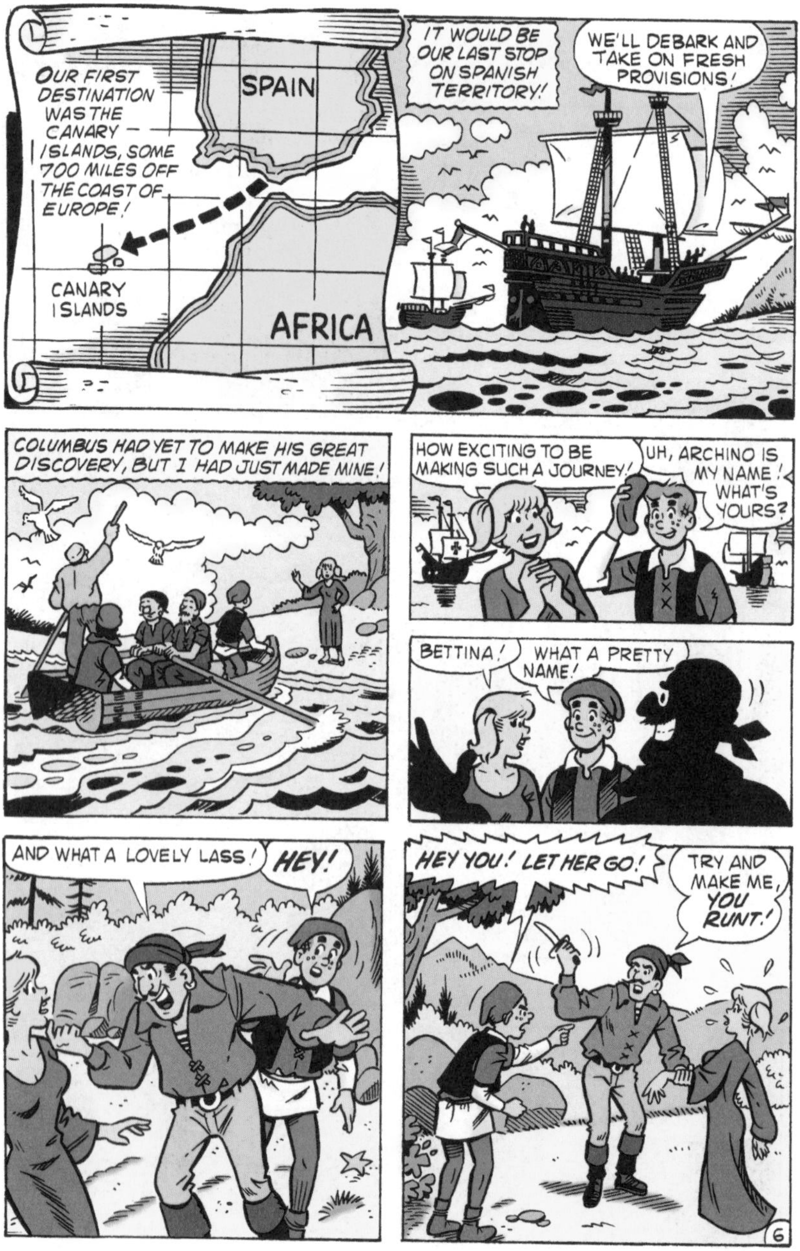

OUR FIRST DESTINATION WAS THE CANARY ISLANDS, SOME 700 MILES OFF THE COAST OF EUROPE!
SPAIN
CANARY ISLANDS
AFRICA
IT WOULD BE OUR LAST STOP ON SPANISH TERRITORY!
WE'LL DEBARK AND TAKE ON FRESH PROVISIONS!
COLUMBUS HAD YET TO MAKE HIS GREAT DISCOVERY, BUT I HAD JUST MADE MINE!
HOW EXCITING TO BE MAKING SUCH A JOURNEY!
UH, ARCHINO IS MY NAME! WHAT'S YOURS?
BETTINA!
WHAT A PRETTY NAME!
AND WHAT A LOVELY LASS!
HEY!
HEY YOU! LET HER GO!
TRY AND MAKE ME, YOU RUNT!
6

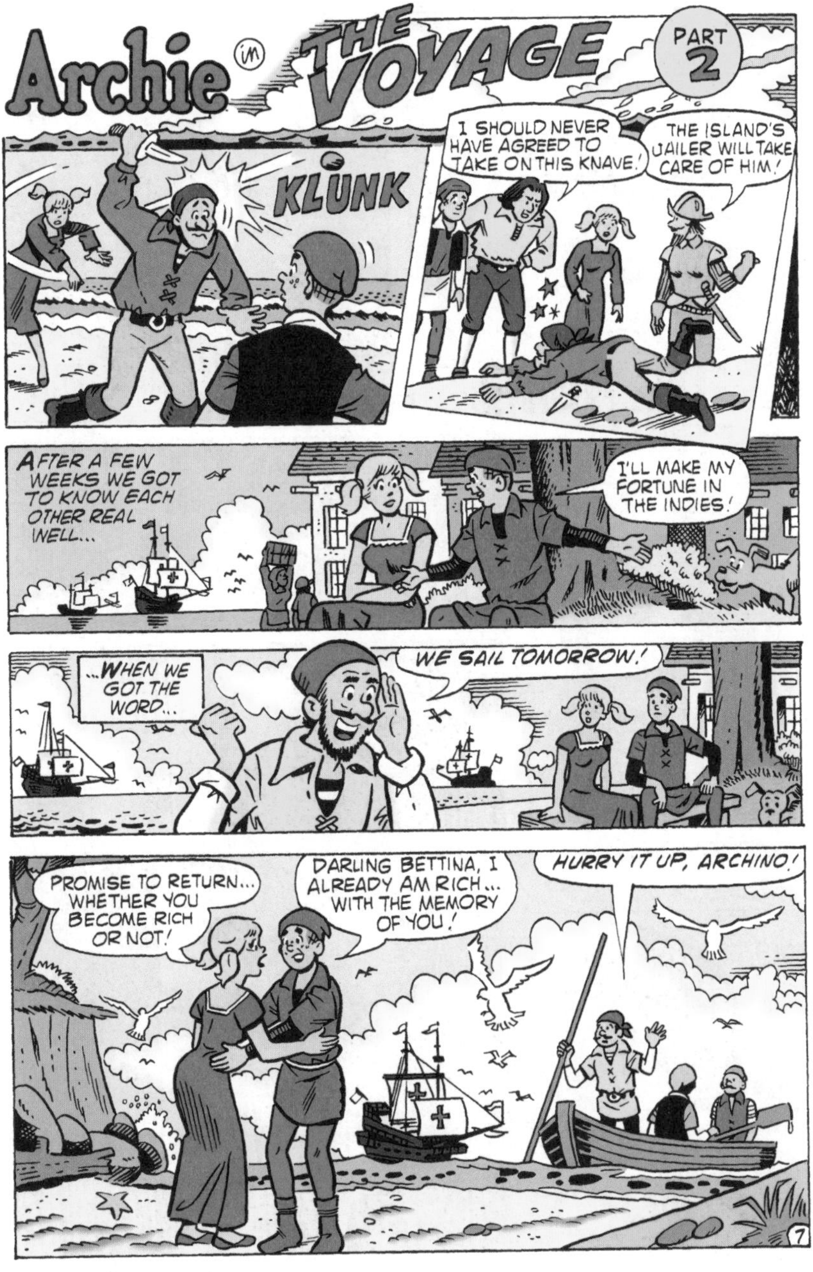

Archie in THE VOYAGE PART 2
KLUNK
I SHOULD NEVER HAVE AGREED TO TAKE ON THIS KNAVE!
THE ISLAND'S JAILER WILL TAKE CARE OF HIM!
AFTER A FEW WEEKS WE GOT TO KNOW EACH OTHER REAL WELL...
I'LL MAKE MY FORTUNE IN THE INDIES!
...WHEN WE GOT THE WORD...
WE SAIL TOMORROW!
PROMISE TO RETURN... WHETHER YOU BECOME RICH OR NOT!
DARLING BETTINA, I ALREADY AM RICH... WITH THE MEMORY OF YOU!
HURRY IT UP, ARCHINO!
7

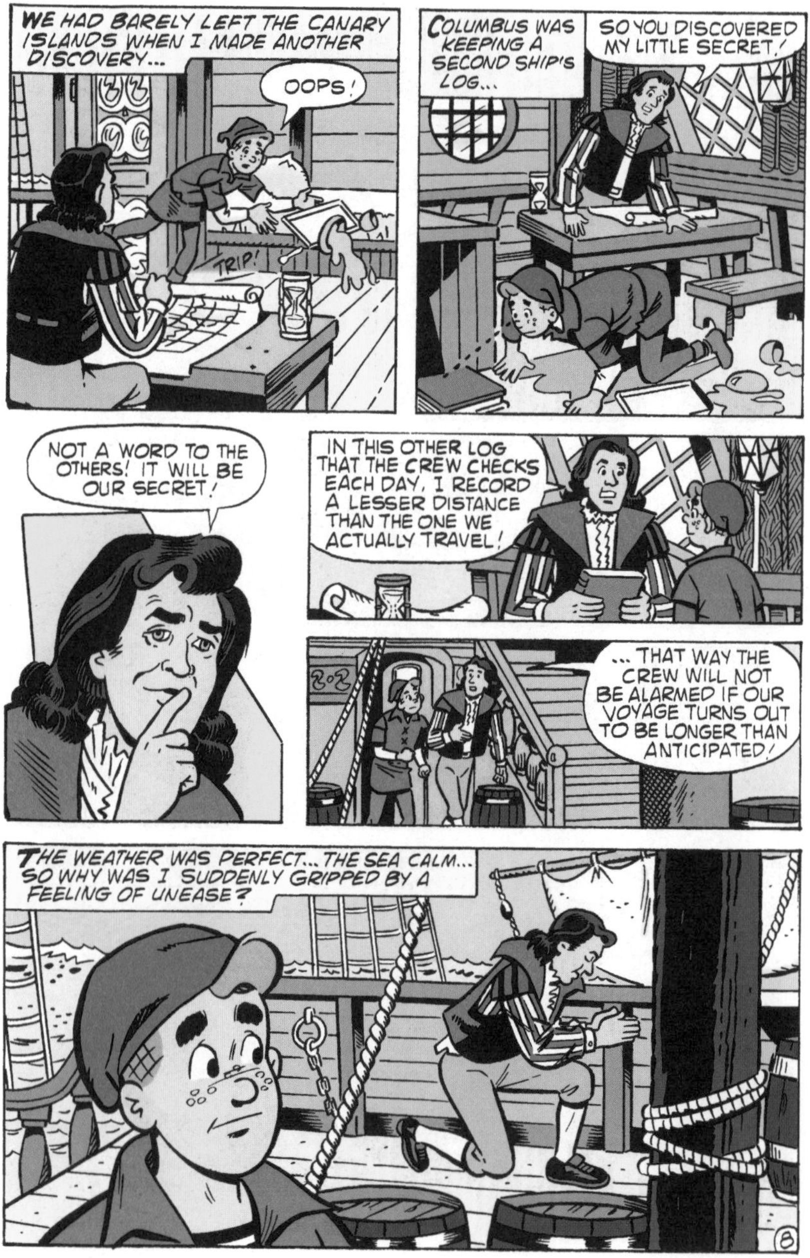
WE HAD BARELY LEFT THE CANARY ISLANDS WHEN I MADE ANOTHER DISCOVERY...
OOPS!
TRIP!
COLUMBUS WAS KEEPING A SECOND SHIP'S LOG...
SO YOU DISCOVERED MY LITTLE SECRET!
NOT A WORD TO THE OTHERS! IT WILL BE OUR SECRET!
IN THIS OTHER LOG THAT THE CREW CHECKS EACH DAY, I RECORD A LESSER DISTANCE THAN THE ONE WE ACTUALLY TRAVEL!
... THAT WAY THE CREW WILL NOT BE ALARMED IF OUR VOYAGE TURNS OUT TO BE LONGER THAN ANTICIPATED!
THE WEATHER WAS PERFECT... THE SEA CALM... SO WHY WAS I SUDDENLY GRIPPED BY A FEELING OF UNEASE?
8

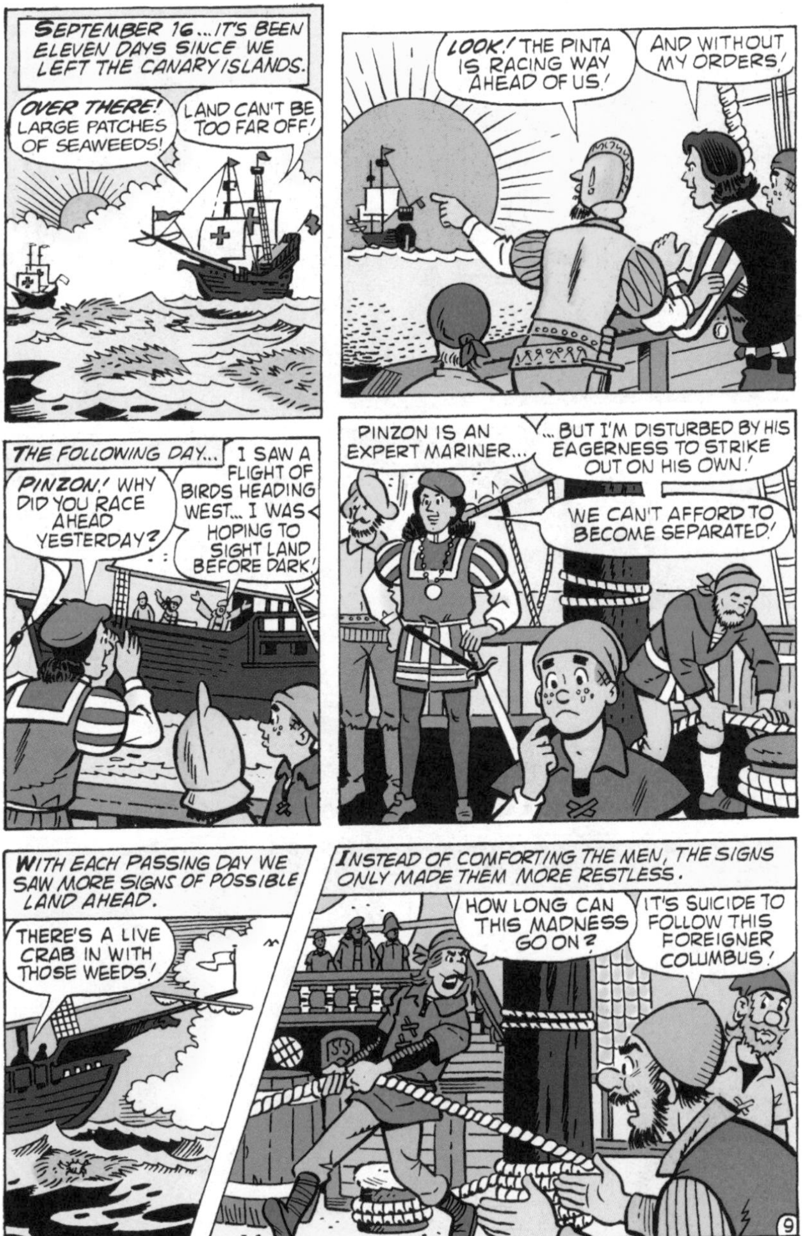
SEPTEMBER 16...IT'S BEEN ELEVEN DAYS SINCE WE LEFT THE CANARY ISLANDS.
OVER THERE! LARGE PATCHES OF SEAWEEDS!
LAND CAN'T BE TOO FAR OFF!
LOOK! THE PINTA IS RACING WAY AHEAD OF US!
AND WITHOUT MY ORDERS!
THE FOLLOWING DAY...
PINZON! WHY DID YOU RACE AHEAD YESTERDAY?
I SAW A FLIGHT OF BIRDS HEADING WEST... I WAS HOPING TO SIGHT LAND BEFORE DARK!
PINZON IS AN EXPERT MARINER...
...BUT I'M DISTURBED BY HIS EAGERNESS TO STRIKE OUT ON HIS OWN!
WE CAN'T AFFORD TO BECOME SEPARATED!
WITH EACH PASSING DAY WE SAW MORE SIGNS OF POSSIBLE LAND AHEAD.
THERE'S A LIVE CRAB IN WITH THOSE WEEDS!
INSTEAD OF COMFORTING THE MEN, THE SIGNS ONLY MADE THEM MORE RESTLESS.
HOW LONG CAN THIS MADNESS GO ON?
IT'S SUICIDE TO FOLLOW THIS FOREIGNER COLUMBUS!
9

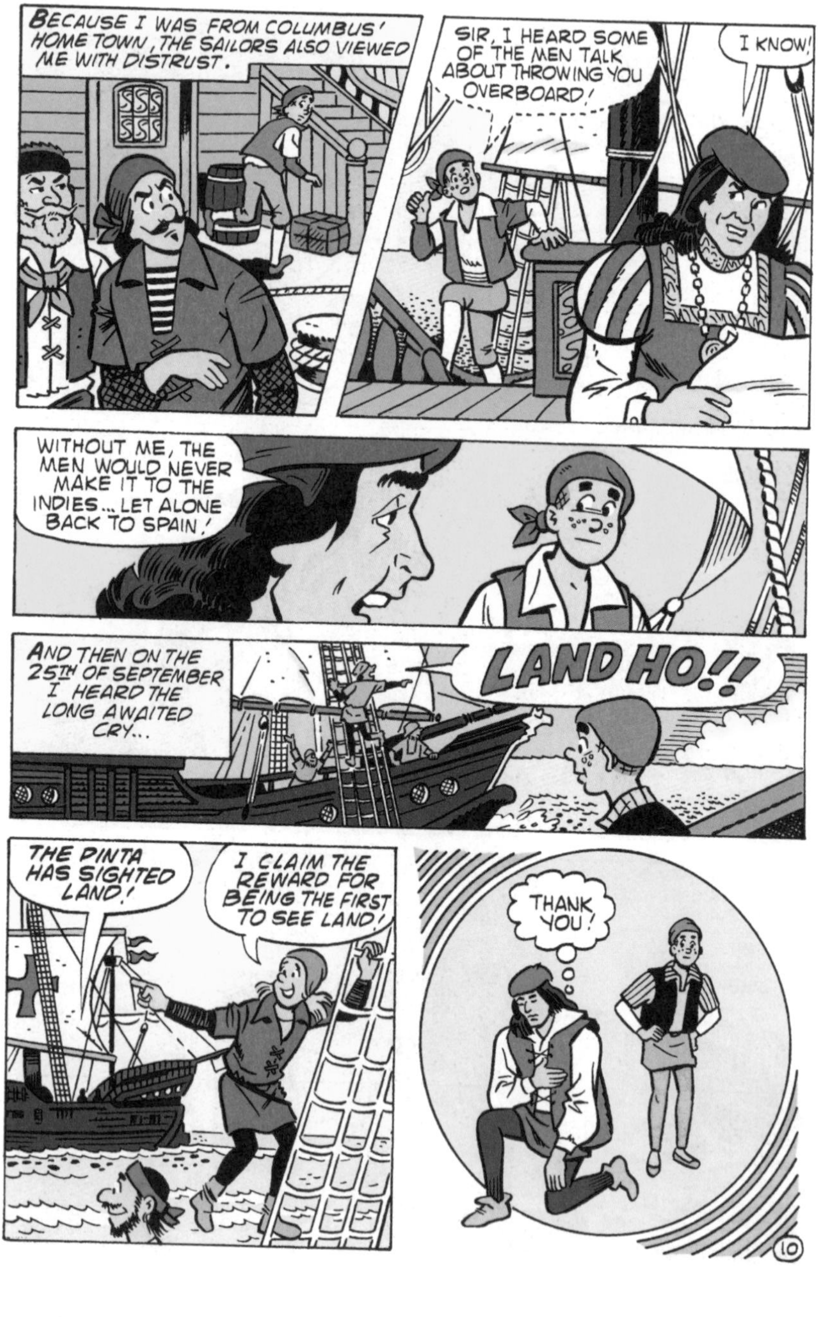

BECAUSE I WAS FROM COLUMBUS' HOME TOWN, THE SAILORS ALSO VIEWED ME WITH DISTRUST.
SIR, I HEARD SOME OF THE MEN TALK ABOUT THROWING YOU OVERBOARD!
I KNOW!
WITHOUT ME, THE MEN WOULD NEVER MAKE IT TO THE INDIES... LET ALONE BACK TO SPAIN!
AND THEN ON THE 25TH OF SEPTEMBER I HEARD THE LONG AWAITED CRY...
LAND HO!!
THE PINTA HAS SIGHTED LAND!
I CLAIM THE REWARD FOR BEING THE FIRST TO SEE LAND!
THANK YOU!
10

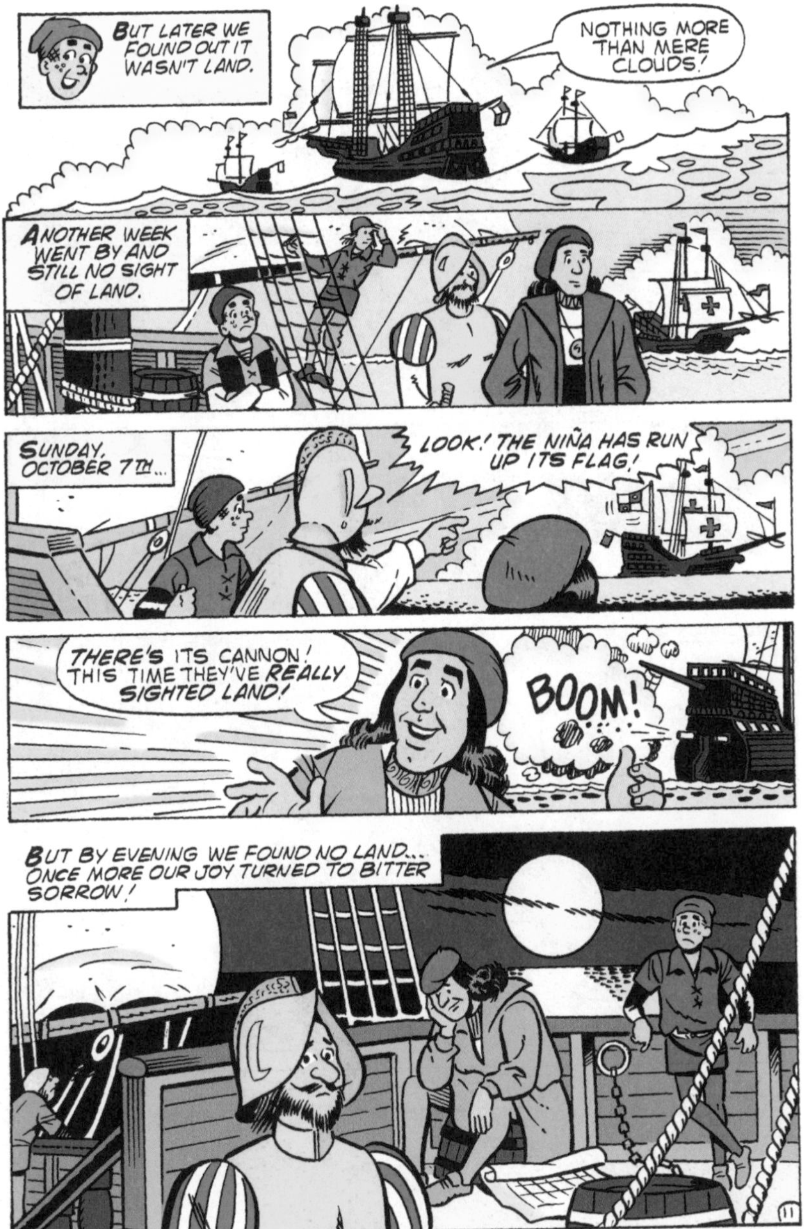
BUT LATER WE FOUND OUT IT WASN'T LAND.
NOTHING MORE THAN MERE CLOUDS!
ANOTHER WEEK WENT BY AND STILL NO SIGHT OF LAND.
SUNDAY, OCTOBER 7TH...
LOOK! THE NIÑA HAS RUN UP ITS FLAG!
THERE'S ITS CANNON! THIS TIME THEY'VE REALLY SIGHTED LAND!
BOOM!
BUT BY EVENING WE FOUND NO LAND... ONCE MORE OUR JOY TURNED TO BITTER SORROW!

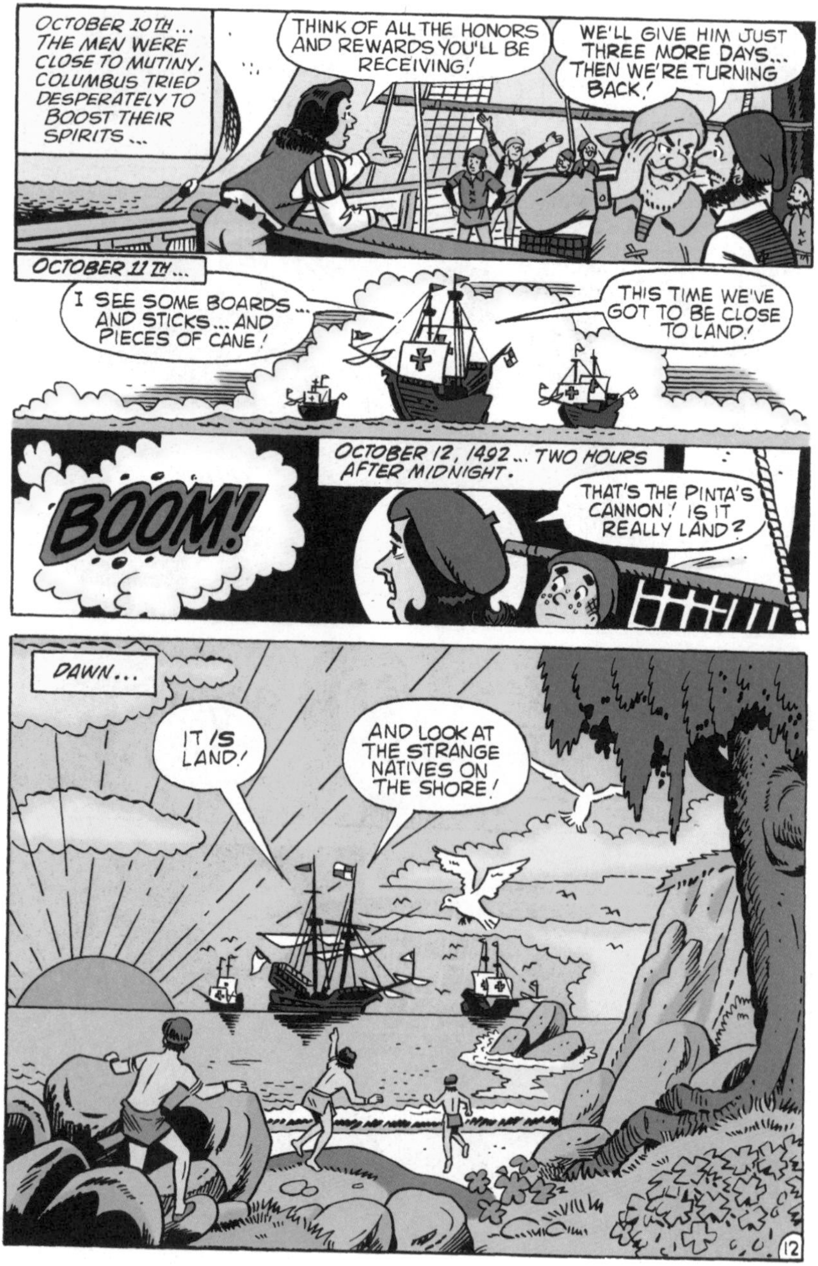
OCTOBER 10TH... THE MEN WERE CLOSE TO MUTINY. COLUMBUS TRIED DESPERATELY TO BOOST THEIR SPIRITS...
THINK OF ALL THE HONORS AND REWARDS YOU'LL BE RECEIVING!
WE'LL GIVE HIM JUST THREE MORE DAYS... THEN WE'RE TURNING BACK!
OCTOBER 11TH...
I SEE SOME BOARDS... AND STICKS... AND PIECES OF CANE!
THIS TIME WE'VE GOT TO BE CLOSE TO LAND!
BOOM!
OCTOBER 12, 1492... TWO HOURS AFTER MIDNIGHT.
THAT'S THE PINTA'S CANNON! IS IT REALLY LAND?
DAWN...
IT IS LAND!
AND LOOK AT THE STRANGE NATIVES ON THE SHORE!
12

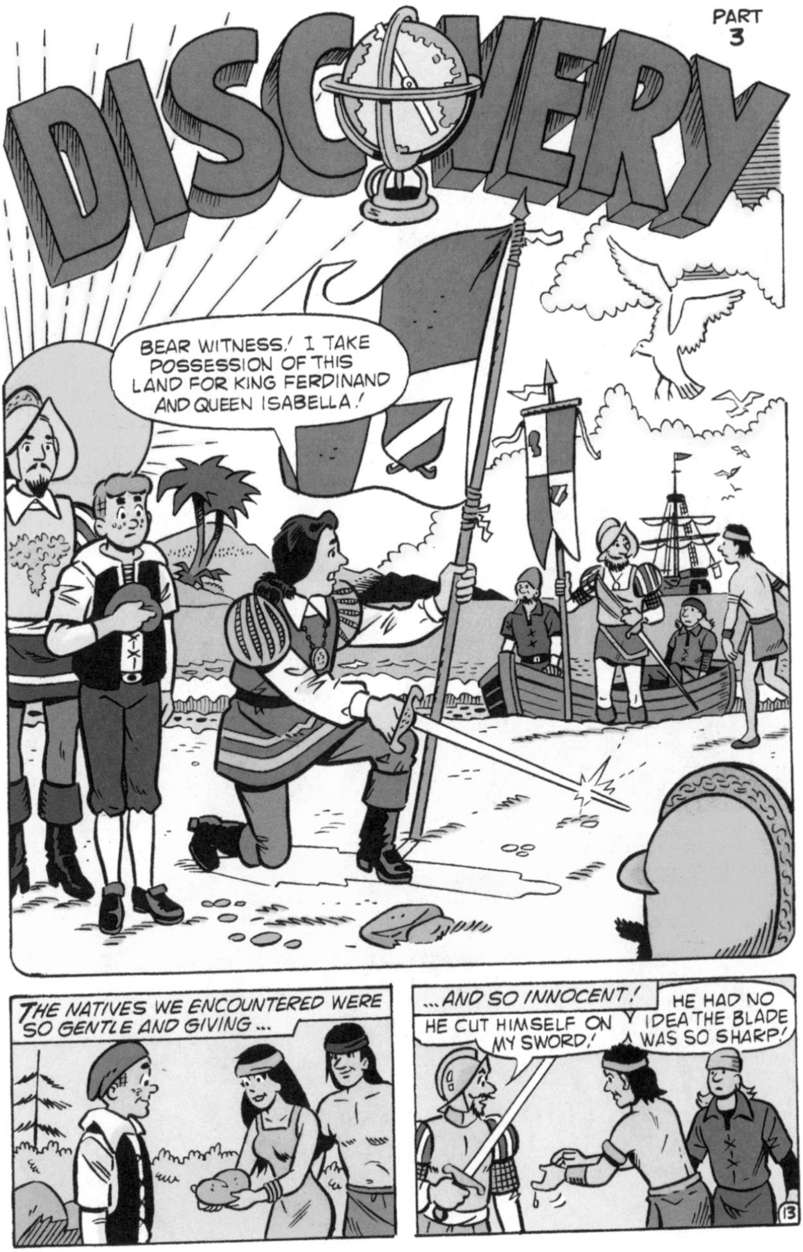
PART 3
DISCOVERY
BEAR WITNESS! I TAKE POSSESSION OF THIS LAND FOR KING FERDINAND AND QUEEN ISABELLA!
THE NATIVES WE ENCOUNTERED WERE SO GENTLE AND GIVING...
...AND SO INNOCENT!
HE CUT HIMSELF ON MY SWORD!
HE HAD NO IDEA THE BLADE WAS SO SHARP!
13

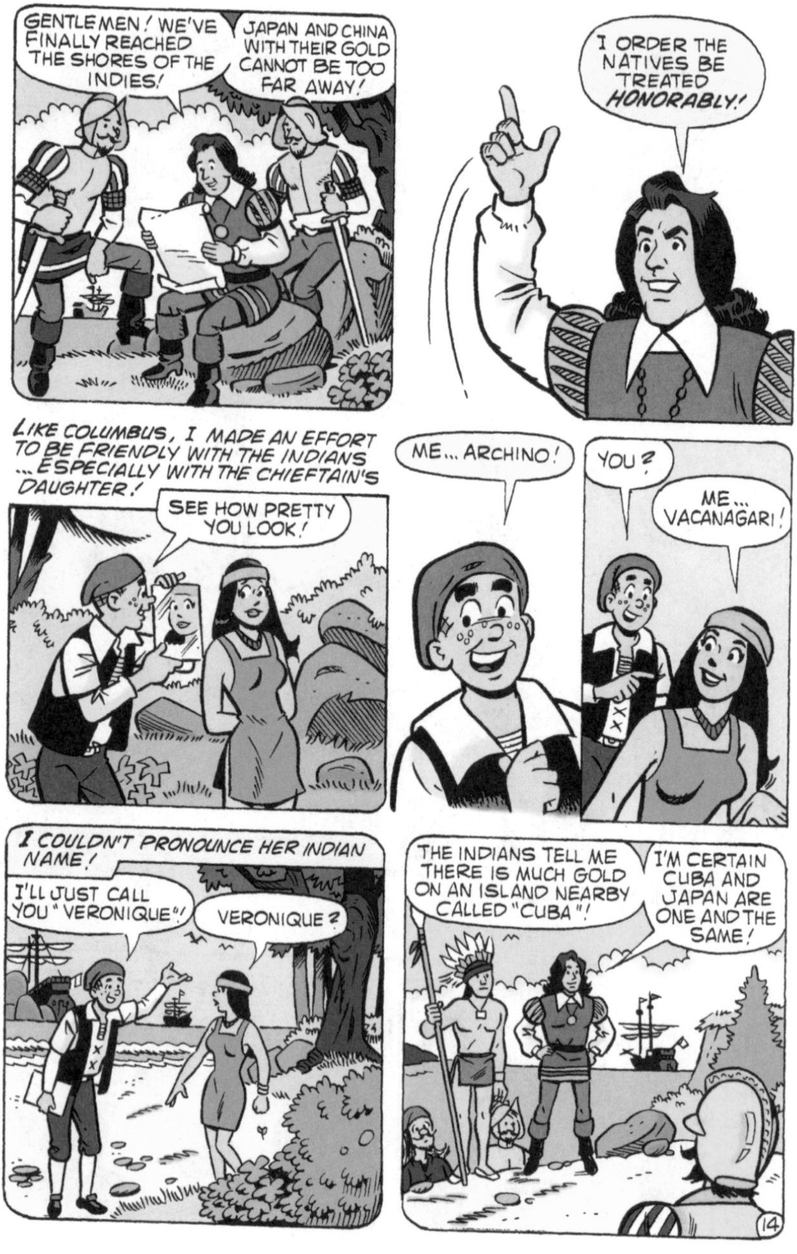
GENTLEMEN! WE'VE FINALLY REACHED THE SHORES OF THE INDIES!
JAPAN AND CHINA WITH THEIR GOLD CANNOT BE TOO FAR AWAY!
I ORDER THE NATIVES BE TREATED *HONORABLY!*
LIKE COLUMBUS, I MADE AN EFFORT TO BE FRIENDLY WITH THE INDIANS ...ESPECIALLY WITH THE CHIEFTAIN'S DAUGHTER!
SEE HOW PRETTY YOU LOOK!
ME... ARCHINO!
YOU?
ME... VACANAGARI!
I COULDN'T PRONOUNCE HER INDIAN NAME!
I'LL JUST CALL YOU "VERONIQUE"!
VERONIQUE?
THE INDIANS TELL ME THERE IS MUCH GOLD ON AN ISLAND NEARBY CALLED "CUBA"!
I'M CERTAIN CUBA AND JAPAN ARE ONE AND THE SAME!
14

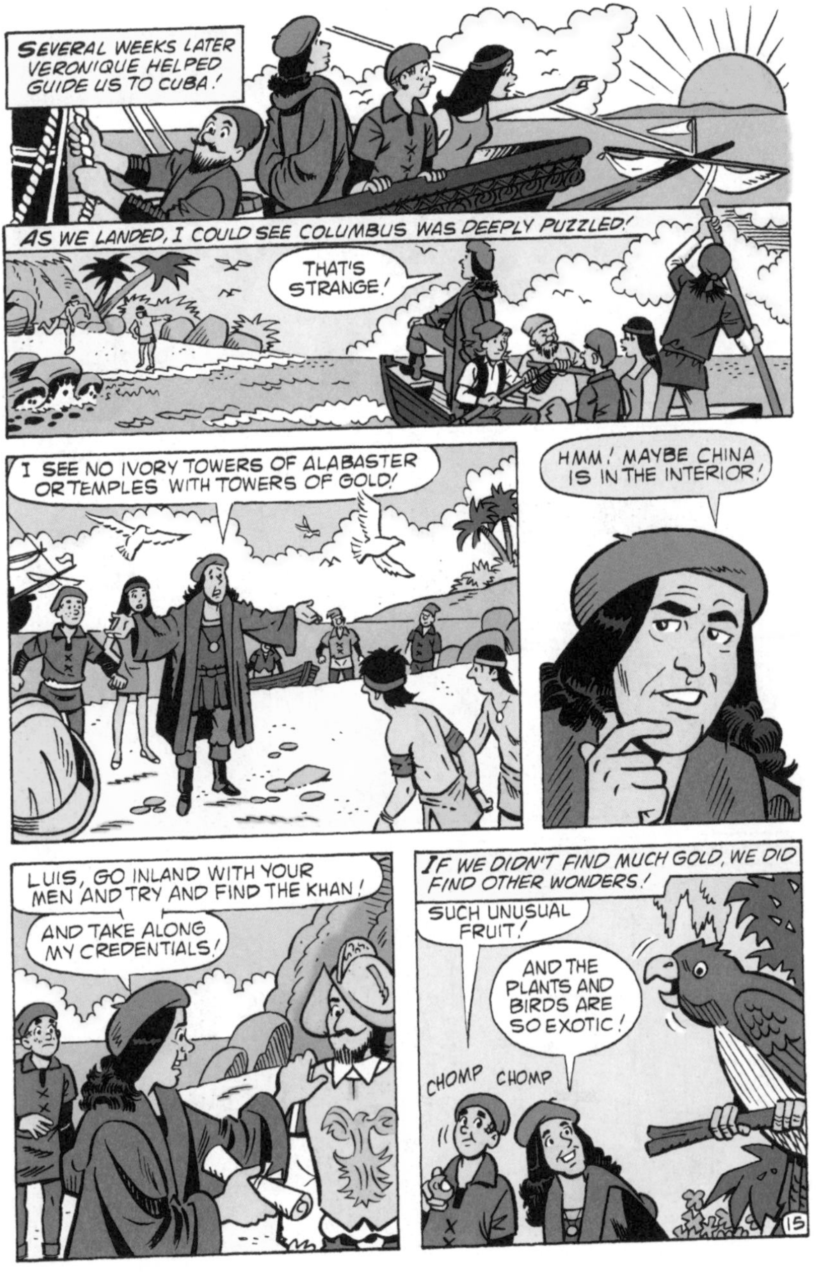
SEVERAL WEEKS LATER VERONIQUE HELPED GUIDE US TO CUBA!
AS WE LANDED, I COULD SEE COLUMBUS WAS DEEPLY PUZZLED!
THAT'S STRANGE!
I SEE NO IVORY TOWERS OF ALABASTER OR TEMPLES WITH TOWERS OF GOLD!
HMM! MAYBE CHINA IS IN THE INTERIOR!
LUIS, GO INLAND WITH YOUR MEN AND TRY AND FIND THE KHAN!
AND TAKE ALONG MY CREDENTIALS!
IF WE DIDN'T FIND MUCH GOLD, WE DID FIND OTHER WONDERS!
SUCH UNUSUAL FRUIT!
AND THE PLANTS AND BIRDS ARE SO EXOTIC!
CHOMP CHOMP
15

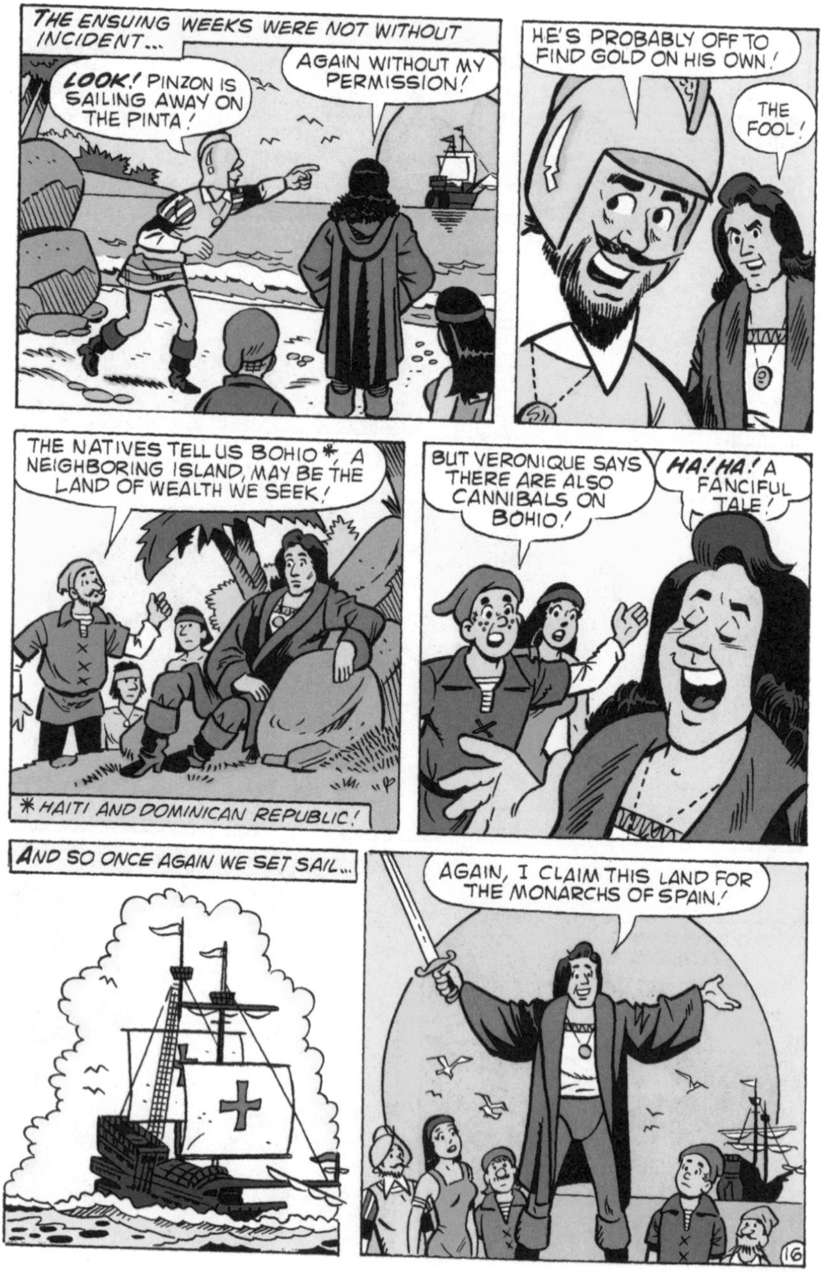
THE ENSUING WEEKS WERE NOT WITHOUT INCIDENT...
LOOK! PINZON IS SAILING AWAY ON THE PINTA!
AGAIN WITHOUT MY PERMISSION!
HE'S PROBABLY OFF TO FIND GOLD ON HIS OWN!
THE FOOL!
THE NATIVES TELL US BOHIO*, A NEIGHBORING ISLAND, MAY BE THE LAND OF WEALTH WE SEEK!
* HAITI AND DOMINICAN REPUBLIC!
BUT VERONIQUE SAYS THERE ARE ALSO CANNIBALS ON BOHIO!
HA! HA! A FANCIFUL TALE!
AND SO ONCE AGAIN WE SET SAIL...
AGAIN, I CLAIM THIS LAND FOR THE MONARCHS OF SPAIN!
16

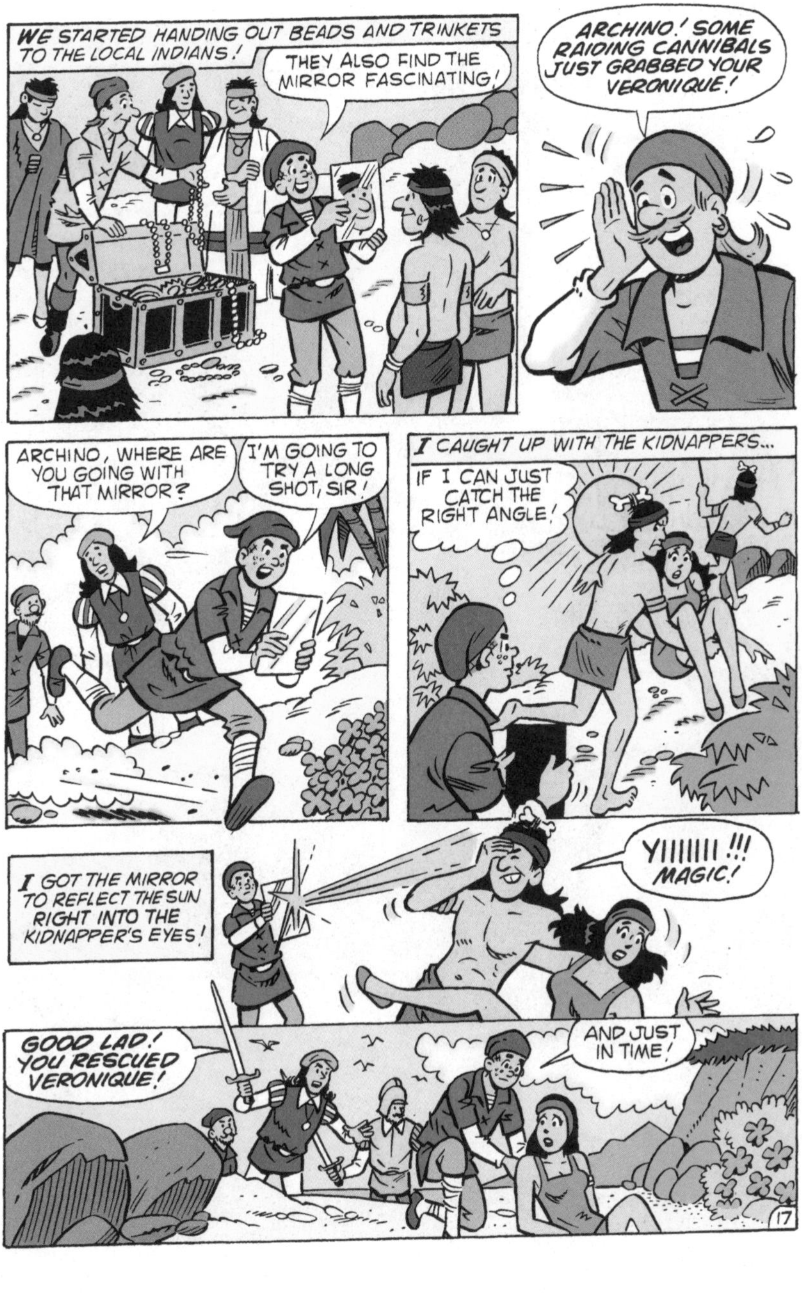
WE STARTED HANDING OUT BEADS AND TRINKETS TO THE LOCAL INDIANS!
THEY ALSO FIND THE MIRROR FASCINATING!
ARCHINO! SOME RAIDING CANNIBALS JUST GRABBED YOUR VERONIQUE!
ARCHINO, WHERE ARE YOU GOING WITH THAT MIRROR?
I'M GOING TO TRY A LONG SHOT, SIR!
I CAUGHT UP WITH THE KIDNAPPERS...
IF I CAN JUST CATCH THE RIGHT ANGLE!
I GOT THE MIRROR TO REFLECT THE SUN RIGHT INTO THE KIDNAPPER'S EYES!
YIIIIIII!!! MAGIC!
GOOD LAD! YOU RESCUED VERONIQUE!
AND JUST IN TIME!
17

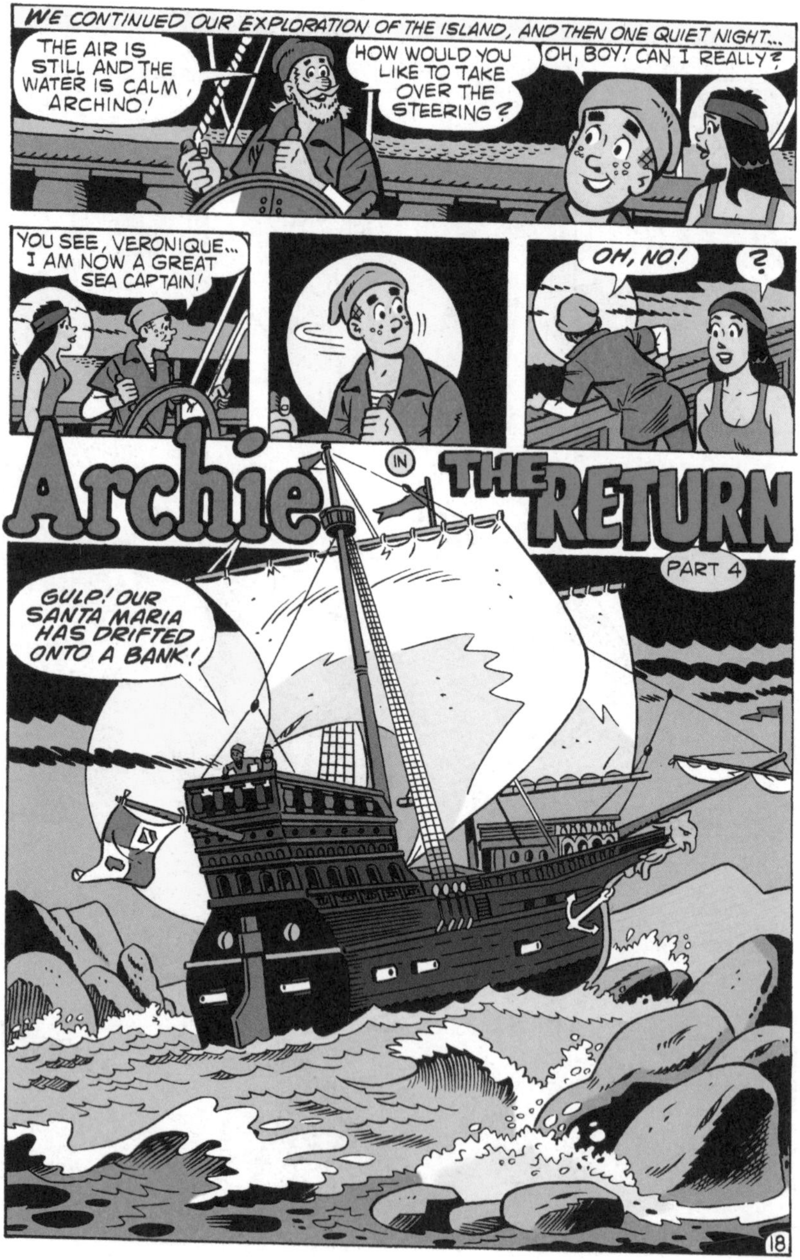
WE CONTINUED OUR EXPLORATION OF THE ISLAND, AND THEN ONE QUIET NIGHT...
THE AIR IS STILL AND THE WATER IS CALM, ARCHINO!
HOW WOULD YOU LIKE TO TAKE OVER THE STEERING?
OH, BOY! CAN I REALLY?
YOU SEE, VERONIQUE... I AM NOW A GREAT SEA CAPTAIN!
OH, NO!
?
Archie IN THE RETURN
PART 4
GULP! OUR SANTA MARIA HAS DRIFTED ONTO A BANK!
18

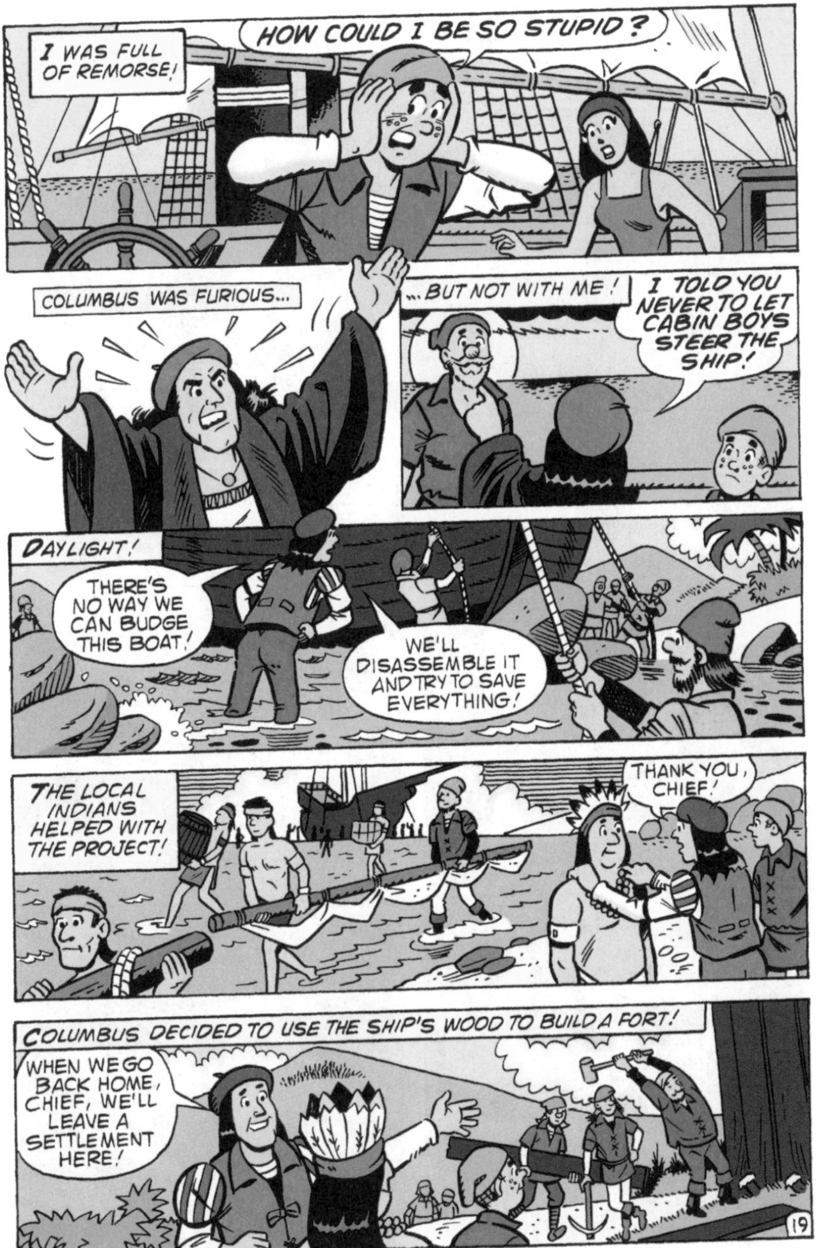
I WAS FULL OF REMORSE!
HOW COULD I BE SO STUPID?
COLUMBUS WAS FURIOUS...
...BUT NOT WITH ME!
I TOLD YOU NEVER TO LET CABIN BOYS STEER THE SHIP!
DAYLIGHT!
THERE'S NO WAY WE CAN BUDGE THIS BOAT!
WE'LL DISASSEMBLE IT AND TRY TO SAVE EVERYTHING!
THE LOCAL INDIANS HELPED WITH THE PROJECT!
THANK YOU, CHIEF!
COLUMBUS DECIDED TO USE THE SHIP'S WOOD TO BUILD A FORT!
WHEN WE GO BACK HOME, CHIEF, WE'LL LEAVE A SETTLEMENT HERE!
19

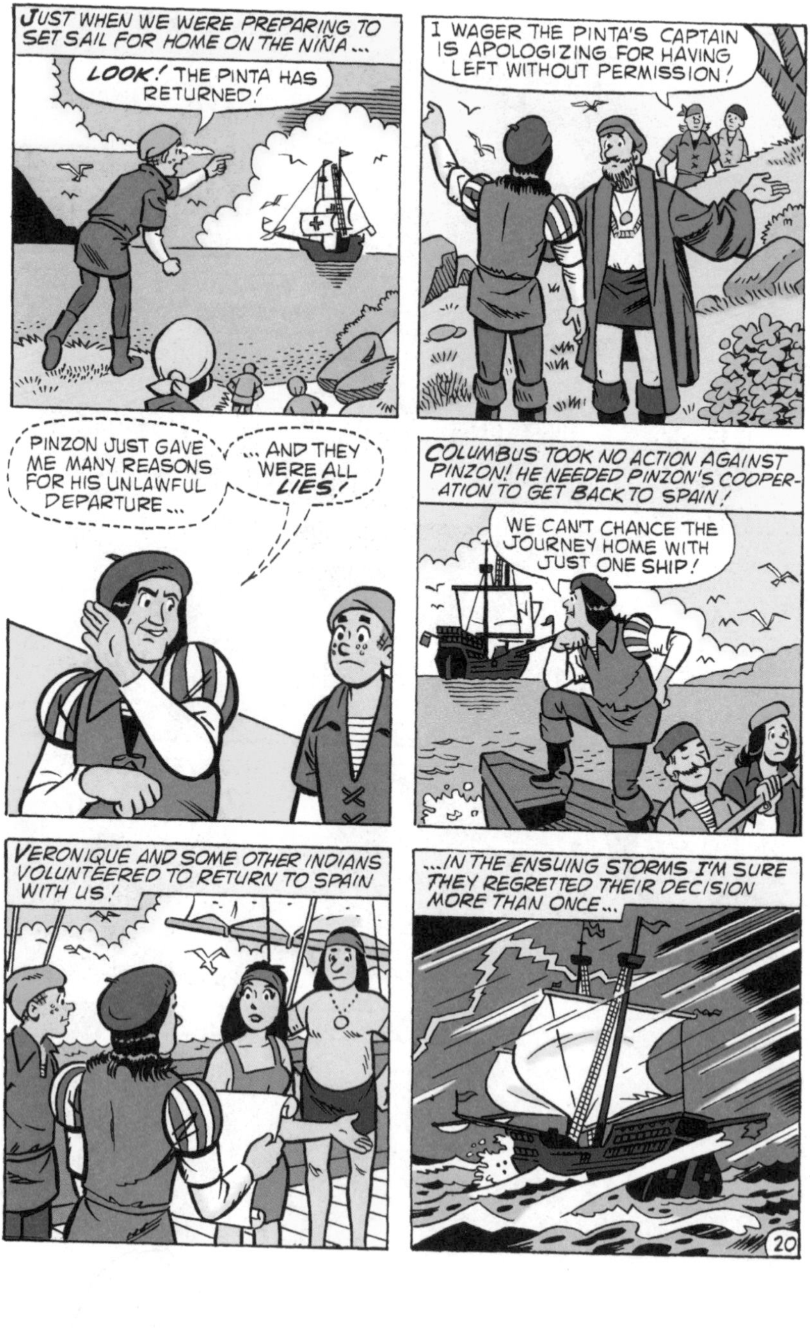
JUST WHEN WE WERE PREPARING TO SET SAIL FOR HOME ON THE NIÑA...
LOOK! THE PINTA HAS RETURNED!
I WAGER THE PINTA'S CAPTAIN IS APOLOGIZING FOR HAVING LEFT WITHOUT PERMISSION!
PINZON JUST GAVE ME MANY REASONS FOR HIS UNLAWFUL DEPARTURE...
...AND THEY WERE ALL LIES!
COLUMBUS TOOK NO ACTION AGAINST PINZON! HE NEEDED PINZON'S COOPERATION TO GET BACK TO SPAIN!
WE CAN'T CHANCE THE JOURNEY HOME WITH JUST ONE SHIP!
VERONIQUE AND SOME OTHER INDIANS VOLUNTEERED TO RETURN TO SPAIN WITH US!
...IN THE ENSUING STORMS I'M SURE THEY REGRETTED THEIR DECISION MORE THAN ONCE...
20

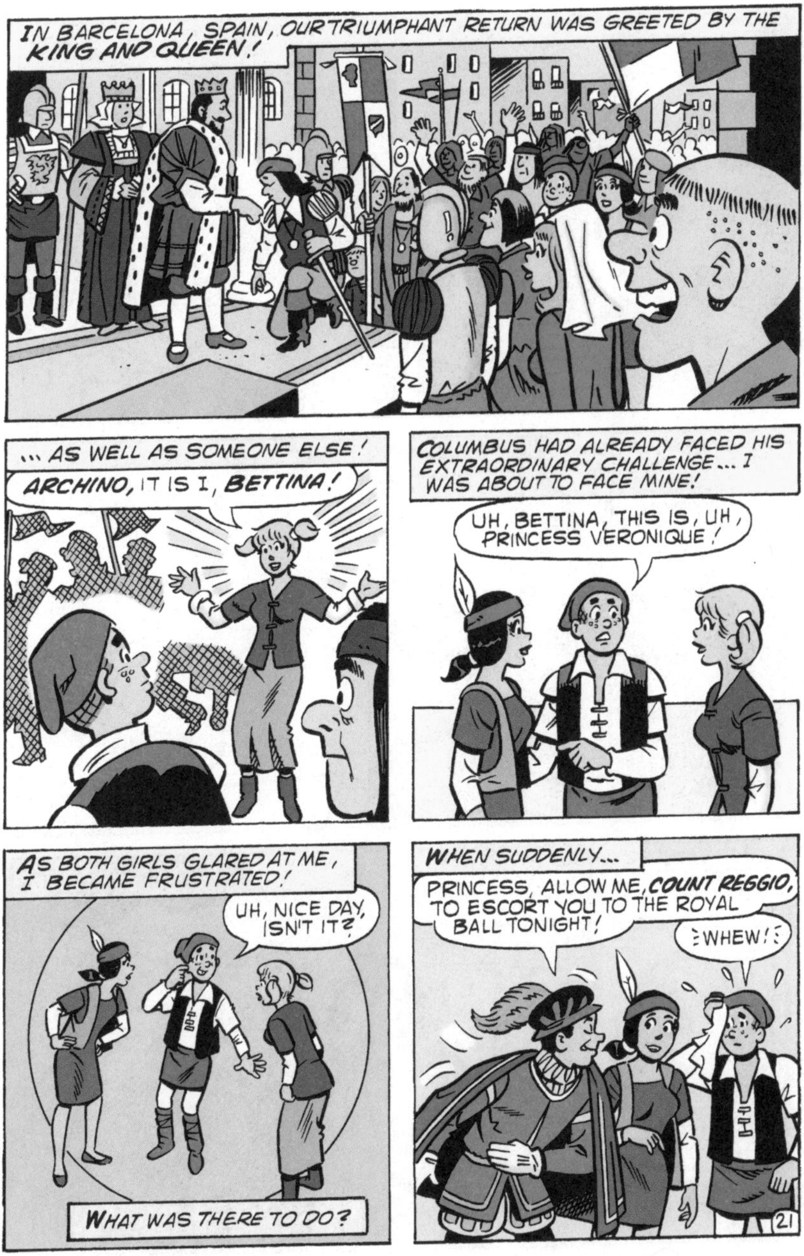
IN BARCELONA, SPAIN, OUR TRIUMPHANT RETURN WAS GREETED BY THE KING AND QUEEN!
... AS WELL AS SOMEONE ELSE!
ARCHINO, IT IS I, BETTINA!
COLUMBUS HAD ALREADY FACED HIS EXTRAORDINARY CHALLENGE... I WAS ABOUT TO FACE MINE!
UH, BETTINA, THIS IS, UH, PRINCESS VERONIQUE!
AS BOTH GIRLS GLARED AT ME, I BECAME FRUSTRATED!
UH, NICE DAY, ISN'T IT?
WHAT WAS THERE TO DO?
WHEN SUDDENLY...
PRINCESS, ALLOW ME, COUNT REGGIO, TO ESCORT YOU TO THE ROYAL BALL TONIGHT!
WHEW!
21

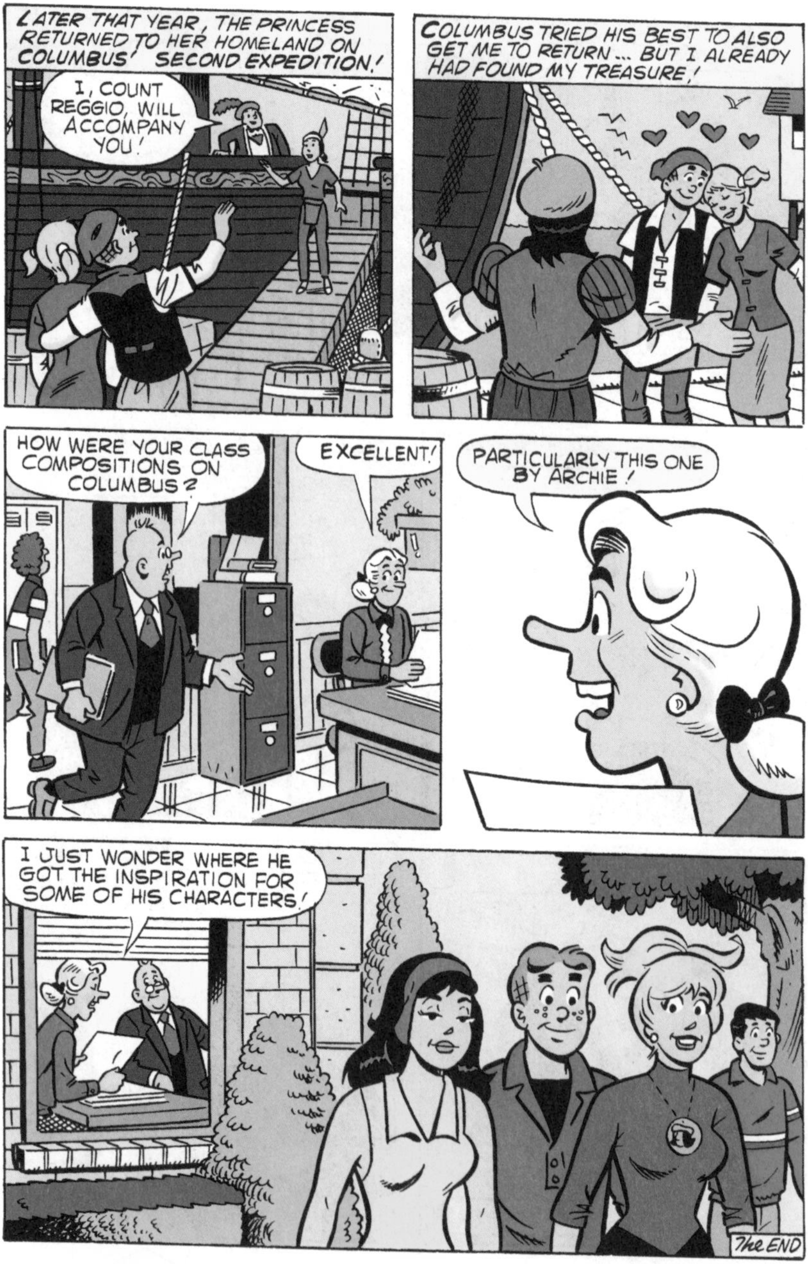
LATER THAT YEAR, THE PRINCESS RETURNED TO HER HOMELAND ON COLUMBUS' SECOND EXPEDITION!
I, COUNT REGGIO, WILL ACCOMPANY YOU!
COLUMBUS TRIED HIS BEST TO ALSO GET ME TO RETURN ... BUT I ALREADY HAD FOUND MY TREASURE!
HOW WERE YOUR CLASS COMPOSITIONS ON COLUMBUS?
EXCELLENT!
PARTICULARLY THIS ONE BY ARCHIE!
I JUST WONDER WHERE HE GOT THE INSPIRATION FOR SOME OF HIS CHARACTERS!
The END

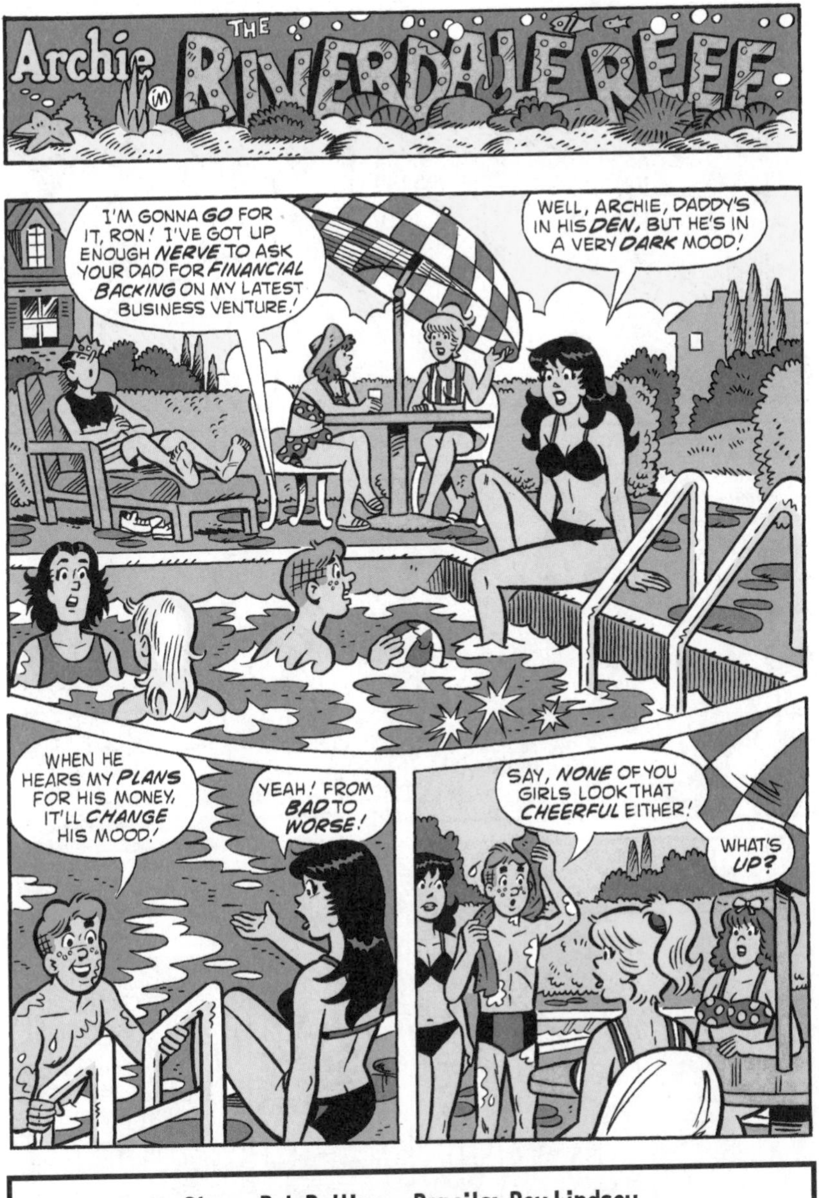
Archie in THE RIVERDALE REEF
I'M GONNA GO FOR IT, RON! I'VE GOT UP ENOUGH NERVE TO ASK YOUR DAD FOR FINANCIAL BACKING ON MY LATEST BUSINESS VENTURE!
WELL, ARCHIE, DADDY'S IN HIS DEN, BUT HE'S IN A VERY DARK MOOD!
WHEN HE HEARS MY PLANS FOR HIS MONEY, IT'LL CHANGE HIS MOOD!
YEAH! FROM BAD TO WORSE!
SAY, NONE OF YOU GIRLS LOOK THAT CHEERFUL EITHER!
WHAT'S UP?

Story: Bob Bolling Pencils: Rex Lindsey
Inks: Rudy Lapick Letters: Bill Yoshida Colors: Dan Parent

Originally printed in WORLD OF ARCHIE #2, NOVEMBER 1992

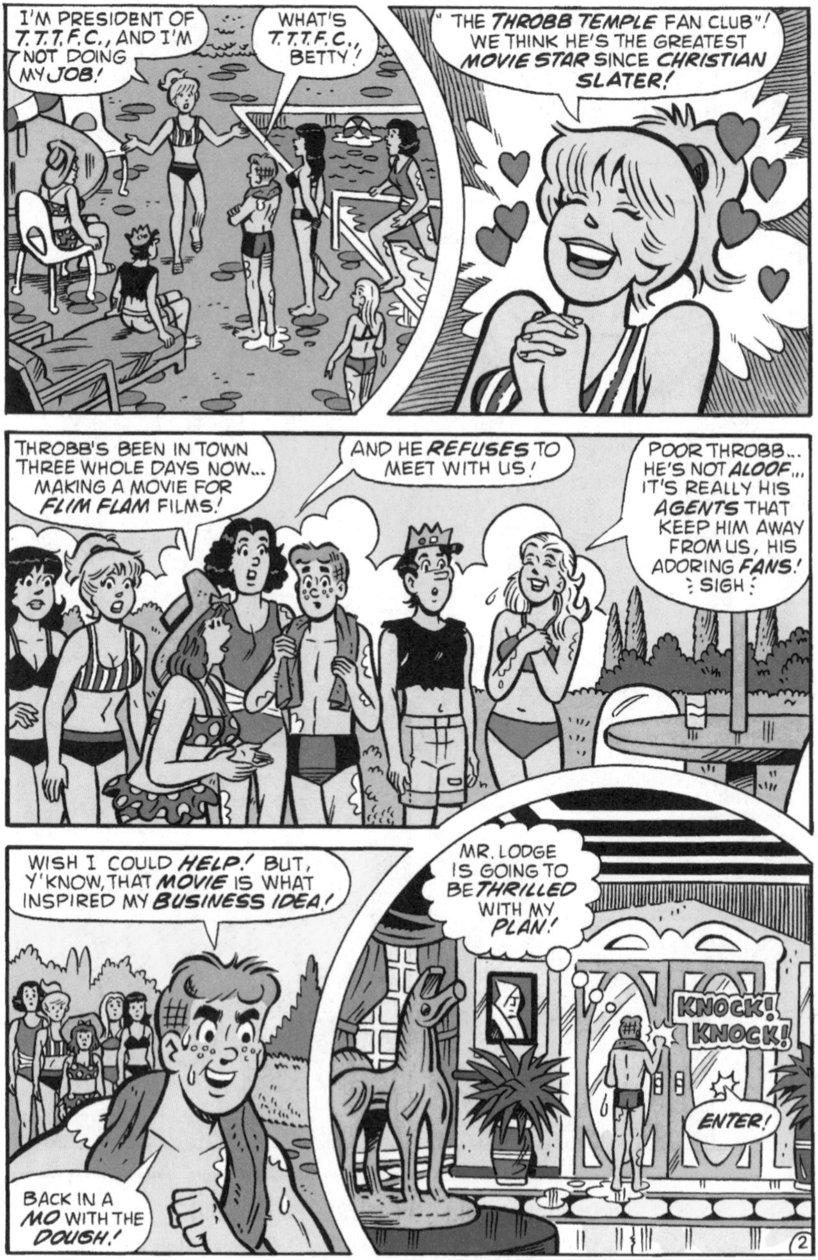
I'M PRESIDENT OF T.T.T.F.C., AND I'M NOT DOING MY JOB!
WHAT'S T.T.T.F.C., BETTY?
" THE THROBB TEMPLE FAN CLUB"! WE THINK HE'S THE GREATEST MOVIE STAR SINCE CHRISTIAN SLATER!
THROBB'S BEEN IN TOWN THREE WHOLE DAYS NOW... MAKING A MOVIE FOR FLIM FLAM FILMS!
AND HE REFUSES TO MEET WITH US!
POOR THROBB... HE'S NOT ALOOF... IT'S REALLY HIS AGENTS THAT KEEP HIM AWAY FROM US, HIS ADORING FANS!
SIGH
WISH I COULD HELP! BUT, Y'KNOW, THAT MOVIE IS WHAT INSPIRED MY BUSINESS IDEA!
BACK IN A MO WITH THE DOUGH!
MR. LODGE IS GOING TO BE THRILLED WITH MY PLAN!
KNOCK! KNOCK!
ENTER!
2

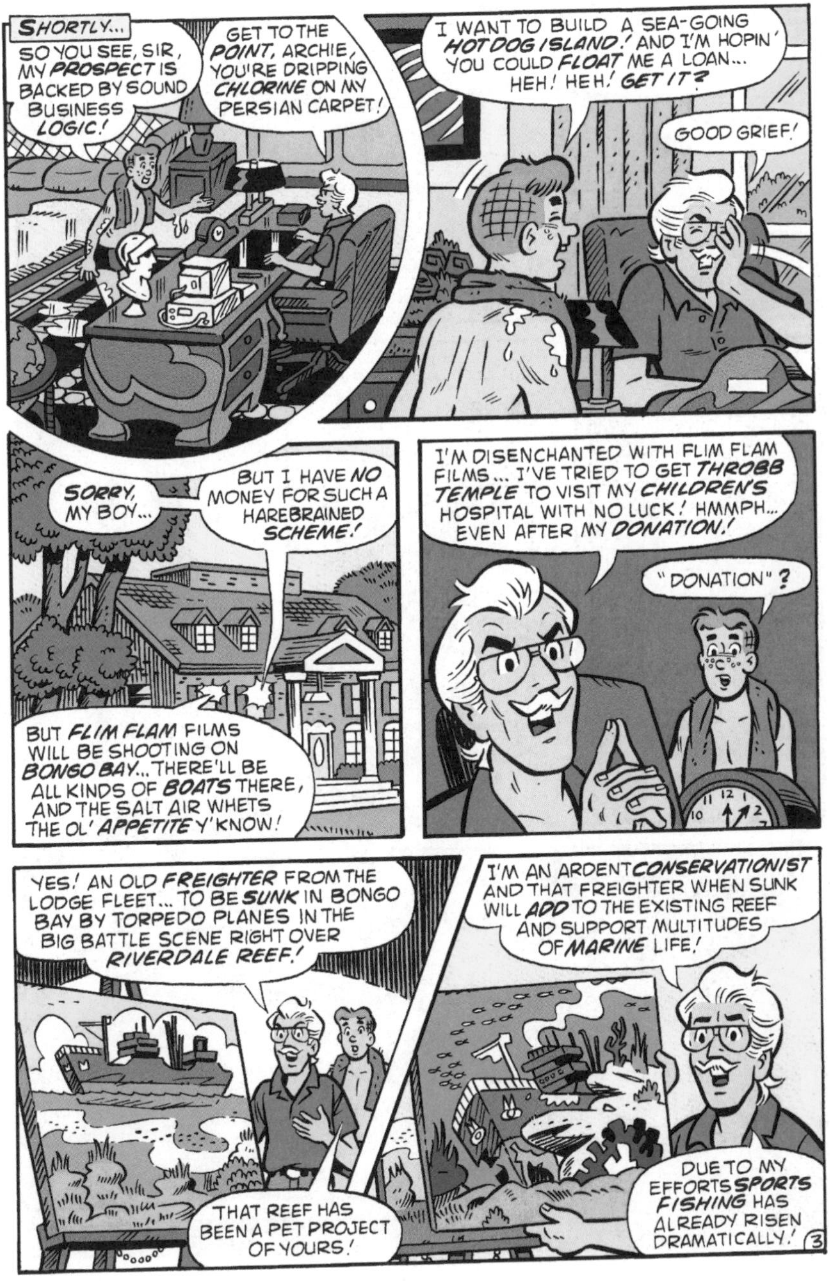
SHORTLY...
SO YOU SEE, SIR, MY PROSPECT IS BACKED BY SOUND BUSINESS LOGIC!
GET TO THE POINT, ARCHIE, YOU'RE DRIPPING CHLORINE ON MY PERSIAN CARPET!
I WANT TO BUILD A SEA-GOING HOT DOG ISLAND! AND I'M HOPIN' YOU COULD FLOAT ME A LOAN... HEH! HEH! GET IT?
GOOD GRIEF!
SORRY, MY BOY...
BUT I HAVE NO MONEY FOR SUCH A HAREBRAINED SCHEME!
BUT FLIM FLAM FILMS WILL BE SHOOTING ON BONGO BAY... THERE'LL BE ALL KINDS OF BOATS THERE, AND THE SALT AIR WHETS THE OL' APPETITE Y'KNOW!
I'M DISENCHANTED WITH FLIM FLAM FILMS... I'VE TRIED TO GET THROBB TEMPLE TO VISIT MY CHILDREN'S HOSPITAL WITH NO LUCK! HMMPH... EVEN AFTER MY DONATION!
"DONATION"?
YES! AN OLD FREIGHTER FROM THE LODGE FLEET... TO BE SUNK IN BONGO BAY BY TORPEDO PLANES IN THE BIG BATTLE SCENE RIGHT OVER RIVERDALE REEF!
THAT REEF HAS BEEN A PET PROJECT OF YOURS!
I'M AN ARDENT CONSERVATIONIST AND THAT FREIGHTER WHEN SUNK WILL ADD TO THE EXISTING REEF AND SUPPORT MULTITUDES OF MARINE LIFE!
DUE TO MY EFFORTS SPORTS FISHING HAS ALREADY RISEN DRAMATICALLY!
3

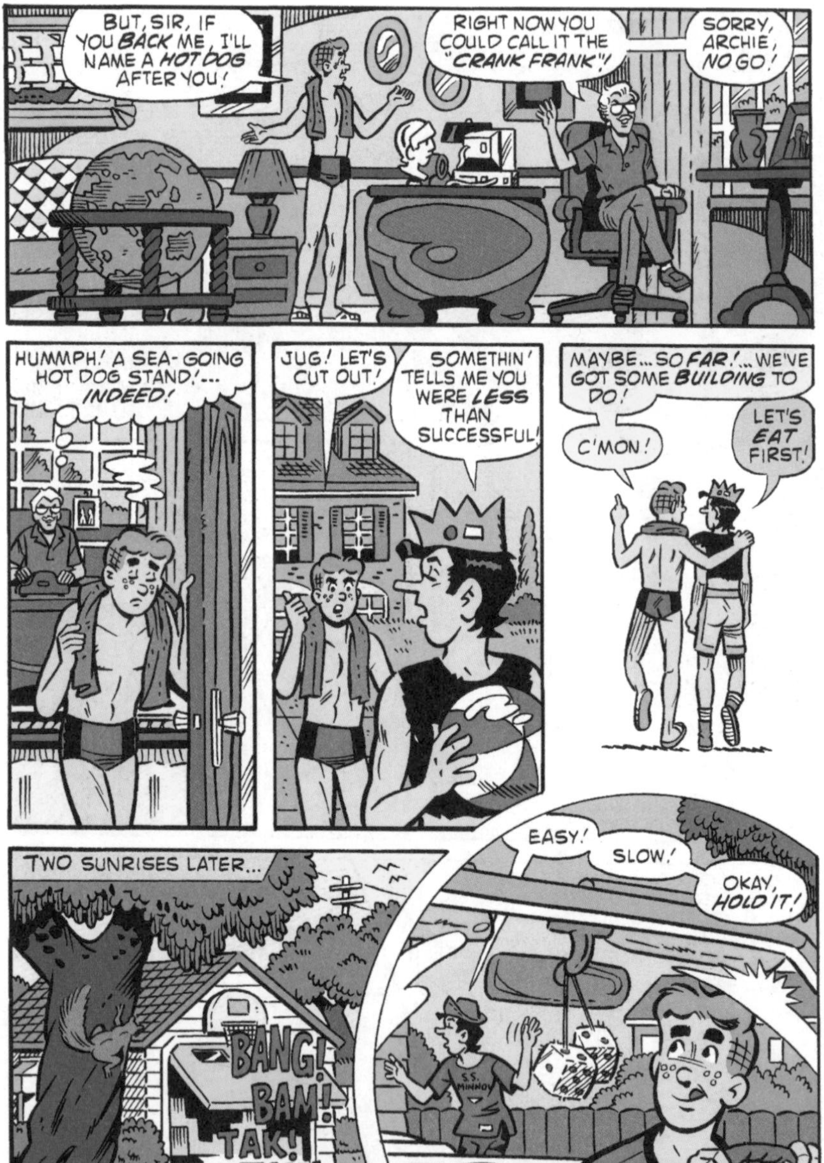
BUT, SIR, IF YOU BACK ME, I'LL NAME A HOT DOG AFTER YOU!
RIGHT NOW YOU COULD CALL IT THE "CRANK FRANK"!
SORRY, ARCHIE, NO GO!
HUMMPH! A SEA-GOING HOT DOG STAND!... INDEED!
JUG! LET'S CUT OUT!
SOMETHIN' TELLS ME YOU WERE LESS THAN SUCCESSFUL!
MAYBE... SO FAR!... WE'VE GOT SOME BUILDING TO DO!
C'MON!
LET'S EAT FIRST!
TWO SUNRISES LATER...
BANG! BAM! TAK! TAK!
EASY!
SLOW!
OKAY, HOLD IT!
S.S. MINNOW
4

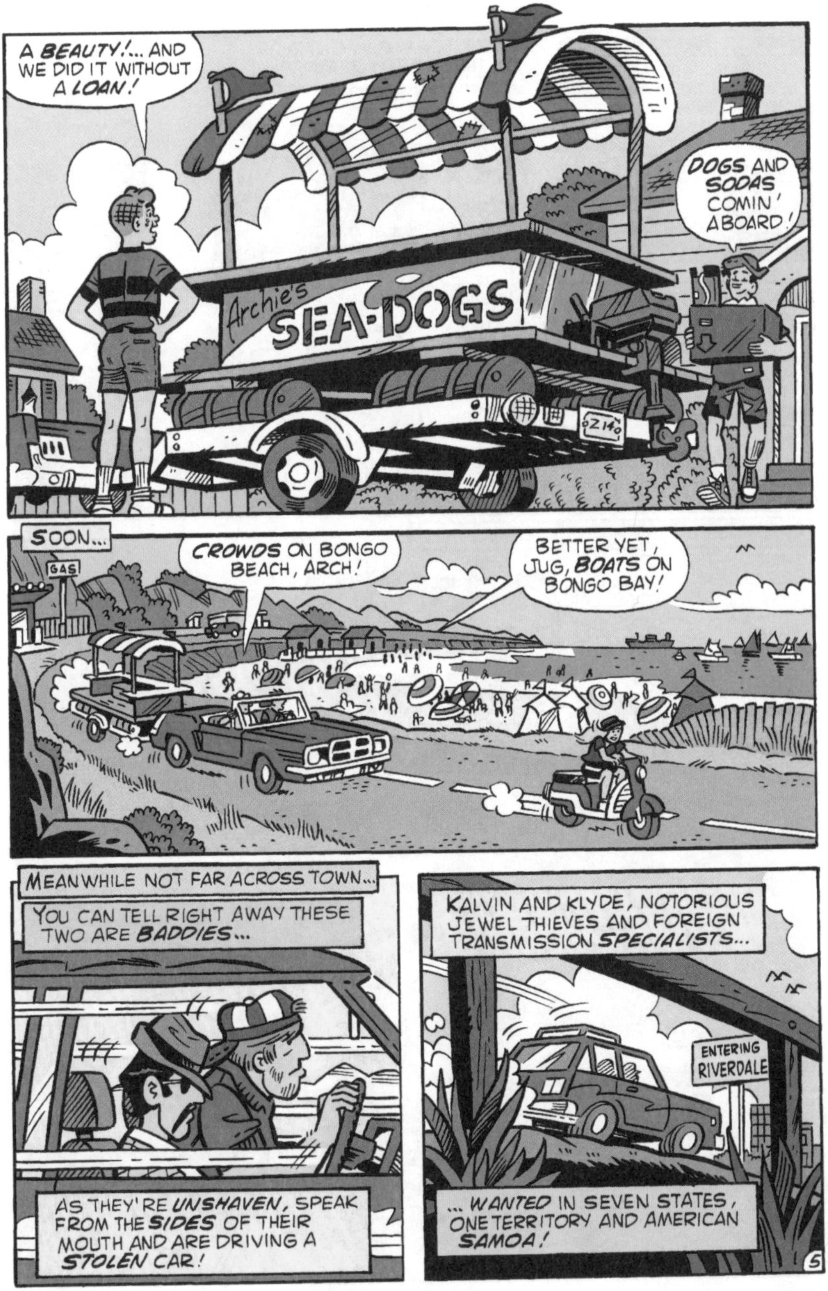
A BEAUTY!... AND WE DID IT WITHOUT A LOAN!
Archie's SEA-DOGS
Z 14
DOGS AND SODAS COMIN' ABOARD!
SOON...
GAS
CROWDS ON BONGO BEACH, ARCH!
BETTER YET, JUG, BOATS ON BONGO BAY!
MEANWHILE NOT FAR ACROSS TOWN...
YOU CAN TELL RIGHT AWAY THESE TWO ARE BADDIES...
AS THEY'RE UNSHAVEN, SPEAK FROM THE SIDES OF THEIR MOUTH AND ARE DRIVING A STOLEN CAR!
KALVIN AND KLYDE, NOTORIOUS JEWEL THIEVES AND FOREIGN TRANSMISSION SPECIALISTS...
ENTERING RIVERDALE
...WANTED IN SEVEN STATES, ONE TERRITORY AND AMERICAN SAMOA!
5

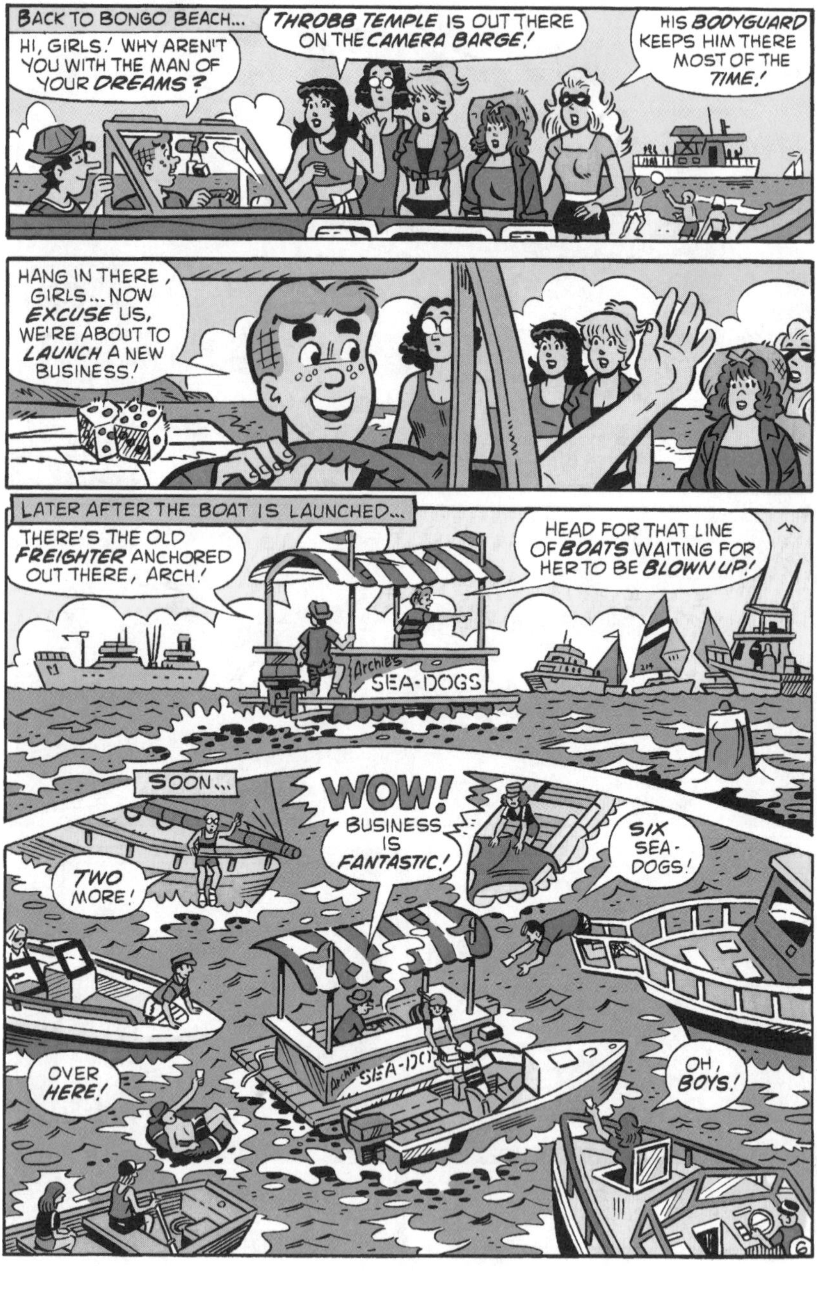
BACK TO BONGO BEACH...
HI, GIRLS! WHY AREN'T YOU WITH THE MAN OF YOUR DREAMS?
THROBB TEMPLE IS OUT THERE ON THE CAMERA BARGE!
HIS BODYGUARD KEEPS HIM THERE MOST OF THE TIME!
HANG IN THERE, GIRLS... NOW EXCUSE US, WE'RE ABOUT TO LAUNCH A NEW BUSINESS!
LATER AFTER THE BOAT IS LAUNCHED...
THERE'S THE OLD FREIGHTER ANCHORED OUT THERE, ARCH!
HEAD FOR THAT LINE OF BOATS WAITING FOR HER TO BE BLOWN UP!
Archie's SEA-DOGS
SOON...
WOW! BUSINESS IS FANTASTIC!
TWO MORE!
SIX SEA-DOGS!
OVER HERE!
OH, BOYS!

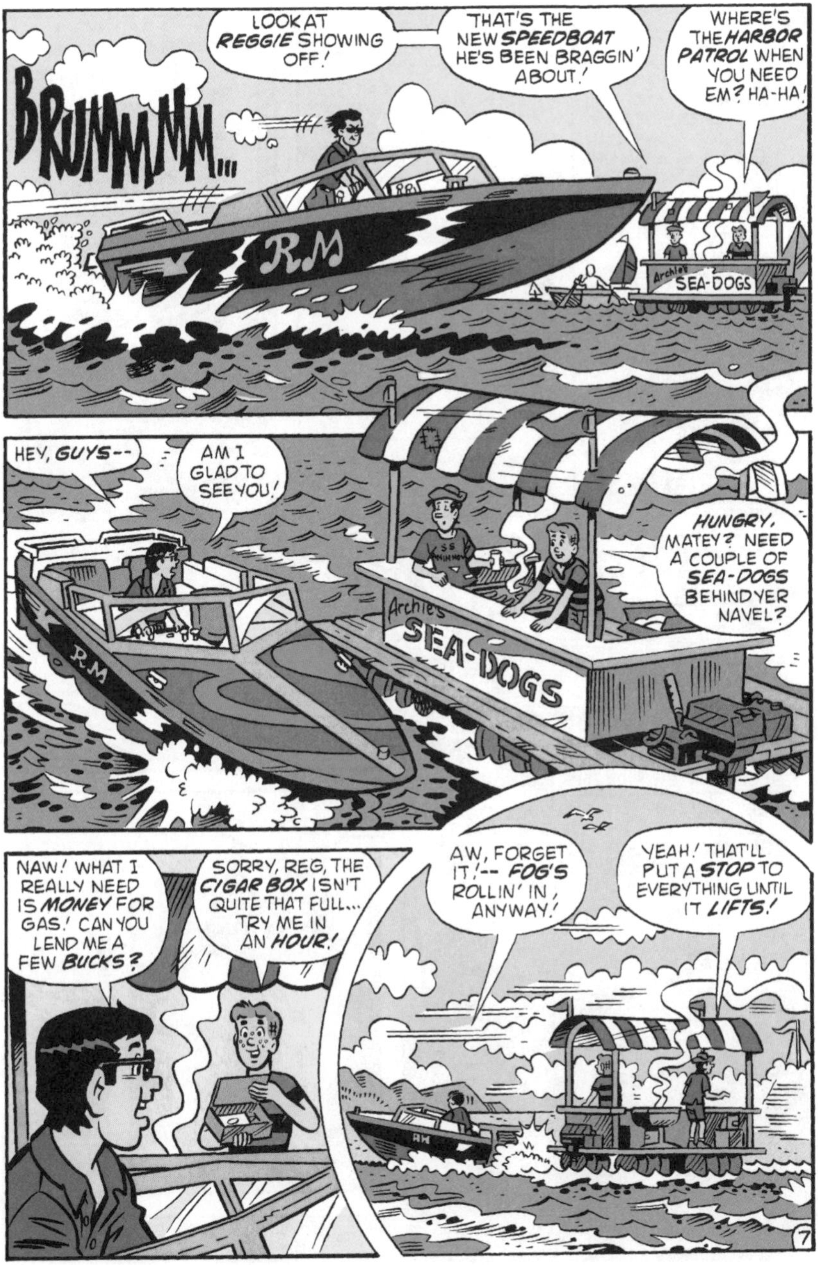
BRUMMMM...
LOOK AT REGGIE SHOWING OFF!
THAT'S THE NEW SPEEDBOAT HE'S BEEN BRAGGIN' ABOUT!
WHERE'S THE HARBOR PATROL WHEN YOU NEED EM? HA-HA!
Archie's SEA-DOGS
HEY, GUYS--
AM I GLAD TO SEE YOU!
HUNGRY, MATEY? NEED A COUPLE OF SEA-DOGS BEHIND YER NAVEL?
Archie's SEA-DOGS
NAW! WHAT I REALLY NEED IS MONEY FOR GAS! CAN YOU LEND ME A FEW BUCKS?
SORRY, REG, THE CIGAR BOX ISN'T QUITE THAT FULL... TRY ME IN AN HOUR!
AW, FORGET IT!-- FOG'S ROLLIN' IN, ANYWAY!
YEAH! THAT'LL PUT A STOP TO EVERYTHING UNTIL IT LIFTS!
7

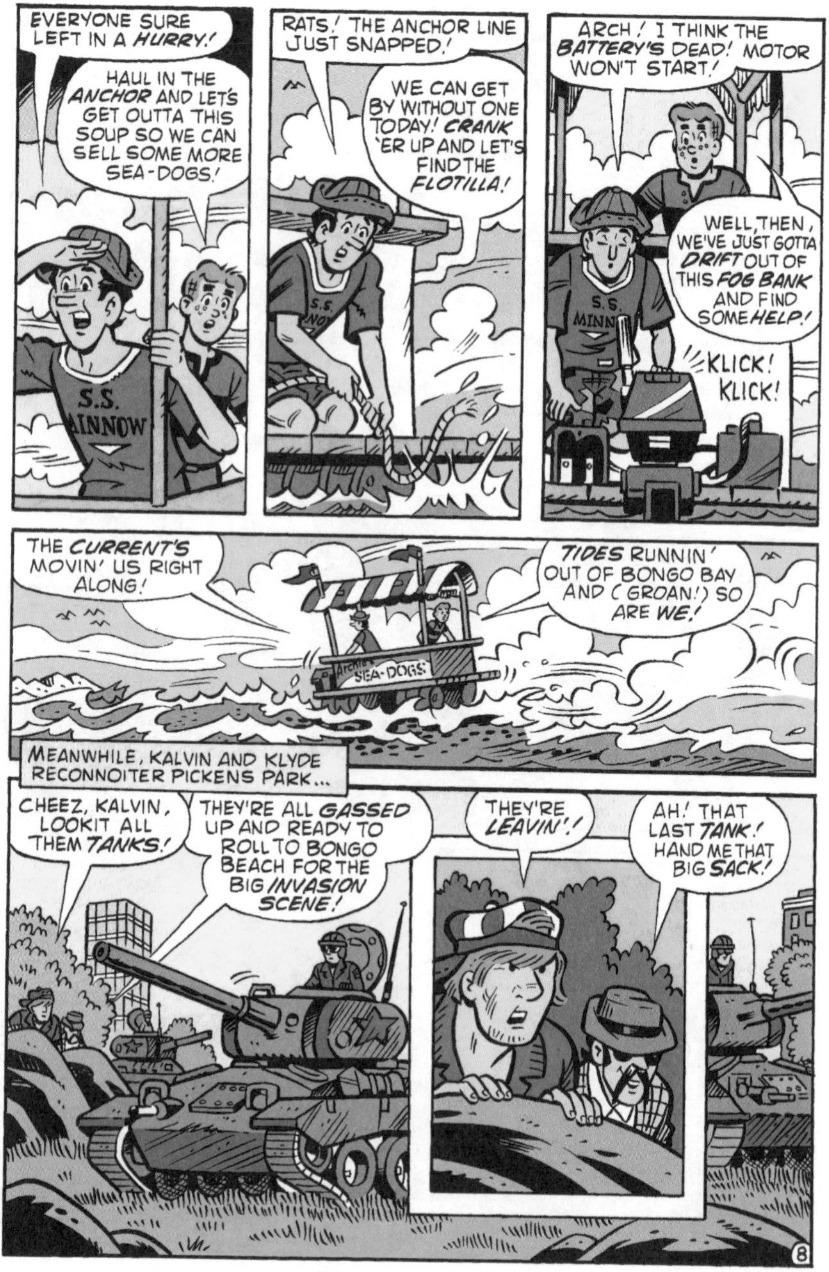
EVERYONE SURE LEFT IN A *HURRY!*
HAUL IN THE *ANCHOR* AND LET'S GET OUTTA THIS SOUP SO WE CAN SELL SOME MORE SEA-DOGS!
S.S. MINNOW
RATS! THE ANCHOR LINE JUST SNAPPED!
WE CAN GET BY WITHOUT ONE TODAY! *CRANK* 'ER UP AND LET'S FIND THE *FLOTILLA!*
ARCH! I THINK THE *BATTERY'S* DEAD! MOTOR WON'T START!
WELL, THEN, WE'VE JUST GOTTA *DRIFT* OUT OF THIS *FOG BANK* AND FIND SOME *HELP!*
KLICK! KLICK!
THE *CURRENT'S* MOVIN' US RIGHT ALONG!
TIDES RUNNIN' OUT OF BONGO BAY AND (GROAN!) SO ARE *WE!*
Archie's SEA-DOGS
MEANWHILE, KALVIN AND KLYDE RECONNOITER PICKENS PARK...
CHEEZ, KALVIN, LOOKIT ALL THEM *TANKS!*
THEY'RE ALL *GASSED* UP AND READY TO ROLL TO BONGO BEACH FOR THE BIG *INVASION SCENE!*
THEY'RE *LEAVIN'!*
AH! THAT LAST *TANK!* HAND ME THAT BIG *SACK!*
8

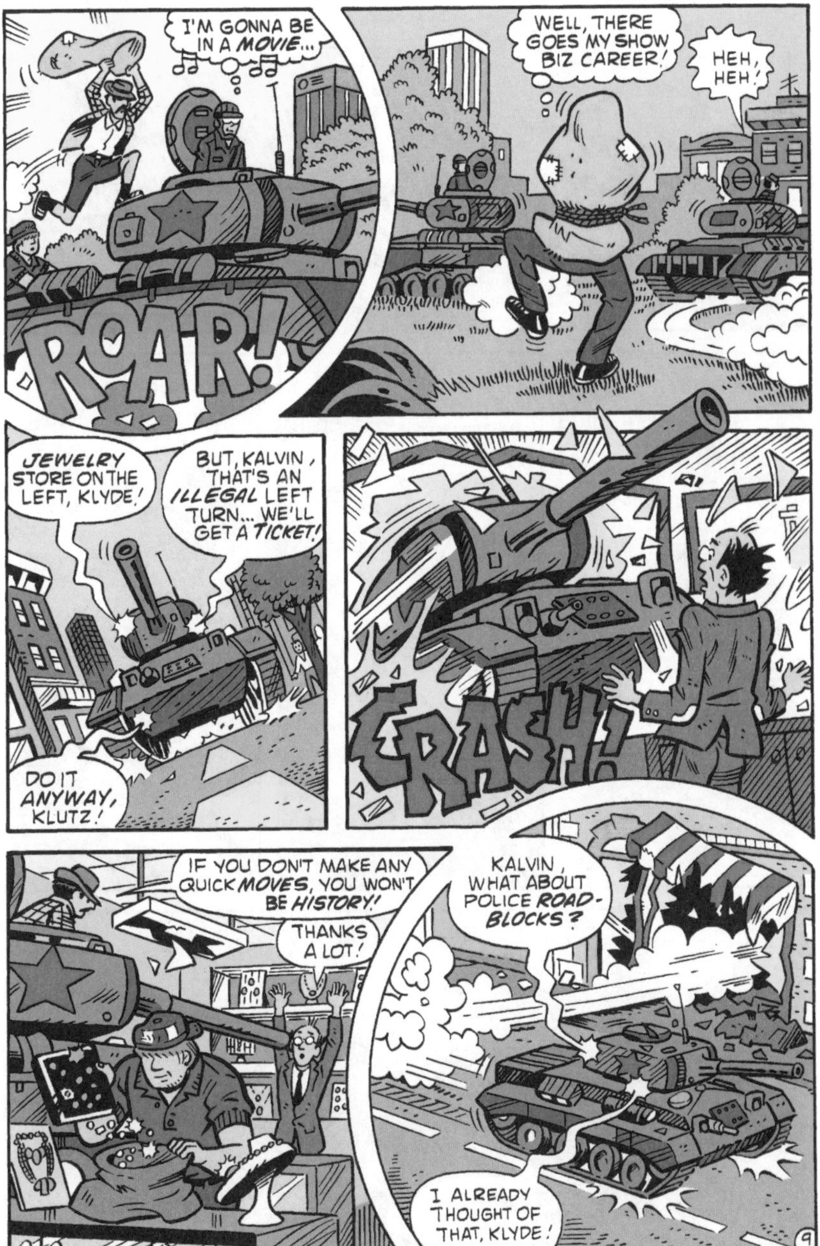
I'M GONNA BE IN A MOVIE...
ROAR!
WELL, THERE GOES MY SHOW BIZ CAREER!
HEH, HEH!
JEWELRY STORE ON THE LEFT, KLYDE!
BUT, KALVIN, THAT'S AN ILLEGAL LEFT TURN... WE'LL GET A TICKET!
DO IT ANYWAY, KLUTZ!
CRASH!
IF YOU DON'T MAKE ANY QUICK MOVES, YOU WON'T BE HISTORY!
THANKS A LOT!
KALVIN, WHAT ABOUT POLICE ROAD-BLOCKS?
I ALREADY THOUGHT OF THAT, KLYDE!
9

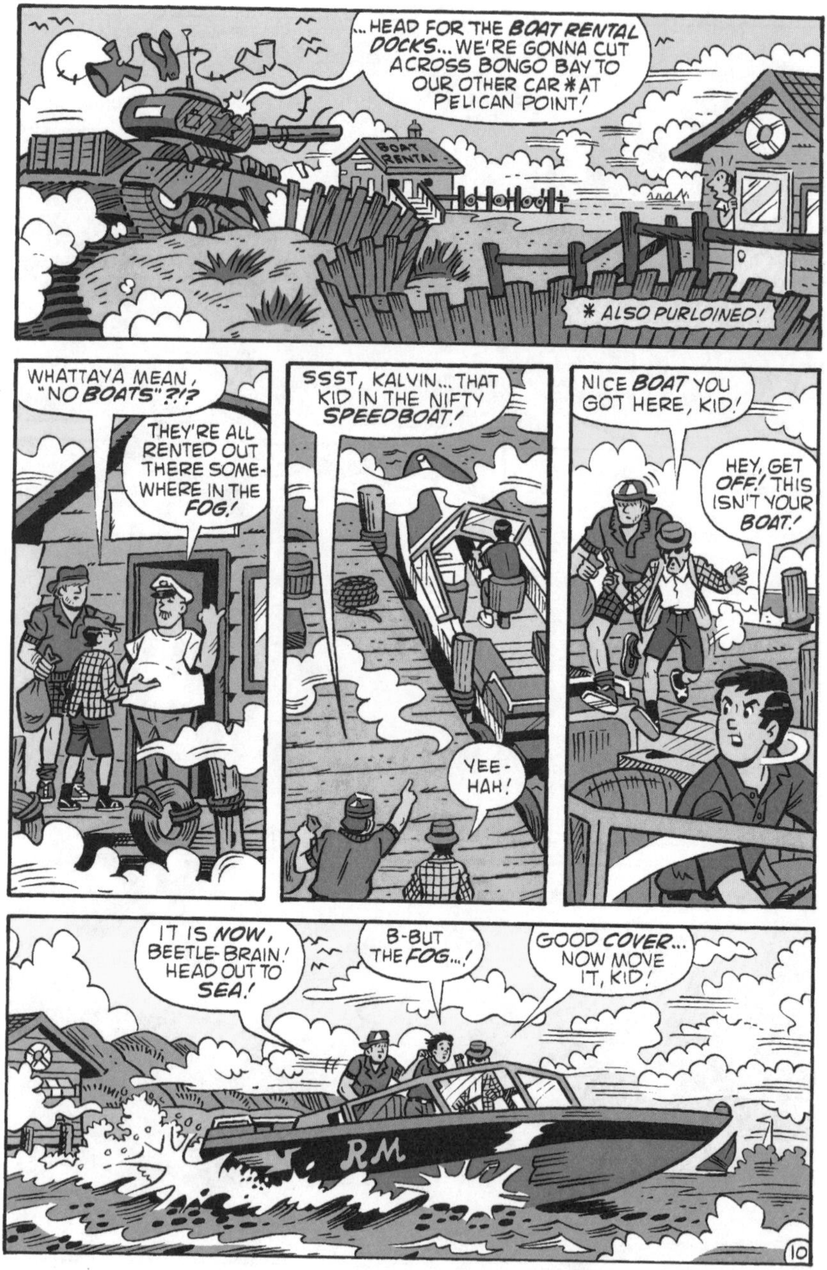
...HEAD FOR THE BOAT RENTAL DOCKS... WE'RE GONNA CUT ACROSS BONGO BAY TO OUR OTHER CAR* AT PELICAN POINT!
BOAT RENTAL
* ALSO PURLOINED!
WHATTAYA MEAN, "NO BOATS"?!?
THEY'RE ALL RENTED OUT THERE SOMEWHERE IN THE FOG!
SSST, KALVIN... THAT KID IN THE NIFTY SPEEDBOAT!
YEE-HAH!
NICE BOAT YOU GOT HERE, KID!
HEY, GET OFF! THIS ISN'T YOUR BOAT!
IT IS NOW, BEETLE-BRAIN! HEAD OUT TO SEA!
B-BUT THE FOG...!
GOOD COVER... NOW MOVE IT, KID!
RM
10

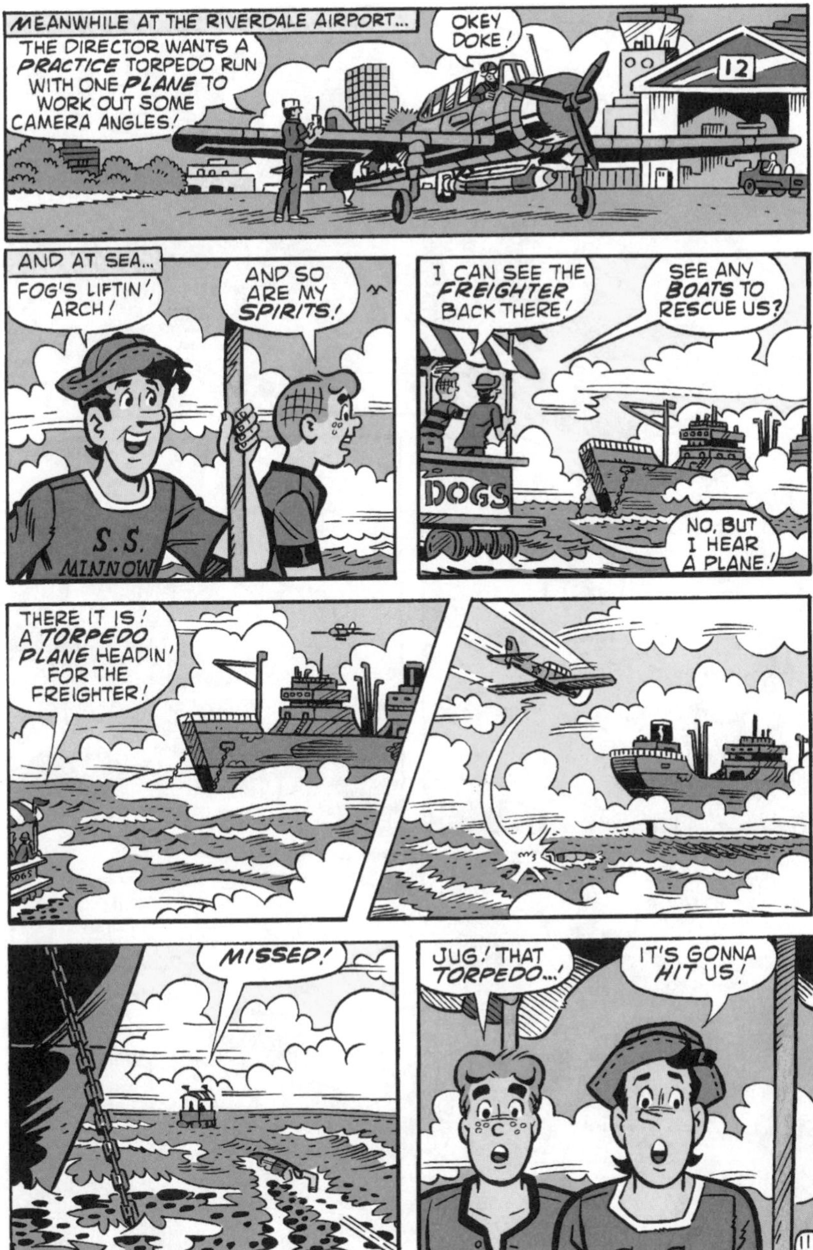
MEANWHILE AT THE RIVERDALE AIRPORT...
THE DIRECTOR WANTS A PRACTICE TORPEDO RUN WITH ONE PLANE TO WORK OUT SOME CAMERA ANGLES!
OKEY DOKE!
12
AND AT SEA...
FOG'S LIFTIN', ARCH!
AND SO ARE MY SPIRITS!
S.S. MINNOW
I CAN SEE THE FREIGHTER BACK THERE!
SEE ANY BOATS TO RESCUE US?
DOGS
NO, BUT I HEAR A PLANE!
THERE IT IS! A TORPEDO PLANE HEADIN' FOR THE FREIGHTER!
MISSED!
JUG! THAT TORPEDO...!
IT'S GONNA HIT US!
11

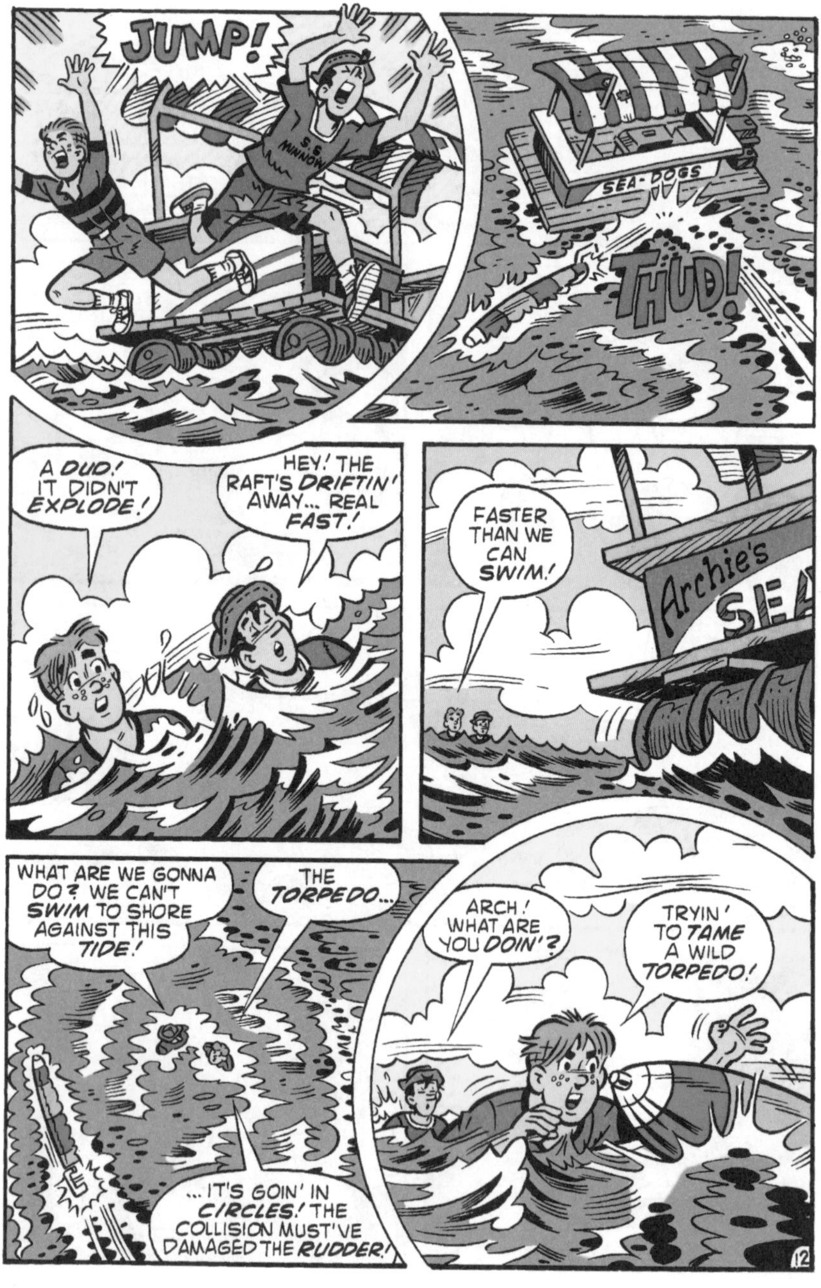
JUMP!
S.S. MINNOW
SEA-DOGS
THUD!
A DUD! IT DIDN'T EXPLODE!
HEY! THE RAFT'S DRIFTIN' AWAY... REAL FAST!
FASTER THAN WE CAN SWIM!
Archie's SEA
WHAT ARE WE GONNA DO? WE CAN'T SWIM TO SHORE AGAINST THIS TIDE!
THE TORPEDO...
...IT'S GOIN' IN CIRCLES! THE COLLISION MUST'VE DAMAGED THE RUDDER!
ARCH! WHAT ARE YOU DOIN'?
TRYIN' TO TAME A WILD TORPEDO!
12

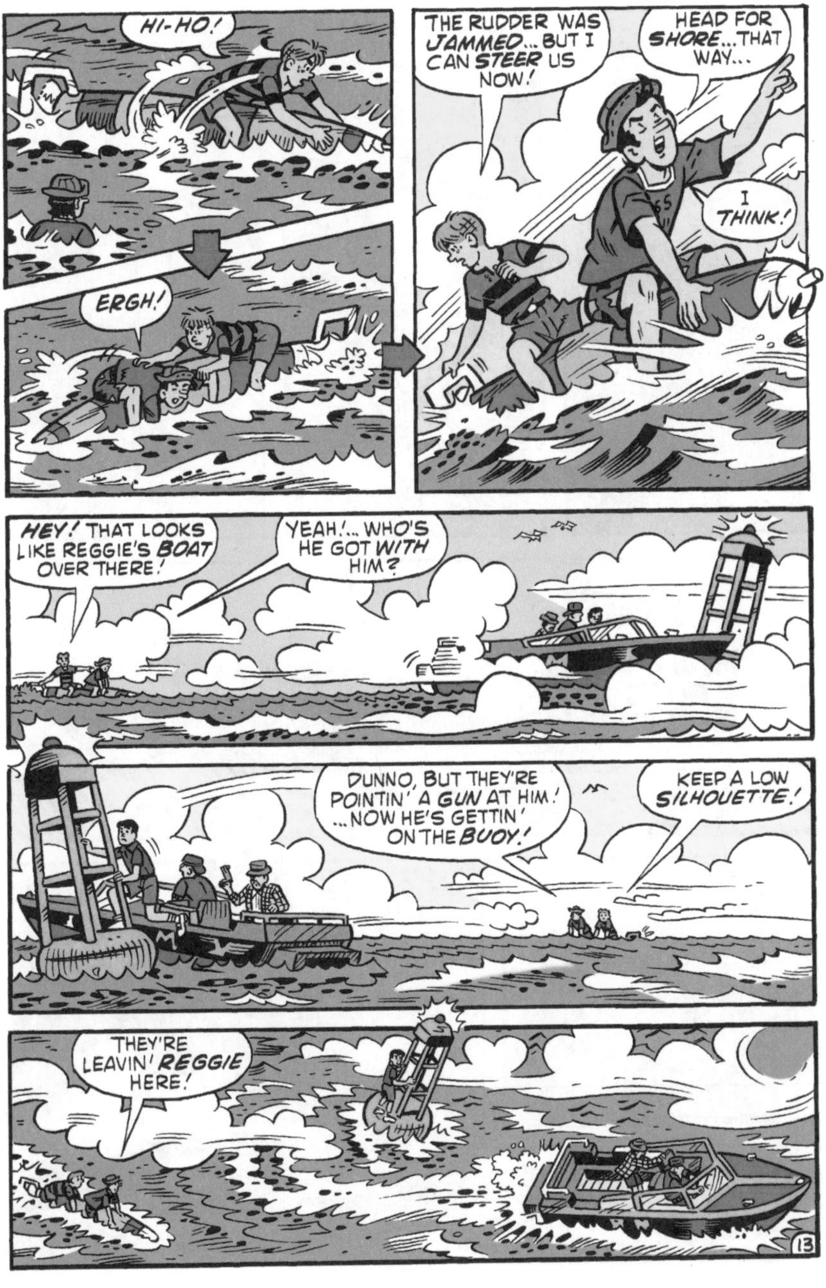
HI-HO!
ERGH!
THE RUDDER WAS JAMMED... BUT I CAN STEER US NOW!
HEAD FOR SHORE...THAT WAY...
I THINK!
HEY! THAT LOOKS LIKE REGGIE'S BOAT OVER THERE!
YEAH!... WHO'S HE GOT WITH HIM?
DUNNO, BUT THEY'RE POINTIN' A GUN AT HIM! ...NOW HE'S GETTIN' ON THE BUOY!
KEEP A LOW SILHOUETTE!
THEY'RE LEAVIN' REGGIE HERE!
13

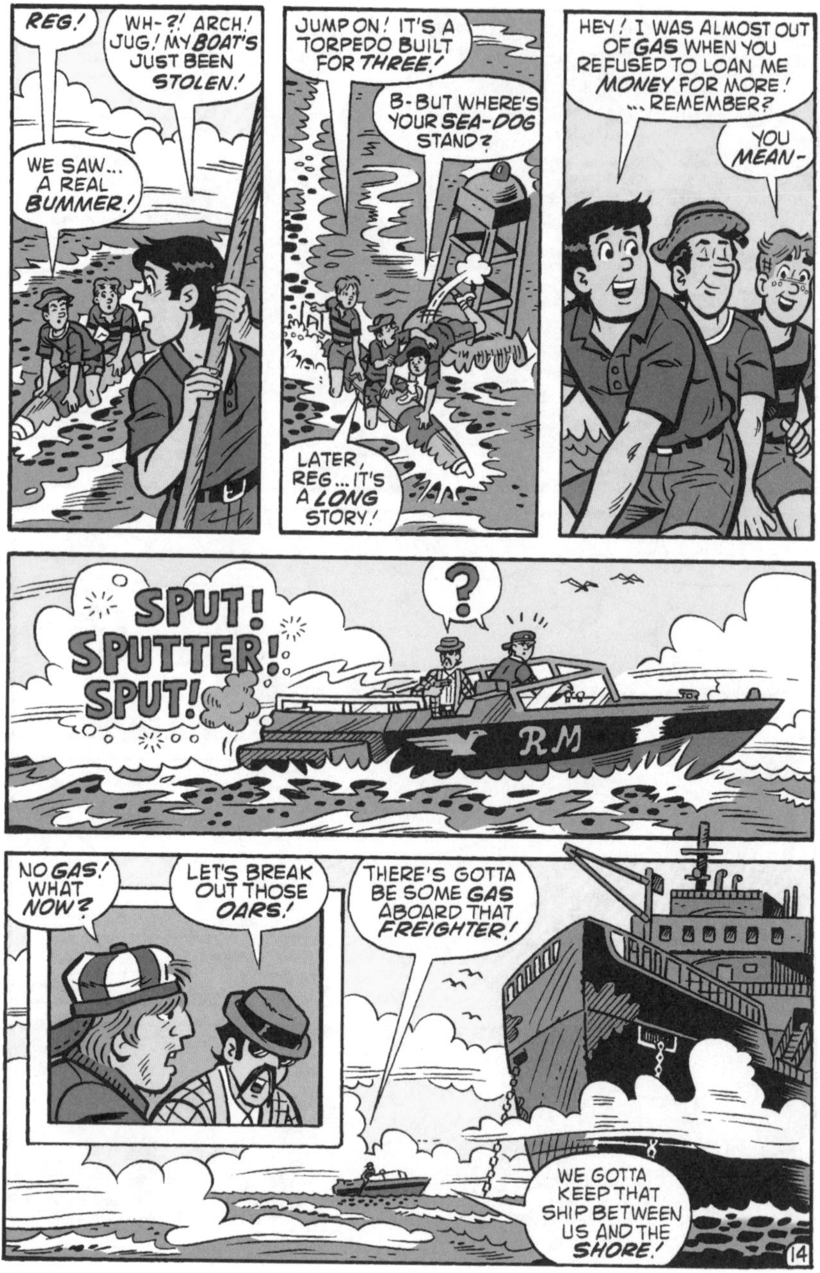
REG!
WH-?! ARCH! JUG! MY BOAT'S JUST BEEN STOLEN!
WE SAW... A REAL BUMMER!
JUMP ON! IT'S A TORPEDO BUILT FOR THREE!
B-BUT WHERE'S YOUR SEA-DOG STAND?
LATER, REG... IT'S A LONG STORY!
HEY! I WAS ALMOST OUT OF GAS WHEN YOU REFUSED TO LOAN ME MONEY FOR MORE! ...REMEMBER?
YOU MEAN-
SPUT! SPUTTER! SPUT!
?
RM
NO GAS! WHAT NOW?
LET'S BREAK OUT THOSE OARS!
THERE'S GOTTA BE SOME GAS ABOARD THAT FREIGHTER!
WE GOTTA KEEP THAT SHIP BETWEEN US AND THE SHORE!
14

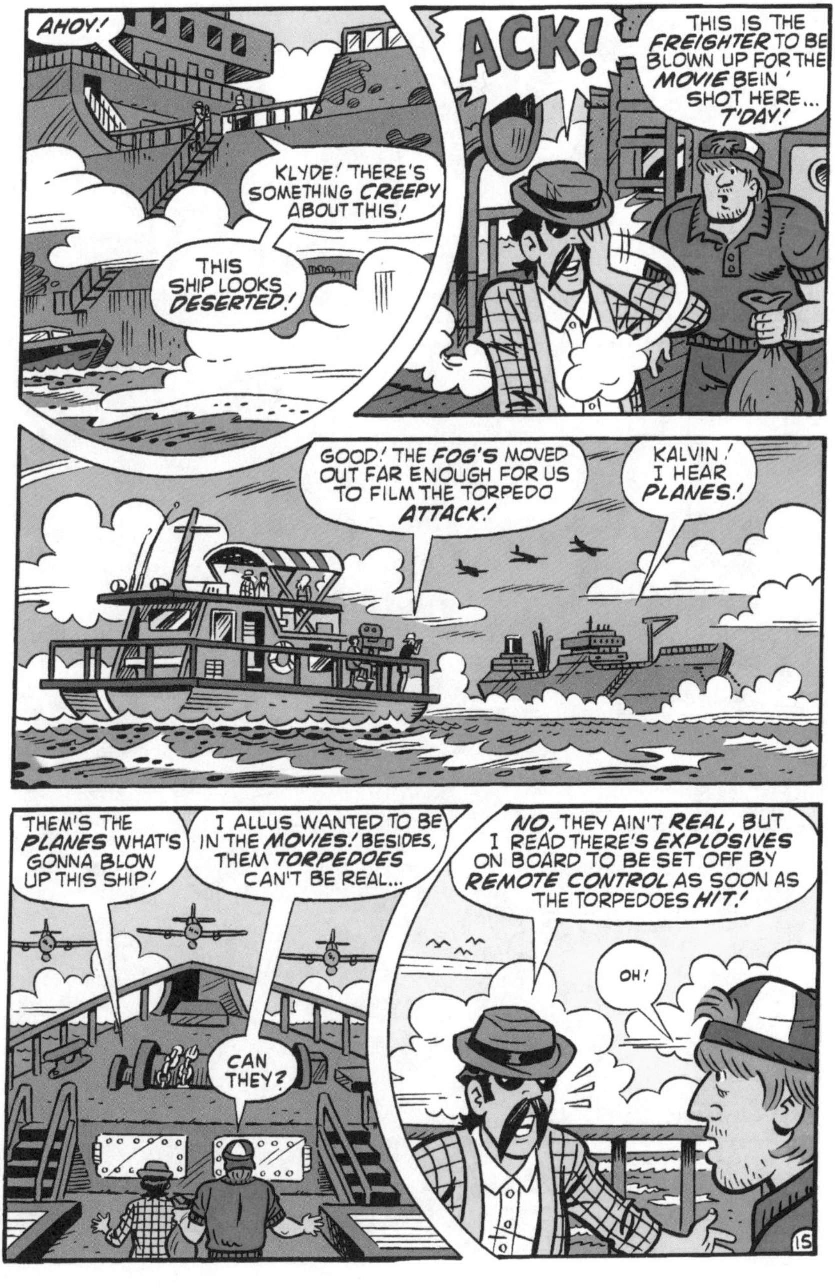
AHOY!
KLYDE! THERE'S SOMETHING CREEPY ABOUT THIS!
THIS SHIP LOOKS DESERTED!
ACK!
THIS IS THE FREIGHTER TO BE BLOWN UP FOR THE MOVIE BEIN' SHOT HERE... T'DAY!
GOOD! THE FOG'S MOVED OUT FAR ENOUGH FOR US TO FILM THE TORPEDO ATTACK!
KALVIN! I HEAR PLANES!
THEM'S THE PLANES WHAT'S GONNA BLOW UP THIS SHIP!
I ALLUS WANTED TO BE IN THE MOVIES! BESIDES, THEM TORPEDOES CAN'T BE REAL...
CAN THEY?
NO, THEY AIN'T REAL, BUT I READ THERE'S EXPLOSIVES ON BOARD TO BE SET OFF BY REMOTE CONTROL AS SOON AS THE TORPEDOES HIT!
OH!
15

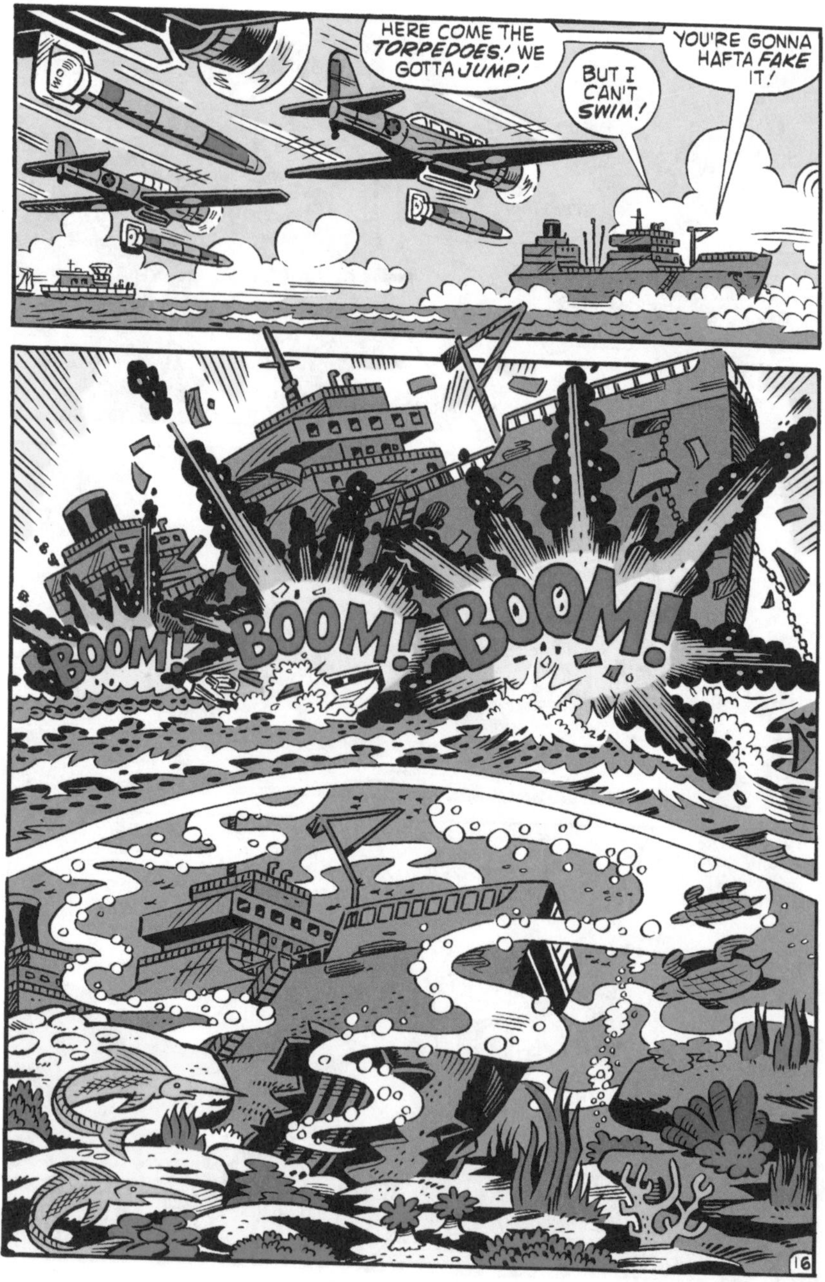
HERE COME THE TORPEDOES! WE GOTTA JUMP!
BUT I CAN'T SWIM!
YOU'RE GONNA HAFTA FAKE IT!
BOOM!
BOOM!
BOOM!
16

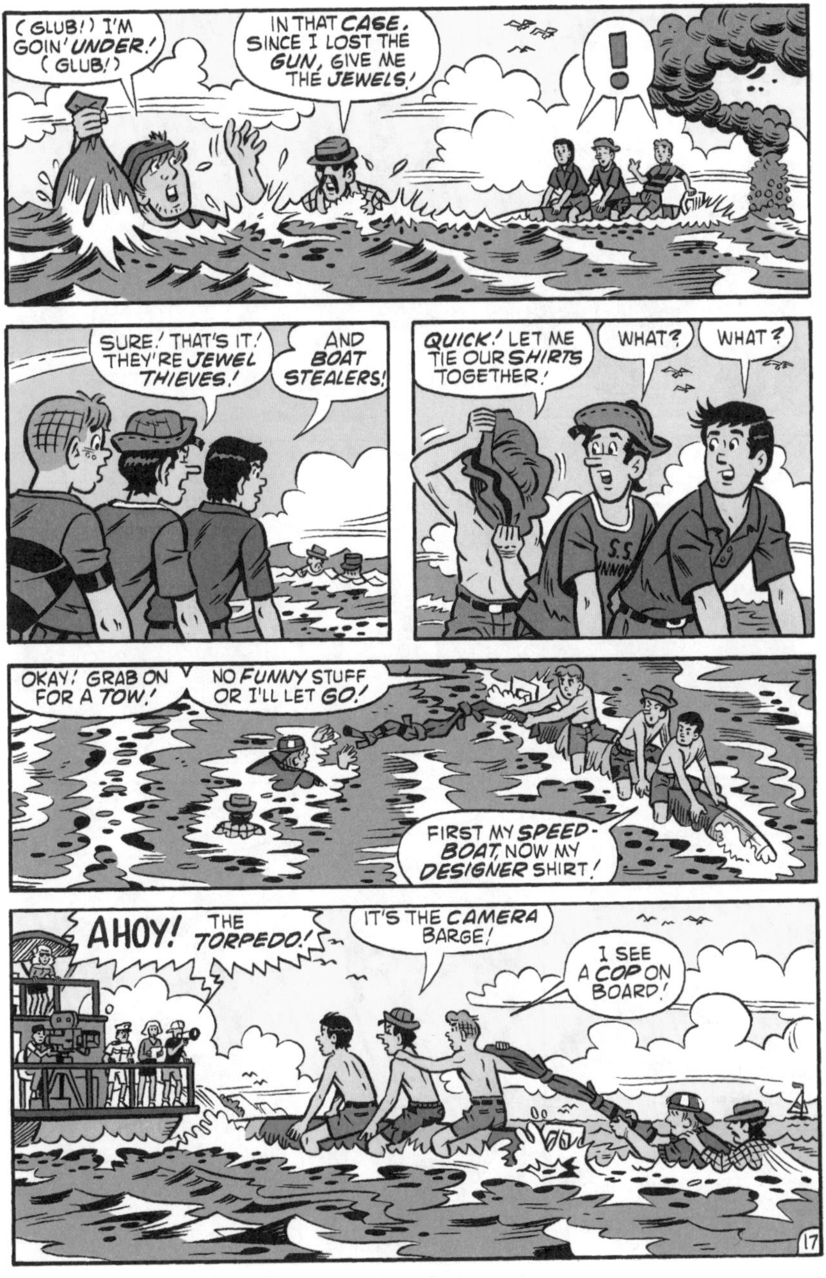

(GLUB!) I'M GOIN' UNDER! (GLUB!)
IN THAT CASE, SINCE I LOST THE GUN, GIVE ME THE JEWELS!
!
SURE! THAT'S IT! THEY'RE JEWEL THIEVES!
AND BOAT STEALERS!
QUICK! LET ME TIE OUR SHIRTS TOGETHER!
WHAT?
WHAT?
S.S.
OKAY! GRAB ON FOR A TOW!
NO FUNNY STUFF OR I'LL LET GO!
FIRST MY SPEED-BOAT, NOW MY DESIGNER SHIRT!
AHOY!
THE TORPEDO!
IT'S THE CAMERA BARGE!
I SEE A COP ON BOARD!
17

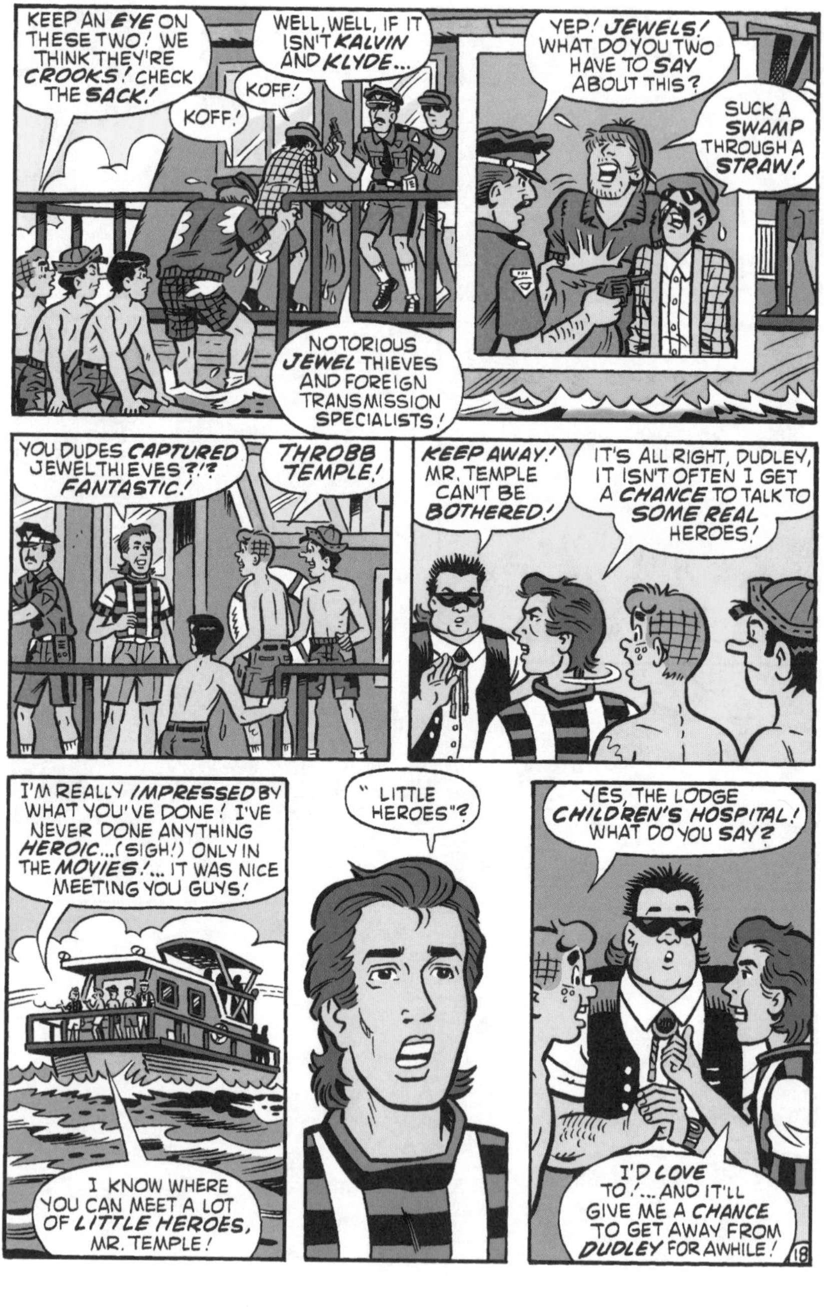
KEEP AN EYE ON THESE TWO! WE THINK THEY'RE CROOKS! CHECK THE SACK!
WELL, WELL, IF IT ISN'T KALVIN AND KLYDE...
KOFF!
KOFF!
NOTORIOUS JEWEL THIEVES AND FOREIGN TRANSMISSION SPECIALISTS!
YEP! JEWELS! WHAT DO YOU TWO HAVE TO SAY ABOUT THIS?
SUCK A SWAMP THROUGH A STRAW!
YOU DUDES CAPTURED JEWEL THIEVES?!? FANTASTIC!
THROBB TEMPLE!
KEEP AWAY! MR. TEMPLE CAN'T BE BOTHERED!
IT'S ALL RIGHT, DUDLEY, IT ISN'T OFTEN I GET A CHANCE TO TALK TO SOME REAL HEROES!
I'M REALLY IMPRESSED BY WHAT YOU'VE DONE! I'VE NEVER DONE ANYTHING HEROIC...(SIGH!) ONLY IN THE MOVIES!... IT WAS NICE MEETING YOU GUYS!
I KNOW WHERE YOU CAN MEET A LOT OF LITTLE HEROES, MR. TEMPLE!
"LITTLE HEROES"?
YES, THE LODGE CHILDREN'S HOSPITAL! WHAT DO YOU SAY?
I'D LOVE TO!... AND IT'LL GIVE ME A CHANCE TO GET AWAY FROM DUDLEY FOR AWHILE!
18

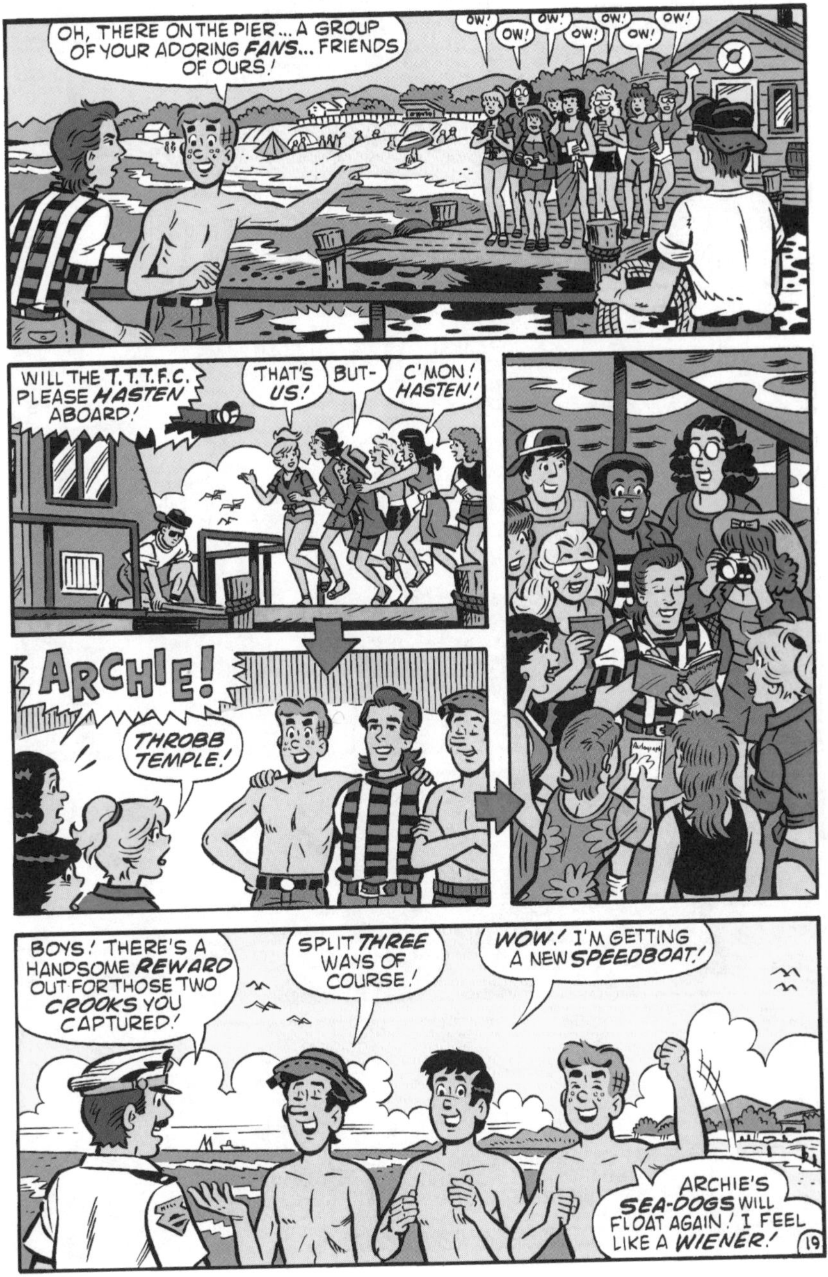
OH, THERE ON THE PIER... A GROUP OF YOUR ADORING FANS... FRIENDS OF OURS!
OW!
OW!
OW!
OW!
OW!
OW!
OW!
WILL THE T.T.T.F.C. PLEASE HASTEN ABOARD!
THAT'S US!
BUT-
C'MON! HASTEN!
ARCHIE!
THROBB TEMPLE!
BOYS! THERE'S A HANDSOME REWARD OUT FOR THOSE TWO CROOKS YOU CAPTURED!
SPLIT THREE WAYS OF COURSE!
WOW! I'M GETTING A NEW SPEEDBOAT!
ARCHIE'S SEA-DOGS WILL FLOAT AGAIN! I FEEL LIKE A WIENER!
19

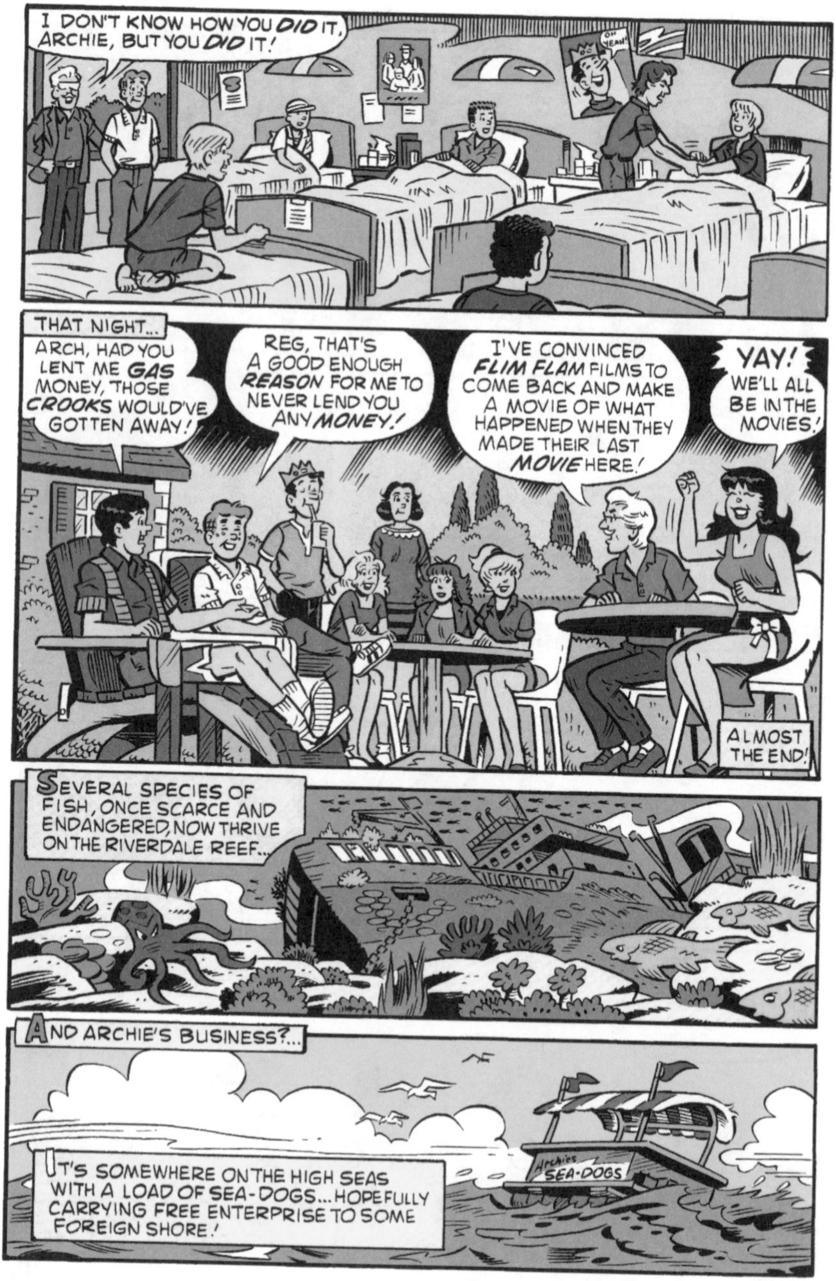
I DON'T KNOW HOW YOU DID IT, ARCHIE, BUT YOU DID IT!
OH YEAH!
THAT NIGHT...
ARCH, HAD YOU LENT ME GAS MONEY, THOSE CROOKS WOULD'VE GOTTEN AWAY!
REG, THAT'S A GOOD ENOUGH REASON FOR ME TO NEVER LEND YOU ANY MONEY!
I'VE CONVINCED FLIM FLAM FILMS TO COME BACK AND MAKE A MOVIE OF WHAT HAPPENED WHEN THEY MADE THEIR LAST MOVIE HERE!
YAY! WE'LL ALL BE IN THE MOVIES!
ALMOST THE END!
SEVERAL SPECIES OF FISH, ONCE SCARCE AND ENDANGERED, NOW THRIVE ON THE RIVERDALE REEF...
AND ARCHIE'S BUSINESS?...
IT'S SOMEWHERE ON THE HIGH SEAS WITH A LOAD OF SEA-DOGS... HOPEFULLY CARRYING FREE ENTERPRISE TO SOME FOREIGN SHORE!
Archie's SEA-DOGS

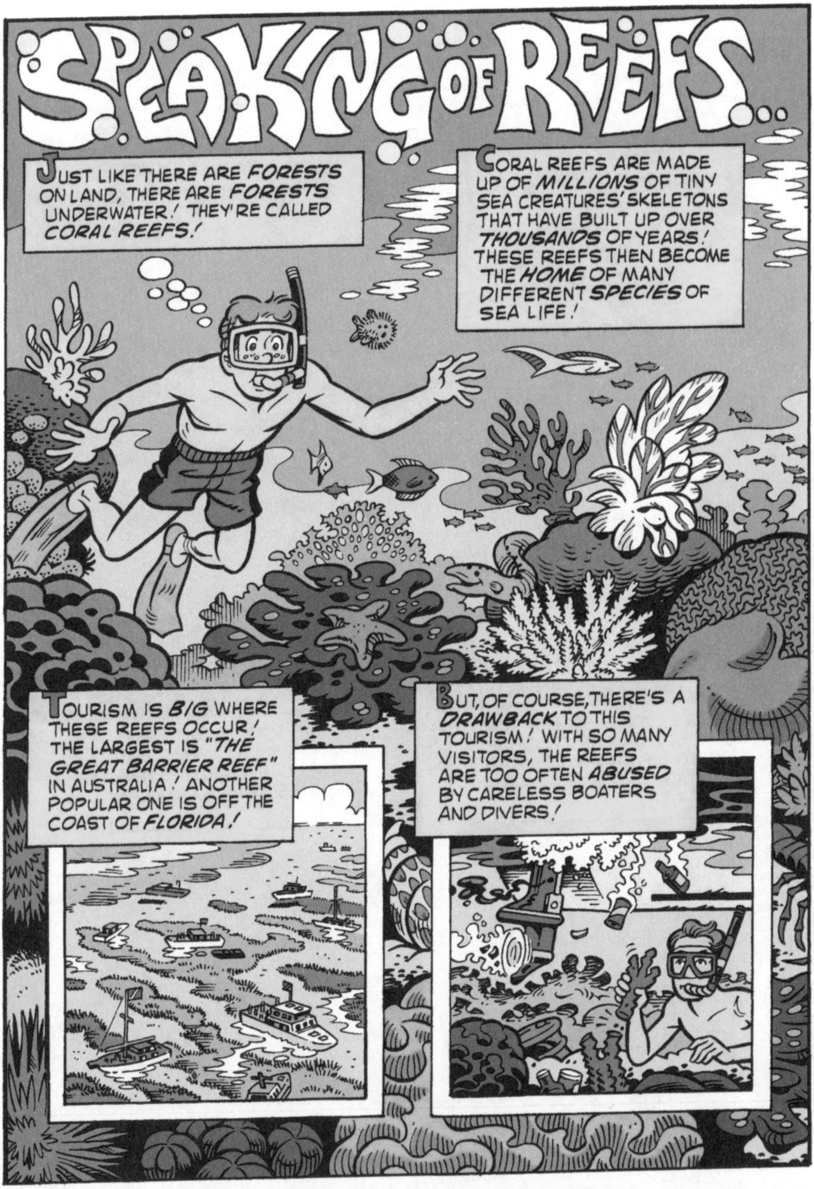
SPEAKING OF REEFS...
JUST LIKE THERE ARE FORESTS ON LAND, THERE ARE FORESTS UNDERWATER! THEY'RE CALLED CORAL REEFS!
CORAL REEFS ARE MADE UP OF MILLIONS OF TINY SEA CREATURES' SKELETONS THAT HAVE BUILT UP OVER THOUSANDS OF YEARS! THESE REEFS THEN BECOME THE HOME OF MANY DIFFERENT SPECIES OF SEA LIFE!
TOURISM IS BIG WHERE THESE REEFS OCCUR! THE LARGEST IS "THE GREAT BARRIER REEF" IN AUSTRALIA! ANOTHER POPULAR ONE IS OFF THE COAST OF FLORIDA!
BUT, OF COURSE, THERE'S A DRAWBACK TO THIS TOURISM! WITH SO MANY VISITORS, THE REEFS ARE TOO OFTEN ABUSED BY CARELESS BOATERS AND DIVERS!

Story: Bob Bolling Pencils: Rex Lindsey
Inks: Rudy Lapick Letters: Bill Yoshida Colors: Dan Parent

Originally printed in WORLD OF ARCHIE #2, NOVEMBER 1992

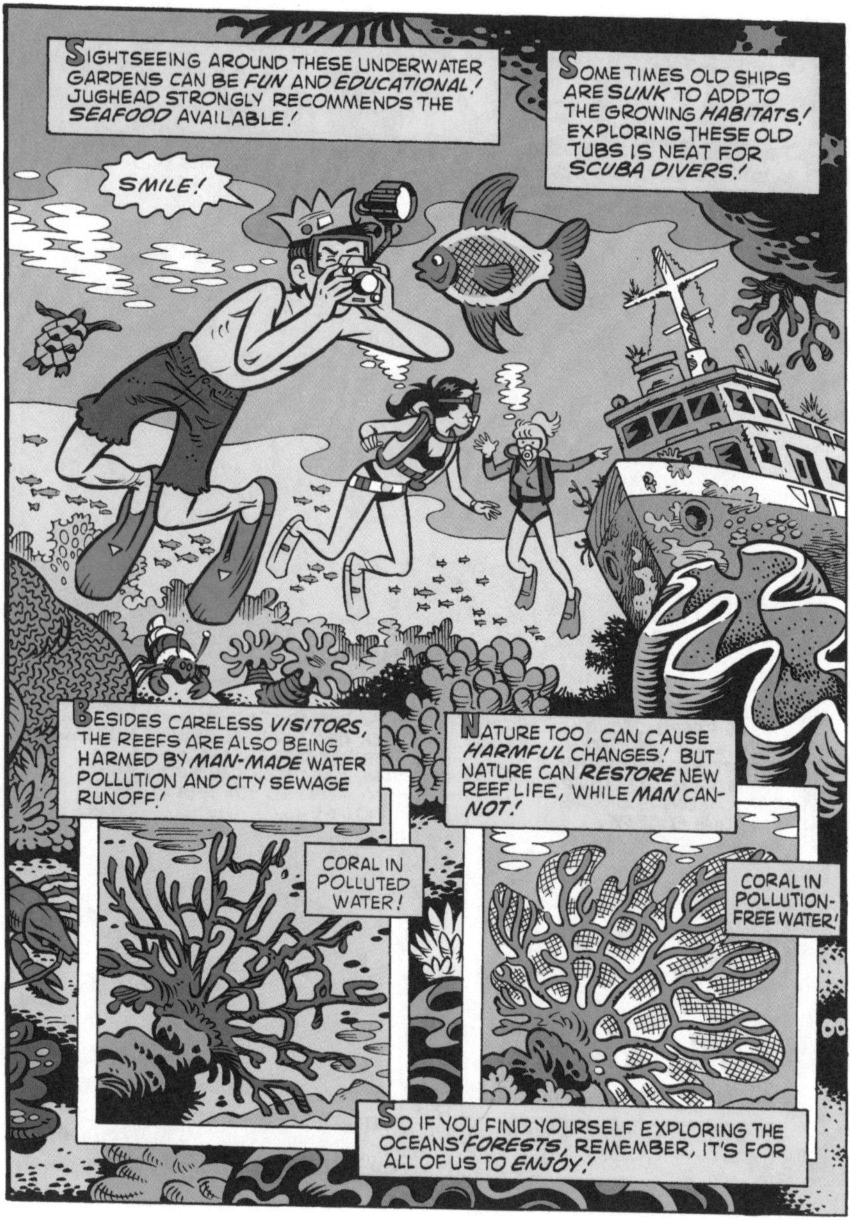
SIGHTSEEING AROUND THESE UNDERWATER GARDENS CAN BE FUN AND EDUCATIONAL! JUGHEAD STRONGLY RECOMMENDS THE SEAFOOD AVAILABLE!
SOMETIMES OLD SHIPS ARE SUNK TO ADD TO THE GROWING HABITATS! EXPLORING THESE OLD TUBS IS NEAT FOR SCUBA DIVERS!
SMILE!
BESIDES CARELESS VISITORS, THE REEFS ARE ALSO BEING HARMED BY MAN-MADE WATER POLLUTION AND CITY SEWAGE RUNOFF!
CORAL IN POLLUTED WATER!
NATURE TOO, CAN CAUSE HARMFUL CHANGES! BUT NATURE CAN RESTORE NEW REEF LIFE, WHILE MAN CAN-NOT!
CORAL IN POLLUTION-FREE WATER!
SO IF YOU FIND YOURSELF EXPLORING THE OCEANS' FORESTS, REMEMBER, IT'S FOR ALL OF US TO ENJOY!

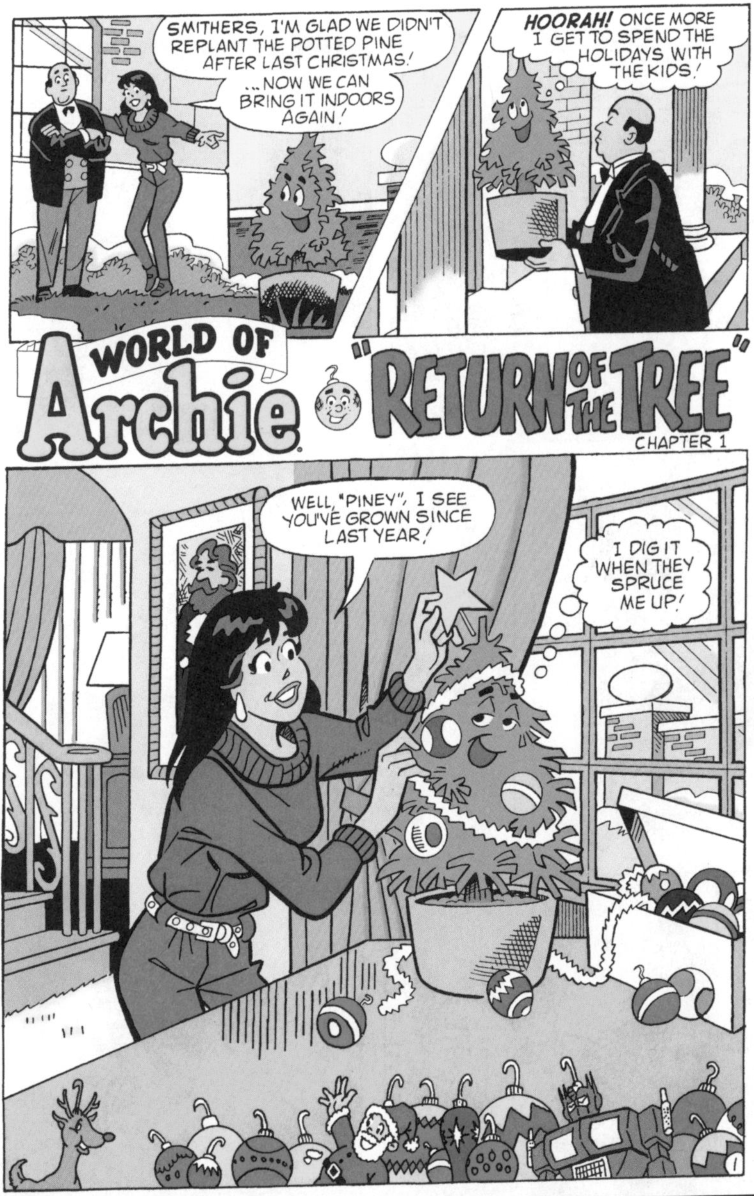
SMITHERS, I'M GLAD WE DIDN'T REPLANT THE POTTED PINE AFTER LAST CHRISTMAS! ...NOW WE CAN BRING IT INDOORS AGAIN!
HOORAH! ONCE MORE I GET TO SPEND THE HOLIDAYS WITH THE KIDS!
WORLD OF Archie
"RETURN OF THE TREE"
CHAPTER 1
WELL, "PINEY", I SEE YOU'VE GROWN SINCE LAST YEAR!
I DIG IT WHEN THEY SPRUCE ME UP!

Story: George Gladir Pencils: Stan Goldberg
Inks: Henry Scarpelli Letters: Bill Yoshida Colors: Barry Grossman

Originally printed in WORLD OF ARCHIE #3, FEBRUARY 1993

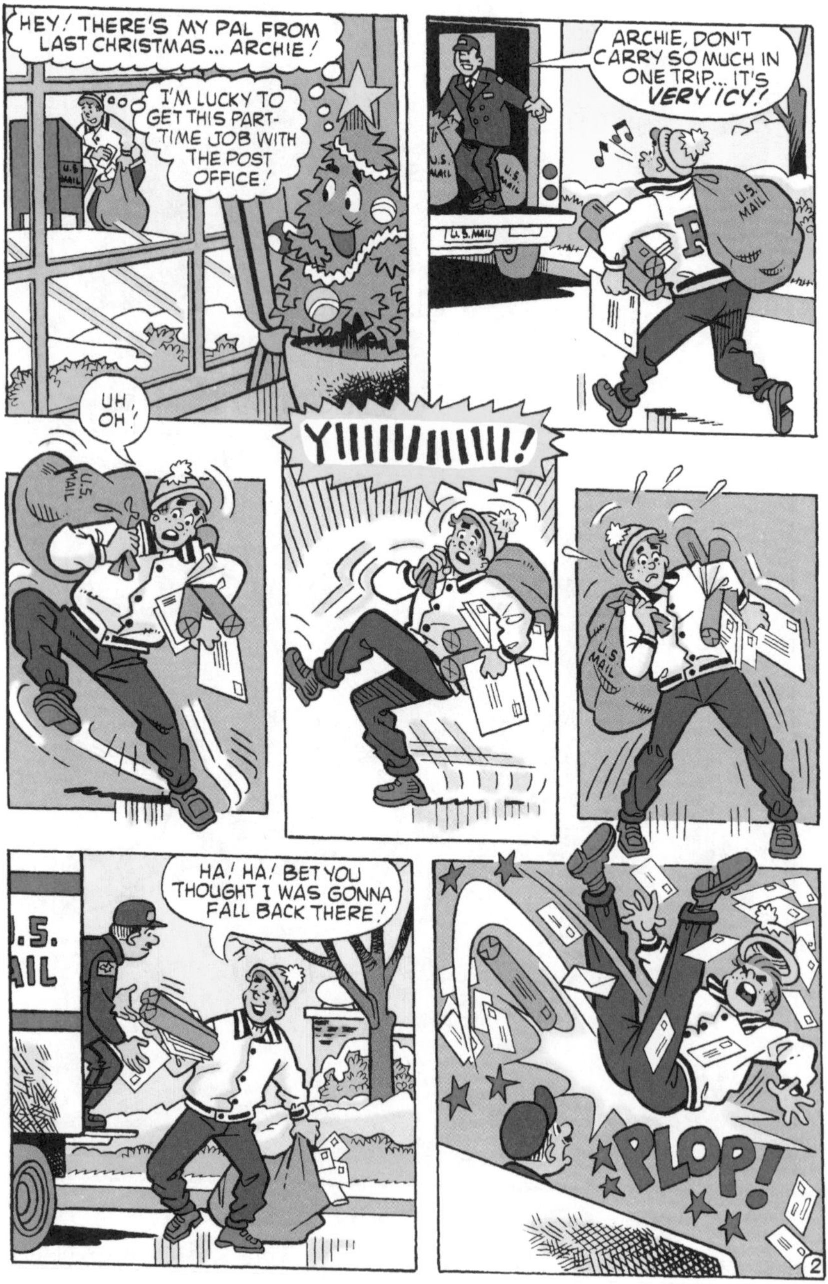
HEY! THERE'S MY PAL FROM LAST CHRISTMAS... ARCHIE!
U.S. MAIL
I'M LUCKY TO GET THIS PART-TIME JOB WITH THE POST OFFICE!
ARCHIE, DON'T CARRY SO MUCH IN ONE TRIP... IT'S VERY ICY!
U.S. MAIL
U.S. MAIL
U.S. MAIL
U.S. MAIL
UH, OH!
U.S. MAIL
YIIIIIIIIIII!
U.S. MAIL
HA! HA! BET YOU THOUGHT I WAS GONNA FALL BACK THERE!
U.S.
AIL
PLOP!
2

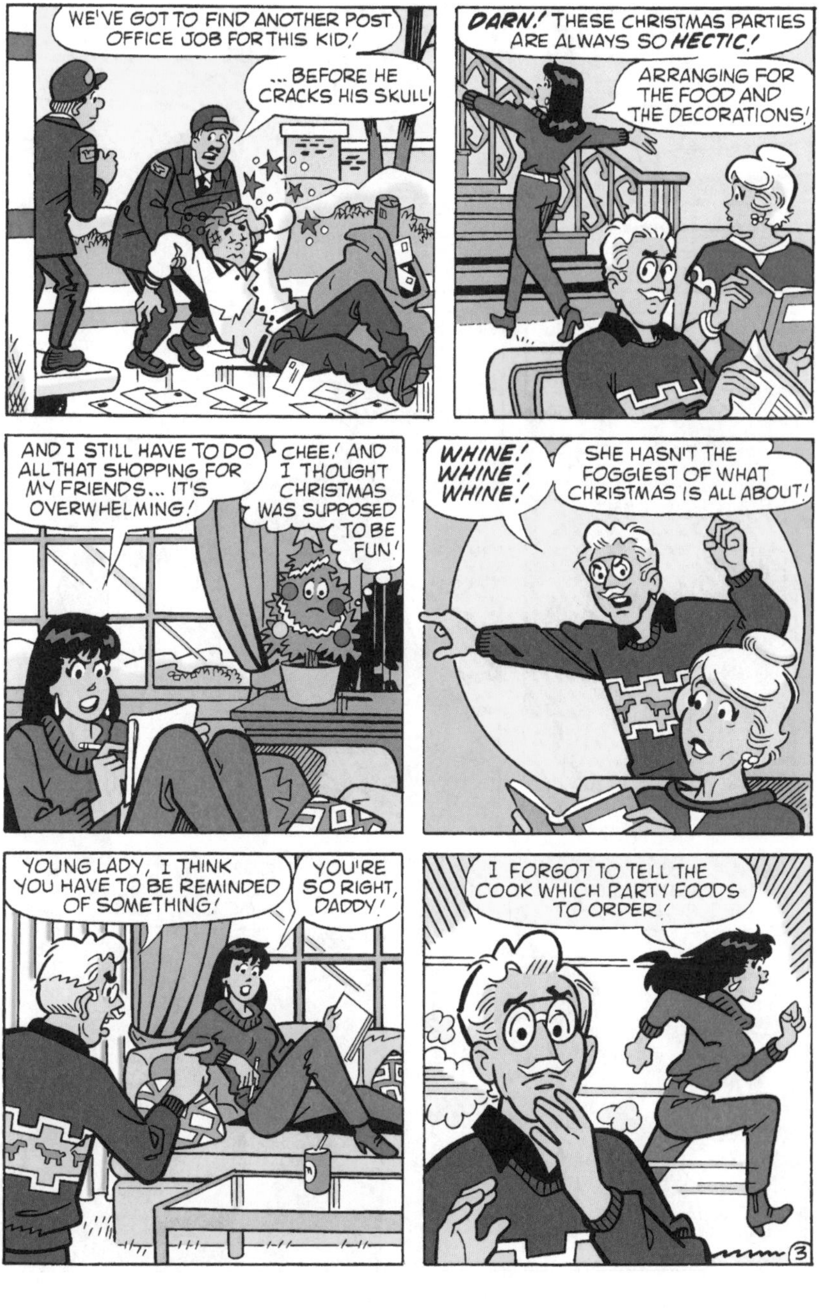
WE'VE GOT TO FIND ANOTHER POST OFFICE JOB FOR THIS KID!
... BEFORE HE CRACKS HIS SKULL!
DARN! THESE CHRISTMAS PARTIES ARE ALWAYS SO HECTIC!
ARRANGING FOR THE FOOD AND THE DECORATIONS!
AND I STILL HAVE TO DO ALL THAT SHOPPING FOR MY FRIENDS... IT'S OVERWHELMING!
CHEE! AND I THOUGHT CHRISTMAS WAS SUPPOSED TO BE FUN!
WHINE! WHINE! WHINE!
SHE HASN'T THE FOGGIEST OF WHAT CHRISTMAS IS ALL ABOUT!
YOUNG LADY, I THINK YOU HAVE TO BE REMINDED OF SOMETHING!
YOU'RE SO RIGHT, DADDY!
I FORGOT TO TELL THE COOK WHICH PARTY FOODS TO ORDER!
3

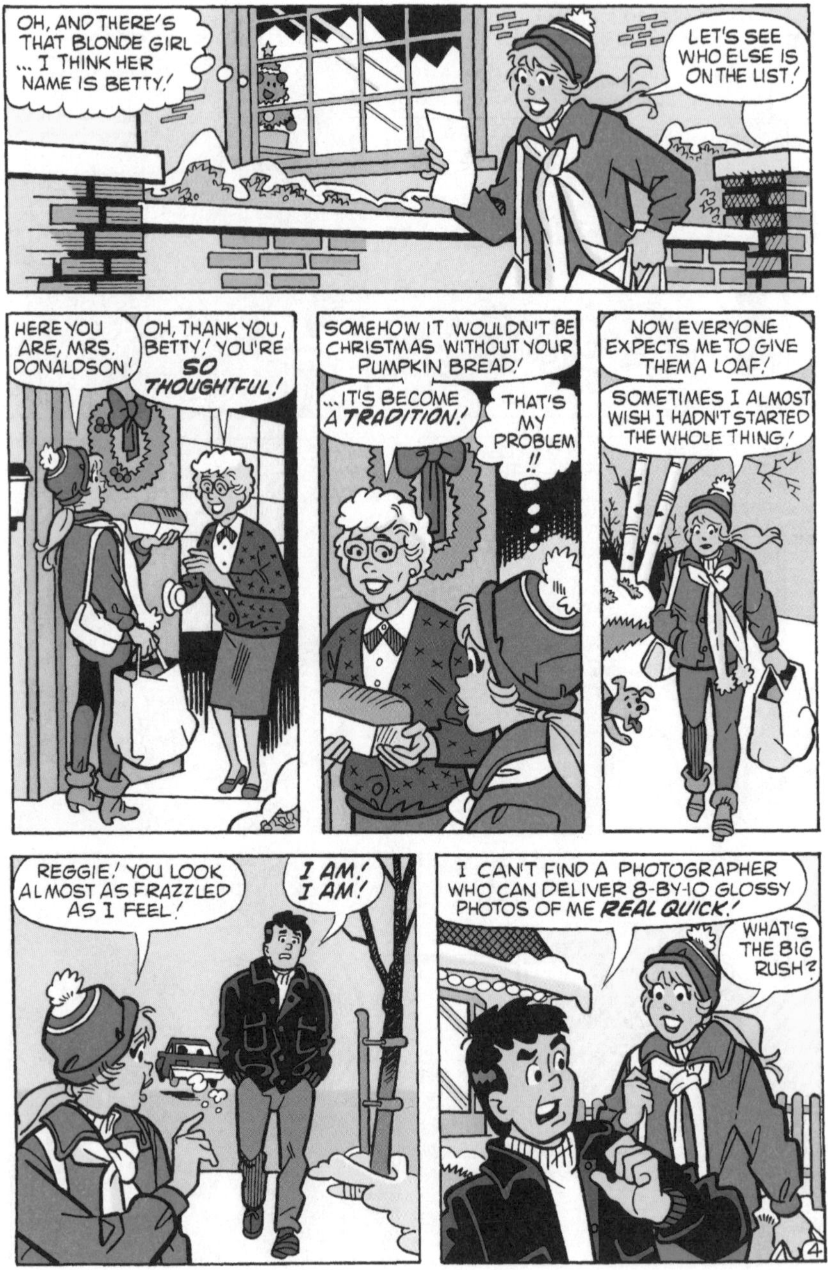
OH, AND THERE'S THAT BLONDE GIRL ... I THINK HER NAME IS BETTY!
LET'S SEE WHO ELSE IS ON THE LIST!
HERE YOU ARE, MRS. DONALDSON!
OH, THANK YOU, BETTY! YOU'RE SO THOUGHTFUL!
SOMEHOW IT WOULDN'T BE CHRISTMAS WITHOUT YOUR PUMPKIN BREAD!
...IT'S BECOME A TRADITION!
THAT'S MY PROBLEM!!
NOW EVERYONE EXPECTS ME TO GIVE THEM A LOAF!
SOMETIMES I ALMOST WISH I HADN'T STARTED THE WHOLE THING!
REGGIE! YOU LOOK ALMOST AS FRAZZLED AS I FEEL!
I AM! I AM!
WHAT'S THE BIG RUSH?
I CAN'T FIND A PHOTOGRAPHER WHO CAN DELIVER 8-BY-10 GLOSSY PHOTOS OF ME REAL QUICK!
4

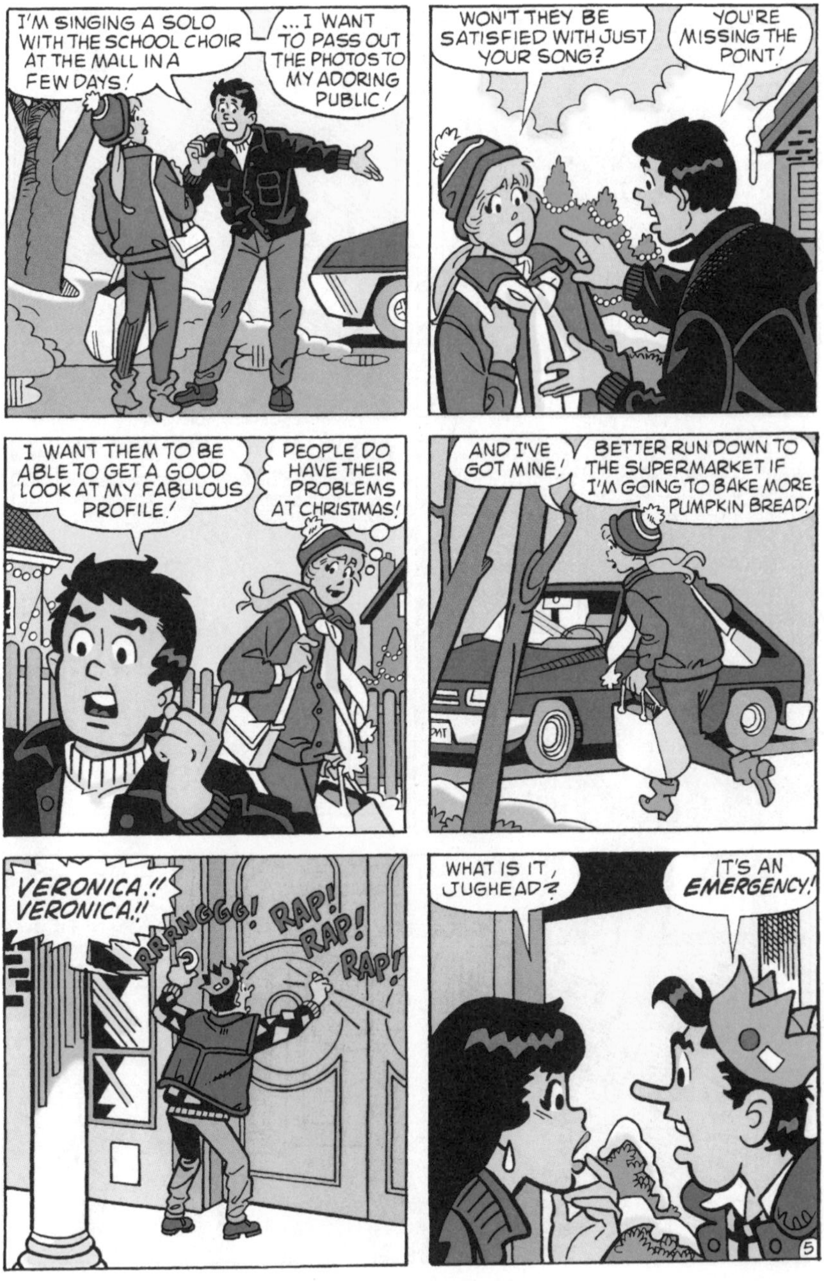
I'M SINGING A SOLO WITH THE SCHOOL CHOIR AT THE MALL IN A FEW DAYS!
...I WANT TO PASS OUT THE PHOTOS TO MY ADORING PUBLIC!
WON'T THEY BE SATISFIED WITH JUST YOUR SONG?
YOU'RE MISSING THE POINT!
I WANT THEM TO BE ABLE TO GET A GOOD LOOK AT MY FABULOUS PROFILE!
PEOPLE DO HAVE THEIR PROBLEMS AT CHRISTMAS!
AND I'VE GOT MINE!
BETTER RUN DOWN TO THE SUPERMARKET IF I'M GOING TO BAKE MORE PUMPKIN BREAD!
VERONICA!! VERONICA!!
RRRNGGG!
RAP! RAP! RAP!
WHAT IS IT, JUGHEAD?
IT'S AN EMERGENCY!
5

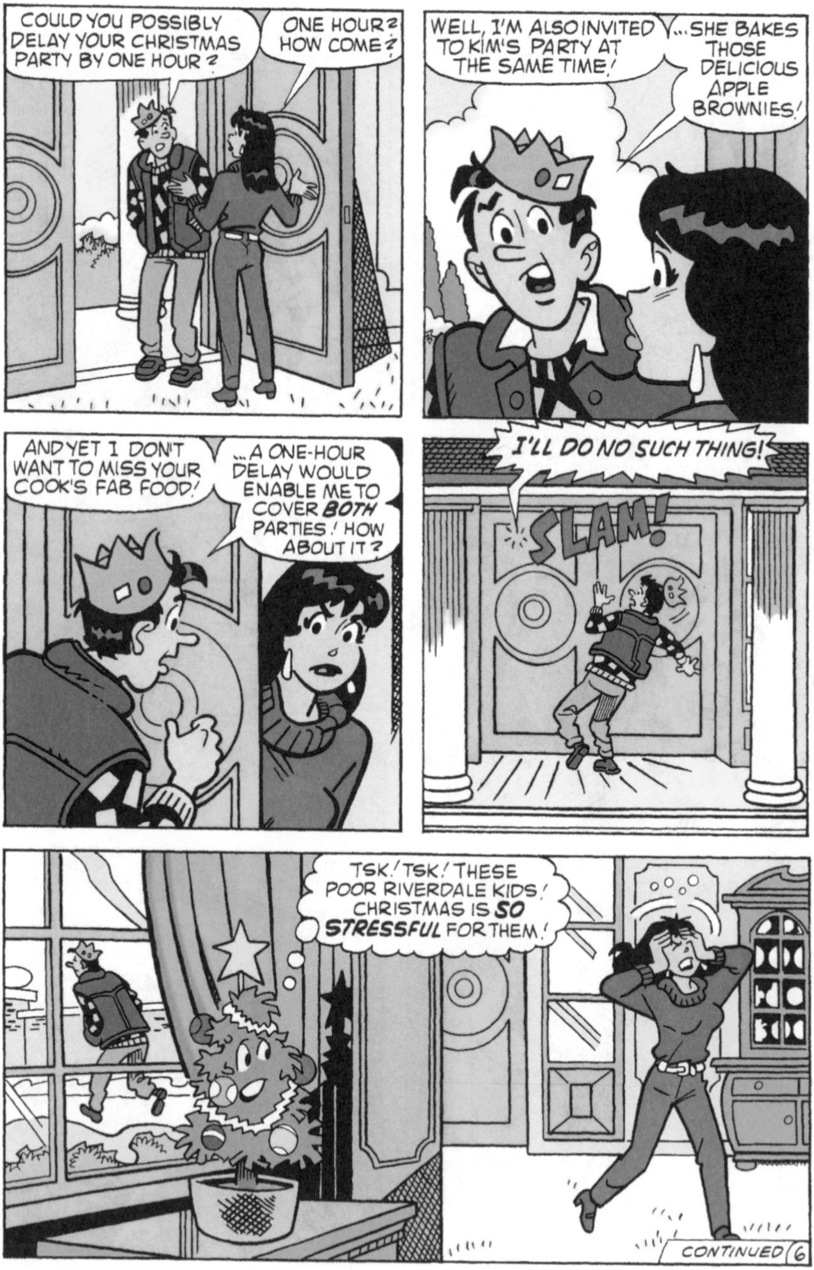
COULD YOU POSSIBLY DELAY YOUR CHRISTMAS PARTY BY ONE HOUR?
ONE HOUR? HOW COME?
WELL, I'M ALSO INVITED TO KIM'S PARTY AT THE SAME TIME!
...SHE BAKES THOSE DELICIOUS APPLE BROWNIES!
AND YET I DON'T WANT TO MISS YOUR COOK'S FAB FOOD!
...A ONE-HOUR DELAY WOULD ENABLE ME TO COVER BOTH PARTIES! HOW ABOUT IT?
I'LL DO NO SUCH THING!
SLAM!
TSK! TSK! THESE POOR RIVERDALE KIDS! CHRISTMAS IS SO STRESSFUL FOR THEM!
CONTINUED
6

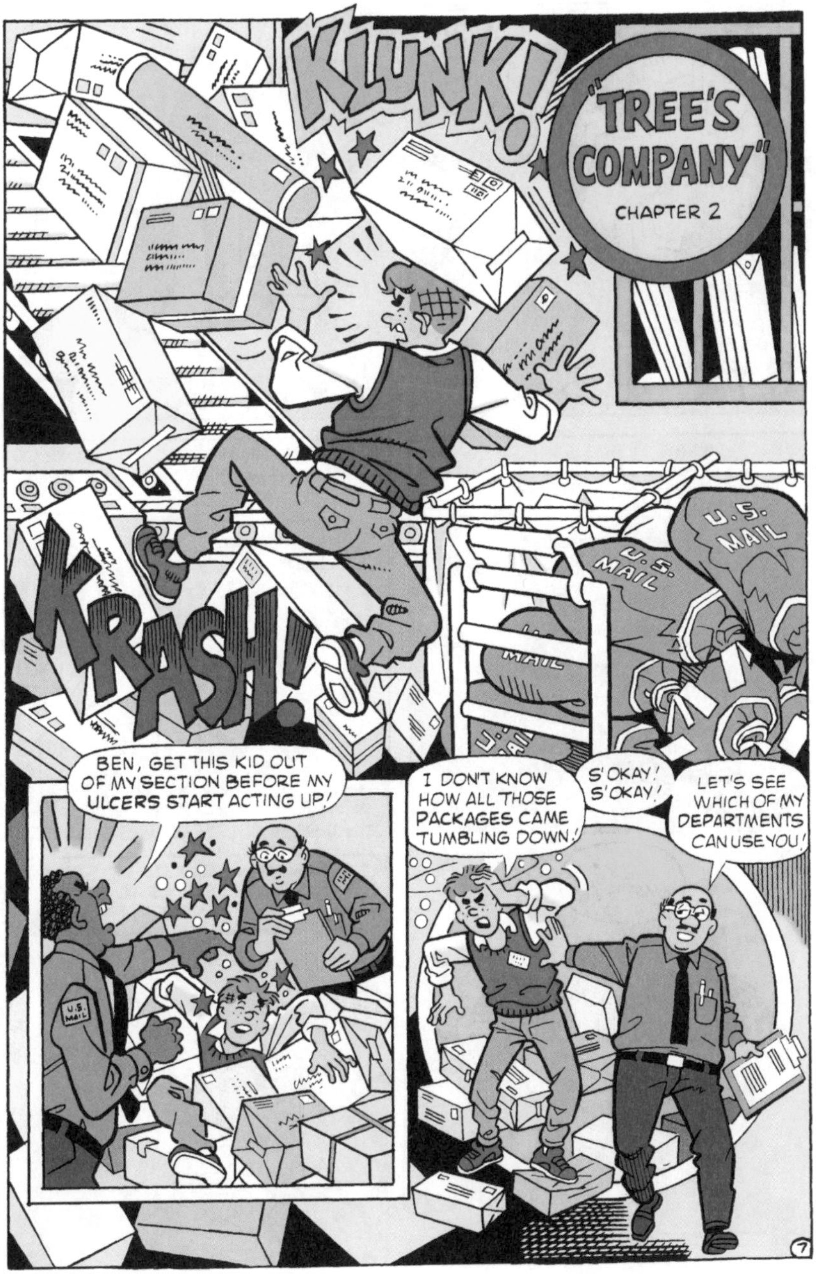
KLUNK!
"TREE'S COMPANY"
CHAPTER 2
KRASH!
U.S. MAIL
U.S. MAIL
BEN, GET THIS KID OUT OF MY SECTION BEFORE MY ULCERS START ACTING UP!
I DON'T KNOW HOW ALL THOSE PACKAGES CAME TUMBLING DOWN!
S'OKAY! S'OKAY!
LET'S SEE WHICH OF MY DEPARTMENTS CAN USE YOU!
U.S. MAIL
7

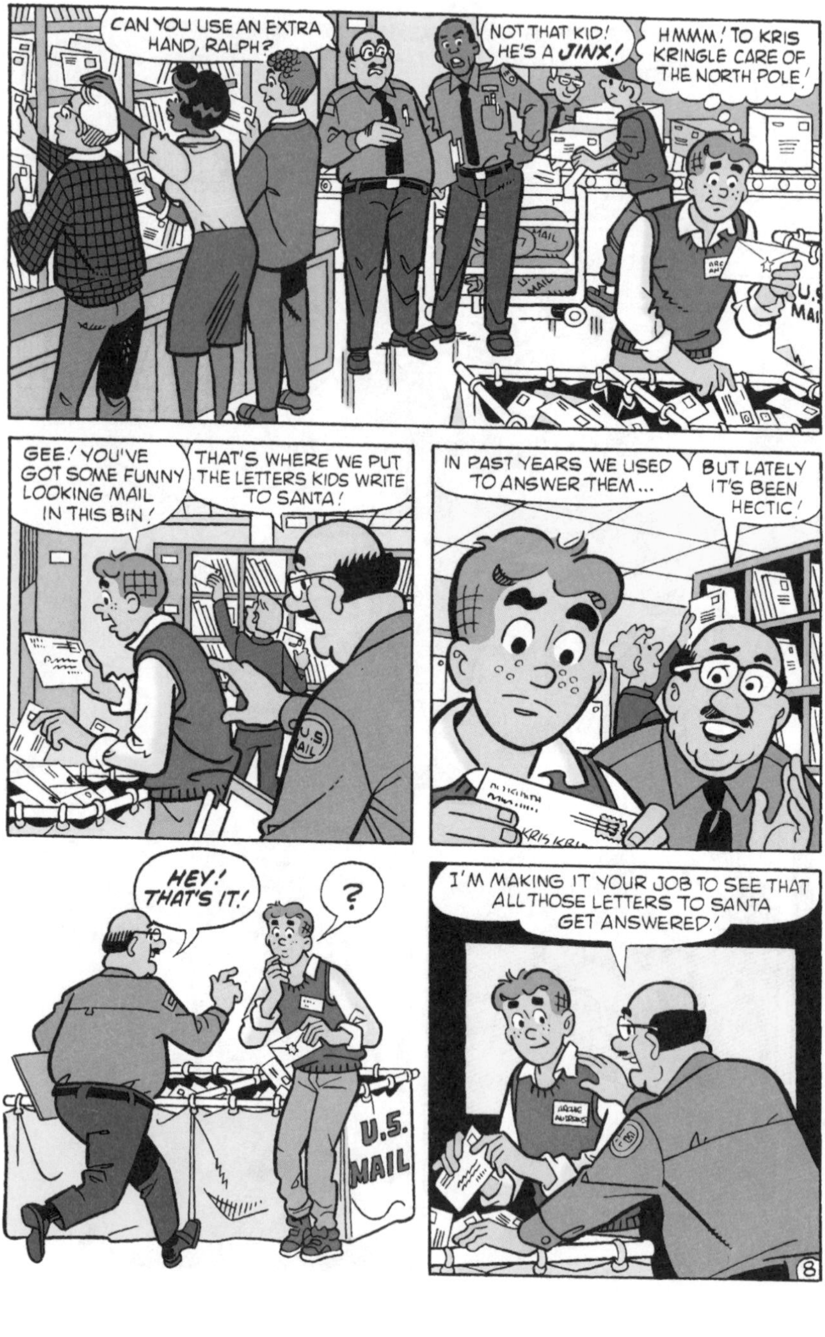
CAN YOU USE AN EXTRA HAND, RALPH?
NOT THAT KID! HE'S A JINX!
HMMM! TO KRIS KRINGLE CARE OF THE NORTH POLE!
U.S. MAIL
GEE! YOU'VE GOT SOME FUNNY LOOKING MAIL IN THIS BIN!
THAT'S WHERE WE PUT THE LETTERS KIDS WRITE TO SANTA!
IN PAST YEARS WE USED TO ANSWER THEM...
BUT LATELY IT'S BEEN HECTIC!
HEY! THAT'S IT!
?
U.S. MAIL
I'M MAKING IT YOUR JOB TO SEE THAT ALL THOSE LETTERS TO SANTA GET ANSWERED!
8

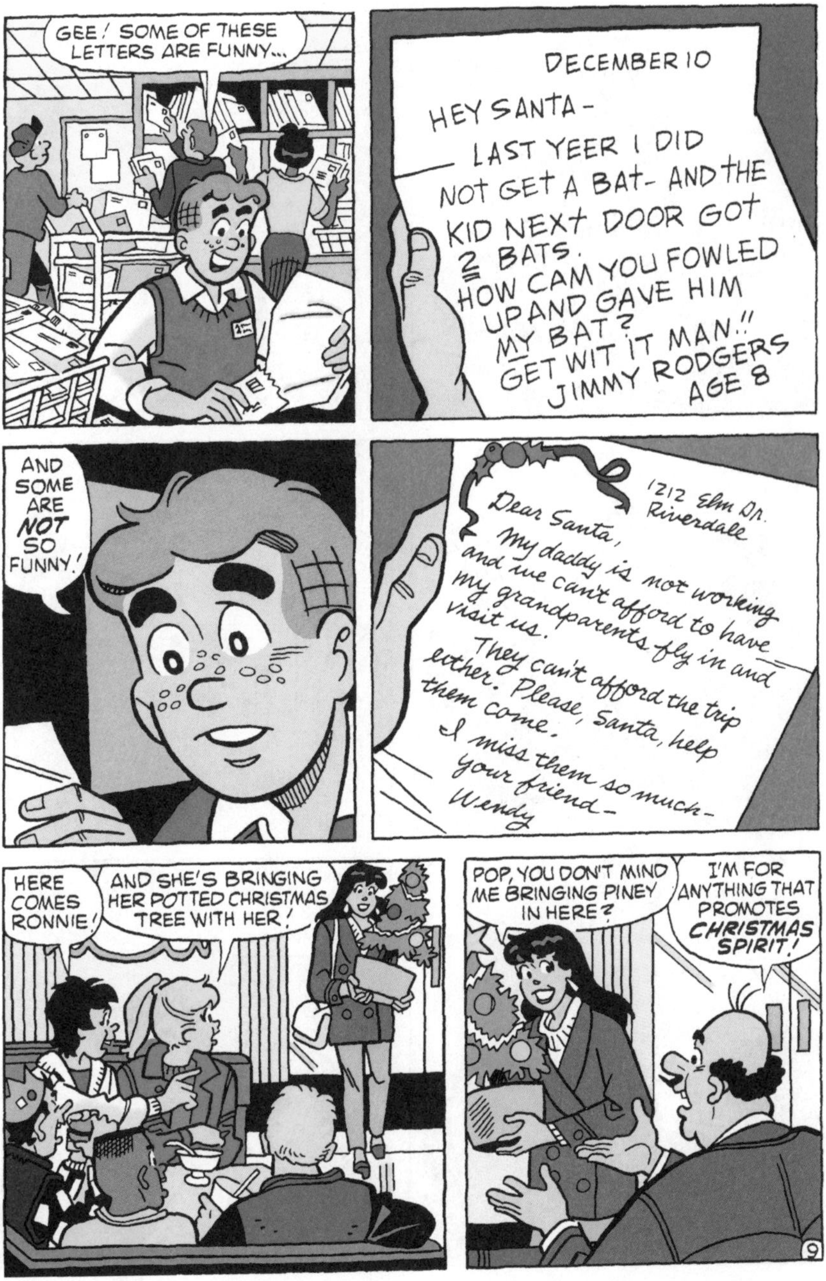
GEE! SOME OF THESE LETTERS ARE FUNNY...
DECEMBER 10
HEY SANTA -
LAST YEER I DID NOT GET A BAT- AND THE KID NEXT DOOR GOT 2 BATS.
HOW CAM YOU FOWLED UP AND GAVE HIM MY BAT?
GET WIT IT MAN!!
JIMMY RODGERS
AGE 8
AND SOME ARE NOT SO FUNNY!
1212 Elm Dr.
Riverdale
Dear Santa,
My daddy is not working and we can't afford to have my grandparents fly in and visit us.
They can't afford the trip either. Please, Santa, help them come.
I miss them so much -
your friend -
Wendy
HERE COMES RONNIE!
AND SHE'S BRINGING HER POTTED CHRISTMAS TREE WITH HER!
POP, YOU DON'T MIND ME BRINGING PINEY IN HERE?
I'M FOR ANYTHING THAT PROMOTES CHRISTMAS SPIRIT!
9

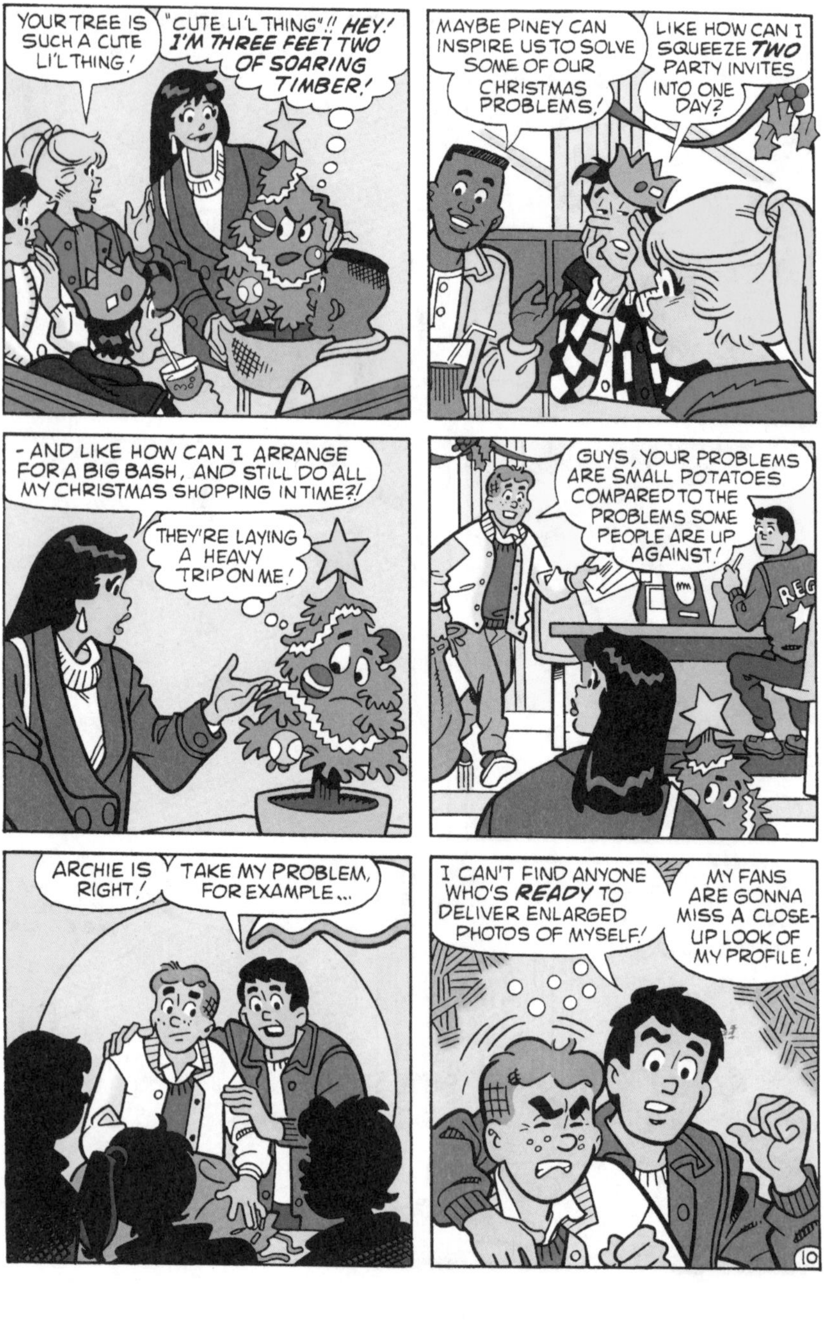
YOUR TREE IS SUCH A CUTE LI'L THING!
"CUTE LI'L THING"!! HEY! I'M THREE FEET TWO OF SOARING TIMBER!
MAYBE PINEY CAN INSPIRE US TO SOLVE SOME OF OUR CHRISTMAS PROBLEMS!
LIKE HOW CAN I SQUEEZE TWO PARTY INVITES INTO ONE DAY?
- AND LIKE HOW CAN I ARRANGE FOR A BIG BASH, AND STILL DO ALL MY CHRISTMAS SHOPPING IN TIME?!
THEY'RE LAYING A HEAVY TRIP ON ME!
GUYS, YOUR PROBLEMS ARE SMALL POTATOES COMPARED TO THE PROBLEMS SOME PEOPLE ARE UP AGAINST!
REG
ARCHIE IS RIGHT!
TAKE MY PROBLEM, FOR EXAMPLE...
I CAN'T FIND ANYONE WHO'S READY TO DELIVER ENLARGED PHOTOS OF MYSELF!
MY FANS ARE GONNA MISS A CLOSE-UP LOOK OF MY PROFILE!
10

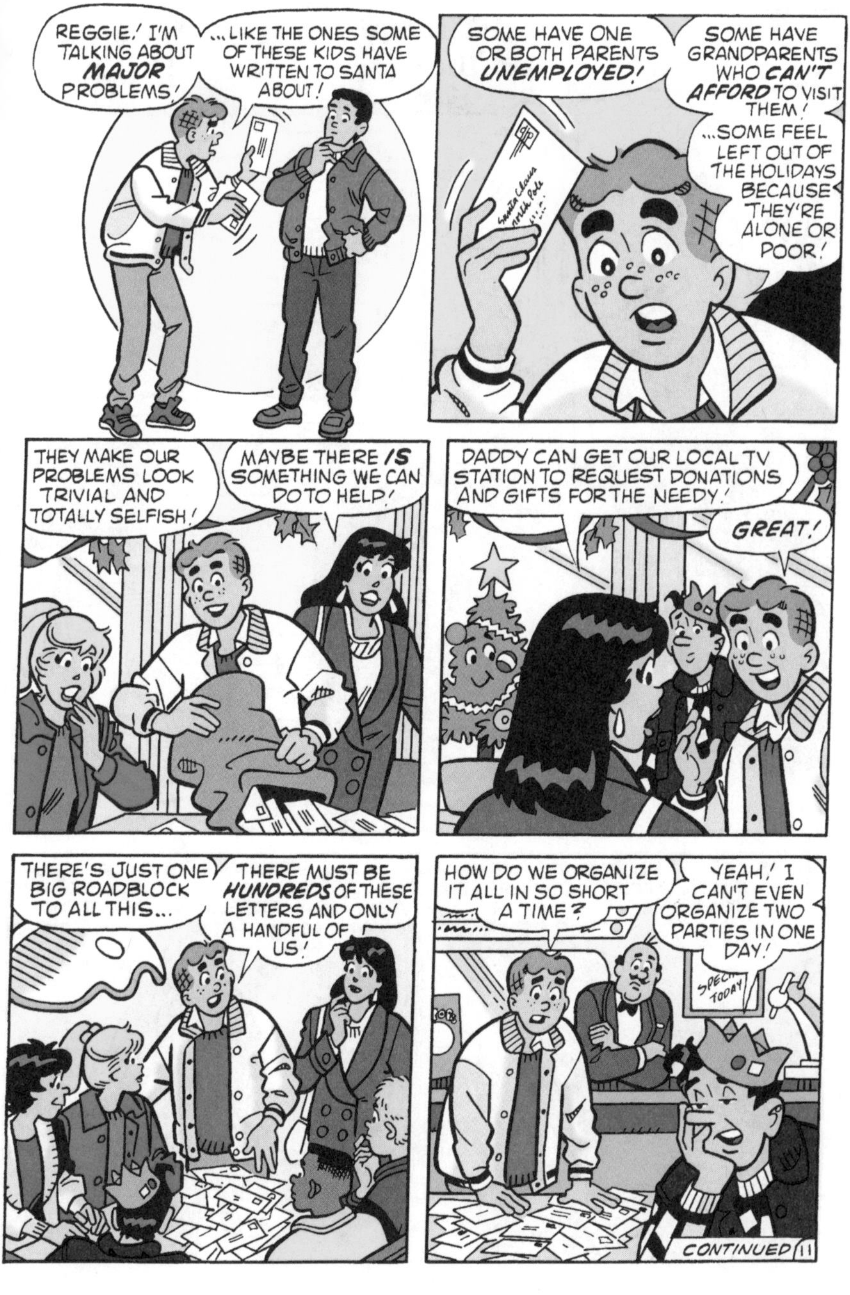
REGGIE! I'M TALKING ABOUT MAJOR PROBLEMS!
...LIKE THE ONES SOME OF THESE KIDS HAVE WRITTEN TO SANTA ABOUT!
SOME HAVE ONE OR BOTH PARENTS UNEMPLOYED!
SOME HAVE GRANDPARENTS WHO CAN'T AFFORD TO VISIT THEM!
...SOME FEEL LEFT OUT OF THE HOLIDAYS BECAUSE THEY'RE ALONE OR POOR!
THEY MAKE OUR PROBLEMS LOOK TRIVIAL AND TOTALLY SELFISH!
MAYBE THERE IS SOMETHING WE CAN DO TO HELP!
DADDY CAN GET OUR LOCAL TV STATION TO REQUEST DONATIONS AND GIFTS FOR THE NEEDY!
GREAT!
THERE'S JUST ONE BIG ROADBLOCK TO ALL THIS...
THERE MUST BE HUNDREDS OF THESE LETTERS AND ONLY A HANDFUL OF US!
HOW DO WE ORGANIZE IT ALL IN SO SHORT A TIME?
YEAH! I CAN'T EVEN ORGANIZE TWO PARTIES IN ONE DAY!
CONTINUED
11

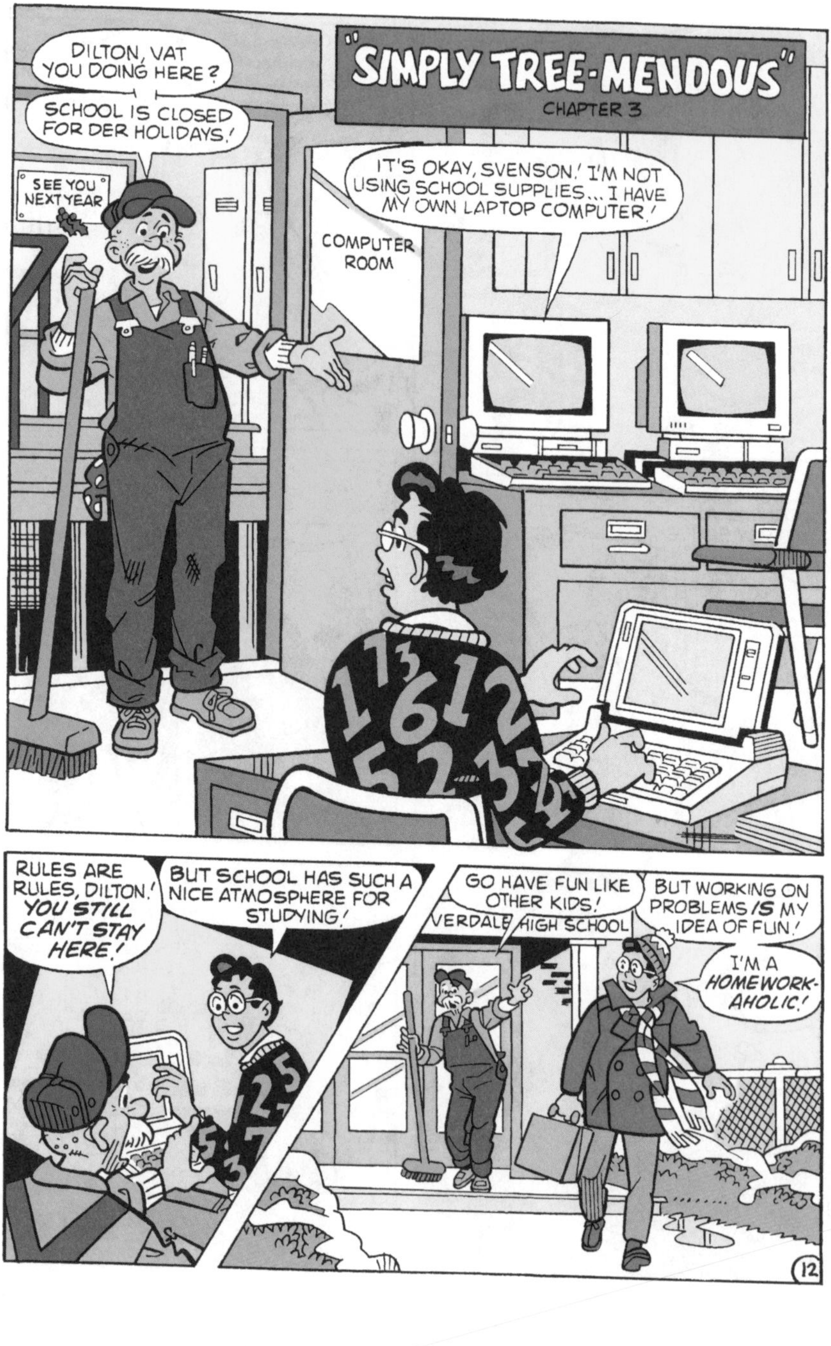
"SIMPLY TREE-MENDOUS"
CHAPTER 3
DILTON, VAT YOU DOING HERE?
SCHOOL IS CLOSED FOR DER HOLIDAYS!
SEE YOU NEXT YEAR
IT'S OKAY, SVENSON! I'M NOT USING SCHOOL SUPPLIES... I HAVE MY OWN LAPTOP COMPUTER!
COMPUTER ROOM
RULES ARE RULES, DILTON! YOU STILL CAN'T STAY HERE!
BUT SCHOOL HAS SUCH A NICE ATMOSPHERE FOR STUDYING!
GO HAVE FUN LIKE OTHER KIDS!
VERDALE HIGH SCHOOL
BUT WORKING ON PROBLEMS IS MY IDEA OF FUN!
I'M A HOMEWORK-AHOLIC!
12

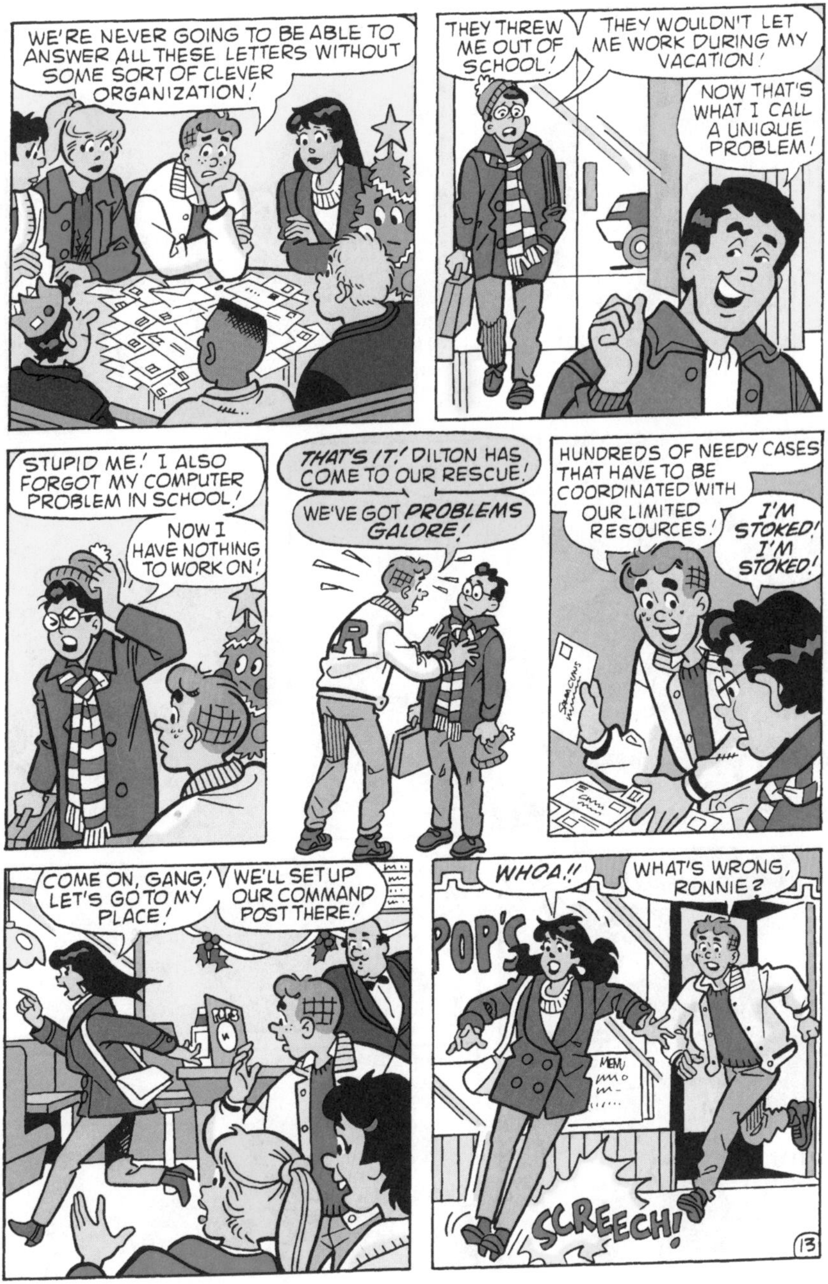
WE'RE NEVER GOING TO BE ABLE TO ANSWER ALL THESE LETTERS WITHOUT SOME SORT OF CLEVER ORGANIZATION!
THEY THREW ME OUT OF SCHOOL!
THEY WOULDN'T LET ME WORK DURING MY VACATION!
NOW THAT'S WHAT I CALL A UNIQUE PROBLEM!
STUPID ME! I ALSO FORGOT MY COMPUTER PROBLEM IN SCHOOL!
NOW I HAVE NOTHING TO WORK ON!
THAT'S IT! DILTON HAS COME TO OUR RESCUE!
WE'VE GOT PROBLEMS GALORE!
HUNDREDS OF NEEDY CASES THAT HAVE TO BE COORDINATED WITH OUR LIMITED RESOURCES!
I'M STOKED! I'M STOKED!
COME ON, GANG! LET'S GO TO MY PLACE!
WE'LL SET UP OUR COMMAND POST THERE!
WHOA!!
WHAT'S WRONG, RONNIE?
POP'S
MENU
SCREECH!
13

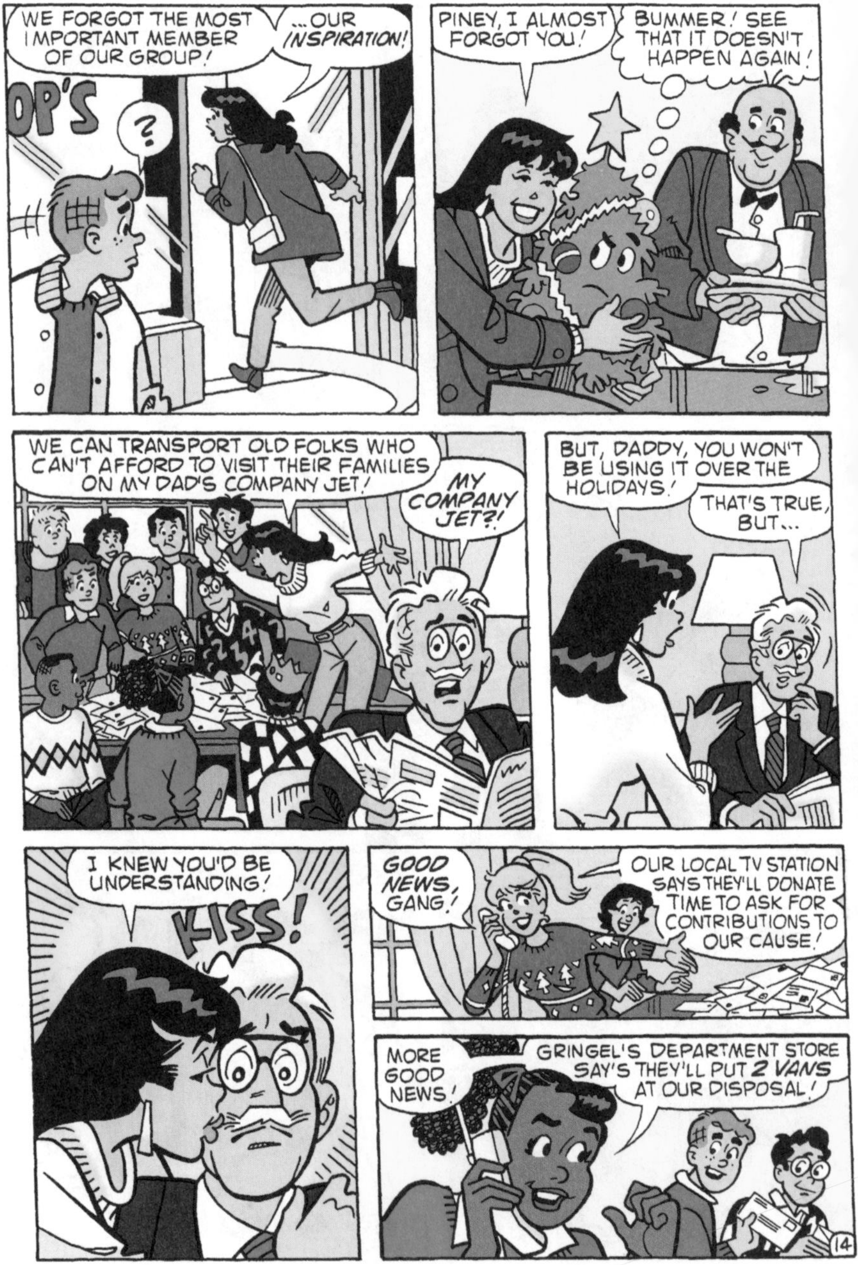
WE FORGOT THE MOST IMPORTANT MEMBER OF OUR GROUP!
...OUR INSPIRATION!
OP'S
?
PINEY, I ALMOST FORGOT YOU!
BUMMER! SEE THAT IT DOESN'T HAPPEN AGAIN!
WE CAN TRANSPORT OLD FOLKS WHO CAN'T AFFORD TO VISIT THEIR FAMILIES ON MY DAD'S COMPANY JET!
MY COMPANY JET?!
BUT, DADDY, YOU WON'T BE USING IT OVER THE HOLIDAYS!
THAT'S TRUE, BUT...
I KNEW YOU'D BE UNDERSTANDING!
KISS!
GOOD NEWS, GANG!
OUR LOCAL TV STATION SAYS THEY'LL DONATE TIME TO ASK FOR CONTRIBUTIONS TO OUR CAUSE!
MORE GOOD NEWS!
GRINGEL'S DEPARTMENT STORE SAY'S THEY'LL PUT 2 VANS AT OUR DISPOSAL!
14

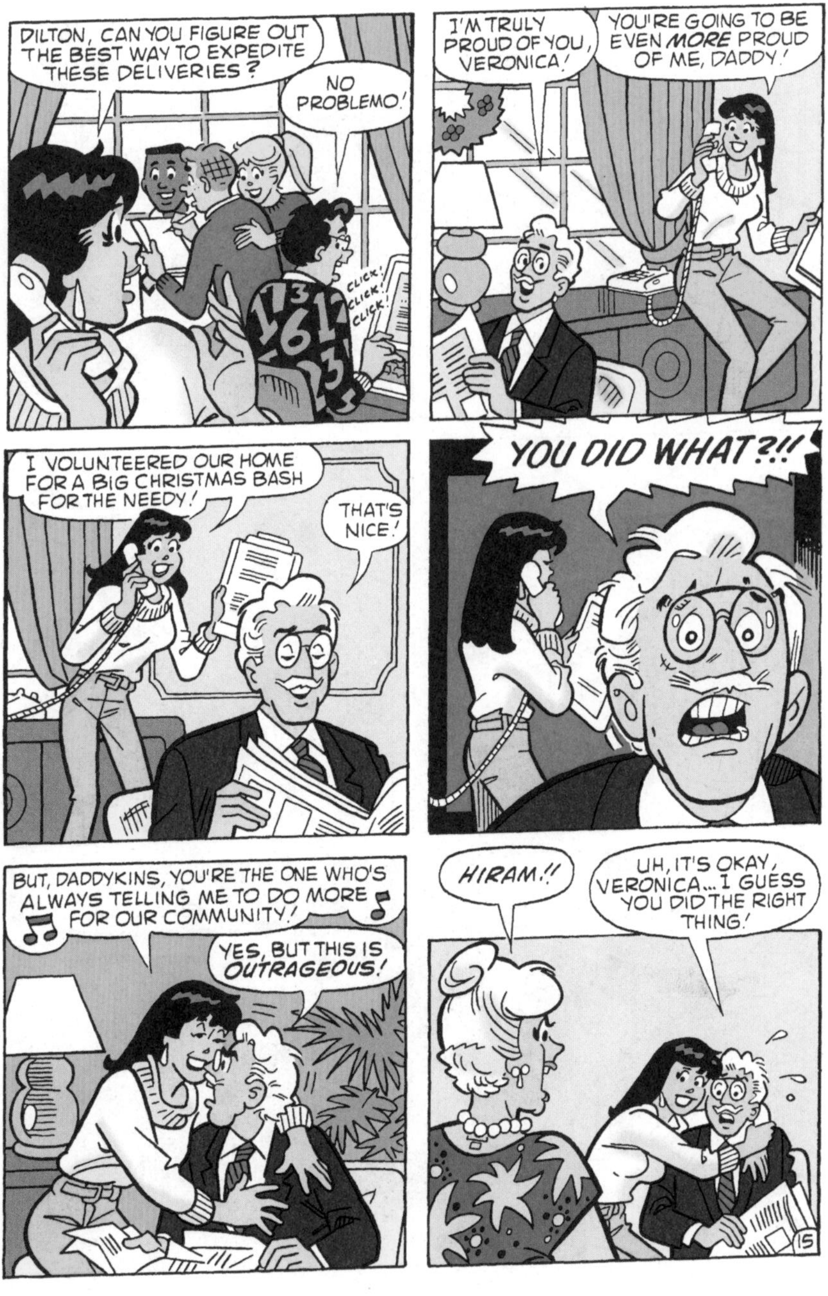
DILTON, CAN YOU FIGURE OUT THE BEST WAY TO EXPEDITE THESE DELIVERIES?
NO PROBLEMO!
CLICK! CLICK! CLICK!
I'M TRULY PROUD OF YOU, VERONICA!
YOU'RE GOING TO BE EVEN MORE PROUD OF ME, DADDY!
I VOLUNTEERED OUR HOME FOR A BIG CHRISTMAS BASH FOR THE NEEDY!
THAT'S NICE!
YOU DID WHAT?!!
BUT, DADDYKINS, YOU'RE THE ONE WHO'S ALWAYS TELLING ME TO DO MORE FOR OUR COMMUNITY!
YES, BUT THIS IS OUTRAGEOUS!
HIRAM!!
UH, IT'S OKAY, VERONICA... I GUESS YOU DID THE RIGHT THING!
15

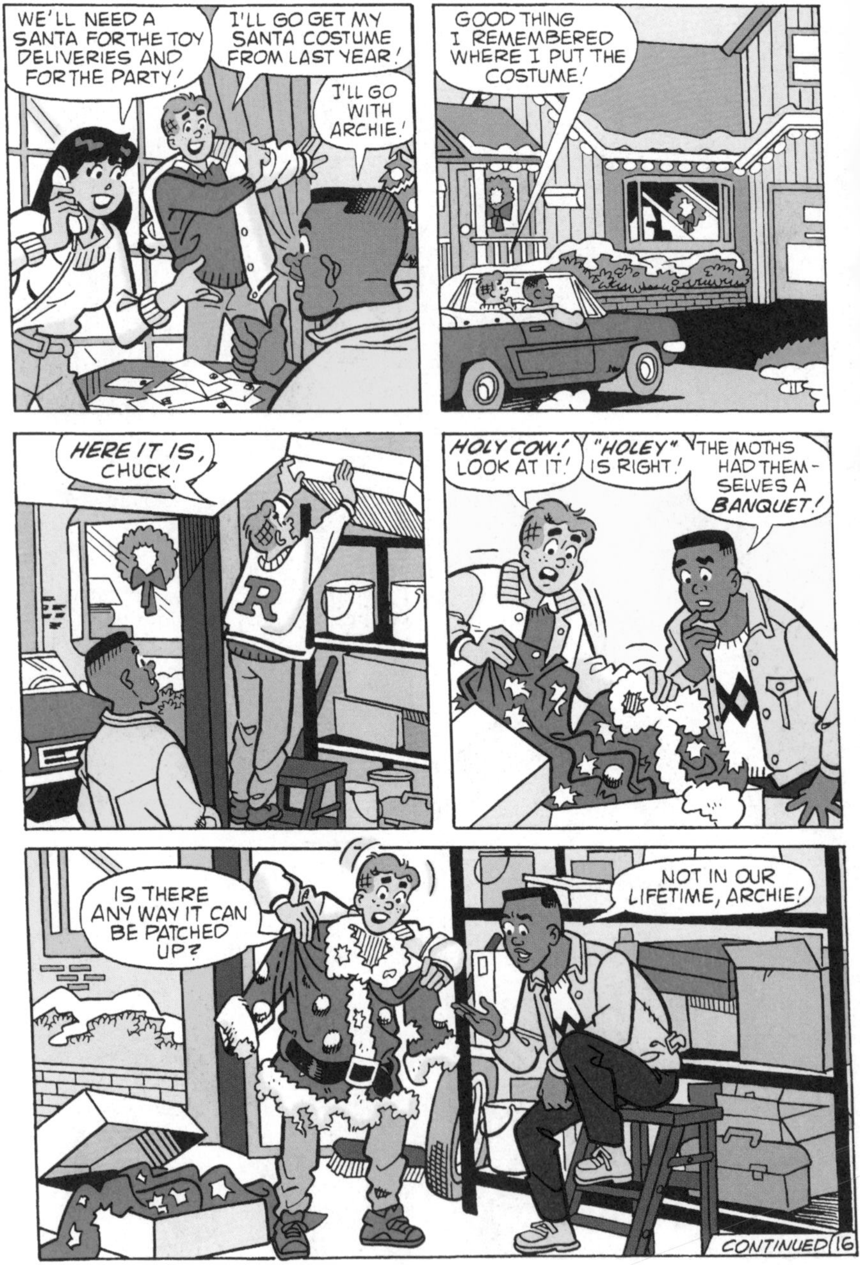
WE'LL NEED A SANTA FOR THE TOY DELIVERIES AND FOR THE PARTY!
I'LL GO GET MY SANTA COSTUME FROM LAST YEAR!
I'LL GO WITH ARCHIE!
GOOD THING I REMEMBERED WHERE I PUT THE COSTUME!
HERE IT IS, CHUCK!
HOLY COW! LOOK AT IT!
"HOLEY" IS RIGHT!
THE MOTHS HAD THEM-SELVES A BANQUET!
IS THERE ANY WAY IT CAN BE PATCHED UP?
NOT IN OUR LIFETIME, ARCHIE!
CONTINUED 16

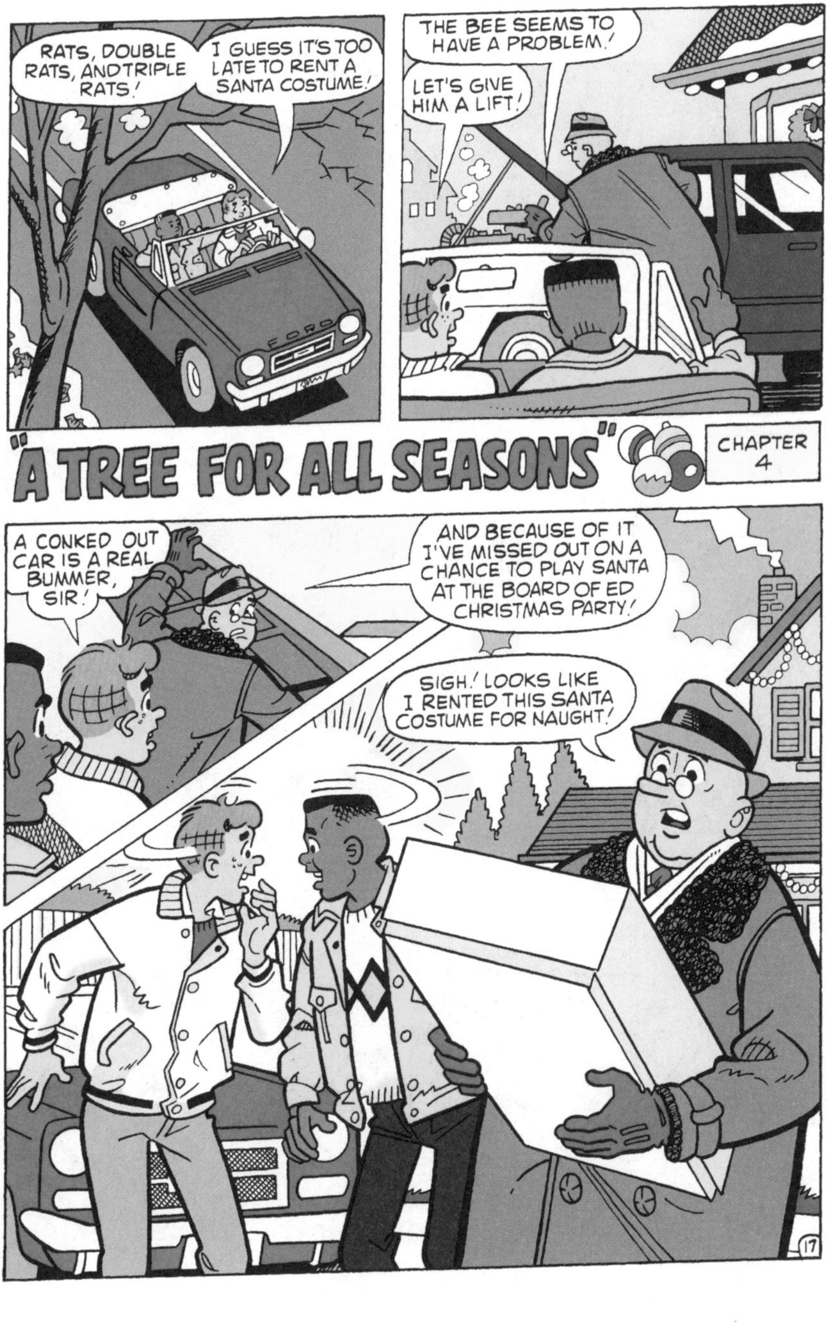
RATS, DOUBLE RATS, AND TRIPLE RATS!
I GUESS IT'S TOO LATE TO RENT A SANTA COSTUME!
THE BEE SEEMS TO HAVE A PROBLEM!
LET'S GIVE HIM A LIFT!
"A TREE FOR ALL SEASONS"
CHAPTER 4
A CONKED OUT CAR IS A REAL BUMMER, SIR!
AND BECAUSE OF IT I'VE MISSED OUT ON A CHANCE TO PLAY SANTA AT THE BOARD OF ED CHRISTMAS PARTY!
SIGH! LOOKS LIKE I RENTED THIS SANTA COSTUME FOR NAUGHT!
17

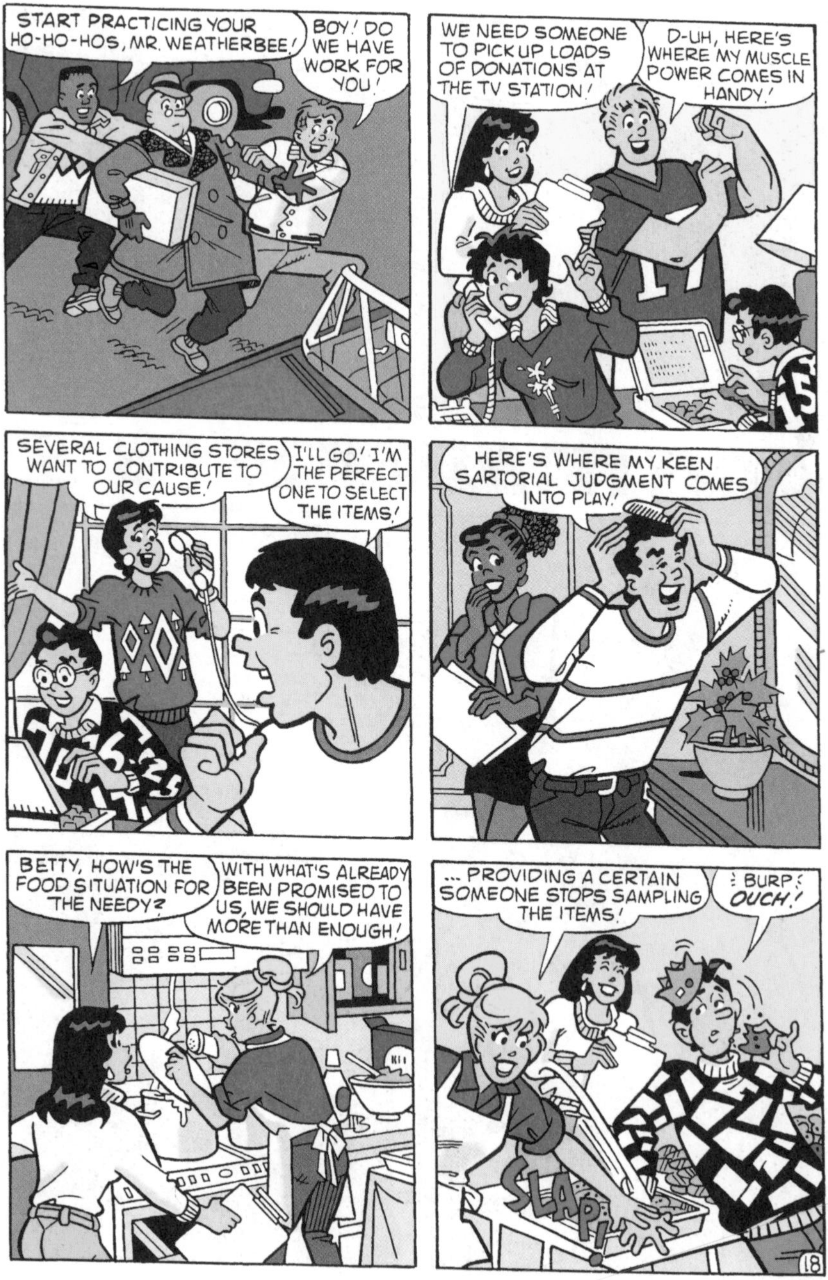
START PRACTICING YOUR HO-HO-HOS, MR. WEATHERBEE!
BOY! DO WE HAVE WORK FOR YOU!
WE NEED SOMEONE TO PICK UP LOADS OF DONATIONS AT THE TV STATION!
D-UH, HERE'S WHERE MY MUSCLE POWER COMES IN HANDY!
SEVERAL CLOTHING STORES WANT TO CONTRIBUTE TO OUR CAUSE!
I'LL GO! I'M THE PERFECT ONE TO SELECT THE ITEMS!
HERE'S WHERE MY KEEN SARTORIAL JUDGMENT COMES INTO PLAY!
BETTY, HOW'S THE FOOD SITUATION FOR THE NEEDY?
WITH WHAT'S ALREADY BEEN PROMISED TO US, WE SHOULD HAVE MORE THAN ENOUGH!
... PROVIDING A CERTAIN SOMEONE STOPS SAMPLING THE ITEMS!
BURP
OUCH!
SLAP!
18

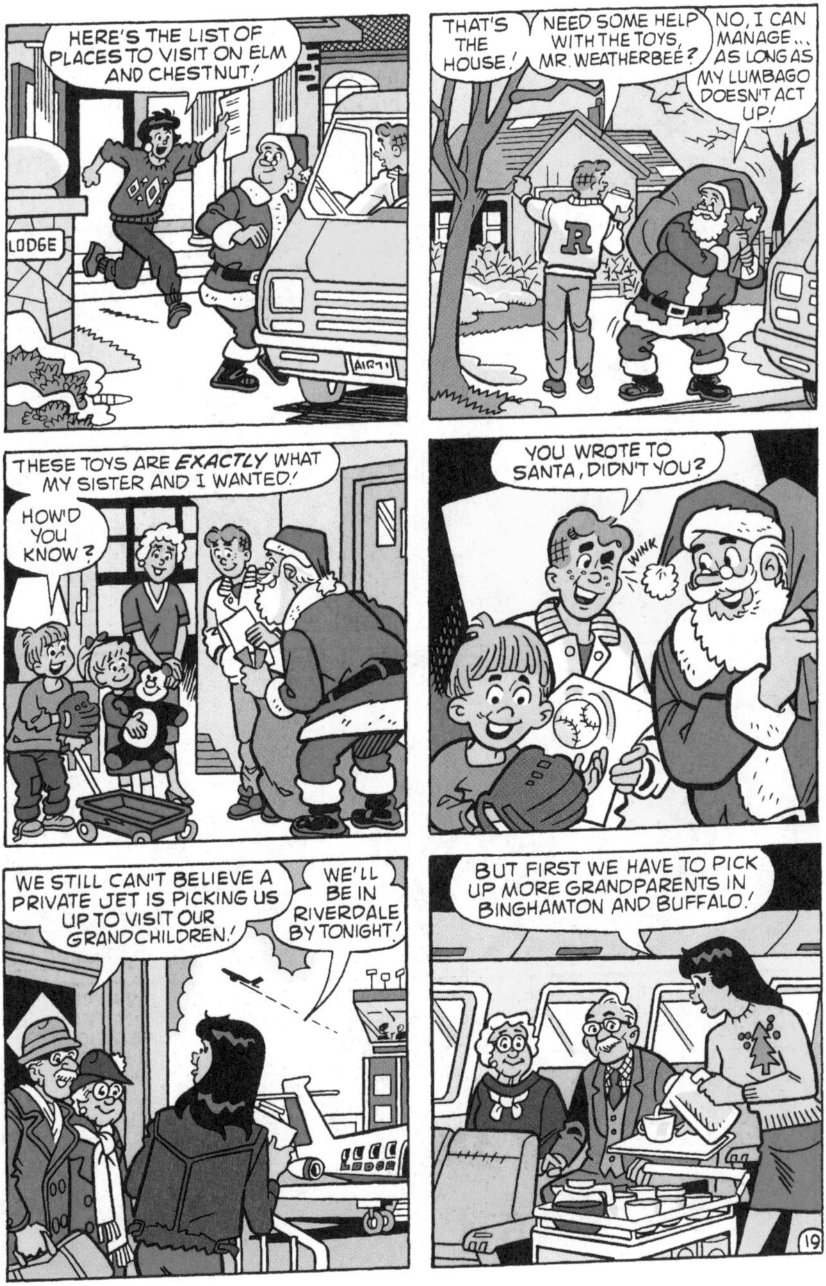
HERE'S THE LIST OF PLACES TO VISIT ON ELM AND CHESTNUT!
LODGE
AIR 1
THAT'S THE HOUSE!
NEED SOME HELP WITH THE TOYS, MR. WEATHERBEE?
NO, I CAN MANAGE... AS LONG AS MY LUMBAGO DOESN'T ACT UP!
THESE TOYS ARE *EXACTLY* WHAT MY SISTER AND I WANTED!
HOW'D YOU KNOW?
YOU WROTE TO SANTA, DIDN'T YOU?
WINK
WE STILL CAN'T BELIEVE A PRIVATE JET IS PICKING US UP TO VISIT OUR GRANDCHILDREN!
WE'LL BE IN RIVERDALE BY TONIGHT!
LODGE
BUT FIRST WE HAVE TO PICK UP MORE GRANDPARENTS IN BINGHAMTON AND BUFFALO!
19

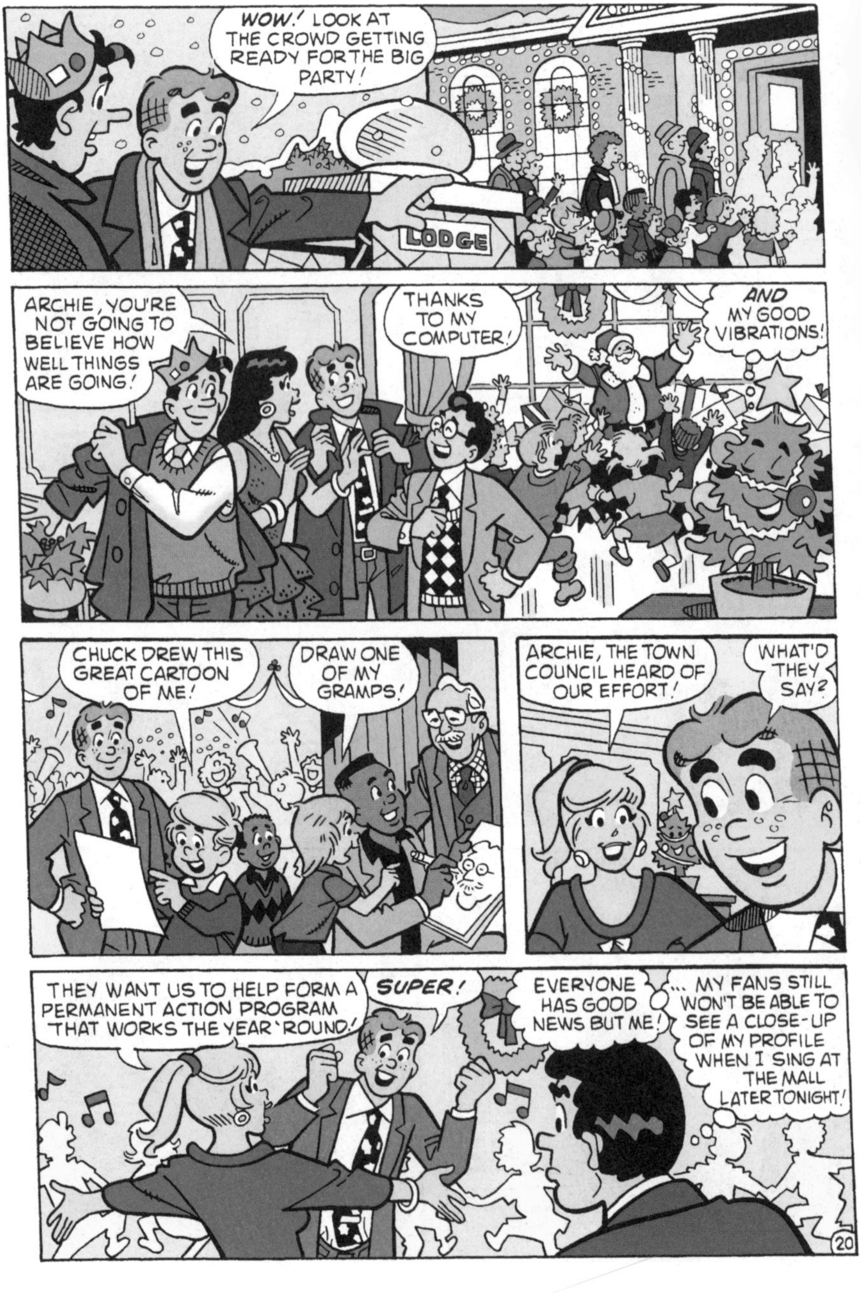
WOW! LOOK AT THE CROWD GETTING READY FOR THE BIG PARTY!
LODGE
ARCHIE, YOU'RE NOT GOING TO BELIEVE HOW WELL THINGS ARE GOING!
THANKS TO MY COMPUTER!
AND MY GOOD VIBRATIONS!
CHUCK DREW THIS GREAT CARTOON OF ME!
DRAW ONE OF MY GRAMPS!
ARCHIE, THE TOWN COUNCIL HEARD OF OUR EFFORT!
WHAT'D THEY SAY?
THEY WANT US TO HELP FORM A PERMANENT ACTION PROGRAM THAT WORKS THE YEAR 'ROUND!
SUPER!
EVERYONE HAS GOOD NEWS BUT ME!
... MY FANS STILL WON'T BE ABLE TO SEE A CLOSE-UP OF MY PROFILE WHEN I SING AT THE MALL LATER TONIGHT!
20

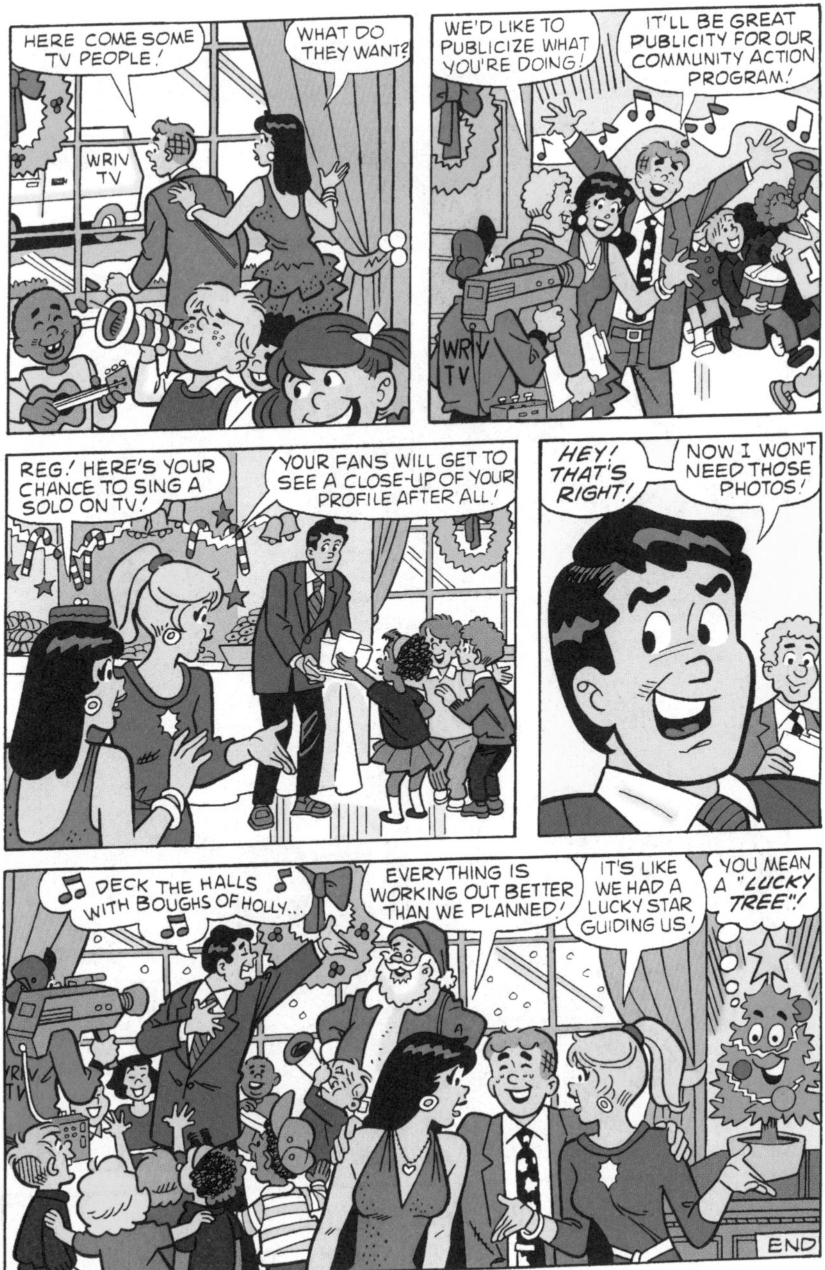
HERE COME SOME TV PEOPLE!
WHAT DO THEY WANT?
WRIV TV
WE'D LIKE TO PUBLICIZE WHAT YOU'RE DOING!
IT'LL BE GREAT PUBLICITY FOR OUR COMMUNITY ACTION PROGRAM!
WRIV TV
REG! HERE'S YOUR CHANCE TO SING A SOLO ON TV!
YOUR FANS WILL GET TO SEE A CLOSE-UP OF YOUR PROFILE AFTER ALL!
HEY! THAT'S RIGHT!
NOW I WON'T NEED THOSE PHOTOS!
DECK THE HALLS WITH BOUGHS OF HOLLY...
EVERYTHING IS WORKING OUT BETTER THAN WE PLANNED!
IT'S LIKE WE HAD A LUCKY STAR GUIDING US!
YOU MEAN A "LUCKY TREE"!
END

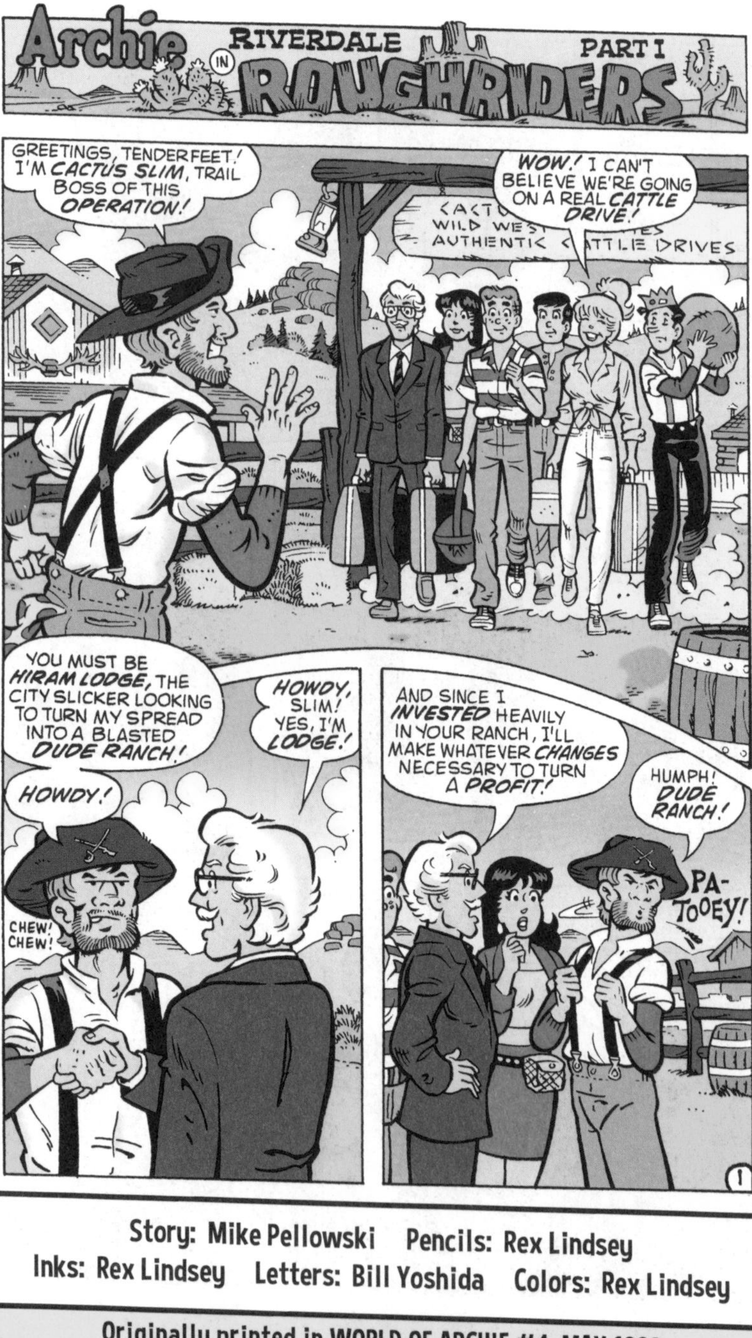
Archie
IN
RIVERDALE
PART I
ROUGHRIDERS
GREETINGS, TENDERFEET! I'M CACTUS SLIM, TRAIL BOSS OF THIS OPERATION!
WOW! I CAN'T BELIEVE WE'RE GOING ON A REAL CATTLE DRIVE!
AUTHENTIC CATTLE DRIVES
YOU MUST BE HIRAM LODGE, THE CITY SLICKER LOOKING TO TURN MY SPREAD INTO A BLASTED DUDE RANCH!
HOWDY, SLIM! YES, I'M LODGE!
HOWDY!
CHEW! CHEW!
AND SINCE I INVESTED HEAVILY IN YOUR RANCH, I'LL MAKE WHATEVER CHANGES NECESSARY TO TURN A PROFIT!
HUMPH! DUDE RANCH!
PA-TOOEY!
1

Story: Mike Pellowski Pencils: Rex Lindsey
Inks: Rex Lindsey Letters: Bill Yoshida Colors: Rex Lindsey

Originally printed in WORLD OF ARCHIE #4, MAY 1993

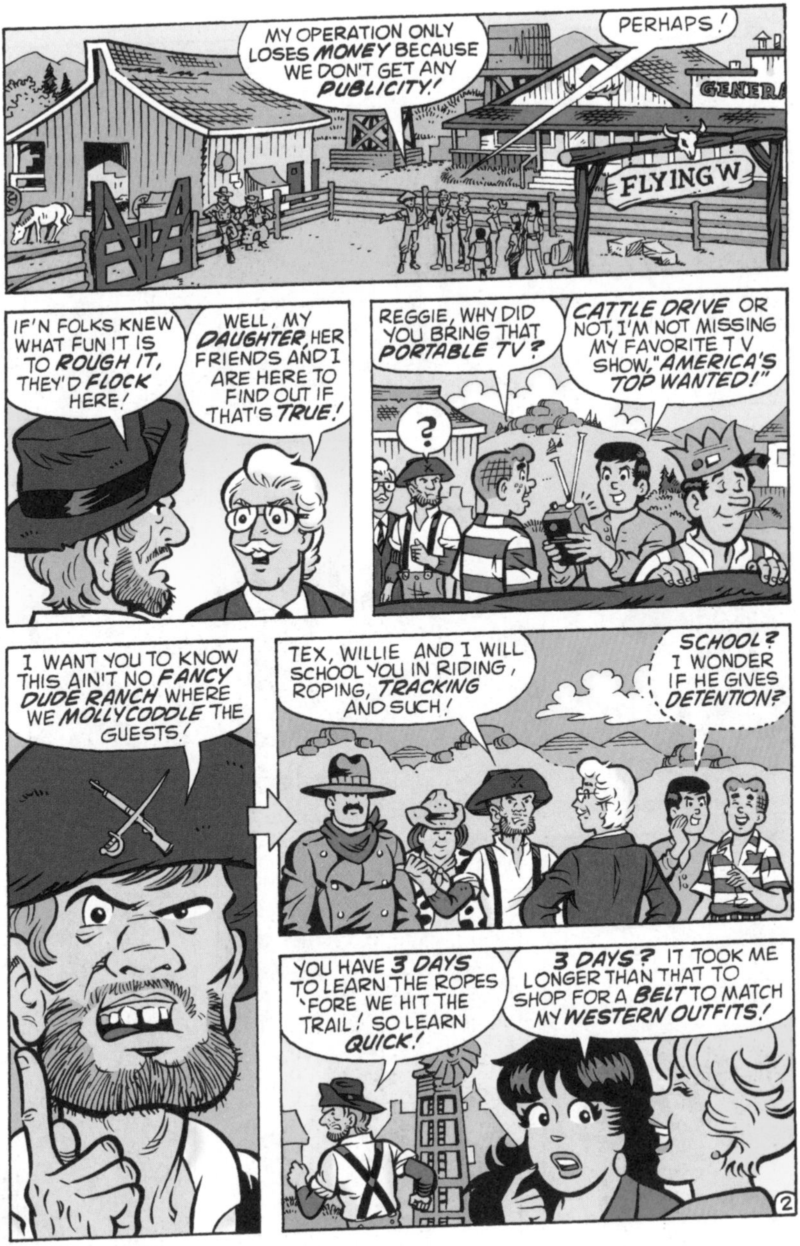

MY OPERATION ONLY LOSES MONEY BECAUSE WE DON'T GET ANY PUBLICITY!
PERHAPS!
GENERA
FLYING W
IF'N FOLKS KNEW WHAT FUN IT IS TO ROUGH IT, THEY'D FLOCK HERE!
WELL, MY DAUGHTER, HER FRIENDS AND I ARE HERE TO FIND OUT IF THAT'S TRUE!
REGGIE, WHY DID YOU BRING THAT PORTABLE TV?
CATTLE DRIVE OR NOT, I'M NOT MISSING MY FAVORITE T V SHOW, "AMERICA'S TOP WANTED!"
?
I WANT YOU TO KNOW THIS AIN'T NO FANCY DUDE RANCH WHERE WE MOLLYCODDLE THE GUESTS!
TEX, WILLIE AND I WILL SCHOOL YOU IN RIDING, ROPING, TRACKING AND SUCH!
SCHOOL? I WONDER IF HE GIVES DETENTION?
YOU HAVE 3 DAYS TO LEARN THE ROPES 'FORE WE HIT THE TRAIL! SO LEARN QUICK!
3 DAYS? IT TOOK ME LONGER THAN THAT TO SHOP FOR A BELT TO MATCH MY WESTERN OUTFITS!
2

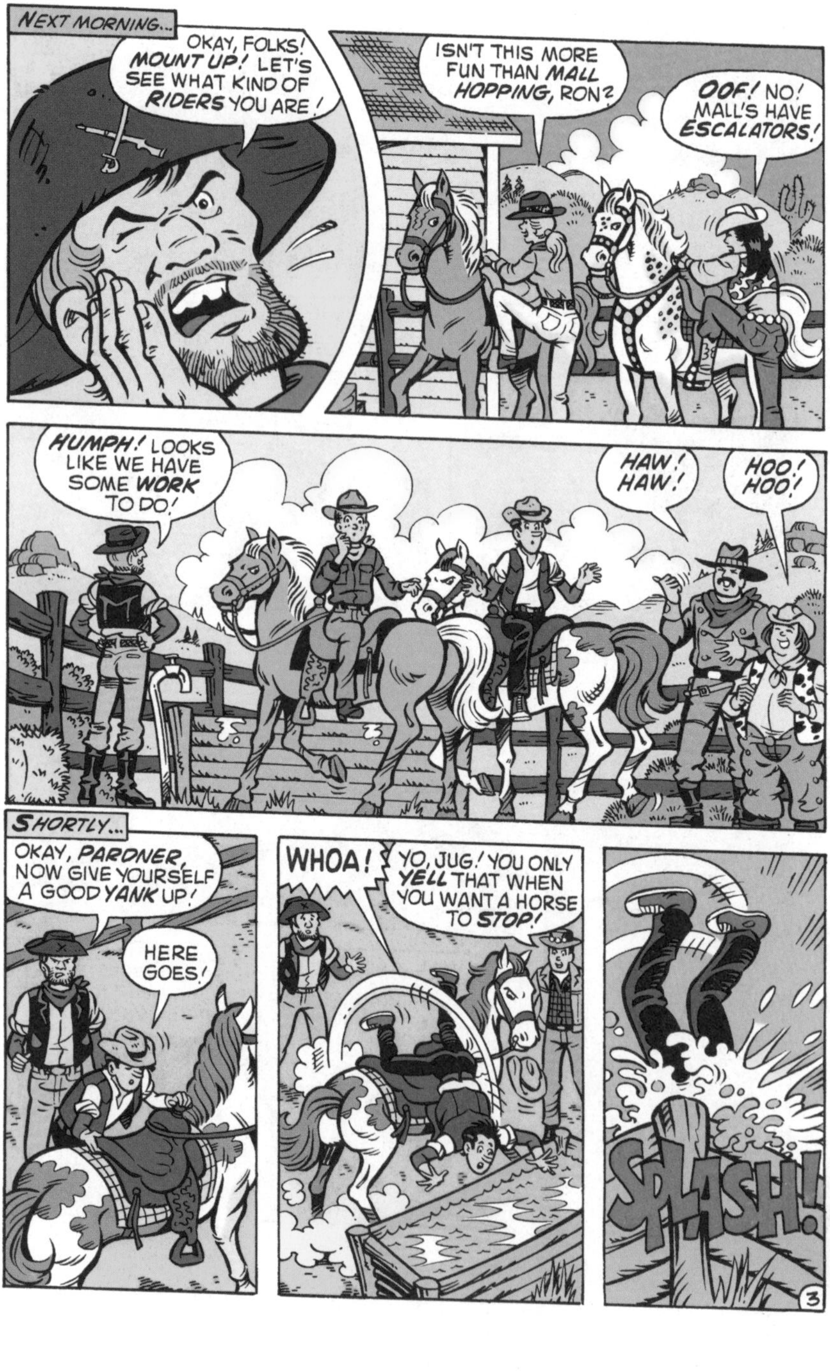
NEXT MORNING...
OKAY, FOLKS! MOUNT UP! LET'S SEE WHAT KIND OF RIDERS YOU ARE!
ISN'T THIS MORE FUN THAN MALL HOPPING, RON?
OOF! NO! MALL'S HAVE ESCALATORS!
HUMPH! LOOKS LIKE WE HAVE SOME WORK TO DO!
HAW! HAW!
HOO! HOO!
SHORTLY...
OKAY, PARDNER, NOW GIVE YOURSELF A GOOD YANK UP!
HERE GOES!
WHOA!
YO, JUG! YOU ONLY YELL THAT WHEN YOU WANT A HORSE TO STOP!
SPLASH!
3

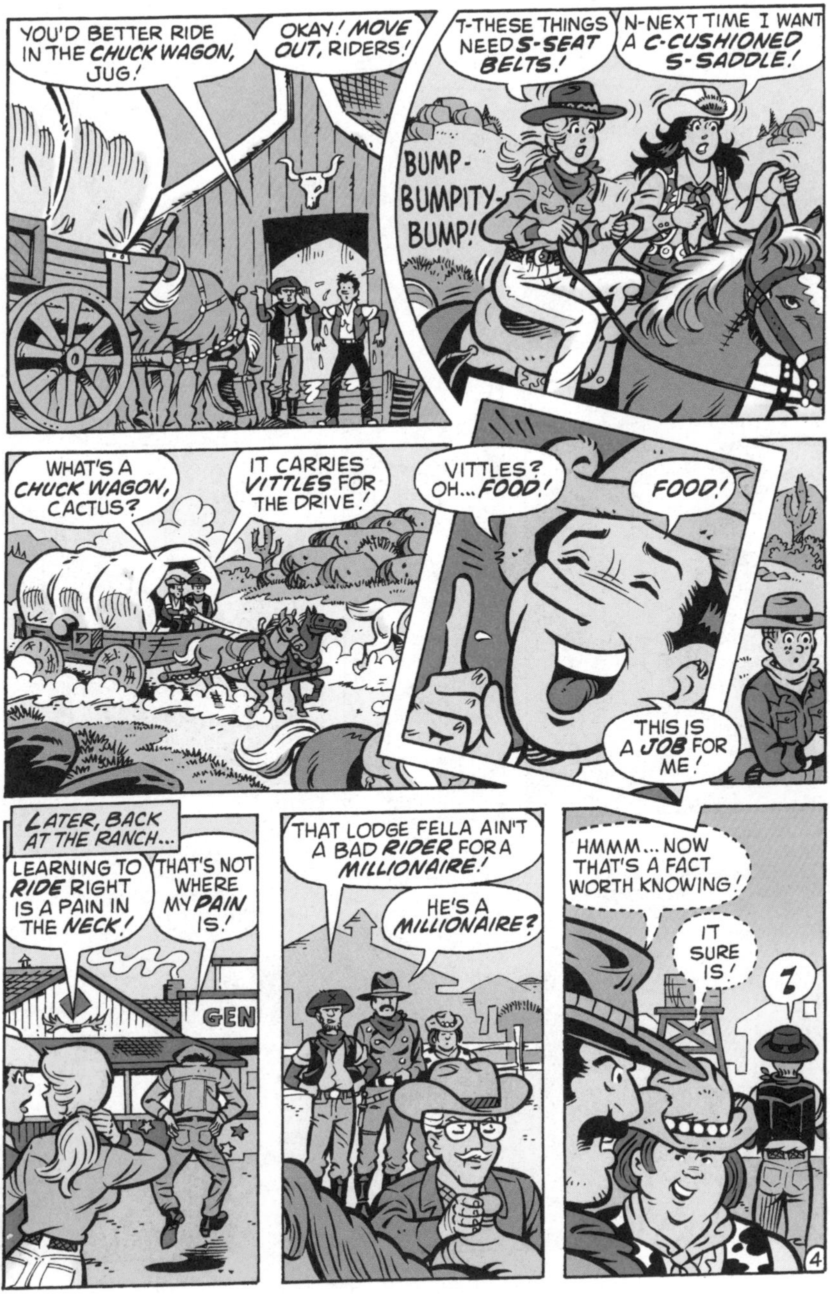
YOU'D BETTER RIDE IN THE CHUCK WAGON, JUG!
OKAY! MOVE OUT, RIDERS!
T-THESE THINGS NEED S-SEAT BELTS!
N-NEXT TIME I WANT A C-CUSHIONED S-SADDLE!
BUMP-BUMPITY-BUMP!
WHAT'S A CHUCK WAGON, CACTUS?
IT CARRIES VITTLES FOR THE DRIVE!
VITTLES? OH... FOOD!
FOOD!
THIS IS A JOB FOR ME!
LATER, BACK AT THE RANCH...
LEARNING TO RIDE RIGHT IS A PAIN IN THE NECK!
THAT'S NOT WHERE MY PAIN IS!
GEN
THAT LODGE FELLA AIN'T A BAD RIDER FOR A MILLIONAIRE!
HE'S A MILLIONAIRE?
HMMM... NOW THAT'S A FACT WORTH KNOWING!
IT SURE IS!
?
4

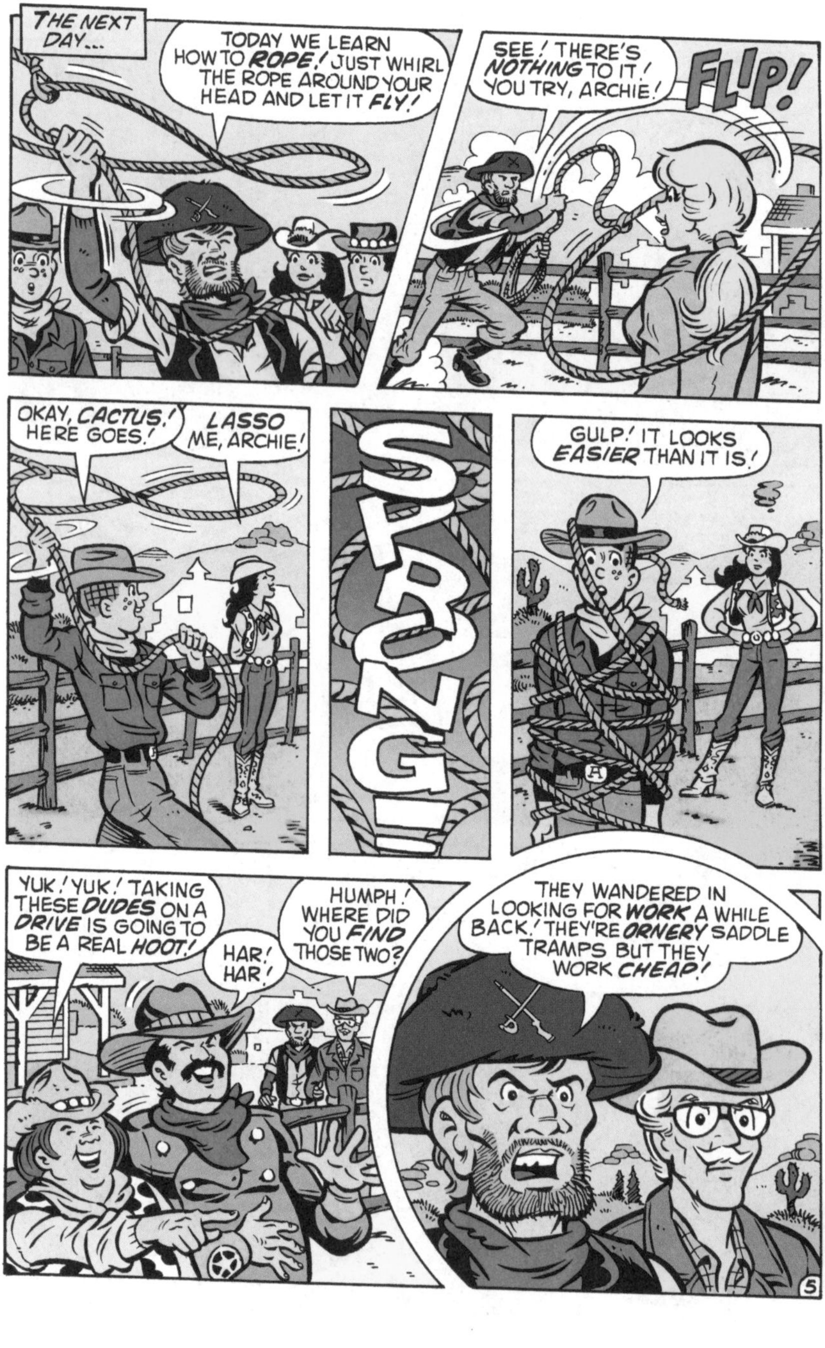
THE NEXT DAY...
TODAY WE LEARN HOW TO ROPE! JUST WHIRL THE ROPE AROUND YOUR HEAD AND LET IT FLY!
SEE! THERE'S NOTHING TO IT! YOU TRY, ARCHIE!
FLIP!
OKAY, CACTUS! HERE GOES!
LASSO ME, ARCHIE!
SPROING!
GULP! IT LOOKS EASIER THAN IT IS!
YUK! YUK! TAKING THESE DUDES ON A DRIVE IS GOING TO BE A REAL HOOT!
HAR! HAR!
HUMPH! WHERE DID YOU FIND THOSE TWO?
THEY WANDERED IN LOOKING FOR WORK A WHILE BACK! THEY'RE ORNERY SADDLE TRAMPS BUT THEY WORK CHEAP!
5

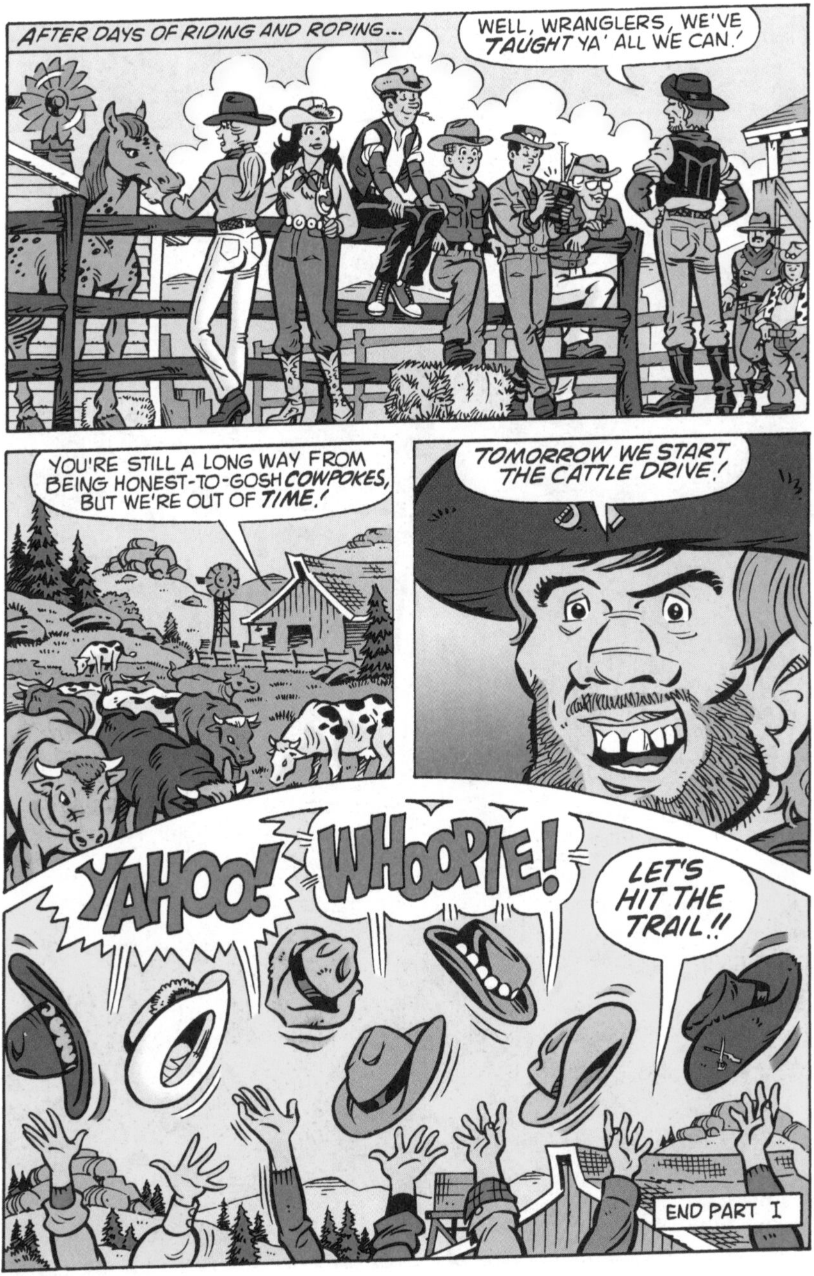
AFTER DAYS OF RIDING AND ROPING...
WELL, WRANGLERS, WE'VE TAUGHT YA' ALL WE CAN.!
YOU'RE STILL A LONG WAY FROM BEING HONEST-TO-GOSH COWPOKES, BUT WE'RE OUT OF TIME.!
TOMORROW WE START THE CATTLE DRIVE.!
YAHOO!
WHOOPIE!
LET'S HIT THE TRAIL!!
END PART I

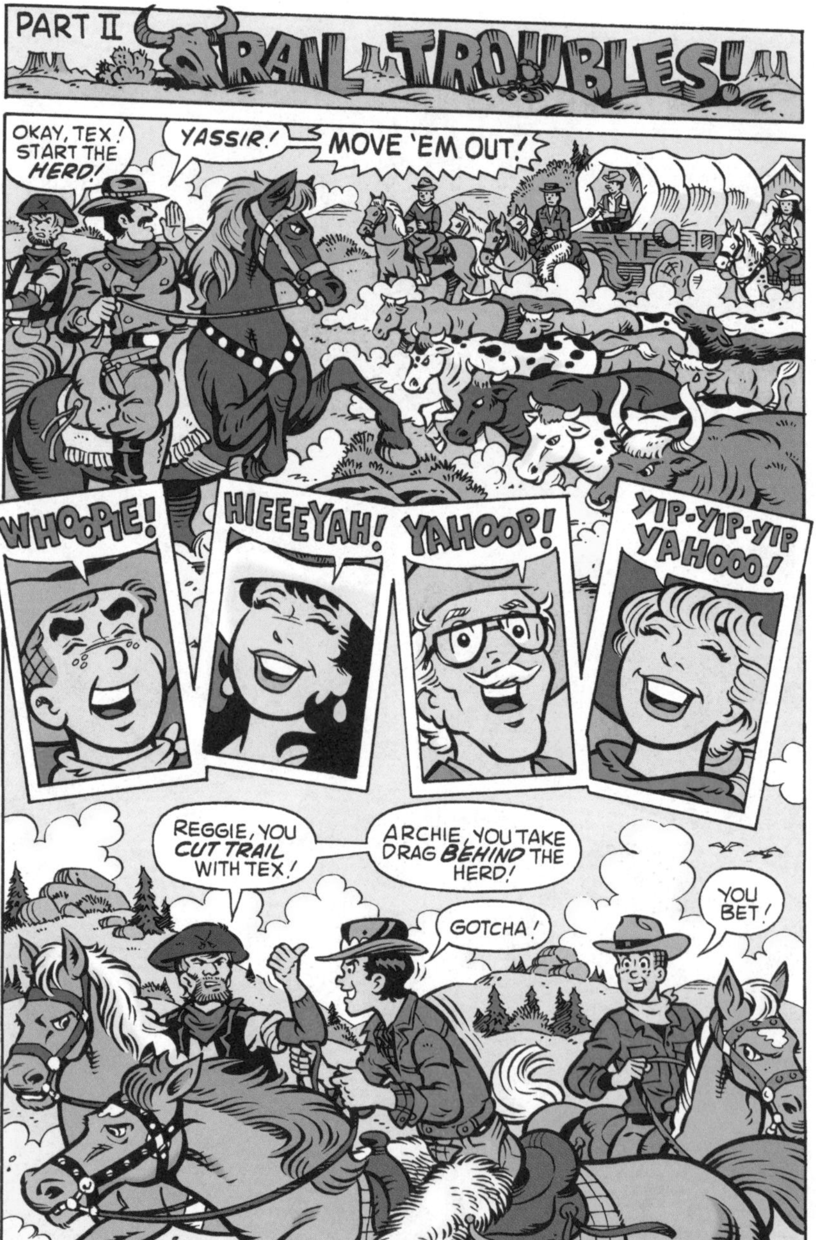
PART II
TRAIL TROUBLES!
OKAY, TEX! START THE HERD!
YASSIR!
MOVE 'EM OUT!
WHOOPIE!
HIEEEYAH!
YAHOOP!
YIP-YIP-YIP YAHOOO!
REGGIE, YOU CUT TRAIL WITH TEX!
ARCHIE, YOU TAKE DRAG BEHIND THE HERD!
GOTCHA!
YOU BET!
7

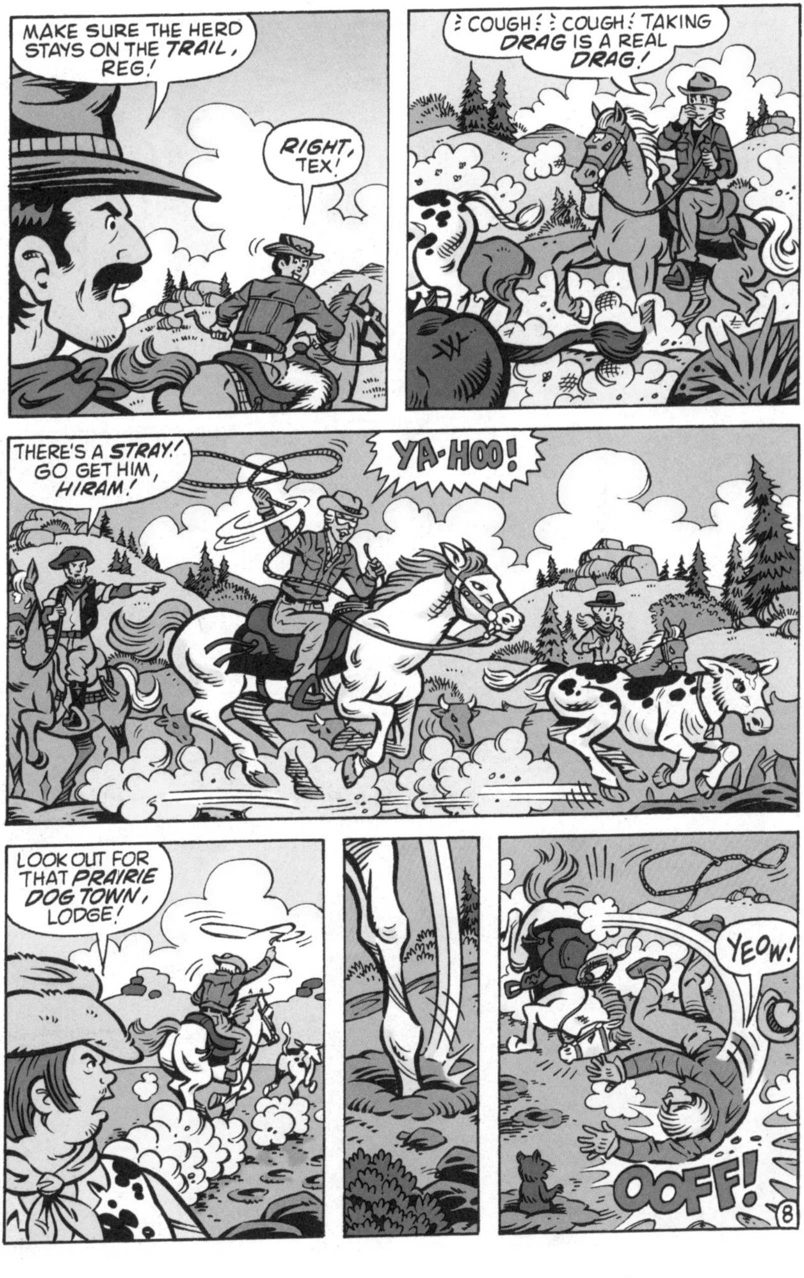
MAKE SURE THE HERD STAYS ON THE TRAIL, REG!
RIGHT, TEX!
COUGH! COUGH! TAKING DRAG IS A REAL DRAG!
THERE'S A STRAY! GO GET HIM, HIRAM!
YA-HOO!
LOOK OUT FOR THAT PRAIRIE DOG TOWN, LODGE!
YEOW!
OOFF!
8

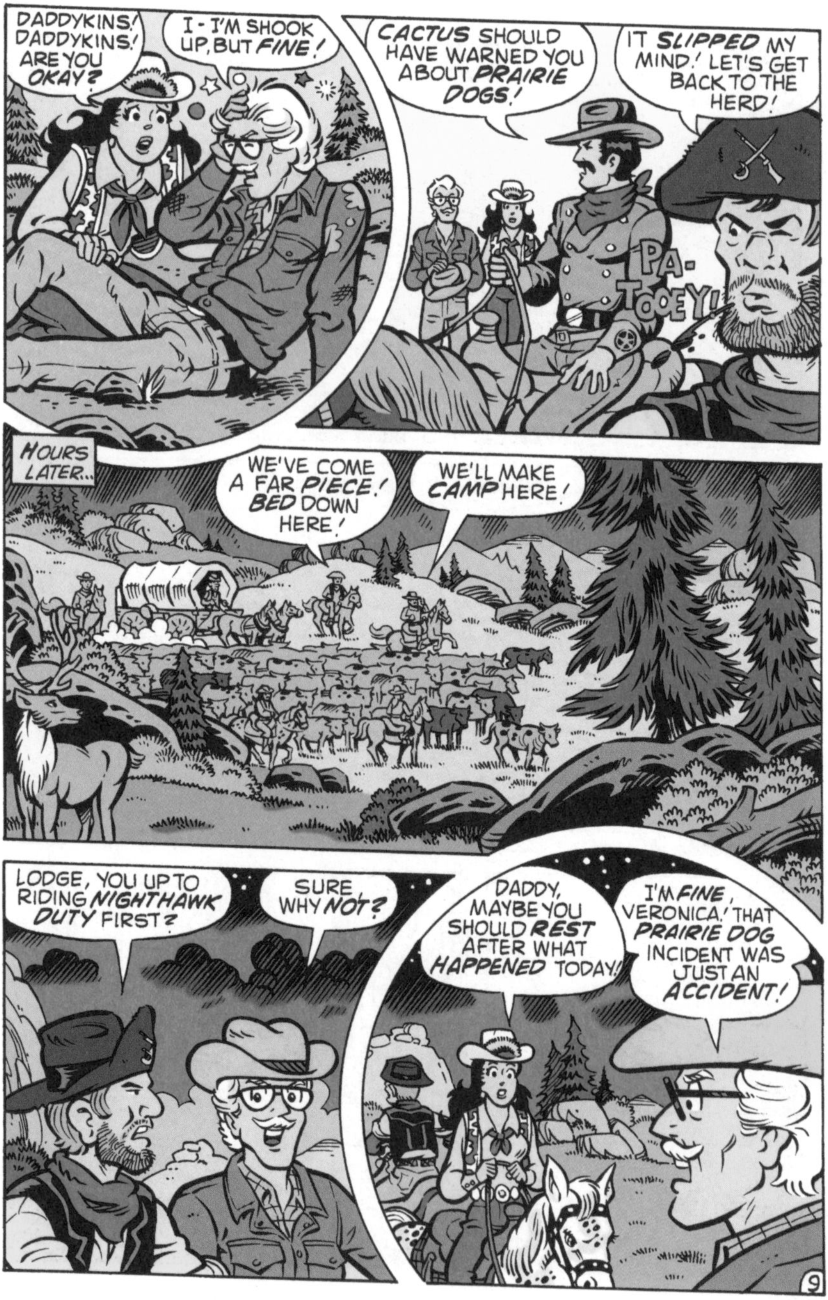
DADDYKINS! DADDYKINS! ARE YOU OKAY?
I - I'M SHOOK UP, BUT FINE!
CACTUS SHOULD HAVE WARNED YOU ABOUT PRAIRIE DOGS!
IT SLIPPED MY MIND! LET'S GET BACK TO THE HERD!
PA-TOOEY!
HOURS LATER...
WE'VE COME A FAR PIECE! BED DOWN HERE!
WE'LL MAKE CAMP HERE!
LODGE, YOU UP TO RIDING NIGHTHAWK DUTY FIRST?
SURE WHY NOT?
DADDY, MAYBE YOU SHOULD REST AFTER WHAT HAPPENED TODAY!
I'M FINE, VERONICA! THAT PRAIRIE DOG INCIDENT WAS JUST AN ACCIDENT!
9

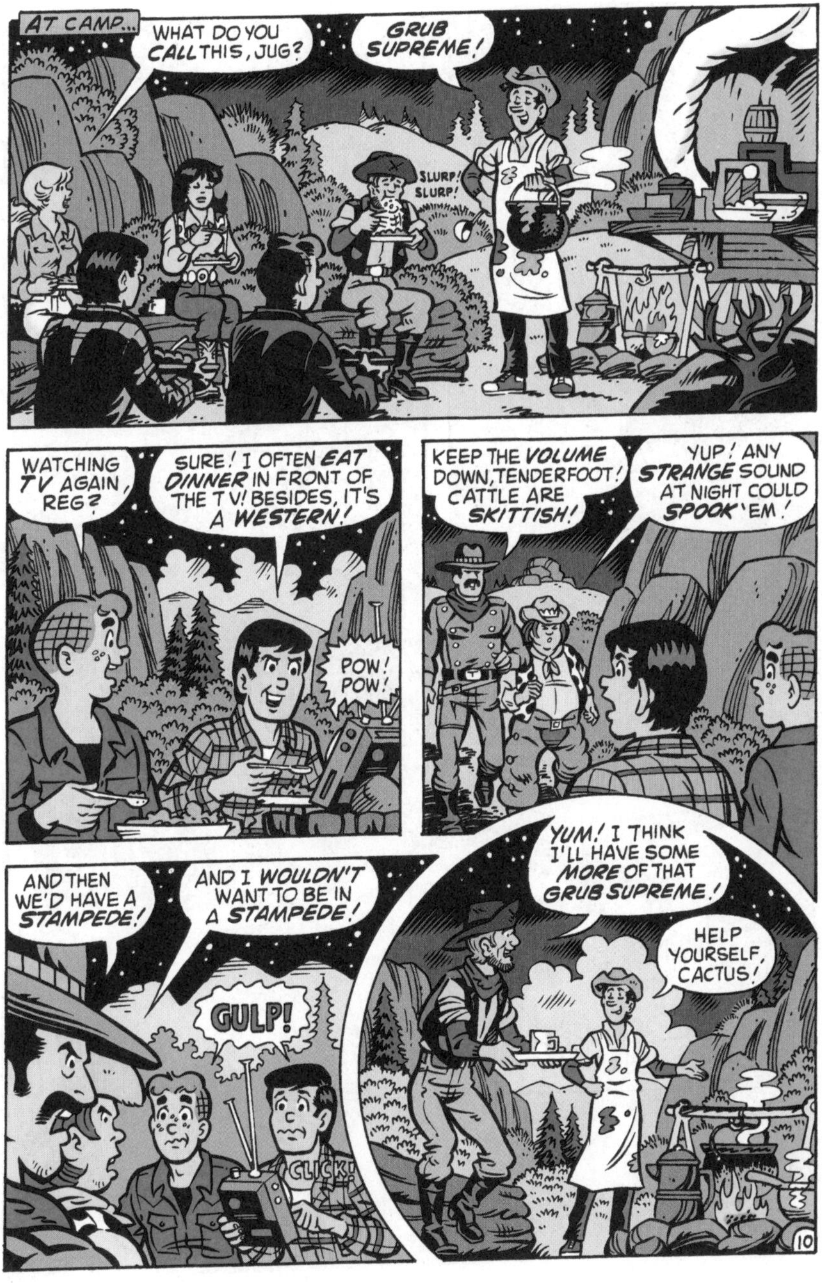
AT CAMP...
WHAT DO YOU CALL THIS, JUG?
GRUB SUPREME!
SLURP! SLURP!
WATCHING TV AGAIN, REG?
SURE! I OFTEN EAT DINNER IN FRONT OF THE TV! BESIDES, IT'S A WESTERN!
POW! POW!
KEEP THE VOLUME DOWN, TENDERFOOT! CATTLE ARE SKITTISH!
YUP! ANY STRANGE SOUND AT NIGHT COULD SPOOK 'EM!
AND THEN WE'D HAVE A STAMPEDE!
AND I WOULDN'T WANT TO BE IN A STAMPEDE!
GULP!
CLICK!
YUM! I THINK I'LL HAVE SOME MORE OF THAT GRUB SUPREME!
HELP YOURSELF, CACTUS!
10

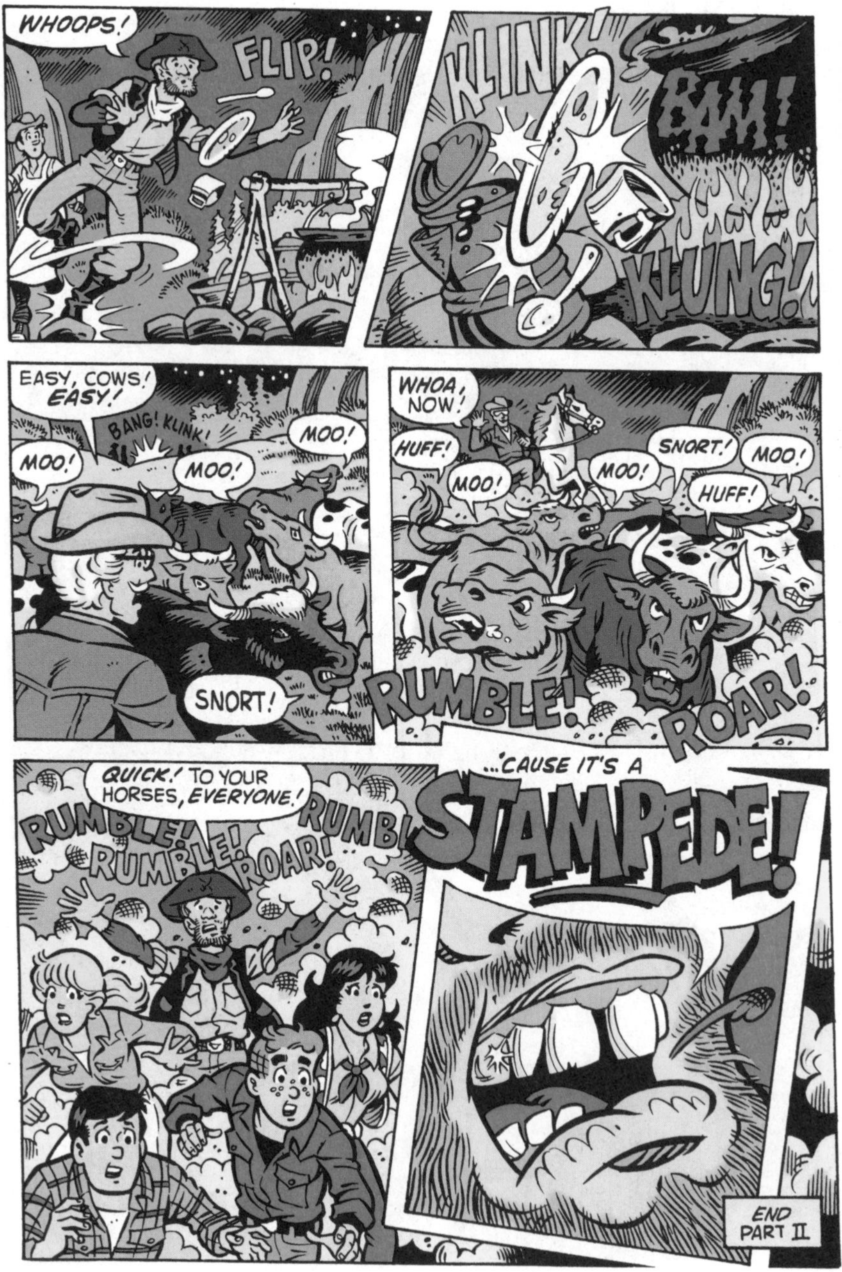
WHOOPS!
FLIP!
KLINK!
BAM!
KLUNG!
EASY, COWS! EASY!
BANG! KLINK!
MOO!
MOO!
MOO!
SNORT!
WHOA, NOW!
HUFF!
MOO!
MOO!
SNORT!
MOO!
HUFF!
RUMBLE!
ROAR!
QUICK! TO YOUR HORSES, EVERYONE!
RUMBLE!
RUMBLE!
ROAR!
RUMBL
...'CAUSE IT'S A
STAMPEDE!
END PART II

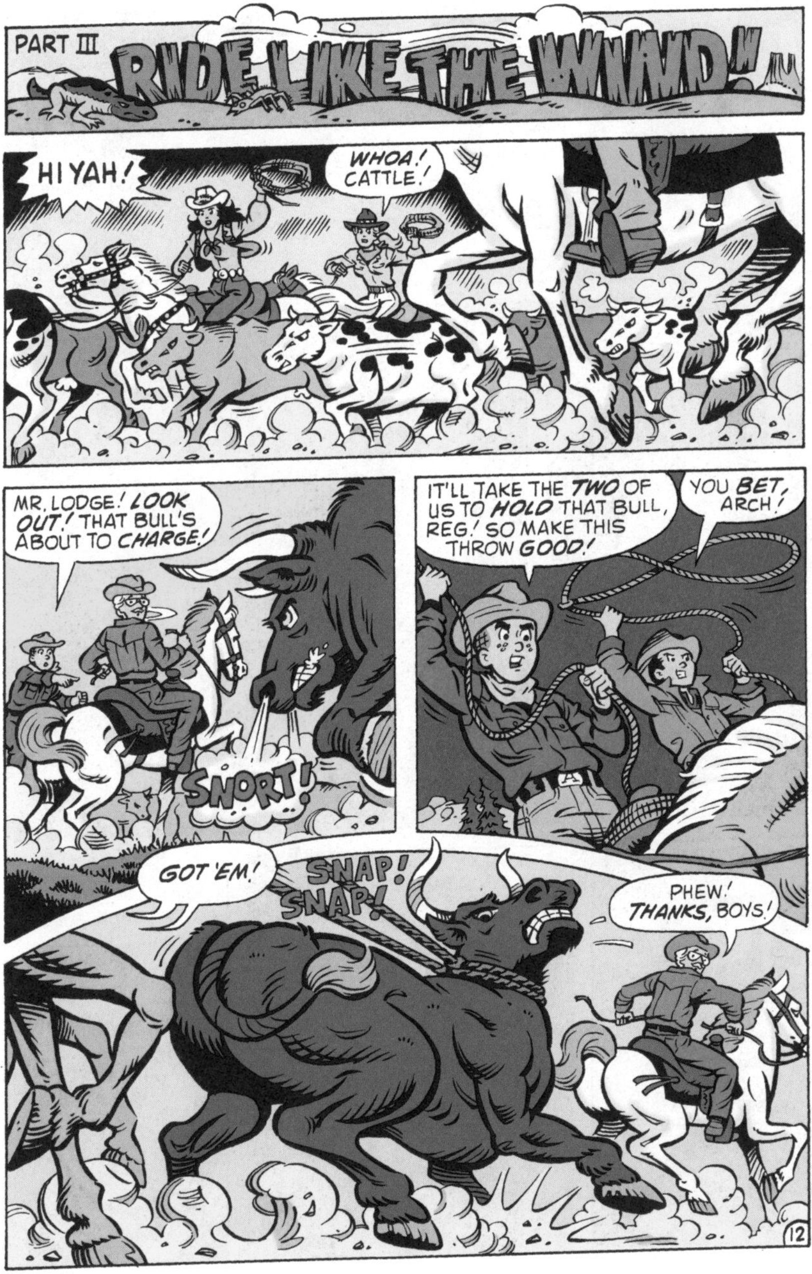
PART III
"RIDE LIKE THE WIND!"
HI YAH!
WHOA! CATTLE!
MR. LODGE! LOOK OUT! THAT BULL'S ABOUT TO CHARGE!
SNORT!
IT'LL TAKE THE TWO OF US TO HOLD THAT BULL, REG! SO MAKE THIS THROW GOOD!
YOU BET, ARCH!
GOT 'EM!
SNAP! SNAP!
PHEW! THANKS, BOYS!
12

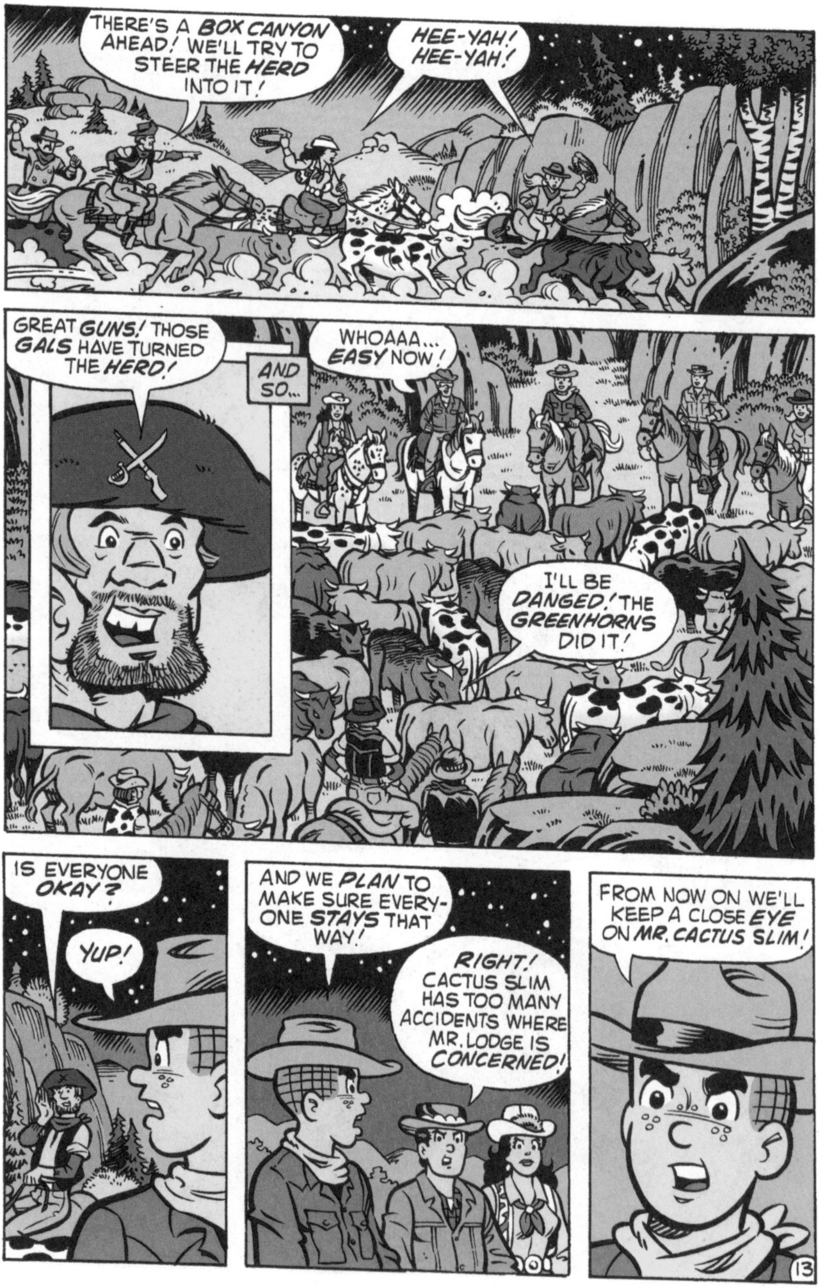
THERE'S A BOX CANYON AHEAD! WE'LL TRY TO STEER THE HERD INTO IT!
HEE-YAH! HEE-YAH!
GREAT GUNS! THOSE GALS HAVE TURNED THE HERD!
AND SO...
WHOAAA... EASY NOW!
I'LL BE DANGED! THE GREENHORNS DID IT!
IS EVERYONE OKAY?
YUP!
AND WE PLAN TO MAKE SURE EVERY-ONE STAYS THAT WAY!
RIGHT! CACTUS SLIM HAS TOO MANY ACCIDENTS WHERE MR. LODGE IS CONCERNED!
FROM NOW ON WE'LL KEEP A CLOSE EYE ON MR. CACTUS SLIM!
13

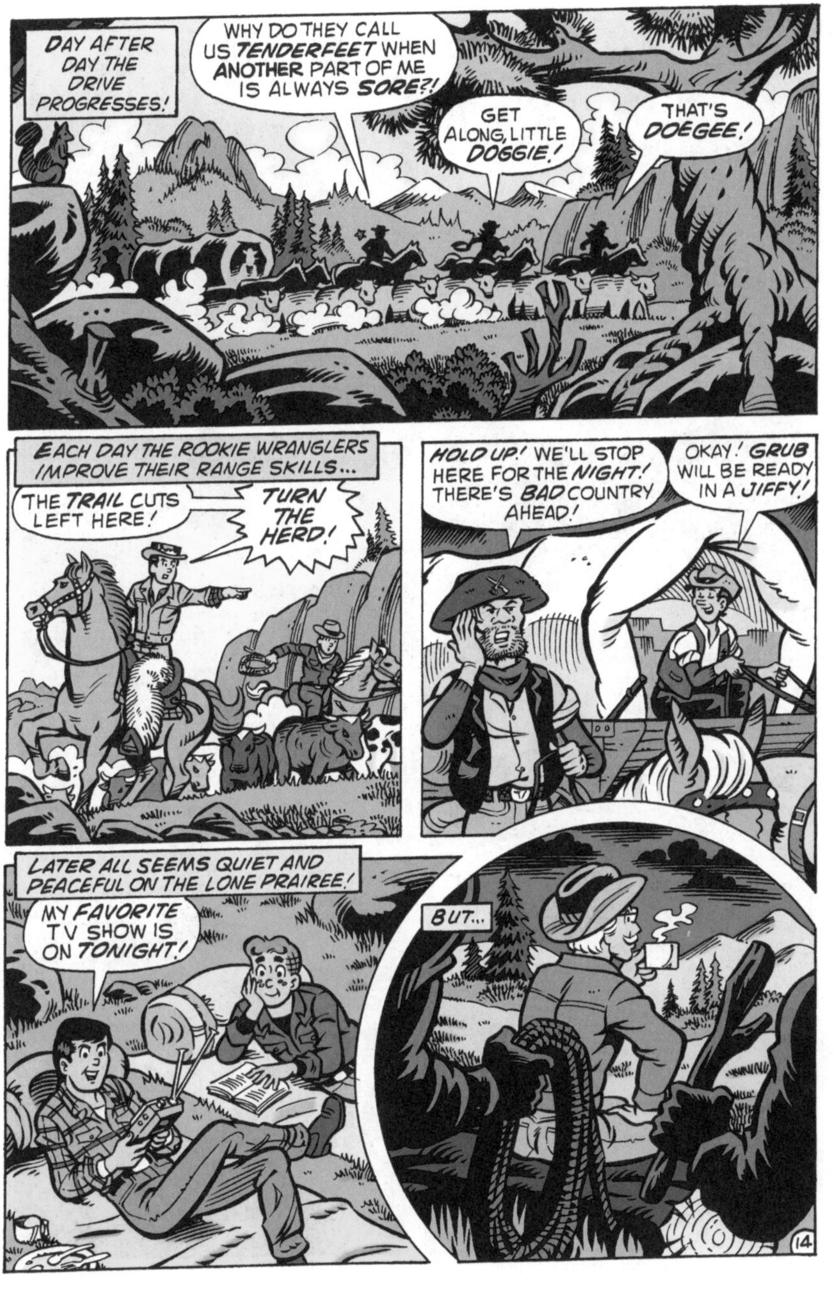
DAY AFTER DAY THE DRIVE PROGRESSES!
WHY DO THEY CALL US TENDERFEET WHEN ANOTHER PART OF ME IS ALWAYS SORE?!
GET ALONG, LITTLE DOGGIE!
THAT'S DOEGEE!
EACH DAY THE ROOKIE WRANGLERS IMPROVE THEIR RANGE SKILLS...
THE TRAIL CUTS LEFT HERE!
TURN THE HERD!
HOLD UP! WE'LL STOP HERE FOR THE NIGHT! THERE'S BAD COUNTRY AHEAD!
OKAY! GRUB WILL BE READY IN A JIFFY!
LATER ALL SEEMS QUIET AND PEACEFUL ON THE LONE PRAIREE!
MY FAVORITE TV SHOW IS ON TONIGHT!
BUT...
14

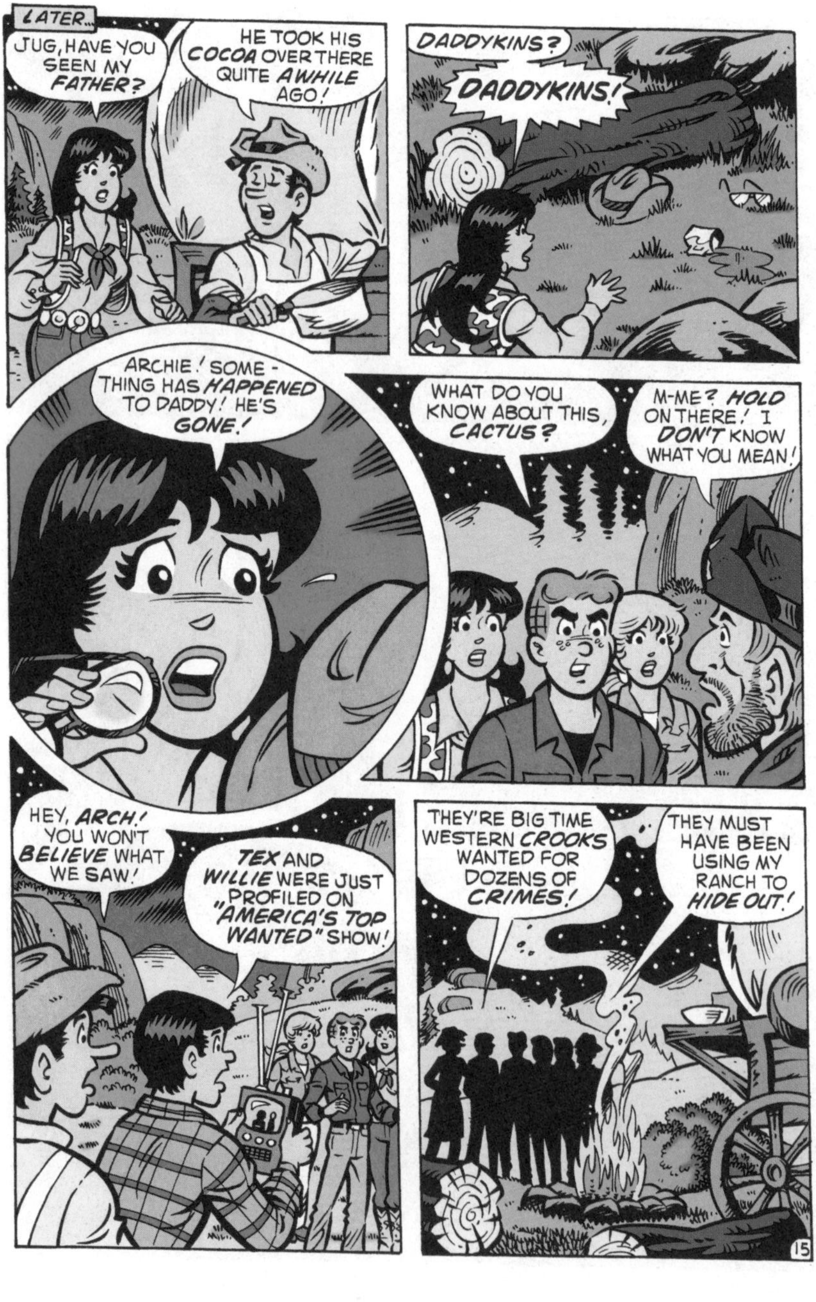
LATER...
JUG, HAVE YOU SEEN MY FATHER?
HE TOOK HIS COCOA OVER THERE QUITE AWHILE AGO!
DADDYKINS?
DADDYKINS!
ARCHIE! SOME-THING HAS HAPPENED TO DADDY! HE'S GONE!
WHAT DO YOU KNOW ABOUT THIS, CACTUS?
M-ME? HOLD ON THERE! I DON'T KNOW WHAT YOU MEAN!
HEY, ARCH! YOU WON'T BELIEVE WHAT WE SAW!
TEX AND WILLIE WERE JUST PROFILED ON "AMERICA'S TOP WANTED" SHOW!
THEY'RE BIG TIME WESTERN CROOKS WANTED FOR DOZENS OF CRIMES!
THEY MUST HAVE BEEN USING MY RANCH TO HIDE OUT!
15

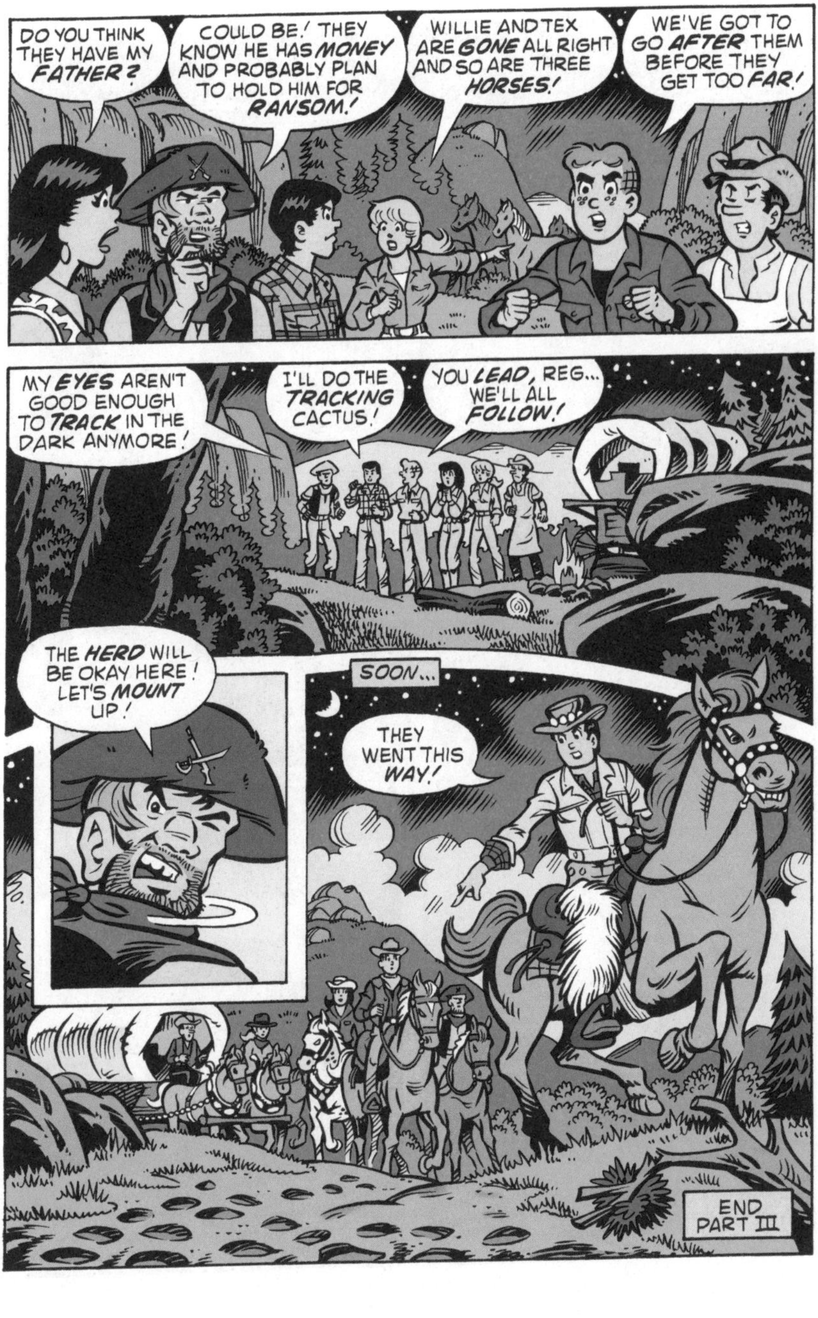
DO YOU THINK THEY HAVE MY FATHER?
COULD BE! THEY KNOW HE HAS MONEY AND PROBABLY PLAN TO HOLD HIM FOR RANSOM!
WILLIE AND TEX ARE GONE ALL RIGHT AND SO ARE THREE HORSES!
WE'VE GOT TO GO AFTER THEM BEFORE THEY GET TOO FAR!
MY EYES AREN'T GOOD ENOUGH TO TRACK IN THE DARK ANYMORE!
I'LL DO THE TRACKING CACTUS!
YOU LEAD, REG... WE'LL ALL FOLLOW!
THE HERD WILL BE OKAY HERE! LET'S MOUNT UP!
SOON...
THEY WENT THIS WAY!
END PART III

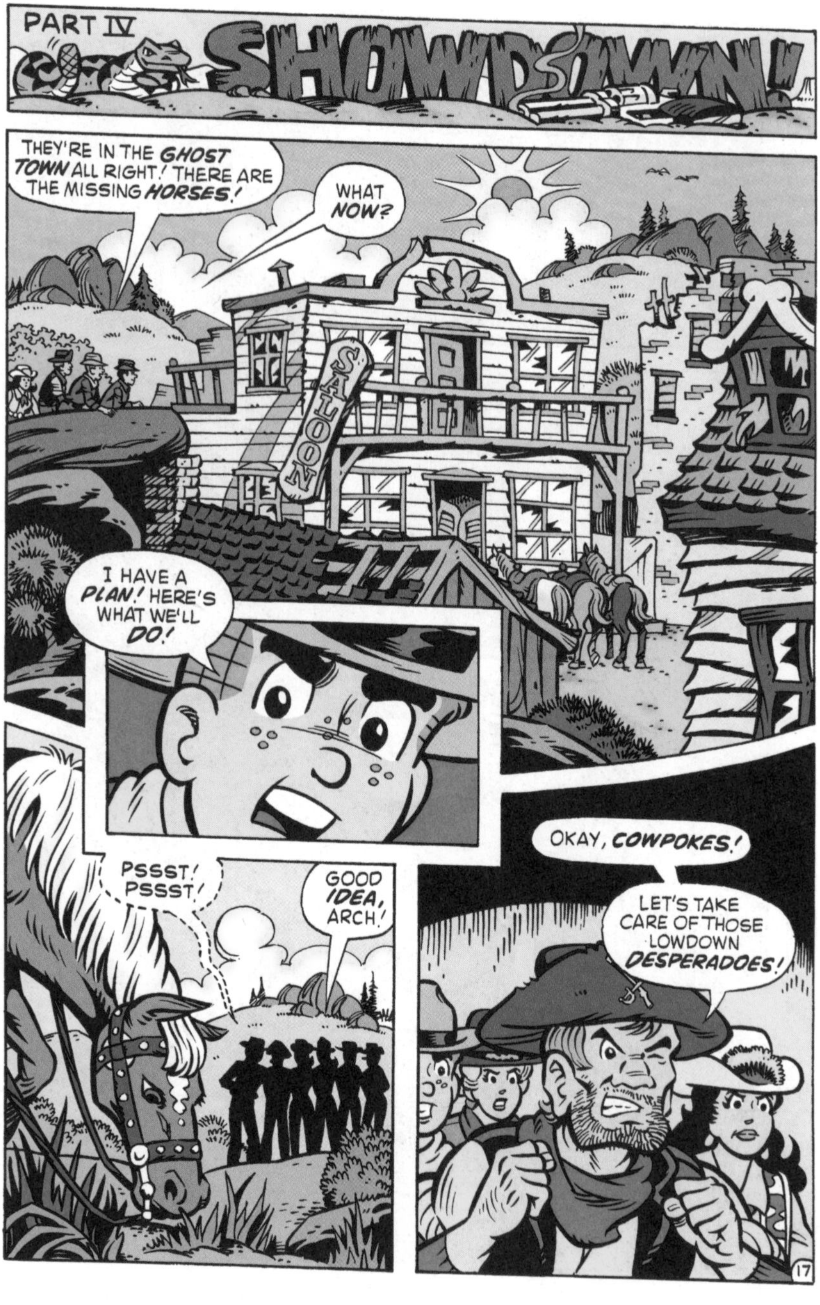
PART IV
SHOWDOWN!
THEY'RE IN THE GHOST TOWN ALL RIGHT! THERE ARE THE MISSING HORSES!
WHAT NOW?
SALOON
I HAVE A PLAN! HERE'S WHAT WE'LL DO!
PSSST! PSSST!
GOOD IDEA, ARCH!
OKAY, COWPOKES!
LET'S TAKE CARE OF THOSE LOWDOWN DESPERADOES!
17

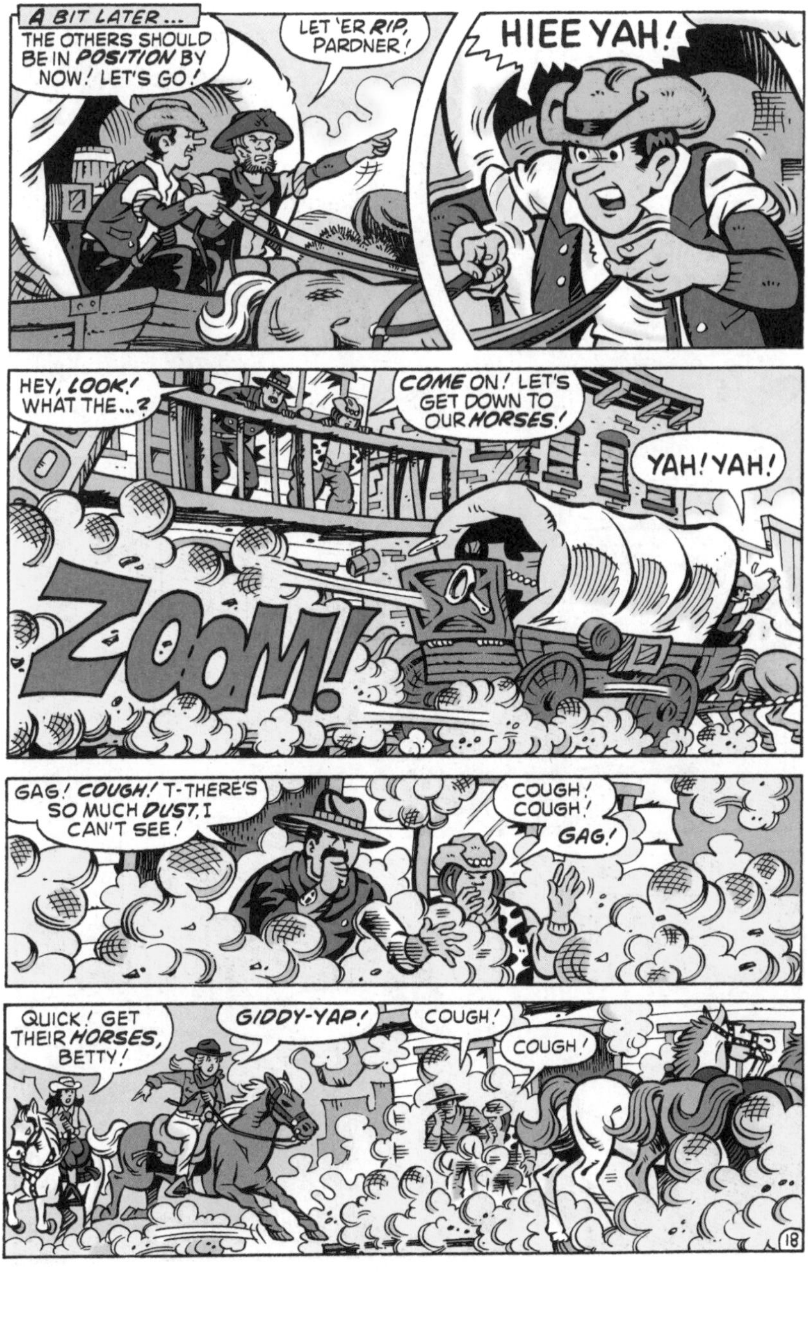
A BIT LATER...
THE OTHERS SHOULD BE IN POSITION BY NOW! LET'S GO!
LET 'ER RIP, PARDNER!
HIEE YAH!
HEY, LOOK! WHAT THE...?
COME ON! LET'S GET DOWN TO OUR HORSES!
YAH! YAH!
ZOOM!
GAG! COUGH! T-THERE'S SO MUCH DUST, I CAN'T SEE!
COUGH! COUGH! GAG!
QUICK! GET THEIR HORSES, BETTY!
GIDDY-YAP!
COUGH!
COUGH!
18

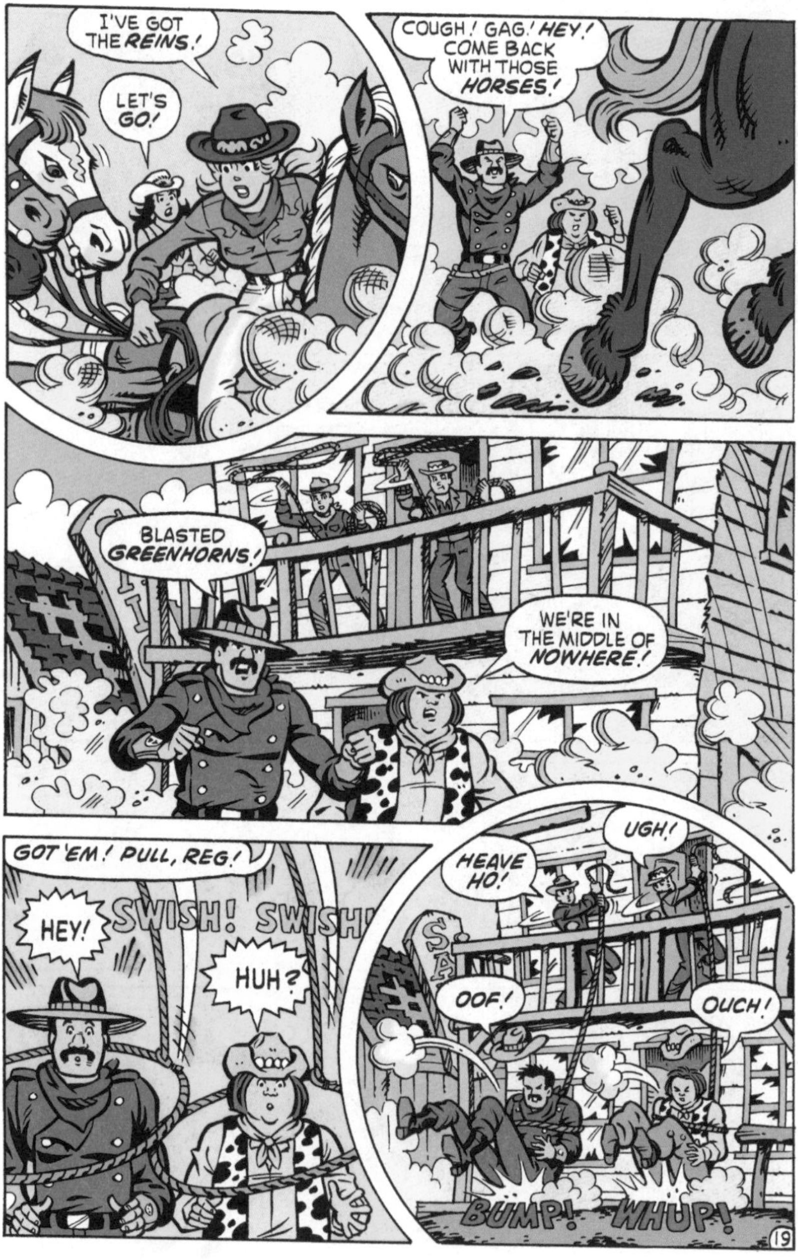
I'VE GOT THE REINS!
LET'S GO!
COUGH! GAG! HEY! COME BACK WITH THOSE HORSES!
BLASTED GREENHORNS!
WE'RE IN THE MIDDLE OF NOWHERE!
GOT 'EM! PULL, REG!
HEY!
SWISH! SWISH!
HUH?
HEAVE HO!
UGH!
OOF!
OUCH!
BUMP! WHUP!
19

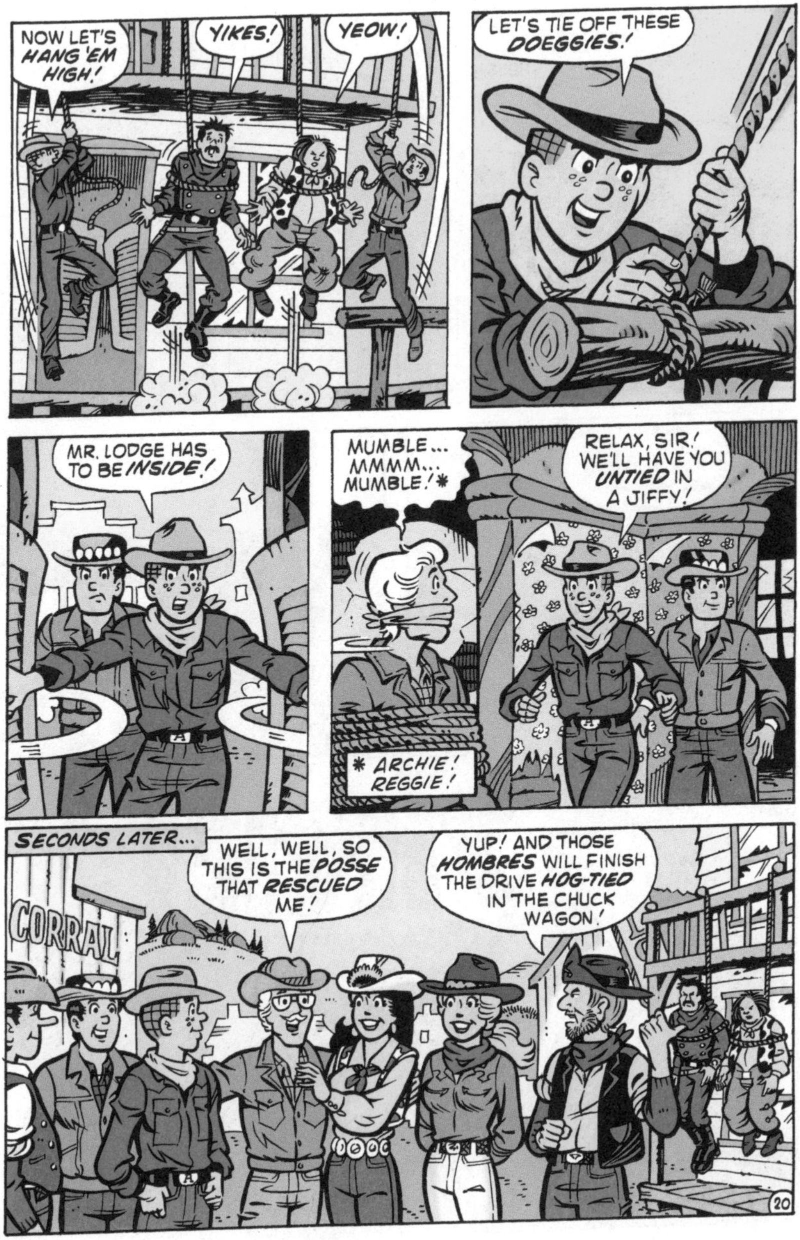
NOW LET'S HANG 'EM HIGH!
YIKES!
YEOW!
LET'S TIE OFF THESE DOEGGIES!
MR. LODGE HAS TO BE INSIDE!
MUMBLE... MMMM... MUMBLE! *
RELAX, SIR! WE'LL HAVE YOU UNTIED IN A JIFFY!
* ARCHIE! REGGIE!
SECONDS LATER...
CORRAL
WELL, WELL, SO THIS IS THE POSSE THAT RESCUED ME!
YUP! AND THOSE HOMBRES WILL FINISH THE DRIVE HOG-TIED IN THE CHUCK WAGON!
20

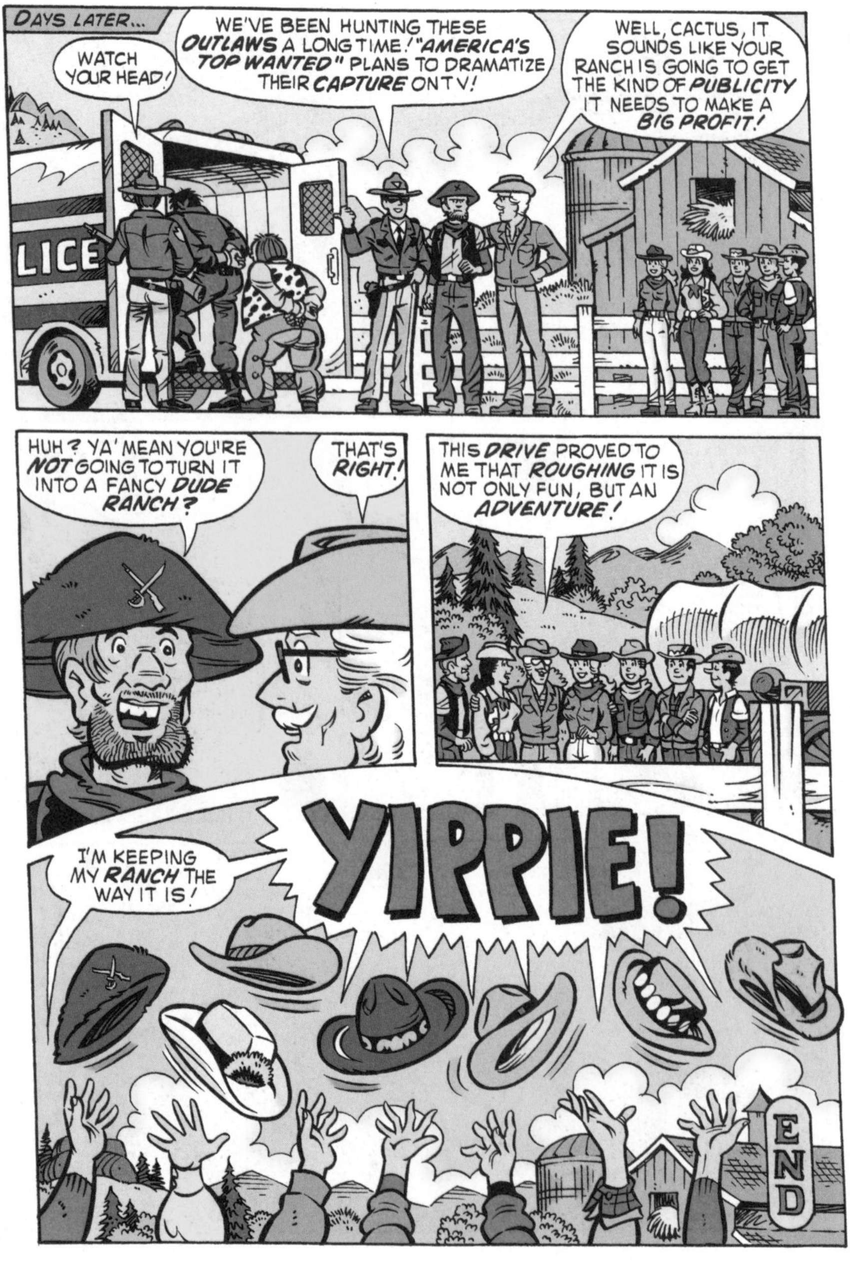
DAYS LATER...
WATCH YOUR HEAD!
WE'VE BEEN HUNTING THESE OUTLAWS A LONG TIME! "AMERICA'S TOP WANTED" PLANS TO DRAMATIZE THEIR CAPTURE ON TV!
WELL, CACTUS, IT SOUNDS LIKE YOUR RANCH IS GOING TO GET THE KIND OF PUBLICITY IT NEEDS TO MAKE A BIG PROFIT!
LICE
HUH? YA' MEAN YOU'RE NOT GOING TO TURN IT INTO A FANCY DUDE RANCH?
THAT'S RIGHT!
THIS DRIVE PROVED TO ME THAT ROUGHING IT IS NOT ONLY FUN, BUT AN ADVENTURE!
I'M KEEPING MY RANCH THE WAY IT IS!
YIPPIE!
END

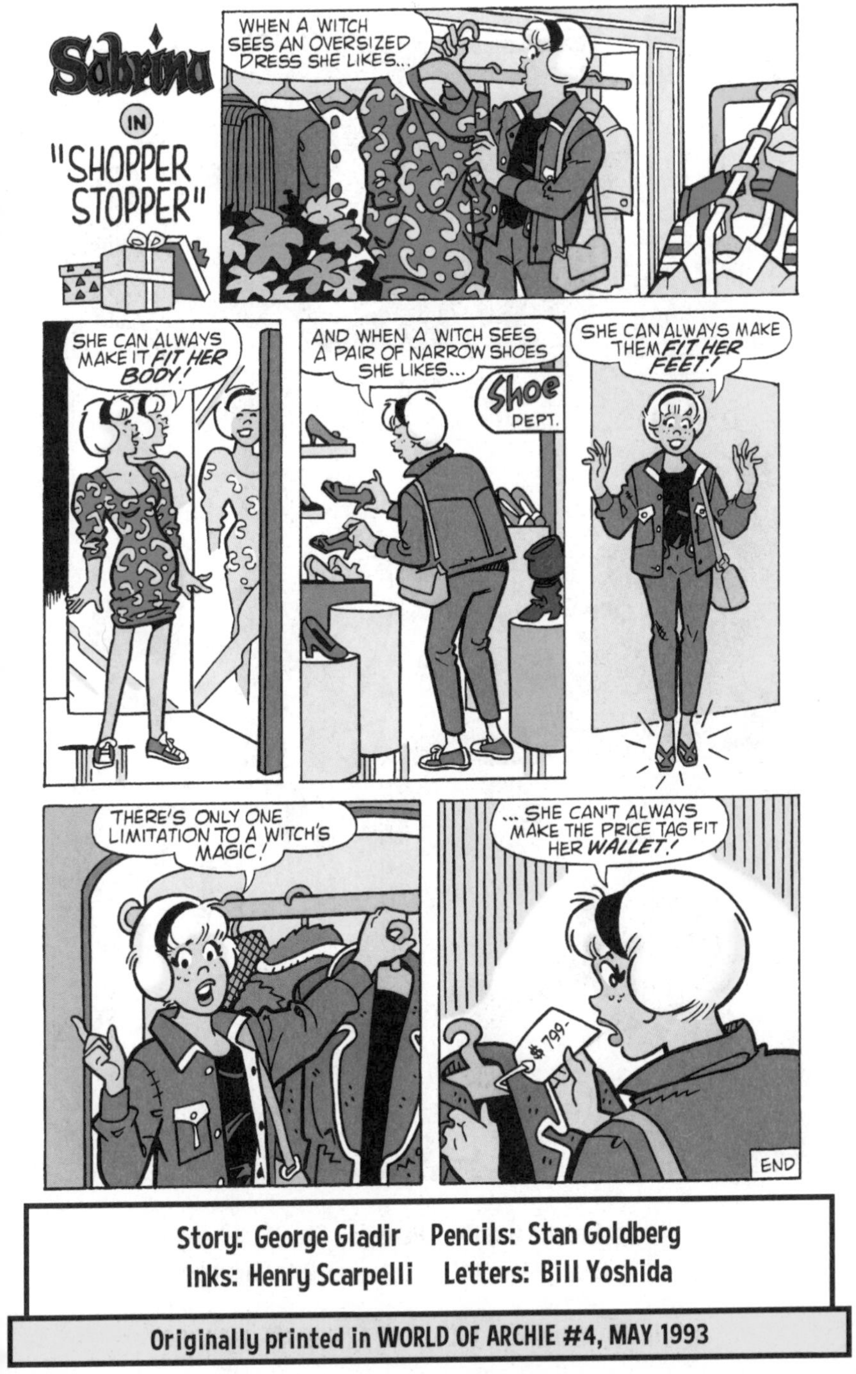
Sabrina
IN
"SHOPPER STOPPER"
WHEN A WITCH SEES AN OVERSIZED DRESS SHE LIKES...
SHE CAN ALWAYS MAKE IT FIT HER BODY!
AND WHEN A WITCH SEES A PAIR OF NARROW SHOES SHE LIKES...
Shoe DEPT.
SHE CAN ALWAYS MAKE THEM FIT HER FEET!
THERE'S ONLY ONE LIMITATION TO A WITCH'S MAGIC!
... SHE CAN'T ALWAYS MAKE THE PRICE TAG FIT HER WALLET!
$799-
END

Story: George Gladir **Pencils:** Stan Goldberg
Inks: Henry Scarpelli **Letters:** Bill Yoshida

Originally printed in WORLD OF ARCHIE #4, MAY 1993

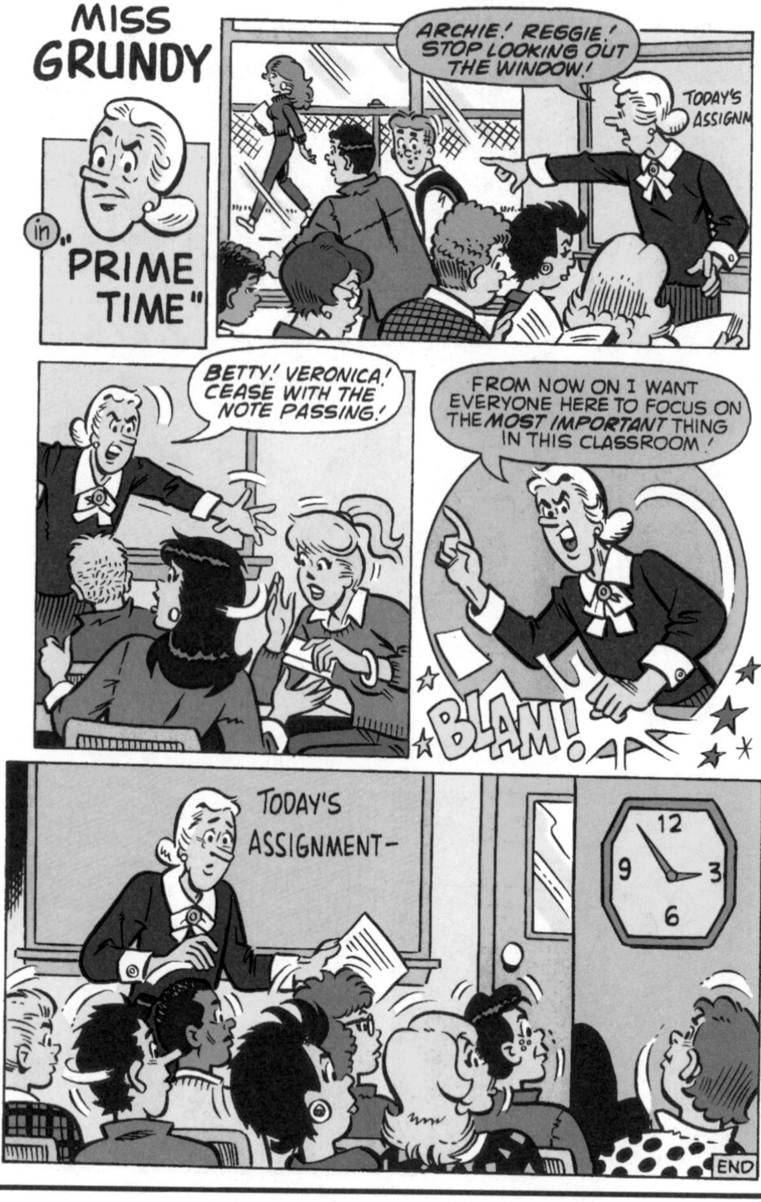
MISS GRUNDY
in "PRIME TIME"
ARCHIE! REGGIE! STOP LOOKING OUT THE WINDOW!
TODAY'S ASSIGNM
BETTY! VERONICA! CEASE WITH THE NOTE PASSING!
FROM NOW ON I WANT EVERYONE HERE TO FOCUS ON THE MOST IMPORTANT THING IN THIS CLASSROOM!
BLAM!
TODAY'S ASSIGNMENT-
12 3 6 9
END

Story: George Gladir Pencils: Stan Goldberg
Inks: Henry Scarpelli Letters: Bill Yoshida

Originally printed in WORLD OF ARCHIE #4, MAY 1993

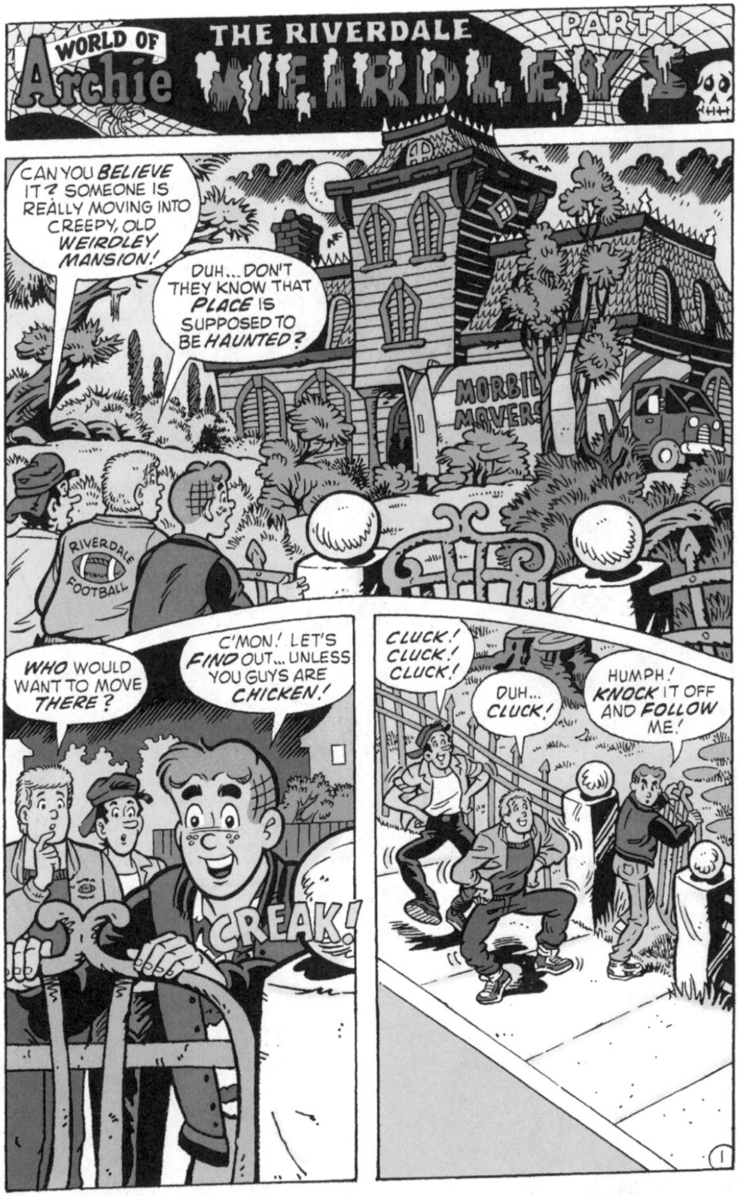
WORLD OF Archie
THE RIVERDALE WEIRDLEYS
PART I
CAN YOU BELIEVE IT? SOMEONE IS REALLY MOVING INTO CREEPY, OLD WEIRDLEY MANSION!
DUH... DON'T THEY KNOW THAT PLACE IS SUPPOSED TO BE HAUNTED?
MORBID MOVERS
RIVERDALE FOOTBALL
WHO WOULD WANT TO MOVE THERE?
C'MON! LET'S FIND OUT... UNLESS YOU GUYS ARE CHICKEN!
CREAK!
CLUCK! CLUCK! CLUCK!
DUH... CLUCK!
HUMPH! KNOCK IT OFF AND FOLLOW ME!
1

Story: Mike Pellowski Pencils: Rex Lindsey
Inks: Rex Lindsey Letters: Bill Yoshida

Originally printed in WORLD OF ARCHIE #5, AUGUST 1993

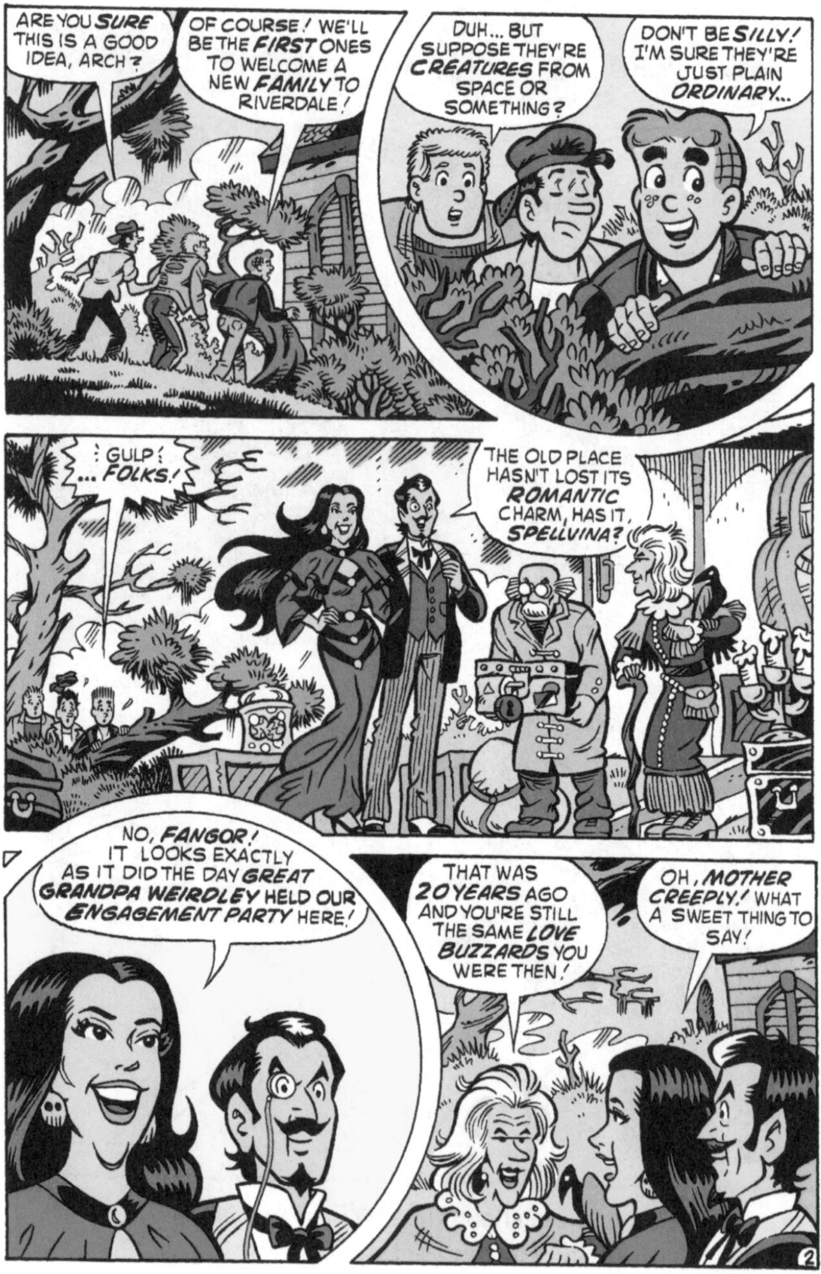
ARE YOU SURE THIS IS A GOOD IDEA, ARCH?
OF COURSE! WE'LL BE THE FIRST ONES TO WELCOME A NEW FAMILY TO RIVERDALE!
DUH... BUT SUPPOSE THEY'RE CREATURES FROM SPACE OR SOMETHING?
DON'T BE SILLY! I'M SURE THEY'RE JUST PLAIN ORDINARY...
GULP! ...FOLKS!
THE OLD PLACE HASN'T LOST ITS ROMANTIC CHARM, HAS IT, SPELLVINA?
NO, FANGOR! IT LOOKS EXACTLY AS IT DID THE DAY GREAT GRANDPA WEIRDLEY HELD OUR ENGAGEMENT PARTY HERE!
THAT WAS 20 YEARS AGO AND YOU'RE STILL THE SAME LOVE BUZZARDS YOU WERE THEN!
OH, MOTHER CREEPLY! WHAT A SWEET THING TO SAY!
2

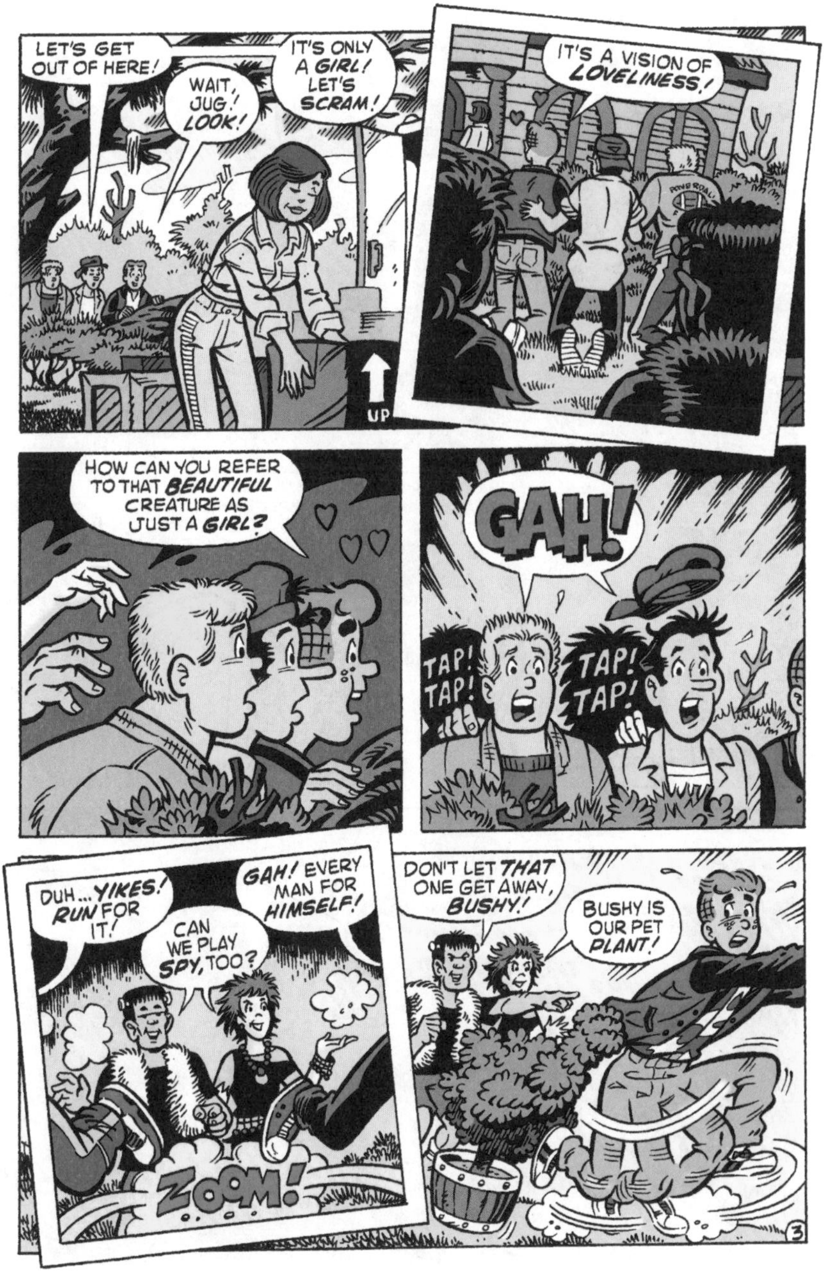
LET'S GET OUT OF HERE!
WAIT, JUG! LOOK!
IT'S ONLY A GIRL! LET'S SCRAM!
UP
IT'S A VISION OF LOVELINESS!
HOW CAN YOU REFER TO THAT BEAUTIFUL CREATURE AS JUST A GIRL?
GAH!
TAP! TAP!
TAP! TAP!
DUH...YIKES! RUN FOR IT!
CAN WE PLAY SPY, TOO?
GAH! EVERY MAN FOR HIMSELF!
ZOOM!
DON'T LET THAT ONE GET AWAY, BUSHY!
BUSHY IS OUR PET PLANT!
3

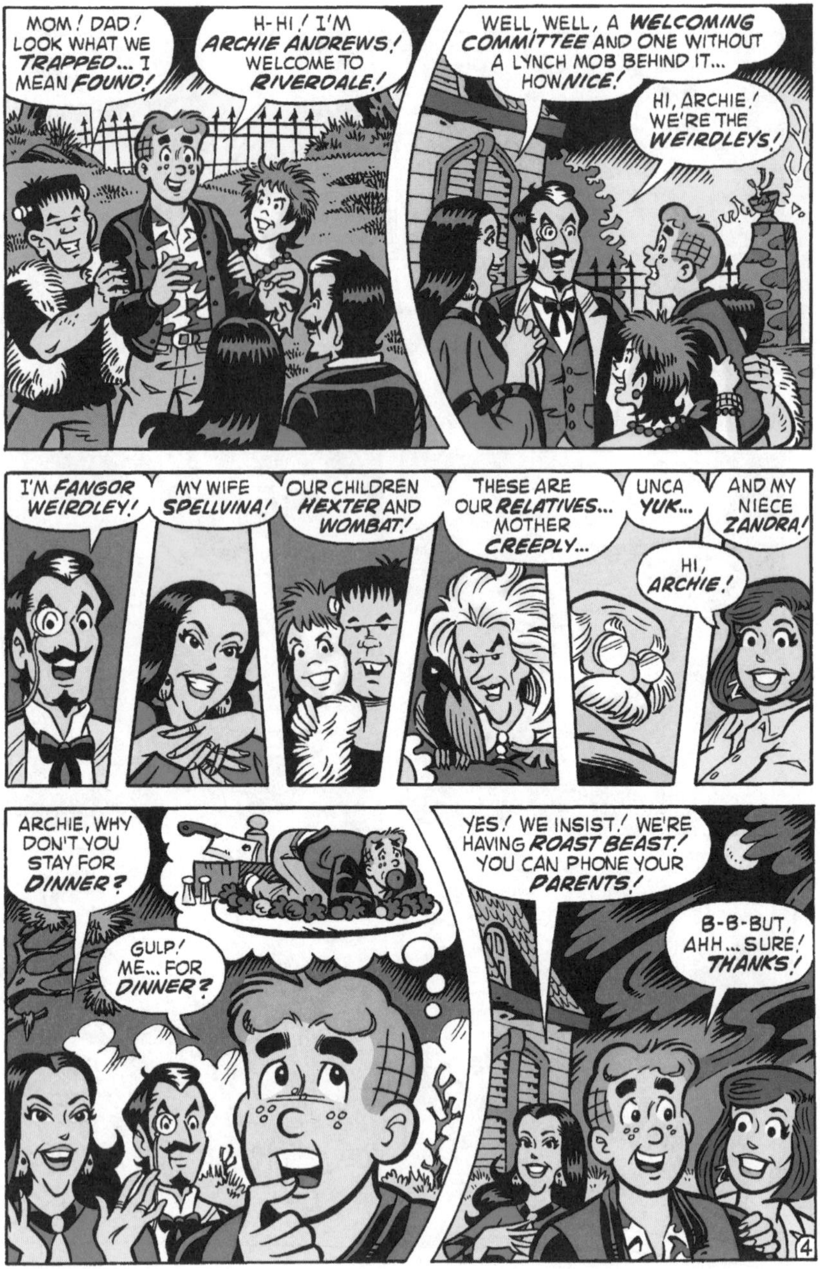
MOM! DAD! LOOK WHAT WE TRAPPED... I MEAN FOUND!
H-HI! I'M ARCHIE ANDREWS! WELCOME TO RIVERDALE!
WELL, WELL, A WELCOMING COMMITTEE AND ONE WITHOUT A LYNCH MOB BEHIND IT... HOW NICE!
HI, ARCHIE! WE'RE THE WEIRDLEYS!
I'M FANGOR WEIRDLEY!
MY WIFE SPELLVINA!
OUR CHILDREN HEXTER AND WOMBAT!
THESE ARE OUR RELATIVES... MOTHER CREEPLY...
UNCA YUK...
AND MY NIECE ZANDRA!
HI, ARCHIE!
ARCHIE, WHY DON'T YOU STAY FOR DINNER?
GULP! ME... FOR DINNER?
YES! WE INSIST! WE'RE HAVING ROAST BEAST! YOU CAN PHONE YOUR PARENTS!
B-B-BUT, AHH... SURE! THANKS!
4

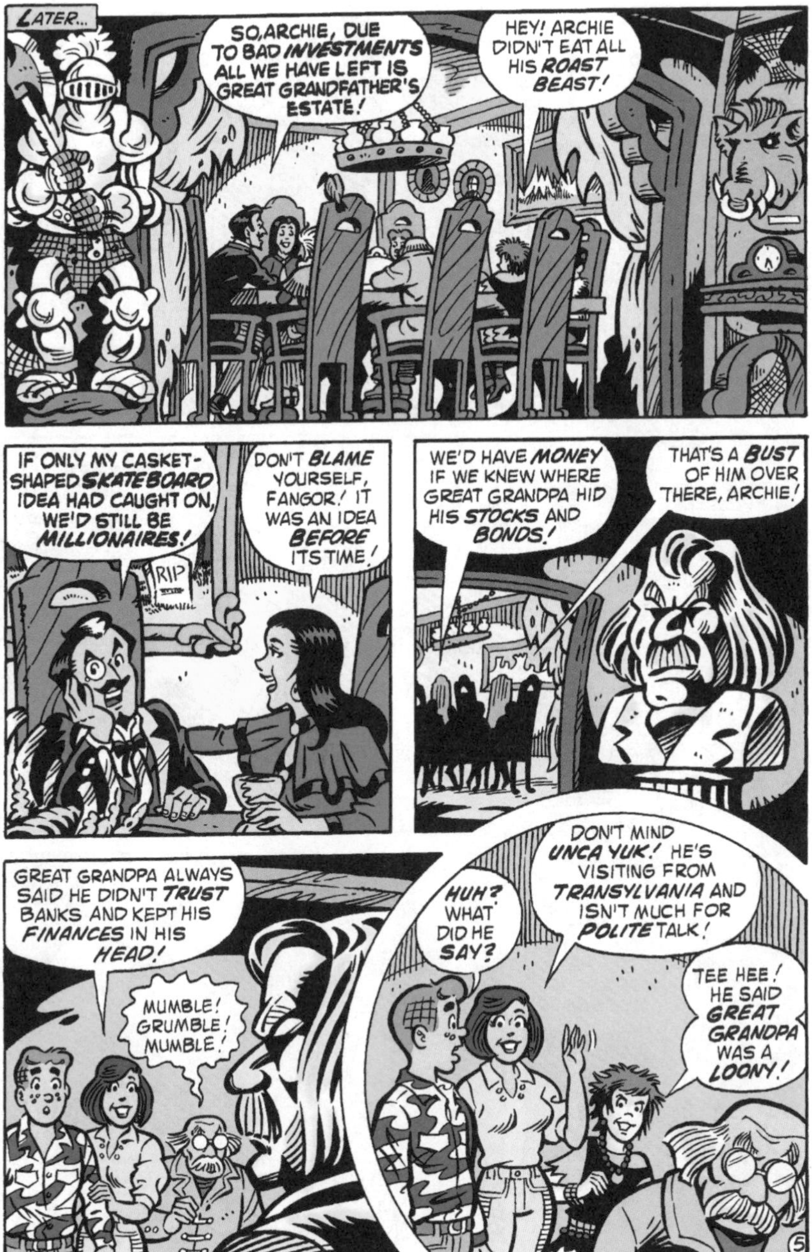
LATER...
SO, ARCHIE, DUE TO BAD INVESTMENTS ALL WE HAVE LEFT IS GREAT GRANDFATHER'S ESTATE!
HEY! ARCHIE DIDN'T EAT ALL HIS ROAST BEAST!
IF ONLY MY CASKET-SHAPED SKATEBOARD IDEA HAD CAUGHT ON, WE'D STILL BE MILLIONAIRES!
DON'T BLAME YOURSELF, FANGOR! IT WAS AN IDEA BEFORE ITS TIME!
RIP
WE'D HAVE MONEY IF WE KNEW WHERE GREAT GRANDPA HID HIS STOCKS AND BONDS!
THAT'S A BUST OF HIM OVER THERE, ARCHIE!
GREAT GRANDPA ALWAYS SAID HE DIDN'T TRUST BANKS AND KEPT HIS FINANCES IN HIS HEAD!
MUMBLE! GRUMBLE! MUMBLE!
HUH? WHAT DID HE SAY?
DON'T MIND UNCA YUK! HE'S VISITING FROM TRANSYLVANIA AND ISN'T MUCH FOR POLITE TALK!
TEE HEE! HE SAID GREAT GRANDPA WAS A LOONY!
5

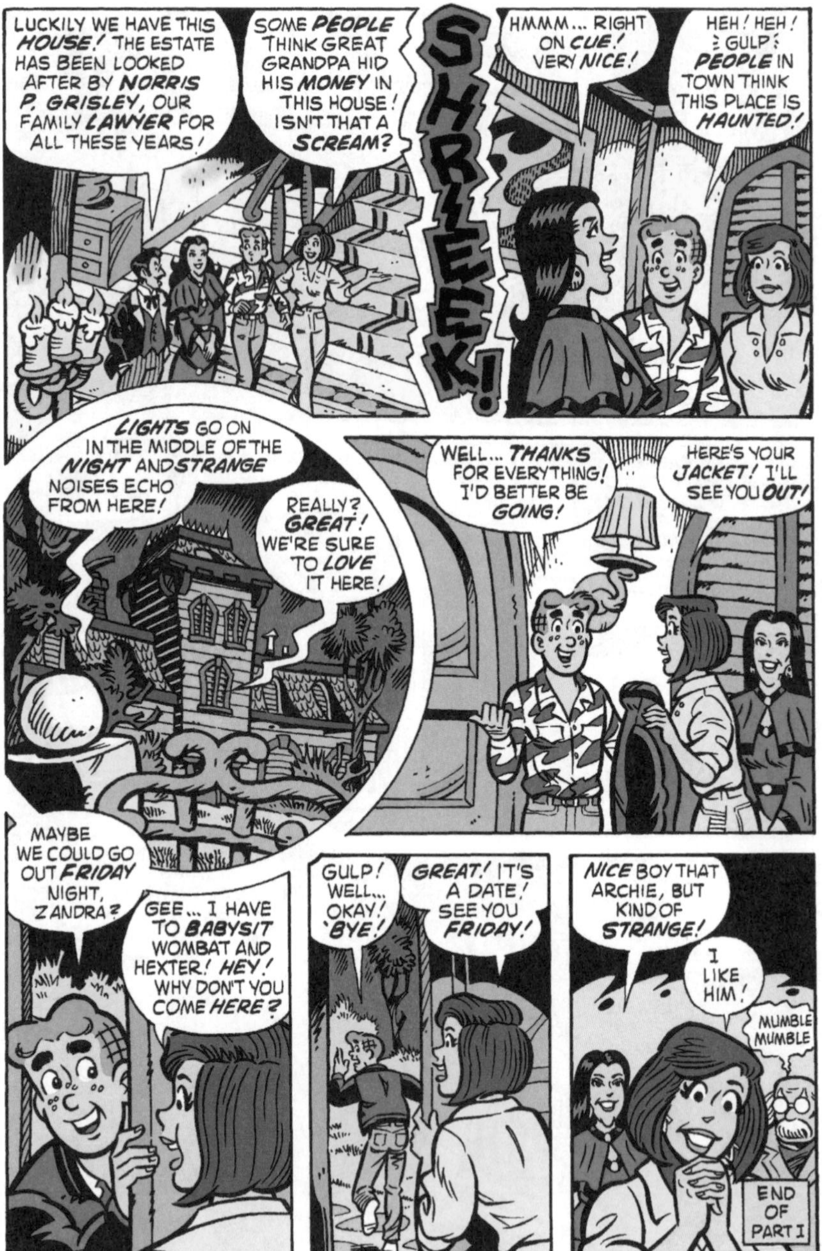
LUCKILY WE HAVE THIS HOUSE! THE ESTATE HAS BEEN LOOKED AFTER BY NORRIS P. GRISLEY, OUR FAMILY LAWYER FOR ALL THESE YEARS!
SOME PEOPLE THINK GREAT GRANDPA HID HIS MONEY IN THIS HOUSE! ISN'T THAT A SCREAM?
SHRIEEEK!
HMMM... RIGHT ON CUE! VERY NICE!
HEH! HEH! GULP! PEOPLE IN TOWN THINK THIS PLACE IS HAUNTED!
LIGHTS GO ON IN THE MIDDLE OF THE NIGHT AND STRANGE NOISES ECHO FROM HERE!
REALLY? GREAT! WE'RE SURE TO LOVE IT HERE!
WELL... THANKS FOR EVERYTHING! I'D BETTER BE GOING!
HERE'S YOUR JACKET! I'LL SEE YOU OUT!
MAYBE WE COULD GO OUT FRIDAY NIGHT, ZANDRA?
GEE... I HAVE TO BABYSIT WOMBAT AND HEXTER! HEY! WHY DON'T YOU COME HERE?
GULP! WELL... OKAY! 'BYE!
GREAT! IT'S A DATE! SEE YOU FRIDAY!
NICE BOY THAT ARCHIE, BUT KIND OF STRANGE!
I LIKE HIM!
MUMBLE MUMBLE
END OF PART I

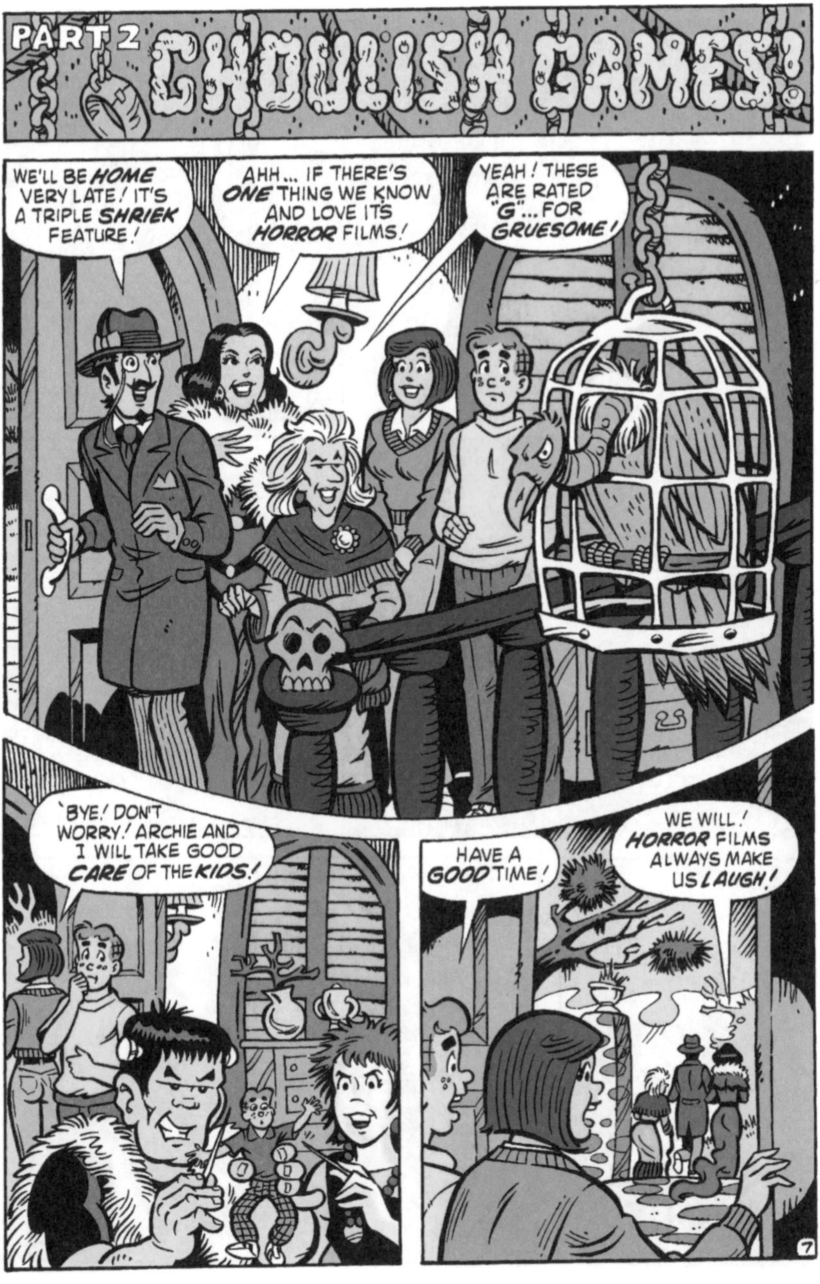
PART 2
GHOULISH GAMES!
WE'LL BE HOME VERY LATE! IT'S A TRIPLE SHRIEK FEATURE!
AHH... IF THERE'S ONE THING WE KNOW AND LOVE IT'S HORROR FILMS!
YEAH! THESE ARE RATED "G"... FOR GRUESOME!
'BYE! DON'T WORRY! ARCHIE AND I WILL TAKE GOOD CARE OF THE KIDS!
HAVE A GOOD TIME!
WE WILL! HORROR FILMS ALWAYS MAKE US LAUGH!
7

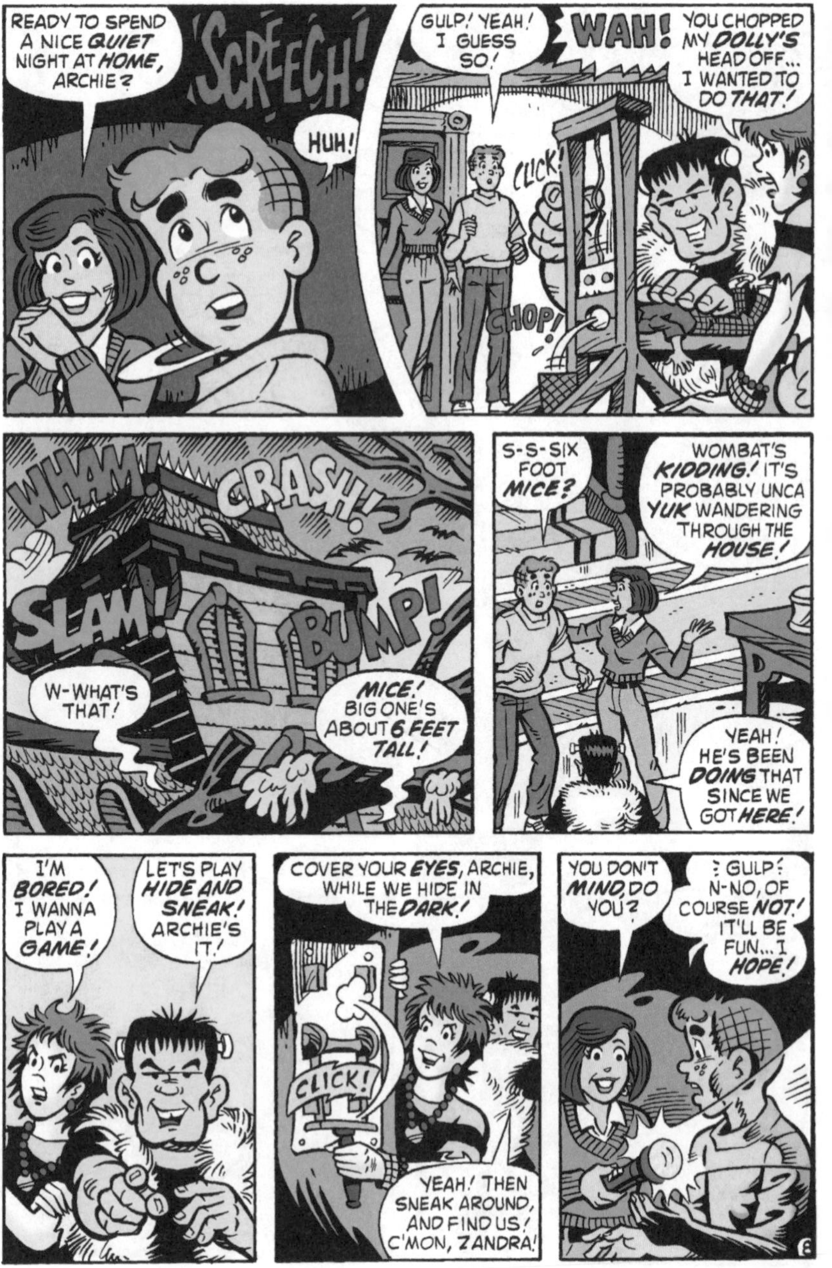
READY TO SPEND A NICE QUIET NIGHT AT HOME, ARCHIE?
SCREECH!
HUH!
GULP! YEAH! I GUESS SO!
WAH! YOU CHOPPED MY DOLLY'S HEAD OFF... I WANTED TO DO THAT!
CLICK!
CHOP!
WHAM!
CRASH!
SLAM!
BUMP!
W-WHAT'S THAT!
MICE! BIG ONE'S ABOUT 6 FEET TALL!
S-S-SIX FOOT MICE?
WOMBAT'S KIDDING! IT'S PROBABLY UNCA YUK WANDERING THROUGH THE HOUSE!
YEAH! HE'S BEEN DOING THAT SINCE WE GOT HERE!
I'M BORED! I WANNA PLAY A GAME!
LET'S PLAY HIDE AND SNEAK! ARCHIE'S IT!
COVER YOUR EYES, ARCHIE, WHILE WE HIDE IN THE DARK!
CLICK!
YEAH! THEN SNEAK AROUND, AND FIND US! C'MON, ZANDRA!
YOU DON'T MIND, DO YOU?
GULP! N-NO, OF COURSE NOT! IT'LL BE FUN... I HOPE!
8

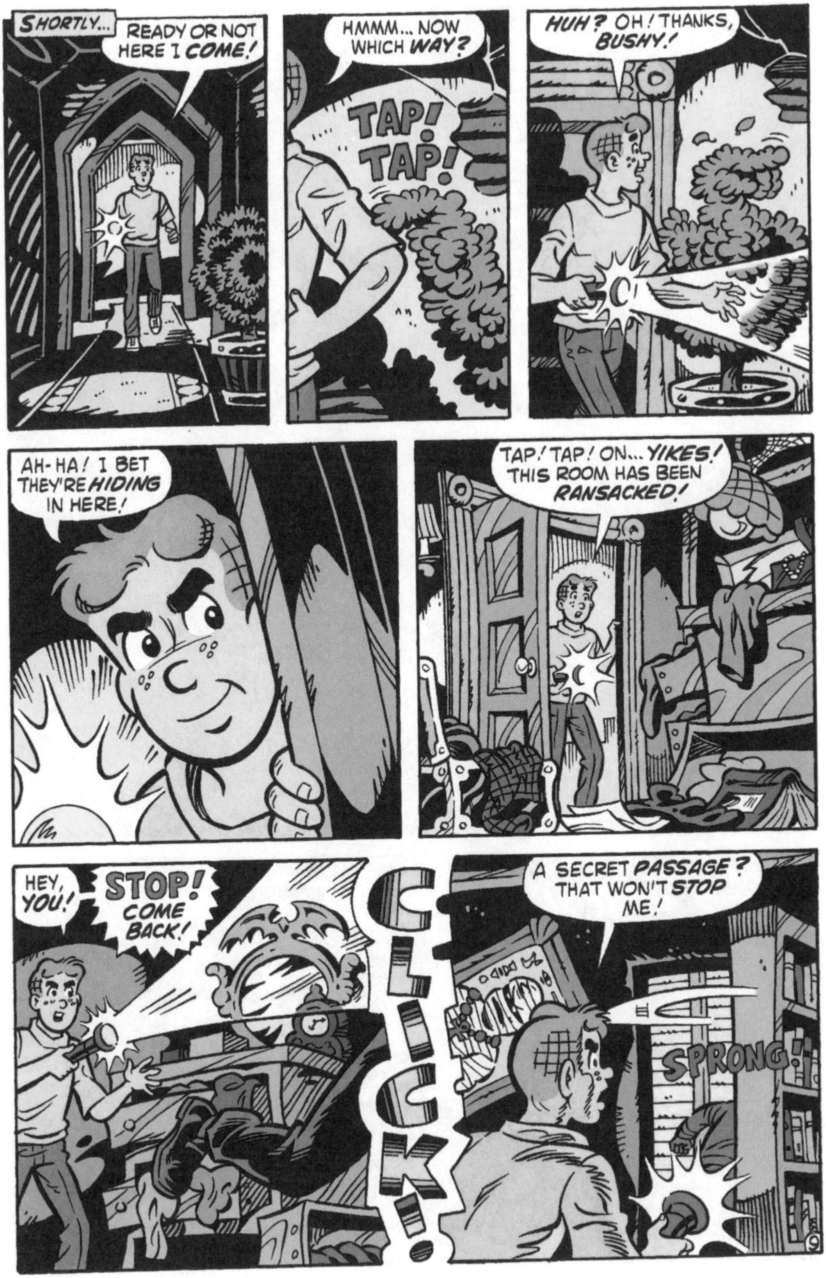
SHORTLY...
READY OR NOT HERE I COME!
HMMM... NOW WHICH WAY?
TAP! TAP!
HUH? OH! THANKS, BUSHY!
AH-HA! I BET THEY'RE HIDING IN HERE!
TAP! TAP! ON... YIKES! THIS ROOM HAS BEEN RANSACKED!
HEY, YOU!
STOP! COME BACK!
CLICK!
A SECRET PASSAGE? THAT WON'T STOP ME!
SPRONG!
9

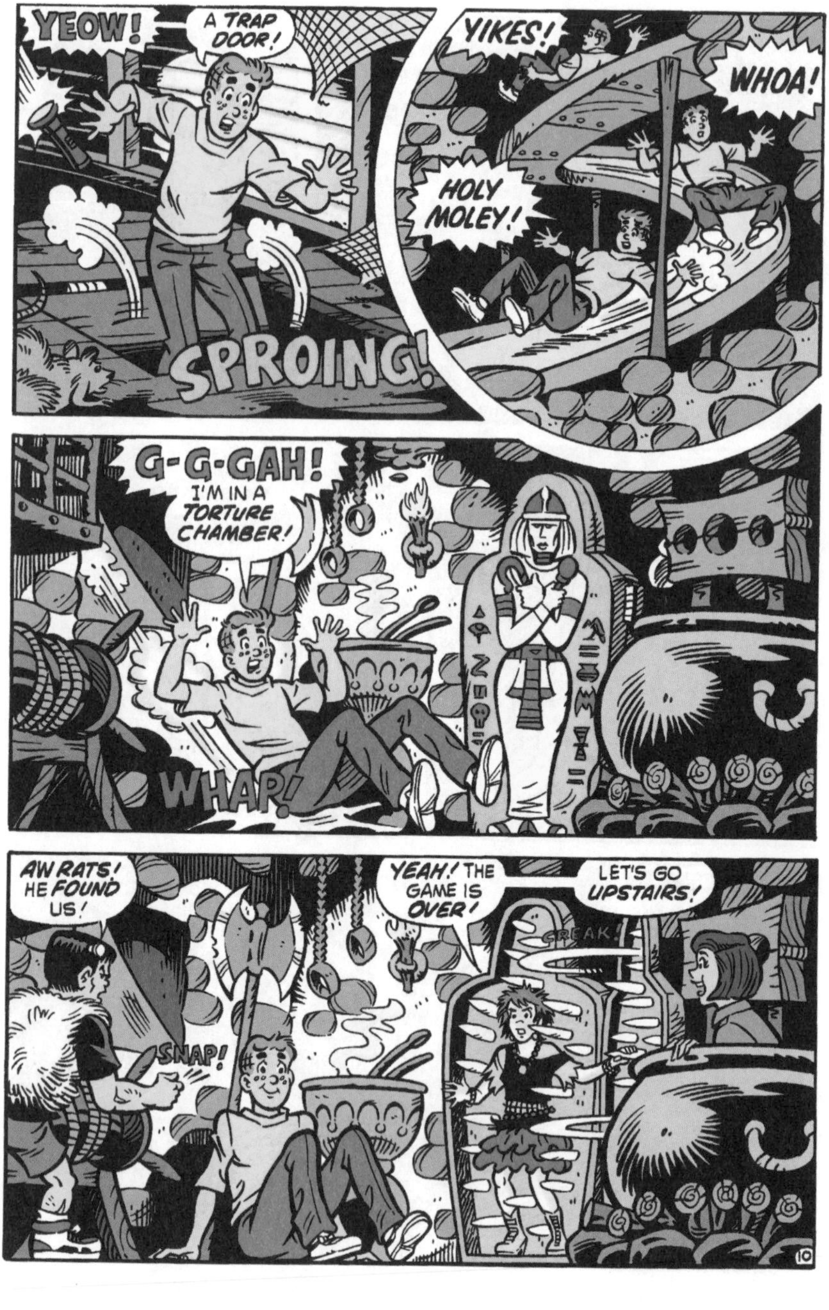
YEOW!
A TRAP DOOR!
SPROING!
YIKES!
WHOA!
HOLY MOLEY!
G-G-GAH! I'M IN A TORTURE CHAMBER!
WHAP!
AW RATS! HE FOUND US!
YEAH! THE GAME IS OVER!
LET'S GO UPSTAIRS!
SNAP!
CREAK!
10

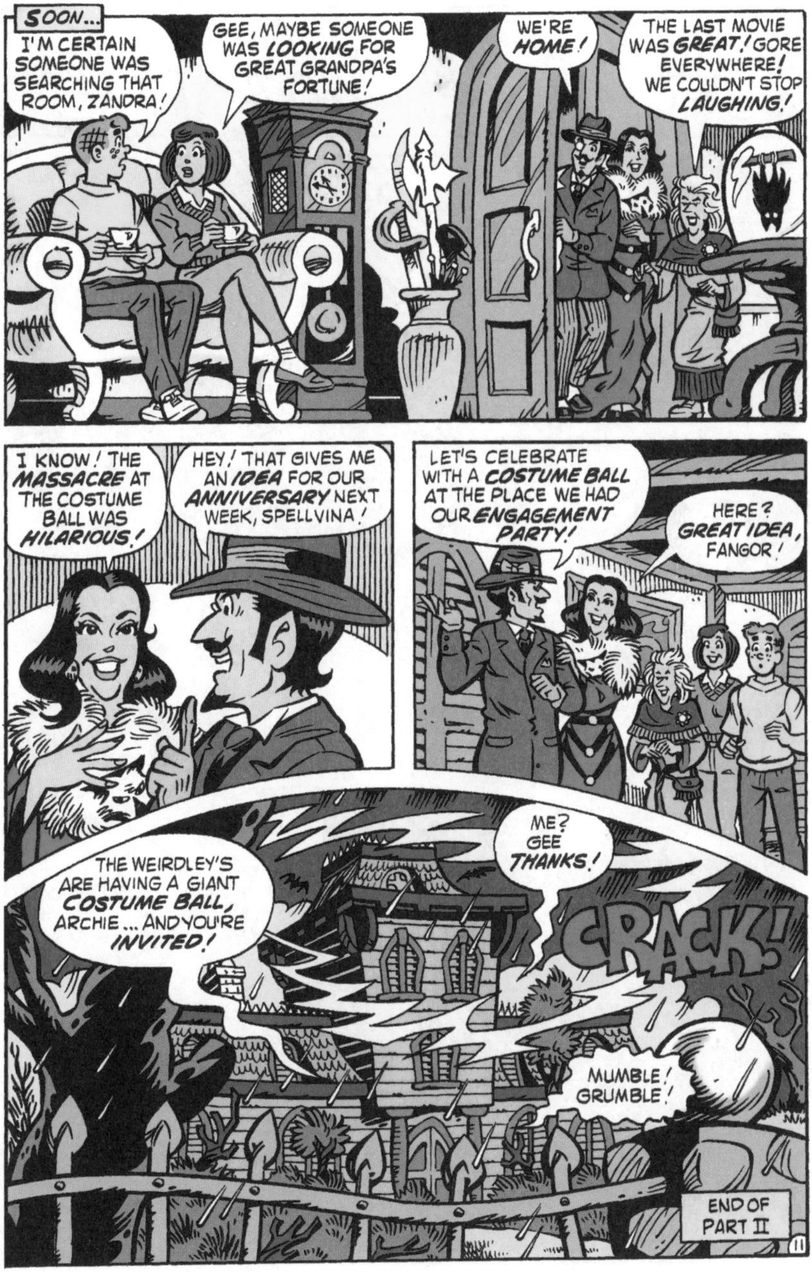
SOON...
I'M CERTAIN SOMEONE WAS SEARCHING THAT ROOM, ZANDRA!
GEE, MAYBE SOMEONE WAS LOOKING FOR GREAT GRANDPA'S FORTUNE!
WE'RE HOME!
THE LAST MOVIE WAS GREAT! GORE EVERYWHERE! WE COULDN'T STOP LAUGHING!
I KNOW! THE MASSACRE AT THE COSTUME BALL WAS HILARIOUS!
HEY! THAT GIVES ME AN IDEA FOR OUR ANNIVERSARY NEXT WEEK, SPELLVINA!
LET'S CELEBRATE WITH A COSTUME BALL AT THE PLACE WE HAD OUR ENGAGEMENT PARTY!
HERE? GREAT IDEA, FANGOR!
THE WEIRDLEY'S ARE HAVING A GIANT COSTUME BALL, ARCHIE... AND YOU'RE INVITED!
ME? GEE THANKS!
CRACK!
MUMBLE! GRUMBLE!
END OF PART II
11

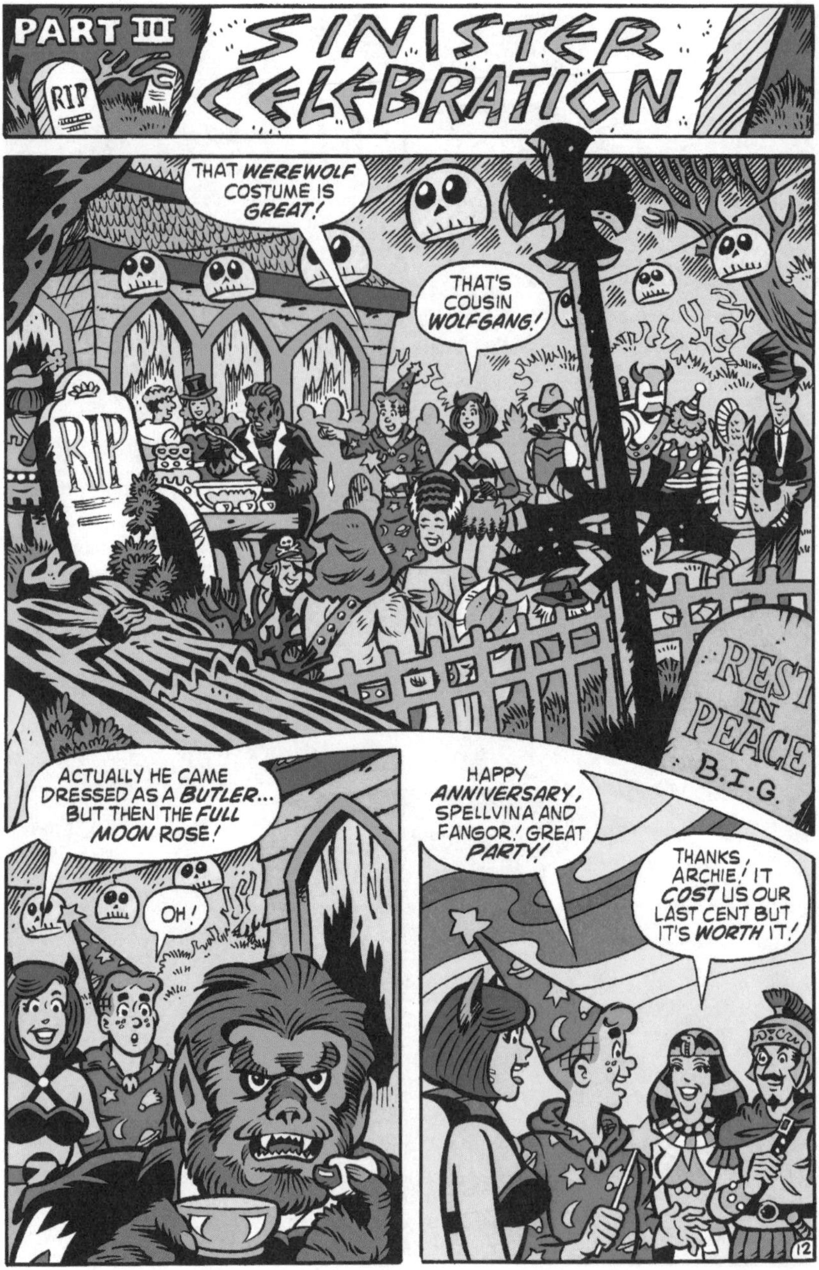
PART III
SINISTER CELEBRATION
THAT WEREWOLF COSTUME IS GREAT!
THAT'S COUSIN WOLFGANG!
REST IN PEACE B.I.G.
ACTUALLY HE CAME DRESSED AS A BUTLER... BUT THEN THE FULL MOON ROSE!
OH!
HAPPY ANNIVERSARY, SPELLVINA AND FANGOR! GREAT PARTY!
THANKS, ARCHIE! IT COST US OUR LAST CENT BUT IT'S WORTH IT!
12

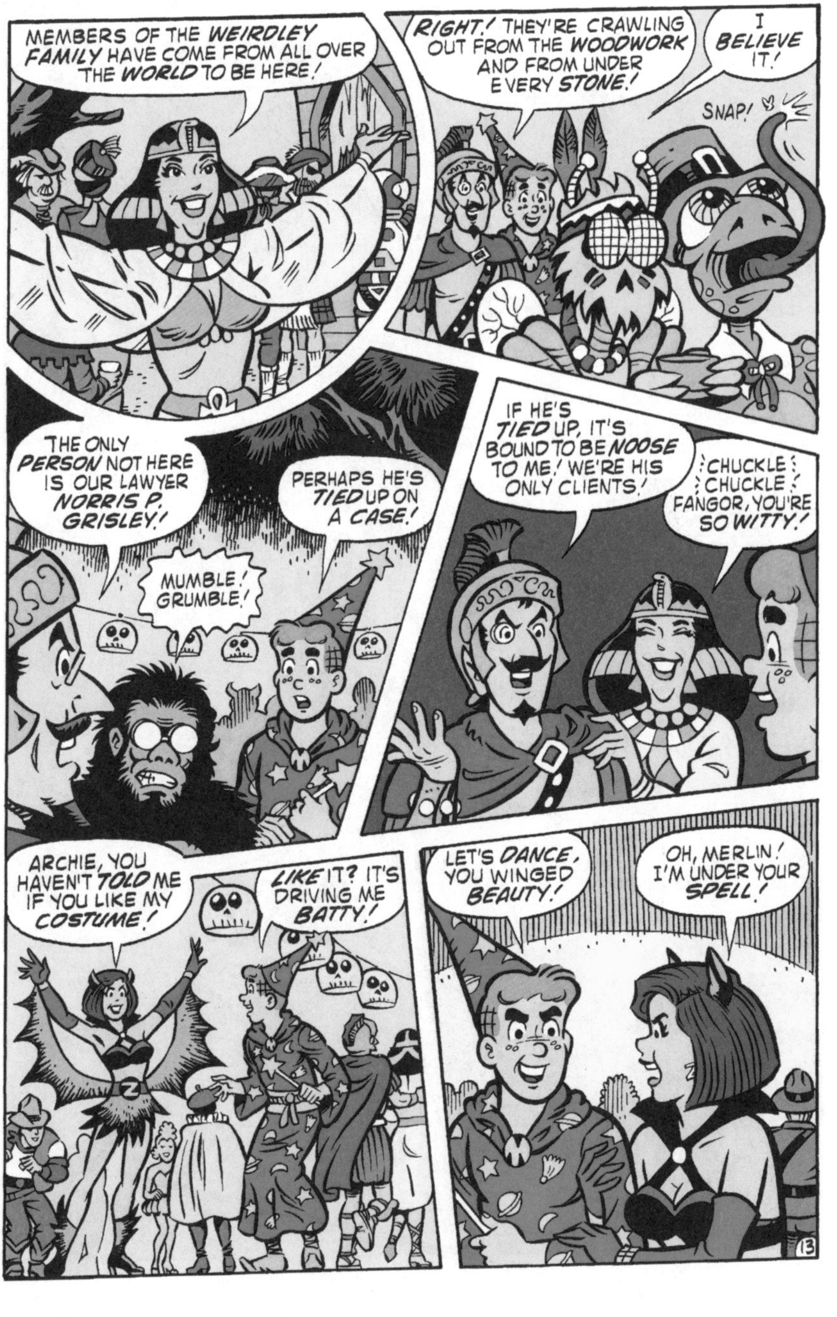
MEMBERS OF THE WEIRDLEY FAMILY HAVE COME FROM ALL OVER THE WORLD TO BE HERE!
RIGHT! THEY'RE CRAWLING OUT FROM THE WOODWORK AND FROM UNDER EVERY STONE!
I BELIEVE IT!
SNAP!
THE ONLY PERSON NOT HERE IS OUR LAWYER NORRIS P. GRISLEY!
PERHAPS HE'S TIED UP ON A CASE!
MUMBLE! GRUMBLE!
IF HE'S TIED UP, IT'S BOUND TO BE NOOSE TO ME! WE'RE HIS ONLY CLIENTS!
CHUCKLE CHUCKLE FANGOR, YOU'RE SO WITTY!
ARCHIE, YOU HAVEN'T TOLD ME IF YOU LIKE MY COSTUME!
LIKE IT? IT'S DRIVING ME BATTY!
LET'S DANCE, YOU WINGED BEAUTY!
OH, MERLIN! I'M UNDER YOUR SPELL!
13

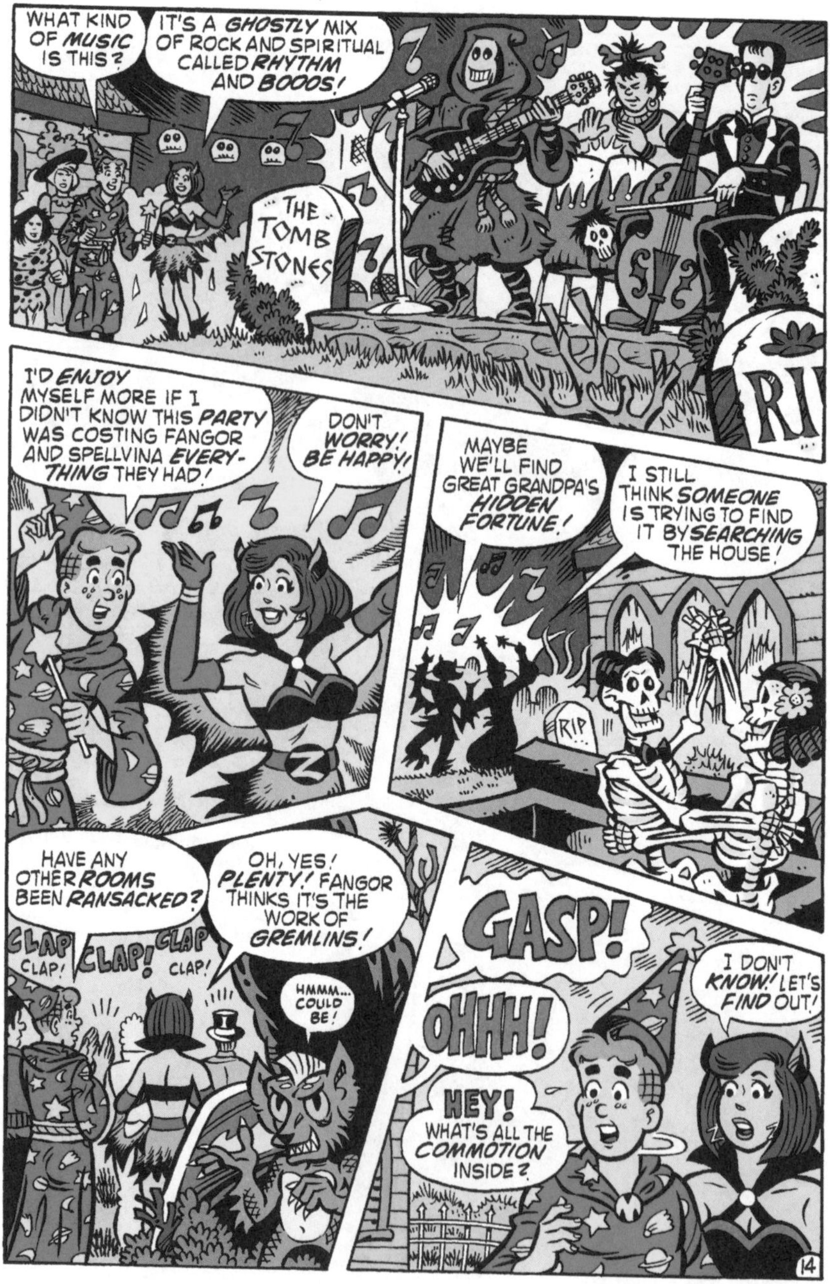
WHAT KIND OF MUSIC IS THIS?
IT'S A GHOSTLY MIX OF ROCK AND SPIRITUAL CALLED RHYTHM AND BOOOS!
THE TOMB STONES
RIP
I'D ENJOY MYSELF MORE IF I DIDN'T KNOW THIS PARTY WAS COSTING FANGOR AND SPELLVINA EVERYTHING THEY HAD!
DON'T WORRY! BE HAPPY!
MAYBE WE'LL FIND GREAT GRANDPA'S HIDDEN FORTUNE!
I STILL THINK SOMEONE IS TRYING TO FIND IT BY SEARCHING THE HOUSE!
RIP
HAVE ANY OTHER ROOMS BEEN RANSACKED?
OH, YES! PLENTY! FANGOR THINKS IT'S THE WORK OF GREMLINS!
CLAP CLAP! CLAP! CLAP CLAP!
HMMM... COULD BE!
GASP!
OHHH!
I DON'T KNOW! LET'S FIND OUT!
HEY! WHAT'S ALL THE COMMOTION INSIDE?
14

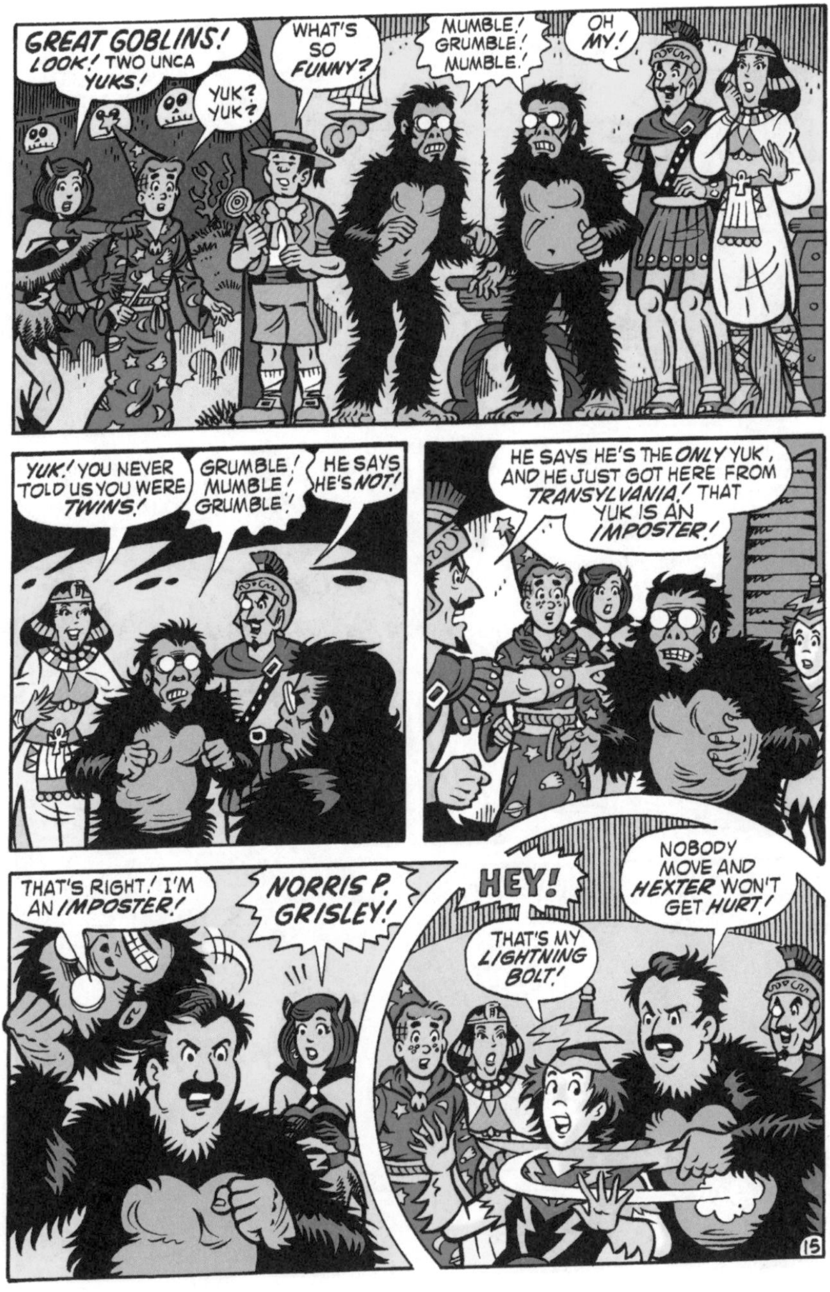
GREAT GOBLINS! LOOK! TWO UNCA YUKS!
YUK? YUK?
WHAT'S SO FUNNY?
MUMBLE! GRUMBLE! MUMBLE!
OH MY!
YUK! YOU NEVER TOLD US YOU WERE TWINS!
GRUMBLE! MUMBLE! GRUMBLE!
HE SAYS HE'S NOT!
HE SAYS HE'S THE ONLY YUK, AND HE JUST GOT HERE FROM TRANSYLVANIA! THAT YUK IS AN IMPOSTER!
THAT'S RIGHT! I'M AN IMPOSTER!
NORRIS P. GRISLEY!
HEY!
THAT'S MY LIGHTNING BOLT!
NOBODY MOVE AND HEXTER WON'T GET HURT!
15

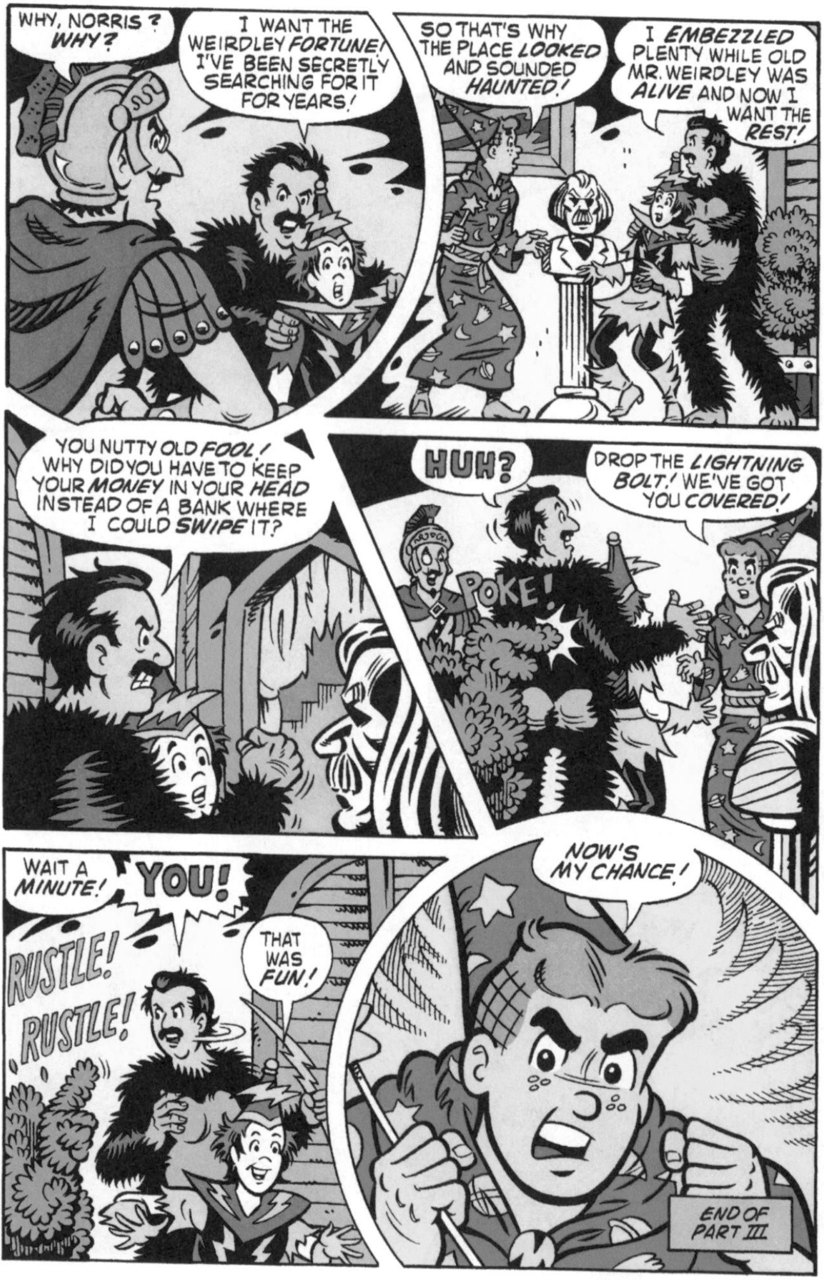
WHY, NORRIS? WHY?
I WANT THE WEIRDLEY FORTUNE! I'VE BEEN SECRETLY SEARCHING FOR IT FOR YEARS!
SO THAT'S WHY THE PLACE LOOKED AND SOUNDED HAUNTED!
I EMBEZZLED PLENTY WHILE OLD MR. WEIRDLEY WAS ALIVE AND NOW I WANT THE REST!
YOU NUTTY OLD FOOL! WHY DID YOU HAVE TO KEEP YOUR MONEY IN YOUR HEAD INSTEAD OF A BANK WHERE I COULD SWIPE IT?
HUH?
DROP THE LIGHTNING BOLT! WE'VE GOT YOU COVERED!
POKE!
WAIT A MINUTE!
YOU!
RUSTLE! RUSTLE!
THAT WAS FUN!
NOW'S MY CHANCE!
END OF PART III

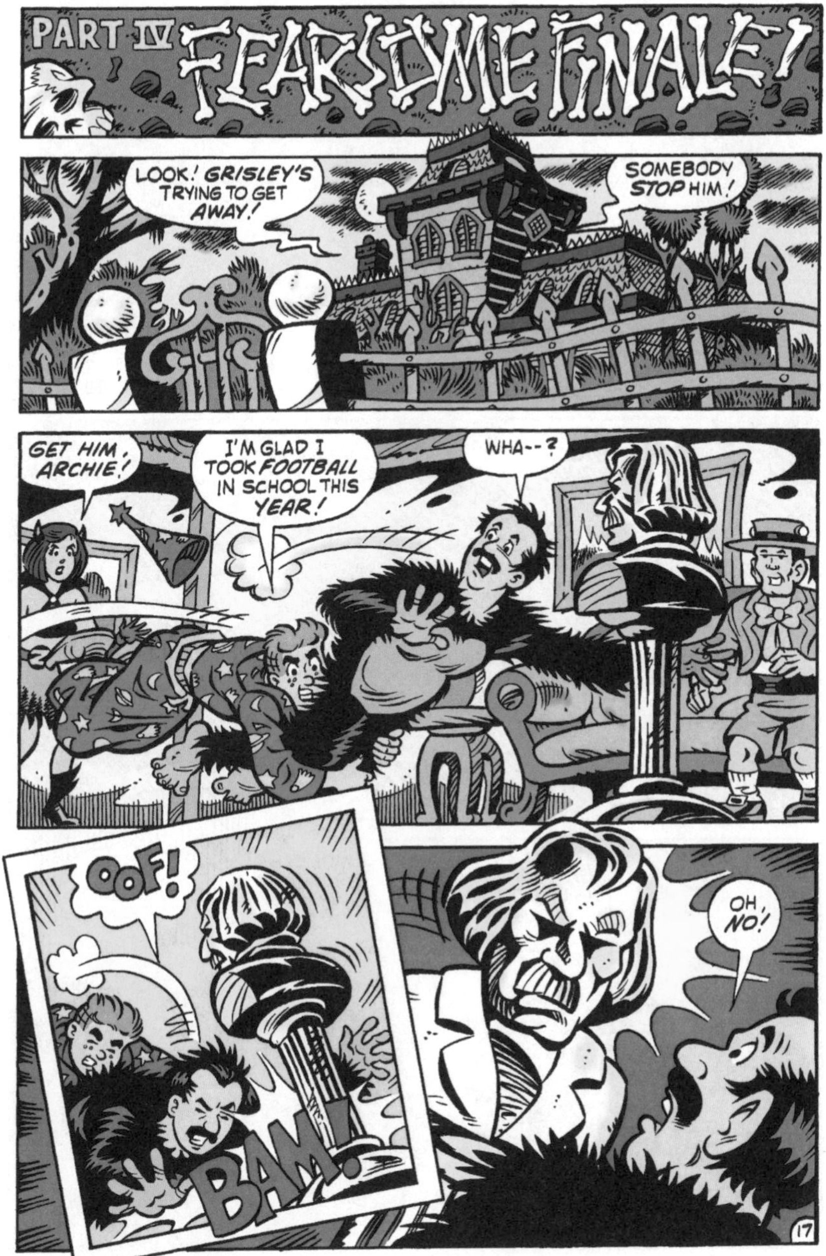
PART IV FEARSOME FINALE!
LOOK! GRISLEY'S TRYING TO GET AWAY!
SOMEBODY STOP HIM!
GET HIM, ARCHIE!
I'M GLAD I TOOK FOOTBALL IN SCHOOL THIS YEAR!
WHA--?
OOF!
BAM!
OH, NO!
17

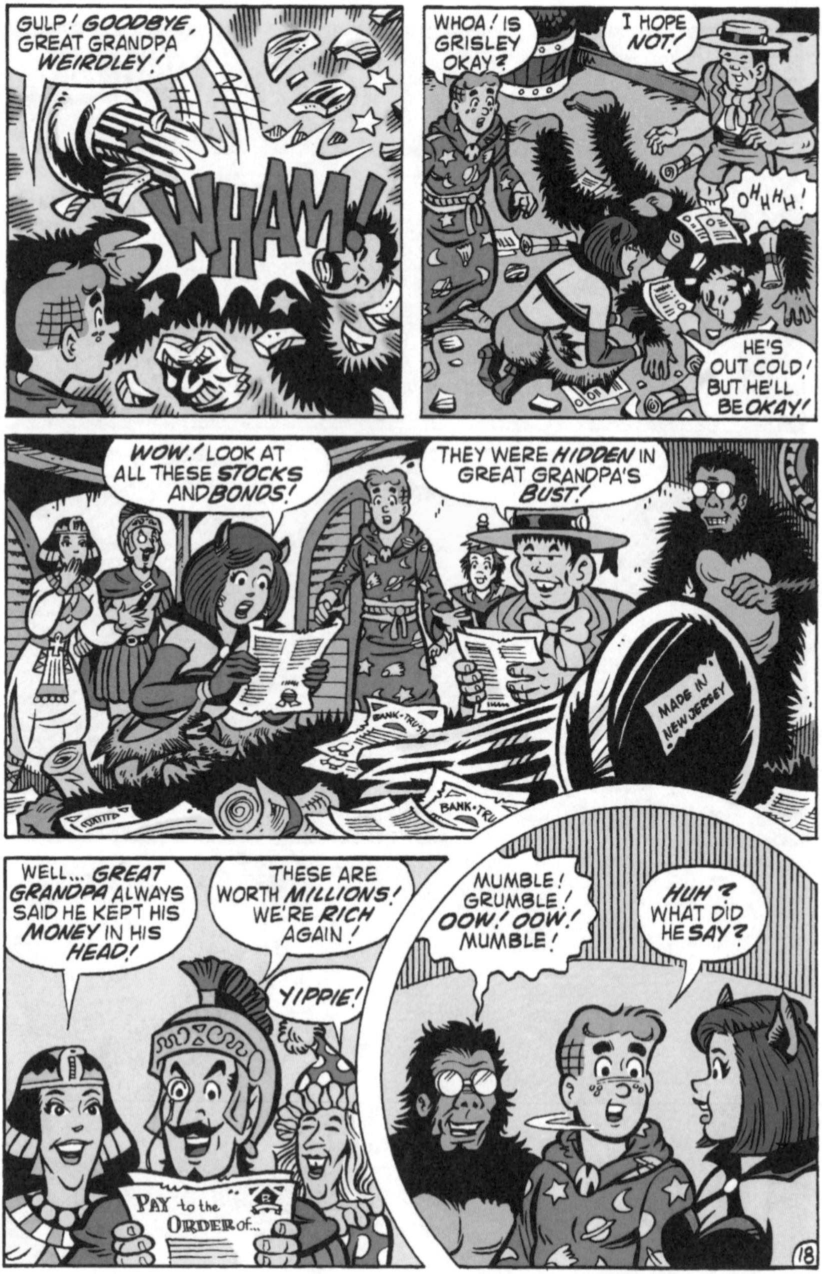
GULP! GOODBYE, GREAT GRANDPA WEIRDLEY!
WHAM!
WHOA! IS GRISLEY OKAY?
I HOPE NOT!
OHHHH!
HE'S OUT COLD! BUT HE'LL BE OKAY!
WOW! LOOK AT ALL THESE STOCKS AND BONDS!
THEY WERE HIDDEN IN GREAT GRANDPA'S BUST!
BANK-TRUST
MADE IN NEW JERSEY
BANK-TRU
WELL... GREAT GRANDPA ALWAYS SAID HE KEPT HIS MONEY IN HIS HEAD!
THESE ARE WORTH MILLIONS! WE'RE RICH AGAIN!
YIPPIE!
PAY to the ORDER of...
MUMBLE! GRUMBLE! OOW! OOW! MUMBLE!
HUH? WHAT DID HE SAY?
18

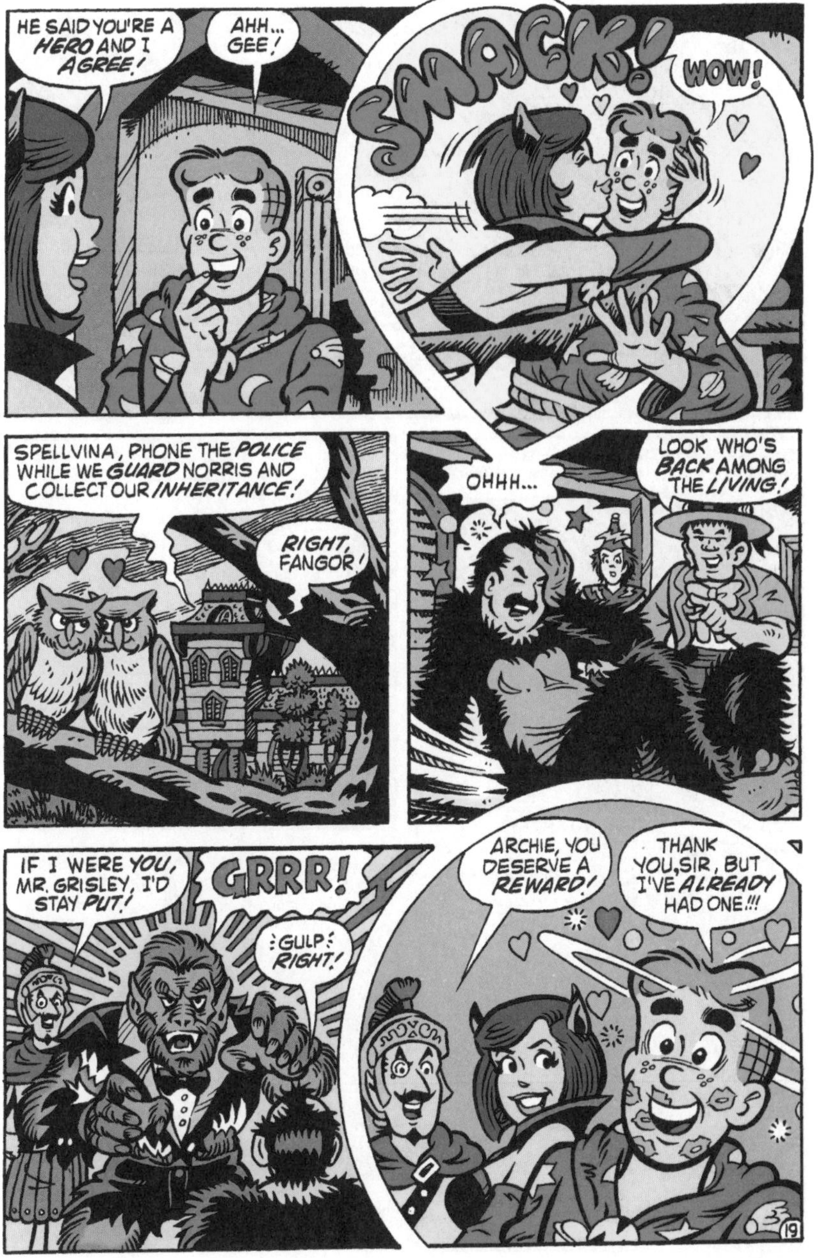
HE SAID YOU'RE A HERO AND I AGREE!
AHH... GEE!
SMACK!
WOW!
SPELLVINA, PHONE THE POLICE WHILE WE GUARD NORRIS AND COLLECT OUR INHERITANCE!
RIGHT, FANGOR!
OHHH...
LOOK WHO'S BACK AMONG THE LIVING!
IF I WERE YOU, MR. GRISLEY, I'D STAY PUT!
GRRR!
GULP RIGHT!
ARCHIE, YOU DESERVE A REWARD!
THANK YOU, SIR, BUT I'VE ALREADY HAD ONE!!!
19

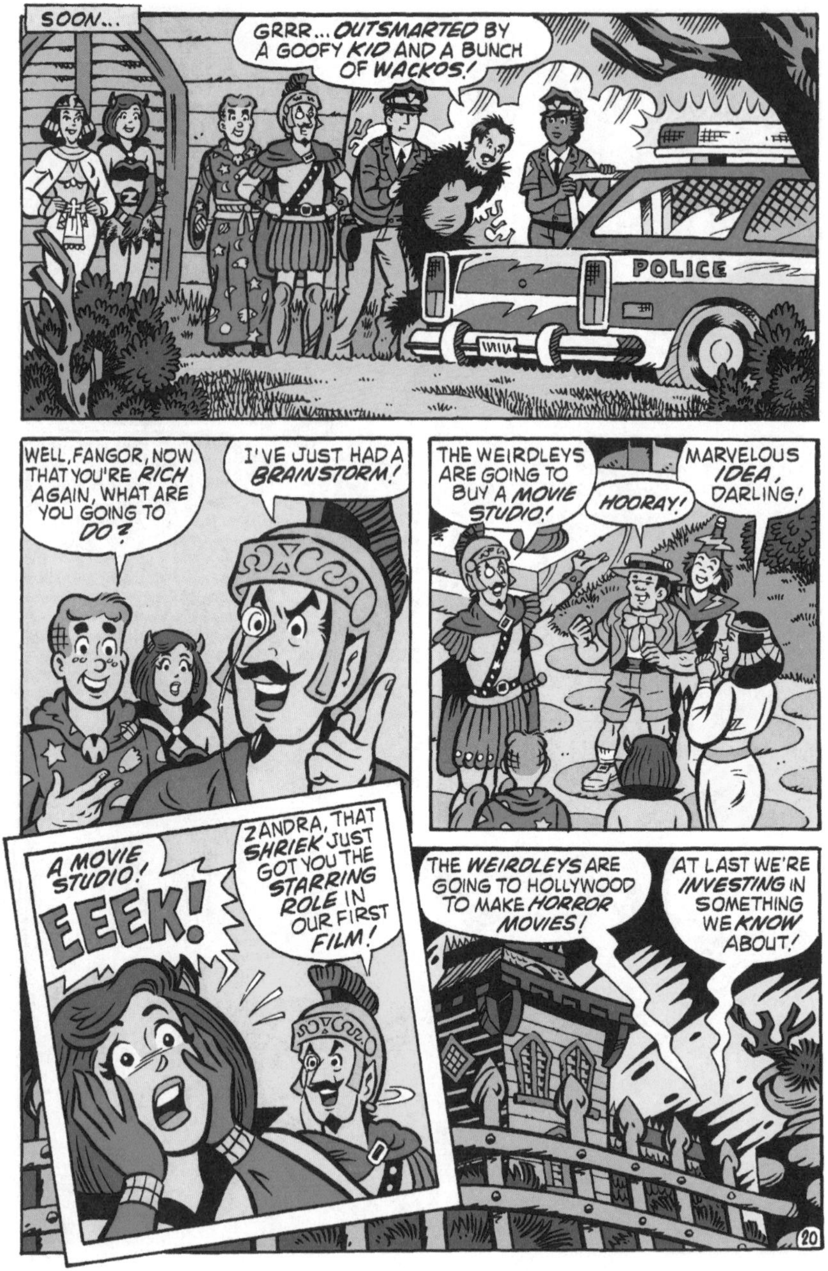
SOON...
GRRR... OUTSMARTED BY A GOOFY KID AND A BUNCH OF WACKOS!
POLICE
WELL, FANGOR, NOW THAT YOU'RE RICH AGAIN, WHAT ARE YOU GOING TO DO?
I'VE JUST HAD A BRAINSTORM!
THE WEIRDLEYS ARE GOING TO BUY A MOVIE STUDIO!
HOORAY!
MARVELOUS IDEA, DARLING!
A MOVIE STUDIO!
EEEK!
ZANDRA, THAT SHRIEK JUST GOT YOU THE STARRING ROLE IN OUR FIRST FILM!
THE WEIRDLEYS ARE GOING TO HOLLYWOOD TO MAKE HORROR MOVIES!
AT LAST WE'RE INVESTING IN SOMETHING WE KNOW ABOUT!
20

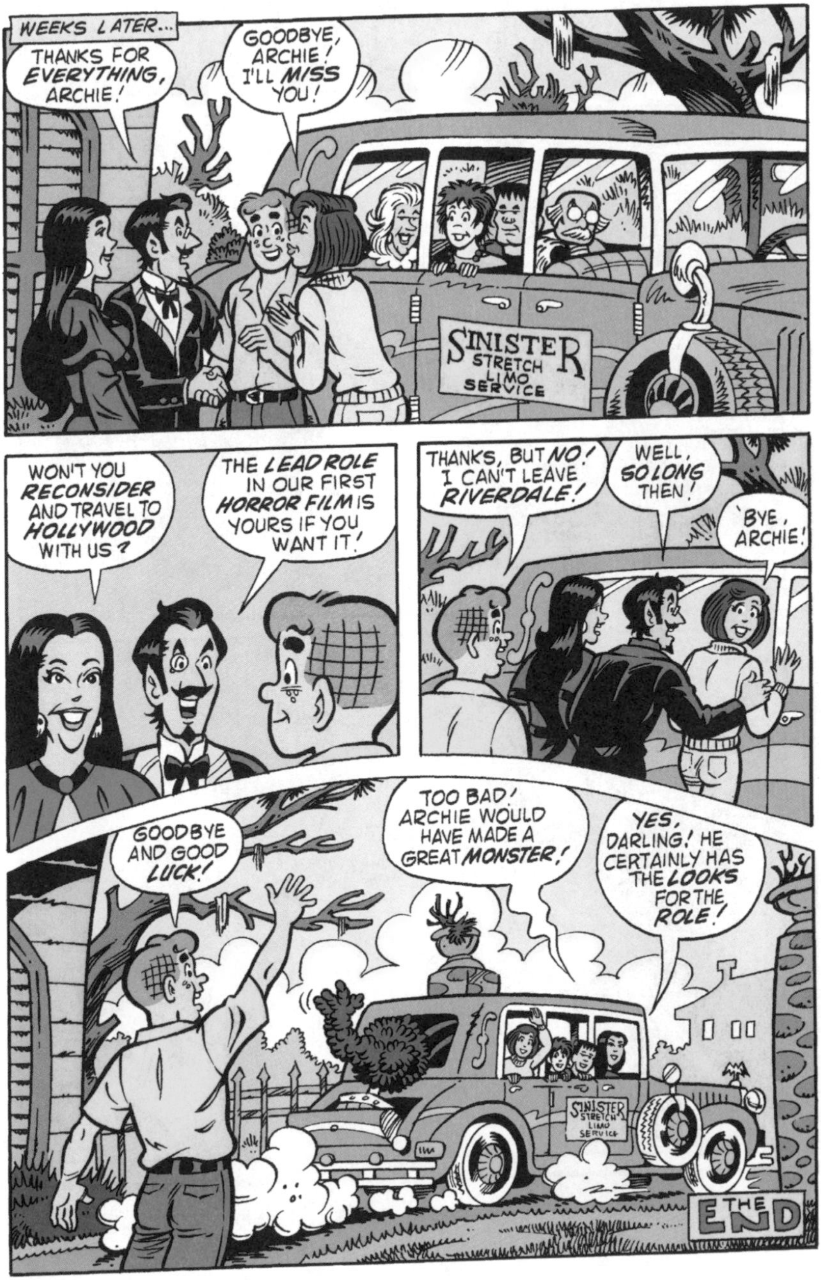
WEEKS LATER...
THANKS FOR EVERYTHING, ARCHIE!
GOODBYE, ARCHIE! I'LL MISS YOU!
SINISTER STRETCH LIMO SERVICE
WON'T YOU RECONSIDER AND TRAVEL TO HOLLYWOOD WITH US?
THE LEAD ROLE IN OUR FIRST HORROR FILM IS YOURS IF YOU WANT IT!
THANKS, BUT NO! I CAN'T LEAVE RIVERDALE!
WELL, SO LONG THEN!
'BYE, ARCHIE!
GOODBYE AND GOOD LUCK!
TOO BAD! ARCHIE WOULD HAVE MADE A GREAT MONSTER!
YES, DARLING! HE CERTAINLY HAS THE LOOKS FOR THE ROLE!
SINISTER STRETCH LIMO SERVICE
THE END

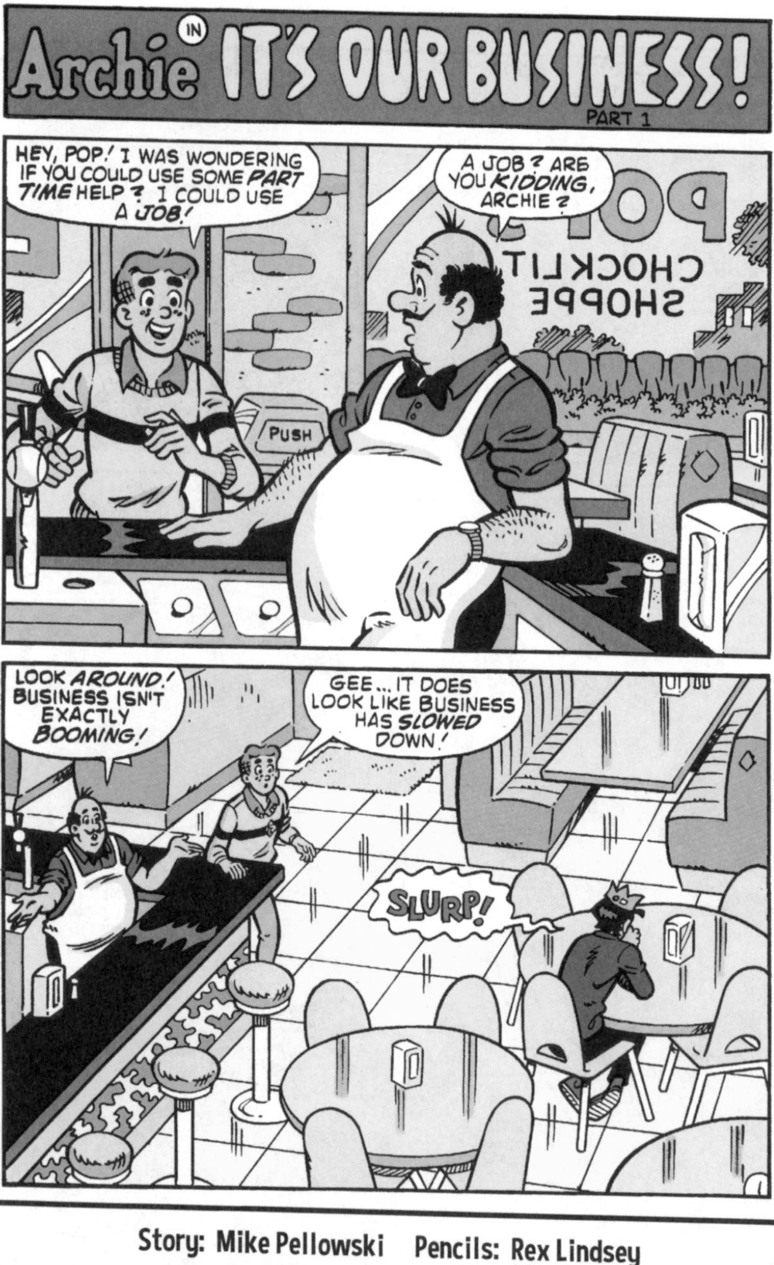
Archie IN IT'S OUR BUSINESS!
PART 1
HEY, POP! I WAS WONDERING IF YOU COULD USE SOME PART TIME HELP? I COULD USE A JOB!
A JOB? ARE YOU KIDDING, ARCHIE?
PUSH
LOOK AROUND! BUSINESS ISN'T EXACTLY BOOMING!
GEE... IT DOES LOOK LIKE BUSINESS HAS SLOWED DOWN!
SLURP!

Story: Mike Pellowski Pencils: Rex Lindsey
Inks: Rex Lindsey Letters: Bill Yoshida

Originally printed in WORLD OF ARCHIE #6, NOVEMBER 1993

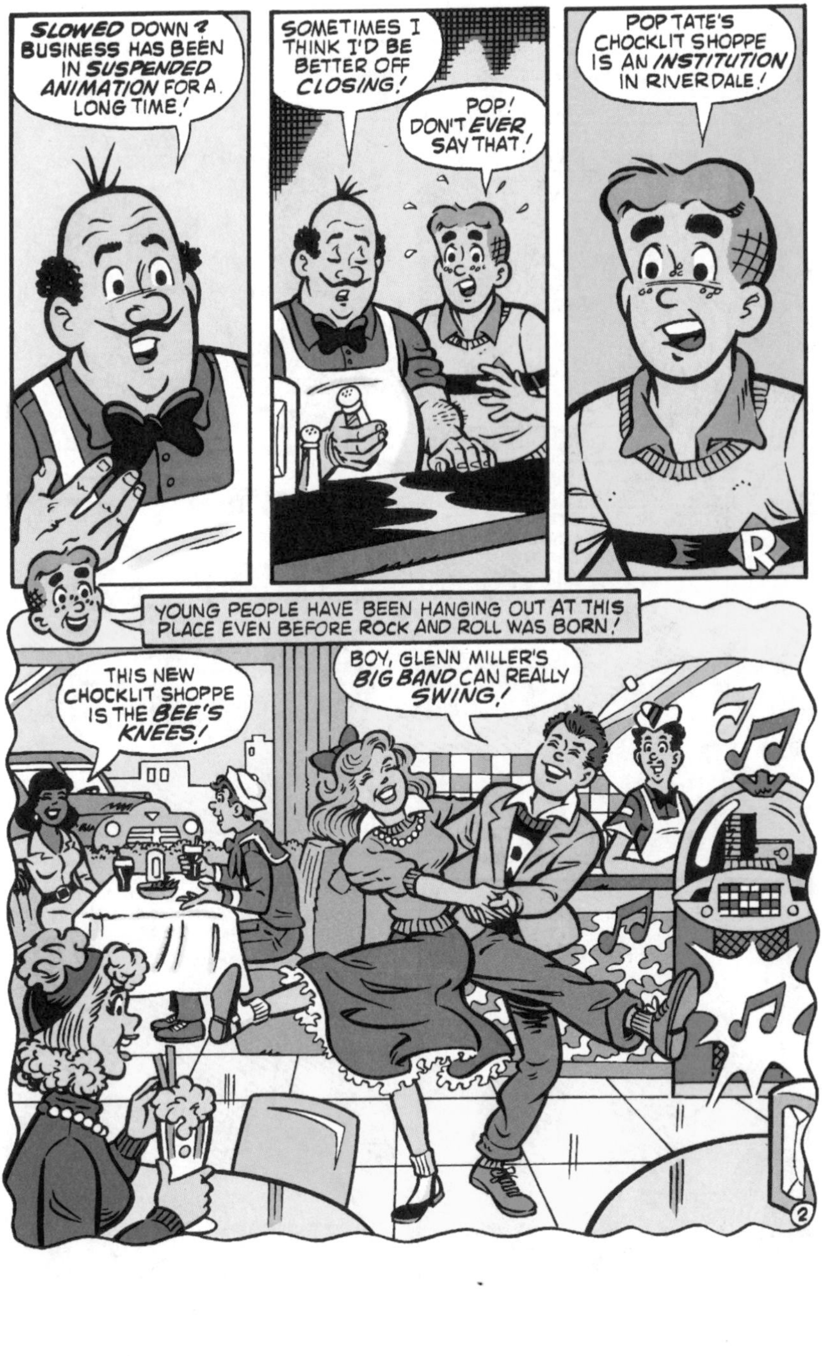
SLOWED DOWN? BUSINESS HAS BEEN IN SUSPENDED ANIMATION FOR A LONG TIME!
SOMETIMES I THINK I'D BE BETTER OFF CLOSING!
POP! DON'T EVER SAY THAT!
POP TATE'S CHOCKLIT SHOPPE IS AN INSTITUTION IN RIVERDALE!
YOUNG PEOPLE HAVE BEEN HANGING OUT AT THIS PLACE EVEN BEFORE ROCK AND ROLL WAS BORN!
THIS NEW CHOCKLIT SHOPPE IS THE BEE'S KNEES!
BOY, GLENN MILLER'S BIG BAND CAN REALLY SWING!
2

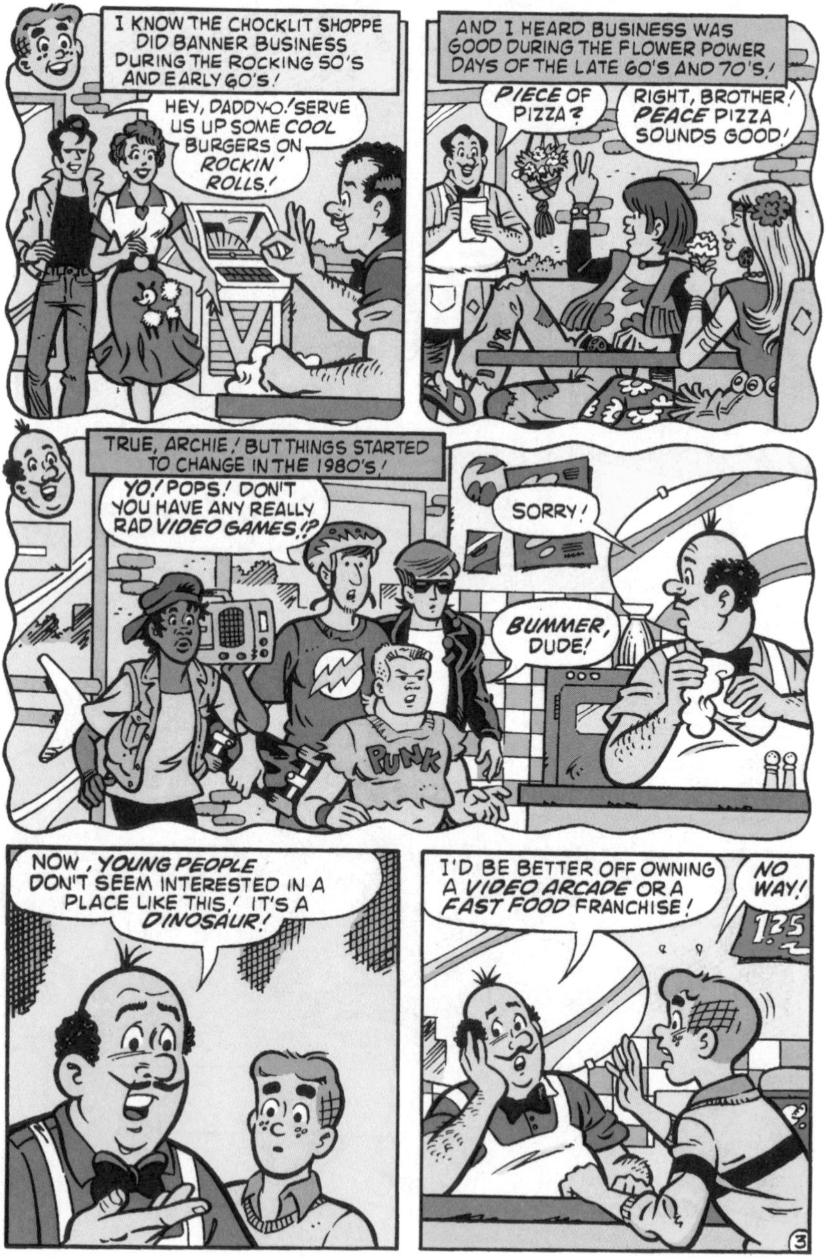
I KNOW THE CHOCKLIT SHOPPE DID BANNER BUSINESS DURING THE ROCKING 50'S AND EARLY 60'S!
HEY, DADDY-O! SERVE US UP SOME COOL BURGERS ON ROCKIN' ROLLS!
AND I HEARD BUSINESS WAS GOOD DURING THE FLOWER POWER DAYS OF THE LATE 60'S AND 70'S!
PIECE OF PIZZA?
RIGHT, BROTHER! PEACE PIZZA SOUNDS GOOD!
TRUE, ARCHIE! BUT THINGS STARTED TO CHANGE IN THE 1980'S!
YO! POPS! DON'T YOU HAVE ANY REALLY RAD VIDEO GAMES!?
SORRY!
BUMMER, DUDE!
PUNK
NOW, YOUNG PEOPLE DON'T SEEM INTERESTED IN A PLACE LIKE THIS! IT'S A DINOSAUR!
I'D BE BETTER OFF OWNING A VIDEO ARCADE OR A FAST FOOD FRANCHISE!
NO WAY!
1.25
3

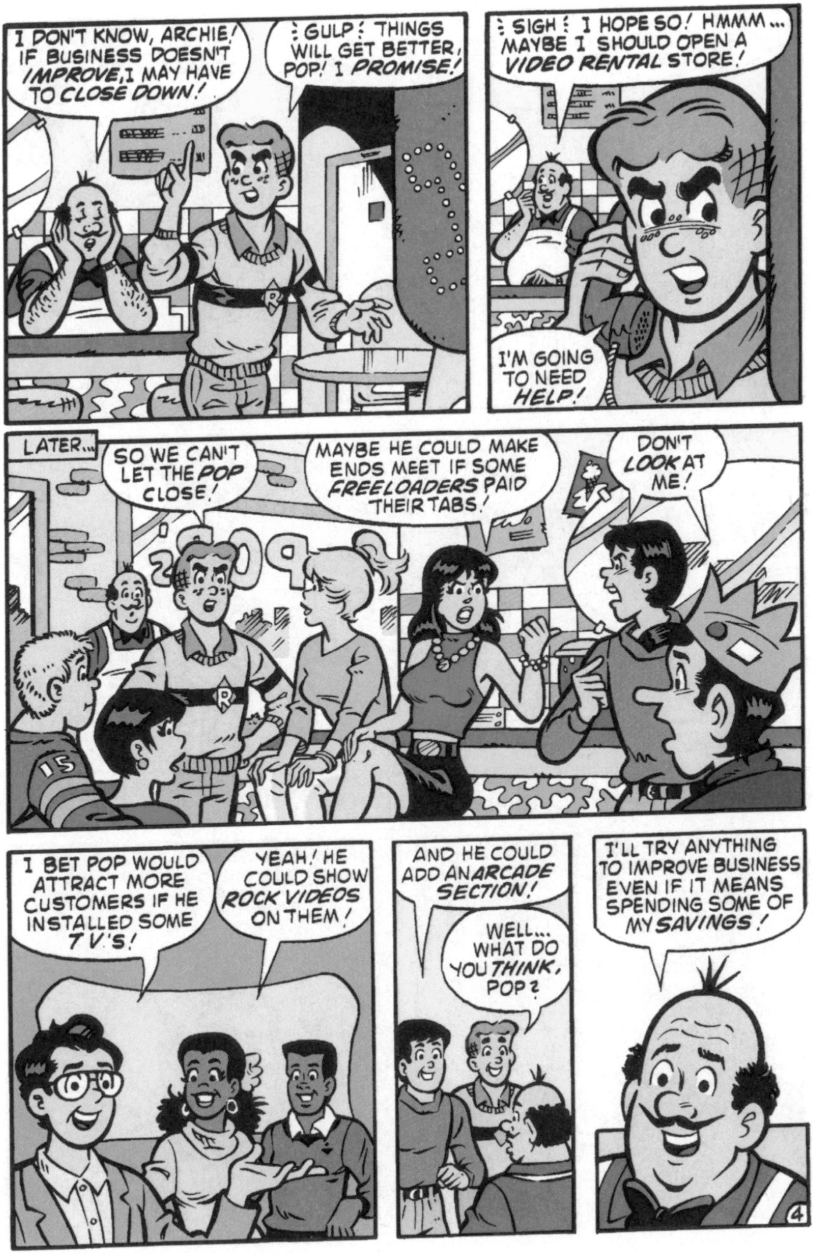
I DON'T KNOW, ARCHIE! IF BUSINESS DOESN'T IMPROVE, I MAY HAVE TO CLOSE DOWN!
GULP! THINGS WILL GET BETTER, POP! I PROMISE!
SIGH! I HOPE SO! HMMM... MAYBE I SHOULD OPEN A VIDEO RENTAL STORE!
I'M GOING TO NEED HELP!
LATER...
SO WE CAN'T LET THE POP CLOSE!
MAYBE HE COULD MAKE ENDS MEET IF SOME FREELOADERS PAID THEIR TABS!
DON'T LOOK AT ME!
I BET POP WOULD ATTRACT MORE CUSTOMERS IF HE INSTALLED SOME TV'S!
YEAH! HE COULD SHOW ROCK VIDEOS ON THEM!
AND HE COULD ADD AN ARCADE SECTION!
WELL... WHAT DO YOU THINK, POP?
I'LL TRY ANYTHING TO IMPROVE BUSINESS EVEN IF IT MEANS SPENDING SOME OF MY SAVINGS!
4

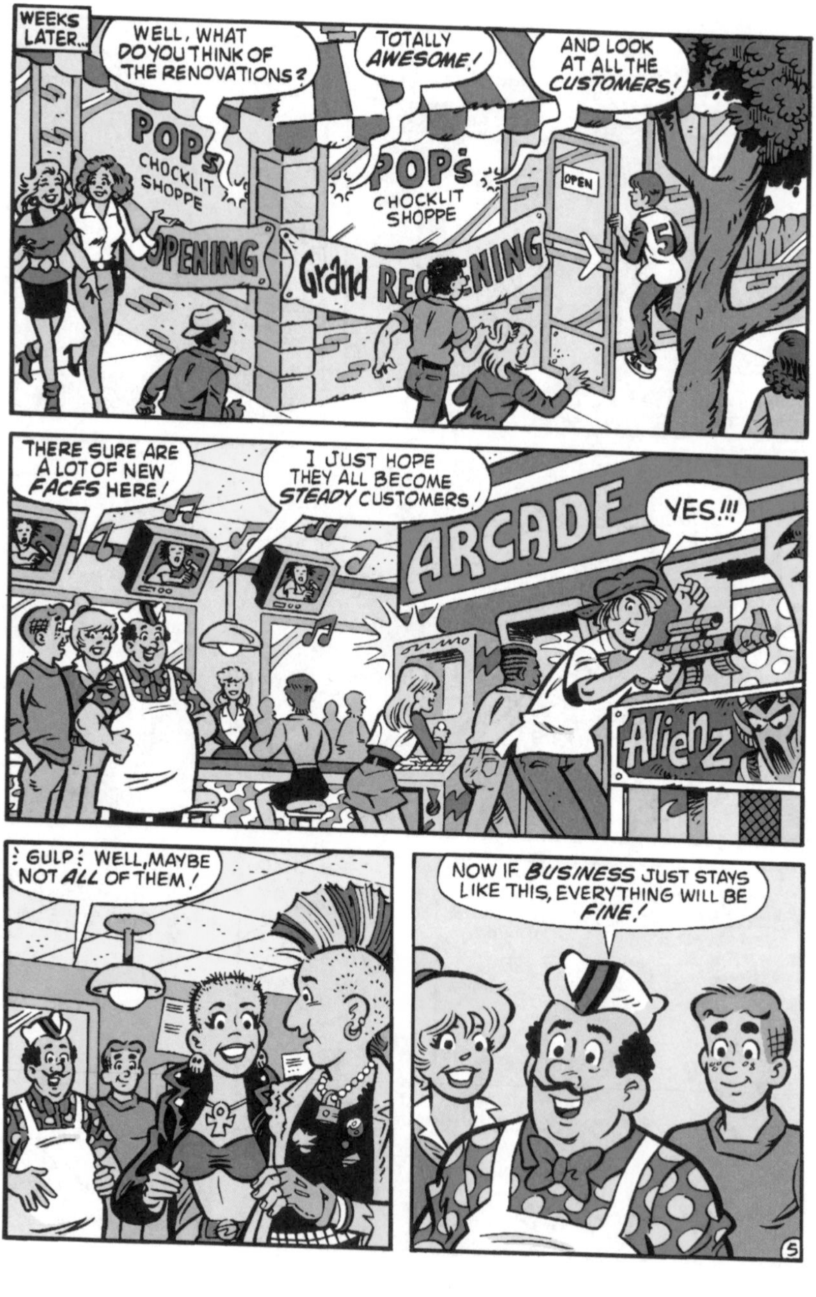
WEEKS LATER...
WELL, WHAT DO YOU THINK OF THE RENOVATIONS?
TOTALLY AWESOME!
AND LOOK AT ALL THE CUSTOMERS!
POP's CHOCKLIT SHOPPE
POP's CHOCKLIT SHOPPE
OPEN
OPENING
Grand RE ENING
THERE SURE ARE A LOT OF NEW FACES HERE!
I JUST HOPE THEY ALL BECOME STEADY CUSTOMERS!
ARCADE
YES!!!
Alienz
GULP! WELL, MAYBE NOT ALL OF THEM!
NOW IF BUSINESS JUST STAYS LIKE THIS, EVERYTHING WILL BE FINE!
5

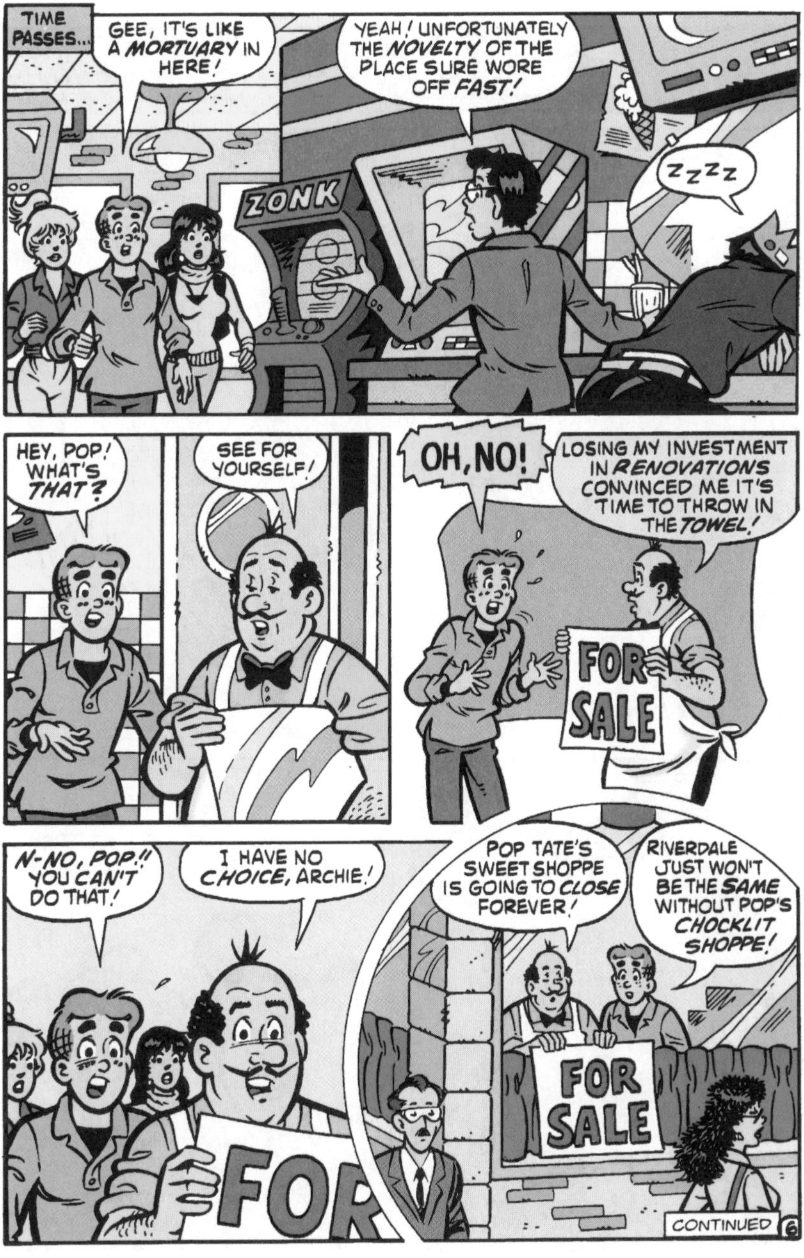
TIME PASSES...
GEE, IT'S LIKE A MORTUARY IN HERE!
YEAH! UNFORTUNATELY THE NOVELTY OF THE PLACE SURE WORE OFF FAST!
ZONK
ZZZZ
HEY, POP! WHAT'S THAT?
SEE FOR YOURSELF!
OH, NO!
LOSING MY INVESTMENT IN RENOVATIONS CONVINCED ME IT'S TIME TO THROW IN THE TOWEL!
FOR SALE
N-NO, POP!! YOU CAN'T DO THAT!
I HAVE NO CHOICE, ARCHIE!
FOR
POP TATE'S SWEET SHOPPE IS GOING TO CLOSE FOREVER!
RIVERDALE JUST WON'T BE THE SAME WITHOUT POP'S CHOCKLIT SHOPPE!
FOR SALE
CONTINUED
6

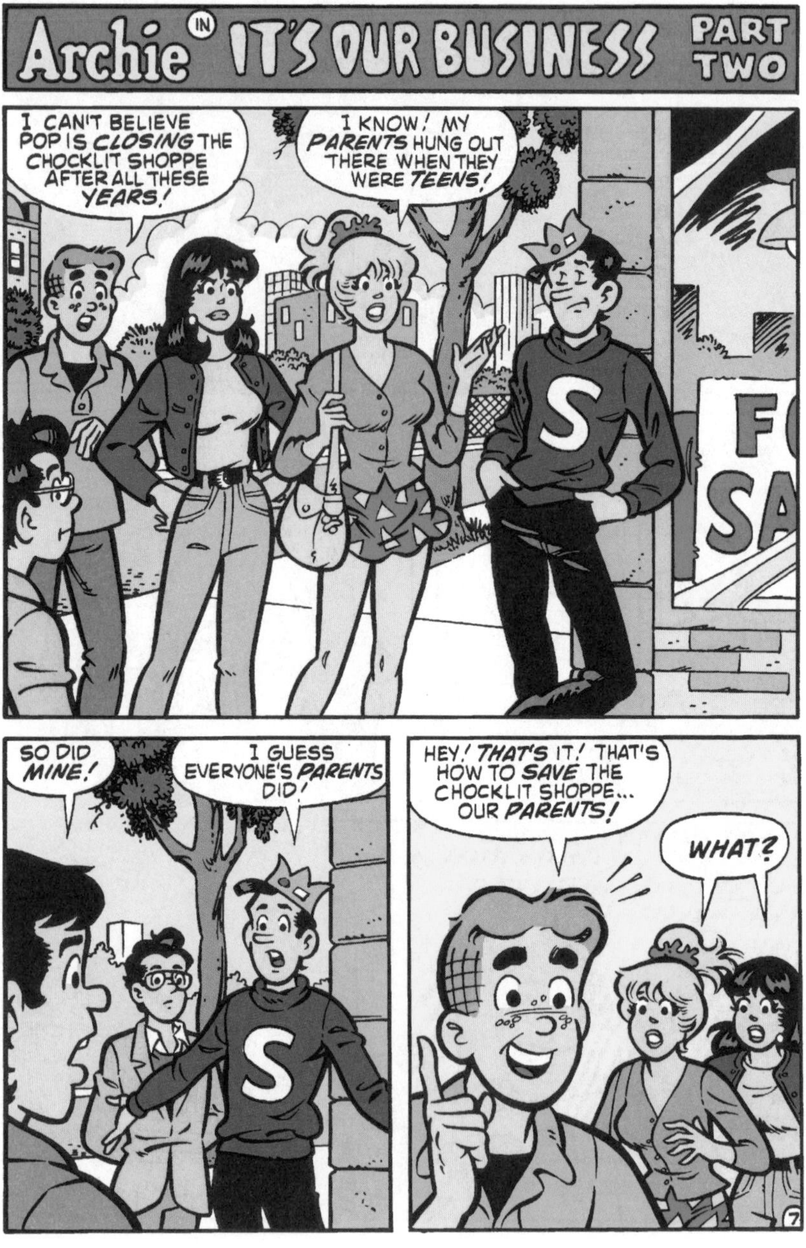
Archie IN IT'S OUR BUSINESS PART TWO
I CAN'T BELIEVE POP IS CLOSING THE CHOCKLIT SHOPPE AFTER ALL THESE YEARS!
I KNOW! MY PARENTS HUNG OUT THERE WHEN THEY WERE TEENS!
SO DID MINE!
I GUESS EVERYONE'S PARENTS DID!
HEY! THAT'S IT! THAT'S HOW TO SAVE THE CHOCKLIT SHOPPE... OUR PARENTS!
WHAT?
7

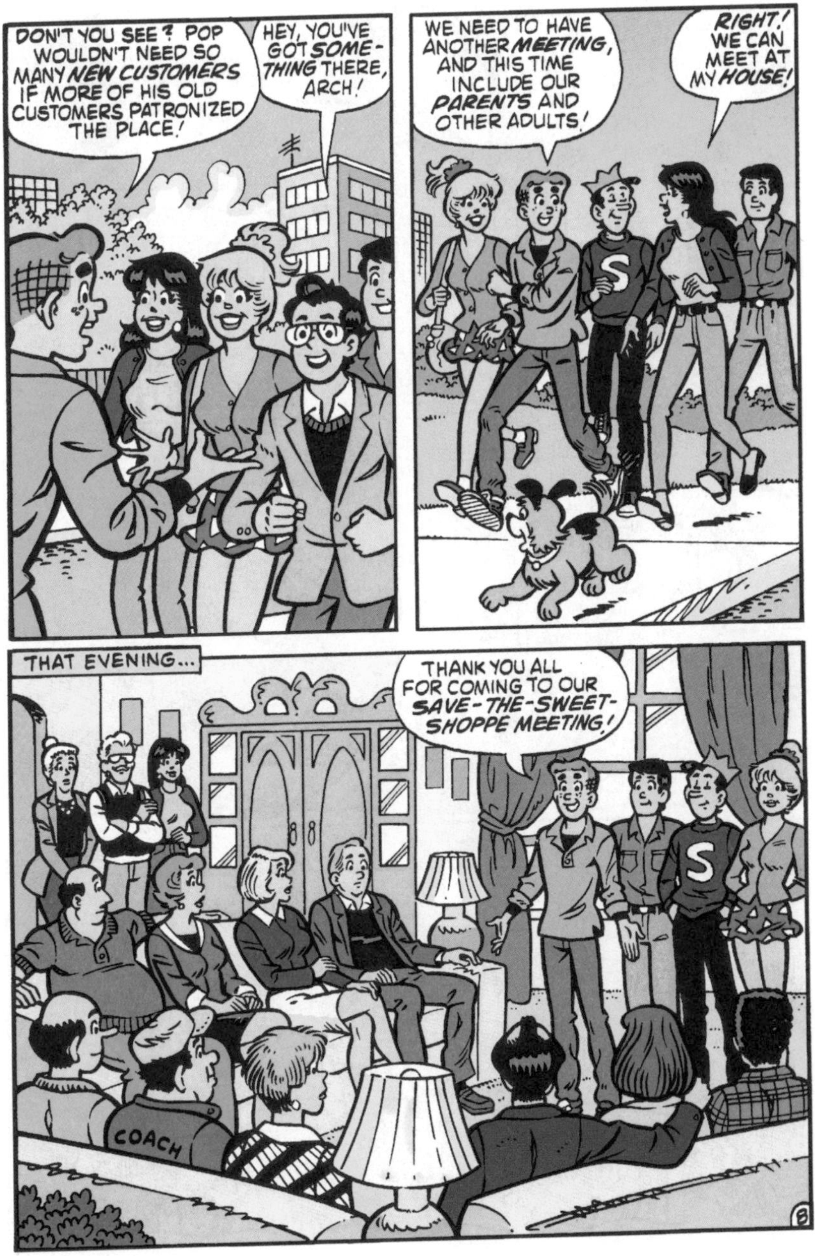
DON'T YOU SEE? POP WOULDN'T NEED SO MANY NEW CUSTOMERS IF MORE OF HIS OLD CUSTOMERS PATRONIZED THE PLACE!
HEY, YOU'VE GOT SOME-THING THERE, ARCH!
WE NEED TO HAVE ANOTHER MEETING, AND THIS TIME INCLUDE OUR PARENTS AND OTHER ADULTS!
RIGHT! WE CAN MEET AT MY HOUSE!
THAT EVENING...
THANK YOU ALL FOR COMING TO OUR SAVE-THE-SWEET-SHOPPE MEETING!
COACH
8

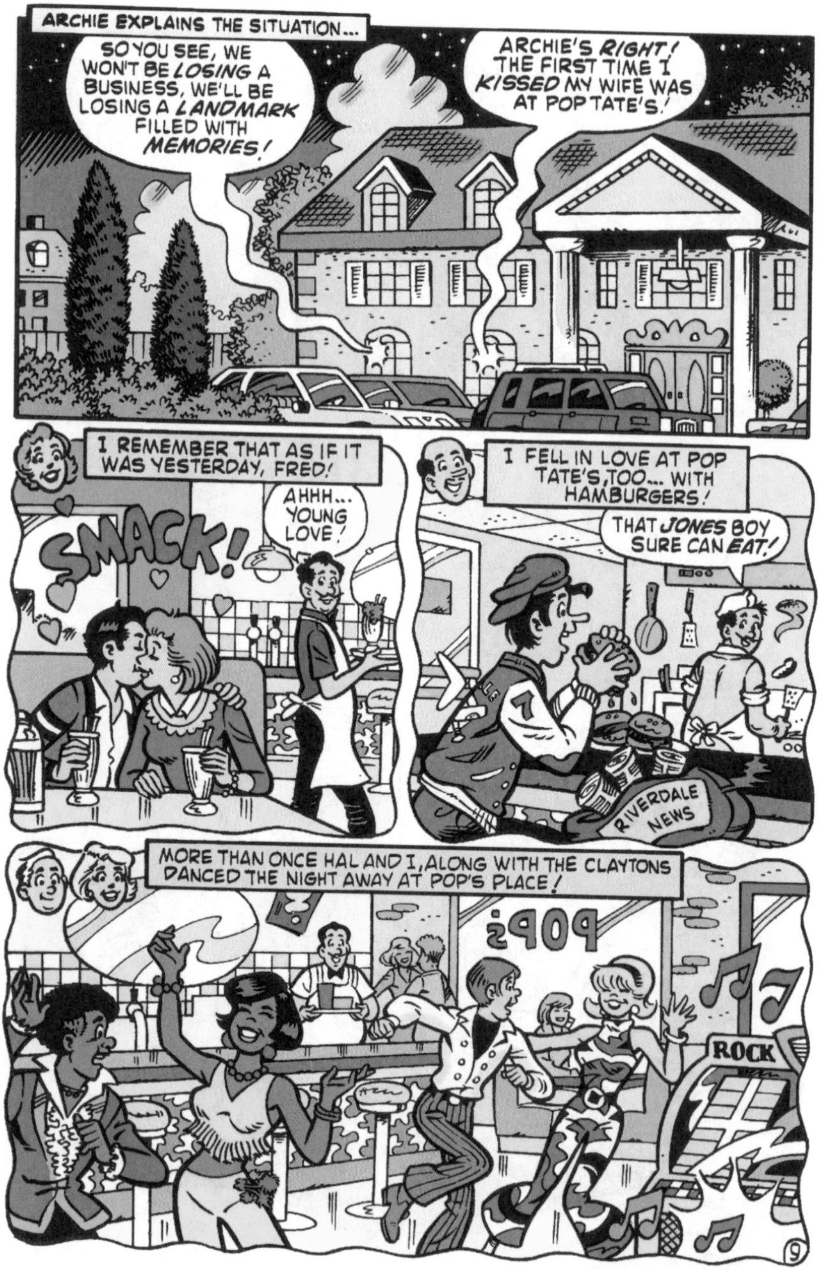
ARCHIE EXPLAINS THE SITUATION...
SO YOU SEE, WE WON'T BE LOSING A BUSINESS, WE'LL BE LOSING A LANDMARK FILLED WITH MEMORIES!
ARCHIE'S RIGHT! THE FIRST TIME I KISSED MY WIFE WAS AT POP TATE'S!
I REMEMBER THAT AS IF IT WAS YESTERDAY, FRED!
SMACK!
AHHH... YOUNG LOVE!
I FELL IN LOVE AT POP TATE'S, TOO... WITH HAMBURGERS!
THAT JONES BOY SURE CAN EAT!
RIVERDALE NEWS
MORE THAN ONCE HAL AND I, ALONG WITH THE CLAYTONS DANCED THE NIGHT AWAY AT POP'S PLACE!
POP'S
ROCK
9

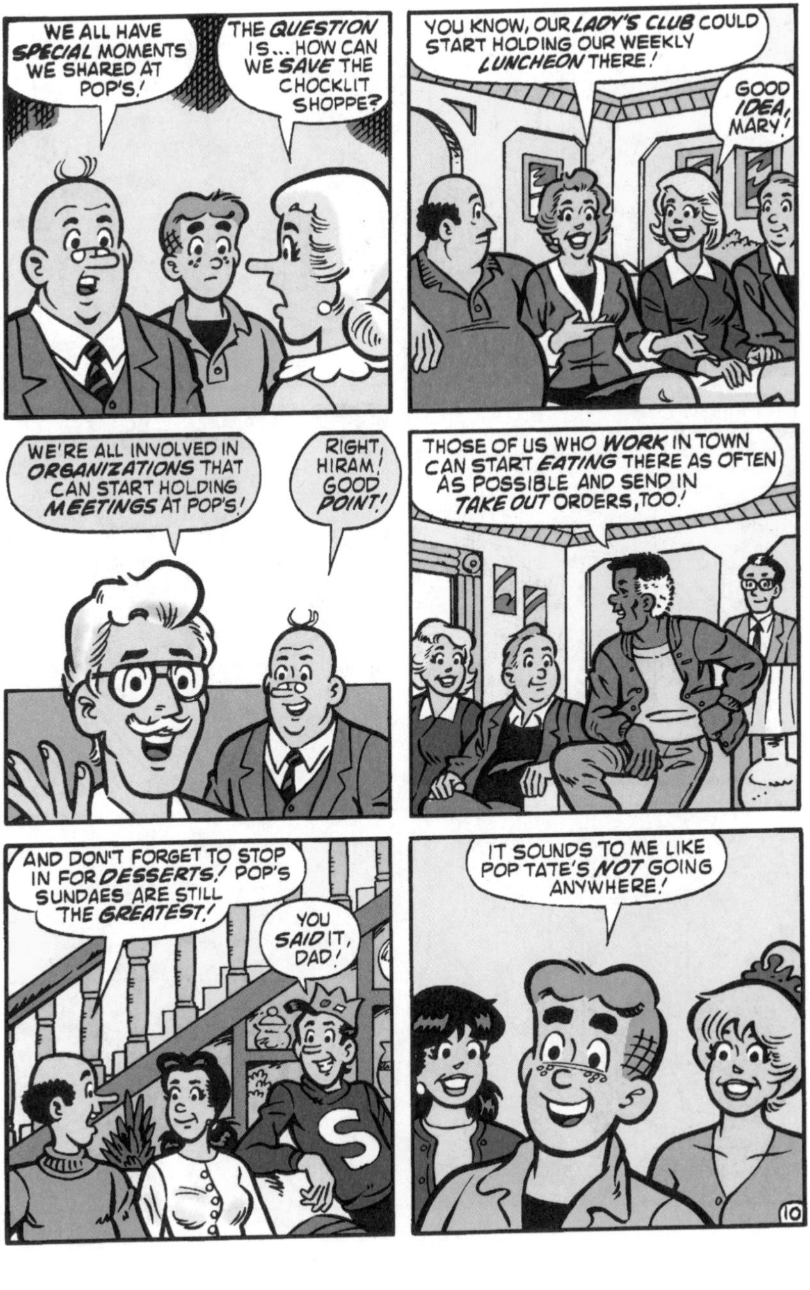
WE ALL HAVE SPECIAL MOMENTS WE SHARED AT POP'S!
THE QUESTION IS... HOW CAN WE SAVE THE CHOCKLIT SHOPPE?
YOU KNOW, OUR LADY'S CLUB COULD START HOLDING OUR WEEKLY LUNCHEON THERE!
GOOD IDEA, MARY!
WE'RE ALL INVOLVED IN ORGANIZATIONS THAT CAN START HOLDING MEETINGS AT POP'S!
RIGHT, HIRAM! GOOD POINT!
THOSE OF US WHO WORK IN TOWN CAN START EATING THERE AS OFTEN AS POSSIBLE AND SEND IN TAKE OUT ORDERS, TOO!
AND DON'T FORGET TO STOP IN FOR DESSERTS! POP'S SUNDAES ARE STILL THE GREATEST!
YOU SAID IT, DAD!
IT SOUNDS TO ME LIKE POP TATE'S NOT GOING ANYWHERE!
10

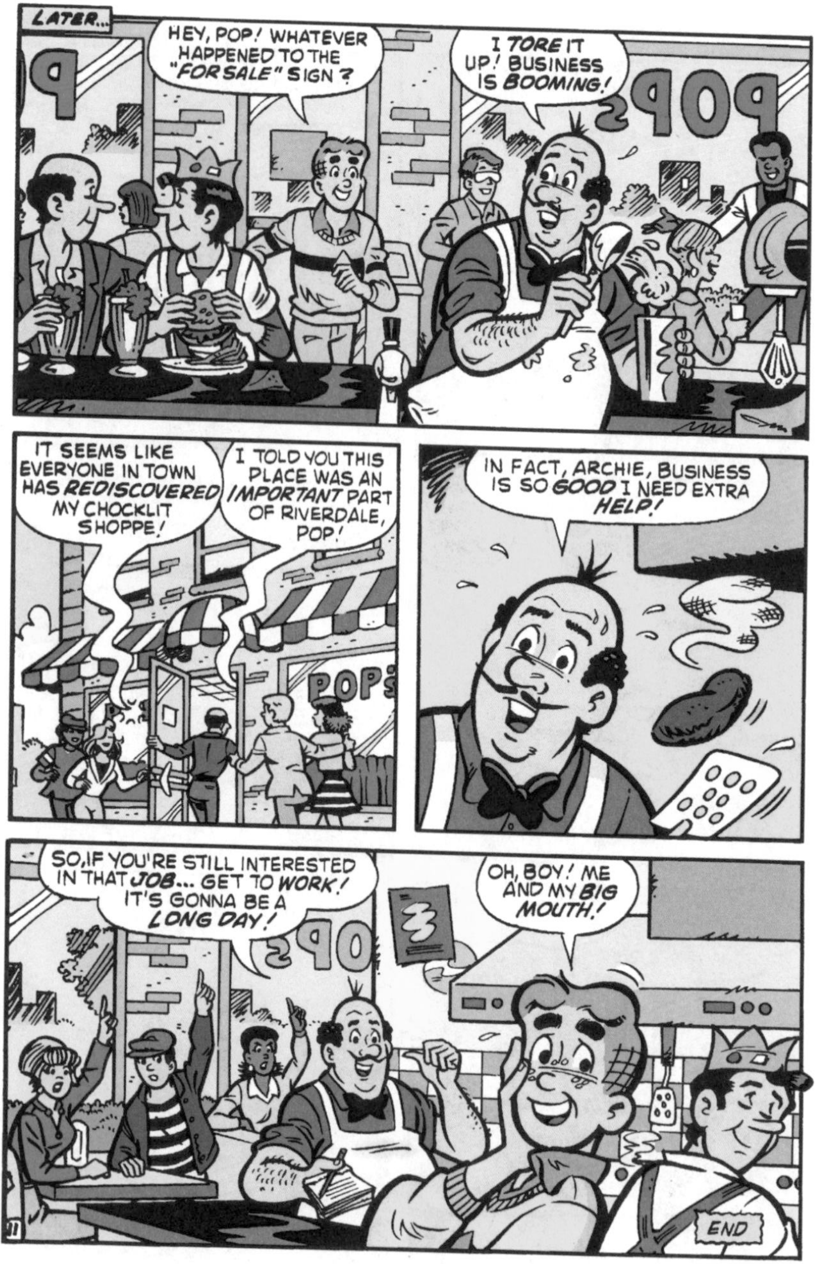
LATER...
HEY, POP! WHATEVER HAPPENED TO THE "FOR SALE" SIGN?
I TORE IT UP! BUSINESS IS BOOMING!
POPS
IT SEEMS LIKE EVERYONE IN TOWN HAS REDISCOVERED MY CHOCKLIT SHOPPE!
I TOLD YOU THIS PLACE WAS AN IMPORTANT PART OF RIVERDALE, POP!
POP'S
IN FACT, ARCHIE, BUSINESS IS SO GOOD I NEED EXTRA HELP!
SO, IF YOU'RE STILL INTERESTED IN THAT JOB... GET TO WORK! IT'S GONNA BE A LONG DAY!
OH, BOY! ME AND MY BIG MOUTH!
END

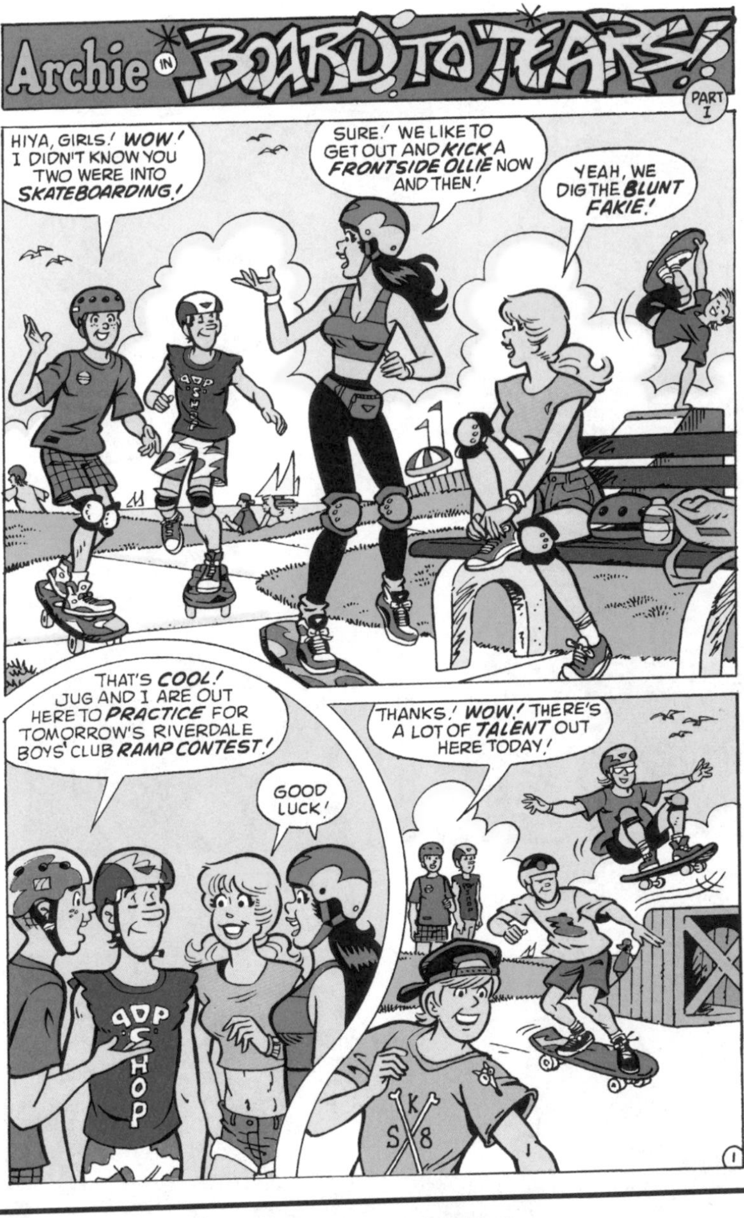
Archie in BOARD TO TEARS!
PART I
HIYA, GIRLS! WOW! I DIDN'T KNOW YOU TWO WERE INTO SKATEBOARDING!
SURE! WE LIKE TO GET OUT AND KICK A FRONTSIDE OLLIE NOW AND THEN!
YEAH, WE DIG THE BLUNT FAKIE!
THAT'S COOL! JUG AND I ARE OUT HERE TO PRACTICE FOR TOMORROW'S RIVERDALE BOYS' CLUB RAMP CONTEST!
GOOD LUCK!
THANKS! WOW! THERE'S A LOT OF TALENT OUT HERE TODAY!
1

Story, Art & Colors: Rex Lindsey
Letters: Bill Yoshida

Originally printed in WORLD OF ARCHIE #6, NOVEMBER 1993

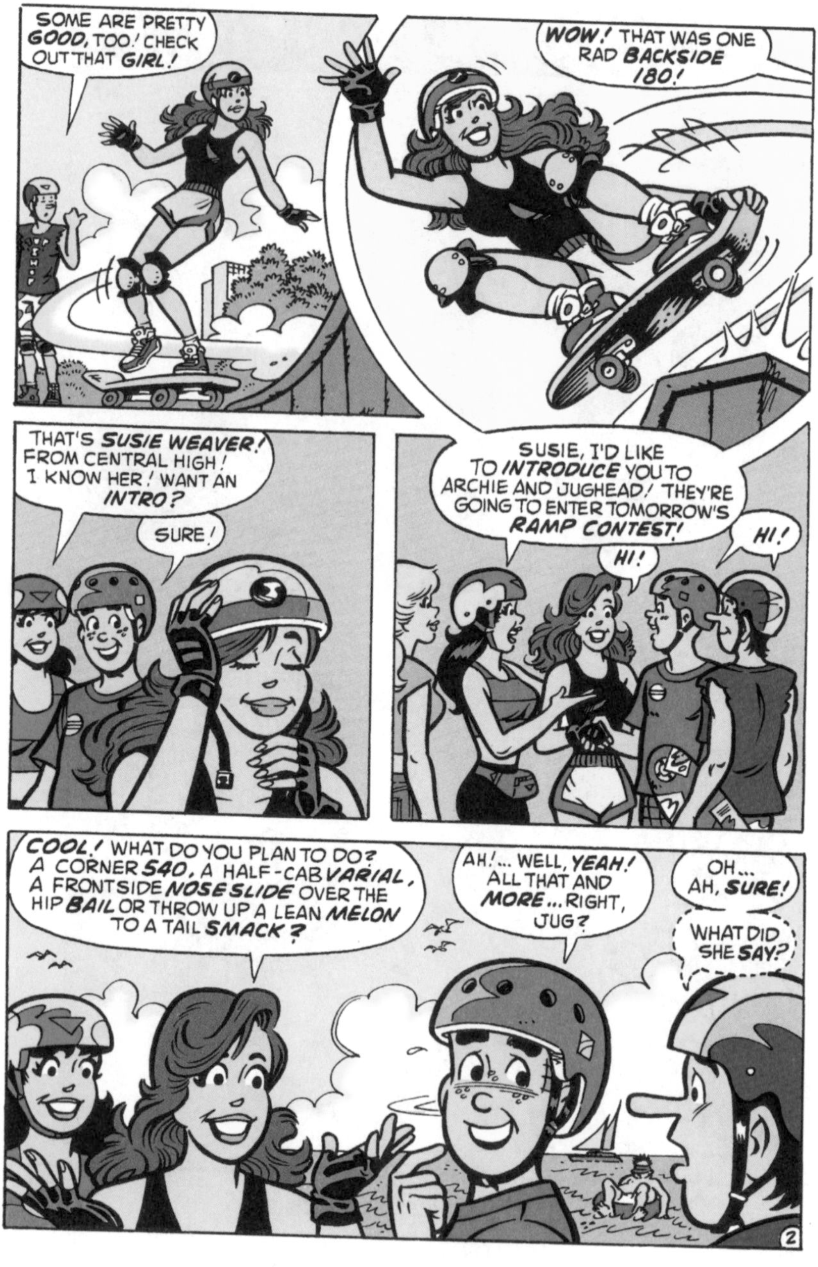
SOME ARE PRETTY GOOD, TOO! CHECK OUT THAT GIRL!
WOW! THAT WAS ONE RAD BACKSIDE 180!
THAT'S SUSIE WEAVER! FROM CENTRAL HIGH! I KNOW HER! WANT AN INTRO?
SURE!
SUSIE, I'D LIKE TO INTRODUCE YOU TO ARCHIE AND JUGHEAD! THEY'RE GOING TO ENTER TOMORROW'S RAMP CONTEST!
HI!
HI!
COOL! WHAT DO YOU PLAN TO DO? A CORNER 540, A HALF-CAB VARIAL, A FRONTSIDE NOSE SLIDE OVER THE HIP BAIL OR THROW UP A LEAN MELON TO A TAIL SMACK?
AH!... WELL, YEAH! ALL THAT AND MORE... RIGHT, JUG?
OH... AH, SURE!
WHAT DID SHE SAY?
2

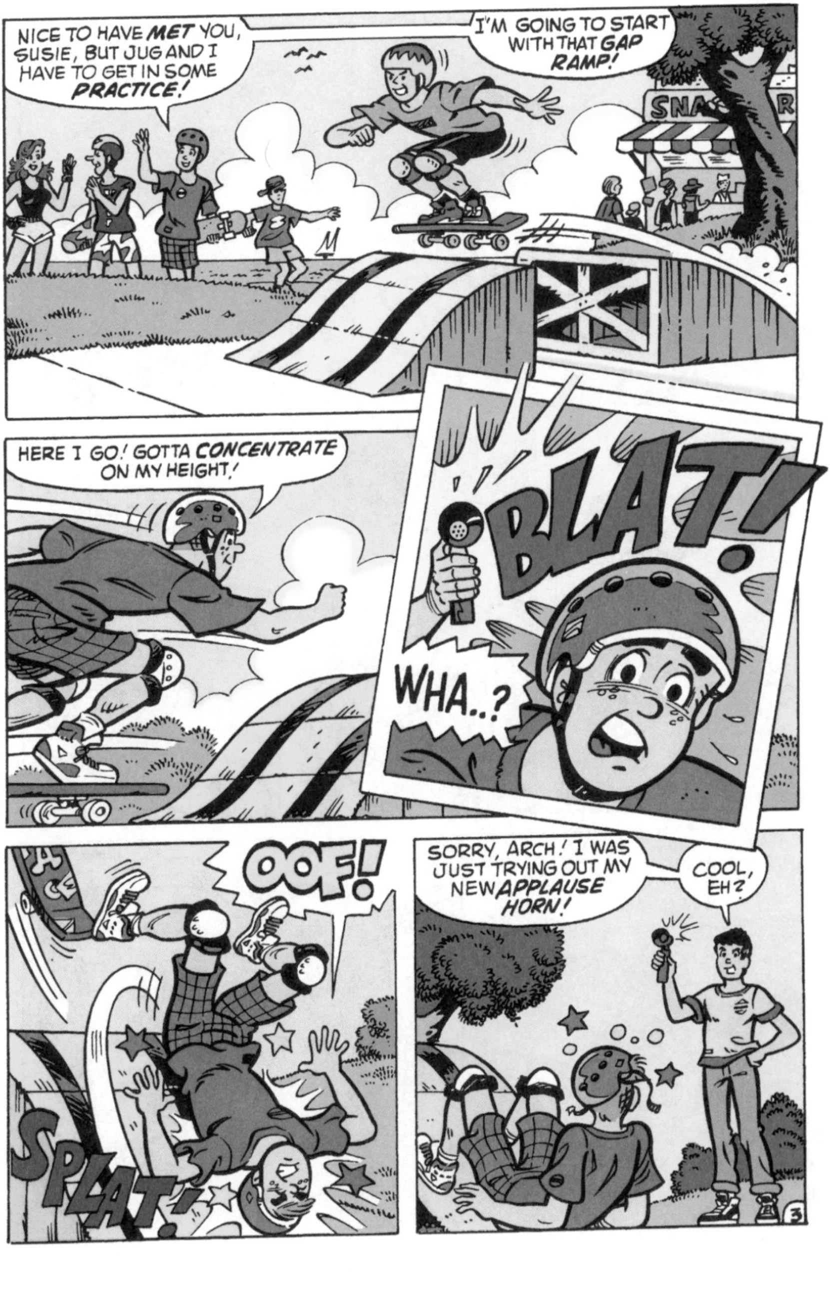
NICE TO HAVE MET YOU, SUSIE, BUT JUG AND I HAVE TO GET IN SOME PRACTICE!
I'M GOING TO START WITH THAT GAP RAMP!
SNA R
HERE I GO! GOTTA CONCENTRATE ON MY HEIGHT!
BLAT!
WHA..?
OOF!
SPLAT!
SORRY, ARCH! I WAS JUST TRYING OUT MY NEW APPLAUSE HORN!
COOL, EH?
3

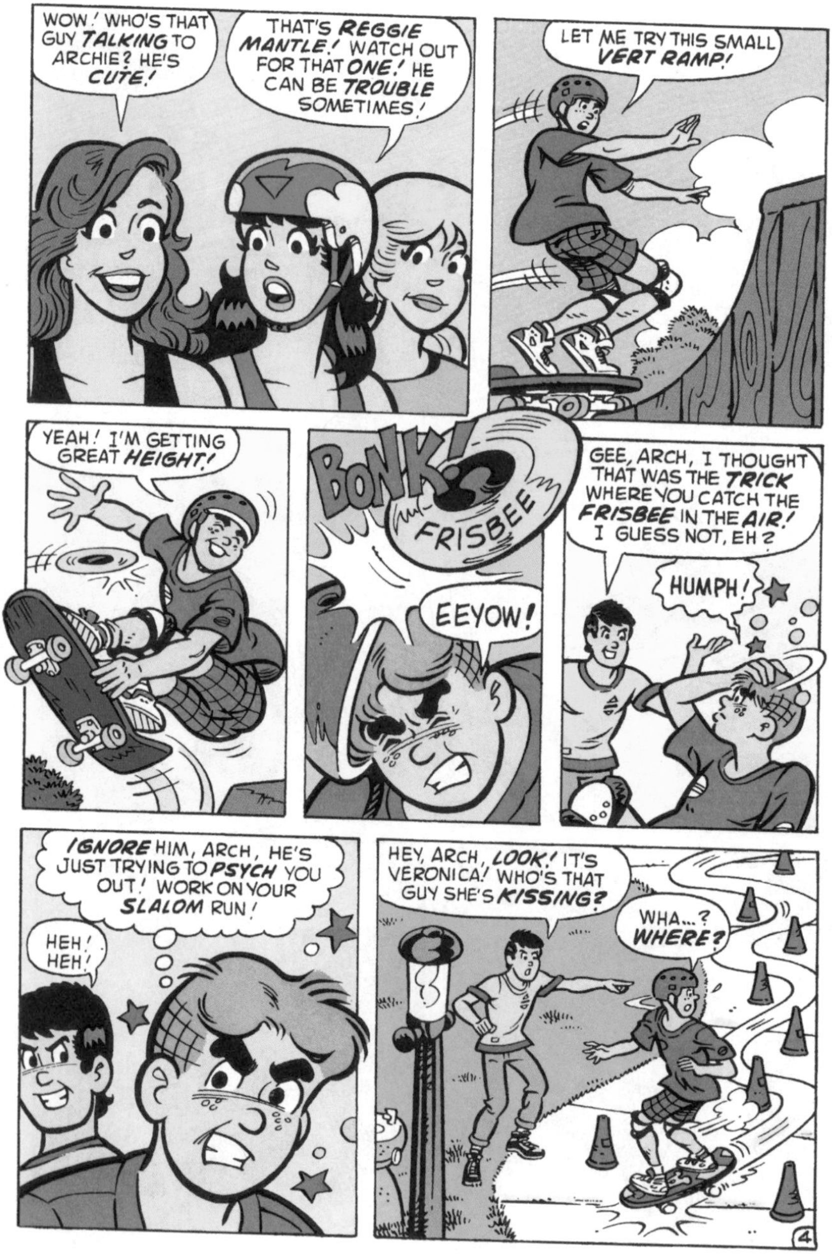
WOW! WHO'S THAT GUY TALKING TO ARCHIE? HE'S CUTE!
THAT'S REGGIE MANTLE! WATCH OUT FOR THAT ONE! HE CAN BE TROUBLE SOMETIMES!
LET ME TRY THIS SMALL VERT RAMP!
YEAH! I'M GETTING GREAT HEIGHT!
BONK!
FRISBEE
EEYOW!
GEE, ARCH, I THOUGHT THAT WAS THE TRICK WHERE YOU CATCH THE FRISBEE IN THE AIR! I GUESS NOT, EH?
HUMPH!
IGNORE HIM, ARCH, HE'S JUST TRYING TO PSYCH YOU OUT! WORK ON YOUR SLALOM RUN!
HEH! HEH!
HEY, ARCH, LOOK! IT'S VERONICA! WHO'S THAT GUY SHE'S KISSING?
WHA...? WHERE?
4

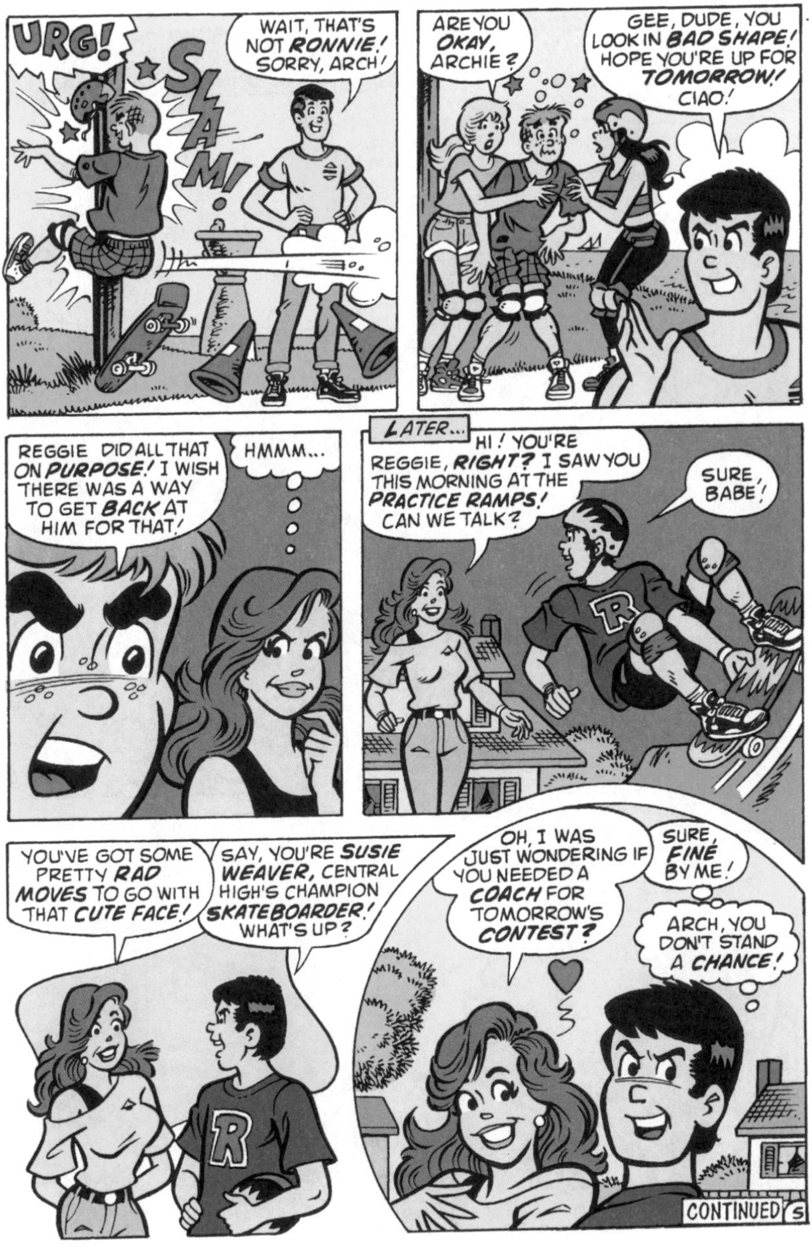
URG!
SLAM!
WAIT, THAT'S NOT RONNIE! SORRY, ARCH!
ARE YOU OKAY, ARCHIE?
GEE, DUDE, YOU LOOK IN BAD SHAPE! HOPE YOU'RE UP FOR TOMORROW! CIAO!
REGGIE DID ALL THAT ON PURPOSE! I WISH THERE WAS A WAY TO GET BACK AT HIM FOR THAT!
HMMM...
LATER...
HI! YOU'RE REGGIE, RIGHT? I SAW YOU THIS MORNING AT THE PRACTICE RAMPS! CAN WE TALK?
SURE, BABE!
YOU'VE GOT SOME PRETTY RAD MOVES TO GO WITH THAT CUTE FACE!
SAY, YOU'RE SUSIE WEAVER, CENTRAL HIGH'S CHAMPION SKATEBOARDER! WHAT'S UP?
OH, I WAS JUST WONDERING IF YOU NEEDED A COACH FOR TOMORROW'S CONTEST?
SURE, FINE BY ME!
ARCH, YOU DON'T STAND A CHANCE!
CONTINUED
5

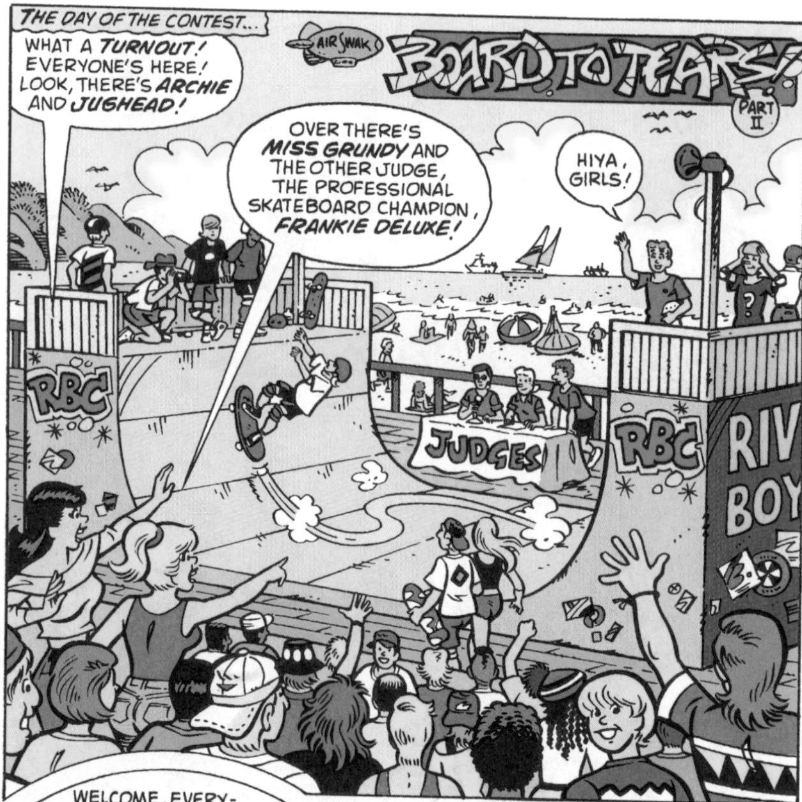
THE DAY OF THE CONTEST...
WHAT A TURNOUT! EVERYONE'S HERE! LOOK, THERE'S ARCHIE AND JUGHEAD!
AIR SWAK
BOARD TO TEARS! PART II
OVER THERE'S MISS GRUNDY AND THE OTHER JUDGE, THE PROFESSIONAL SKATEBOARD CHAMPION, FRANKIE DELUXE!
HIYA, GIRLS!
RBC
JUDGES
RBC
RIV BOY

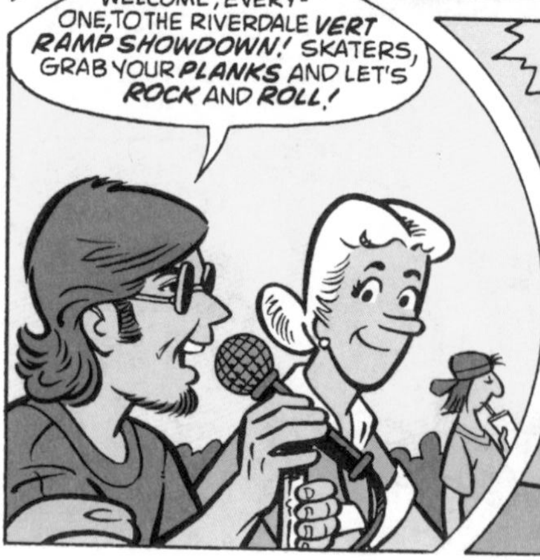
WELCOME, EVERY-ONE, TO THE RIVERDALE VERT RAMP SHOWDOWN! SKATERS, GRAB YOUR PLANKS AND LET'S ROCK AND ROLL!

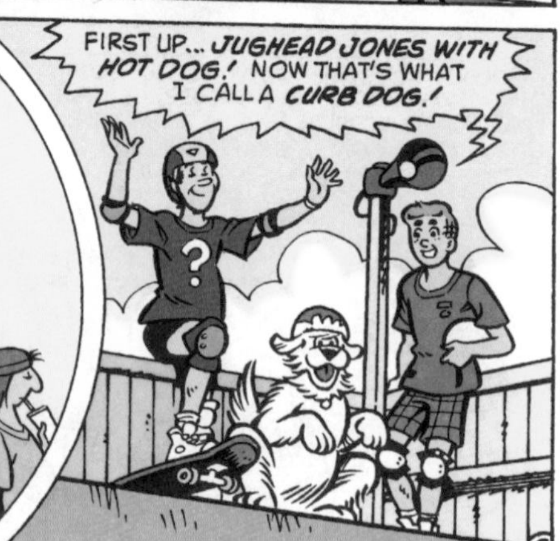
FIRST UP... JUGHEAD JONES WITH HOT DOG! NOW THAT'S WHAT I CALL A CURB DOG!
5

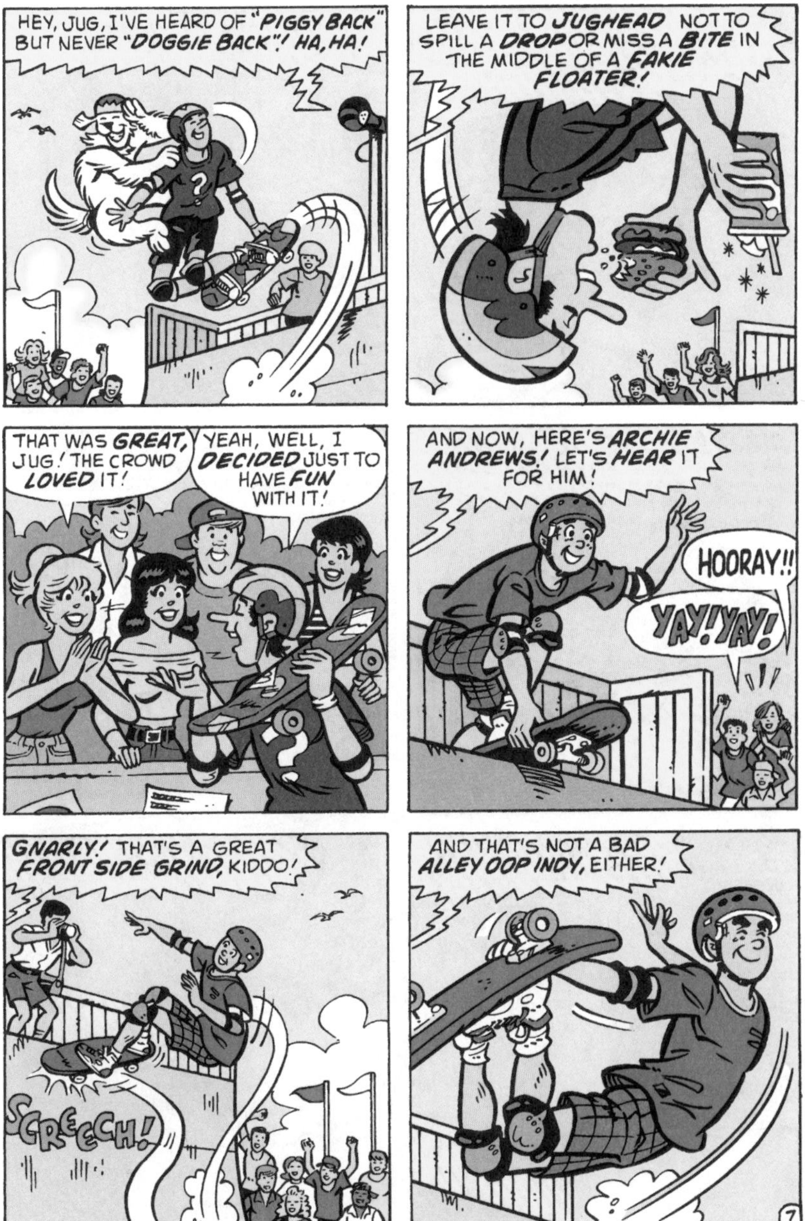
HEY, JUG, I'VE HEARD OF "PIGGY BACK" BUT NEVER "DOGGIE BACK"! HA, HA!
LEAVE IT TO JUGHEAD NOT TO SPILL A DROP OR MISS A BITE IN THE MIDDLE OF A FAKIE FLOATER!
THAT WAS GREAT, JUG! THE CROWD LOVED IT!
YEAH, WELL, I DECIDED JUST TO HAVE FUN WITH IT!
AND NOW, HERE'S ARCHIE ANDREWS! LET'S HEAR IT FOR HIM!
HOORAY!!
YAY! YAY!
GNARLY! THAT'S A GREAT FRONT SIDE GRIND, KIDDO!
SCREECH!
AND THAT'S NOT A BAD ALLEY OOP INDY, EITHER!
7

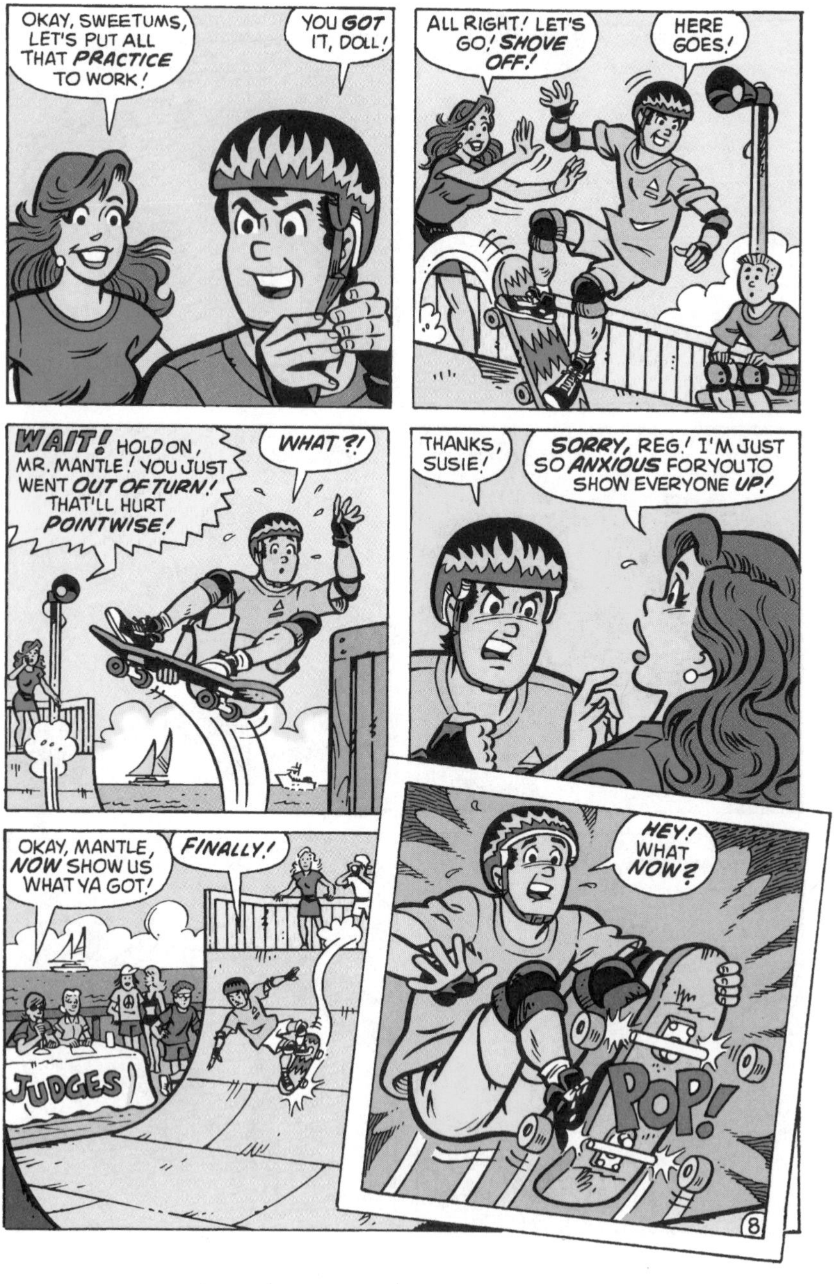

OKAY, SWEETUMS, LET'S PUT ALL THAT PRACTICE TO WORK!
YOU GOT IT, DOLL!
ALL RIGHT! LET'S GO! SHOVE OFF!
HERE GOES!
WAIT! HOLD ON, MR. MANTLE! YOU JUST WENT OUT OF TURN! THAT'LL HURT POINTWISE!
WHAT?!
THANKS, SUSIE!
SORRY, REG.! I'M JUST SO ANXIOUS FOR YOU TO SHOW EVERYONE UP!
OKAY, MANTLE, NOW SHOW US WHAT YA GOT!
FINALLY!
JUDGES
HEY! WHAT NOW?
POP!
8

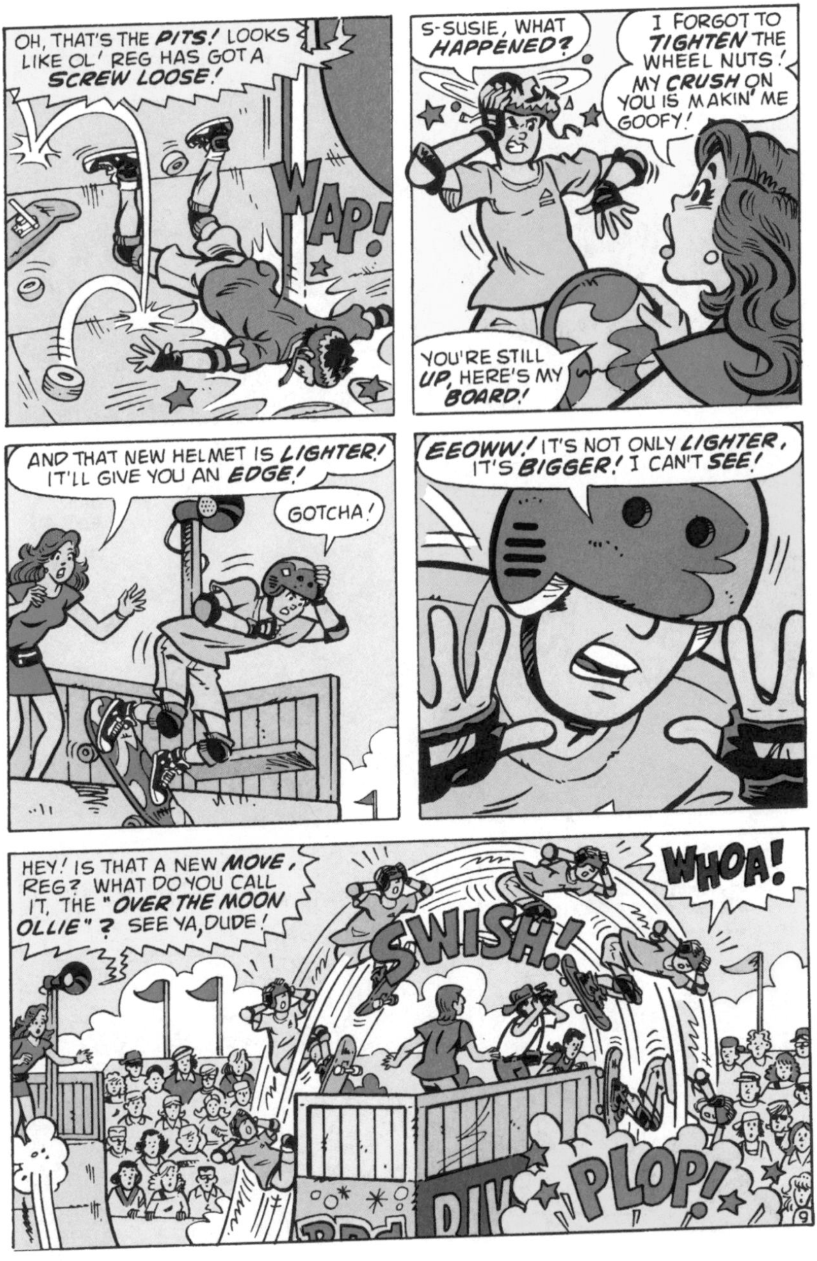

OH, THAT'S THE PITS! LOOKS LIKE OL' REG HAS GOT A SCREW LOOSE!
WAP!
S-SUSIE, WHAT HAPPENED?
I FORGOT TO TIGHTEN THE WHEEL NUTS! MY CRUSH ON YOU IS MAKIN' ME GOOFY!
YOU'RE STILL UP, HERE'S MY BOARD!
AND THAT NEW HELMET IS LIGHTER! IT'LL GIVE YOU AN EDGE!
GOTCHA!
EEOWW! IT'S NOT ONLY LIGHTER, IT'S BIGGER! I CAN'T SEE!
HEY! IS THAT A NEW MOVE, REG? WHAT DO YOU CALL IT, THE "OVER THE MOON OLLIE"? SEE YA, DUDE!
WHOA!
SWISH!
PLOP!
9

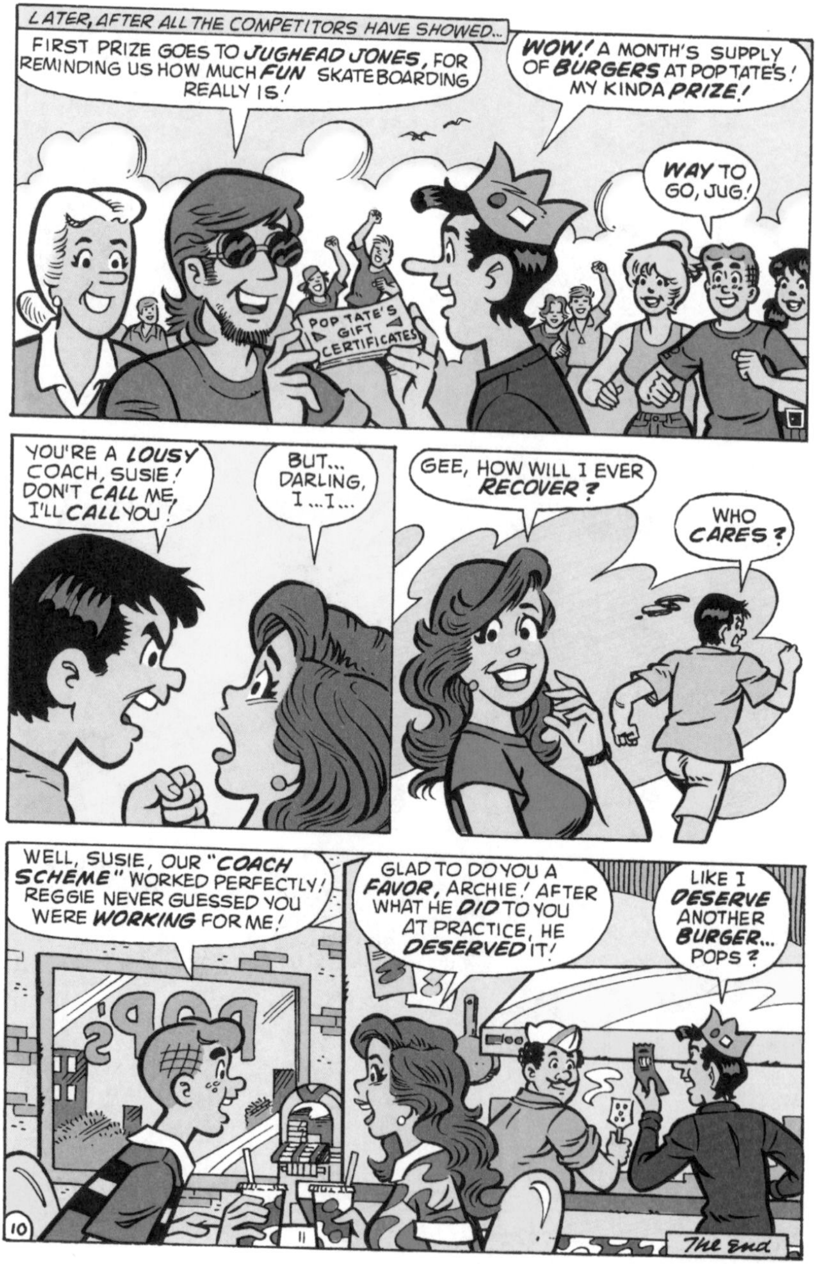
LATER, AFTER ALL THE COMPETITORS HAVE SHOWED...
FIRST PRIZE GOES TO JUGHEAD JONES, FOR REMINDING US HOW MUCH FUN SKATEBOARDING REALLY IS!
WOW! A MONTH'S SUPPLY OF BURGERS AT POP TATE'S! MY KINDA PRIZE!
WAY TO GO, JUG!
POP TATE'S GIFT CERTIFICATES
YOU'RE A LOUSY COACH, SUSIE! DON'T CALL ME, I'LL CALL YOU!
BUT... DARLING, I...I...
GEE, HOW WILL I EVER RECOVER?
WHO CARES?
WELL, SUSIE, OUR "COACH SCHEME" WORKED PERFECTLY! REGGIE NEVER GUESSED YOU WERE WORKING FOR ME!
GLAD TO DO YOU A FAVOR, ARCHIE! AFTER WHAT HE DID TO YOU AT PRACTICE, HE DESERVED IT!
LIKE I DESERVE ANOTHER BURGER... POPS?
POP'S
10
The End

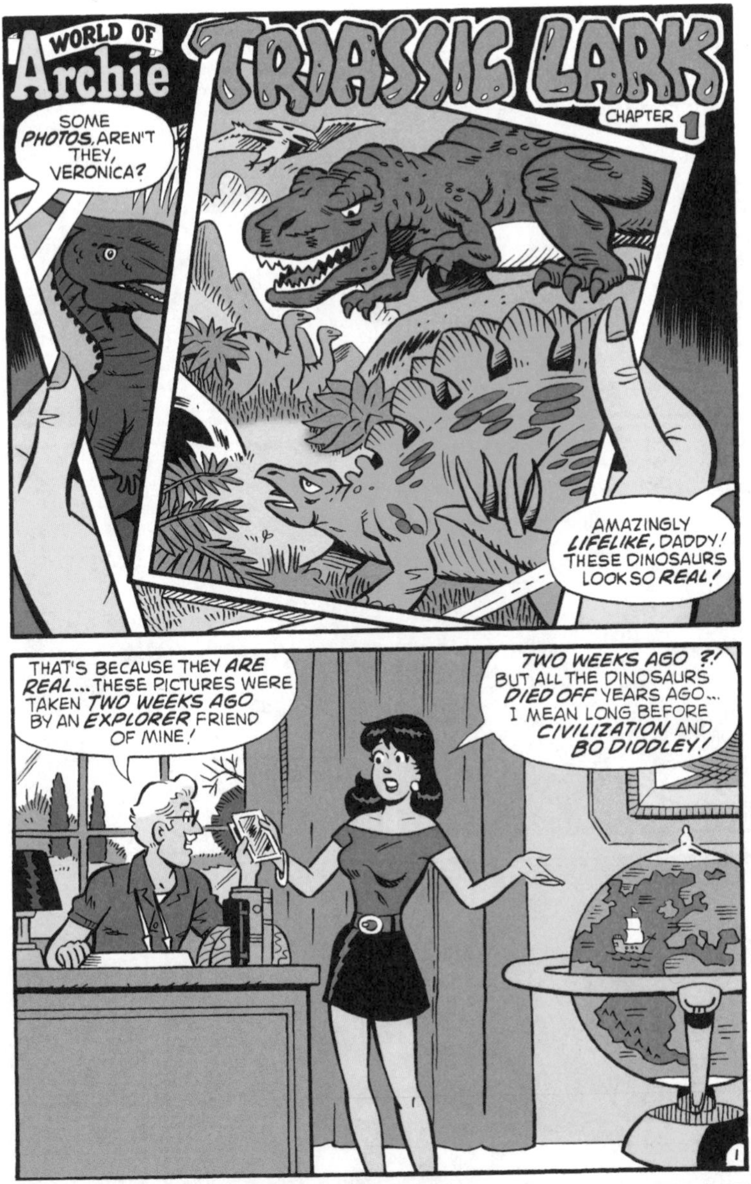
WORLD OF Archie
TRIASSIC LARK
CHAPTER 1
SOME PHOTOS, AREN'T THEY, VERONICA?
AMAZINGLY LIFELIKE, DADDY! THESE DINOSAURS LOOK SO REAL!
THAT'S BECAUSE THEY ARE REAL... THESE PICTURES WERE TAKEN TWO WEEKS AGO BY AN EXPLORER FRIEND OF MINE!
TWO WEEKS AGO ?! BUT ALL THE DINOSAURS DIED OFF YEARS AGO... I MEAN LONG BEFORE CIVILIZATION AND BO DIDDLEY!
1

Story: Bob Bolling Pencils: Rex Lindsey
Inks: Rudy Lapick Letters: Bill Yoshida Colors: Barry Grossman

Originally printed in WORLD OF ARCHIE #7, FEBRUARY 1994

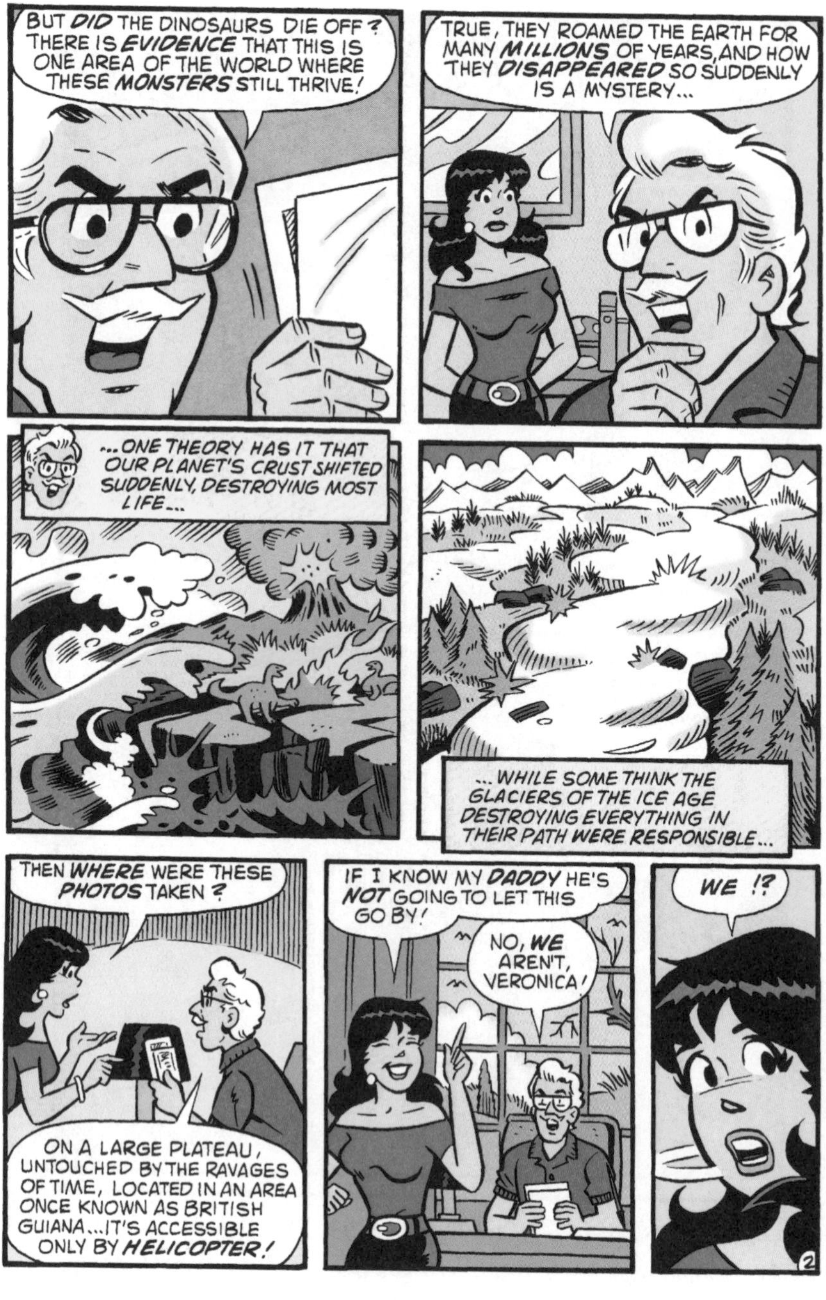
BUT DID THE DINOSAURS DIE OFF? THERE IS EVIDENCE THAT THIS IS ONE AREA OF THE WORLD WHERE THESE MONSTERS STILL THRIVE!
TRUE, THEY ROAMED THE EARTH FOR MANY MILLIONS OF YEARS, AND HOW THEY DISAPPEARED SO SUDDENLY IS A MYSTERY...
...ONE THEORY HAS IT THAT OUR PLANET'S CRUST SHIFTED SUDDENLY, DESTROYING MOST LIFE...
...WHILE SOME THINK THE GLACIERS OF THE ICE AGE DESTROYING EVERYTHING IN THEIR PATH WERE RESPONSIBLE...
THEN WHERE WERE THESE PHOTOS TAKEN?
ON A LARGE PLATEAU, UNTOUCHED BY THE RAVAGES OF TIME, LOCATED IN AN AREA ONCE KNOWN AS BRITISH GUIANA...IT'S ACCESSIBLE ONLY BY HELICOPTER!
IF I KNOW MY DADDY HE'S NOT GOING TO LET THIS GO BY!
NO, WE AREN'T, VERONICA!
WE !?
2

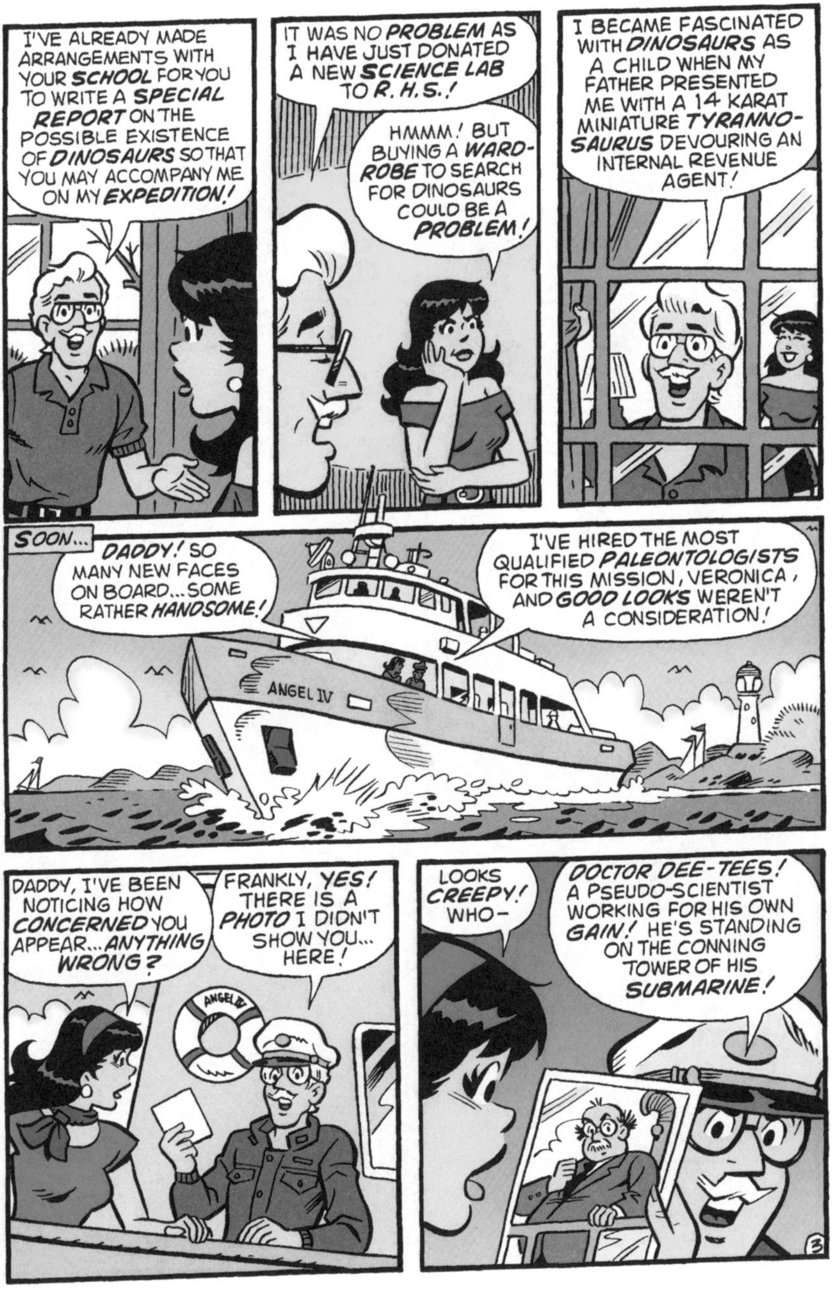
I'VE ALREADY MADE ARRANGEMENTS WITH YOUR SCHOOL FOR YOU TO WRITE A SPECIAL REPORT ON THE POSSIBLE EXISTENCE OF DINOSAURS SO THAT YOU MAY ACCOMPANY ME ON MY EXPEDITION!
IT WAS NO PROBLEM AS I HAVE JUST DONATED A NEW SCIENCE LAB TO R.H.S.!
HMMM! BUT BUYING A WARDROBE TO SEARCH FOR DINOSAURS COULD BE A PROBLEM!
I BECAME FASCINATED WITH DINOSAURS AS A CHILD WHEN MY FATHER PRESENTED ME WITH A 14 KARAT MINIATURE TYRANNOSAURUS DEVOURING AN INTERNAL REVENUE AGENT!
SOON...
DADDY! SO MANY NEW FACES ON BOARD...SOME RATHER HANDSOME!
I'VE HIRED THE MOST QUALIFIED PALEONTOLOGISTS FOR THIS MISSION, VERONICA, AND GOOD LOOKS WEREN'T A CONSIDERATION!
ANGEL IV
DADDY, I'VE BEEN NOTICING HOW CONCERNED YOU APPEAR...ANYTHING WRONG?
FRANKLY, YES! THERE IS A PHOTO I DIDN'T SHOW YOU... HERE!
ANGEL IV
LOOKS CREEPY! WHO–
DOCTOR DEE-TEES! A PSEUDO-SCIENTIST WORKING FOR HIS OWN GAIN! HE'S STANDING ON THE CONNING TOWER OF HIS SUBMARINE!
3

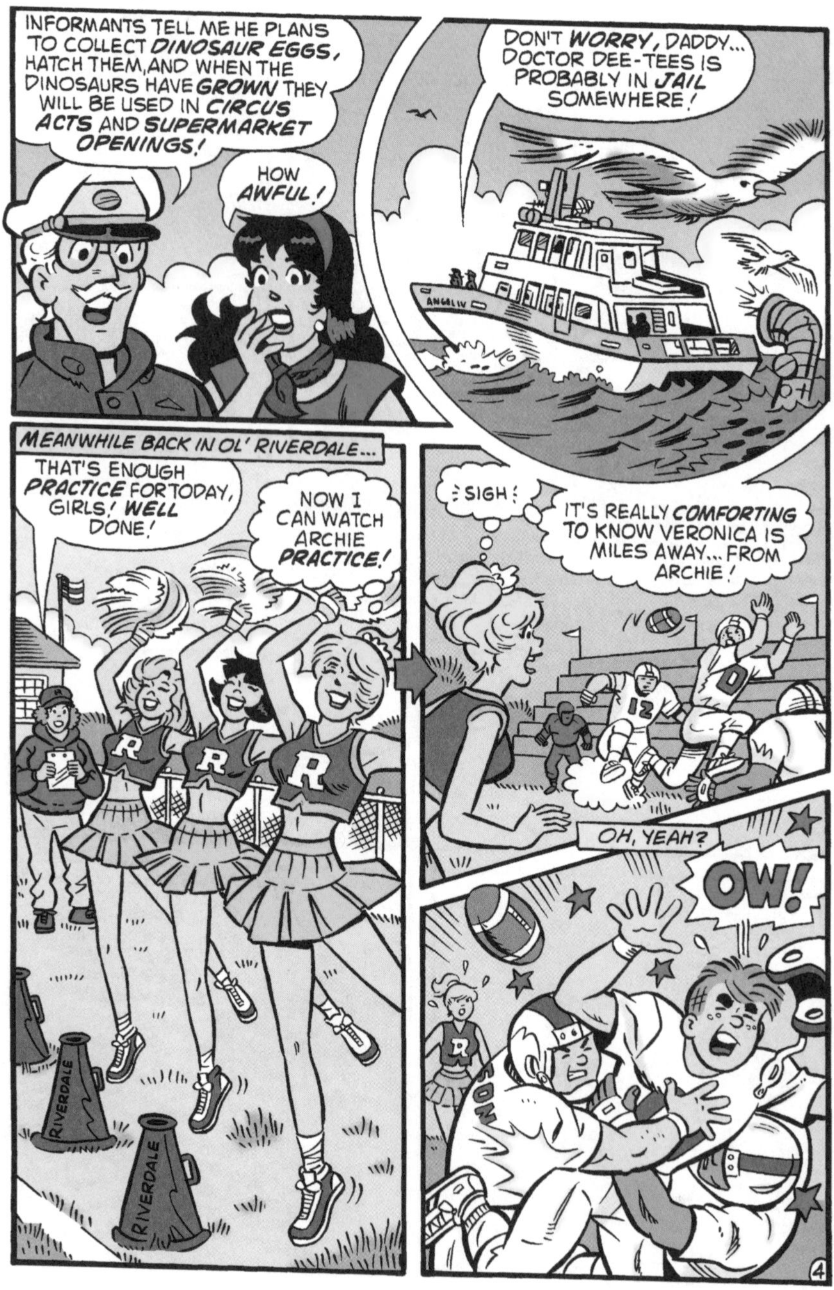
INFORMANTS TELL ME HE PLANS TO COLLECT DINOSAUR EGGS, HATCH THEM, AND WHEN THE DINOSAURS HAVE GROWN THEY WILL BE USED IN CIRCUS ACTS AND SUPERMARKET OPENINGS!
HOW AWFUL!
DON'T WORRY, DADDY... DOCTOR DEE-TEES IS PROBABLY IN JAIL SOMEWHERE!
MEANWHILE BACK IN OL' RIVERDALE...
THAT'S ENOUGH PRACTICE FOR TODAY, GIRLS! WELL DONE!
NOW I CAN WATCH ARCHIE PRACTICE!
RIVERDALE
RIVERDALE
SIGH
IT'S REALLY COMFORTING TO KNOW VERONICA IS MILES AWAY... FROM ARCHIE!
OH, YEAH?
OW!
4

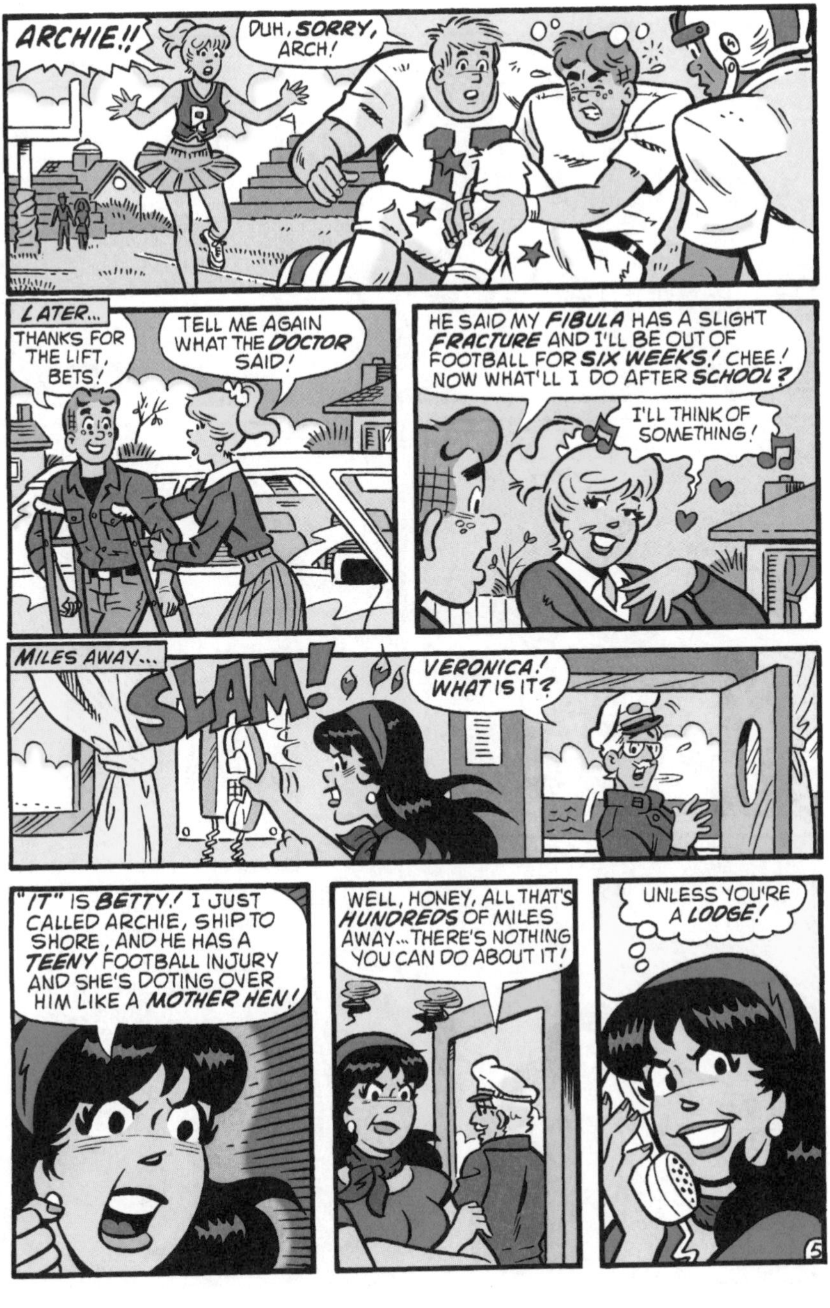
ARCHIE!!
DUH, SORRY, ARCH!
LATER...
THANKS FOR THE LIFT, BETS!
TELL ME AGAIN WHAT THE DOCTOR SAID!
HE SAID MY FIBULA HAS A SLIGHT FRACTURE AND I'LL BE OUT OF FOOTBALL FOR SIX WEEKS! CHEE! NOW WHAT'LL I DO AFTER SCHOOL?
I'LL THINK OF SOMETHING!
MILES AWAY...
SLAM!
VERONICA! WHAT IS IT?
"IT" IS BETTY! I JUST CALLED ARCHIE, SHIP TO SHORE, AND HE HAS A TEENY FOOTBALL INJURY AND SHE'S DOTING OVER HIM LIKE A MOTHER HEN!
WELL, HONEY, ALL THAT'S HUNDREDS OF MILES AWAY... THERE'S NOTHING YOU CAN DO ABOUT IT!
UNLESS YOU'RE A LODGE!
5

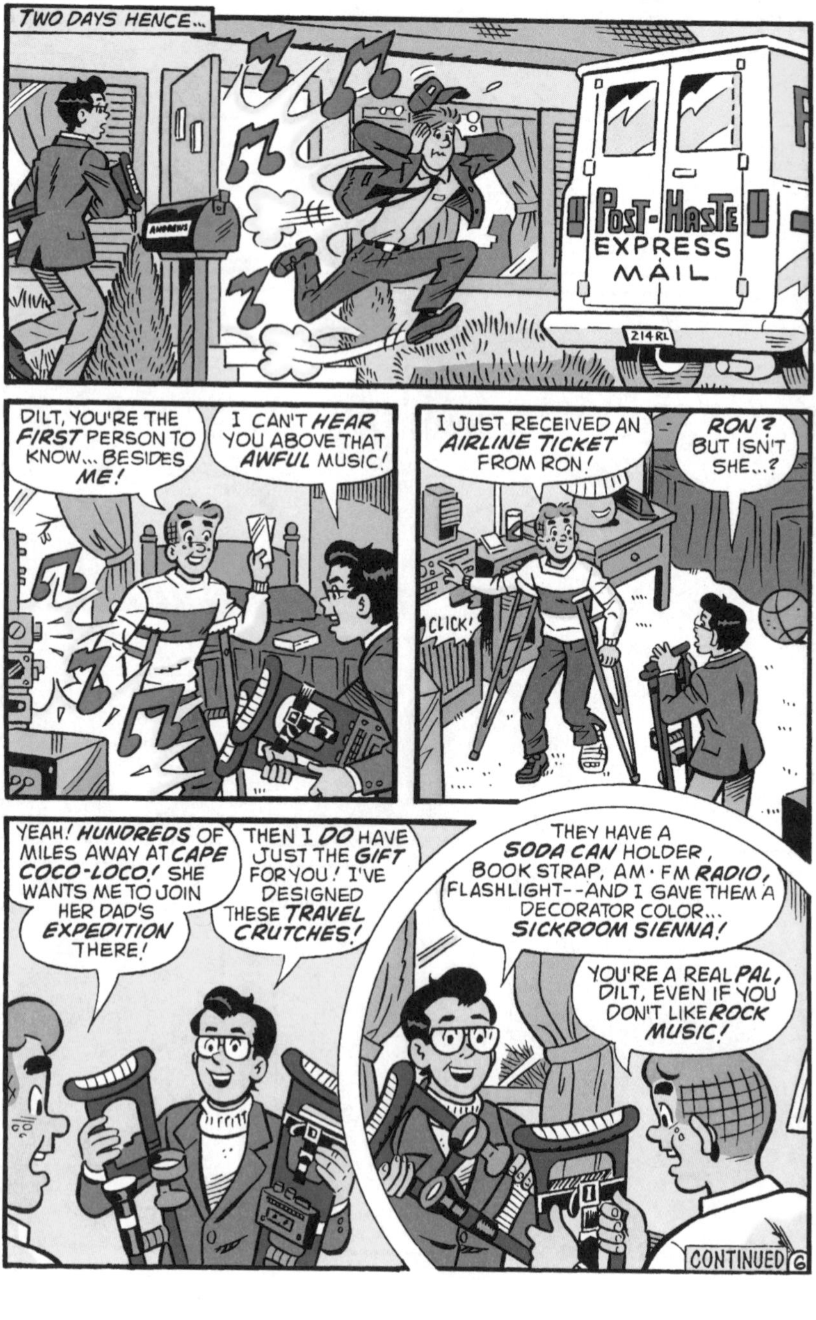
TWO DAYS HENCE...
ANDREWS
POST-HASTE EXPRESS MAIL
214RL
DILT, YOU'RE THE FIRST PERSON TO KNOW... BESIDES ME!
I CAN'T HEAR YOU ABOVE THAT AWFUL MUSIC!
I JUST RECEIVED AN AIRLINE TICKET FROM RON!
RON? BUT ISN'T SHE...?
CLICK!
YEAH! HUNDREDS OF MILES AWAY AT CAPE COCO-LOCO! SHE WANTS ME TO JOIN HER DAD'S EXPEDITION THERE!
THEN I DO HAVE JUST THE GIFT FOR YOU! I'VE DESIGNED THESE TRAVEL CRUTCHES!
THEY HAVE A SODA CAN HOLDER, BOOK STRAP, AM · FM RADIO, FLASHLIGHT--AND I GAVE THEM A DECORATOR COLOR... SICKROOM SIENNA!
YOU'RE A REAL PAL, DILT, EVEN IF YOU DON'T LIKE ROCK MUSIC!
CONTINUED 6

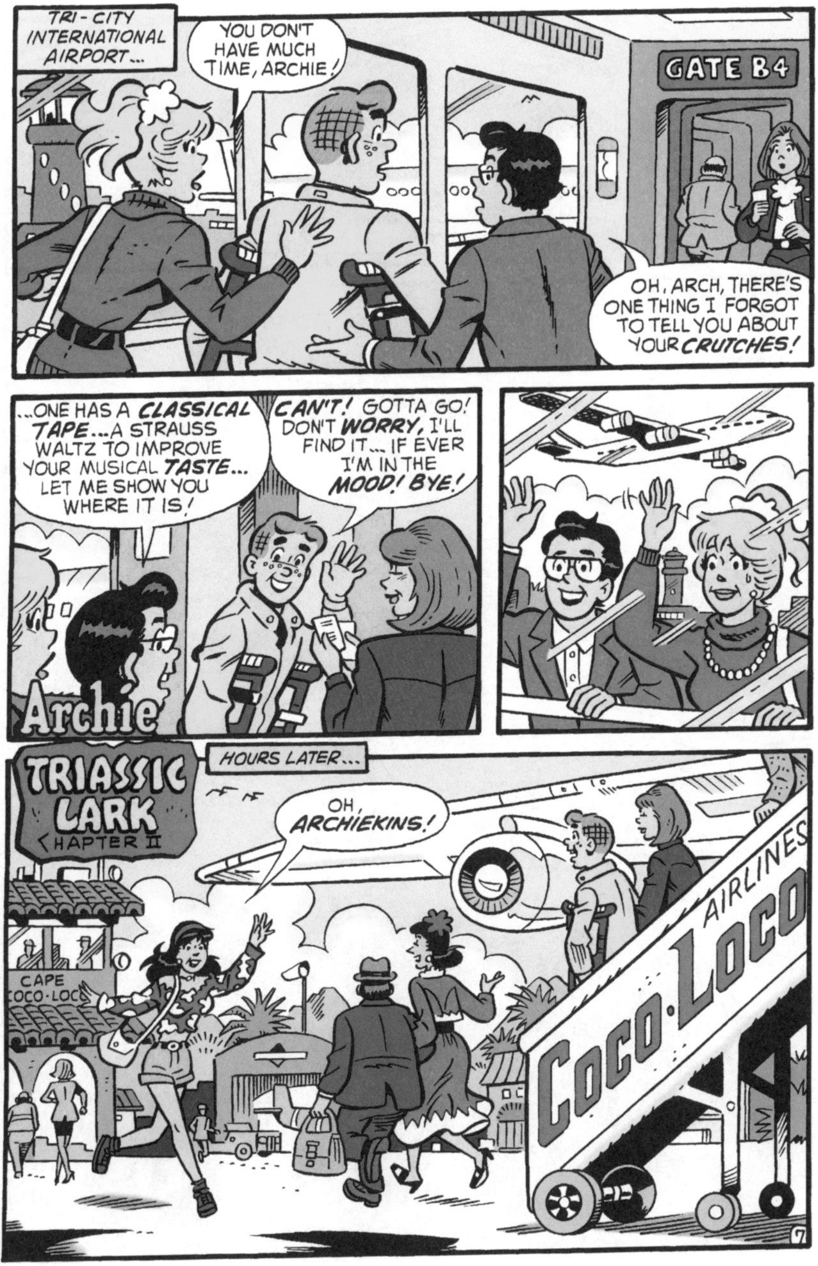
TRI-CITY INTERNATIONAL AIRPORT...
YOU DON'T HAVE MUCH TIME, ARCHIE!
GATE B4
OH, ARCH, THERE'S ONE THING I FORGOT TO TELL YOU ABOUT YOUR CRUTCHES!
...ONE HAS A CLASSICAL TAPE...A STRAUSS WALTZ TO IMPROVE YOUR MUSICAL TASTE... LET ME SHOW YOU WHERE IT IS!
CAN'T! GOTTA GO! DON'T WORRY, I'LL FIND IT... IF EVER I'M IN THE MOOD! BYE!
Archie
TRIASSIC LARK CHAPTER II
HOURS LATER...
OH, ARCHIEKINS!
CAPE COCO·LOCO
AIRLINES
COCO·LOCO
7

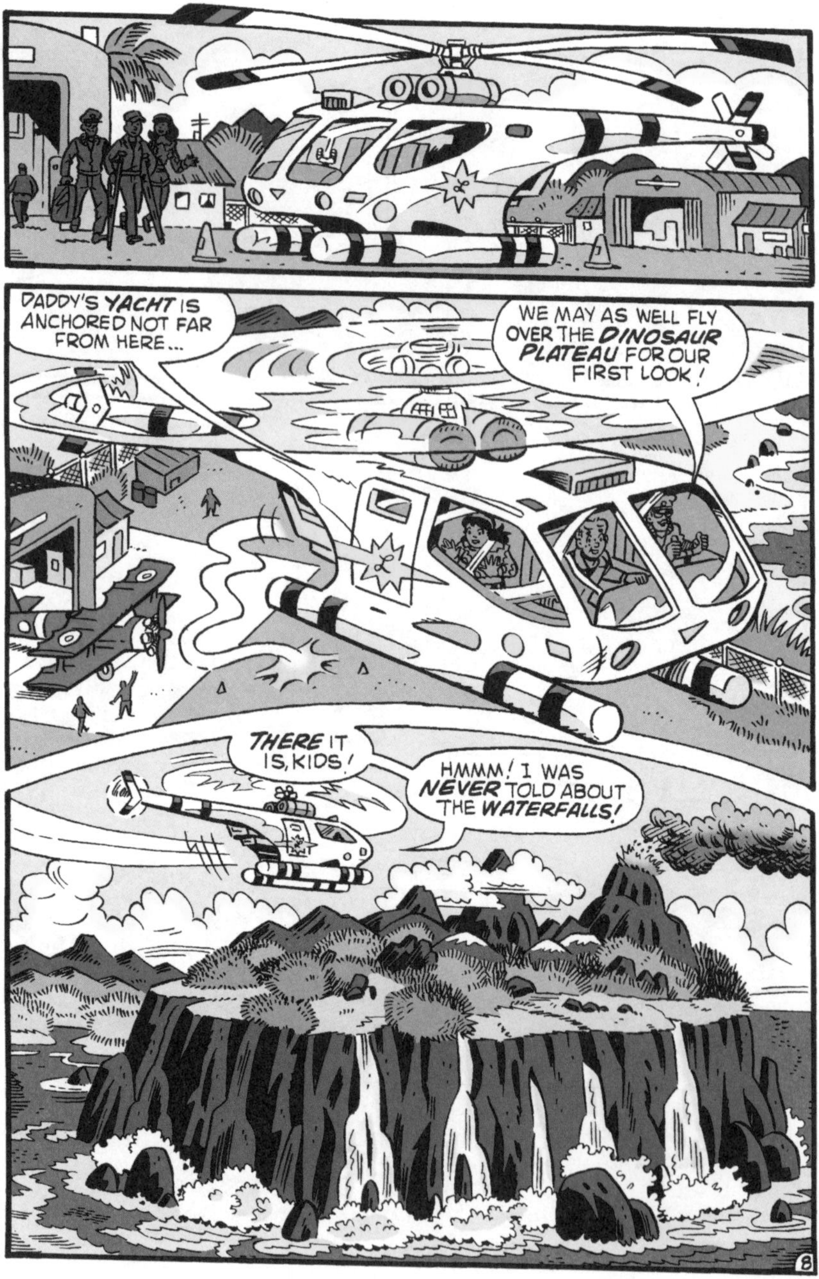
DADDY'S YACHT IS ANCHORED NOT FAR FROM HERE...
WE MAY AS WELL FLY OVER THE DINOSAUR PLATEAU FOR OUR FIRST LOOK!
THERE IT IS, KIDS!
HMMM! I WAS NEVER TOLD ABOUT THE WATERFALLS!
8

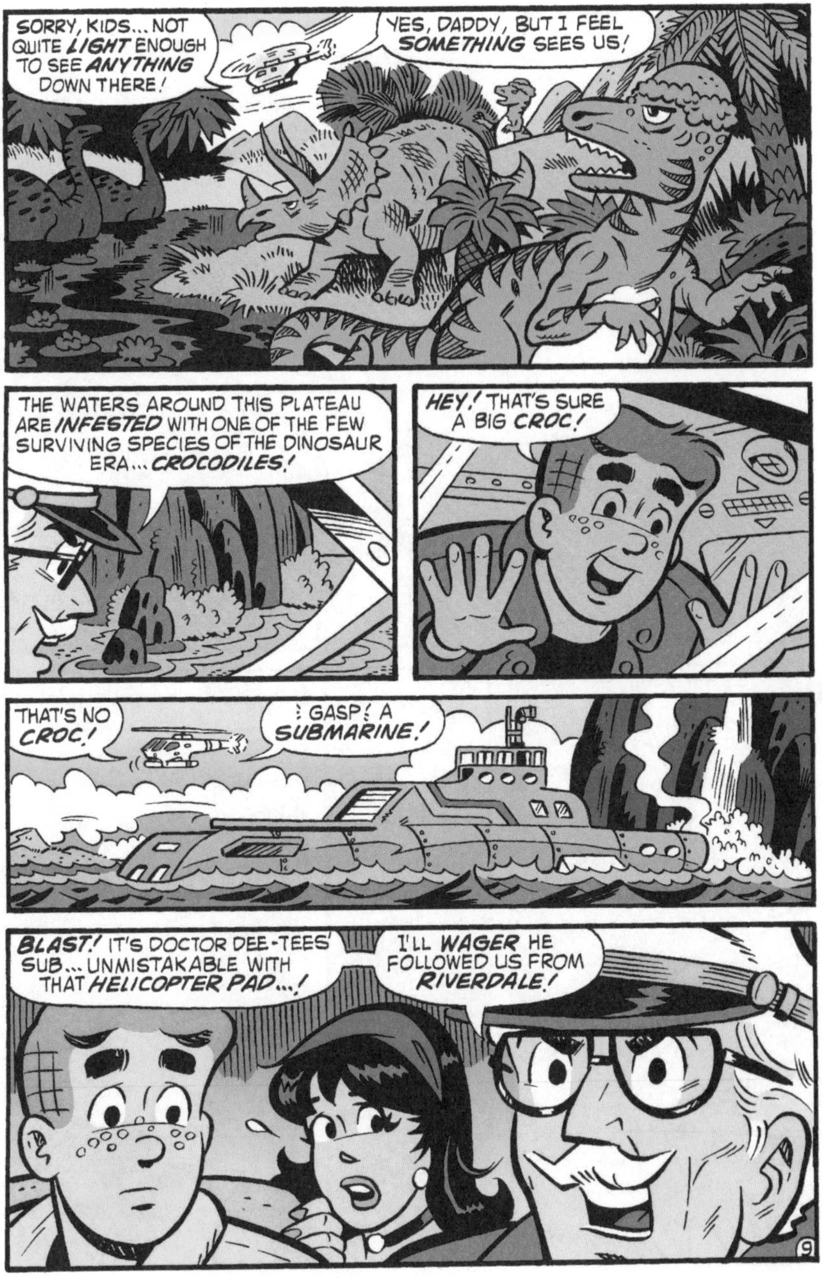
SORRY, KIDS... NOT QUITE LIGHT ENOUGH TO SEE ANYTHING DOWN THERE!
YES, DADDY, BUT I FEEL SOMETHING SEES US!
THE WATERS AROUND THIS PLATEAU ARE INFESTED WITH ONE OF THE FEW SURVIVING SPECIES OF THE DINOSAUR ERA... CROCODILES!
HEY! THAT'S SURE A BIG CROC!
THAT'S NO CROC!
GASP! A SUBMARINE!
BLAST! IT'S DOCTOR DEE-TEES' SUB... UNMISTAKABLE WITH THAT HELICOPTER PAD...!
I'LL WAGER HE FOLLOWED US FROM RIVERDALE!
9

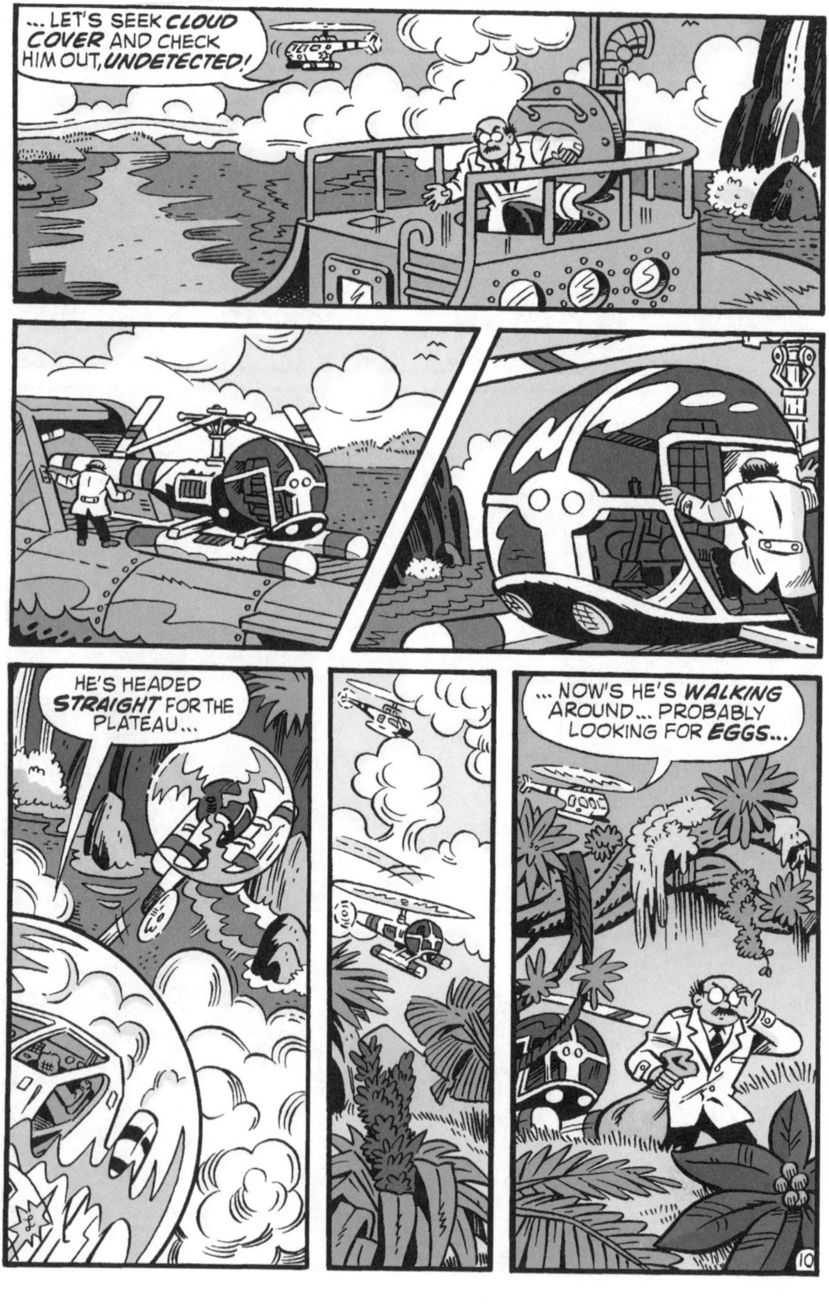
...LET'S SEEK CLOUD COVER AND CHECK HIM OUT, UNDETECTED!
HE'S HEADED STRAIGHT FOR THE PLATEAU...
...NOW'S HE'S WALKING AROUND... PROBABLY LOOKING FOR EGGS...
10

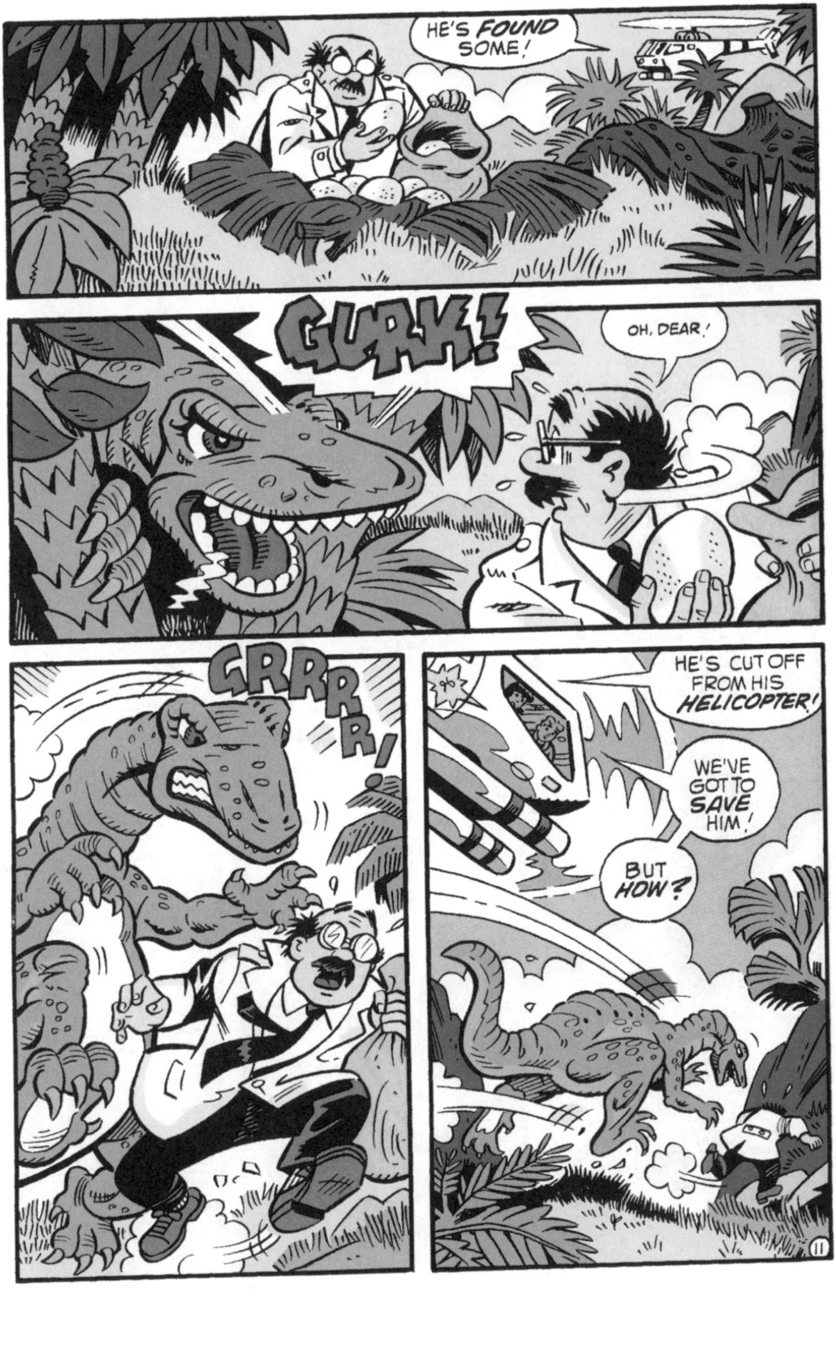
HE'S FOUND SOME!
GURK!
OH, DEAR!
GRRRR!
HE'S CUT OFF FROM HIS HELICOPTER!
WE'VE GOT TO SAVE HIM!
BUT HOW?
11

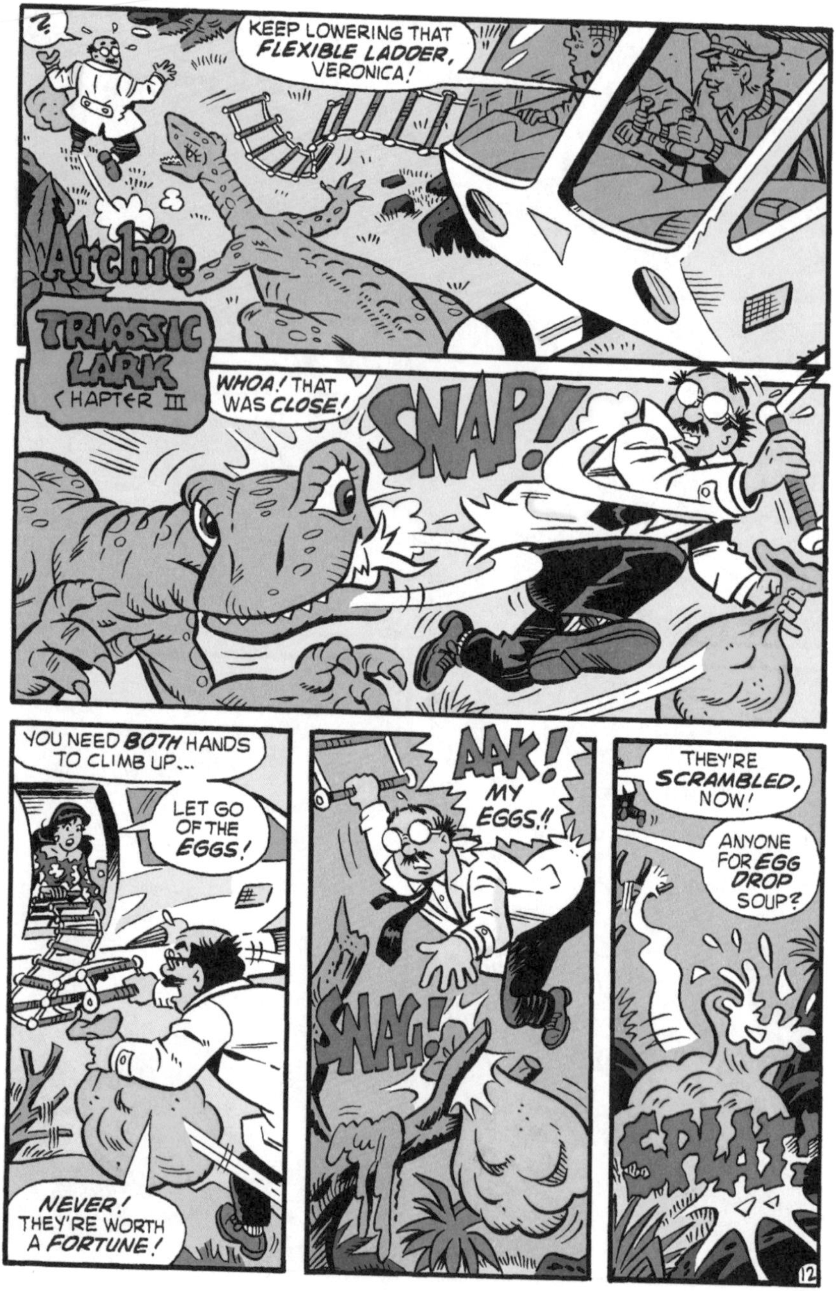
?
KEEP LOWERING THAT FLEXIBLE LADDER, VERONICA!
Archie
TRIASSIC LARK
CHAPTER III
WHOA! THAT WAS CLOSE!
SNAP!
YOU NEED BOTH HANDS TO CLIMB UP...
LET GO OF THE EGGS!
NEVER! THEY'RE WORTH A FORTUNE!
AAK!
MY EGGS!!
SNAG!
THEY'RE SCRAMBLED, NOW!
ANYONE FOR EGG DROP SOUP?
SPLAT!
12

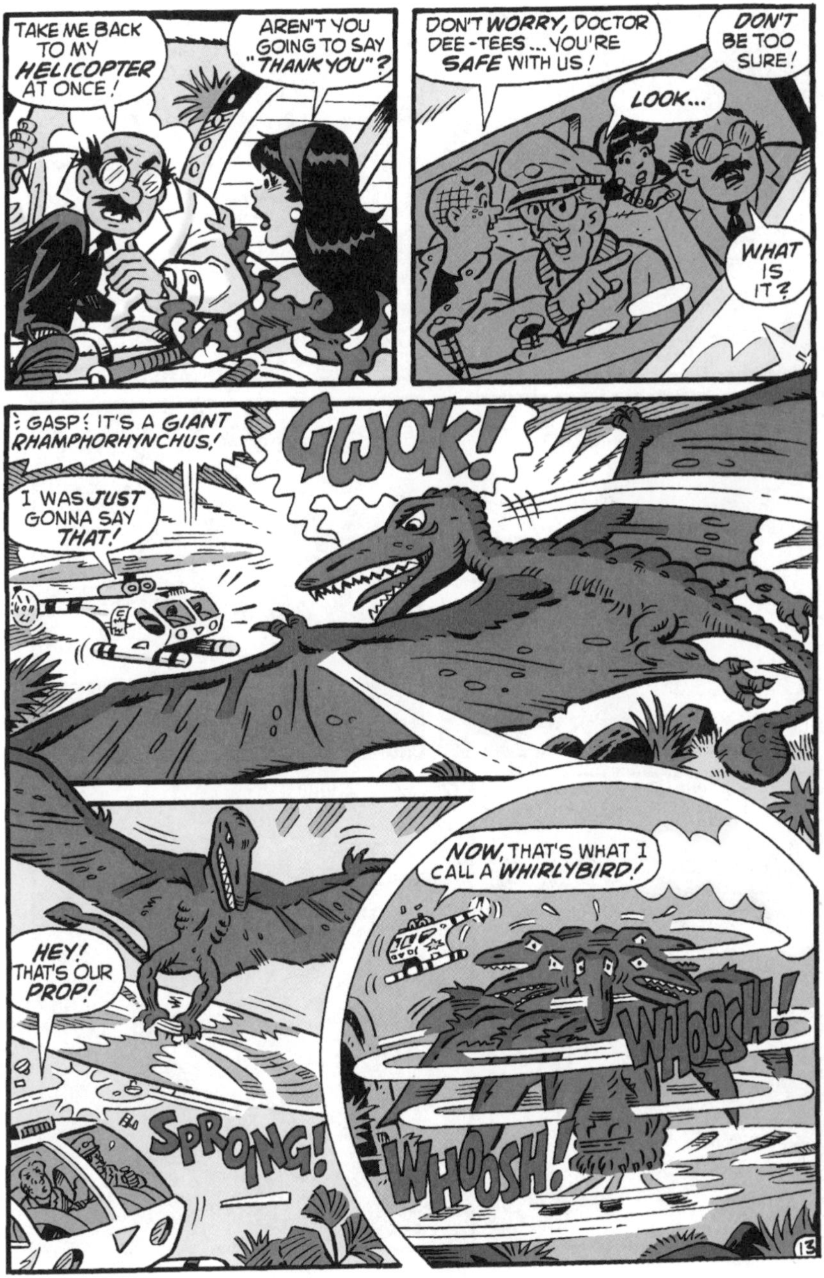
TAKE ME BACK TO MY HELICOPTER AT ONCE!
AREN'T YOU GOING TO SAY "THANK YOU"?
DON'T WORRY, DOCTOR DEE-TEES... YOU'RE SAFE WITH US!
DON'T BE TOO SURE!
LOOK...
WHAT IS IT?
GASP! IT'S A GIANT RHAMPHORHYNCHUS!
GWOK!
I WAS JUST GONNA SAY THAT!
HEY! THAT'S OUR PROP!
SPROING!
NOW, THAT'S WHAT I CALL A WHIRLYBIRD!
WHOOSH!
WHOOSH!
13

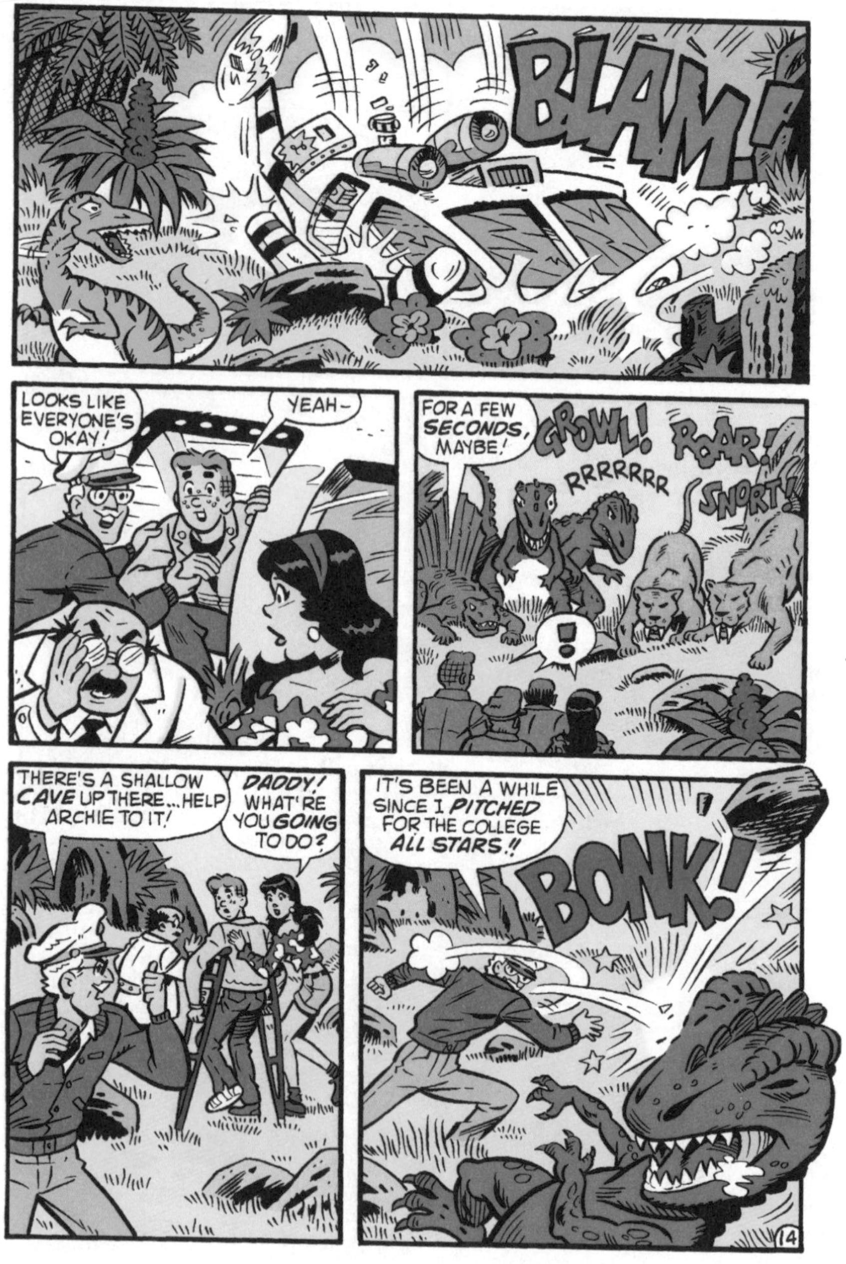
BLAM!!
LOOKS LIKE EVERYONE'S OKAY!
YEAH–
FOR A FEW SECONDS, MAYBE!
GROWL! ROAR!
RRRRRRR
SNORT!
!
THERE'S A SHALLOW CAVE UP THERE... HELP ARCHIE TO IT!
DADDY! WHAT'RE YOU GOING TO DO?
IT'S BEEN A WHILE SINCE I PITCHED FOR THE COLLEGE ALL STARS.!!
BONK!
14

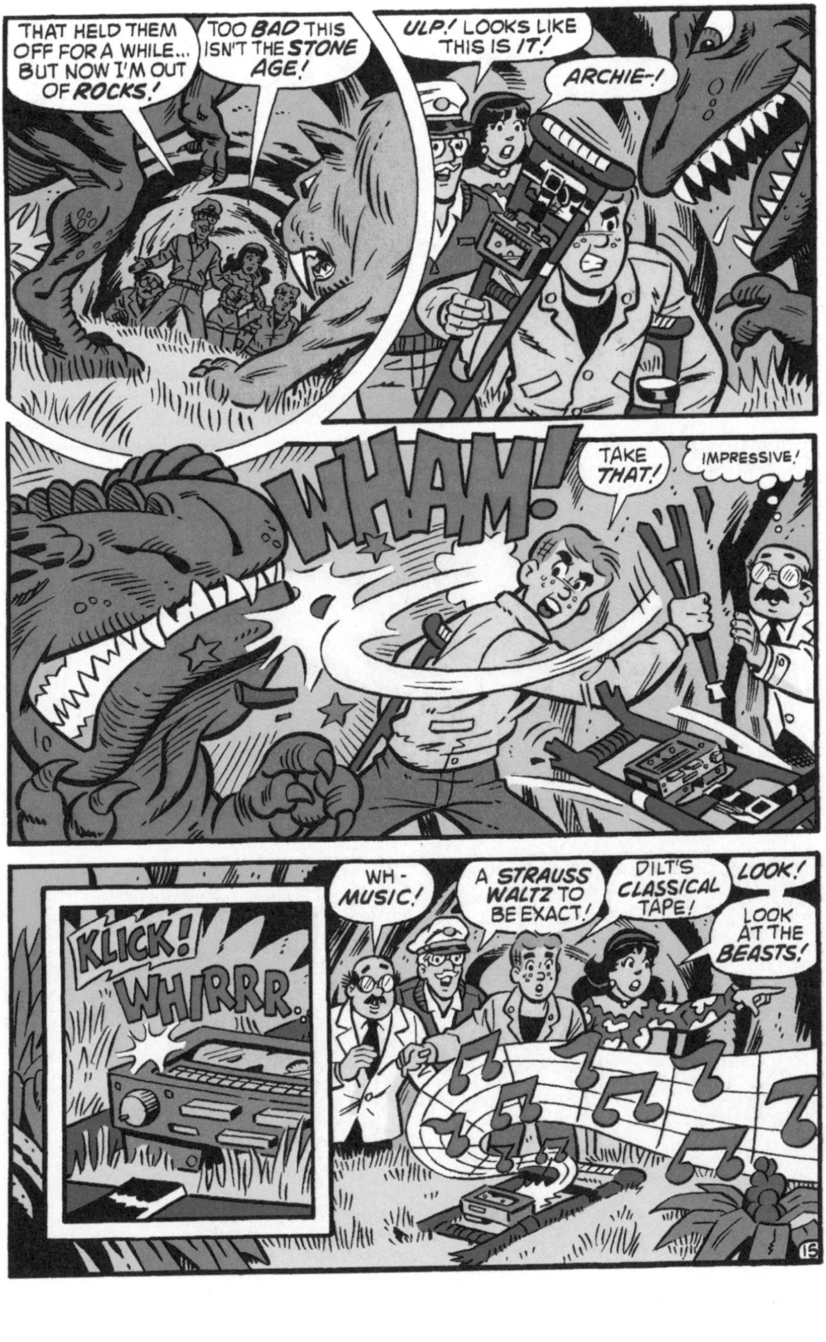
THAT HELD THEM OFF FOR A WHILE... BUT NOW I'M OUT OF ROCKS!
TOO BAD THIS ISN'T THE STONE AGE!
ULP! LOOKS LIKE THIS IS IT!
ARCHIE-!
WHAM!
TAKE THAT!
IMPRESSIVE!
KLICK!
WHIRRR
WH- MUSIC!
A STRAUSS WALTZ TO BE EXACT!
DILT'S CLASSICAL TAPE!
LOOK!
LOOK AT THE BEASTS!
15

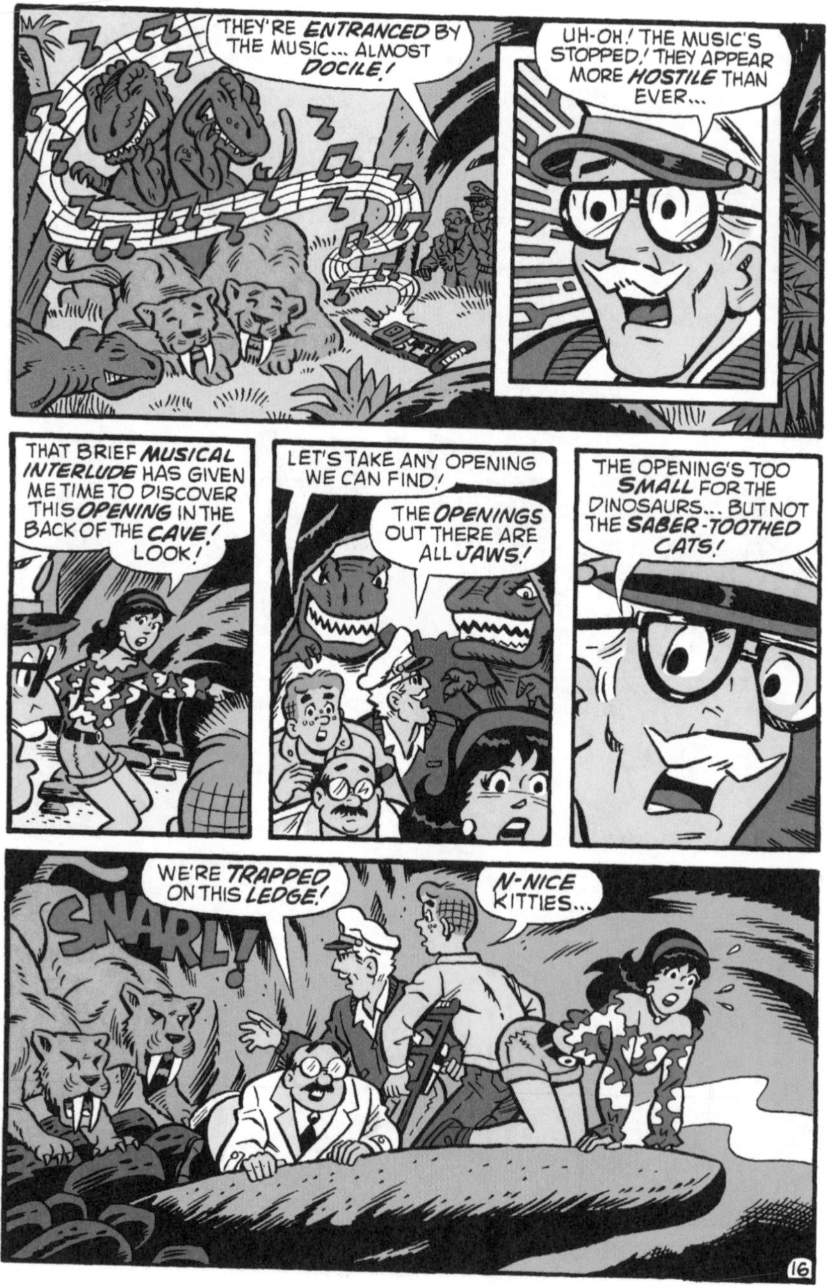
THEY'RE ENTRANCED BY THE MUSIC... ALMOST DOCILE!
UH-OH! THE MUSIC'S STOPPED! THEY APPEAR MORE HOSTILE THAN EVER...
THAT BRIEF MUSICAL INTERLUDE HAS GIVEN ME TIME TO DISCOVER THIS OPENING IN THE BACK OF THE CAVE! LOOK!
LET'S TAKE ANY OPENING WE CAN FIND!
THE OPENINGS OUT THERE ARE ALL JAWS!
THE OPENING'S TOO SMALL FOR THE DINOSAURS... BUT NOT THE SABER-TOOTHED CATS!
SNARL!
WE'RE TRAPPED ON THIS LEDGE!
N-NICE KITTIES...
16

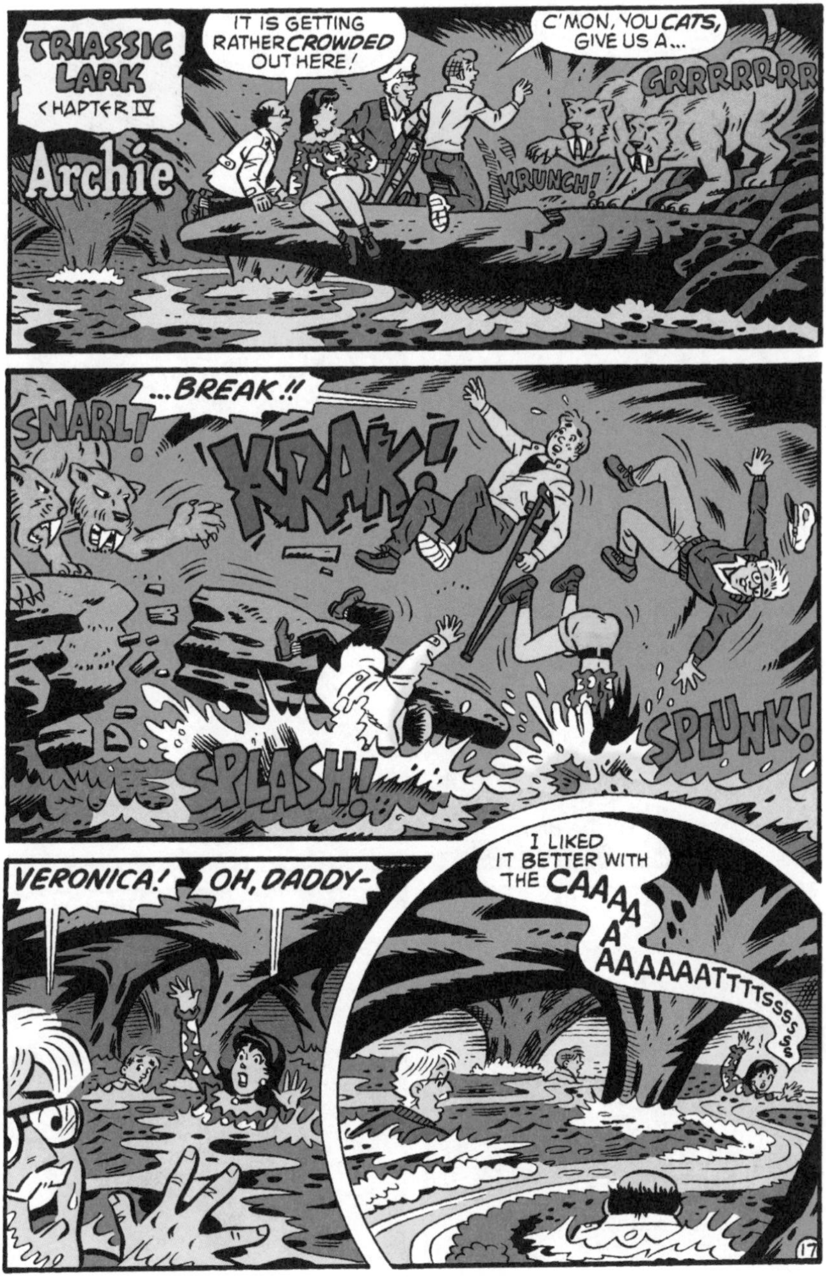
TRIASSIC LARK
CHAPTER IV
Archie
IT IS GETTING RATHER CROWDED OUT HERE!
C'MON, YOU CATS, GIVE US A...
GRRRRRRR
KRUNCH!
...BREAK!!
SNARL!
KRAK!
SPLASH!
SPLUNK!
VERONICA!
OH, DADDY-
I LIKED IT BETTER WITH THE CAAAA A AAAAAATTTTSSSSSS
17

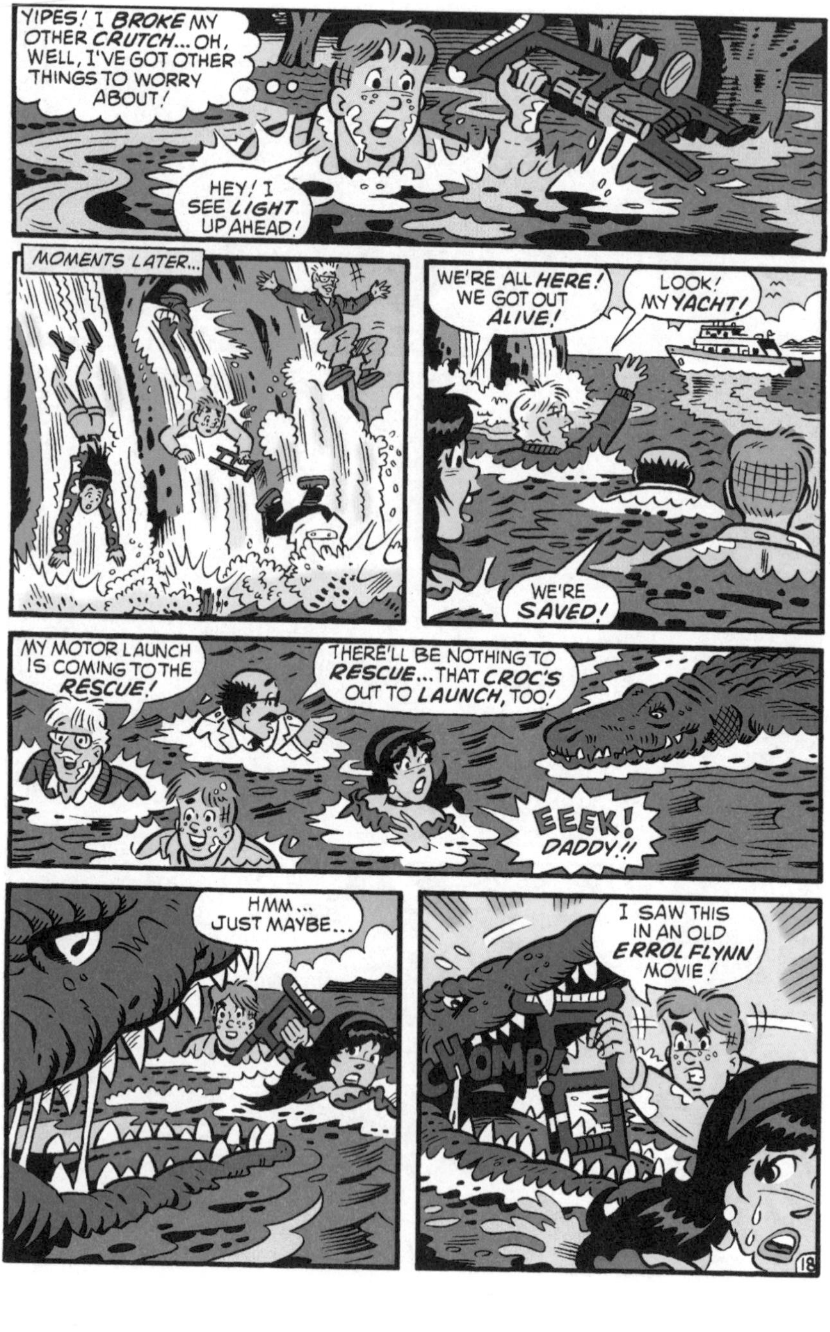
YIPES! I BROKE MY OTHER CRUTCH... OH, WELL, I'VE GOT OTHER THINGS TO WORRY ABOUT!
HEY! I SEE LIGHT UP AHEAD!
MOMENTS LATER...
WE'RE ALL HERE! WE GOT OUT ALIVE!
LOOK! MY YACHT!
WE'RE SAVED!
MY MOTOR LAUNCH IS COMING TO THE RESCUE!
THERE'LL BE NOTHING TO RESCUE... THAT CROC'S OUT TO LAUNCH, TOO!
EEEK! DADDY!!
HMM... JUST MAYBE...
I SAW THIS IN AN OLD ERROL FLYNN MOVIE!
CHOMP!
18

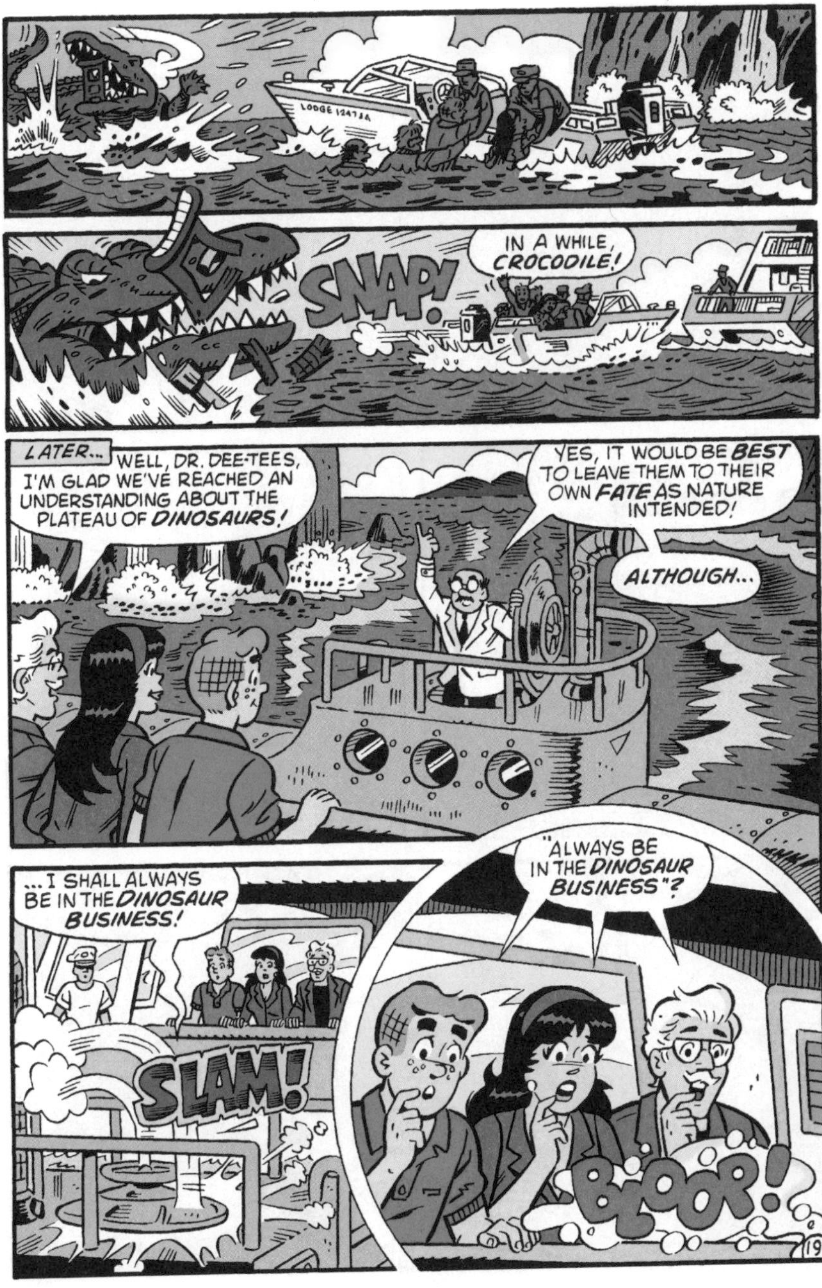
LODGE 1247 SA
IN A WHILE, CROCODILE!
SNAP!
LATER...
WELL, DR. DEE-TEES, I'M GLAD WE'VE REACHED AN UNDERSTANDING ABOUT THE PLATEAU OF DINOSAURS!
YES, IT WOULD BE BEST TO LEAVE THEM TO THEIR OWN FATE AS NATURE INTENDED!
ALTHOUGH...
...I SHALL ALWAYS BE IN THE DINOSAUR BUSINESS!
SLAM!
"ALWAYS BE IN THE DINOSAUR BUSINESS"?
BLOOP!
19

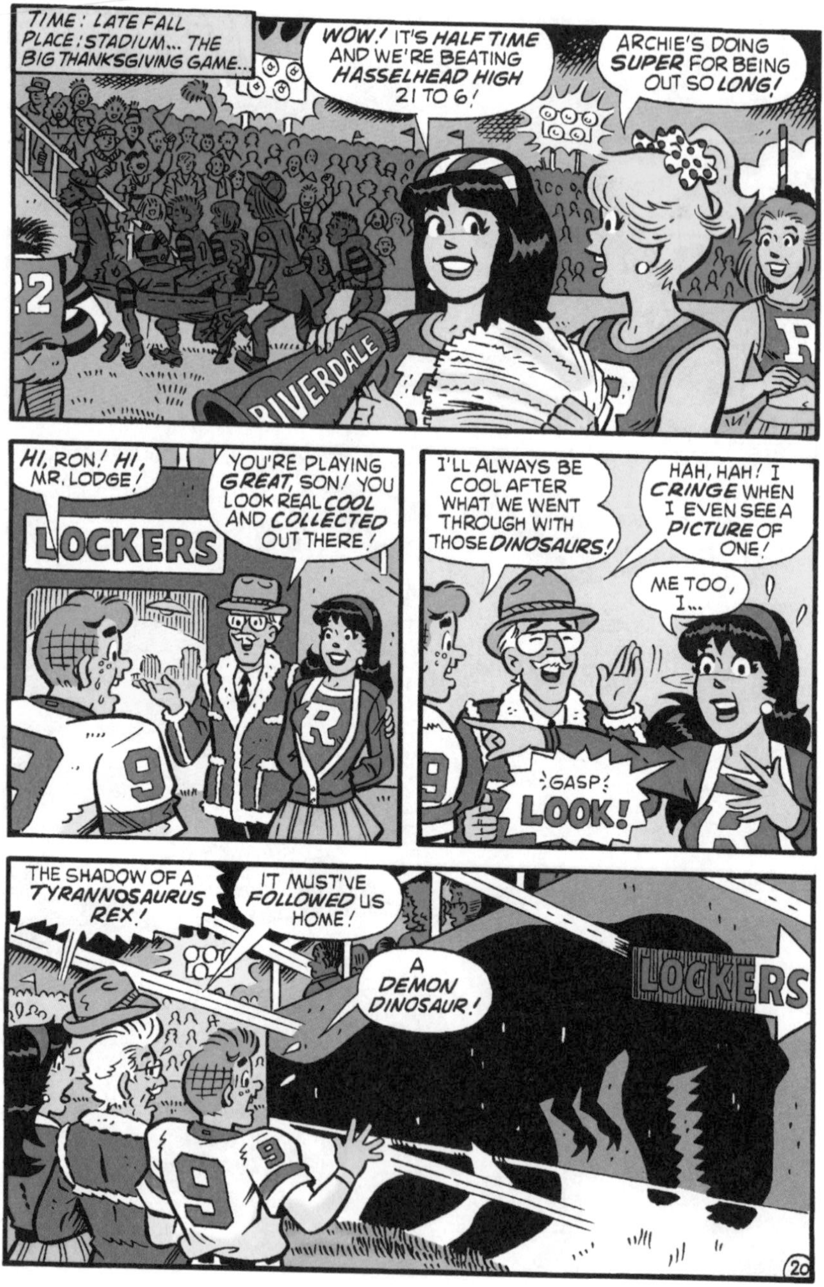
TIME: LATE FALL
PLACE: STADIUM... THE BIG THANKSGIVING GAME...
WOW! IT'S HALF TIME AND WE'RE BEATING HASSELHEAD HIGH 21 TO 6!
ARCHIE'S DOING SUPER FOR BEING OUT SO LONG!
RIVERDALE
HI, RON! HI, MR. LODGE!
LOCKERS
YOU'RE PLAYING GREAT, SON! YOU LOOK REAL COOL AND COLLECTED OUT THERE!
I'LL ALWAYS BE COOL AFTER WHAT WE WENT THROUGH WITH THOSE DINOSAURS!
HAH, HAH! I CRINGE WHEN I EVEN SEE A PICTURE OF ONE!
ME TOO, I...
GASP! LOOK!
THE SHADOW OF A TYRANNOSAURUS REX!
IT MUST'VE FOLLOWED US HOME!
A DEMON DINOSAUR!
LOCKERS
20

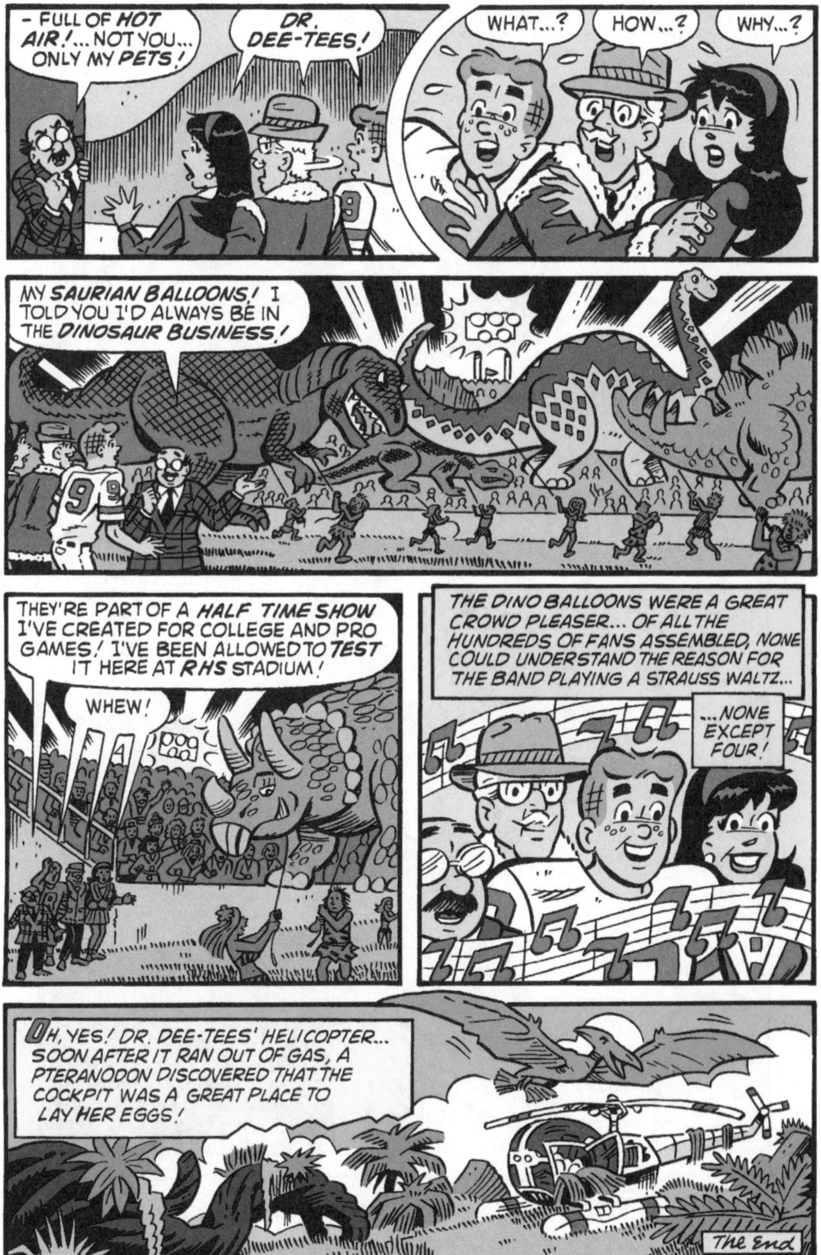
- FULL OF HOT AIR!... NOT YOU... ONLY MY PETS!
DR. DEE-TEES!
WHAT...?
HOW...?
WHY...?
MY SAURIAN BALLOONS! I TOLD YOU I'D ALWAYS BE IN THE DINOSAUR BUSINESS!
THEY'RE PART OF A HALF TIME SHOW I'VE CREATED FOR COLLEGE AND PRO GAMES! I'VE BEEN ALLOWED TO TEST IT HERE AT RHS STADIUM!
WHEW!
THE DINO BALLOONS WERE A GREAT CROWD PLEASER... OF ALL THE HUNDREDS OF FANS ASSEMBLED, NONE COULD UNDERSTAND THE REASON FOR THE BAND PLAYING A STRAUSS WALTZ...
...NONE EXCEPT FOUR!
OH, YES! DR. DEE-TEES' HELICOPTER... SOON AFTER IT RAN OUT OF GAS, A PTERANODON DISCOVERED THAT THE COCKPIT WAS A GREAT PLACE TO LAY HER EGGS!
The End

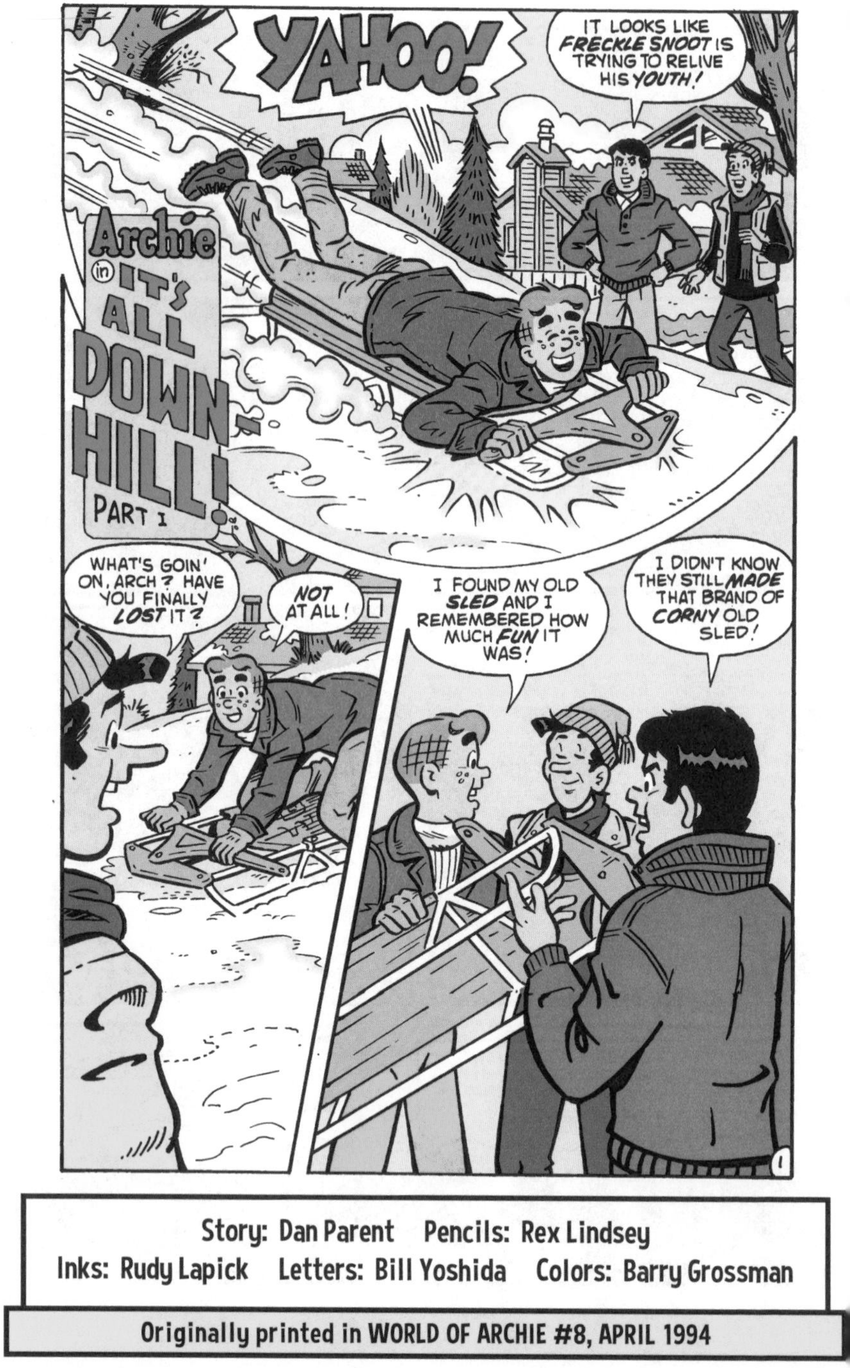
YAHOO!
IT LOOKS LIKE FRECKLE SNOOT IS TRYING TO RELIVE HIS YOUTH!
Archie in IT'S ALL DOWN-HILL! PART 1
WHAT'S GOIN' ON, ARCH? HAVE YOU FINALLY LOST IT?
NOT AT ALL!
I FOUND MY OLD SLED AND I REMEMBERED HOW MUCH FUN IT WAS!
I DIDN'T KNOW THEY STILL MADE THAT BRAND OF CORNY OLD SLED!
1

Story: Dan Parent Pencils: Rex Lindsey
Inks: Rudy Lapick Letters: Bill Yoshida Colors: Barry Grossman

Originally printed in WORLD OF ARCHIE #8, APRIL 1994

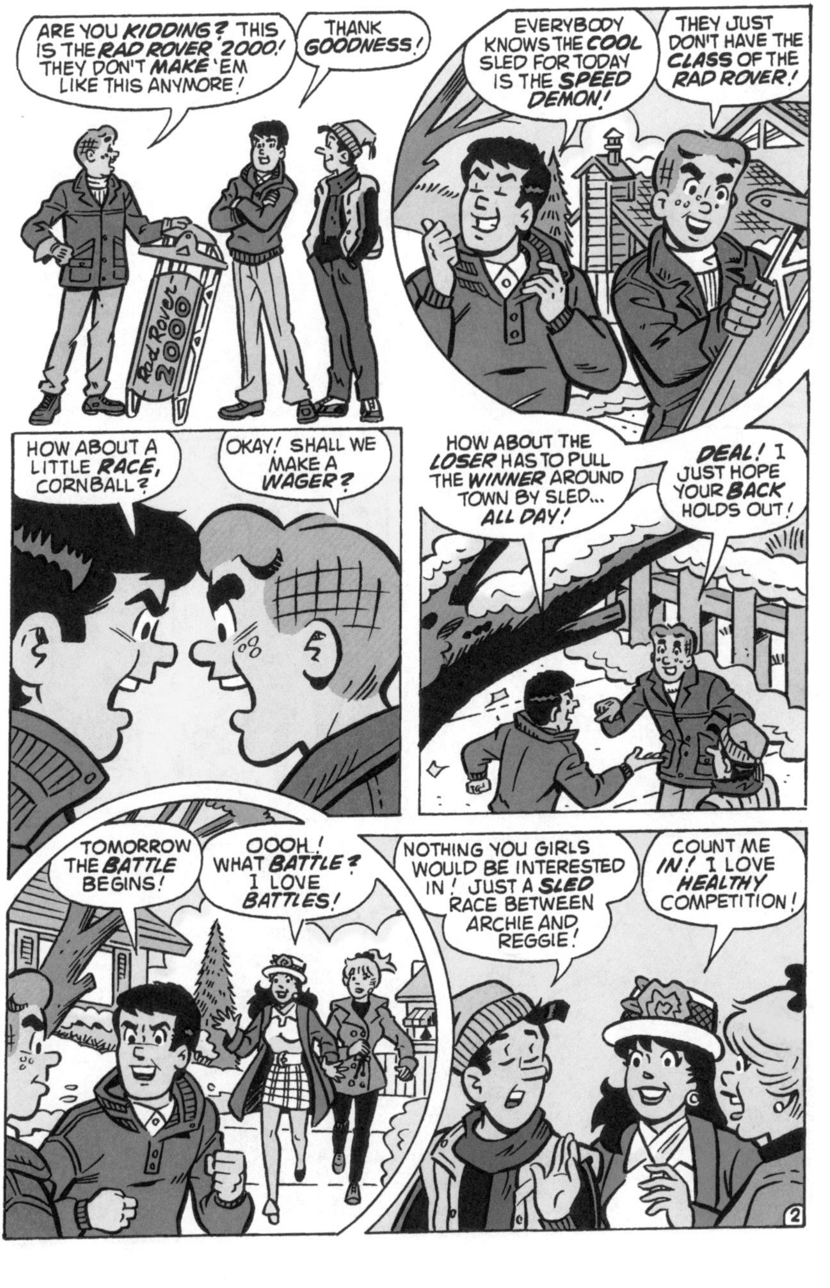
ARE YOU KIDDING? THIS IS THE RAD ROVER 2000! THEY DON'T MAKE 'EM LIKE THIS ANYMORE!
THANK GOODNESS!
Rad Rover 2000
EVERYBODY KNOWS THE COOL SLED FOR TODAY IS THE SPEED DEMON!
THEY JUST DON'T HAVE THE CLASS OF THE RAD ROVER!
HOW ABOUT A LITTLE RACE, CORNBALL?
OKAY! SHALL WE MAKE A WAGER?
HOW ABOUT THE LOSER HAS TO PULL THE WINNER AROUND TOWN BY SLED... ALL DAY!
DEAL! I JUST HOPE YOUR BACK HOLDS OUT!
TOMORROW THE BATTLE BEGINS!
OOOH! WHAT BATTLE? I LOVE BATTLES!
NOTHING YOU GIRLS WOULD BE INTERESTED IN! JUST A SLED RACE BETWEEN ARCHIE AND REGGIE!
COUNT ME IN! I LOVE HEALTHY COMPETITION!
2

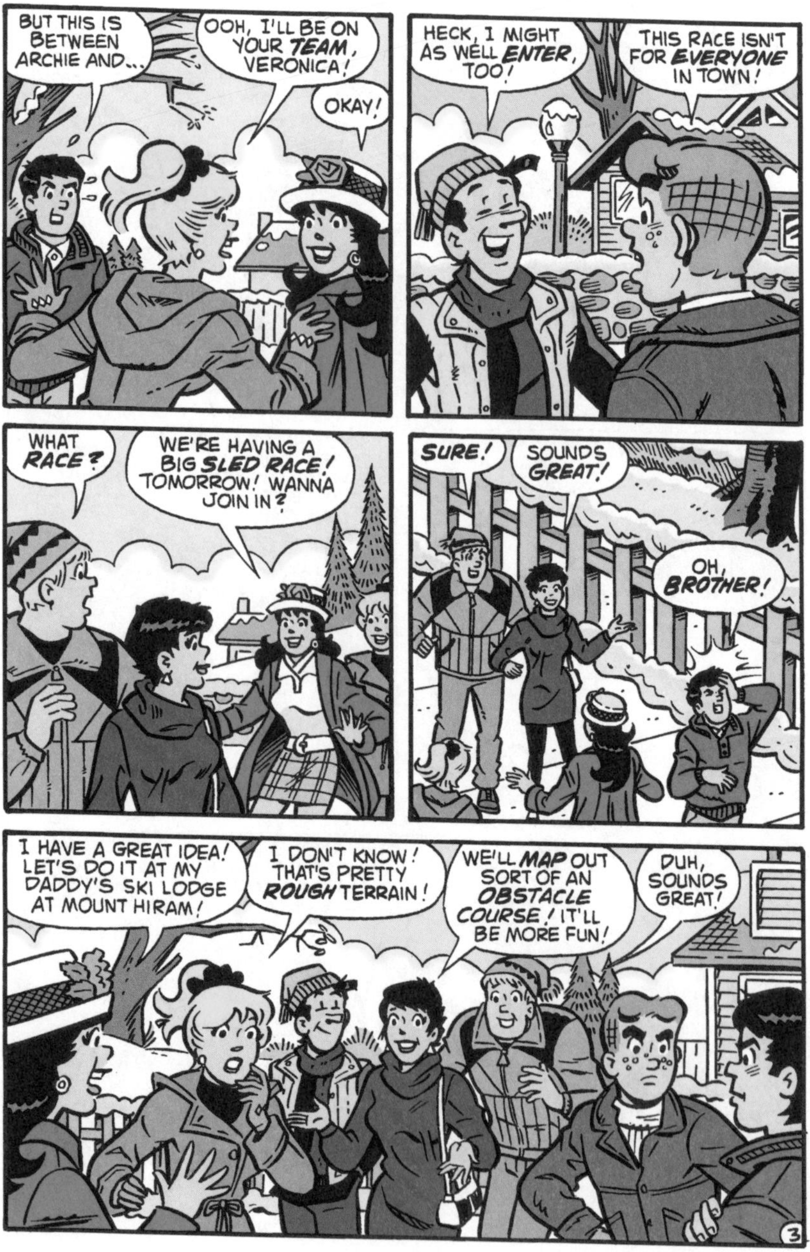
BUT THIS IS BETWEEN ARCHIE AND...
OOH, I'LL BE ON YOUR TEAM, VERONICA!
OKAY!
HECK, I MIGHT AS WELL ENTER, TOO!
THIS RACE ISN'T FOR EVERYONE IN TOWN!
WHAT RACE?
WE'RE HAVING A BIG SLED RACE! TOMORROW! WANNA JOIN IN?
SURE!
SOUNDS GREAT!
OH, BROTHER!
I HAVE A GREAT IDEA! LET'S DO IT AT MY DADDY'S SKI LODGE AT MOUNT HIRAM!
I DON'T KNOW! THAT'S PRETTY ROUGH TERRAIN!
WE'LL MAP OUT SORT OF AN OBSTACLE COURSE! IT'LL BE MORE FUN!
DUH, SOUNDS GREAT!
3

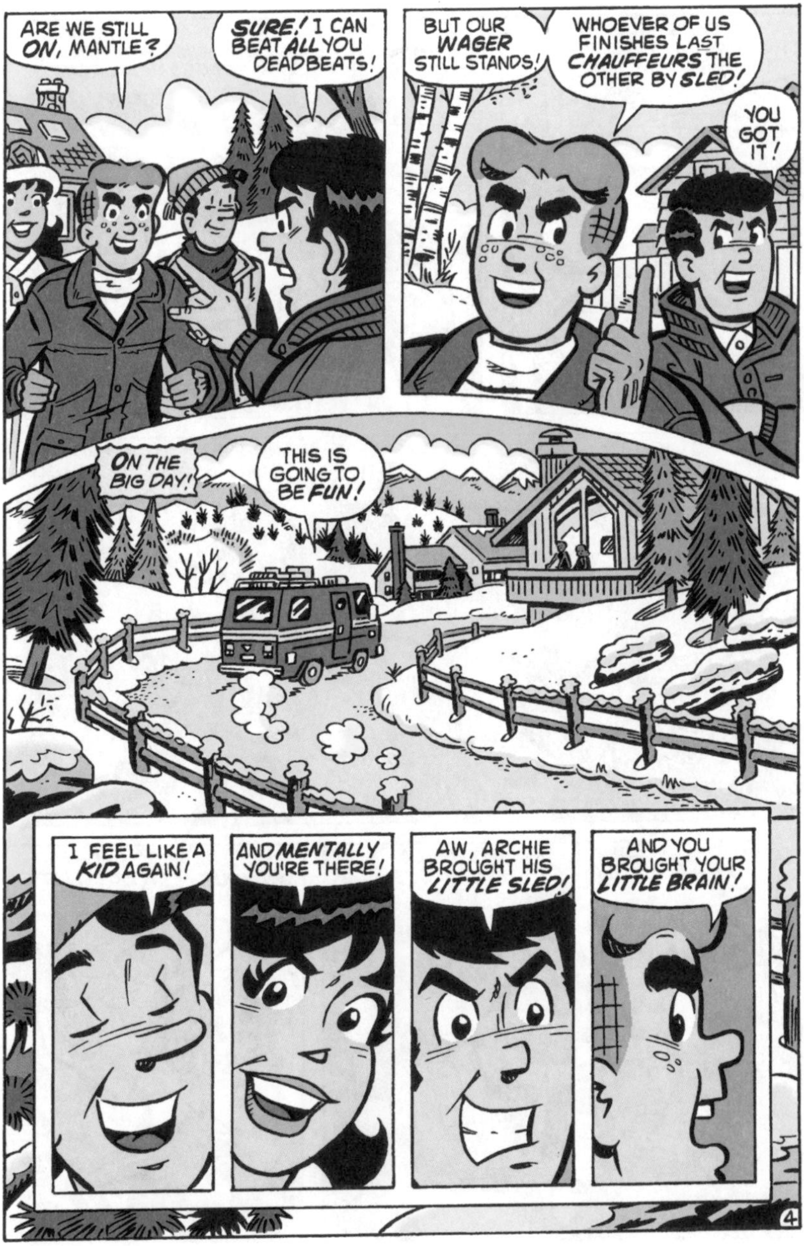
ARE WE STILL ON, MANTLE?
SURE! I CAN BEAT ALL YOU DEADBEATS!
BUT OUR WAGER STILL STANDS!
WHOEVER OF US FINISHES LAST CHAUFFEURS THE OTHER BY SLED!
YOU GOT IT!
ON THE BIG DAY!
THIS IS GOING TO BE FUN!
I FEEL LIKE A KID AGAIN!
AND MENTALLY YOU'RE THERE!
AW, ARCHIE BROUGHT HIS LITTLE SLED!
AND YOU BROUGHT YOUR LITTLE BRAIN!
4

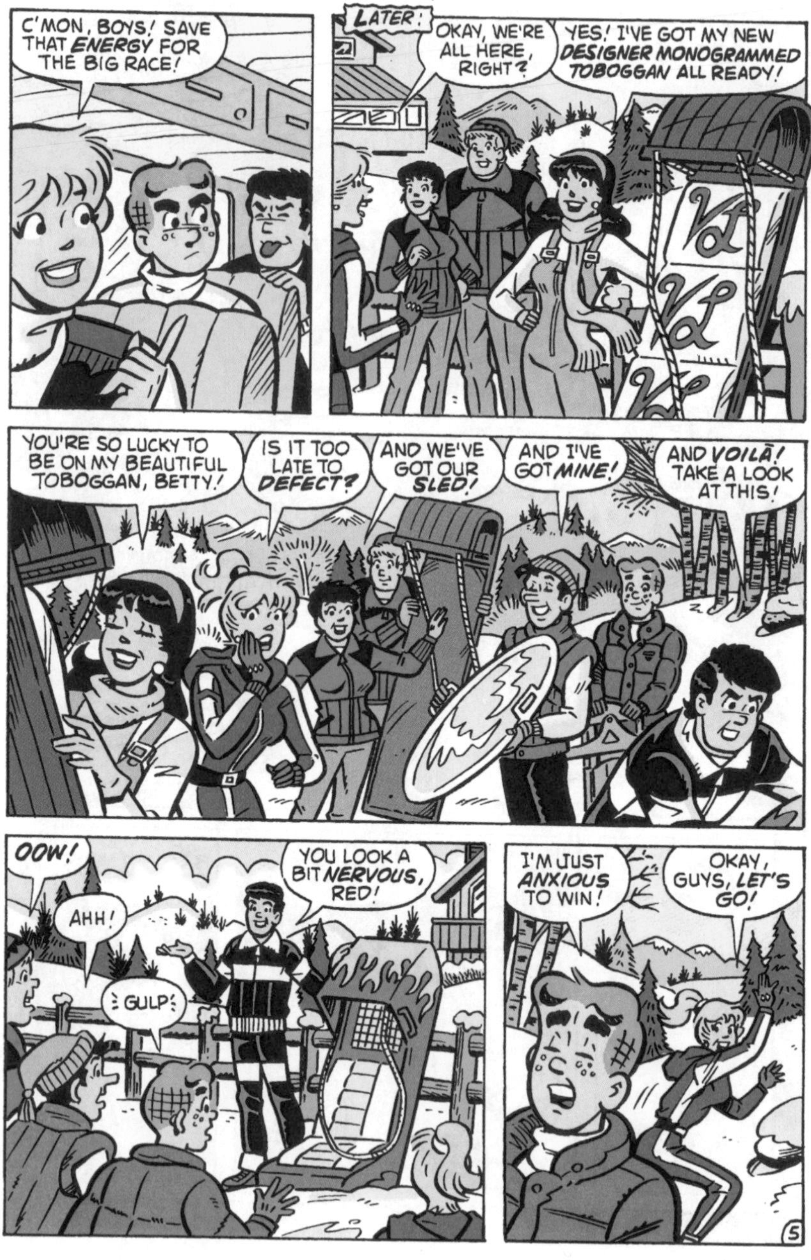
C'MON, BOYS! SAVE THAT ENERGY FOR THE BIG RACE!
LATER:
OKAY, WE'RE ALL HERE, RIGHT?
YES! I'VE GOT MY NEW DESIGNER MONOGRAMMED TOBOGGAN ALL READY!
YOU'RE SO LUCKY TO BE ON MY BEAUTIFUL TOBOGGAN, BETTY!
IS IT TOO LATE TO DEFECT?
AND WE'VE GOT OUR SLED!
AND I'VE GOT MINE!
AND VOILÀ! TAKE A LOOK AT THIS!
OOW!
AHH!
GULP!
YOU LOOK A BIT NERVOUS, RED!
I'M JUST ANXIOUS TO WIN!
OKAY, GUYS, LET'S GO!
5

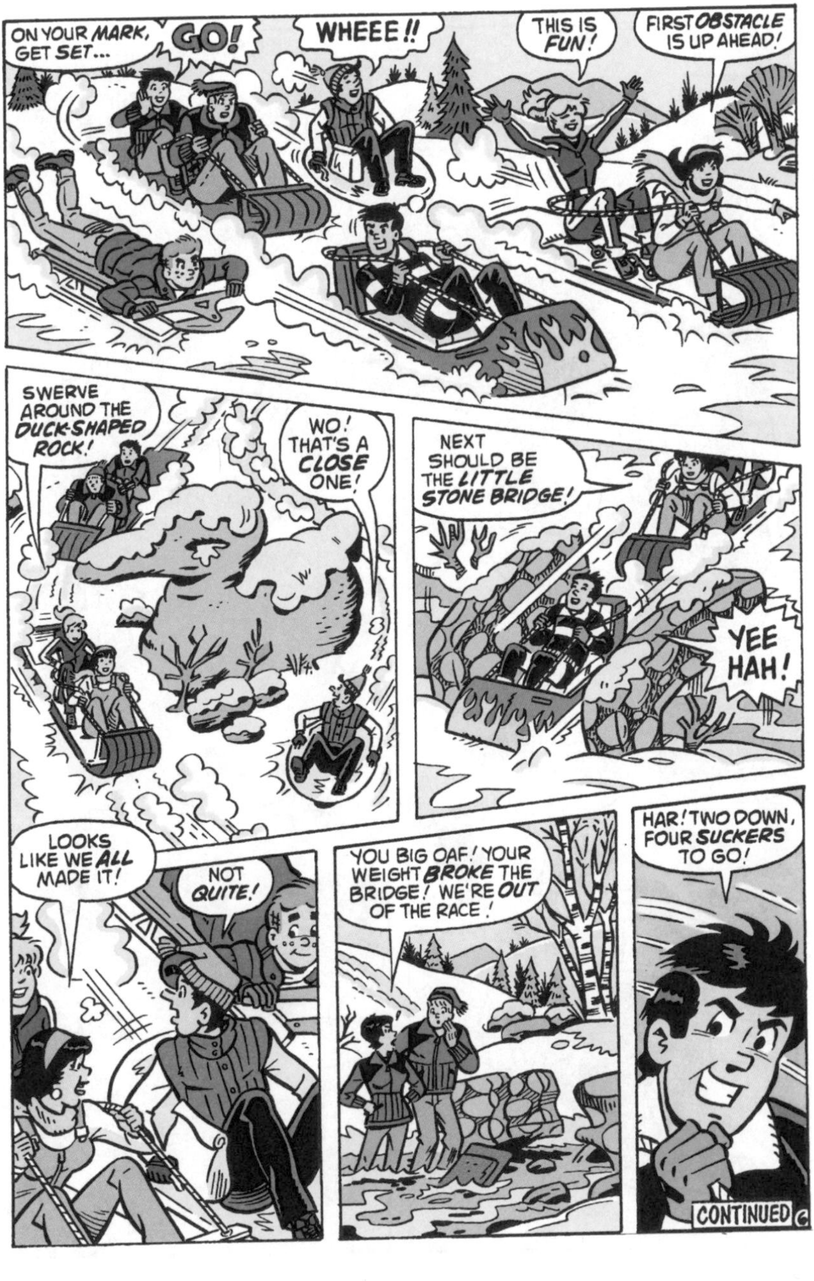
ON YOUR MARK, GET SET...
GO!
WHEEE!!
THIS IS FUN!
FIRST OBSTACLE IS UP AHEAD!
SWERVE AROUND THE DUCK-SHAPED ROCK!
WO! THAT'S A CLOSE ONE!
NEXT SHOULD BE THE LITTLE STONE BRIDGE!
YEE HAH!
LOOKS LIKE WE ALL MADE IT!
NOT QUITE!
YOU BIG OAF! YOUR WEIGHT BROKE THE BRIDGE! WE'RE OUT OF THE RACE!
HAR! TWO DOWN, FOUR SUCKERS TO GO!
CONTINUED
6

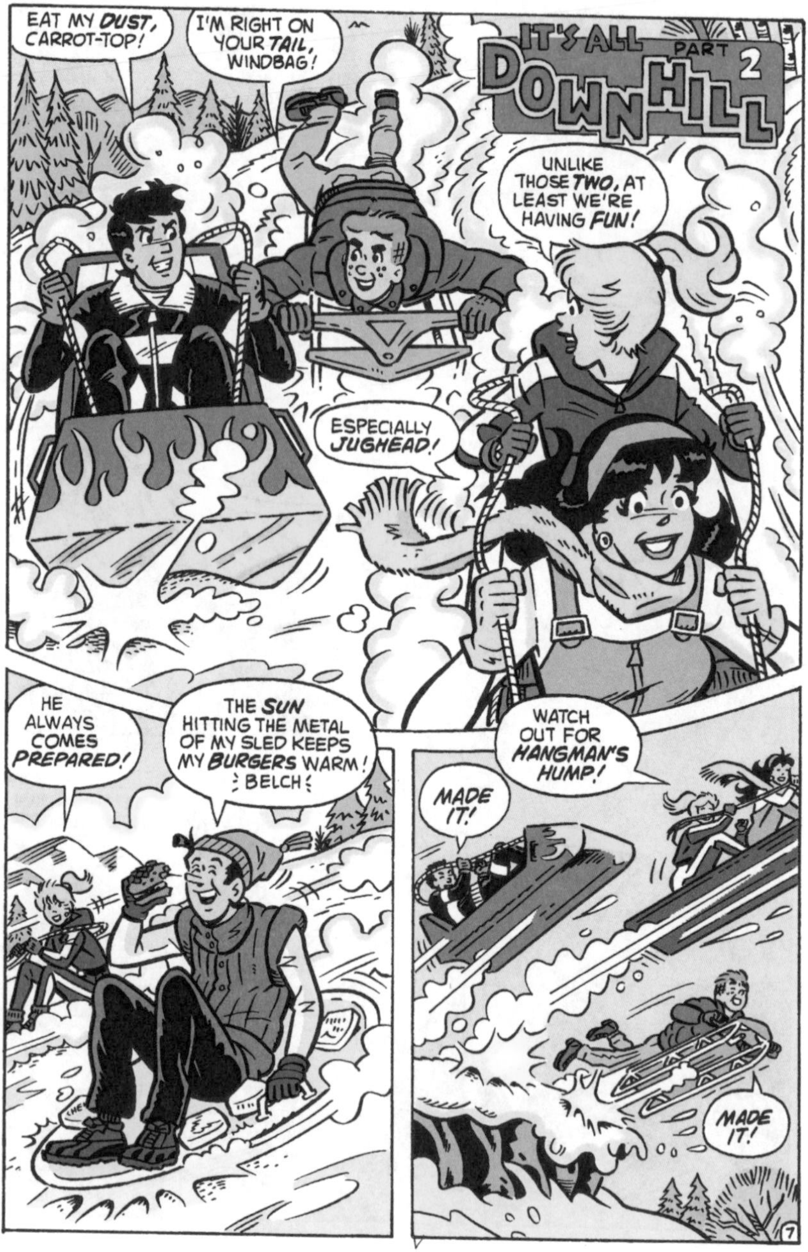
EAT MY DUST, CARROT-TOP!
I'M RIGHT ON YOUR TAIL, WINDBAG!
IT'S ALL DOWNHILL PART 2
UNLIKE THOSE TWO, AT LEAST WE'RE HAVING FUN!
ESPECIALLY JUGHEAD!
HE ALWAYS COMES PREPARED!
THE SUN HITTING THE METAL OF MY SLED KEEPS MY BURGERS WARM! ⁝BELCH⁝
WATCH OUT FOR HANGMAN'S HUMP!
MADE IT!
MADE IT!
7

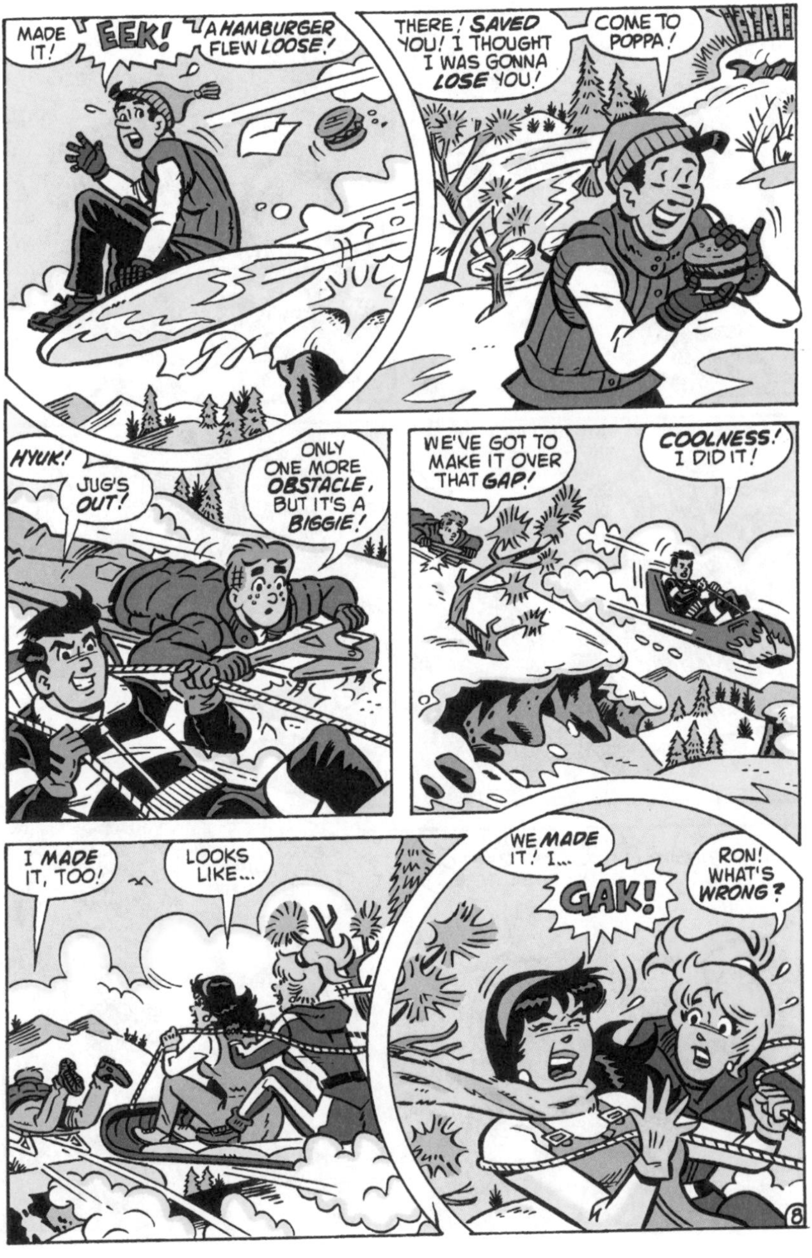
MADE IT!
EEK!
A HAMBURGER FLEW LOOSE!
THERE! SAVED YOU! I THOUGHT I WAS GONNA LOSE YOU!
COME TO POPPA!
HYUK!
JUG'S OUT!
ONLY ONE MORE OBSTACLE, BUT IT'S A BIGGIE!
WE'VE GOT TO MAKE IT OVER THAT GAP!
COOLNESS! I DID IT!
I MADE IT, TOO!
LOOKS LIKE...
WE MADE IT! I...
GAK!
RON! WHAT'S WRONG?
8

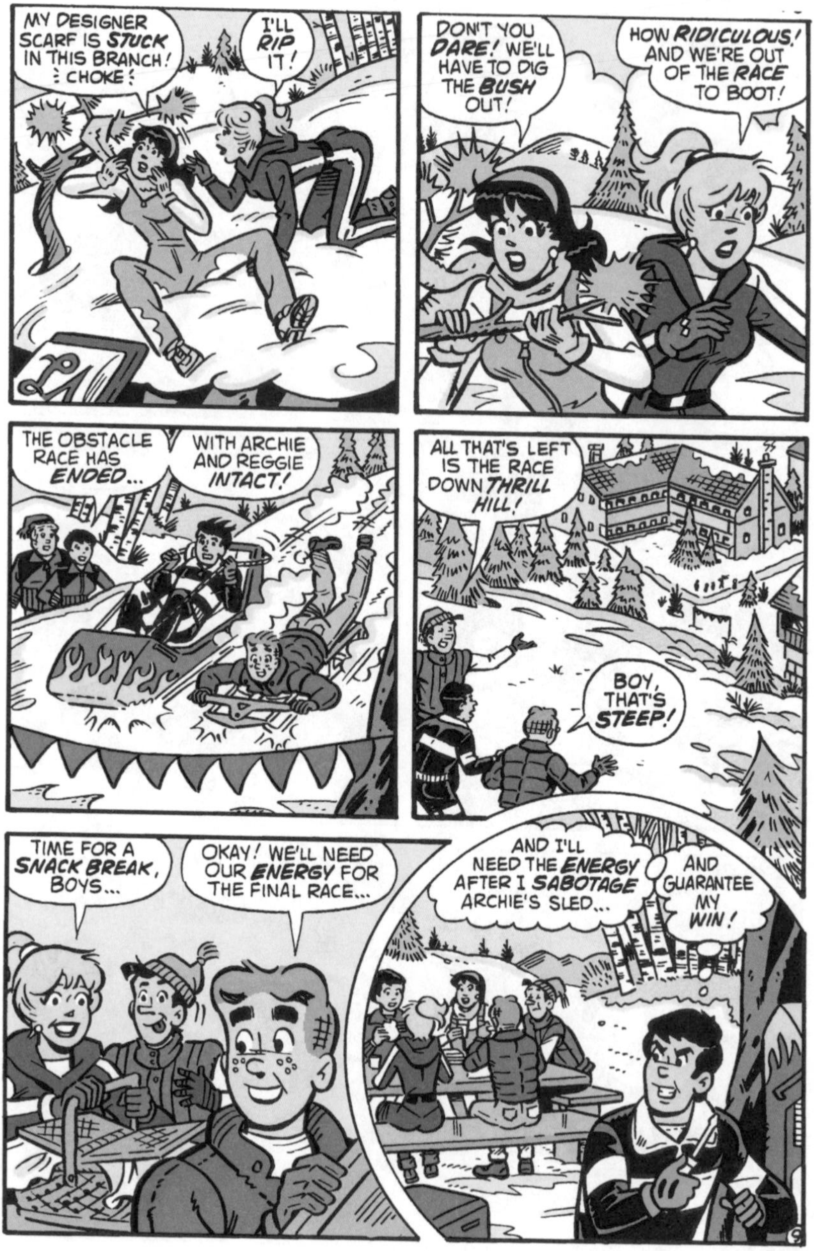
MY DESIGNER SCARF IS STUCK IN THIS BRANCH! CHOKE
I'LL RIP IT!
DON'T YOU DARE! WE'LL HAVE TO DIG THE BUSH OUT!
HOW RIDICULOUS! AND WE'RE OUT OF THE RACE TO BOOT!
THE OBSTACLE RACE HAS ENDED...
WITH ARCHIE AND REGGIE INTACT!
ALL THAT'S LEFT IS THE RACE DOWN THRILL HILL!
BOY, THAT'S STEEP!
TIME FOR A SNACK BREAK, BOYS...
OKAY! WE'LL NEED OUR ENERGY FOR THE FINAL RACE...
AND I'LL NEED THE ENERGY AFTER I SABOTAGE ARCHIE'S SLED...
AND GUARANTEE MY WIN!
9

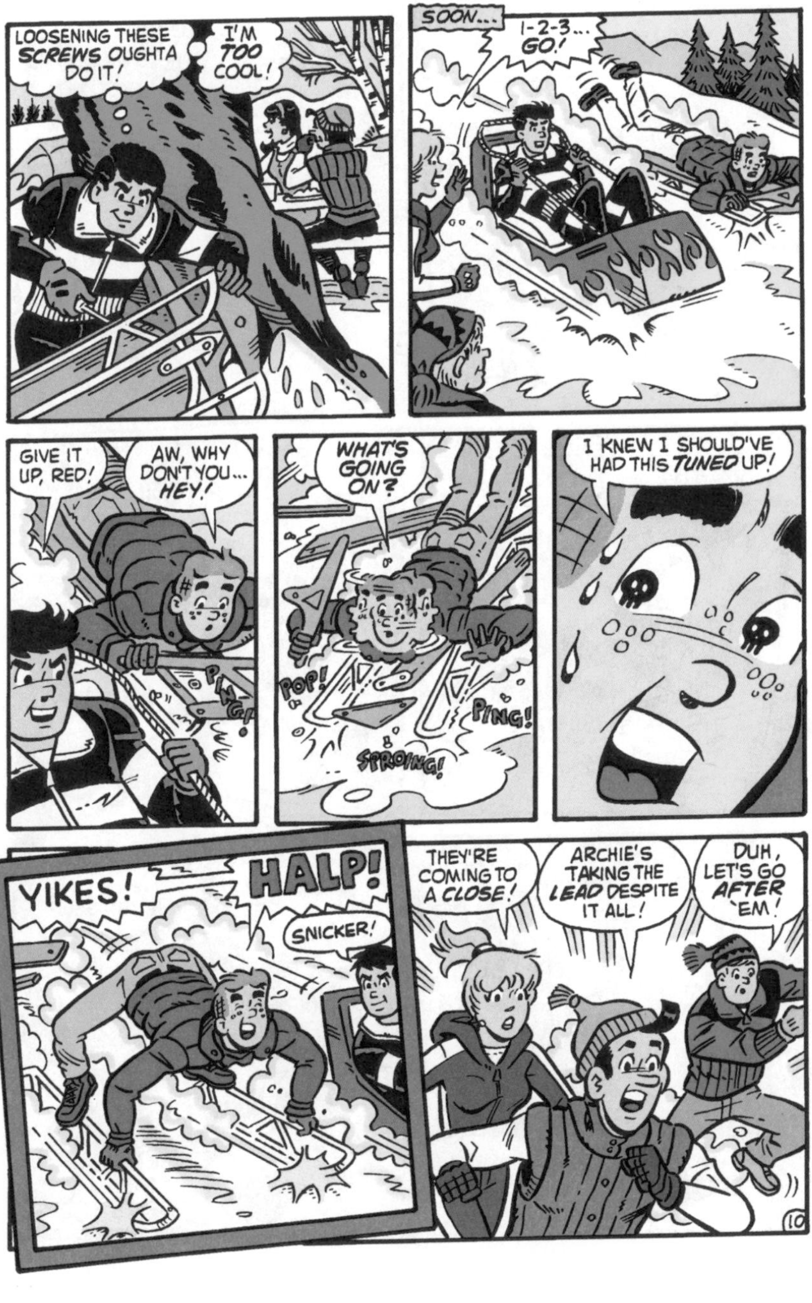
LOOSENING THESE SCREWS OUGHTA DO IT!
I'M TOO COOL!
SOON...
1-2-3... GO!
GIVE IT UP, RED!
AW, WHY DON'T YOU... HEY!
PING!
WHAT'S GOING ON?
POP!
PING!
SPROING!
I KNEW I SHOULD'VE HAD THIS TUNED UP!
YIKES!
HALP!
SNICKER!
THEY'RE COMING TO A CLOSE!
ARCHIE'S TAKING THE LEAD DESPITE IT ALL!
DUH, LET'S GO AFTER 'EM!
10

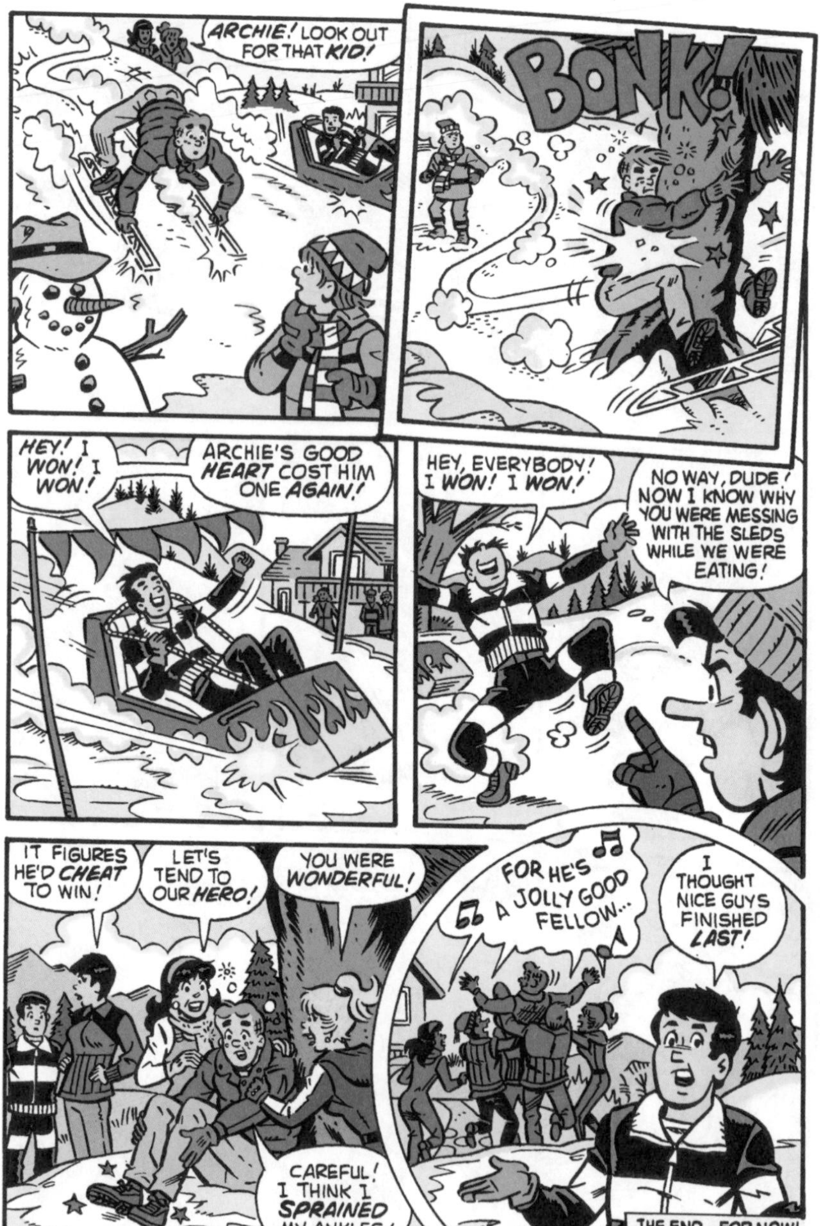
ARCHIE! LOOK OUT FOR THAT KID!
BONK!
HEY! I WON! I WON!
ARCHIE'S GOOD HEART COST HIM ONE AGAIN!
HEY, EVERYBODY! I WON! I WON!
NO WAY, DUDE! NOW I KNOW WHY YOU WERE MESSING WITH THE SLEDS WHILE WE WERE EATING!
IT FIGURES HE'D CHEAT TO WIN!
LET'S TEND TO OUR HERO!
YOU WERE WONDERFUL!
CAREFUL! I THINK I SPRAINED MY ANKLES!
FOR HE'S A JOLLY GOOD FELLOW...
I THOUGHT NICE GUYS FINISHED LAST!
THE END... FOR NOW!

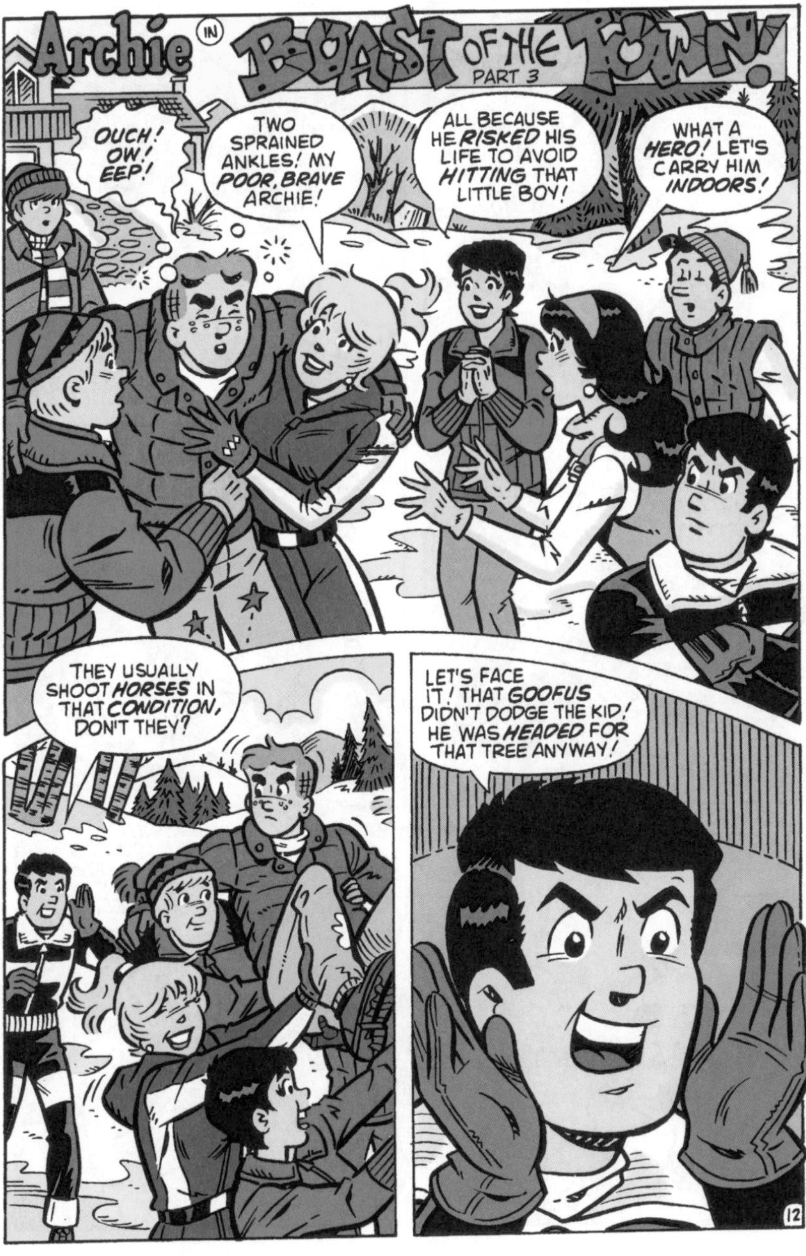
Archie IN BOAST OF THE TOWN!
PART 3
OUCH! OW! EEP!
TWO SPRAINED ANKLES! MY POOR, BRAVE ARCHIE!
ALL BECAUSE HE RISKED HIS LIFE TO AVOID HITTING THAT LITTLE BOY!
WHAT A HERO! LET'S CARRY HIM INDOORS!
THEY USUALLY SHOOT HORSES IN THAT CONDITION, DON'T THEY?
LET'S FACE IT! THAT GOOFUS DIDN'T DODGE THE KID! HE WAS HEADED FOR THAT TREE ANYWAY!
12

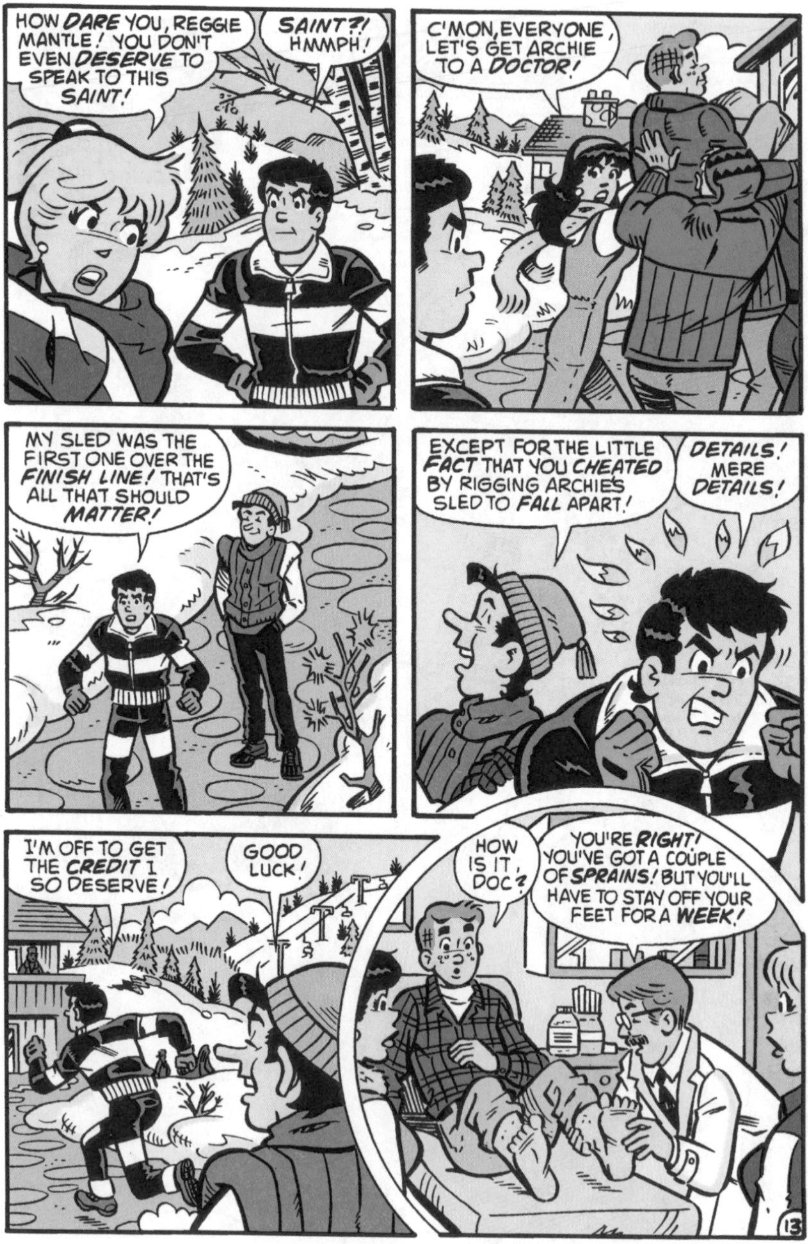
HOW DARE YOU, REGGIE MANTLE! YOU DON'T EVEN DESERVE TO SPEAK TO THIS SAINT!
SAINT?! HMMPH!
C'MON, EVERYONE, LET'S GET ARCHIE TO A DOCTOR!
MY SLED WAS THE FIRST ONE OVER THE FINISH LINE! THAT'S ALL THAT SHOULD MATTER!
EXCEPT FOR THE LITTLE FACT THAT YOU CHEATED BY RIGGING ARCHIE'S SLED TO FALL APART!
DETAILS! MERE DETAILS!
I'M OFF TO GET THE CREDIT I SO DESERVE!
GOOD LUCK!
HOW IS IT, DOC?
YOU'RE RIGHT! YOU'VE GOT A COUPLE OF SPRAINS! BUT YOU'LL HAVE TO STAY OFF YOUR FEET FOR A WEEK!
13

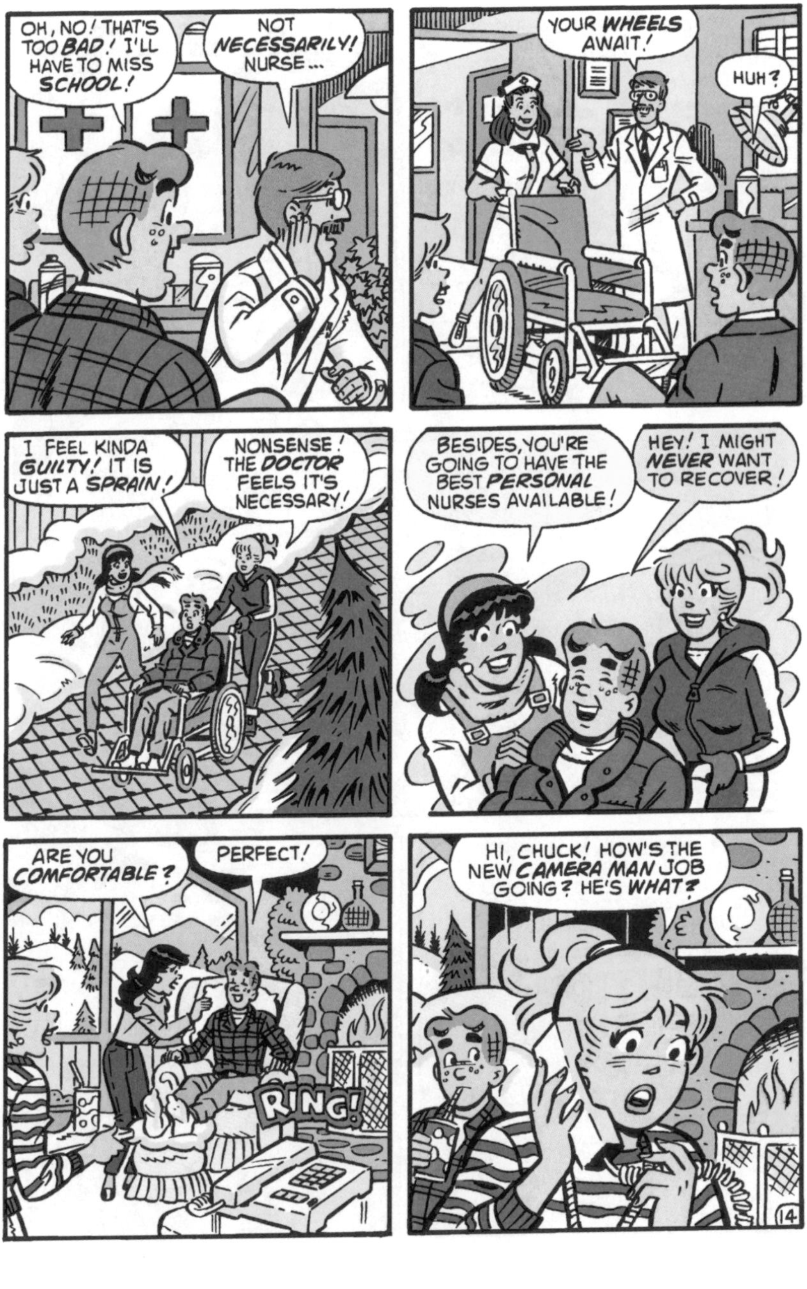
OH, NO! THAT'S TOO BAD! I'LL HAVE TO MISS SCHOOL!
NOT NECESSARILY! NURSE...
YOUR WHEELS AWAIT!
HUH?
I FEEL KINDA GUILTY! IT IS JUST A SPRAIN!
NONSENSE! THE DOCTOR FEELS IT'S NECESSARY!
BESIDES, YOU'RE GOING TO HAVE THE BEST PERSONAL NURSES AVAILABLE!
HEY! I MIGHT NEVER WANT TO RECOVER!
ARE YOU COMFORTABLE?
PERFECT!
RING!
HI, CHUCK! HOW'S THE NEW CAMERA MAN JOB GOING? HE'S WHAT?
14

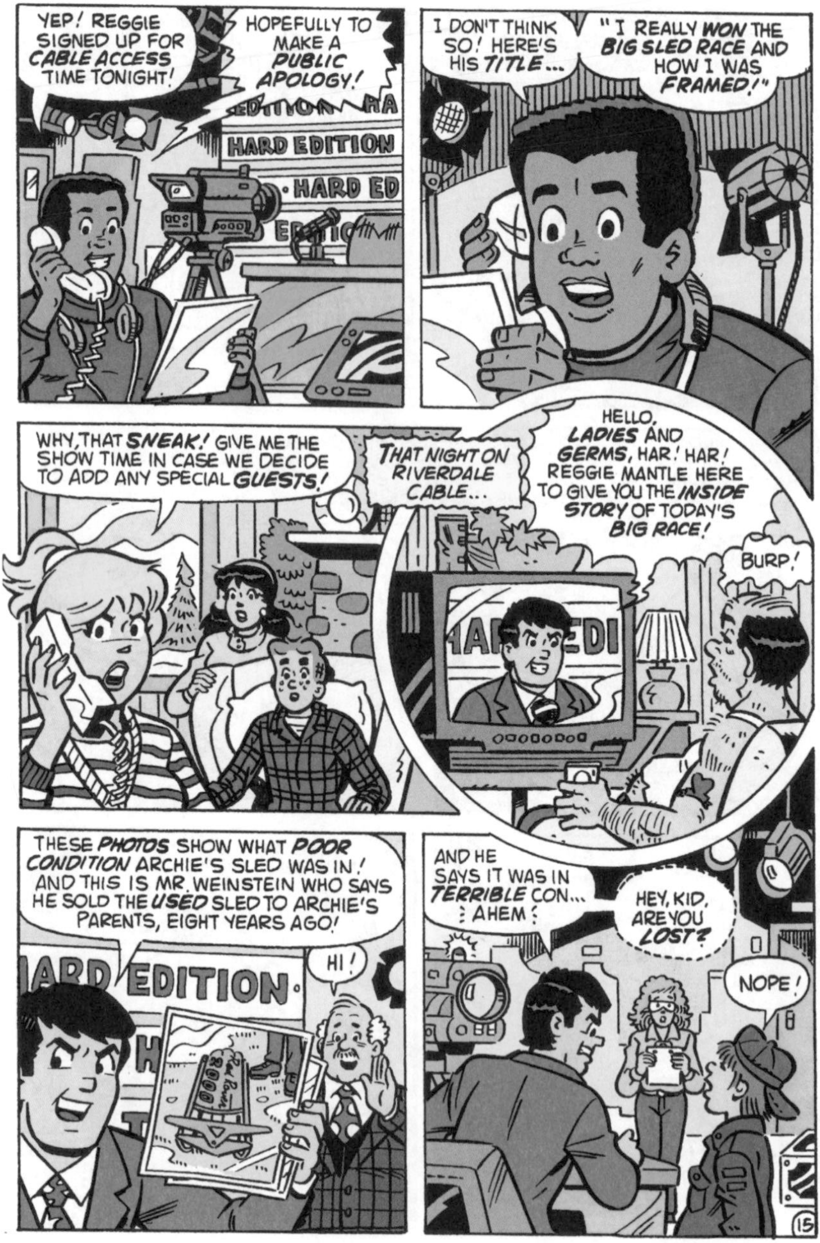
YEP! REGGIE SIGNED UP FOR CABLE ACCESS TIME TONIGHT!
HOPEFULLY TO MAKE A PUBLIC APOLOGY!
HARD EDITION
I DON'T THINK SO! HERE'S HIS TITLE...
"I REALLY WON THE BIG SLED RACE AND HOW I WAS FRAMED!"
WHY, THAT SNEAK! GIVE ME THE SHOW TIME IN CASE WE DECIDE TO ADD ANY SPECIAL GUESTS!
THAT NIGHT ON RIVERDALE CABLE...
HELLO, LADIES AND GERMS, HAR! HAR! REGGIE MANTLE HERE TO GIVE YOU THE INSIDE STORY OF TODAY'S BIG RACE!
BURP!
THESE PHOTOS SHOW WHAT POOR CONDITION ARCHIE'S SLED WAS IN! AND THIS IS MR. WEINSTEIN WHO SAYS HE SOLD THE USED SLED TO ARCHIE'S PARENTS, EIGHT YEARS AGO!
HI!
HARD EDITION
AND HE SAYS IT WAS IN TERRIBLE CON... AHEM
HEY, KID, ARE YOU LOST?
NOPE!
15

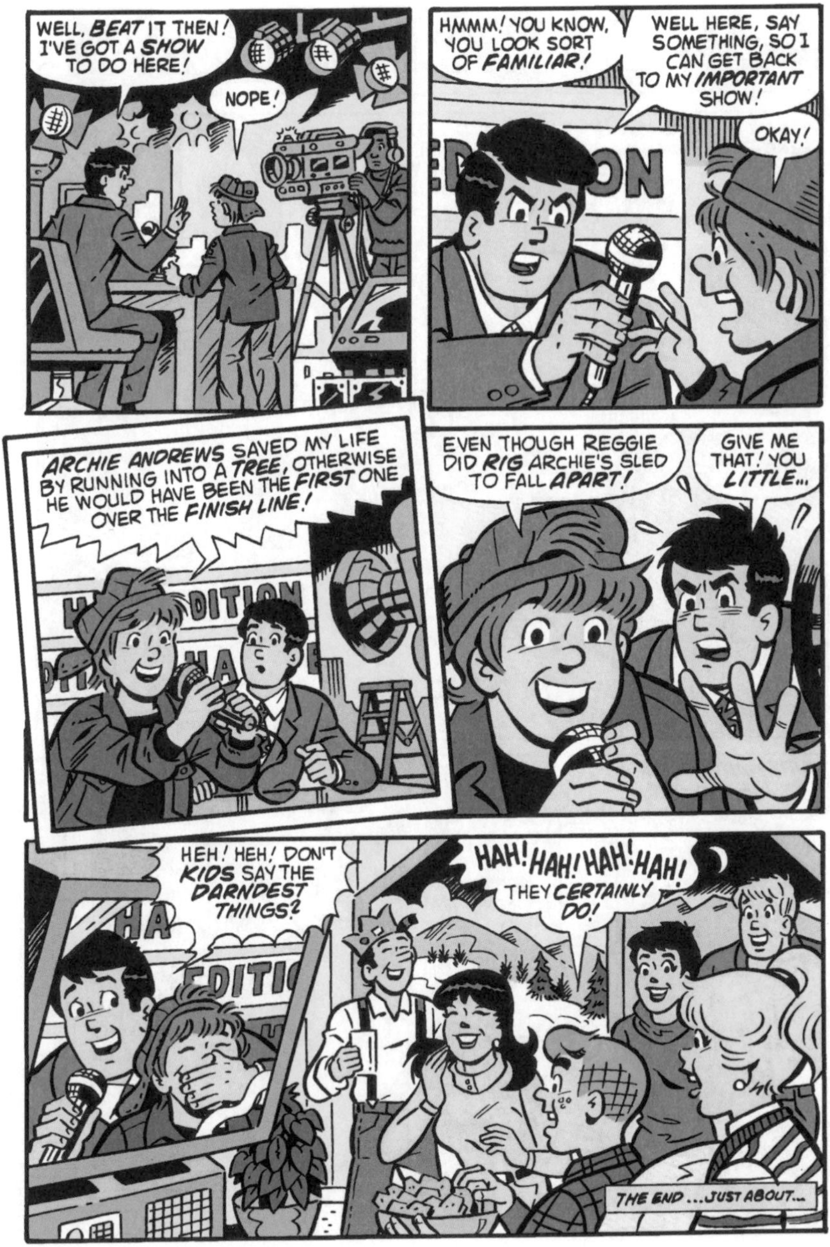
WELL, BEAT IT THEN! I'VE GOT A SHOW TO DO HERE!
NOPE!
HMMM! YOU KNOW, YOU LOOK SORT OF FAMILIAR!
WELL HERE, SAY SOMETHING, SO I CAN GET BACK TO MY IMPORTANT SHOW!
OKAY!
ARCHIE ANDREWS SAVED MY LIFE BY RUNNING INTO A TREE, OTHERWISE HE WOULD HAVE BEEN THE FIRST ONE OVER THE FINISH LINE!
EVEN THOUGH REGGIE DID RIG ARCHIE'S SLED TO FALL APART!
GIVE ME THAT! YOU LITTLE...
HEH! HEH! DON'T KIDS SAY THE DARNDEST THINGS?
HAH! HAH! HAH! HAH! THEY CERTAINLY DO!
THE END ... JUST ABOUT...

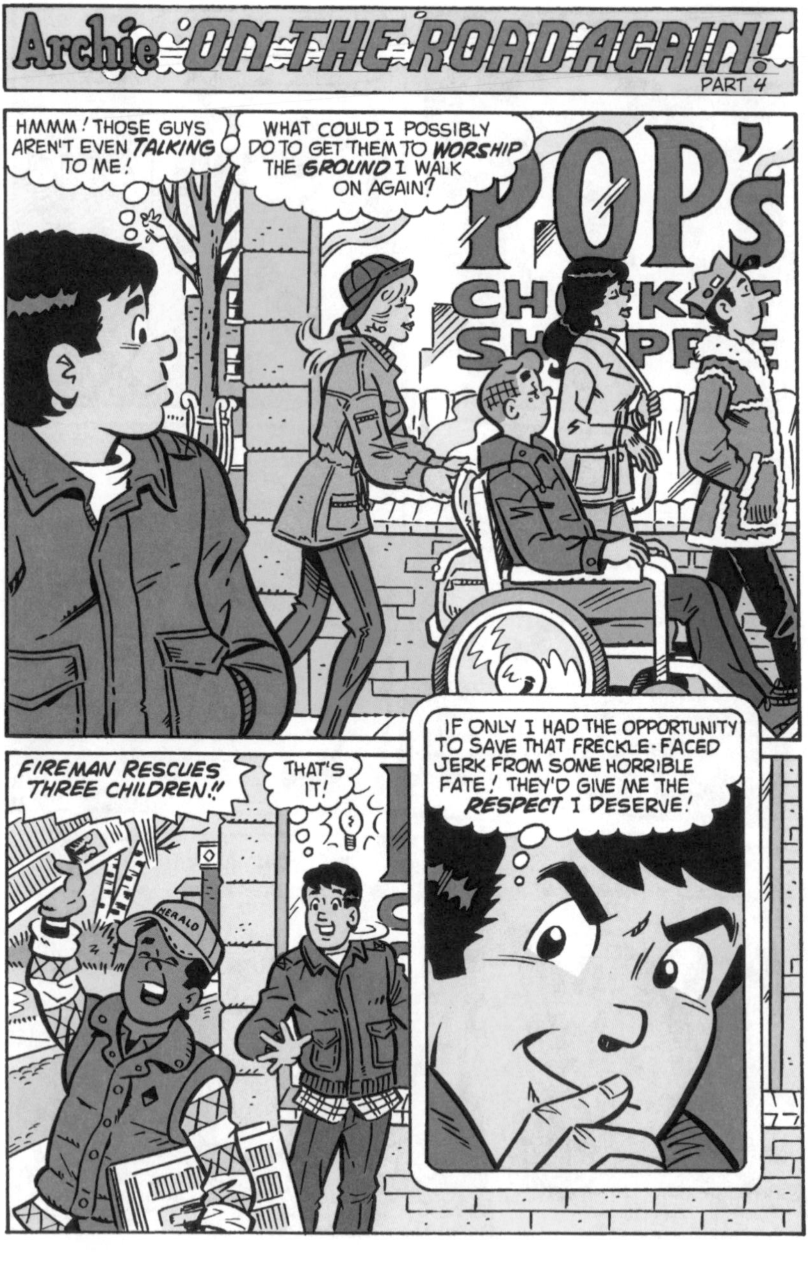
Archie
ON THE ROAD AGAIN!
PART 4
HMMM! THOSE GUYS AREN'T EVEN TALKING TO ME!
WHAT COULD I POSSIBLY DO TO GET THEM TO WORSHIP THE GROUND I WALK ON AGAIN?
POP's
FIREMAN RESCUES THREE CHILDREN!!
THAT'S IT!
IF ONLY I HAD THE OPPORTUNITY TO SAVE THAT FRECKLE-FACED JERK FROM SOME HORRIBLE FATE! THEY'D GIVE ME THE RESPECT I DESERVE!
HERALD

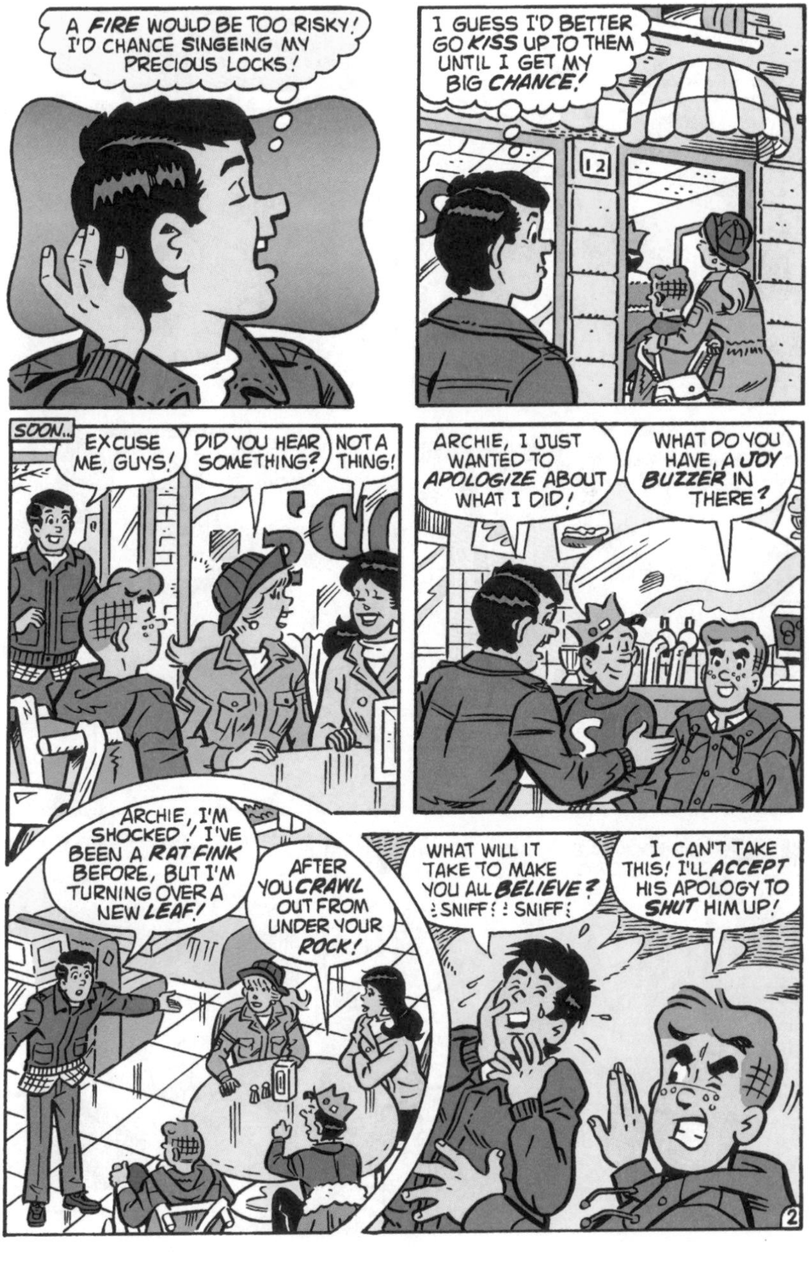
A FIRE WOULD BE TOO RISKY! I'D CHANCE SINGEING MY PRECIOUS LOCKS!
I GUESS I'D BETTER GO KISS UP TO THEM UNTIL I GET MY BIG CHANCE!
12
SOON...
EXCUSE ME, GUYS!
DID YOU HEAR SOMETHING?
NOT A THING!
ARCHIE, I JUST WANTED TO APOLOGIZE ABOUT WHAT I DID!
WHAT DO YOU HAVE, A JOY BUZZER IN THERE?
ARCHIE, I'M SHOCKED! I'VE BEEN A RAT FINK BEFORE, BUT I'M TURNING OVER A NEW LEAF!
AFTER YOU CRAWL OUT FROM UNDER YOUR ROCK!
WHAT WILL IT TAKE TO MAKE YOU ALL BELIEVE? SNIFF! SNIFF!
I CAN'T TAKE THIS! I'LL ACCEPT HIS APOLOGY TO SHUT HIM UP!
2

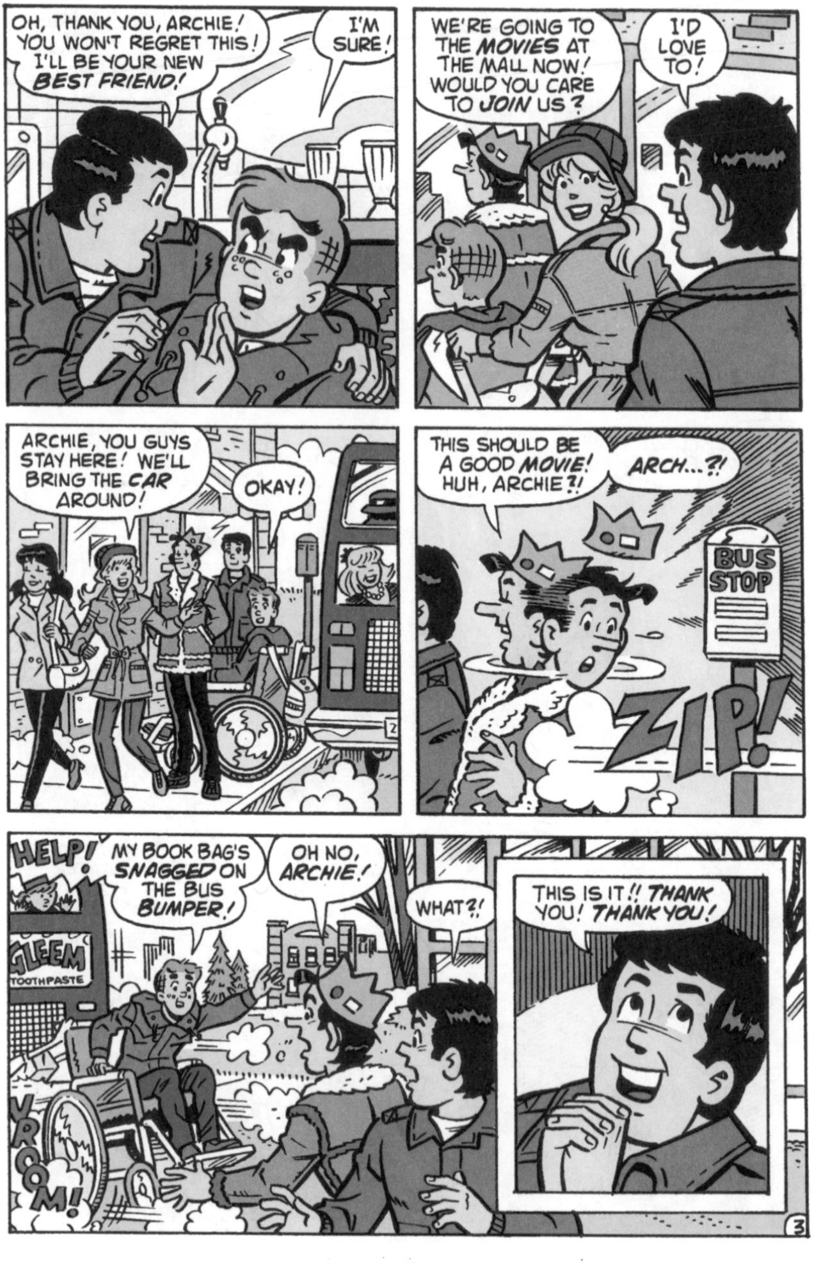
OH, THANK YOU, ARCHIE! YOU WON'T REGRET THIS! I'LL BE YOUR NEW BEST FRIEND!
I'M SURE!
WE'RE GOING TO THE MOVIES AT THE MALL NOW! WOULD YOU CARE TO JOIN US?
I'D LOVE TO!
ARCHIE, YOU GUYS STAY HERE! WE'LL BRING THE CAR AROUND!
OKAY!
THIS SHOULD BE A GOOD MOVIE! HUH, ARCHIE?!
ARCH...?!
BUS STOP
ZIP!
HELP!
MY BOOK BAG'S SNAGGED ON THE BUS BUMPER!
OH NO, ARCHIE!
GLEEM
TOOTHPASTE
VROOM!
WHAT?!
THIS IS IT!! THANK YOU! THANK YOU!
3

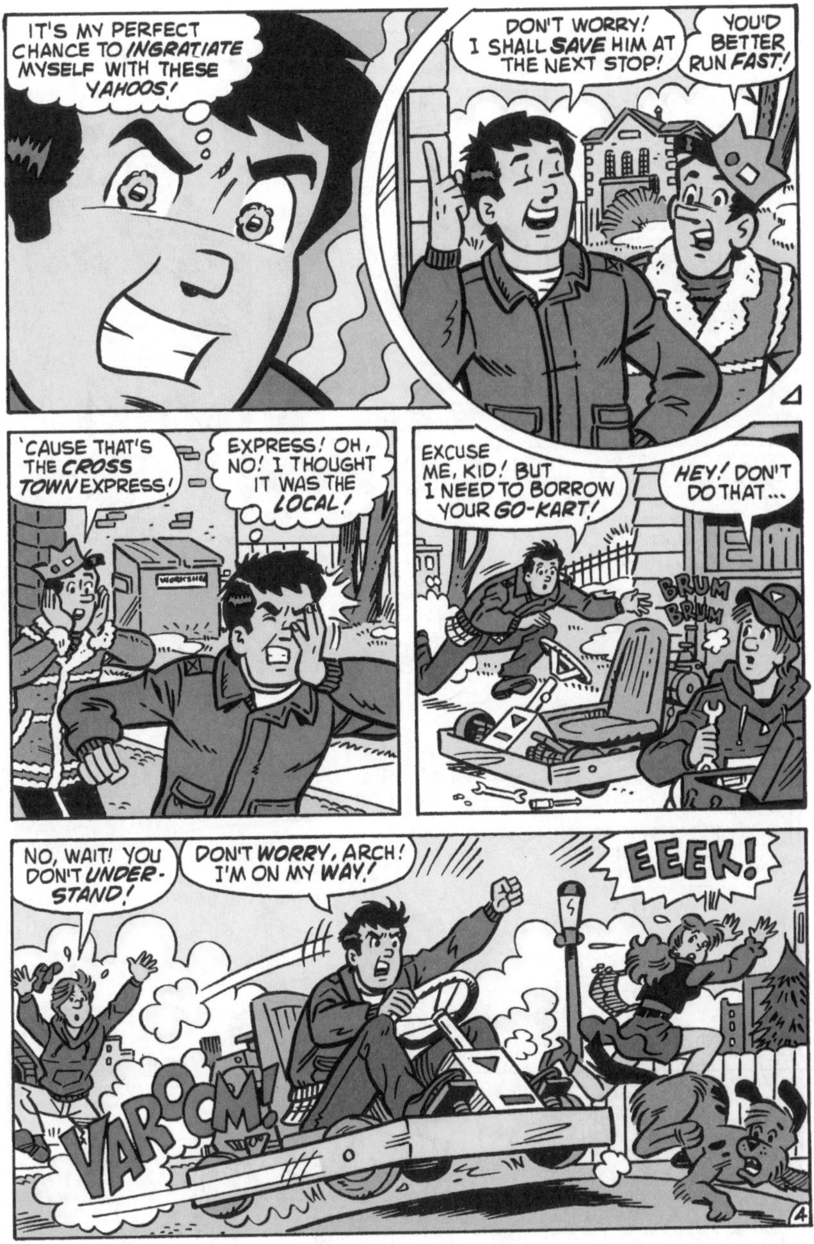
IT'S MY PERFECT CHANCE TO INGRATIATE MYSELF WITH THESE YAHOOS!
DON'T WORRY! I SHALL SAVE HIM AT THE NEXT STOP!
YOU'D BETTER RUN FAST!
'CAUSE THAT'S THE CROSS TOWN EXPRESS!
EXPRESS! OH, NO! I THOUGHT IT WAS THE LOCAL!
EXCUSE ME, KID! BUT I NEED TO BORROW YOUR GO-KART!
HEY! DON'T DO THAT...
BRUM BRUM
NO, WAIT! YOU DON'T UNDER-STAND!
DON'T WORRY, ARCH! I'M ON MY WAY!
EEEK!
VAROOM!
4

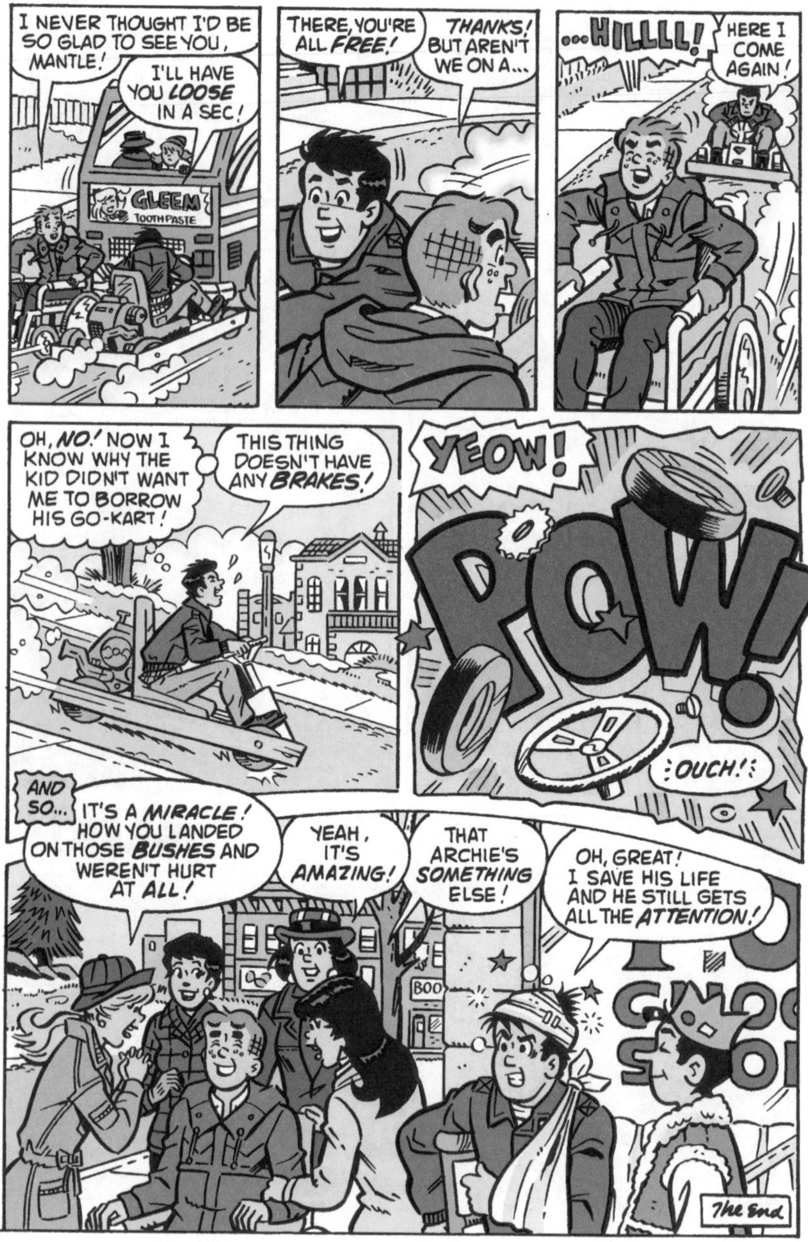
I NEVER THOUGHT I'D BE SO GLAD TO SEE YOU, MANTLE!
I'LL HAVE YOU LOOSE IN A SEC!
GLEEM TOOTHPASTE
THERE, YOU'RE ALL FREE!
THANKS! BUT AREN'T WE ON A...
...HILLLL!
HERE I COME AGAIN!
OH, NO! NOW I KNOW WHY THE KID DIDN'T WANT ME TO BORROW HIS GO-KART!
THIS THING DOESN'T HAVE ANY BRAKES!
YEOW!
POW!
OUCH!
AND SO...
IT'S A MIRACLE! HOW YOU LANDED ON THOSE BUSHES AND WEREN'T HURT AT ALL!
YEAH, IT'S AMAZING!
THAT ARCHIE'S SOMETHING ELSE!
OH, GREAT! I SAVE HIS LIFE AND HE STILL GETS ALL THE ATTENTION!
The End

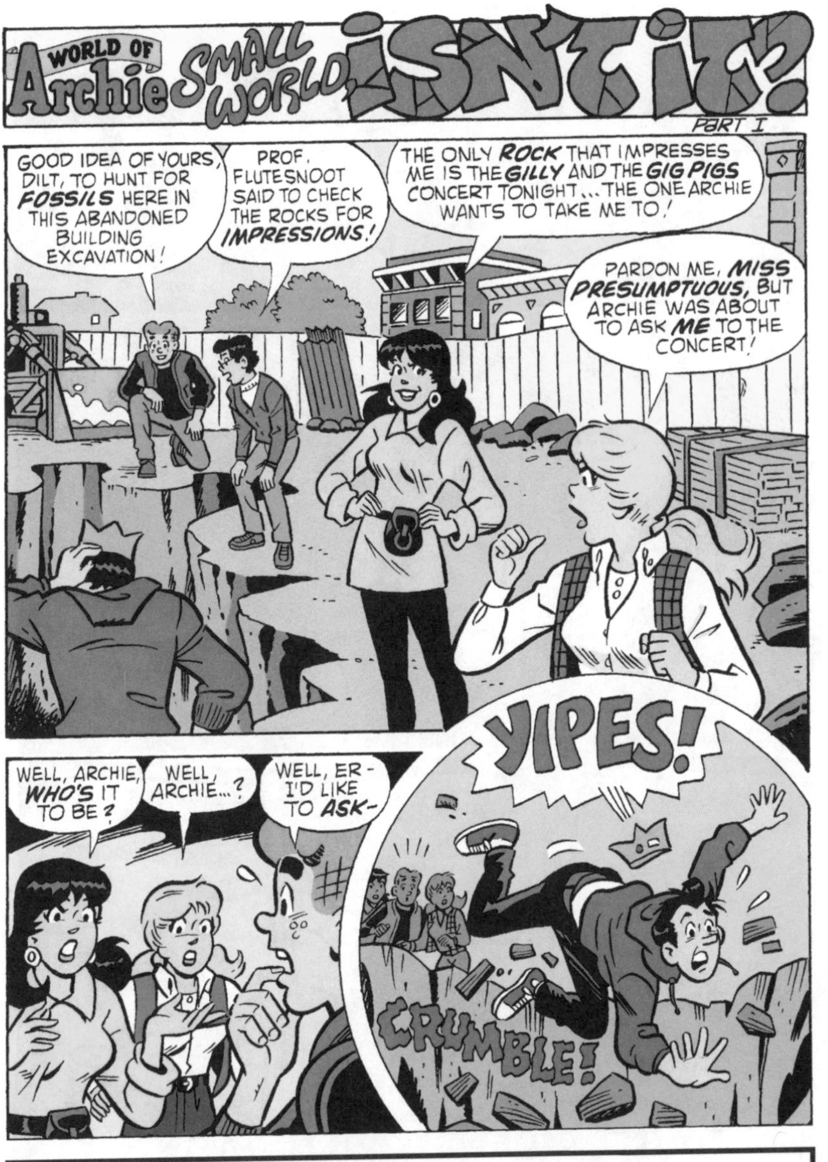

WORLD OF Archie
SMALL WORLD, ISN'T IT?
PART I
GOOD IDEA OF YOURS, DILT, TO HUNT FOR FOSSILS HERE IN THIS ABANDONED BUILDING EXCAVATION!
PROF. FLUTESNOOT SAID TO CHECK THE ROCKS FOR IMPRESSIONS!
THE ONLY ROCK THAT IMPRESSES ME IS THE GILLY AND THE GIG PIGS CONCERT TONIGHT... THE ONE ARCHIE WANTS TO TAKE ME TO!
PARDON ME, MISS PRESUMPTUOUS, BUT ARCHIE WAS ABOUT TO ASK ME TO THE CONCERT!
WELL, ARCHIE, WHO'S IT TO BE?
WELL, ARCHIE...?
WELL, ER- I'D LIKE TO ASK-
YIPES!
CRUMBLE!

Story: Bob Bolling Pencils: Rex Lindsey
Inks: Rudy Lapick Letters: Bill Yoshida

Originally printed in WORLD OF ARCHIE #9, JUNE 1994

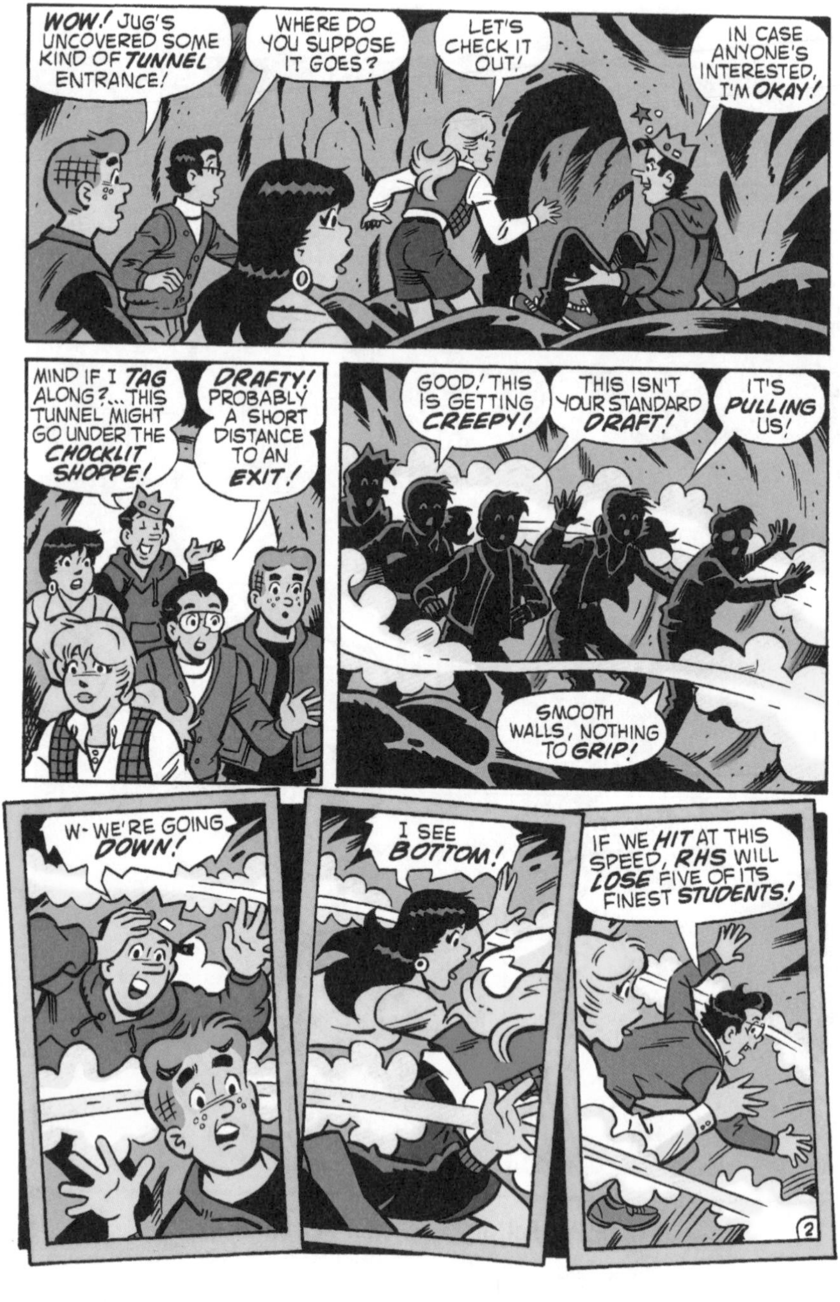
WOW! JUG'S UNCOVERED SOME KIND OF TUNNEL ENTRANCE!
WHERE DO YOU SUPPOSE IT GOES?
LET'S CHECK IT OUT!
IN CASE ANYONE'S INTERESTED, I'M OKAY!
MIND IF I TAG ALONG?... THIS TUNNEL MIGHT GO UNDER THE CHOCKLIT SHOPPE!
DRAFTY! PROBABLY A SHORT DISTANCE TO AN EXIT!
GOOD! THIS IS GETTING CREEPY!
THIS ISN'T YOUR STANDARD DRAFT!
IT'S PULLING US!
SMOOTH WALLS, NOTHING TO GRIP!
W- WE'RE GOING DOWN!
I SEE BOTTOM!
IF WE HIT AT THIS SPEED, RHS WILL LOSE FIVE OF ITS FINEST STUDENTS!
2

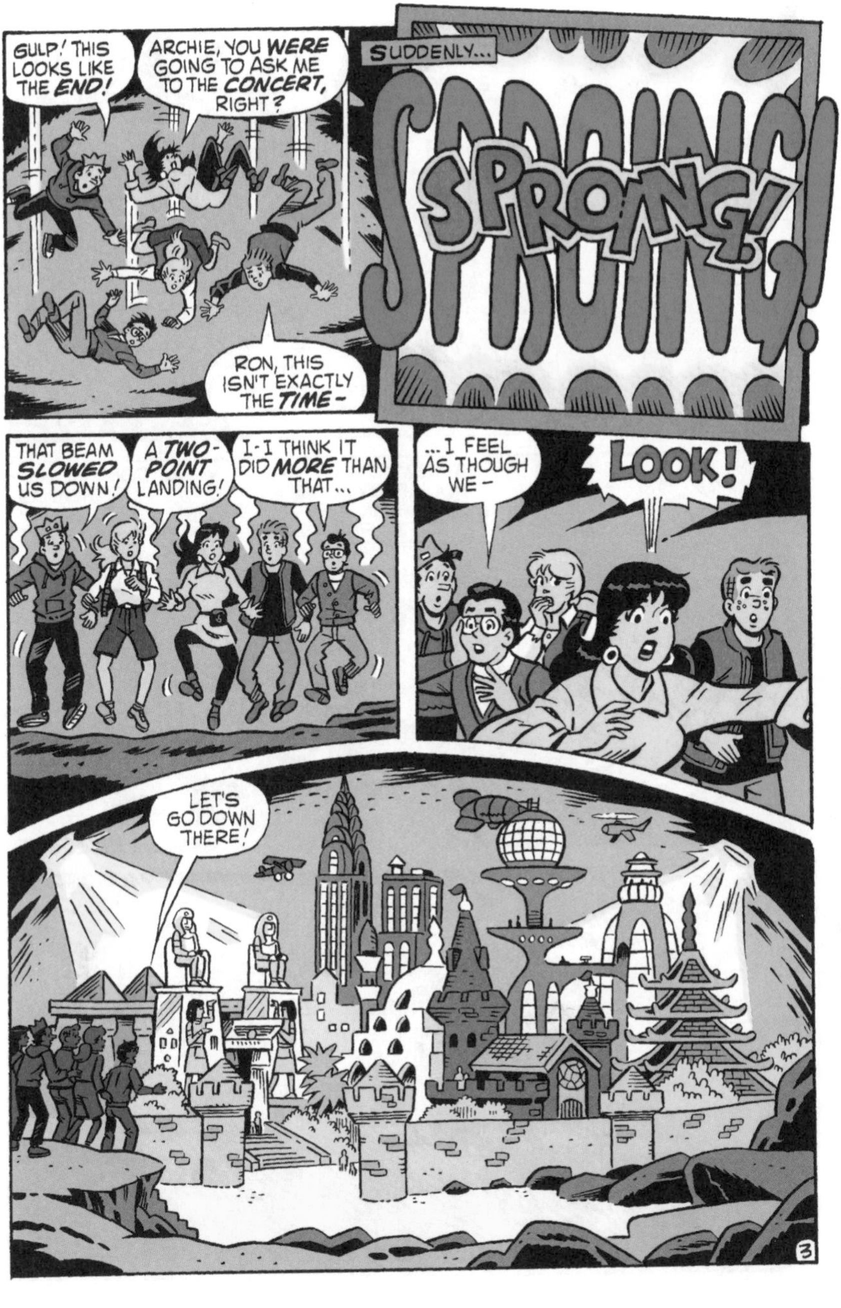
GULP! THIS LOOKS LIKE THE END!
ARCHIE, YOU WERE GOING TO ASK ME TO THE CONCERT, RIGHT?
RON, THIS ISN'T EXACTLY THE TIME -
SUDDENLY...
SPROING!
SPROING!
THAT BEAM SLOWED US DOWN!
A TWO-POINT LANDING!
I-I THINK IT DID MORE THAN THAT...
...I FEEL AS THOUGH WE -
LOOK!
LET'S GO DOWN THERE!
3

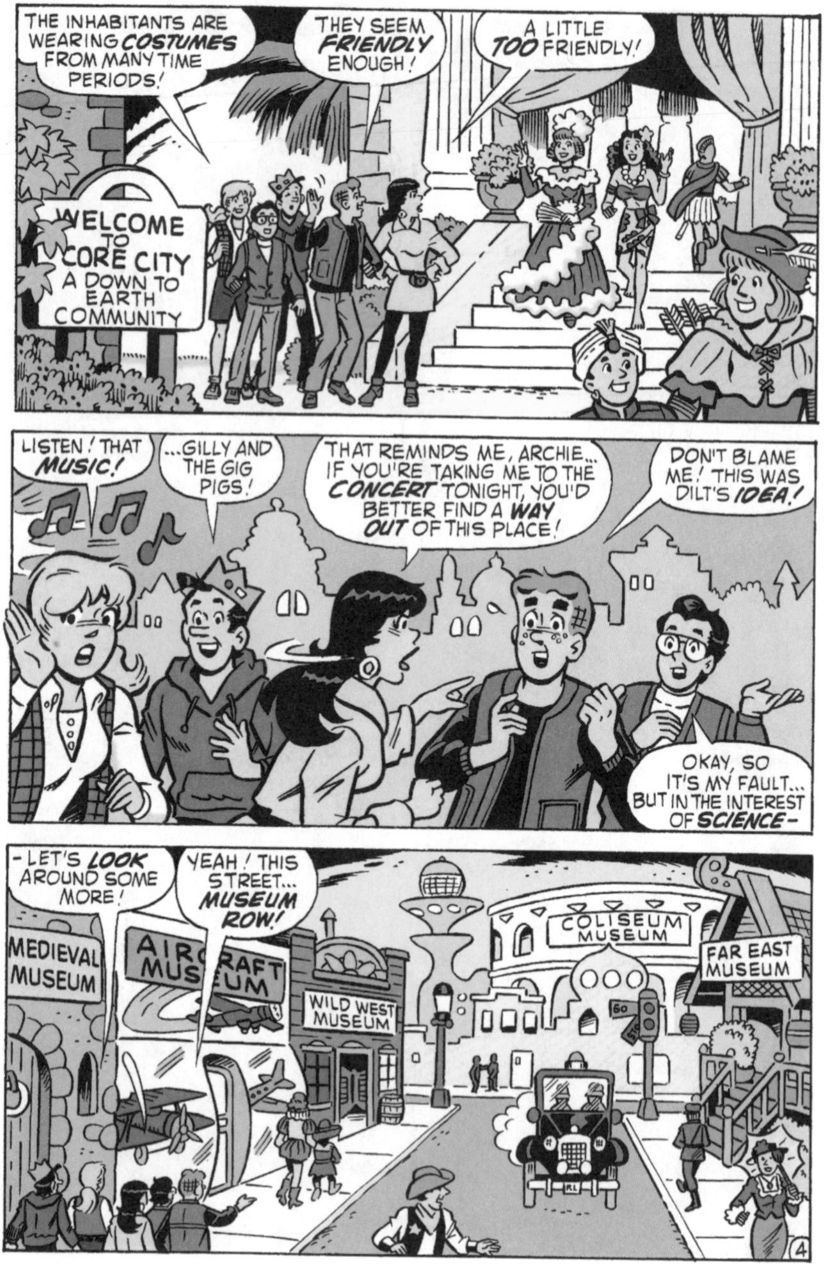
THE INHABITANTS ARE WEARING COSTUMES FROM MANY TIME PERIODS!
THEY SEEM FRIENDLY ENOUGH!
A LITTLE TOO FRIENDLY!
WELCOME TO CORE CITY A DOWN TO EARTH COMMUNITY
LISTEN! THAT MUSIC!
...GILLY AND THE GIG PIGS!
THAT REMINDS ME, ARCHIE... IF YOU'RE TAKING ME TO THE CONCERT TONIGHT, YOU'D BETTER FIND A WAY OUT OF THIS PLACE!
DON'T BLAME ME! THIS WAS DILT'S IDEA!
OKAY, SO IT'S MY FAULT... BUT IN THE INTEREST OF SCIENCE-
-LET'S LOOK AROUND SOME MORE!
YEAH! THIS STREET... MUSEUM ROW!
MEDIEVAL MUSEUM
WILD WEST MUSEUM
COLISEUM MUSEUM
FAR EAST MUSEUM
GO
4

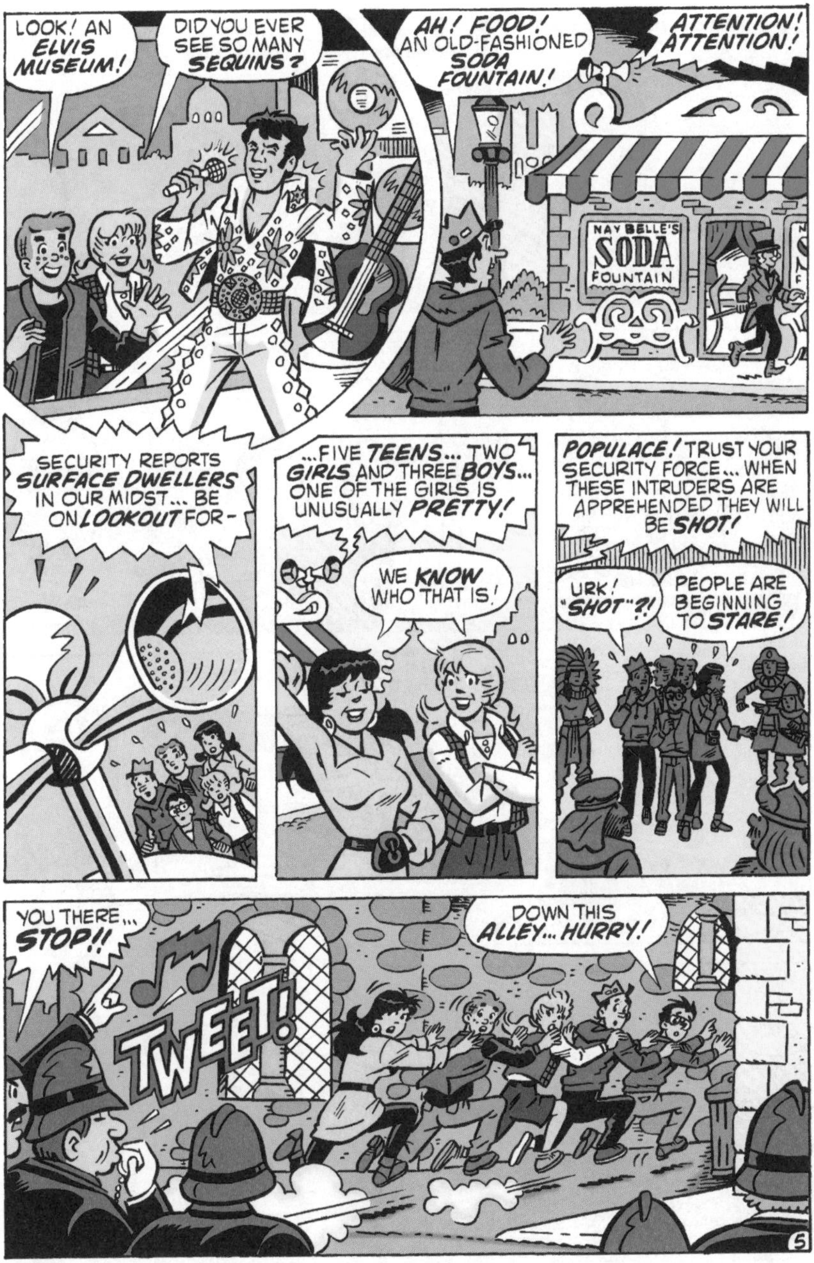
LOOK! AN ELVIS MUSEUM!
DID YOU EVER SEE SO MANY SEQUINS?
AH! FOOD! AN OLD-FASHIONED SODA FOUNTAIN!
NAY BELLE'S SODA FOUNTAIN
ATTENTION! ATTENTION!
SECURITY REPORTS SURFACE DWELLERS IN OUR MIDST... BE ON LOOKOUT FOR-
...FIVE TEENS... TWO GIRLS AND THREE BOYS... ONE OF THE GIRLS IS UNUSUALLY PRETTY!
WE KNOW WHO THAT IS!
POPULACE! TRUST YOUR SECURITY FORCE... WHEN THESE INTRUDERS ARE APPREHENDED THEY WILL BE SHOT!
URK! "SHOT"?!
PEOPLE ARE BEGINNING TO STARE!
YOU THERE... STOP!!
TWEET!
DOWN THIS ALLEY... HURRY!
5

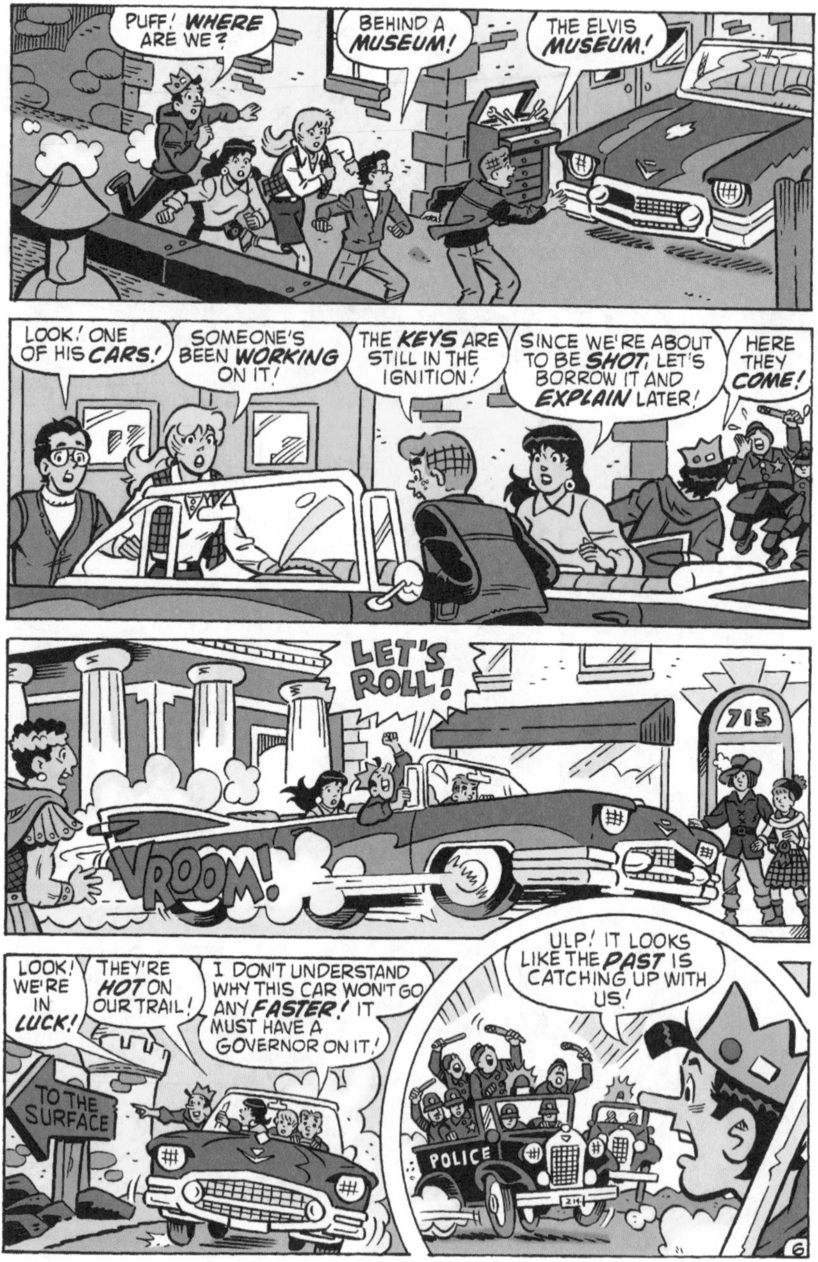
PUFF! WHERE ARE WE?
BEHIND A MUSEUM!
THE ELVIS MUSEUM!
LOOK! ONE OF HIS CARS!
SOMEONE'S BEEN WORKING ON IT!
THE KEYS ARE STILL IN THE IGNITION!
SINCE WE'RE ABOUT TO BE SHOT, LET'S BORROW IT AND EXPLAIN LATER!
HERE THEY COME!
LET'S ROLL!
715
VROOM!
LOOK! WE'RE IN LUCK!
THEY'RE HOT ON OUR TRAIL!
I DON'T UNDERSTAND WHY THIS CAR WON'T GO ANY FASTER! IT MUST HAVE A GOVERNOR ON IT!
TO THE SURFACE
POLICE
ULP! IT LOOKS LIKE THE PAST IS CATCHING UP WITH US!
6

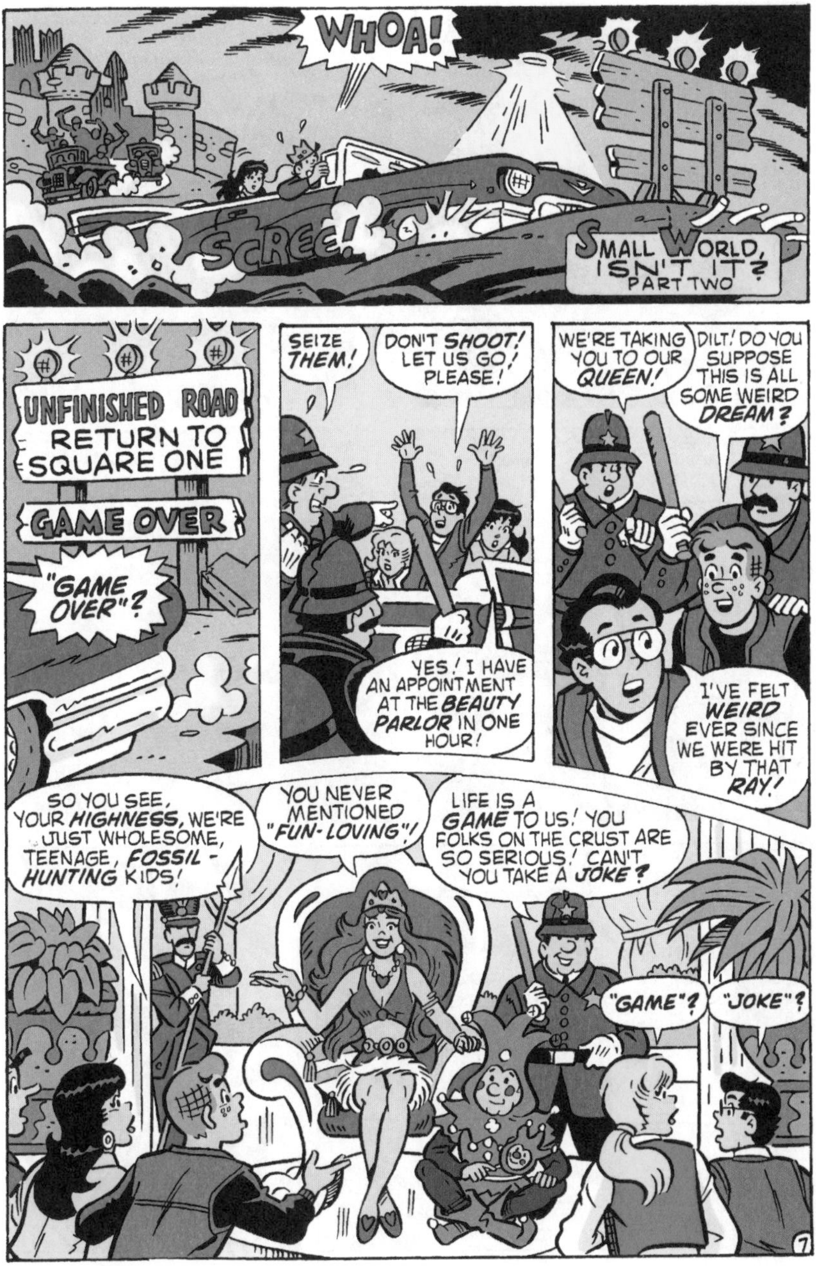
WHOA!
SCREE!
SMALL WORLD, ISN'T IT?
PART TWO
UNFINISHED ROAD
RETURN TO SQUARE ONE
GAME OVER
"GAME OVER"?
SEIZE THEM!
DON'T SHOOT! LET US GO! PLEASE!
YES! I HAVE AN APPOINTMENT AT THE BEAUTY PARLOR IN ONE HOUR!
WE'RE TAKING YOU TO OUR QUEEN!
DILT! DO YOU SUPPOSE THIS IS ALL SOME WEIRD DREAM?
I'VE FELT WEIRD EVER SINCE WE WERE HIT BY THAT RAY!
SO YOU SEE, YOUR HIGHNESS, WE'RE JUST WHOLESOME, TEENAGE, FOSSIL-HUNTING KIDS!
YOU NEVER MENTIONED "FUN-LOVING"!
LIFE IS A GAME TO US! YOU FOLKS ON THE CRUST ARE SO SERIOUS! CAN'T YOU TAKE A JOKE?
"GAME"?
"JOKE"?
7

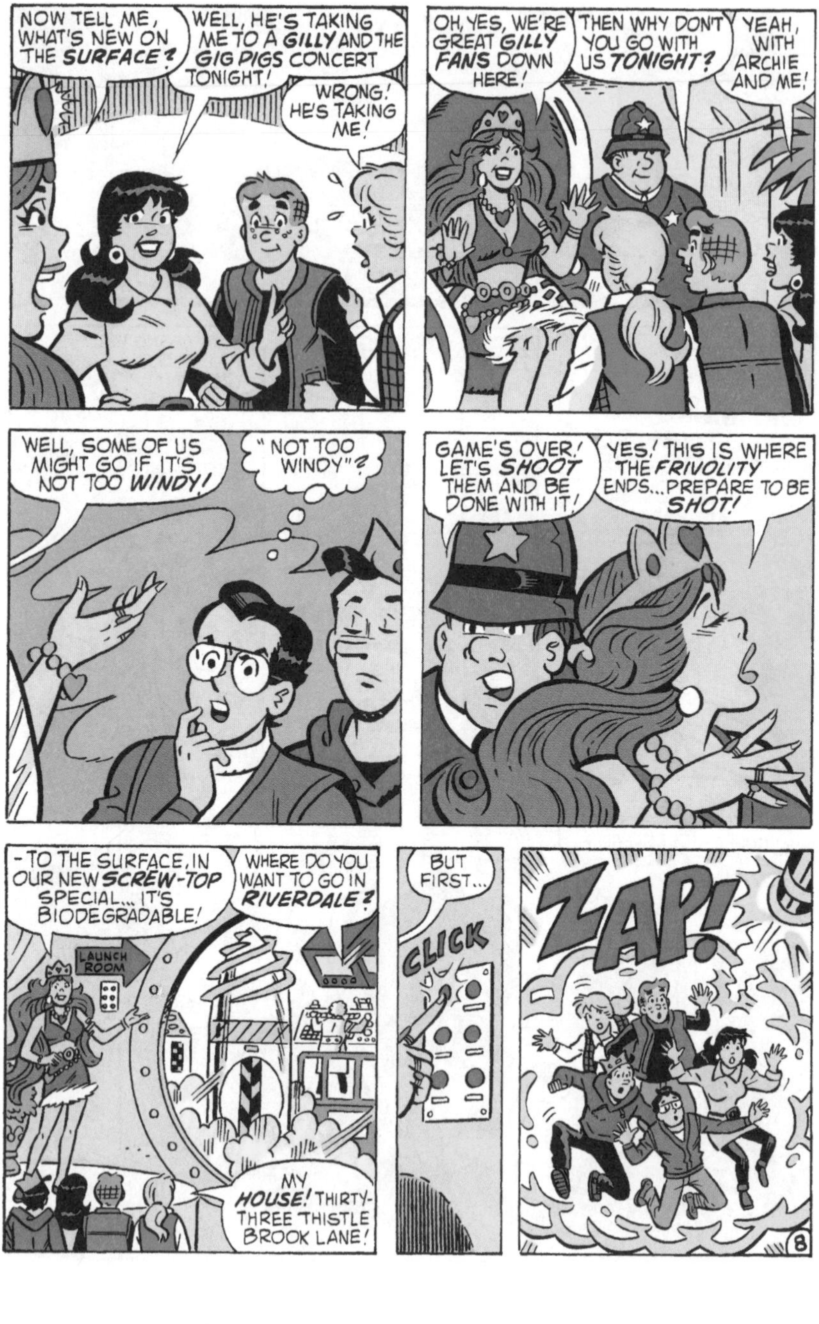
NOW TELL ME, WHAT'S NEW ON THE SURFACE?
WELL, HE'S TAKING ME TO A GILLY AND THE GIG PIGS CONCERT TONIGHT!
WRONG! HE'S TAKING ME!
OH, YES, WE'RE GREAT GILLY FANS DOWN HERE!
THEN WHY DON'T YOU GO WITH US TONIGHT?
YEAH, WITH ARCHIE AND ME!
WELL, SOME OF US MIGHT GO IF IT'S NOT TOO WINDY!
"NOT TOO WINDY"?
GAME'S OVER! LET'S SHOOT THEM AND BE DONE WITH IT!
YES! THIS IS WHERE THE FRIVOLITY ENDS... PREPARE TO BE SHOT!
-TO THE SURFACE, IN OUR NEW SCREW-TOP SPECIAL... IT'S BIODEGRADABLE!
LAUNCH ROOM
WHERE DO YOU WANT TO GO IN RIVERDALE?
MY HOUSE! THIRTY-THREE THISTLE BROOK LANE!
BUT FIRST...
CLICK
ZAP!
8

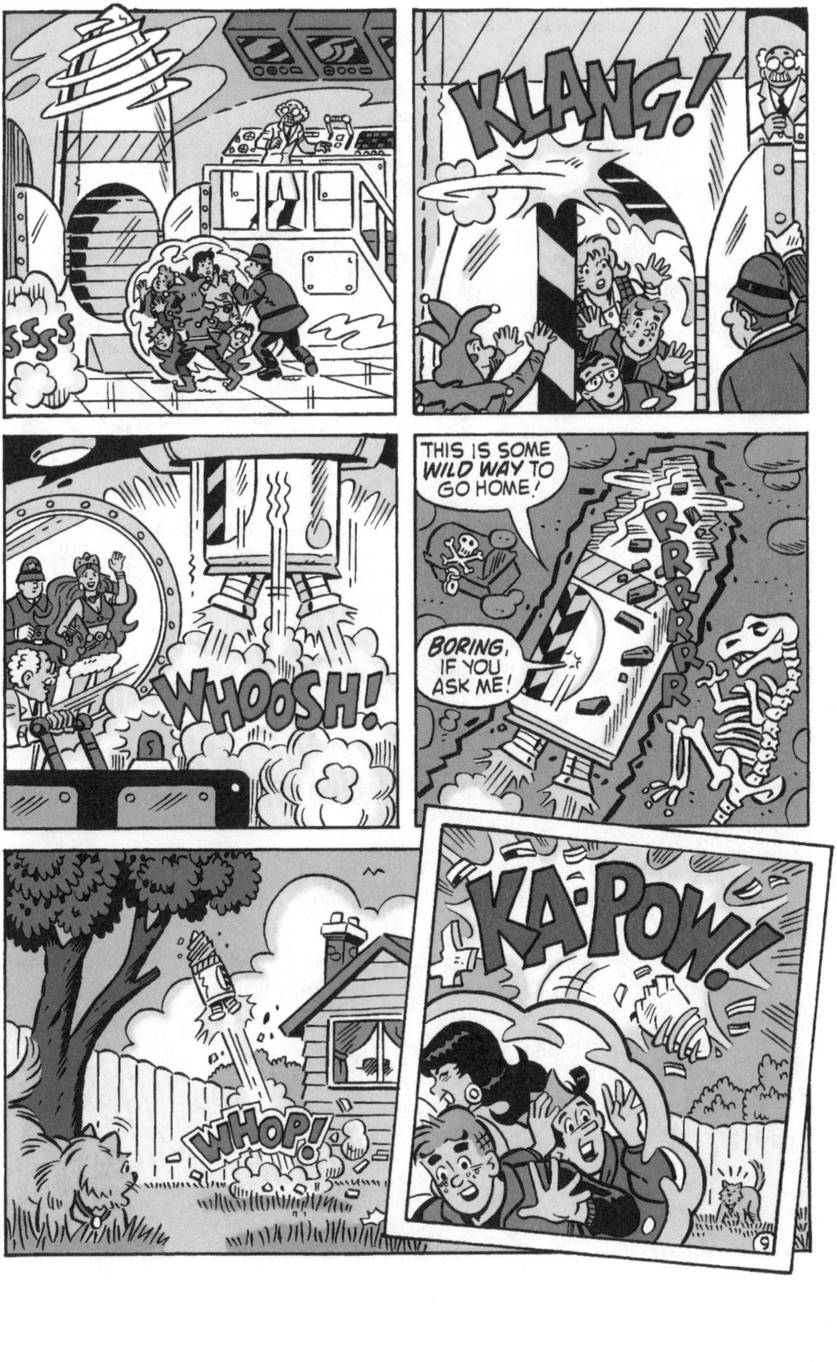
SSSS
KLANG!
THIS IS SOME WILD WAY TO GO HOME!
WHOOSH!
BORING, IF YOU ASK ME!
RRRRRRR
WHOP!
KA-POW!
9

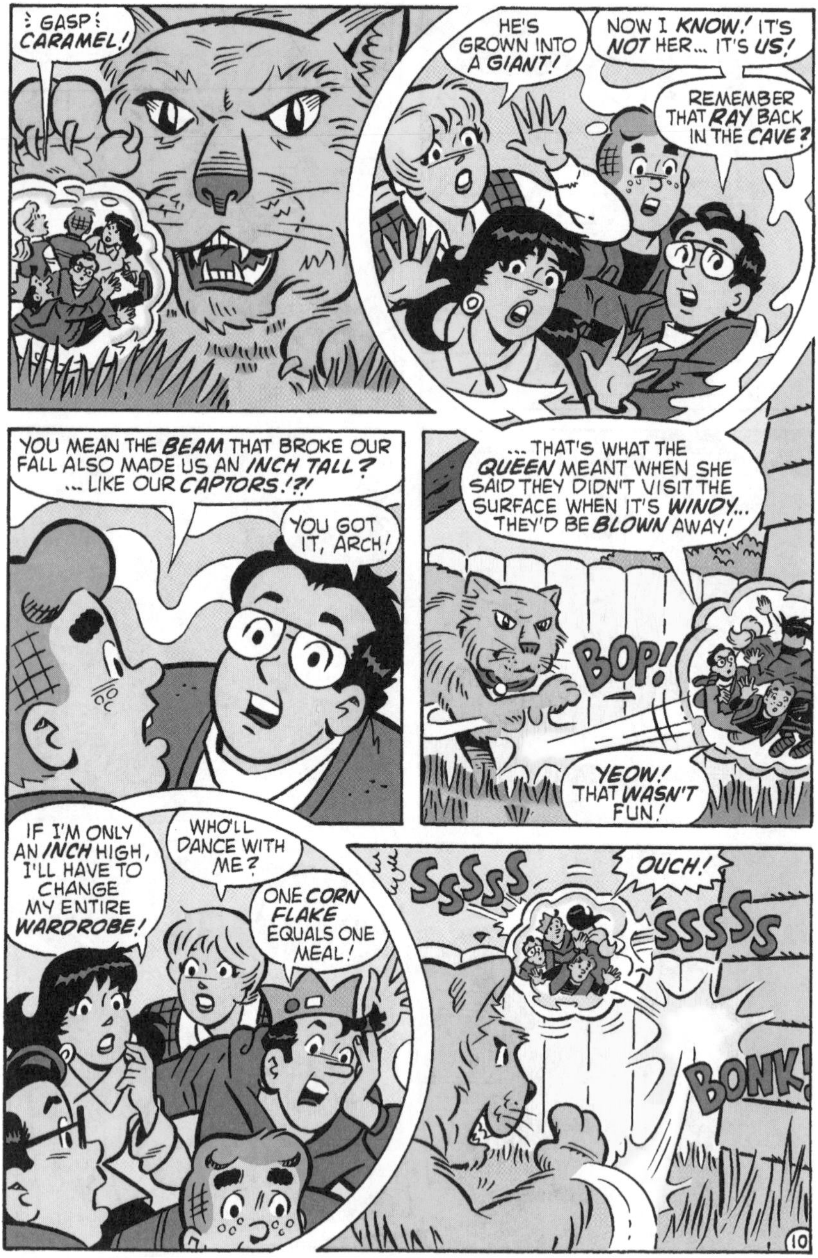
GASP CARAMEL!
HE'S GROWN INTO A GIANT!
NOW I KNOW! IT'S NOT HER... IT'S US!
REMEMBER THAT RAY BACK IN THE CAVE?
YOU MEAN THE BEAM THAT BROKE OUR FALL ALSO MADE US AN INCH TALL? ...LIKE OUR CAPTORS!?!
YOU GOT IT, ARCH!
...THAT'S WHAT THE QUEEN MEANT WHEN SHE SAID THEY DIDN'T VISIT THE SURFACE WHEN IT'S WINDY... THEY'D BE BLOWN AWAY!
BOP!
YEOW! THAT WASN'T FUN!
IF I'M ONLY AN INCH HIGH, I'LL HAVE TO CHANGE MY ENTIRE WARDROBE!
WHO'LL DANCE WITH ME?
ONE CORN FLAKE EQUALS ONE MEAL!
SSSSS
OUCH!
SSSSS
BONK!
10

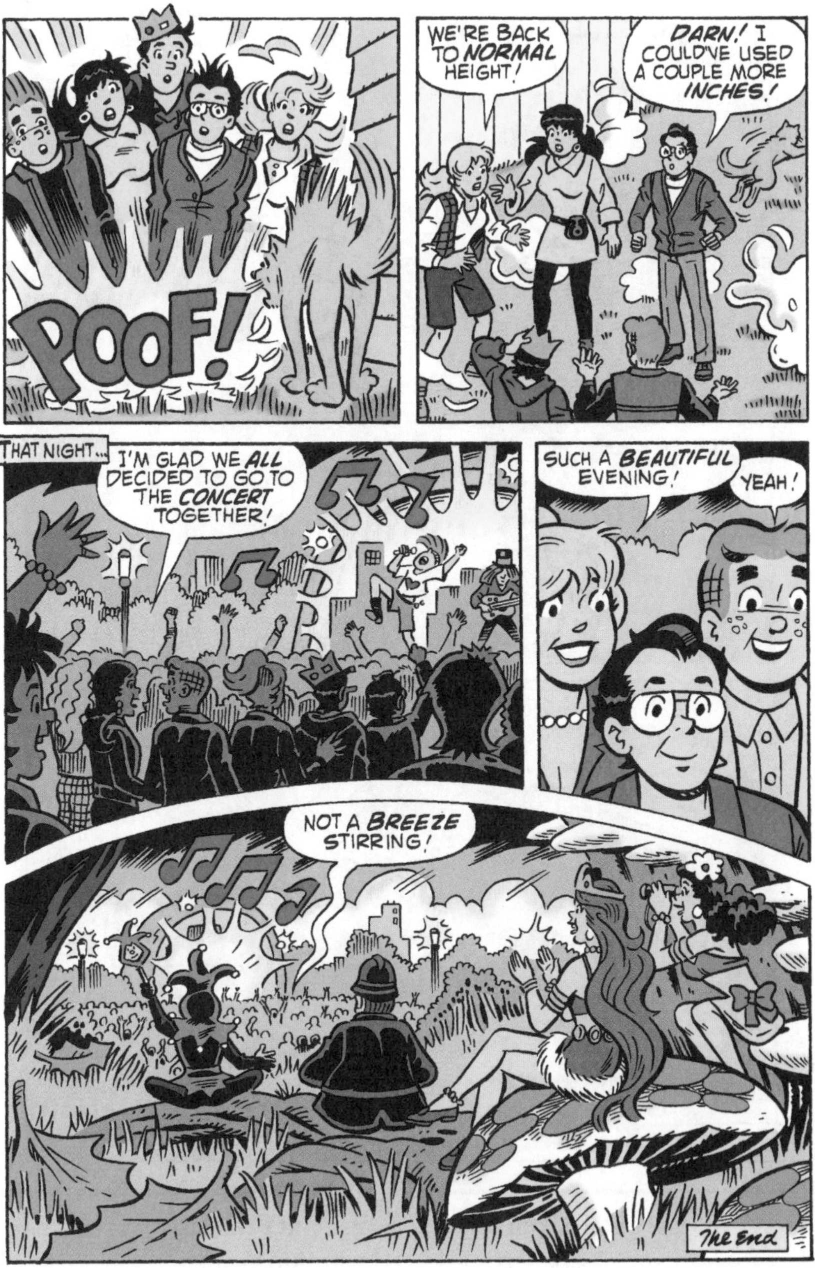
POOF!
WE'RE BACK TO NORMAL HEIGHT!
DARN! I COULD'VE USED A COUPLE MORE INCHES!
THAT NIGHT...
I'M GLAD WE ALL DECIDED TO GO TO THE CONCERT TOGETHER!
SUCH A BEAUTIFUL EVENING!
YEAH!
NOT A BREEZE STIRRING!
The End

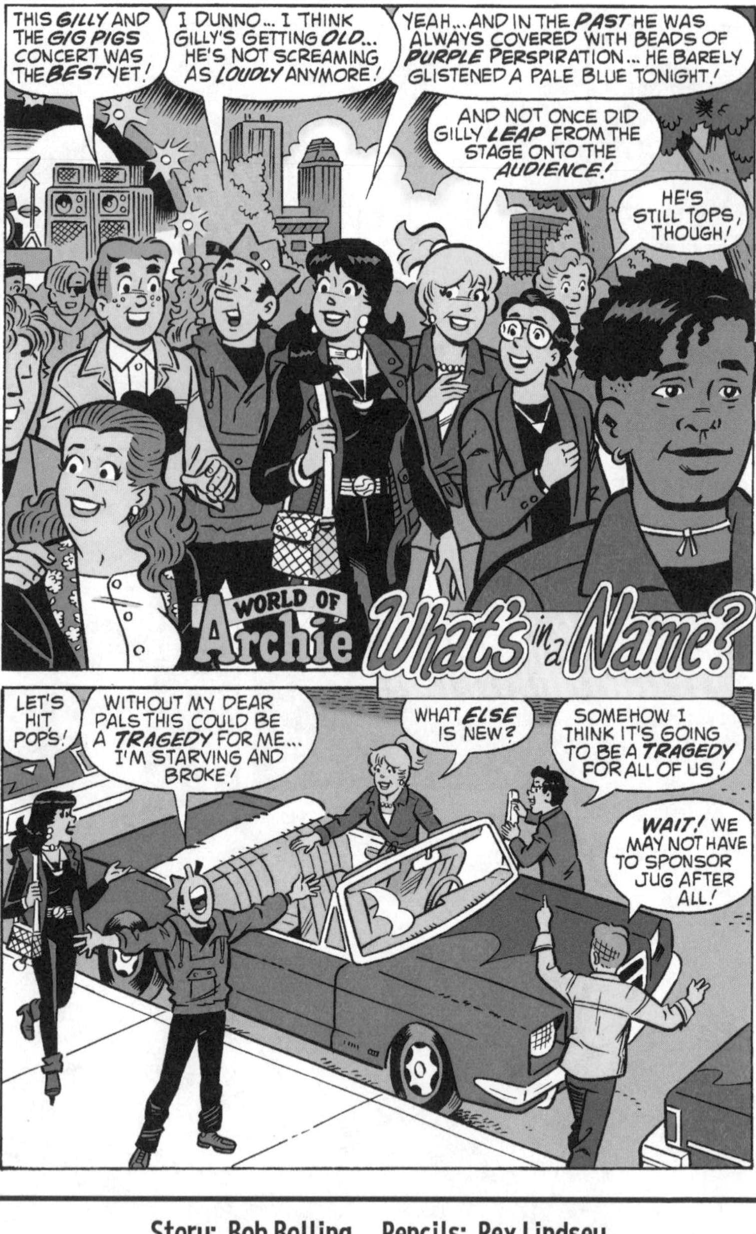
THIS GILLY AND THE GIG PIGS CONCERT WAS THE BEST YET!
I DUNNO... I THINK GILLY'S GETTING OLD... HE'S NOT SCREAMING AS LOUDLY ANYMORE!
YEAH... AND IN THE PAST HE WAS ALWAYS COVERED WITH BEADS OF PURPLE PERSPIRATION... HE BARELY GLISTENED A PALE BLUE TONIGHT!
AND NOT ONCE DID GILLY LEAP FROM THE STAGE ONTO THE AUDIENCE!
HE'S STILL TOPS, THOUGH!
WORLD OF Archie
What's in a Name?
LET'S HIT POP'S!
WITHOUT MY DEAR PALS THIS COULD BE A TRAGEDY FOR ME... I'M STARVING AND BROKE!
WHAT ELSE IS NEW?
SOMEHOW I THINK IT'S GOING TO BE A TRAGEDY FOR ALL OF US!
WAIT! WE MAY NOT HAVE TO SPONSOR JUG AFTER ALL!

Story: Bob Bolling Pencils: Rex Lindsey
Inks: Rudy Lapick Letters: Bill Yoshida

Originally printed in WORLD OF ARCHIE #9, JUNE 1994

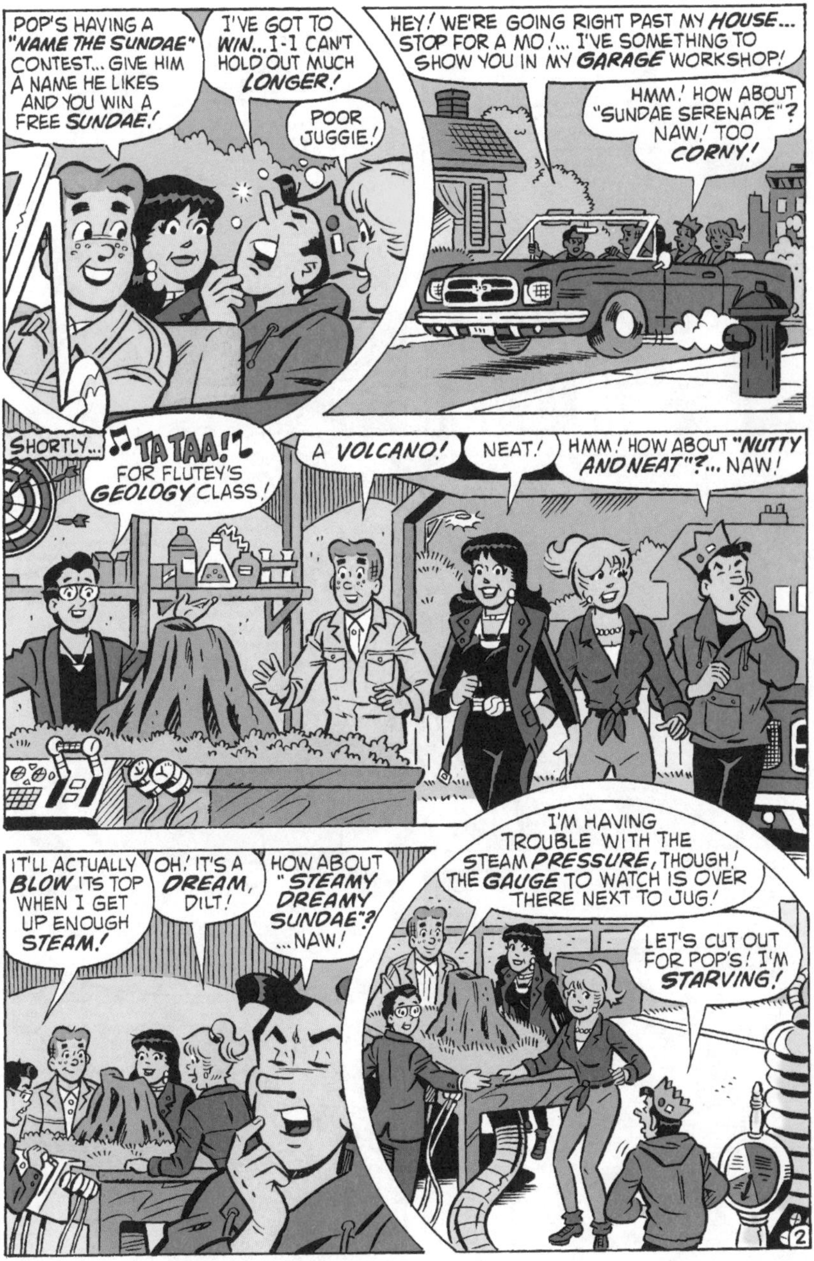
POP'S HAVING A "NAME THE SUNDAE" CONTEST... GIVE HIM A NAME HE LIKES AND YOU WIN A FREE SUNDAE!
I'VE GOT TO WIN... I-I CAN'T HOLD OUT MUCH LONGER!
POOR JUGGIE!
HEY! WE'RE GOING RIGHT PAST MY HOUSE... STOP FOR A MO!... I'VE SOMETHING TO SHOW YOU IN MY GARAGE WORKSHOP!
HMM! HOW ABOUT "SUNDAE SERENADE"? NAW! TOO CORNY!
SHORTLY...
TATAA! FOR FLUTEY'S GEOLOGY CLASS!
A VOLCANO!
NEAT!
HMM! HOW ABOUT "NUTTY AND NEAT"?... NAW!
IT'LL ACTUALLY BLOW ITS TOP WHEN I GET UP ENOUGH STEAM!
OH! IT'S A DREAM, DILT!
HOW ABOUT "STEAMY DREAMY SUNDAE"? ...NAW!
I'M HAVING TROUBLE WITH THE STEAM PRESSURE, THOUGH! THE GAUGE TO WATCH IS OVER THERE NEXT TO JUG!
LET'S CUT OUT FOR POP'S! I'M STARVING!
2

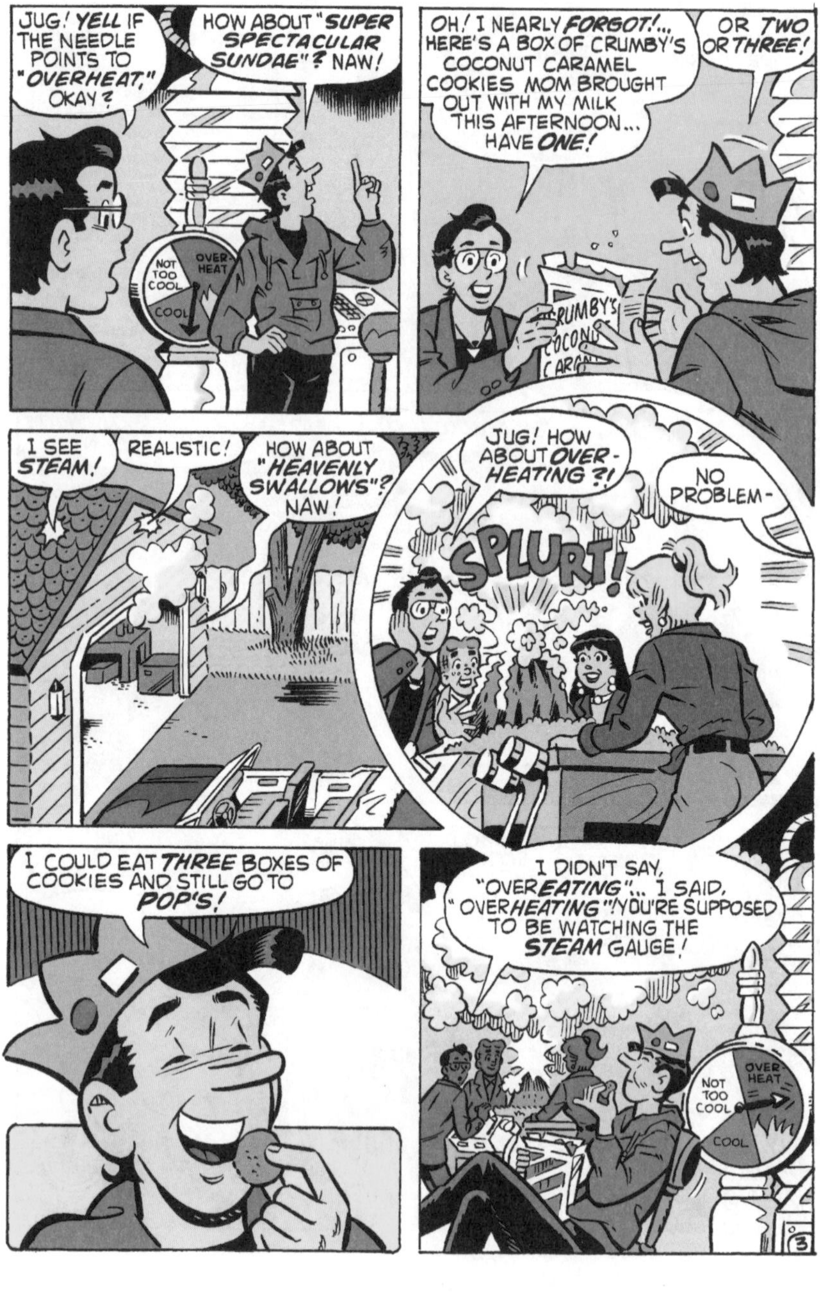
JUG! YELL IF THE NEEDLE POINTS TO "OVERHEAT," OKAY?
HOW ABOUT "SUPER SPECTACULAR SUNDAE"? NAW!
NOT TOO COOL
OVER-HEAT
COOL
OH! I NEARLY FORGOT!... HERE'S A BOX OF CRUMBY'S COCONUT CARAMEL COOKIES MOM BROUGHT OUT WITH MY MILK THIS AFTERNOON... HAVE ONE!
OR TWO OR THREE!
I SEE STEAM!
REALISTIC!
HOW ABOUT "HEAVENLY SWALLOWS"? NAW!
JUG! HOW ABOUT OVER-HEATING?!
NO PROBLEM-
SPLURT!
I COULD EAT THREE BOXES OF COOKIES AND STILL GO TO POP'S!
I DIDN'T SAY, "OVEREATING"... I SAID, "OVERHEATING"! YOU'RE SUPPOSED TO BE WATCHING THE STEAM GAUGE!
NOT TOO COOL
OVER-HEAT
COOL
3

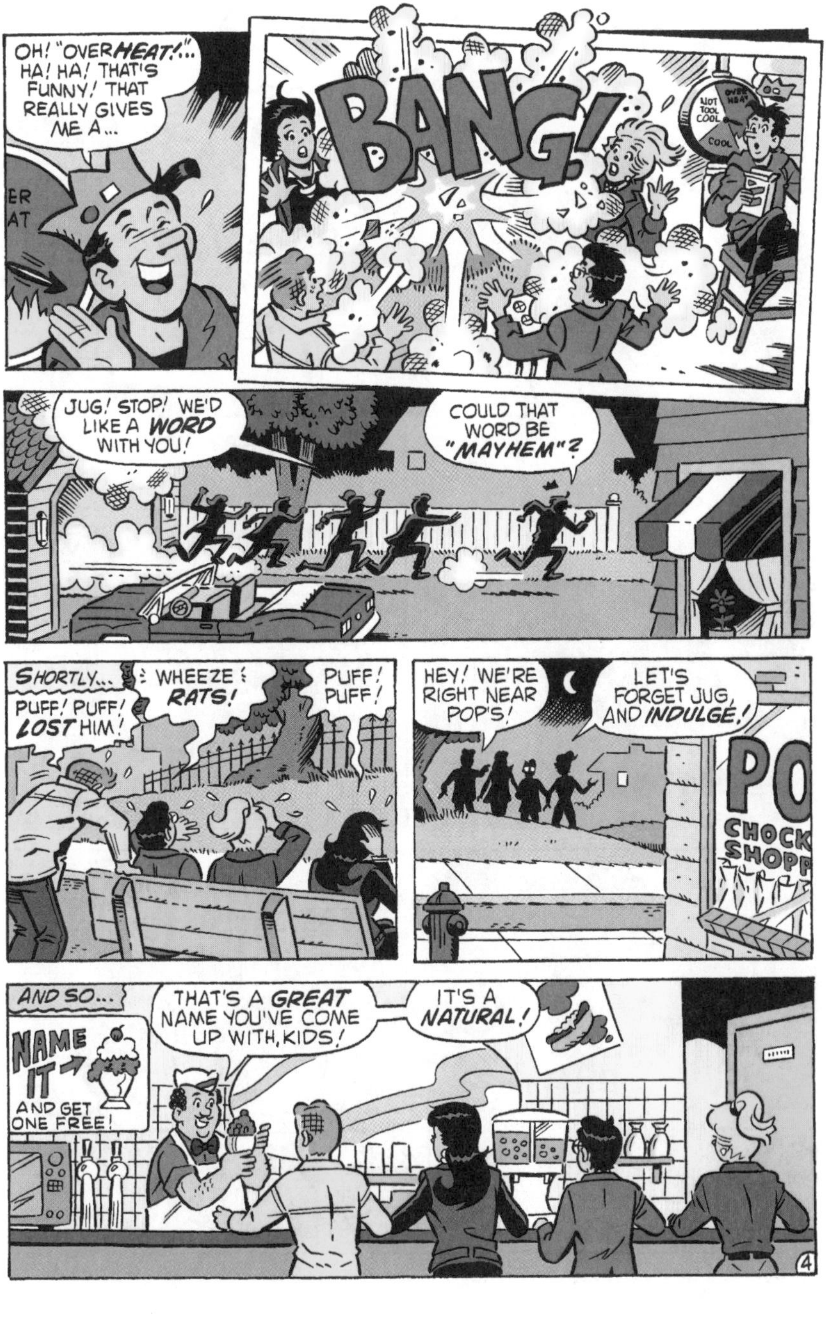
OH! "OVERHEAT!"... HA! HA! THAT'S FUNNY! THAT REALLY GIVES ME A...
BANG!
NOT TOO COOL
OVER HEAT
COOL
JUG! STOP! WE'D LIKE A WORD WITH YOU!
COULD THAT WORD BE "MAYHEM"?
SHORTLY...
PUFF! PUFF! LOST HIM!
WHEEZE RATS!
PUFF! PUFF!
HEY! WE'RE RIGHT NEAR POP'S!
LET'S FORGET JUG, AND INDULGE!
PO
CHOCK
SHOPP
AND SO...
NAME IT AND GET ONE FREE!
THAT'S A GREAT NAME YOU'VE COME UP WITH, KIDS!
IT'S A NATURAL!
4

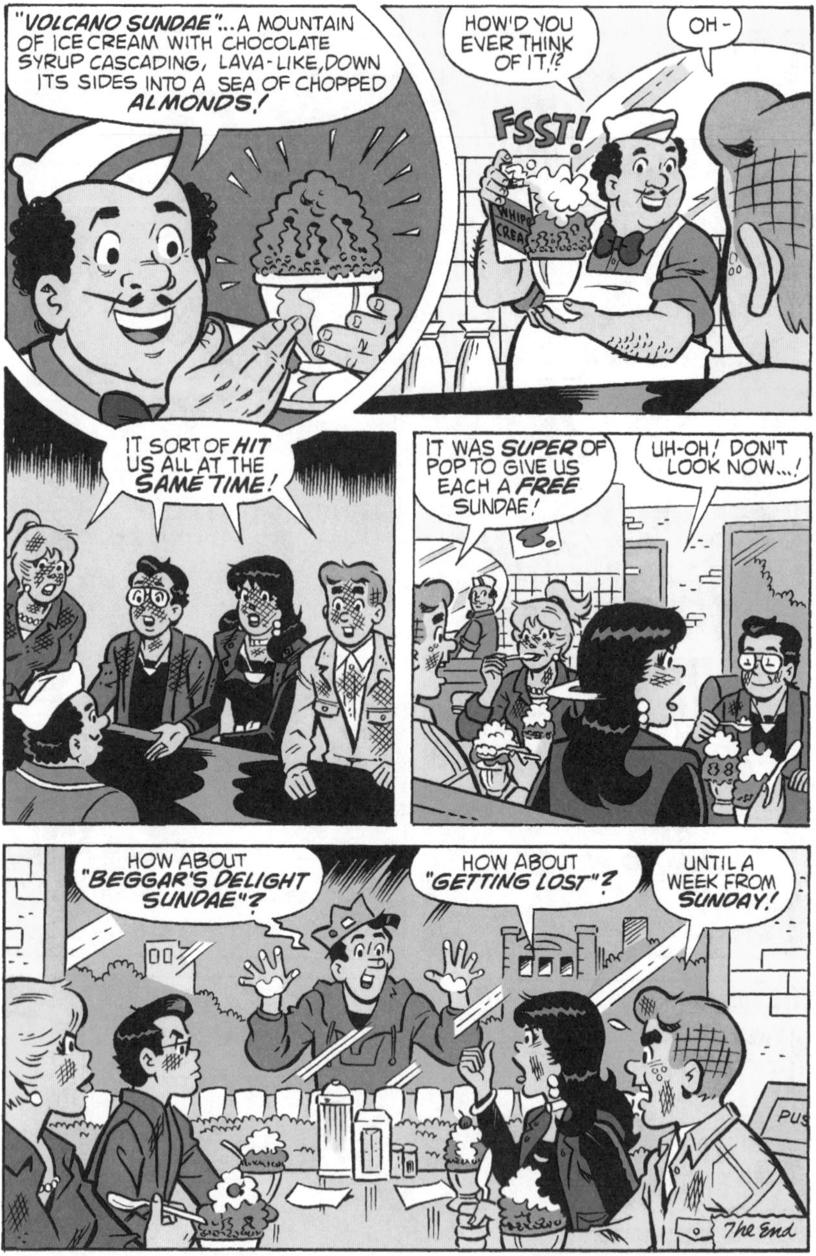
"VOLCANO SUNDAE"...A MOUNTAIN OF ICE CREAM WITH CHOCOLATE SYRUP CASCADING, LAVA-LIKE, DOWN ITS SIDES INTO A SEA OF CHOPPED ALMONDS!
HOW'D YOU EVER THINK OF IT!?
OH -
FSST!
WHIPP
CREA
IT SORT OF HIT US ALL AT THE SAME TIME!
IT WAS SUPER OF POP TO GIVE US EACH A FREE SUNDAE!
UH-OH! DON'T LOOK NOW...!
HOW ABOUT "BEGGAR'S DELIGHT SUNDAE"?
HOW ABOUT "GETTING LOST"?
UNTIL A WEEK FROM SUNDAY!
PUS
The End

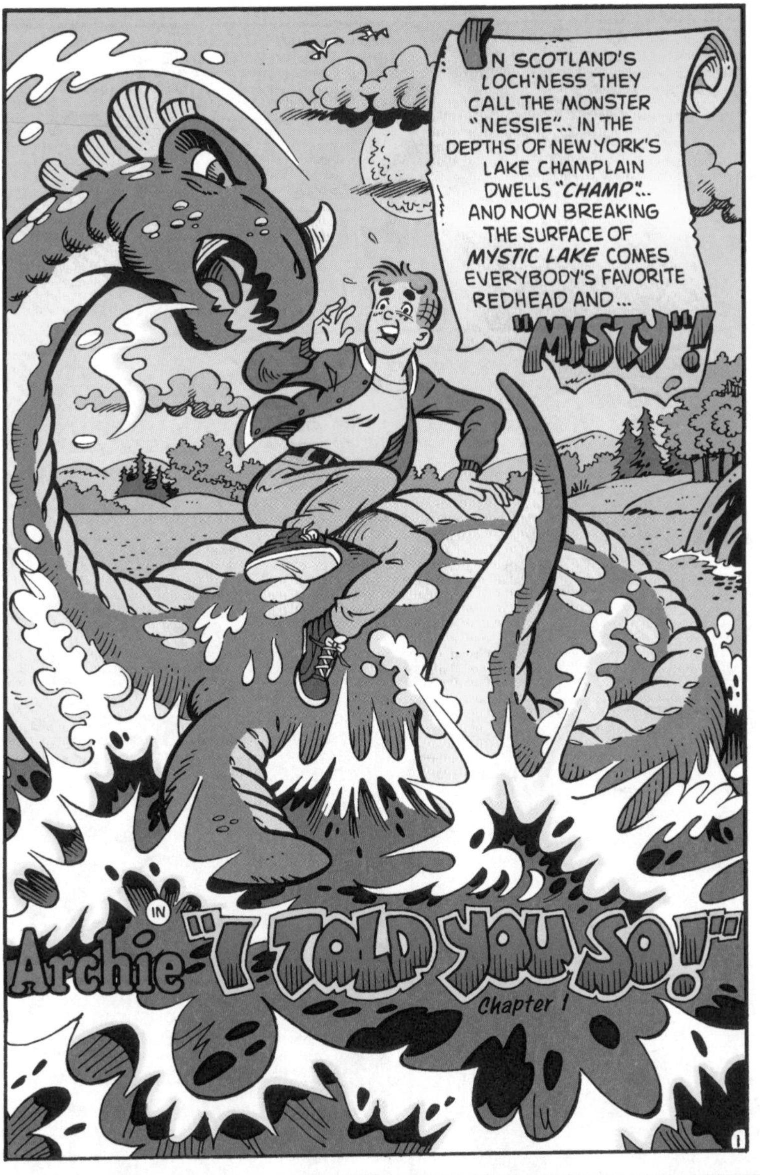
IN SCOTLAND'S LOCH NESS THEY CALL THE MONSTER "NESSIE"... IN THE DEPTHS OF NEW YORK'S LAKE CHAMPLAIN DWELLS "CHAMP"... AND NOW BREAKING THE SURFACE OF MYSTIC LAKE COMES EVERYBODY'S FAVORITE REDHEAD AND...
"MISTY"!
Archie IN "I TOLD YOU SO!"
Chapter 1

Story: Bob Bolling Pencils, Inks & Colors: Rex Lindsey
Letters: Bill Yoshida

Originally printed in WORLD OF ARCHIE #10, JULY 1994

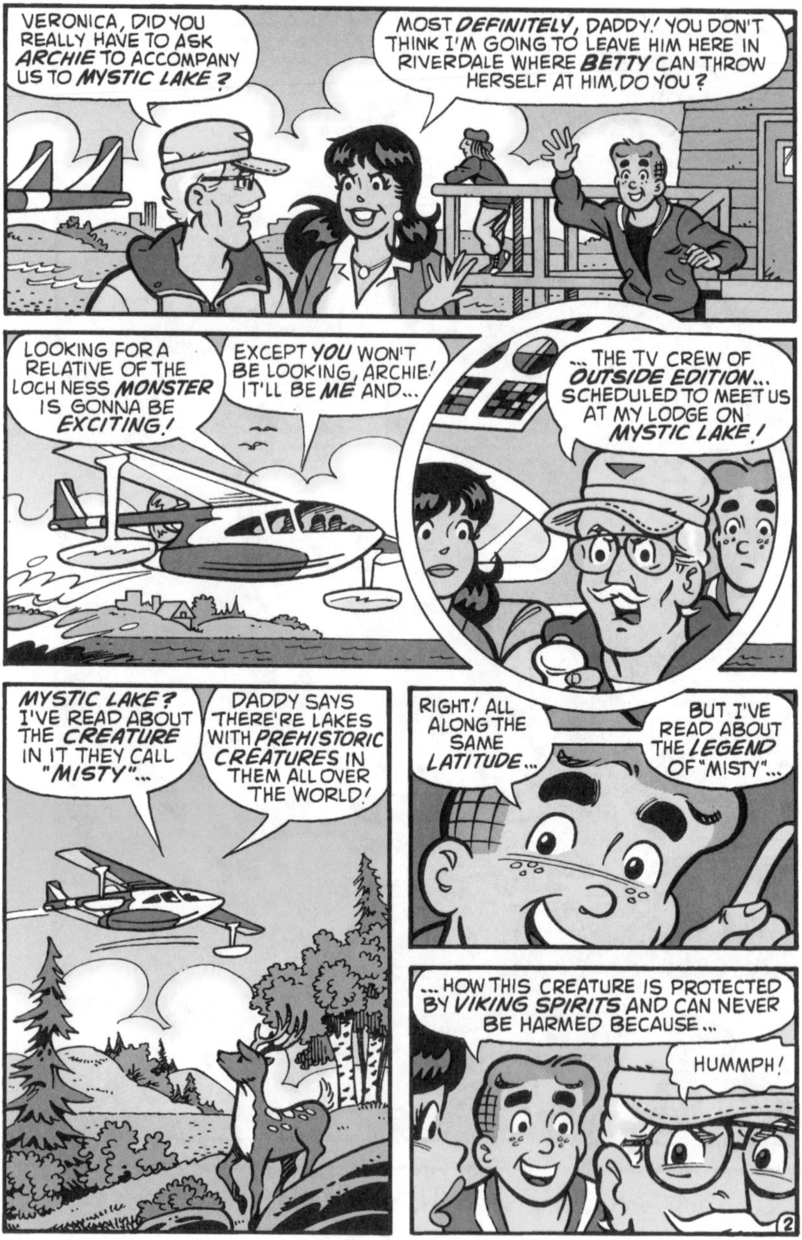
VERONICA, DID YOU REALLY HAVE TO ASK ARCHIE TO ACCOMPANY US TO MYSTIC LAKE?
MOST DEFINITELY, DADDY! YOU DON'T THINK I'M GOING TO LEAVE HIM HERE IN RIVERDALE WHERE BETTY CAN THROW HERSELF AT HIM, DO YOU?
LOOKING FOR A RELATIVE OF THE LOCH NESS MONSTER IS GONNA BE EXCITING!
EXCEPT YOU WON'T BE LOOKING, ARCHIE! IT'LL BE ME AND...
...THE TV CREW OF OUTSIDE EDITION... SCHEDULED TO MEET US AT MY LODGE ON MYSTIC LAKE!
MYSTIC LAKE? I'VE READ ABOUT THE CREATURE IN IT THEY CALL "MISTY"...
DADDY SAYS THERE'RE LAKES WITH PREHISTORIC CREATURES IN THEM ALL OVER THE WORLD!
RIGHT! ALL ALONG THE SAME LATITUDE...
BUT I'VE READ ABOUT THE LEGEND OF "MISTY"...
...HOW THIS CREATURE IS PROTECTED BY VIKING SPIRITS AND CAN NEVER BE HARMED BECAUSE...
HUMMPH!
2

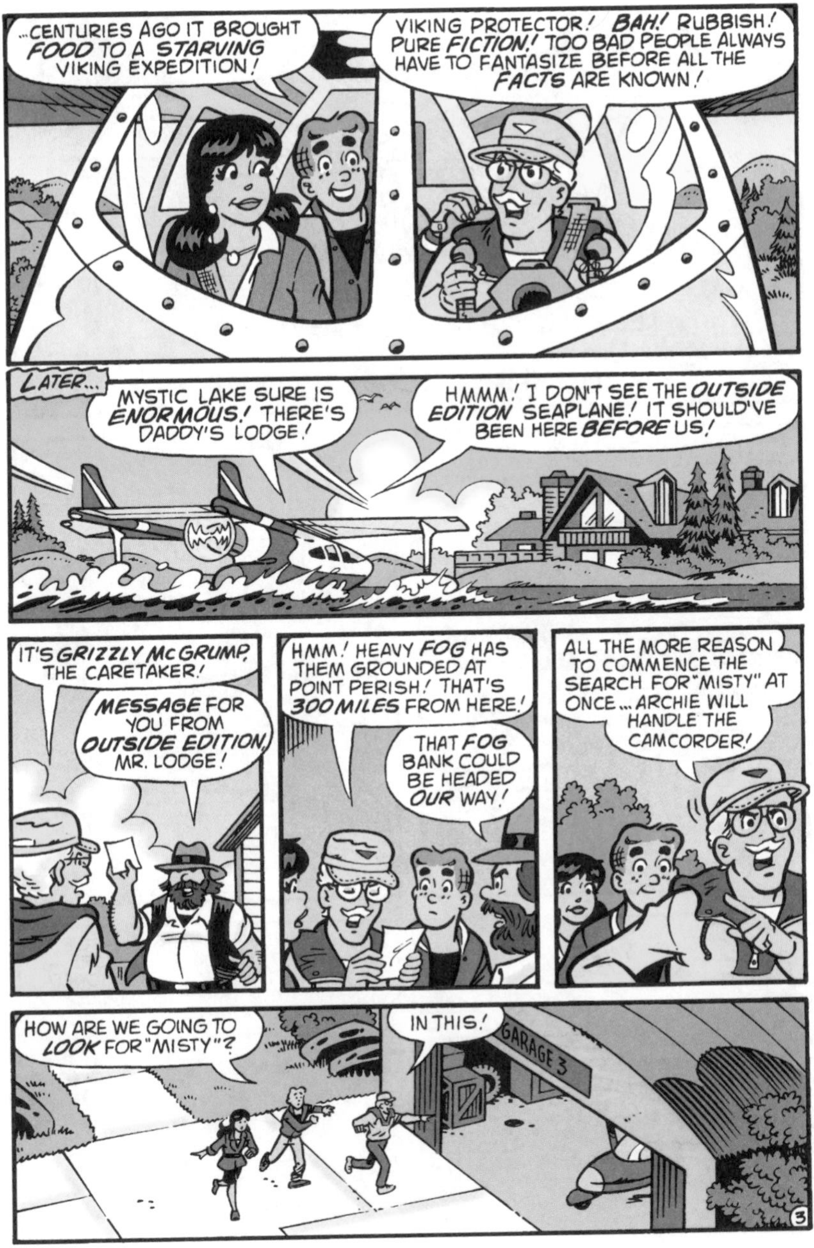
...CENTURIES AGO IT BROUGHT FOOD TO A STARVING VIKING EXPEDITION!
VIKING PROTECTOR! BAH! RUBBISH! PURE FICTION! TOO BAD PEOPLE ALWAYS HAVE TO FANTASIZE BEFORE ALL THE FACTS ARE KNOWN!
LATER...
MYSTIC LAKE SURE IS ENORMOUS! THERE'S DADDY'S LODGE!
HMMM! I DON'T SEE THE OUTSIDE EDITION SEAPLANE! IT SHOULD'VE BEEN HERE BEFORE US!
IT'S GRIZZLY McGRUMP, THE CARETAKER!
MESSAGE FOR YOU FROM OUTSIDE EDITION, MR. LODGE!
HMM! HEAVY FOG HAS THEM GROUNDED AT POINT PERISH! THAT'S 300 MILES FROM HERE!
THAT FOG BANK COULD BE HEADED OUR WAY!
ALL THE MORE REASON TO COMMENCE THE SEARCH FOR "MISTY" AT ONCE ... ARCHIE WILL HANDLE THE CAMCORDER!
HOW ARE WE GOING TO LOOK FOR "MISTY"?
IN THIS!
GARAGE 3
3

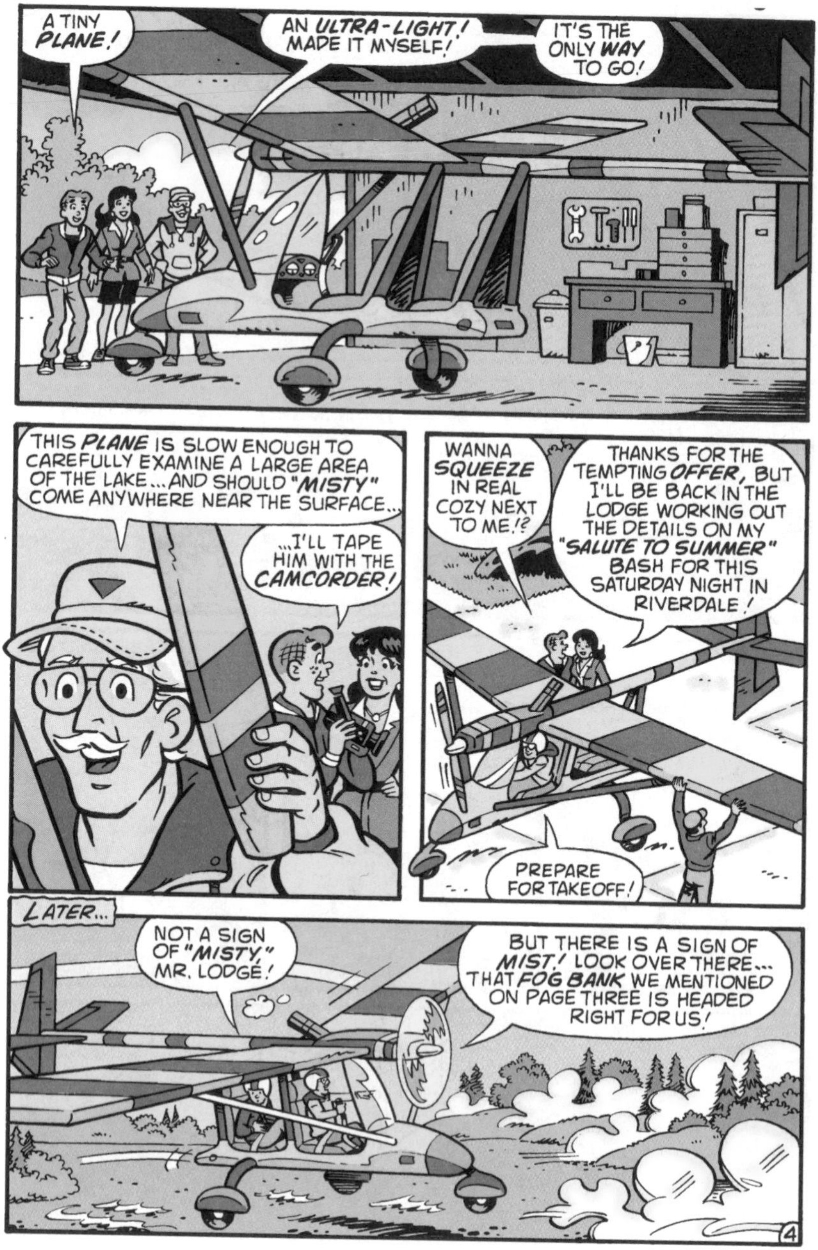
A TINY PLANE!
AN ULTRA-LIGHT! MADE IT MYSELF!
IT'S THE ONLY WAY TO GO!
THIS PLANE IS SLOW ENOUGH TO CAREFULLY EXAMINE A LARGE AREA OF THE LAKE... AND SHOULD "MISTY" COME ANYWHERE NEAR THE SURFACE...
...I'LL TAPE HIM WITH THE CAMCORDER!
WANNA SQUEEZE IN REAL COZY NEXT TO ME!?
THANKS FOR THE TEMPTING OFFER, BUT I'LL BE BACK IN THE LODGE WORKING OUT THE DETAILS ON MY "SALUTE TO SUMMER" BASH FOR THIS SATURDAY NIGHT IN RIVERDALE!
PREPARE FOR TAKEOFF!
LATER...
NOT A SIGN OF "MISTY," MR. LODGE!
BUT THERE IS A SIGN OF MIST! LOOK OVER THERE... THAT FOG BANK WE MENTIONED ON PAGE THREE IS HEADED RIGHT FOR US!
4

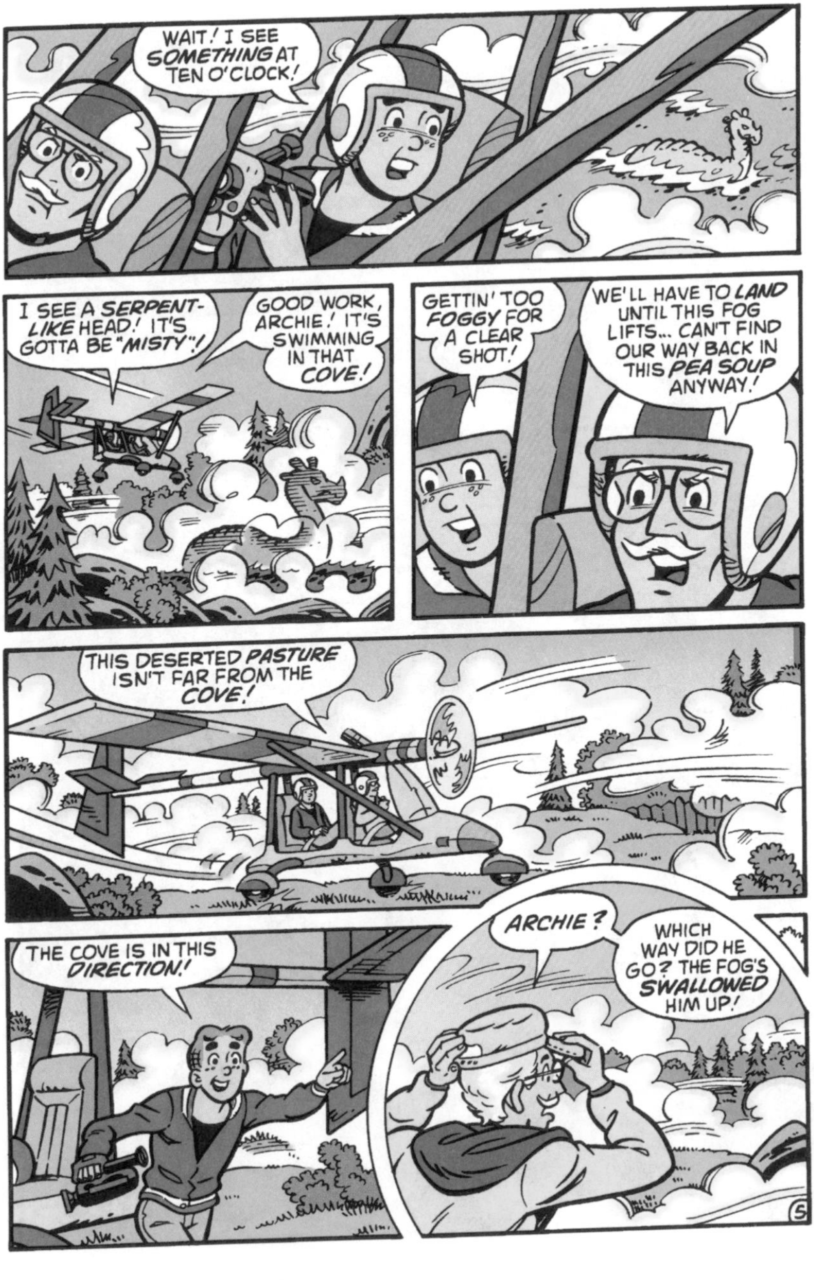
WAIT! I SEE SOMETHING AT TEN O'CLOCK!
I SEE A SERPENT-LIKE HEAD! IT'S GOTTA BE "MISTY"!
GOOD WORK, ARCHIE! IT'S SWIMMING IN THAT COVE!
GETTIN' TOO FOGGY FOR A CLEAR SHOT!
WE'LL HAVE TO LAND UNTIL THIS FOG LIFTS... CAN'T FIND OUR WAY BACK IN THIS PEA SOUP ANYWAY!
THIS DESERTED PASTURE ISN'T FAR FROM THE COVE!
THE COVE IS IN THIS DIRECTION!
ARCHIE?
WHICH WAY DID HE GO? THE FOG'S SWALLOWED HIM UP!
5

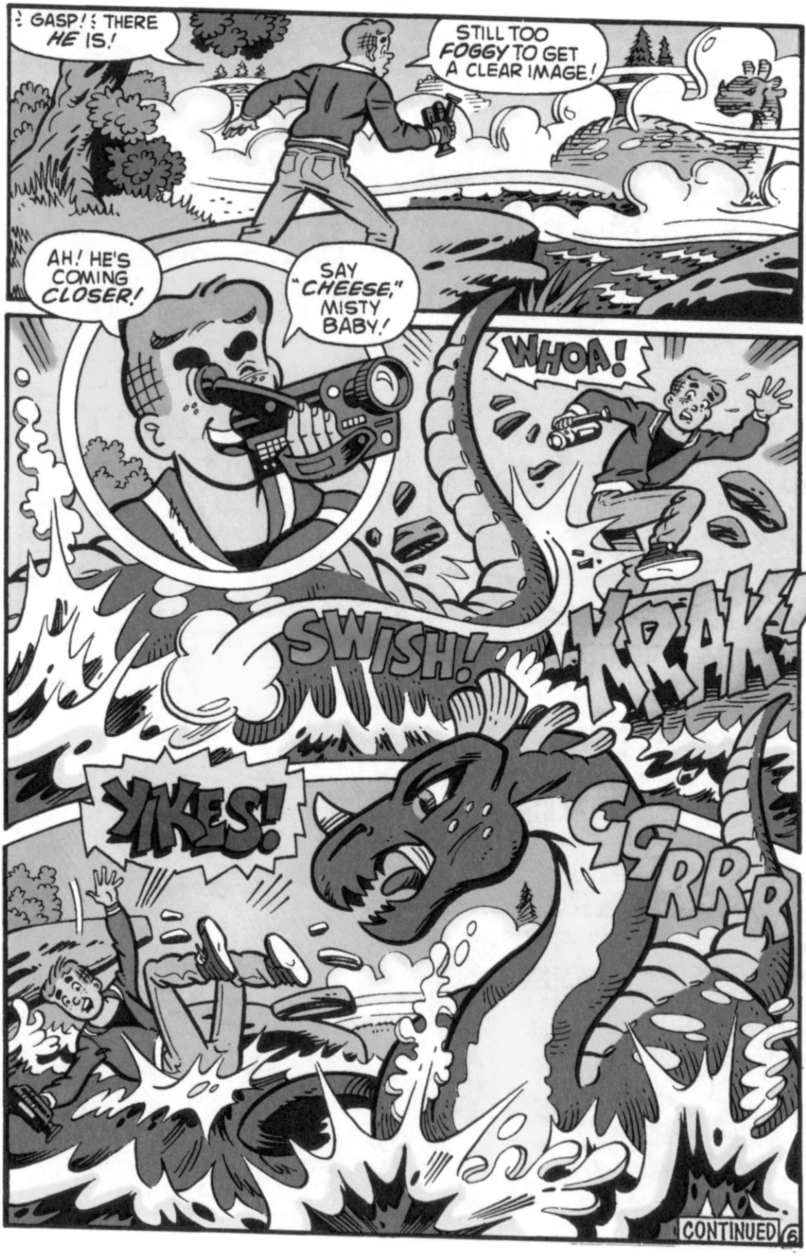
GASP! THERE HE IS!
STILL TOO FOGGY TO GET A CLEAR IMAGE!
AH! HE'S COMING CLOSER!
SAY "CHEESE," MISTY BABY!
WHOA!
SWISH!
KRAK!
YIKES!
GGRRRR
CONTINUED 6

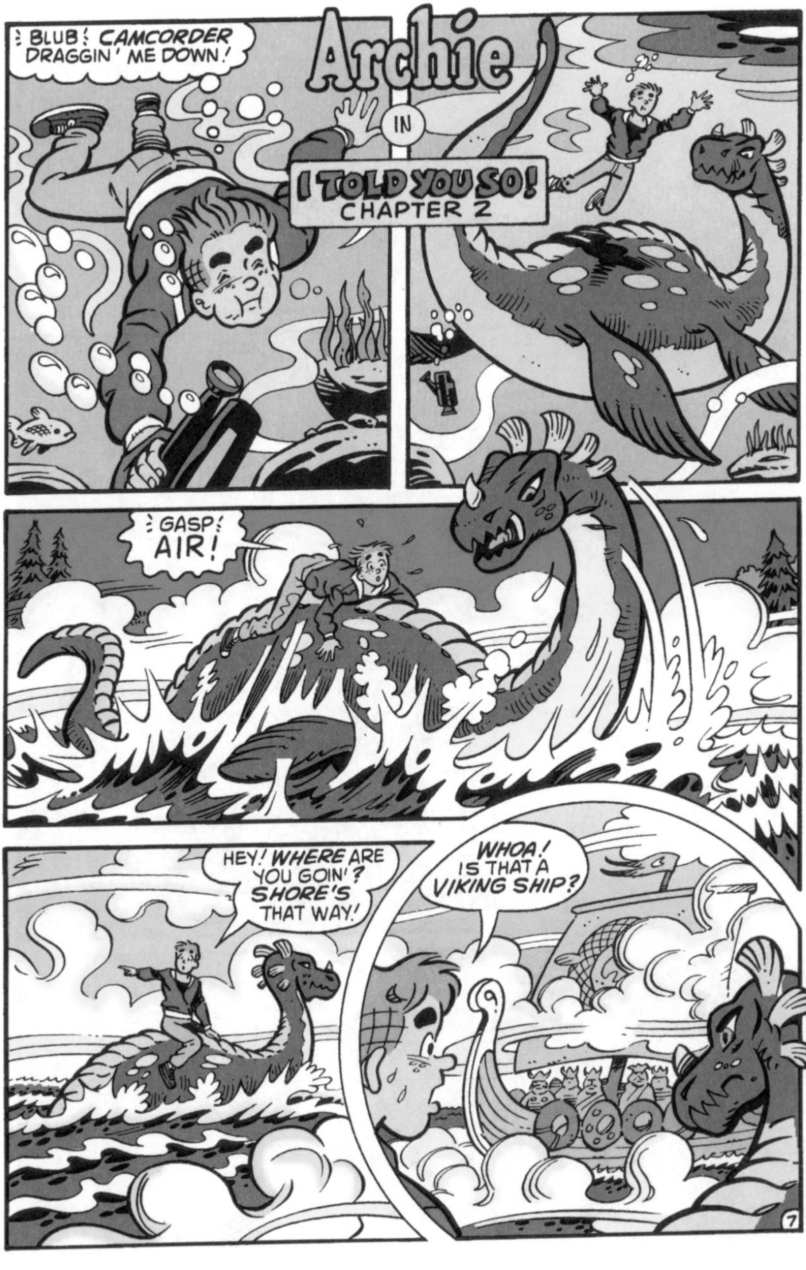
Archie
IN
I TOLD YOU SO!
CHAPTER 2
BLUB! CAMCORDER DRAGGIN' ME DOWN!
GASP! AIR!
HEY! WHERE ARE YOU GOIN'? SHORE'S THAT WAY!
WHOA! IS THAT A VIKING SHIP?
7

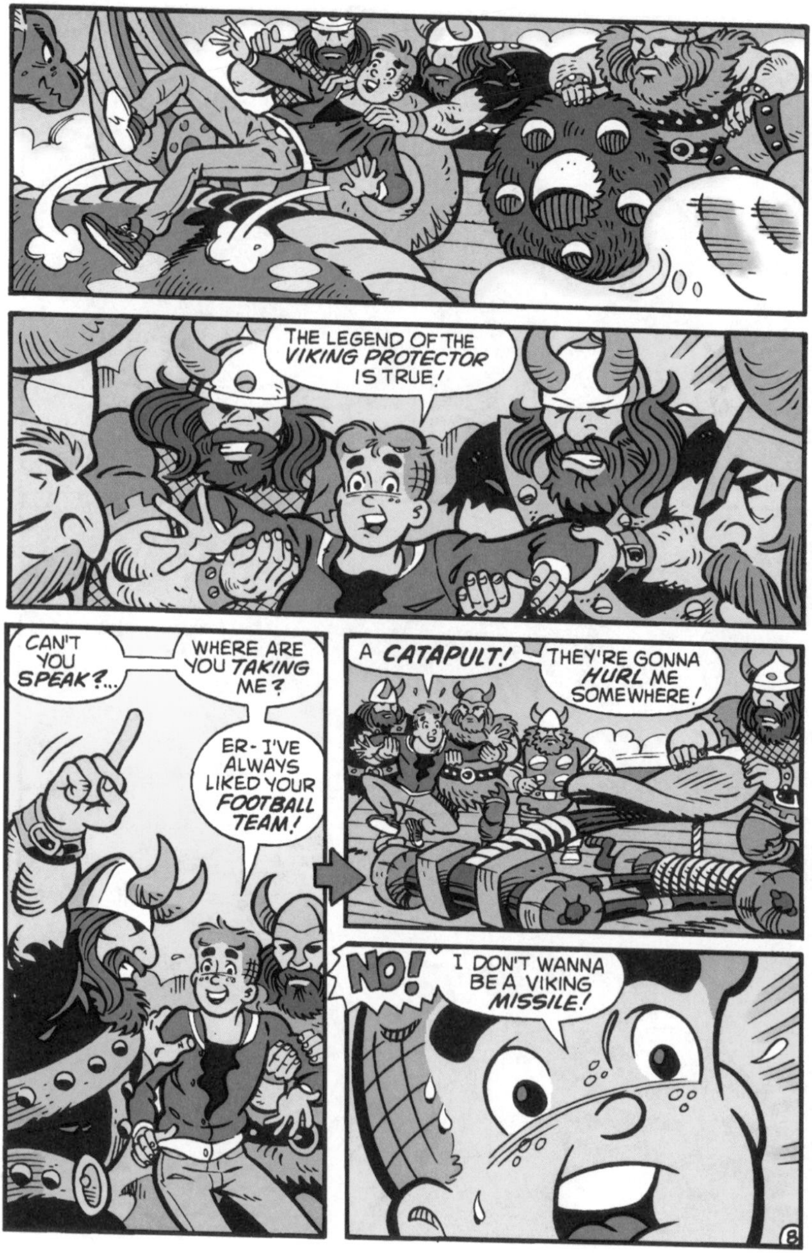
THE LEGEND OF THE VIKING PROTECTOR IS TRUE!
CAN'T YOU SPEAK?...
WHERE ARE YOU TAKING ME?
ER- I'VE ALWAYS LIKED YOUR FOOTBALL TEAM!
A CATAPULT!
THEY'RE GONNA HURL ME SOMEWHERE!
NO!
I DON'T WANNA BE A VIKING MISSILE!
8

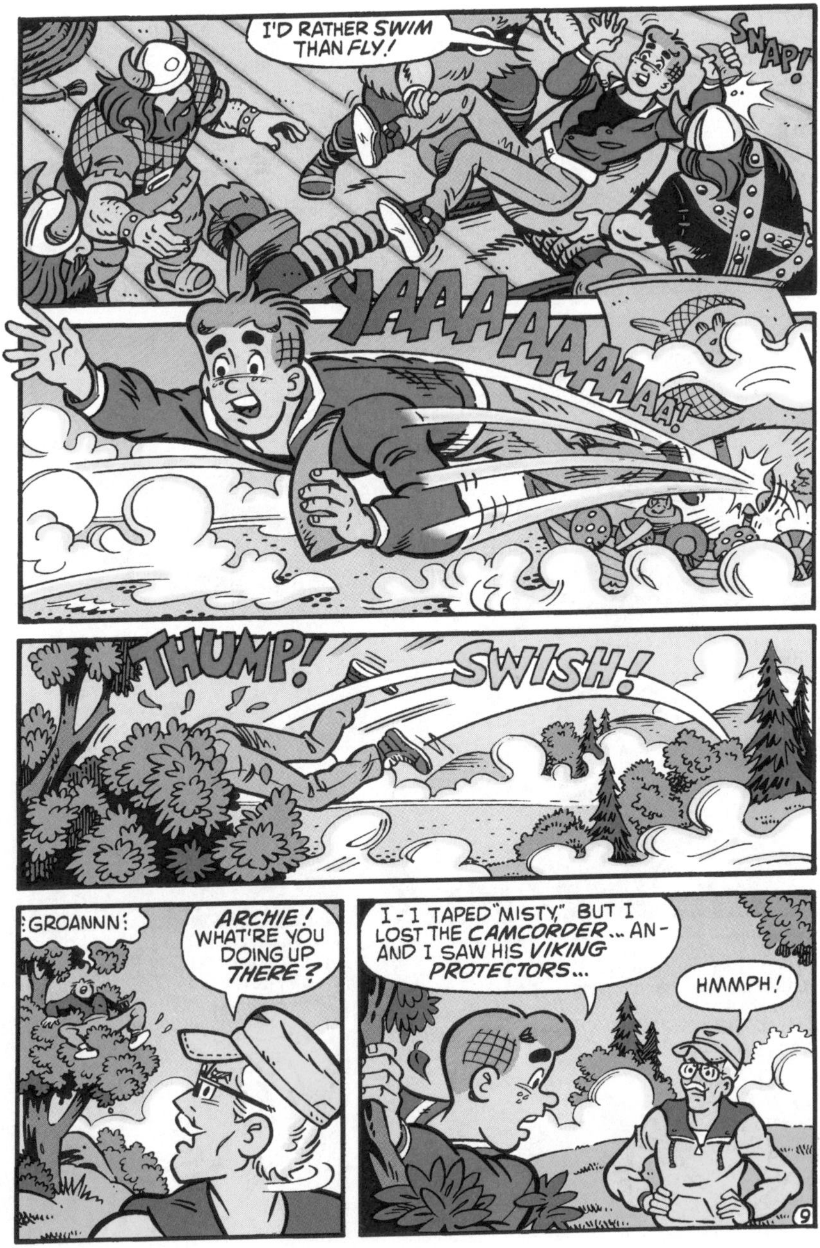
I'D RATHER SWIM THAN FLY!
SNAP!
YAAAAAAAAAAA!
THUMP!
SWISH!
GROANNN
ARCHIE! WHAT'RE YOU DOING UP THERE?
I-I TAPED "MISTY," BUT I LOST THE CAMCORDER... AN- AND I SAW HIS VIKING PROTECTORS...
HMMPH!
9

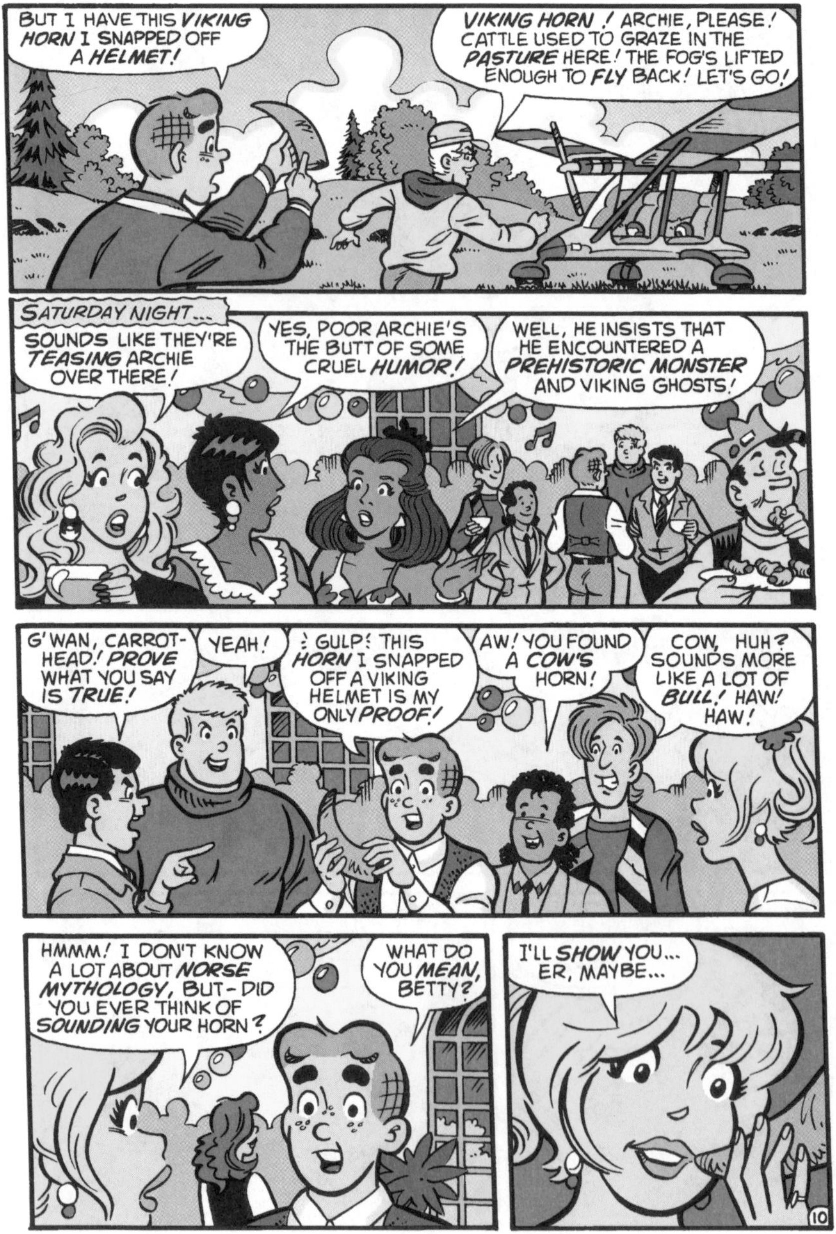
BUT I HAVE THIS VIKING HORN I SNAPPED OFF A HELMET!
VIKING HORN! ARCHIE, PLEASE! CATTLE USED TO GRAZE IN THE PASTURE HERE! THE FOG'S LIFTED ENOUGH TO FLY BACK! LET'S GO!
SATURDAY NIGHT...
SOUNDS LIKE THEY'RE TEASING ARCHIE OVER THERE!
YES, POOR ARCHIE'S THE BUTT OF SOME CRUEL HUMOR!
WELL, HE INSISTS THAT HE ENCOUNTERED A PREHISTORIC MONSTER AND VIKING GHOSTS!
G'WAN, CARROT-HEAD! PROVE WHAT YOU SAY IS TRUE!
YEAH!
GULP! THIS HORN I SNAPPED OFF A VIKING HELMET IS MY ONLY PROOF!
AW! YOU FOUND A COW'S HORN!
COW, HUH? SOUNDS MORE LIKE A LOT OF BULL! HAW! HAW!
HMMM! I DON'T KNOW A LOT ABOUT NORSE MYTHOLOGY, BUT- DID YOU EVER THINK OF SOUNDING YOUR HORN?
WHAT DO YOU MEAN, BETTY?
I'LL SHOW YOU... ER, MAYBE...
10

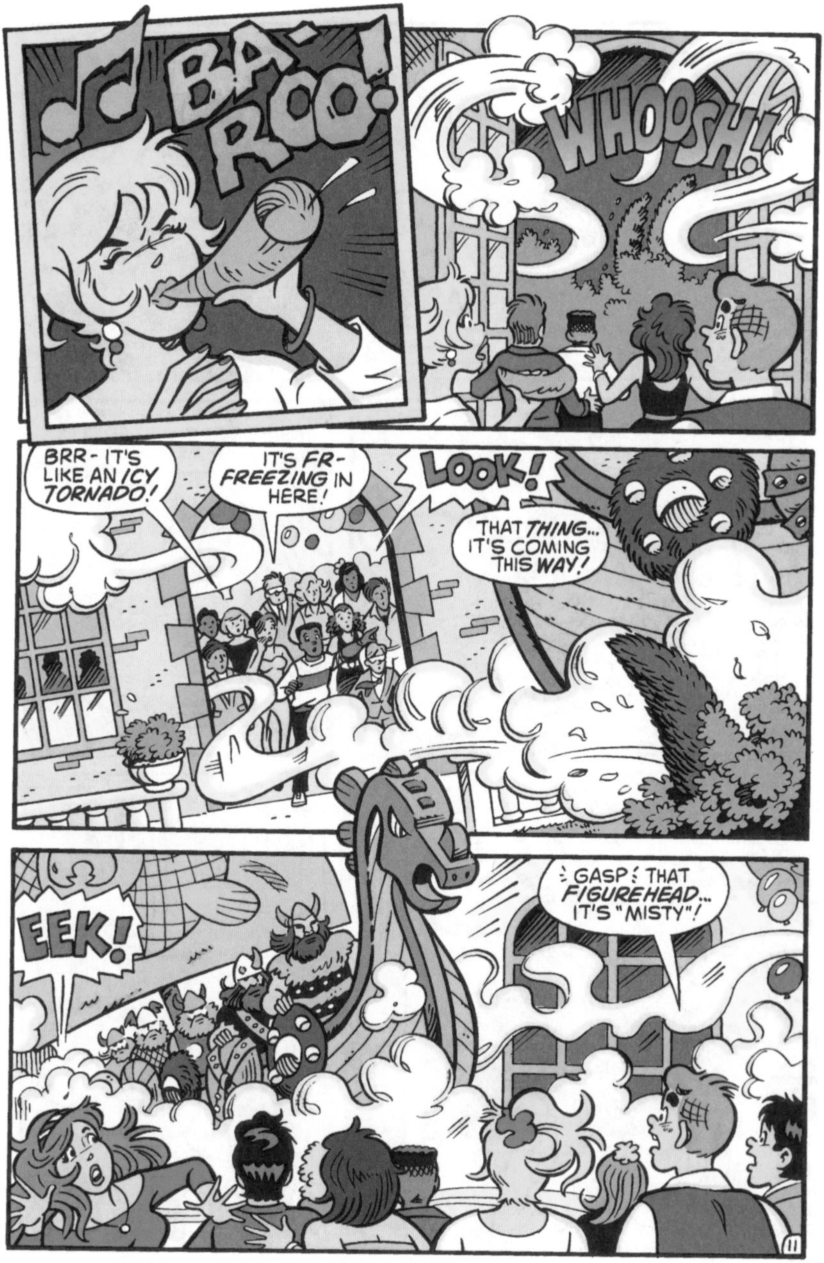
BA-ROO!
WHOOSH!
BRR- IT'S LIKE AN ICY TORNADO!
IT'S FR-FREEZING IN HERE!
LOOK!
THAT THING... IT'S COMING THIS WAY!
EEK!
GASP! THAT FIGUREHEAD... IT'S "MISTY"!
11

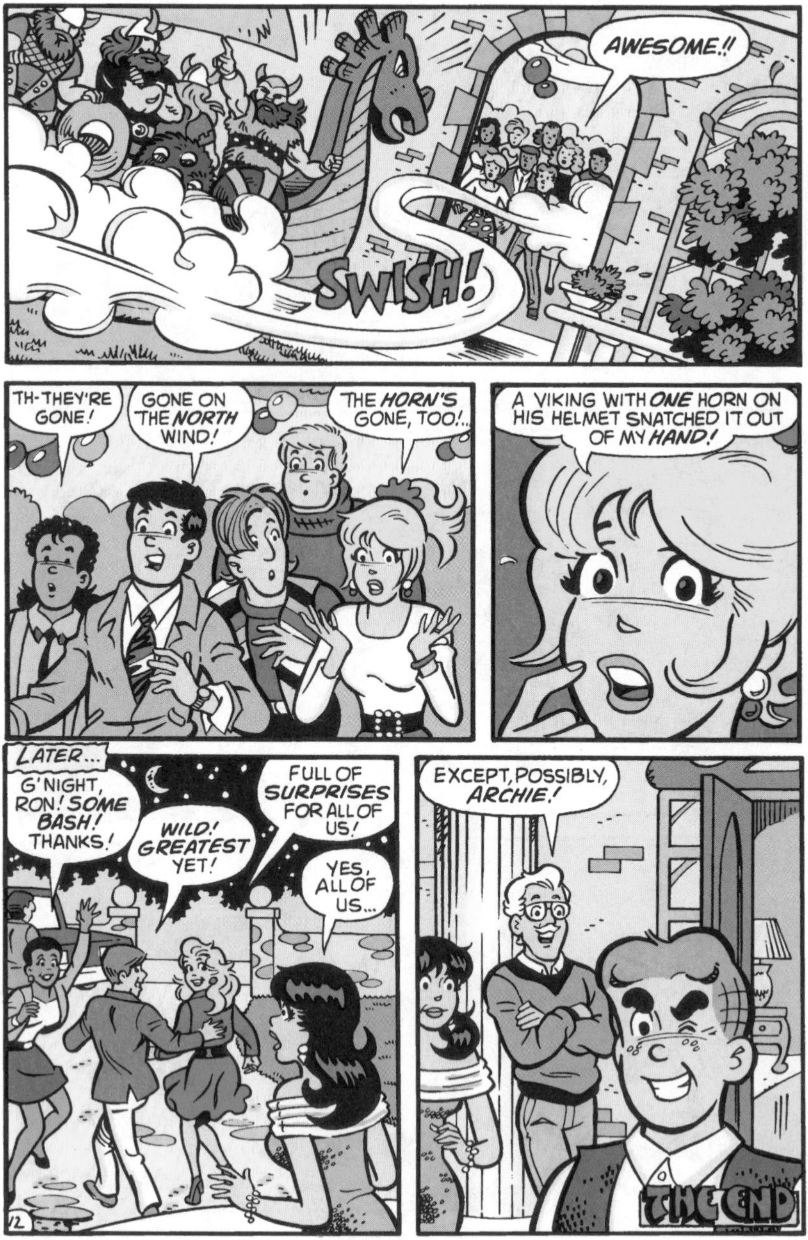
AWESOME!!
SWISH!
TH-THEY'RE GONE!
GONE ON THE NORTH WIND!
THE HORN'S GONE, TOO!..
A VIKING WITH ONE HORN ON HIS HELMET SNATCHED IT OUT OF MY HAND!
LATER...
G'NIGHT, RON! SOME BASH! THANKS!
WILD! GREATEST YET!
FULL OF SURPRISES FOR ALL OF US!
YES, ALL OF US...
12
EXCEPT, POSSIBLY, ARCHIE!
THE END

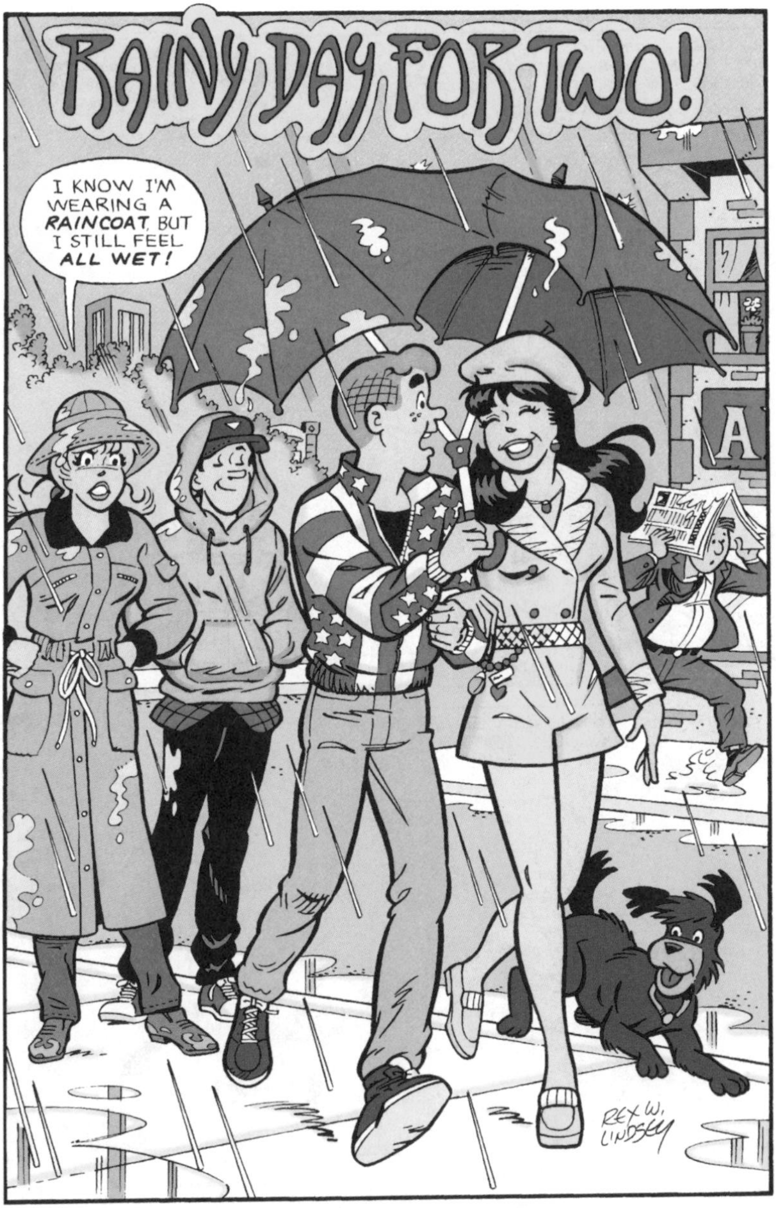
RAINY DAY FOR TWO!
I KNOW I'M WEARING A RAINCOAT, BUT I STILL FEEL ALL WET!
REX W. LINDSEY

Art: Rex Lindsey

Originally printed in WORLD OF ARCHIE #10, JULY 1994

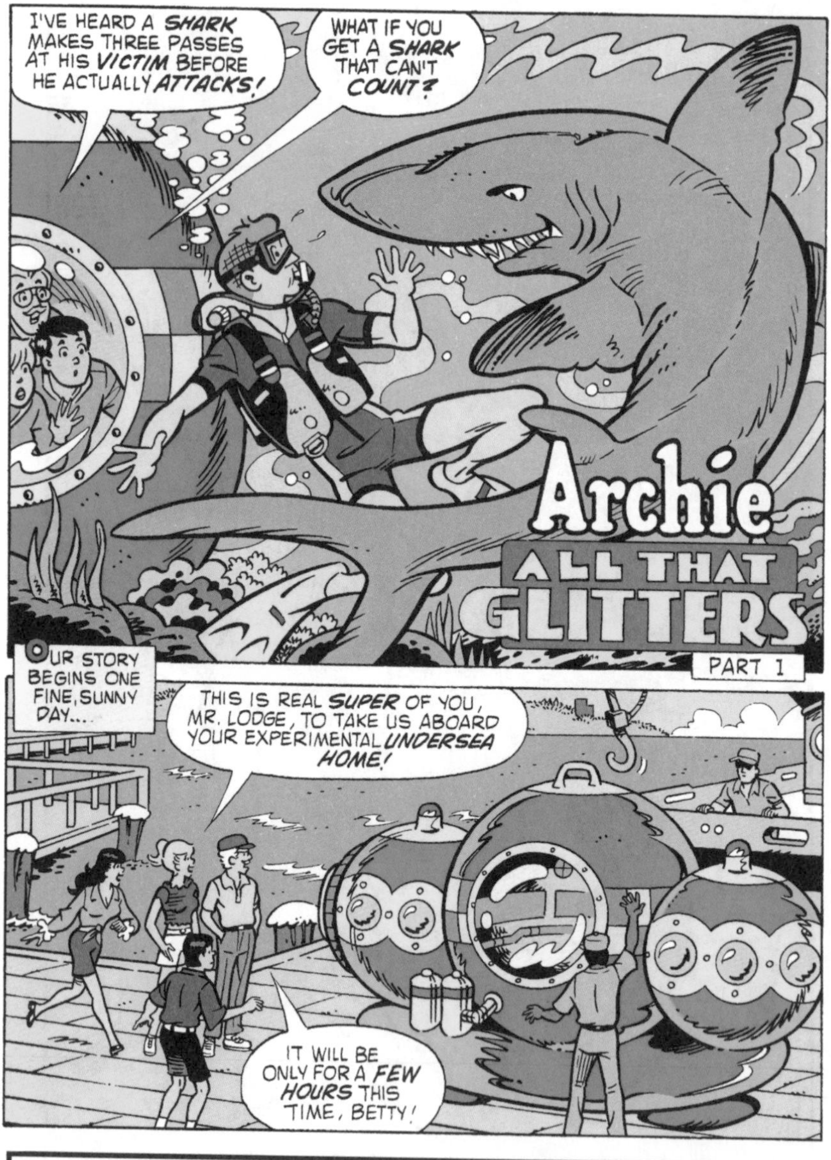
I'VE HEARD A SHARK MAKES THREE PASSES AT HIS VICTIM BEFORE HE ACTUALLY ATTACKS!
WHAT IF YOU GET A SHARK THAT CAN'T COUNT?
Archie
ALL THAT GLITTERS
PART 1
OUR STORY BEGINS ONE FINE, SUNNY DAY...
THIS IS REAL SUPER OF YOU, MR. LODGE, TO TAKE US ABOARD YOUR EXPERIMENTAL UNDERSEA HOME!
IT WILL BE ONLY FOR A FEW HOURS THIS TIME, BETTY!

Story: Bob Bolling Pencils: Rex Lindsey
Inks: Rex Lindsey Letters: Bill Yoshida Colors: Barry Grossman

Originally printed in WORLD OF ARCHIE #11, SEPTEMBER 1994

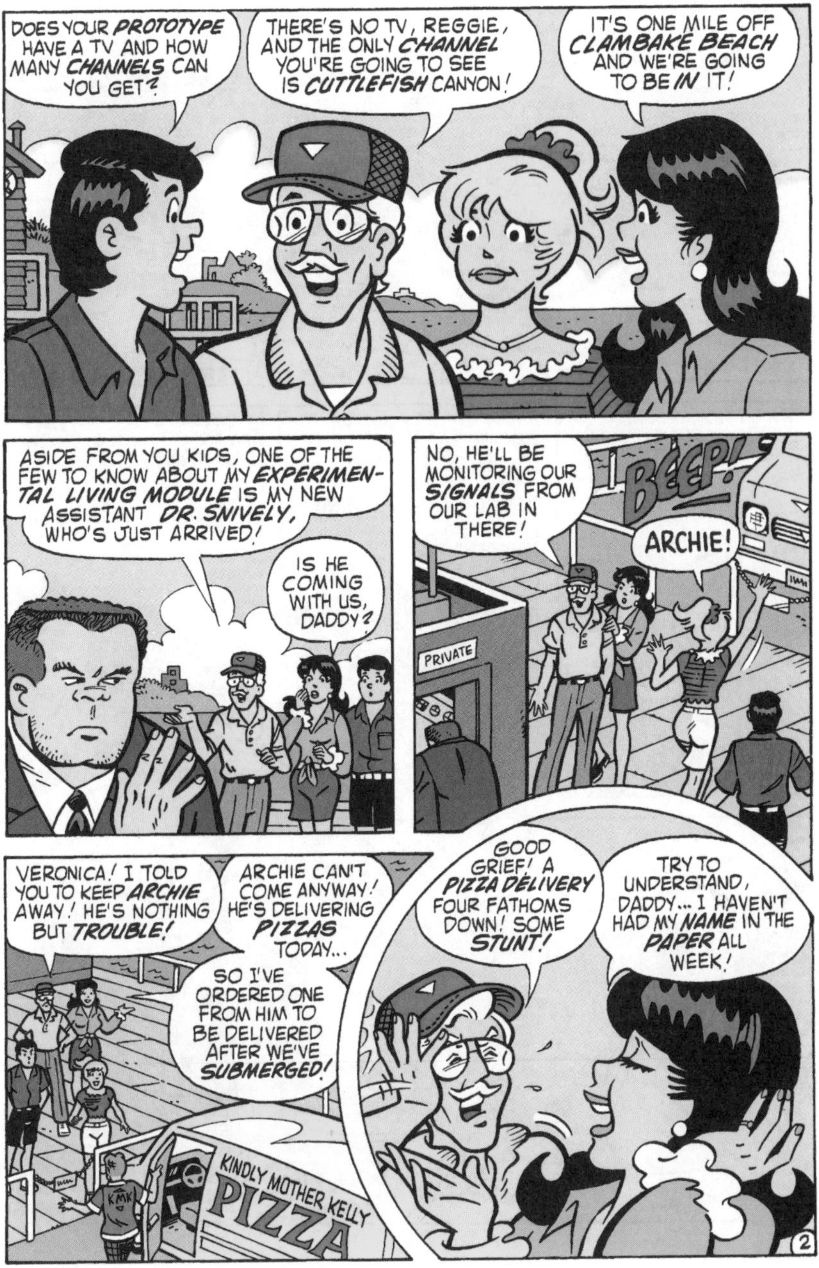
DOES YOUR PROTOTYPE HAVE A TV AND HOW MANY CHANNELS CAN YOU GET?
THERE'S NO TV, REGGIE, AND THE ONLY CHANNEL YOU'RE GOING TO SEE IS CUTTLEFISH CANYON!
IT'S ONE MILE OFF CLAMBAKE BEACH AND WE'RE GOING TO BE IN IT!
ASIDE FROM YOU KIDS, ONE OF THE FEW TO KNOW ABOUT MY EXPERIMENTAL LIVING MODULE IS MY NEW ASSISTANT DR. SNIVELY, WHO'S JUST ARRIVED!
IS HE COMING WITH US, DADDY?
NO, HE'LL BE MONITORING OUR SIGNALS FROM OUR LAB IN THERE!
BEEP!
ARCHIE!
PRIVATE
VERONICA! I TOLD YOU TO KEEP ARCHIE AWAY! HE'S NOTHING BUT TROUBLE!
ARCHIE CAN'T COME ANYWAY! HE'S DELIVERING PIZZAS TODAY...
SO I'VE ORDERED ONE FROM HIM TO BE DELIVERED AFTER WE'VE SUBMERGED!
KMK
KINDLY MOTHER KELLY PIZZA
GOOD GRIEF! A PIZZA DELIVERY FOUR FATHOMS DOWN! SOME STUNT!
TRY TO UNDERSTAND, DADDY... I HAVEN'T HAD MY NAME IN THE PAPER ALL WEEK!
2

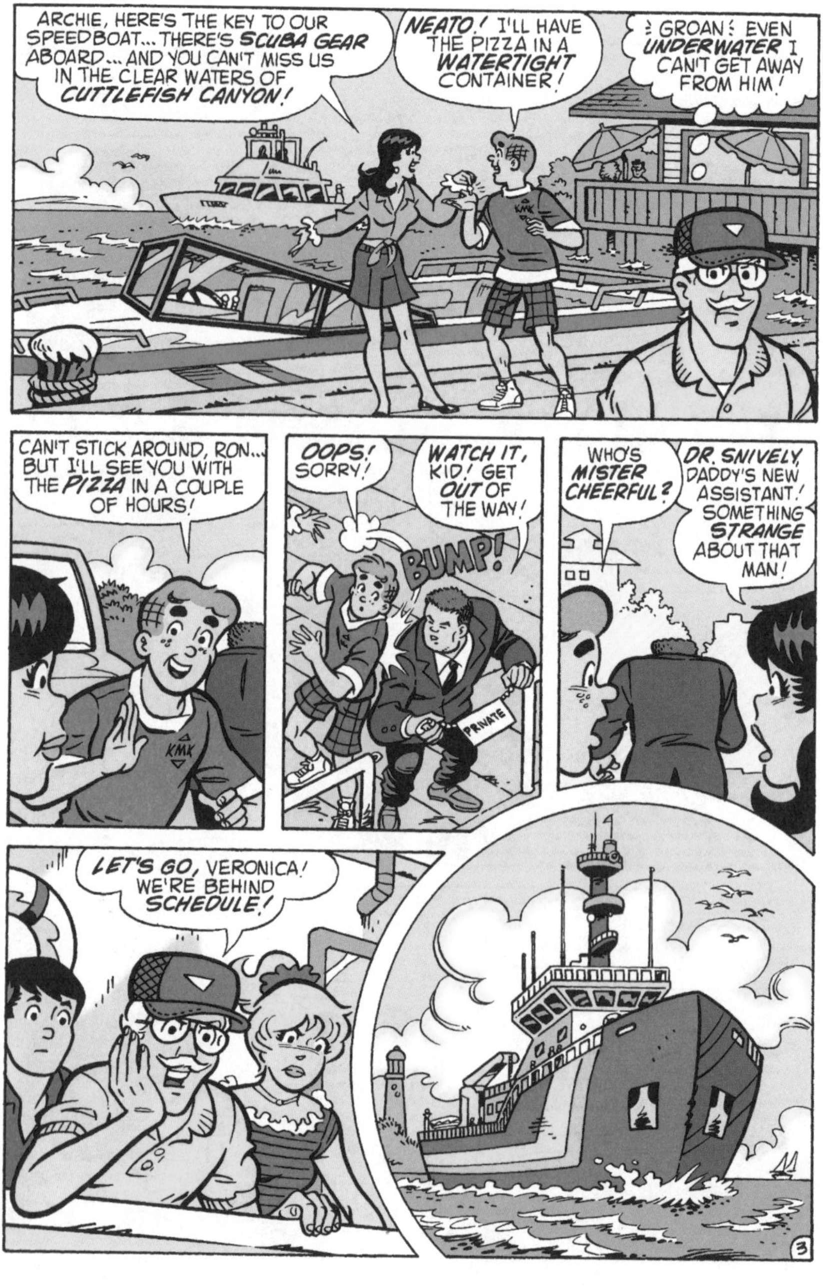
ARCHIE, HERE'S THE KEY TO OUR SPEEDBOAT... THERE'S SCUBA GEAR ABOARD... AND YOU CAN'T MISS US IN THE CLEAR WATERS OF CUTTLEFISH CANYON!
NEATO! I'LL HAVE THE PIZZA IN A WATERTIGHT CONTAINER!
GROAN! EVEN UNDERWATER I CAN'T GET AWAY FROM HIM!
CAN'T STICK AROUND, RON... BUT I'LL SEE YOU WITH THE PIZZA IN A COUPLE OF HOURS!
OOPS! SORRY!
WATCH IT, KID! GET OUT OF THE WAY!
BUMP!
PRIVATE
WHO'S MISTER CHEERFUL?
DR. SNIVELY, DADDY'S NEW ASSISTANT! SOMETHING STRANGE ABOUT THAT MAN!
LET'S GO, VERONICA! WE'RE BEHIND SCHEDULE!
3

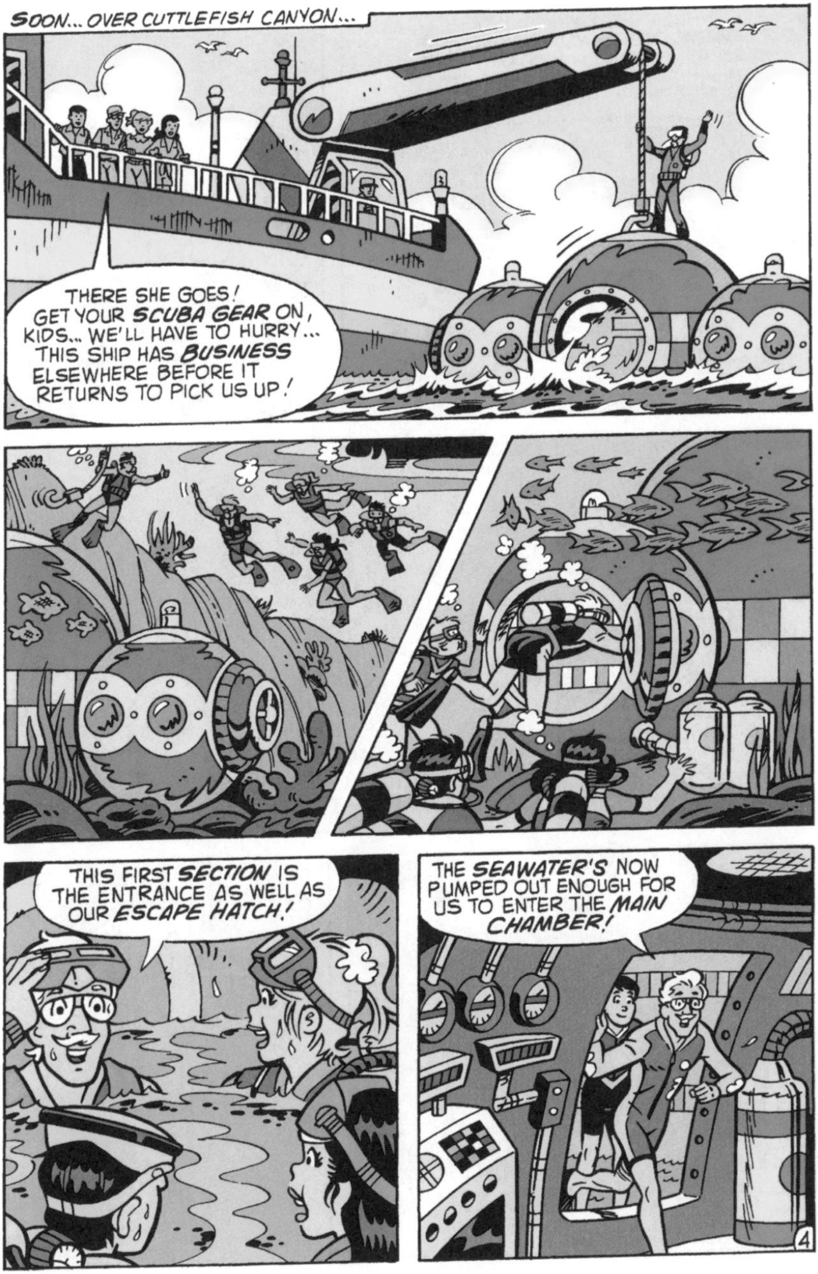
SOON... OVER CUTTLEFISH CANYON...
THERE SHE GOES! GET YOUR SCUBA GEAR ON, KIDS... WE'LL HAVE TO HURRY... THIS SHIP HAS BUSINESS ELSEWHERE BEFORE IT RETURNS TO PICK US UP!
THIS FIRST SECTION IS THE ENTRANCE AS WELL AS OUR ESCAPE HATCH!
THE SEAWATER'S NOW PUMPED OUT ENOUGH FOR US TO ENTER THE MAIN CHAMBER!
4

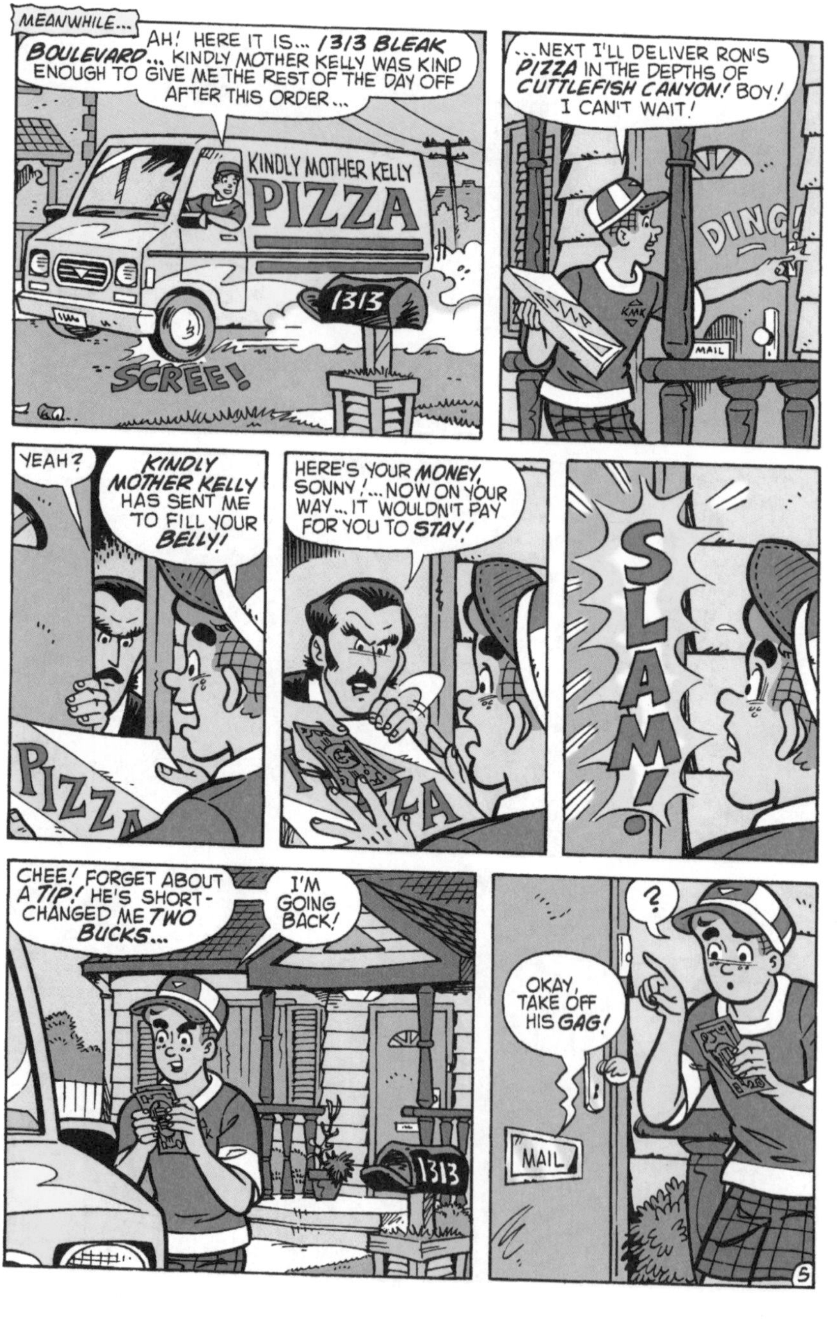
MEANWHILE...
AH! HERE IT IS... 1313 BLEAK BOULEVARD... KINDLY MOTHER KELLY WAS KIND ENOUGH TO GIVE ME THE REST OF THE DAY OFF AFTER THIS ORDER...
KINDLY MOTHER KELLY PIZZA
1313
SCREEE!
...NEXT I'LL DELIVER RON'S PIZZA IN THE DEPTHS OF CUTTLEFISH CANYON! BOY! I CAN'T WAIT!
DING!
MAIL
YEAH?
KINDLY MOTHER KELLY HAS SENT ME TO FILL YOUR BELLY!
HERE'S YOUR MONEY, SONNY!... NOW ON YOUR WAY... IT WOULDN'T PAY FOR YOU TO STAY!
SLAM!
CHEE! FORGET ABOUT A TIP! HE'S SHORT-CHANGED ME TWO BUCKS...
I'M GOING BACK!
1313
?
OKAY, TAKE OFF HIS GAG!
MAIL
5

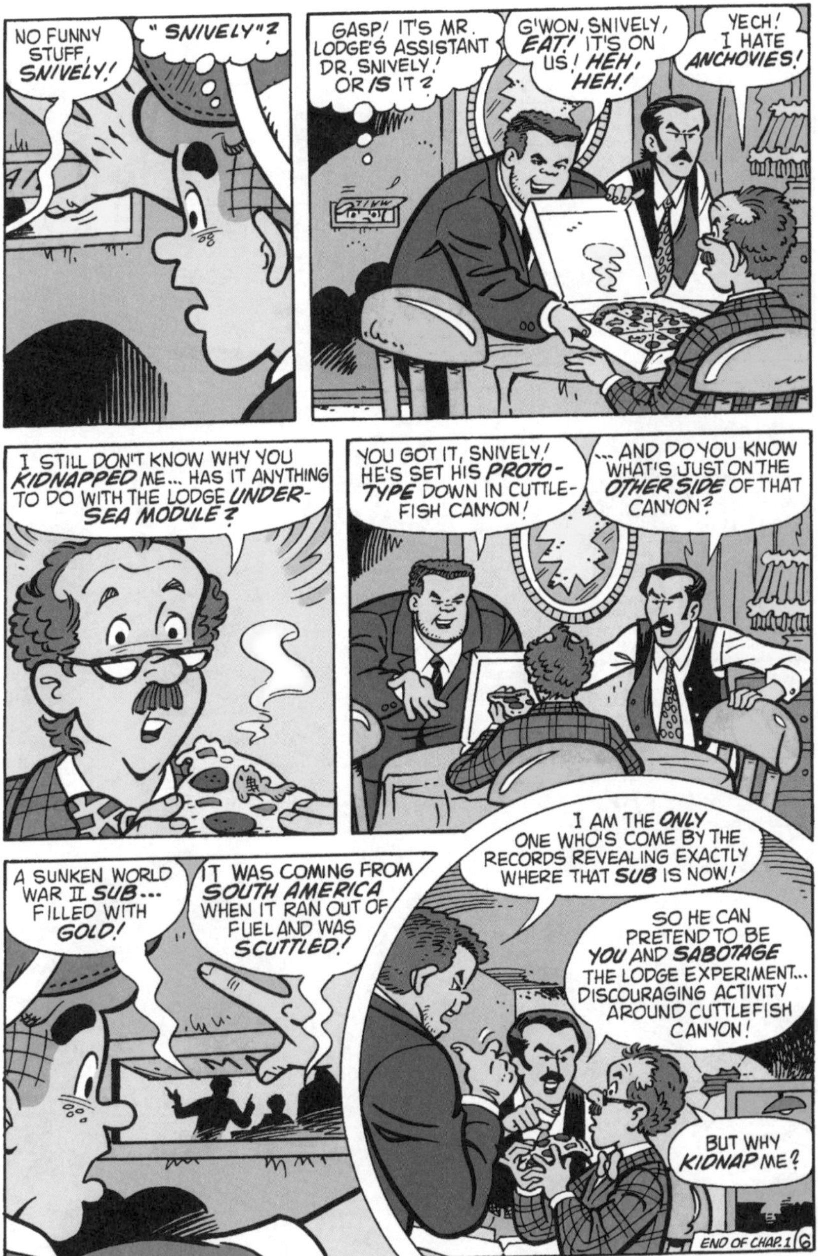
NO FUNNY STUFF, SNIVELY!
"SNIVELY"?
GASP! IT'S MR. LODGE'S ASSISTANT DR. SNIVELY! OR IS IT?
G'WON, SNIVELY, EAT! IT'S ON US! HEH, HEH!
YECH! I HATE ANCHOVIES!
I STILL DON'T KNOW WHY YOU KIDNAPPED ME... HAS IT ANYTHING TO DO WITH THE LODGE UNDER-SEA MODULE?
YOU GOT IT, SNIVELY! HE'S SET HIS PROTO-TYPE DOWN IN CUTTLE-FISH CANYON!
...AND DO YOU KNOW WHAT'S JUST ON THE OTHER SIDE OF THAT CANYON?
A SUNKEN WORLD WAR II SUB... FILLED WITH GOLD!
IT WAS COMING FROM SOUTH AMERICA WHEN IT RAN OUT OF FUEL AND WAS SCUTTLED!
I AM THE ONLY ONE WHO'S COME BY THE RECORDS REVEALING EXACTLY WHERE THAT SUB IS NOW!
SO HE CAN PRETEND TO BE YOU AND SABOTAGE THE LODGE EXPERIMENT... DISCOURAGING ACTIVITY AROUND CUTTLEFISH CANYON!
BUT WHY KIDNAP ME?
END OF CHAP. 1
6

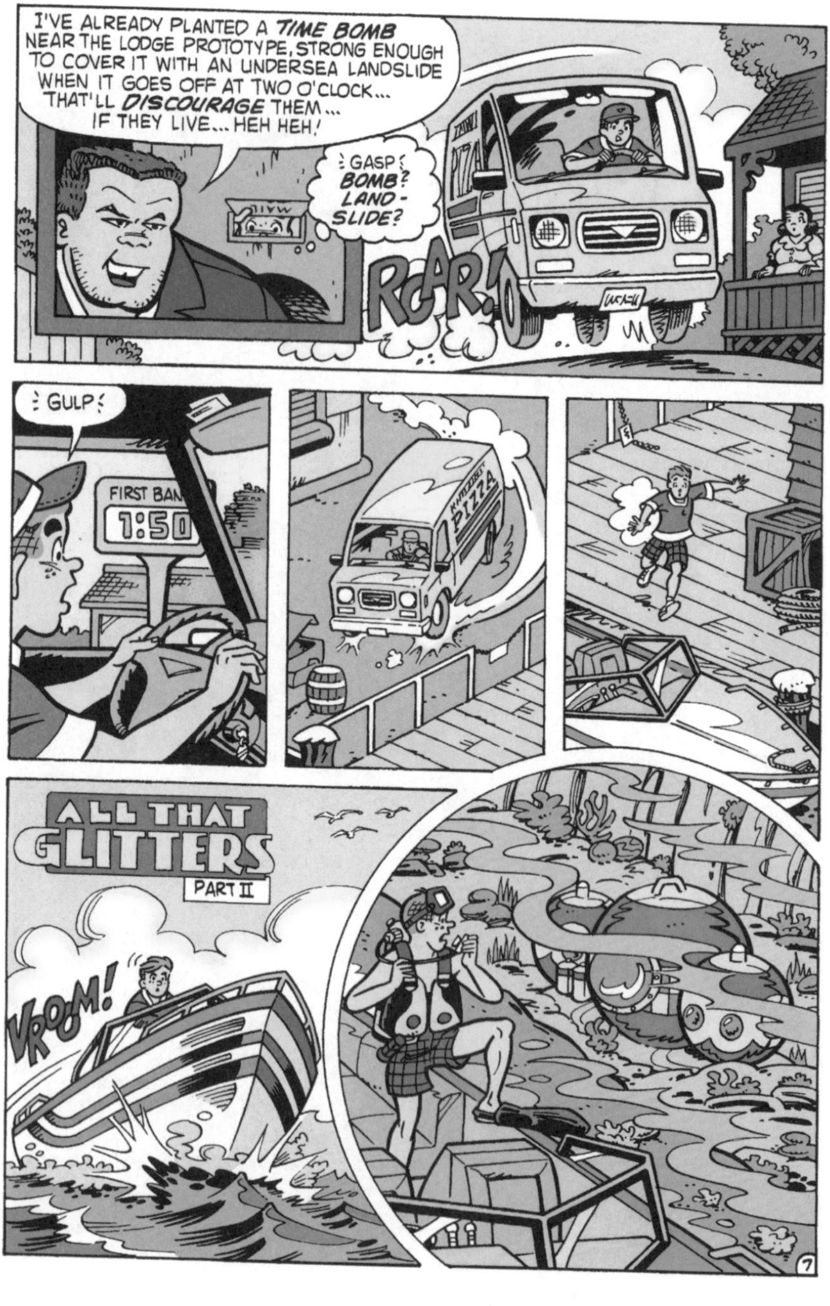
I'VE ALREADY PLANTED A TIME BOMB NEAR THE LODGE PROTOTYPE, STRONG ENOUGH TO COVER IT WITH AN UNDERSEA LANDSLIDE WHEN IT GOES OFF AT TWO O'CLOCK... THAT'LL DISCOURAGE THEM... IF THEY LIVE... HEH HEH!
GASP BOMB? LAND-SLIDE?
ROAR!
GULP
FIRST BAN
1:50
ALL THAT GLITTERS
PART II
VROOM!
7

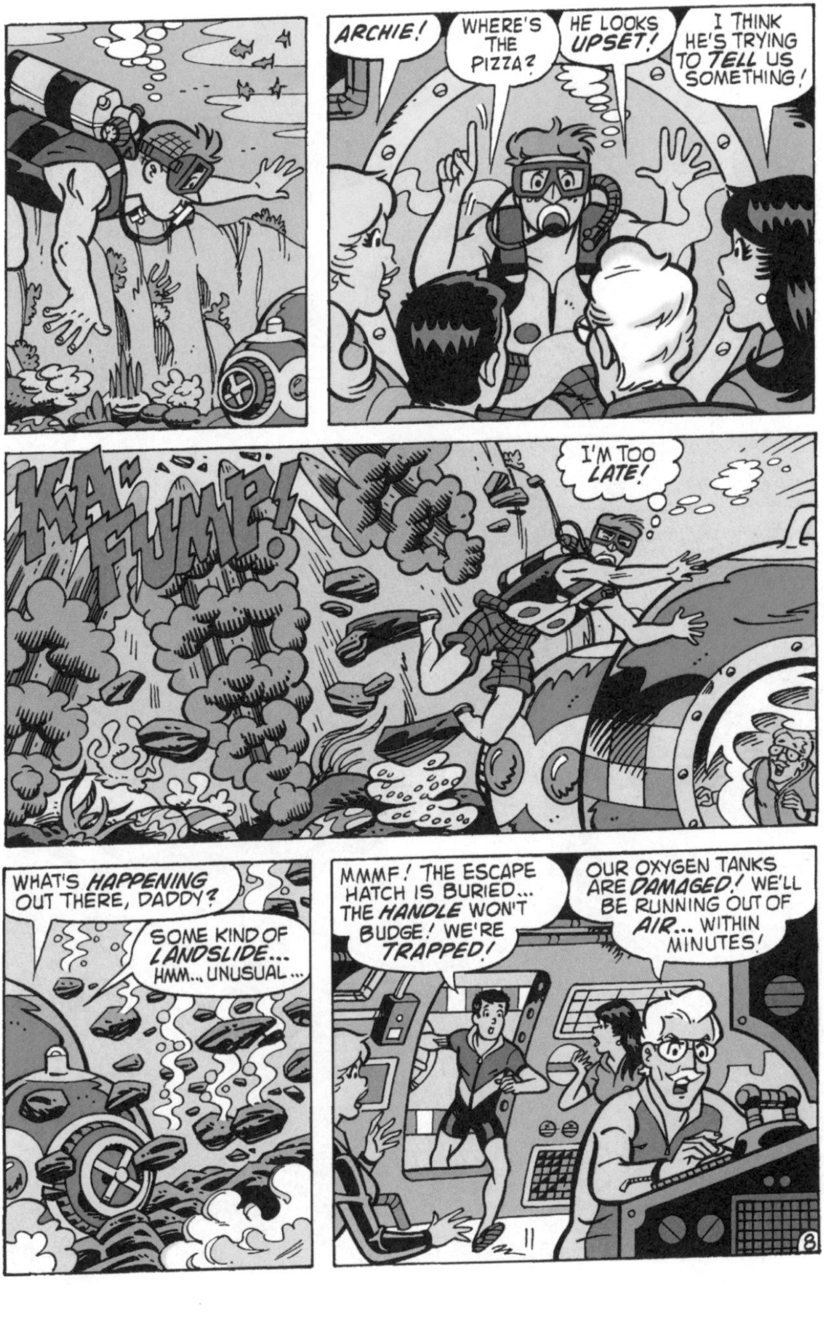
ARCHIE!
WHERE'S THE PIZZA?
HE LOOKS UPSET!
I THINK HE'S TRYING TO TELL US SOMETHING!
KA-FUMP!
I'M TOO LATE!
WHAT'S HAPPENING OUT THERE, DADDY?
SOME KIND OF LANDSLIDE... HMM... UNUSUAL...
MMMF! THE ESCAPE HATCH IS BURIED... THE HANDLE WON'T BUDGE! WE'RE TRAPPED!
OUR OXYGEN TANKS ARE DAMAGED! WE'LL BE RUNNING OUT OF AIR... WITHIN MINUTES!
8

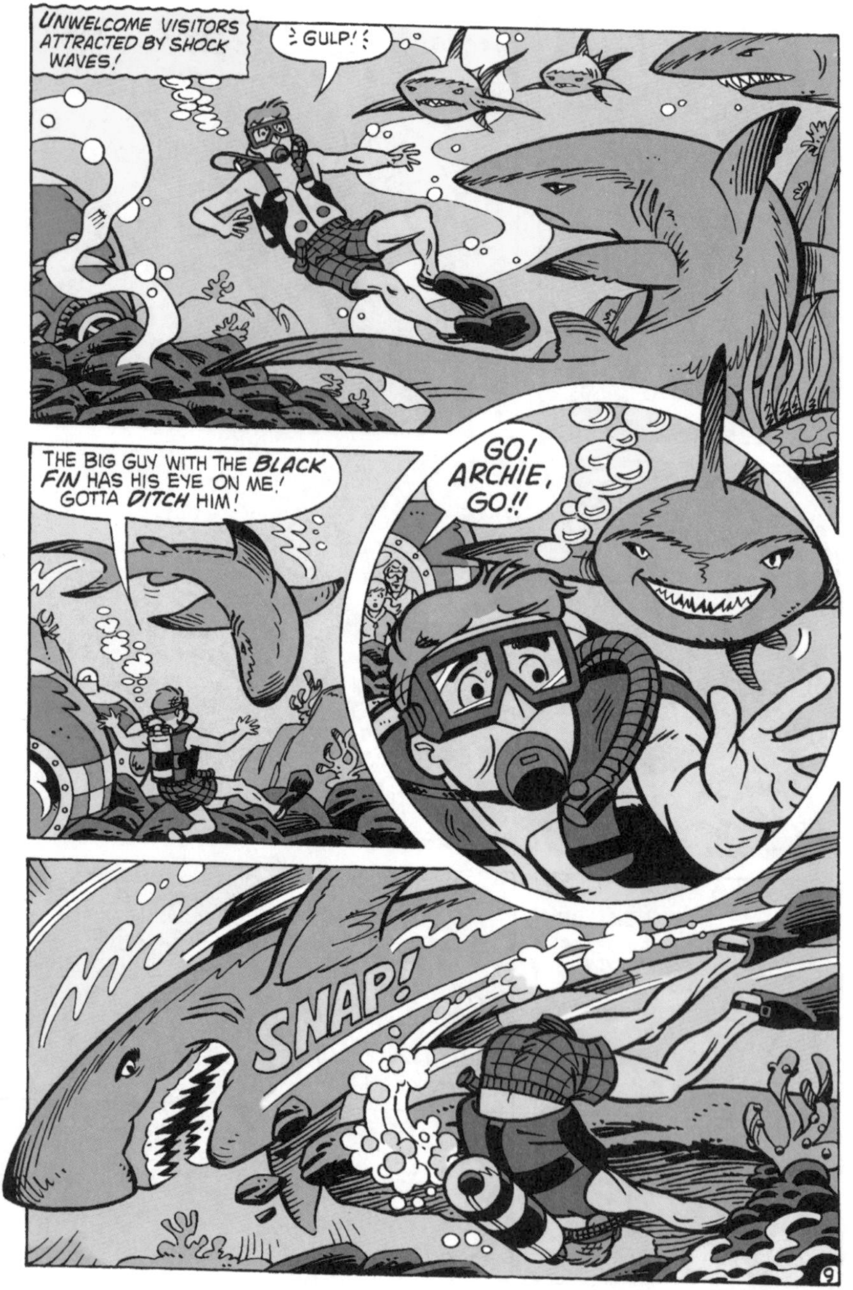
UNWELCOME VISITORS ATTRACTED BY SHOCK WAVES!
GULP!
THE BIG GUY WITH THE BLACK FIN HAS HIS EYE ON ME! GOTTA DITCH HIM!
GO! ARCHIE, GO!!
SNAP!
9

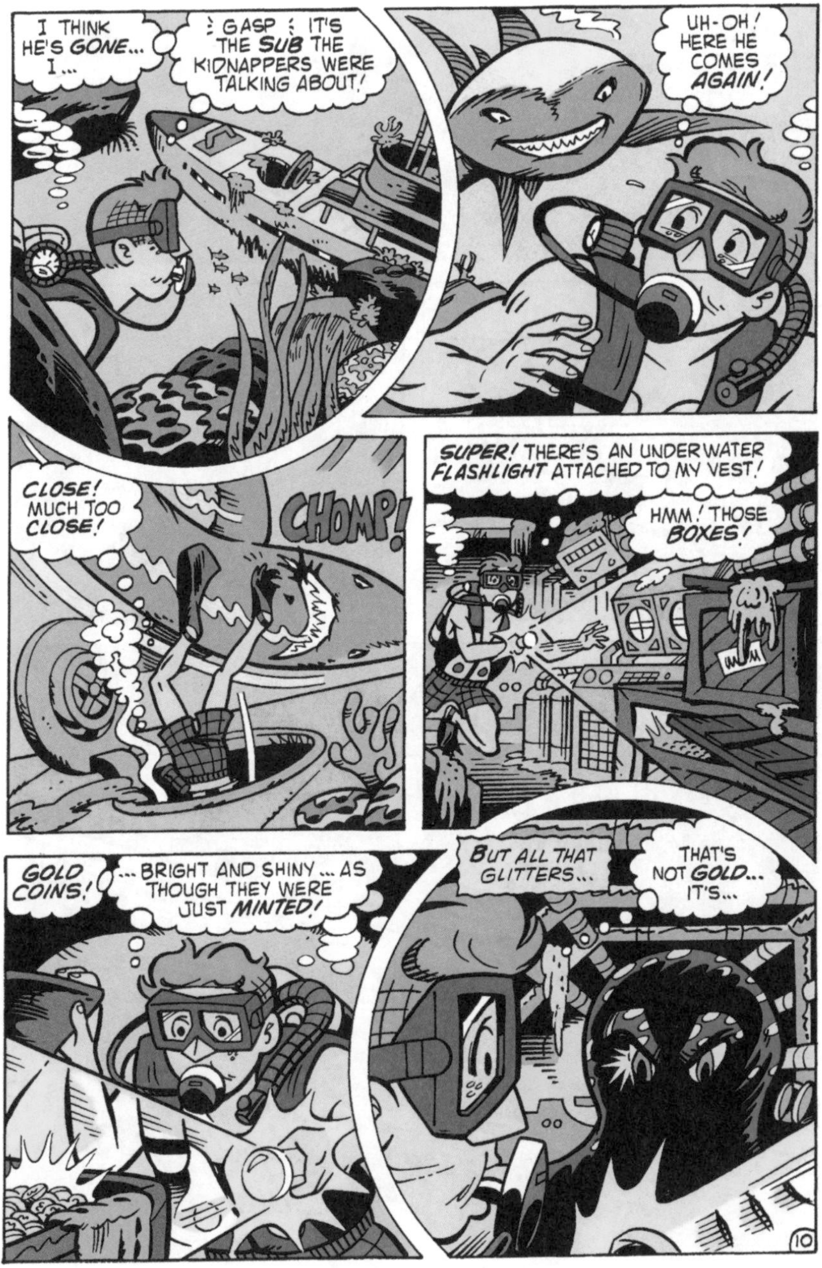
I THINK HE'S GONE... I...
⁝ GASP ⁝ IT'S THE SUB THE KIDNAPPERS WERE TALKING ABOUT!
UH-OH! HERE HE COMES AGAIN!
CLOSE! MUCH TOO CLOSE!
CHOMP!
SUPER! THERE'S AN UNDERWATER FLASHLIGHT ATTACHED TO MY VEST!
HMM! THOSE BOXES!
GOLD COINS!
... BRIGHT AND SHINY ... AS THOUGH THEY WERE JUST MINTED!
BUT ALL THAT GLITTERS...
THAT'S NOT GOLD... IT'S...
10

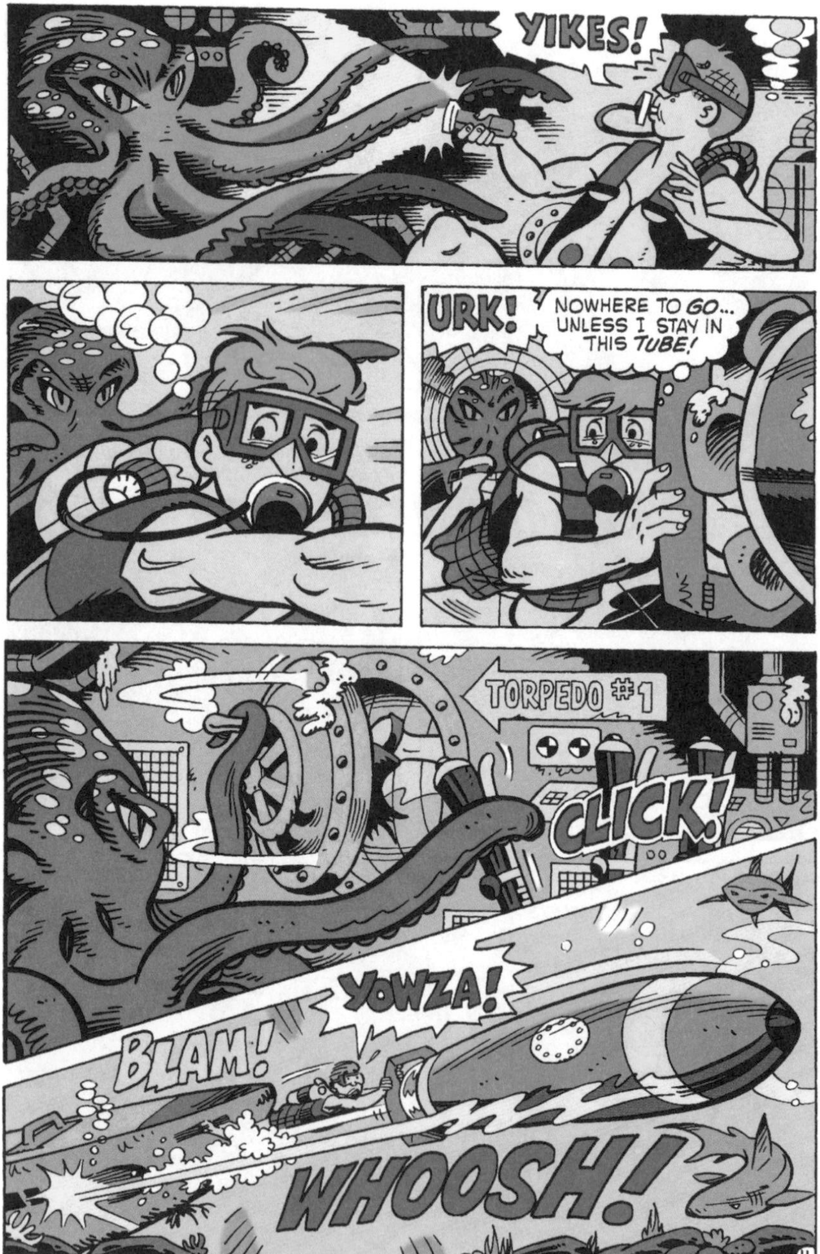
YIKES!
URK!
NOWHERE TO GO... UNLESS I STAY IN THIS TUBE!
TORPEDO #1
CLICK!
YOWZA!
BLAM!
WHOOSH!
11

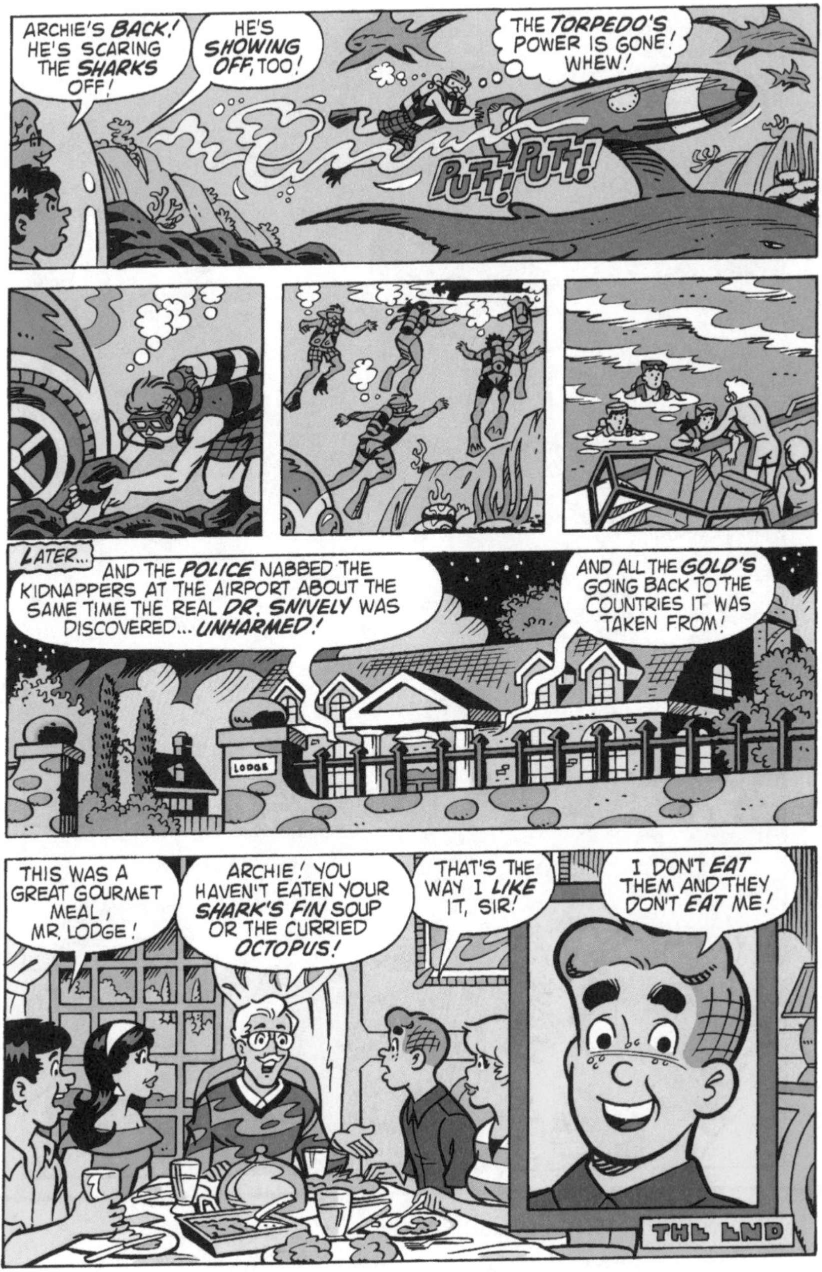
ARCHIE'S BACK! HE'S SCARING THE SHARKS OFF!
HE'S SHOWING OFF, TOO!
THE TORPEDO'S POWER IS GONE! WHEW!
PUTT! PUTT!
LATER...
AND THE POLICE NABBED THE KIDNAPPERS AT THE AIRPORT ABOUT THE SAME TIME THE REAL DR. SNIVELY WAS DISCOVERED... UNHARMED!
AND ALL THE GOLD'S GOING BACK TO THE COUNTRIES IT WAS TAKEN FROM!
LODGE
THIS WAS A GREAT GOURMET MEAL, MR. LODGE!
ARCHIE! YOU HAVEN'T EATEN YOUR SHARK'S FIN SOUP OR THE CURRIED OCTOPUS!
THAT'S THE WAY I LIKE IT, SIR!
I DON'T EAT THEM AND THEY DON'T EAT ME!
THE END

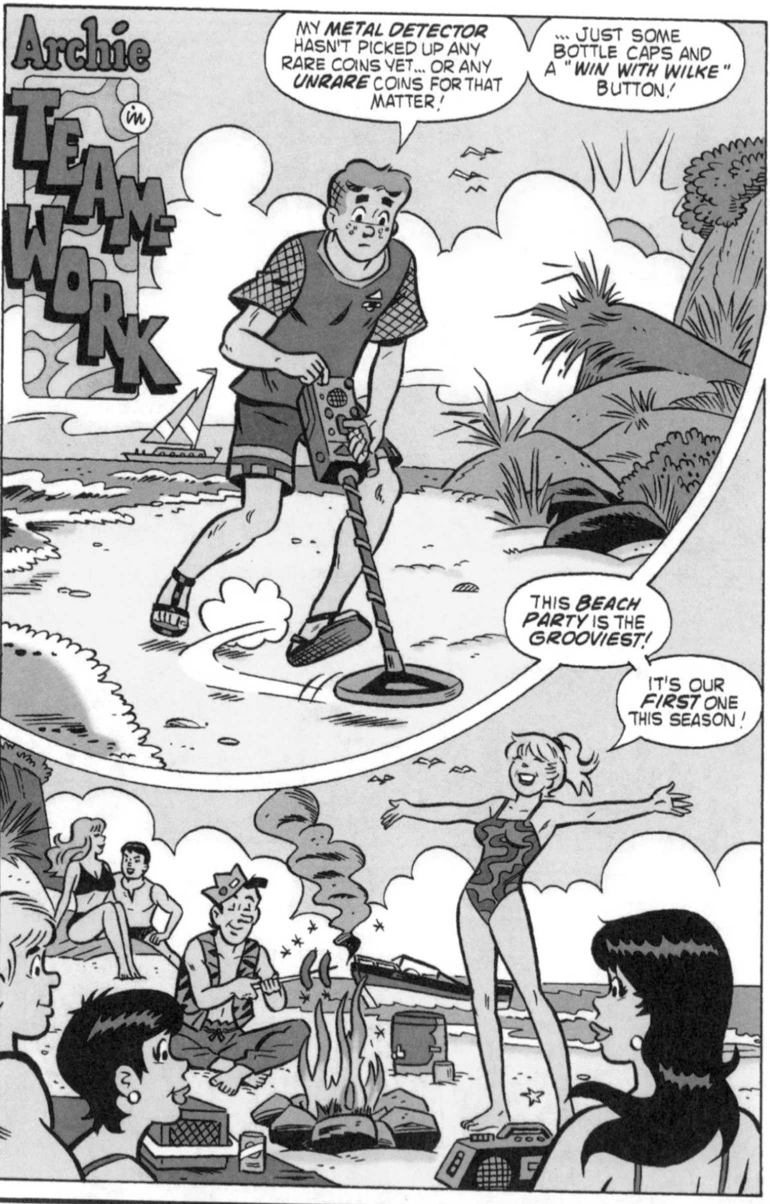
Archie
in
TEAM-WORK
MY METAL DETECTOR HASN'T PICKED UP ANY RARE COINS YET... OR ANY UNRARE COINS FOR THAT MATTER!
... JUST SOME BOTTLE CAPS AND A "WIN WITH WILKE" BUTTON!
THIS BEACH PARTY IS THE GROOVIEST!
IT'S OUR FIRST ONE THIS SEASON!

Story: Bob Bolling Pencils: Rex Lindsey
Inks: Rudy Lapick Letters: Bill Yoshida

Originally printed in WORLD OF ARCHIE #11, SEPTEMBER 1994

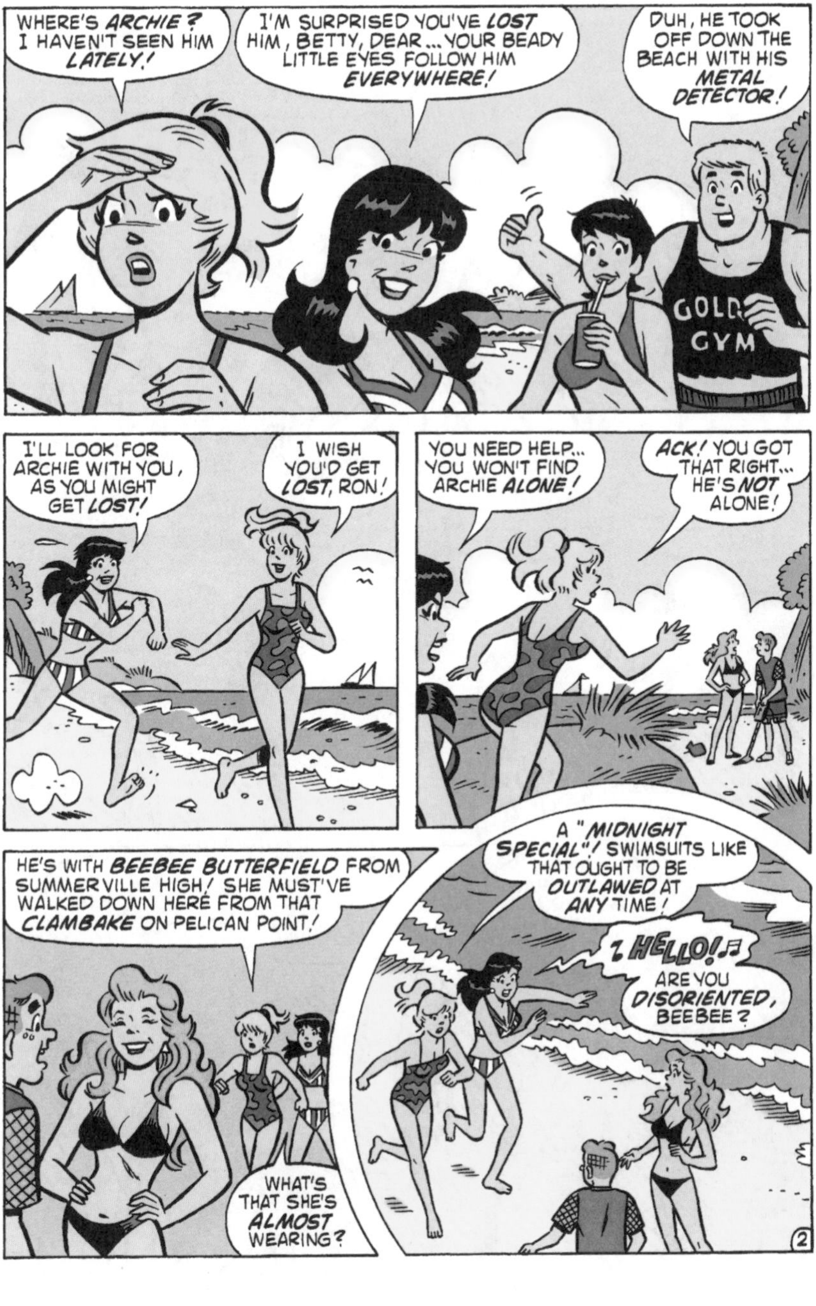
WHERE'S ARCHIE? I HAVEN'T SEEN HIM LATELY!
I'M SURPRISED YOU'VE LOST HIM, BETTY, DEAR ... YOUR BEADY LITTLE EYES FOLLOW HIM EVERYWHERE!
DUH, HE TOOK OFF DOWN THE BEACH WITH HIS METAL DETECTOR!
GOLD GYM
I'LL LOOK FOR ARCHIE WITH YOU, AS YOU MIGHT GET LOST!
I WISH YOU'D GET LOST, RON!
YOU NEED HELP... YOU WON'T FIND ARCHIE ALONE!
ACK! YOU GOT THAT RIGHT... HE'S NOT ALONE!
HE'S WITH BEEBEE BUTTERFIELD FROM SUMMERVILLE HIGH! SHE MUST'VE WALKED DOWN HERE FROM THAT CLAMBAKE ON PELICAN POINT!
WHAT'S THAT SHE'S ALMOST WEARING?
A "MIDNIGHT SPECIAL"! SWIMSUITS LIKE THAT OUGHT TO BE OUTLAWED AT ANY TIME!
HELLO!
ARE YOU DISORIENTED, BEEBEE?
2

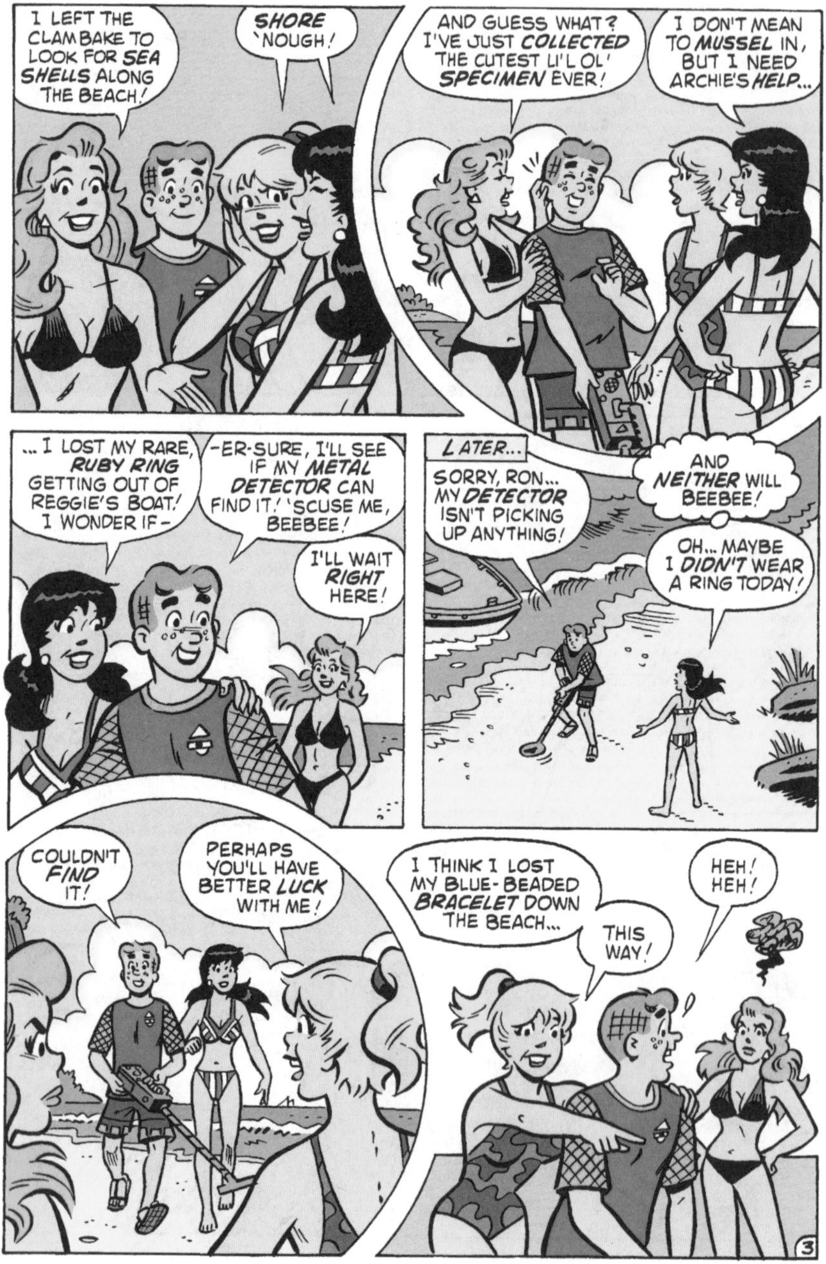
I LEFT THE CLAMBAKE TO LOOK FOR SEA SHELLS ALONG THE BEACH!
SHORE 'NOUGH!
AND GUESS WHAT? I'VE JUST COLLECTED THE CUTEST LI'L OL' SPECIMEN EVER!
I DON'T MEAN TO MUSSEL IN, BUT I NEED ARCHIE'S HELP...
... I LOST MY RARE, RUBY RING GETTING OUT OF REGGIE'S BOAT! I WONDER IF -
-ER-SURE, I'LL SEE IF MY METAL DETECTOR CAN FIND IT! 'SCUSE ME, BEEBEE!
I'LL WAIT RIGHT HERE!
LATER...
SORRY, RON... MY DETECTOR ISN'T PICKING UP ANYTHING!
AND NEITHER WILL BEEBEE!
OH... MAYBE I DIDN'T WEAR A RING TODAY!
COULDN'T FIND IT!
PERHAPS YOU'LL HAVE BETTER LUCK WITH ME!
I THINK I LOST MY BLUE-BEADED BRACELET DOWN THE BEACH...
THIS WAY!
HEH! HEH!
3

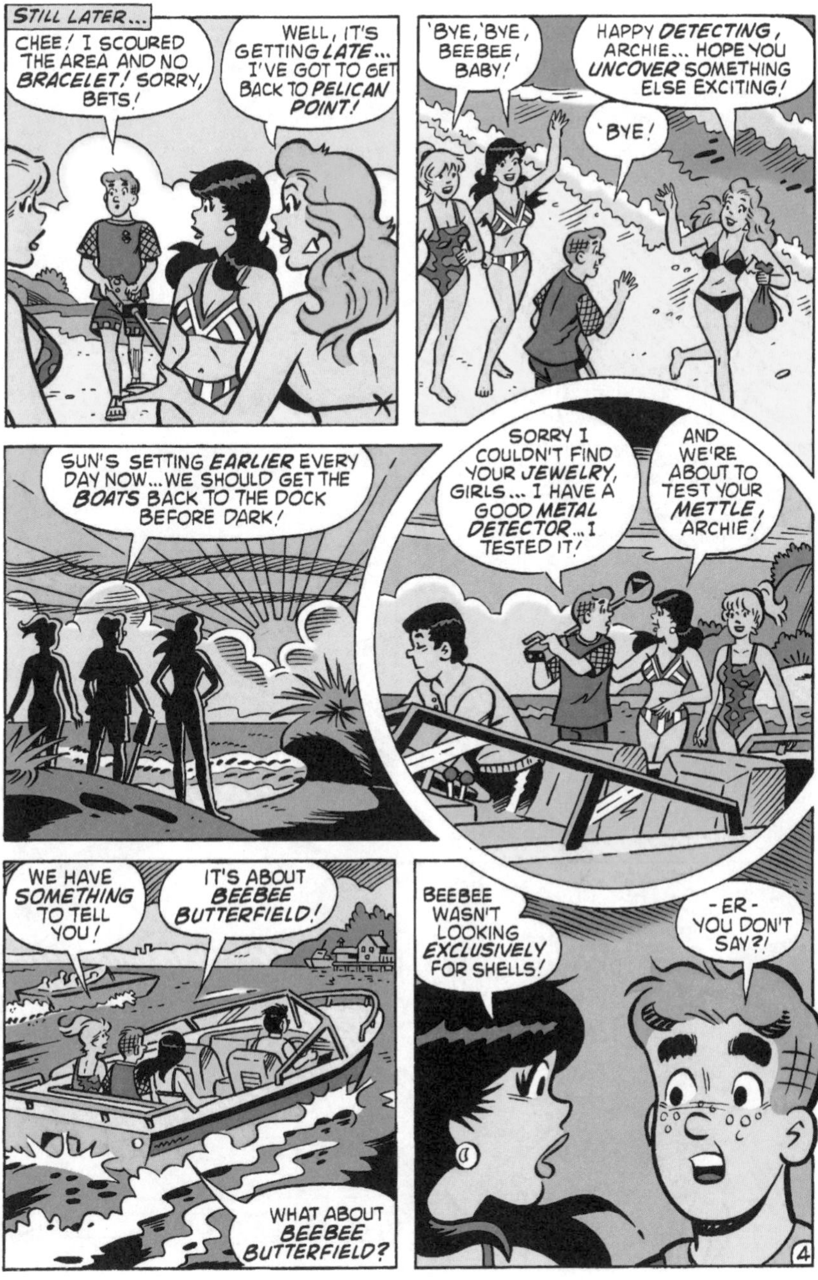
STILL LATER...
CHEE! I SCOURED THE AREA AND NO BRACELET! SORRY, BETS!
WELL, IT'S GETTING LATE... I'VE GOT TO GET BACK TO PELICAN POINT!
'BYE, 'BYE, BEEBEE, BABY!
HAPPY DETECTING, ARCHIE... HOPE YOU UNCOVER SOMETHING ELSE EXCITING!
'BYE!
SUN'S SETTING EARLIER EVERY DAY NOW...WE SHOULD GET THE BOATS BACK TO THE DOCK BEFORE DARK!
SORRY I COULDN'T FIND YOUR JEWELRY, GIRLS... I HAVE A GOOD METAL DETECTOR...I TESTED IT!
AND WE'RE ABOUT TO TEST YOUR METTLE, ARCHIE!
WE HAVE SOMETHING TO TELL YOU!
IT'S ABOUT BEEBEE BUTTERFIELD!
WHAT ABOUT BEEBEE BUTTERFIELD?
BEEBEE WASN'T LOOKING EXCLUSIVELY FOR SHELLS!
-ER- YOU DON'T SAY?!
4

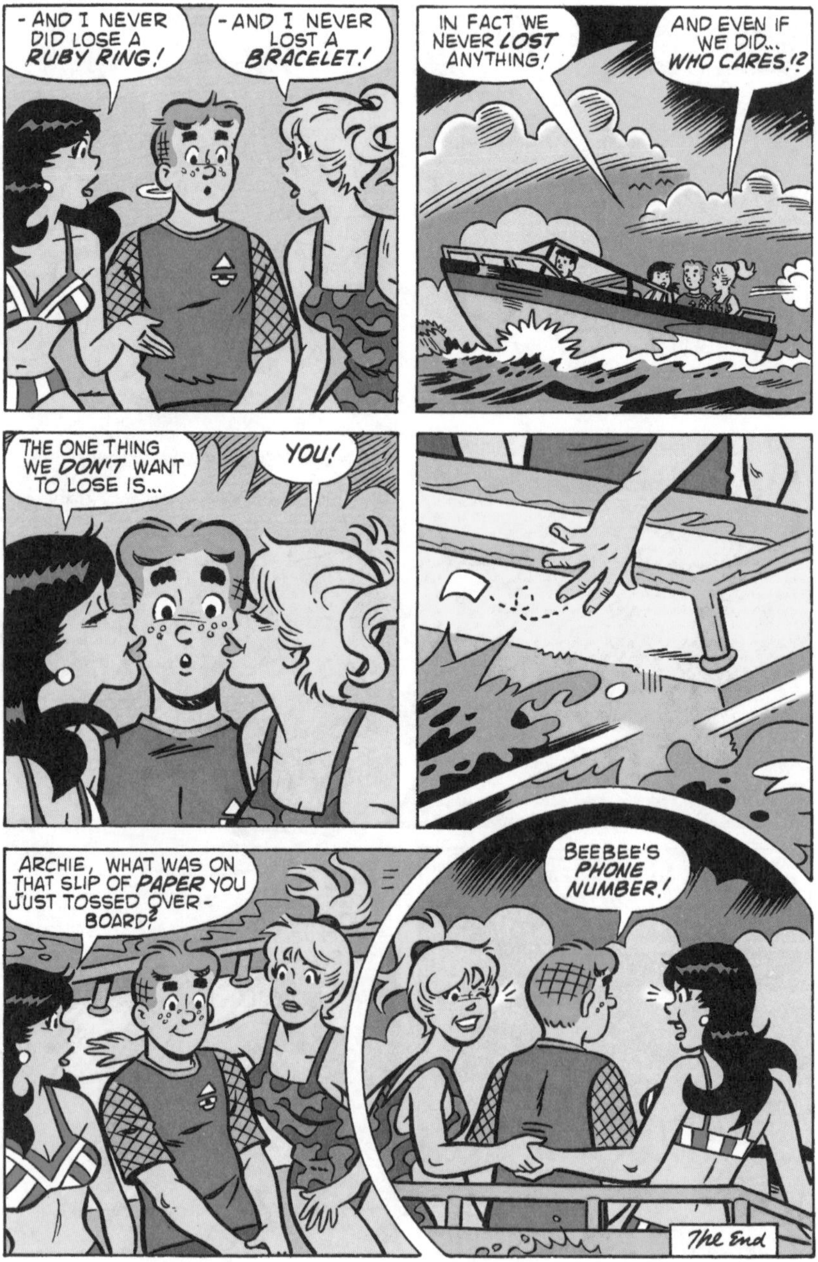
- AND I NEVER DID LOSE A RUBY RING!
- AND I NEVER LOST A BRACELET!
IN FACT WE NEVER LOST ANYTHING!
AND EVEN IF WE DID... WHO CARES!?
THE ONE THING WE DON'T WANT TO LOSE IS...
YOU!
ARCHIE, WHAT WAS ON THAT SLIP OF PAPER YOU JUST TOSSED OVER-BOARD?
BEEBEE'S PHONE NUMBER!
The End